SLIEVGALL'ION

THE
GODDESS
WARS

RIPP BLACK

Slievgall'ion: The Goddess Wars

Copyright © 2021. **Ripp Black**

Because of the dynamic nature of the Internet, any web addresses or links contained in this book may have changed since publication and may no longer be valid. The views expressed in this work are solely those of the author and do not necessarily reflect the views of the publisher, and the publisher hereby disclaims any responsibility for them.

Library of Congress Control Number: 2021912295
ISBN Paperback: 978-1-7368512-6-5
eBook: 978-1-7368512-7-2

Printed in the United States of America

CONTENTS

GRANDMOTHER'S SONG

The circle turns, dance all the way, though once returned we cannot stay.
Ever round and begin again, moving on there is no end.
The Spell is cast and calls me to sleep.
Hiding the secret, the spell holds deep.
Those who remember, yet do they weep
For the loss of the hidden bound in my keep.
The circle turns while the drum does sound, and dancing feet do tread the ground.
Red runs blood, fear stalks the night.
Through visions dark, need stirs the sight
Of treasure hidden far from light.
Heed the warnings. Souls take flight.
The circle turns while the drum does sound, and dancing feet do tread the ground.
Hush in darkness. Hold the sleep.
While the circle moves, the secret we keep.
Stir not the hidden from slumber deep,
Though soul to soul the visions creep.
The circle turns while the drum does sound, and dancing feet do tread the ground.
Through blood and fire, the oath once bound,
Yields the spell when the way is found.
Dance in darkness, the battle to sound,
And bring the promise of abundance unbound.
The circle turns while the drum does sound, and dancing feet do tread the ground.
Ever turning, the circle must spin,
As moving round, new hands join in.
Circle and song see peace to win,
Yet hidden in darkness still lives the sin.
The circle turns while the drum does sound, and dancing feet do tread the ground.

The circle turns, dance all the way, though once returned we cannot stay.

Ever round and begin again, moving on there is no end.

PROLOGUE

Abred - Struggle and evolve
Gwynfyd - Purity
Ceugant - Infinity

She awoke, drenched and shivering, her scream swallowed before it broke the night's silence. The nightmare lingered, as it always did, filled with the roar and rattle and cries of battle, thick with the scent of blood and death. Her age-old grief weighed down, crushing her. Tears streamed, mixing with the cold sweat. Gone. All dead. Her hand reached for her necklace. Closed on emptiness. Sobs shook her as her stifled scream at last gurgled out her cry of deepest anguish.

"Grandmother. Be at peace. No one may harm you, here." The voice in her head failed to calm her. Even as the images of blood and death slowly faded, her heart continued to throb its panic and its tortured sorrow, raising twisted knots of nausea.

"Grandmother." Tine's voice came gently, not in her head, this time, but aloud. Once again, her distress had roused him from his sleep. Guilt joined her grief.

"I am here." His silhouette moved silently across the room, set against the soft light filtering in from the open door. The warmth of his hand brushed her cheek. "Was it the same dream, or did a vision offer something more?"

"Yes. No." The words barely croaked past her stifled sobs. "Both."

"Tell me," Tine coaxed. "What more did you see?"

Grandmother drew a ragged breath, her mind rejecting her attempt to return to the dark dream.

"You must shut out the past, dear one. You cannot change it. And you keep it too long in your soul. Look past the nightmare. Identify what is new. See what is different."

Her darted glance cast him as a blur through her tears. She swiped at them with the backs of her hands before lifting her gaze to him again. Tall like his father and as beautifully dark-skinned as his mother, he stood at her bedside, his bearing calm. The creases at the corners of his eyes were the only signs of the burden of his losses. He wore his centuries and his tragedies with quiet reserve, though she knew his grief was as profound as her own.

She closed her eyes, pushing back the hated dream. What was new? What was different? Through force of will, Grandmother held the nightmare at bay, calling up what her gift of sight had provided. "Voices," she managed. "Too…too many voices. Like all the…the dead clamoring to be heard." A shudder wracked her.

"What did the vision show?"

"A glimpse." She took a moment, forcing a slow breath, concentrating. "It hovered at…at the fringes of the dream. A woman. In white robes. She was… arguing, I think…with a man." The next part she had seen before, though she made no mention of it to Tine. Now, she felt she owed him the knowledge. "They are…they are sending another."

"Another from Brightwater? To search for you?"

"Perhaps," she hedged. She took another measured breath. "Or… or to seek the aid of the guardians."

"You always see what pertains to you. That should tell you whom he seeks."

She breathed in to steady her words, her exhale measured. "Not all visions. Sometimes they come as warnings of danger to those I love."

"Because their deaths would affect you. This one. Did it offer a warning?"

Grandmother's shrug was lost in the remnants of her trembling. "The vision was confused. It carried a sense of anticipation, but also the subtle hint of foreboding."

Tine's lips pinched as he considered. "The others sent to find you failed. So, too, they failed to reach Knife Point Keep. No one from Brightwater has ever succeeded in pressing so deep into the mountains alone." He rubbed his forehead in thought, at last declaring, "We should delay our plans and remain here. At least until you discover the meaning of the vision."

"This one will find me," Grandmother murmured. "Whether he searches for me or not, he will find me. The vision did not show it, but I feel it in my soul."

More than that. After her first vision of of this new seeker, she set plans in motion to guarantee it.

Tine brushed the strands of snowy hair from her face. "Not so long as we are here. Can I bring you something? Some tea, perhaps?" She could only shake her head.

"Then I will sit with you for a moment." Retrieving a chair from beneath the shuttered window, he sat leaning forward and taking Grandmother's hand. He remained longer than a moment, mute and watchful in the stillness of the night. The bond between them served far better than anything he might say. At length, he rose, laying her hand at her side. She knew he would stay longer if she asked it.

"Try to sleep," he offered. "Try to keep the past harbored in that place deep in your mind where it may lie hidden. If you need me, I will come."

Grandmother's gaze followed him. "We must do as we planned." He moved through the shadows, his stride one of contemplation. Turning, he nodded. "Then I have much to do, today. Rest while you can. I will return when it is time."

His absence left an ocean of anguished emptiness.

"We are ever with you."

How common, those words running through her head. She almost believed them. Almost believed that the souls of those she loved could speak to her. Only the sisters' souls possessed that ability. Or did at one time. Long ago, Roisin's voice was a constant companion. Dana's less frequently. Dana's voice came rarely, now. Roisin's had grown distant. Faint. Nemhain's remained the only other voice she might hear. And that one she forbade, maintaining strong spells to keep the Witch out.

"Grandmother?" The sending was so thin and timid she was not entirely certain of it. *"Grandmother?"* A little stronger, this time. Its gentle sweetness was unmistakable.

"Child. I am sorry," she returned, her remorse drawing tears, again. *"I must strengthen my shielding to prevent my nightmares from seeping through to you. How much did you see?"*

"I saw nothing, Grandmother," returned with less hesitation. *"Nothing of your visions. I felt…"*

Grandmother's sigh came on a choked breath. *"How can I keep my pain…my sorrow from you? You bear enough of your own."*

"Far less than you. That is not why I am reaching out, though. He is coming, Grandmother. This one is now within our sacred grove. It is as you said. He is a Soldier of Damsa Dana."

For a long moment, Grandmother lay in silence, her eyes closed tight against the world. *"You know what to do?"*

"I will do as you have asked and as my visions instruct."

"Beware of the visions, child. They do not always speak with sufficient clarity to ascertain the truth of their revelations."

The silence left by Whisper's retreat from her mind opened an even darker void than Tine's physical departure. How long had it been since she last saw the child? A year? Three? Five? Surely, no more than that.

"Abred." The word stung Grandmother's tongue. The first word that prefaced many a spell. And she needed a spell. One of protection to cast around Whisper. Around Shadow and Serenity, as well.

"Should not be a proper way to start any enchantment," she grumbled. "Abred. Struggle and evolve. All my days have been Abred. Where is Gwynfyd? Where is the Purity?" Her huff was agitated and weary. "Ceugant. Infinity. Like Abred, you are all too familiar. Life is Abred and Ceugant. Struggle infinitely. There is no Gwynfyd. I wish for other words to preface my spells." No others came to her.

Venting a weary exhale, she repeated the three. Abred. Gwynfyd. Ceugant. Then with eyes closed, she formed and sent out her spell of protection, praying it would hold. That done, she curled beneath her blankets, hoping to sleep, once more. Instead, her head filled with her song. She was no Adriane Starn…no Amhranai Fearalite, as the Alainn knew him. Her efforts at song writing were clumsy, the music borrowed from an ancient bard whose name was lost to time. But the words carried on the music were the story of her past, of her fears. It both grieved her and shimmered with hope. It was the hope that drew her song to mind. She must cling to the hope.

B randel's nerves twitched at the silence. No birdsong. No rustle in the leaves. No snap of a twig as some creature moved through the shadows beneath the trees. The only indication of his stalkers, aside from the utter lack of sound from anything else, was the sense of their presence. They were out there. Two of them. Always together. Not Red Moon Warriors. Nemhain's murderers had not yet pressed across Brightwater's border into Knife Point. The Soldiers of Damsa Dana prevented it. A couple of highwaymen, perhaps, though it was curious that they did not attack.

Feet braced, his back to a tree, Brandel shifted his bow across his shoulder, his hand settling on the grip of his long knife. Eight days, this pair had followed him. Three days back, when the wild wood gave way to the massive oaks, his sense of them grew stronger, meaning the two followed more closely, now. The early autumn dappling of sunlight, however, produced no sign of them in the shifting shadows along the ground nor within the overlapping branches above. They were good, no question.

"I do not like stalkers," he announced to the air. "Especially when they interfere with my hunt."

A faint and musically mocking laugh responded from high in the canopy, setting the boughs of every tree in a gentle ripple.

"Show yourselves!"

The laugh came again, taunting. Closer but still high up.

"Who are you? What do you want?" he demanded.

"Ah." This sound lacked the music of the laughter. So, too, it lacked volume, coming soft as a sigh. "The question is, what do you want?"

"To be left unhampered. To hunt so that I can eat."

"And what else?"

"Nothing."

An edge trilled through the musical voice. "Not true." Seemingly in response, the sway of every branch ceased. "You seek Grandmother."

Still, he searched the woods and the canopy, looking for the slightest hint of movement. Female, these stalkers. That much was evident. "I seek no one."

The second voice, still as quiet as before, countered, "But you do."

"Indeed," sang the other.

"What would you know of my purpose? Who are you? If you wish some business with me, then have the decency to face me. Otherwise, be on your way."

The creak of branches in the oak behind him spun him away from the tree that backed him. Through the shifting play of light and dark in the lower boughs, he glimpsed the figure. Tall and thin and wearing a hooded gray tunic over snug black leggings tucked at the knees into supple black leather boots, she moved with delicate grace and skilled balance. There was purpose in her carriage as she slipped between the limbs and leaves, shadows seeming to trail with her. At last, she settled on a perch, still well above him.

"You seek the Guardians of Ciuin Rose, and you also seek Grandmother." Branches and leaves danced delicately in cadence with the girl's song. The shock of her black-as-midnight eyes as they fixed on him brought his breath up short. Her brow creased, daring him to deny her accusation a second time. "Why?" As her voice fell silent, so, again, did the subtle dance of the leaves.

"Where is the other?" he pressed. "I do not chat with people I cannot see."

"You do, you know," filtered down from higher above. "You beckoned us to show ourselves."

She stood near the top of the tree. The breeze rippled her camouflage mottled tunic, her red hair glinting each time the sunlight found a space between the shimmer of leaves. Her features, however, remained hidden. The shifting dapples of light also made it difficult to track her as she descended. His first clear look at the girl came when she emerged on the bough next to her companion. This is what stalked him? Children? The dark-eyed, onyx-haired one looked to be no older than fifteen, the smaller, red-haired waif little more than twelve.

"There," the first girl sang. "You see us. Now, tell us why you seek Grandmother."

Brandel averted his gaze under the combined scrutiny of the older girl's flashing dark eyes and the bright emerald of the little redhead's, watching, instead, the motion within the canopy each time the darkhaired girl spoke. He kept his silence, however. It was no business of theirs who he sought or why.

"Fine!" The older girl dropped to the ground, the deeper grays along the floor of the oak forest promptly wrapping round her. Brandel sucked in as she vanished in the shadows. That she remained near, however, was obvious from his sense of her. The younger girl climbed back up the tree, disappearing as her clothing blended in with the oak's mix of remaining greens and autumn's first flare of golds and russets.

"Fine!" he repeated. "Now, let me hunt in peace while I wait for the Guardians of Ciuin Rose to pass this way."

The faint murmur from above proclaimed, "The guardians have not passed this way for more than a year. And you cannot hunt here! Not in this sacred place. We will allow no creature to show itself so long as you remain within the grove."

Brandel dropped his bow from his shoulder to his hand, glaring up in the direction of the diminutive girl's thin voice, though he could find no indication of her. "You expect me starve and foul this place with my corpse?"

"Your death would feed other life," the older girl sang with an edge. The whole of the woodland's vegetation fluttered at the sound. "Besides, you do not look like you are starving. You ate well enough before you entered the grove. The wild wood provided you with three rabbits and a quail, the last of which you finished just last night. Still…" The girl slipped again from the shadows, peering around a massive tree trunk several removed from where he stood. "We do not wish your death on our consciences. If we show you the way to food, you will tell us your business."

"I need no help from you to provide for myself. I will leave your precious grove and return to my hunt."

From above drifted, "You will be lost."

"I do not get lost." Having completed the statement, Brandel realized, with no small amount of chagrin, that he could not, in fact, determine the way back to his camp. In truth, he could determine no direction at all.

"Leave off with your spells of confusion!" he demanded. "Let me find my way out if you are so keen to be rid of me.

"We are doing nothing of the sort!" Resentment grated along the melodic tone. "It is the ancient magic set within the grove that conceals your way. Not lightly does it permit outsiders to penetrate so close to the grove's heart. Nor will it yield them back to the world unless respectfully requested."

Brandel re-shouldered his bow, suppressing a snarl. "Grove, may I pass through and back to my camp so that I might seek for the guardians elsewhere?"

The high titter joined by a rich and musical giggle curled his lip in irritation.

"You will get nowhere with such an attitude. Follow the trail," whispered through Brandel's mind, apparently from the younger child. Turning, he scanned the woodland floor. "What trail?"

"There."

Before him, a small whirlwind stirred, swirling up dust and moldy leaves to clear a path. *"Follow,"* breathed within his head. *"It will lead you. You will find food and shelter from the coming storm."*

"I can shelter well enough in my tent."

The melodic flow of the older girl's words took on a darker tone. "Not on this night. You would do well to accept the offer, though personally, I would prefer to leave you to wander."

"What guarantee do I have that I can trust…" his unfinished question hung on the air, his senses suddenly empty of any presence. "Now, you leave me!" he snorted. Only the sound of stiffening breezes through the trees remained. Muttering, Brandel glanced up, noting the dark clouds thickening above, annoyed that he had not detected the change, himself. A storm was, indeed, brewing. Thunder rolled in the distance and the growing chill carried the heavy scent of rain mixed with ozone. Noble would be caught in it. May his horse possess the good sense to stay sheltered next to the boulders at his camp.

"Very well "Brandel growled at the spinning dust devil. "Lead me to the inn."

It continued to spin in place until he stepped toward it. In turn, it moved, sweeping bare a narrow path. He followed. It moved. He considered picking up the pace when lightning flashed, the sound of thunder rolling closer. The darkening shadows with roots and rocks and sudden holes underfoot, however, dictated he restrain the urge. The trudge grew more difficult when the rain came, turning the holes into sucking mud traps that threatened to hold him fast. Above, lightning flashed again, the peel of thunder nearly on top of him, now. The rain turned to a deluge.

Ducking blowing twigs and leaves, Brandel stopped with each near crack and crash of a branch. The whirlwind paused when he halted, continued when he moved toward it. Each stretch of the grove looked like the last, leaving him to fear the girls had tricked him, using their magic to lead him in circles. Leaning into the wind, the string of his bow humming in his ear, he nevertheless kept his whirling guide in sight and distinguished from the blowing woodland detritus. It came as some relief when the oaks gave way to natural forest and the ground began to climb. He cleared a rise; slid his way down; cleared another. At the bottom of the second, the little whirlwind vanished.

Swearing, Brandel turned in search of it before realizing he stood at the edge of a clearing. Perhaps five hundred meters out rose a dark cliff, the top disappearing against the stormy sky. At its base nestled a cottage, thin light glimmering through the interior curtains of the windows that flanked a single door. Somewhere in the darkness, the crash and roar of a waterfall could be heard over the now near constant rumble of the sky.

Brandel turned his attention back to the building. A cottage. Not an inn. He crouched, still within the trees, wary of approaching. People who lived in such isolation generally did not warm to strangers.

Rapidly shifting eddies of wind created by the rock face, the surrounding woodlands, and the waterfall sent intermittent wafts of cooking meat, baking bread, and burning wood to him. Scowling, he glanced back, dismayed but unsurprised to find no sign of the path that brought him here.

"Welcome."

Startled, Brandel's hand went instantly to his knife.

"You need no weapons, here. We pose no threat."

"So say many who prove, in the end, to wish harm."

"I dare say, you found no suggestion of a lie in my words."

Brandel's lips pinched. "No," he acknowledged. "No lie."

"Then accept our welcome."

Still, he hesitated. As the rain blew more fiercely sideways, needling into his face, he at last closed the distance to the cottage, raising his hand to knock.

"Come," replied before he could complete the motion.

The door creaked as he pushed it open enough to peer in. Beyond it lay a room of fair size. A metal chandelier hung from the center of the ceiling, its lights flickering as it swayed in the fitful draft. Lights. Not candles. Not oil lamps.

"Come," he was urged, again. "And do close the door before this foul night brings in trouble."

Brandel complied but remained near the exit. Moving about the open kitchen was a well-tanned woman of indeterminate age whose short hair and dark eyes were almost as black as those of the girl with the musical voice. The woman stopped next to a large hearth, her fists on her hips as she gave him a curious once-over. Behind her, a rack of meat cooked at the back of the hearth fire, while a large pot simmered on top of a nearby woodstove.

"You look as though you are ready to bolt," she said. "Please. You are welcome, here. We have been expecting you. Dinner is almost ready. A washroom lies there," she added, nodding toward a hallway cut into the cliff face that served as the cottage's back wall. "You may leave your things on the hooks near where you stand. No one will trouble you, here."

"I need directions."

"To find your camp, I assume, since I just gave you directions to clean up." The woman turned to the pot on the stove, giving it a brief stir. "It is unsafe to travel while the storm rages. And it will not abate before daylight. I will not be responsible for losing a stranger to the woods and weather. So, you may as well accept a meal." When Brandel still made no move, she straightened and faced him with cocked brow. "What have you to lose? You will be drier, warmer, and will have a full stomach when you set out, again."

Brandel relinquished, hanging his quiver and bow from one of several hooks and his dripping coat from another. "You expected me, you said. The two girls in the woods sent that I was coming?"

"More or less."

"Who are you?"

Her smile was bright. "Serenity."

"I am…"

"Brandel Journeyson. Your name precedes you, soldier. A lieutenant, I believe. Your honor precedes you, as well. Now, if you please, do wash up."

Brandel leveled a more thorough scrutiny on her. Why should this woman know anything about him?

"Questions later," the woman decreed, returning to her pot for another stir. "Dinner will grow cold if you stand rooted much longer."

His return from the washroom was laden with more questions. Serenity glanced up from setting the meal on the table. "Your expression suggests you did not expect such comforts in so wild a place."

"When I was told I would find shelter, I expected an inn. Yet, even had this been an inn…" His gaze went to the lights overhead before he glanced back down the hall. "I would not have expected electricity. Plumbing, perhaps. The hot water, however, is a bonus."

"Rare luxuries," she admitted. "You are familiar with such, though."

"In the Sisters' Cloister at the Temple of Damsa Dana and at the Lord of Brightwater's Manor House within the keep, both in our capital of Riversong. If electricity exits elsewhere in Brightwater, I have not found it. Plumbing to provide cold water is common enough. Was the hot water that proved a surprise." Again, he flicked a glance at the chandelier. "As for those... I would like to meet the Witch who possesses the extraordinary magic of technology. I believe that is what Strongbow, Lord of Brightwater calls it."

The woman laughed outright. "The magic of technology! It is no magic, Master Journeyson, but compliments of the waterfall and machinery. These luxuries are rare because few have access to the machinery required or the materials to make them. The tales say that our most ancient ancestors knew much about a great many technologies even more remarkable than electricity. They even knew how to employ electricity to heat entire buildings."

"I am familiar with the stories. They say the Goddesses brought some of these strange magics with them from the realm of their birth. That sometime prior to their disappearance before their souls were returned to us, Damsa Dana and Roisin banned much of it, later granting some minor exceptions to the heroes who came to fight with them."

"So say the stories," Serenity nodded. "One of my ancestors was among the heroes. Was he who built this home." She motioned to the table. "Now, please sit. As I said, the meal will grow cold."

Brandel took the nearest chair, watching the woman as she pulled fresh bread from the oven. "Why do you help me?"

"By 'help', you mean providing you a meal and a warm bed for the night, I take it."

"You need not include board for the night. But yes."

Before the woman could answer, the cottage door blew open, admitting a pair of drenched and bedraggled girls, one looking like a dark apparition in the tattered layers of gray and black mist that wrapped her. The fair skin and red hair of the smaller waif made her appear to glow, by comparison.

Serenity set a disgruntled gaze to them and the puddles of mud collecting at their feet. "Honestly! Can the pair of you not return home without making a mess of things? Did you fall in a ditch before coming in? Go! Clean yourselves. You are late for dinner. I will not keep our guest waiting for you. And Shadow! Leave off with the play of your magic. It is impolite to intimidate our guest."

The girl glowered, but released the last strands of darkness, her own fair skin a sharp contrast to the blue-black of her hair and eyes. Together, the two disappeared down the hall, a door slamming in their wake. Serenity shook her head once more as she collected the pot from the stove and ladled soup into the bowl on Brandel's plate. "Please. Eat. You have had a long journey." Sighing at his hesitation, she ladled a bowl for herself, blowing on it before lifting a spoon to her mouth.

"There. You see? The food is safe. We mean you no harm."

Brandel flushed. "I did not mean to suggest I thought otherwise."

"Of course, you did," the woman harrumphed. "You suggested as much with your doubt of us. We are strangers. Why should we invite you in and share our meal? It is a sad time when simple kindnesses are suspect."

"We find enemies where we least expect them."

"We are not your enemy, Master Journeyson."

Brandel ate in quiet thought, his brow furrowing. "You said you know me. How?"

"Know of you, sir. Whisper had a vision of your coming. Grandmother asked us to watch for you. To see that you make it safely to Knife Point Keep."

Brandel returned his spoon to the bowl, the crevice of his brow deepening. "How would your grandmother know my business?"

"Grandmother," Serenity emphasized the single word. "She is a Seer. She knows many things."

Lips pinched, Brandel reflected on Serenity's intimation that she referred not to a personal relation. Was the woman mentioned the one he was sent to find? "Grandmother, then. She has seen that I look for her?"

"She suspects. Now, no more questions. We can talk tomorrow. Eat while the food is still hot."

He considered pressing the matter, but the warmth of the room and the taste of food impressed on him the extent of his fatigue and hunger. With a short nod, he returned to the meal, expressing his thanks as Serenity set a stein of ale beside his plate.

The girls returned, clean and dry, to take their places at the table as Brandel was finishing. Both set to devouring their dinner as though they had eaten nothing for a month.

"Ladies!" Serenity scowled. "Mind your manners!"

The older one brushed her hair from her face, flipping it back from its short drape over her shoulders as she raised her dark eyes to regard their guest. "He should mind his," she sang. "Hunting, he was. In the grove."

"How was he to know otherwise?"

"The oak groves are sacred. They are to be honored."

The smaller girl was also regarding him, now. When she spoke, her voice was sweet and delicate, and still held no more volume than a faint breeze on the air. "He is a soldier from the lowlands. Brightwater's sacred groves no longer stand. He and his people have forgotten."

Brandel bristled at their speculations.

The little one fixed her emerald gaze squarely on him. "Even if my visions had not said as much, your clothes give you away. You wear the emblem of the Soldiers of Damsa Dana on the breast of your coat and your shirt. Hence, you are a soldier, unless you stole the clothes. In addition, your linens and leather tell us you are from the lowlands. You will not last long in the mountains dressed like that. And you cannot deny that the oak groves are gone from Brightwater."

The older girl flipped a hand toward the door, her tone once again discordant. "Give him some woolens and send him on his way. He brings the darkness and trouble with him."

"You directed me here," Brandel remarked.

"Only because we were instructed to do so."

Serenity waved the girl silent. "It may be that darkness and trouble follow him. That does not make him responsible for their coming. Trouble is spreading throughout our world. You know that well enough, Shadow. Leave the man in peace."

"But he does not belong here. He is…"

Serenity cut the girl short with a stern glance. "He is a stranger, here. He is not versed in our ways. You judge him when you should be instructing."

Brandel shifted uncomfortably. "The judging has been on both sides. I mistrusted them, as well."

"I dare say they gave you no reason to trust. Hiding in the trees, I would guess. They were sent to greet you. They should have done so openly."

"He carries weapons," Shadow objected. "How were we to know he would be safe to approach?"

"Everyone carries weapons. Even you. Do you not trust Grandmother? Was she who told us to greet and welcome him."

Shadow dropped her gaze, her face flushing. "Of course, I do. I just…"

The smaller girl pushed her chair from the table, brushing her long hair back from her shoulders before gathering up her dishes and setting them in the sink. Swiping a red curl from her face, she eyed Brandel with such intensity that it raised the hair on the back of his neck. At last, venturing the faintest suggestion of a smile, she offered a curtsey before heading down the hall to disappear somewhere beyond the washroom.

"My turn to do the dishes, I suppose." Shadow's mutter rumbled at odds with the music inherent in her voice.

Serenity waved her away with a sigh. "Go on. To bed with you. I will clean up tonight. See that Whisper is alright."

Shadow dipped Brandel a reluctant curtsey, then dashed down the long hall after the one called Whisper.

"Your daughters are quite the pair," Brandel observed, rising to assist with the cleanup.

Serenity turned from him, busying herself at the sink where water steamed from the faucet. For several long moments, she remained silent. "Shadow is my granddaughter," she said, at last. "Whisper is my…distant niece. They have grown up together and are as inseparable as petals from a flower."

"Cousins, then," Brandel said.

"Close enough."

He considered, wondering why Serenity had both girls in her charge and why she would choose to raise them in such isolation.

The woman's softly spoken, "I am sure you are weary from your travels," interrupted his thoughts. "The third room down on your right is prepared for you. I trust you will find it comfortable enough."

Brandel set his pile of collected dishes on the counter next to the sink. "I thank you for your hospitality, but I need to find the way back to my camp."

"This is no night for traveling in unfamiliar woods. Your horse and your belongings are here. The girls collected them and left them in the stable for you."

Brandel cast a surprised glance toward the door.

"Go," the woman encouraged. "The stable is by the river, just inside the tree line. See to your horse if you wish. I can assure you he is warm and dry and well fed. Shadow may never outgrow her mischief, but neither she nor Whisper would ever neglect your horse or your belongings."

2

The light from the room's corner fireplace glistened off the polished granite walls. Strange walls. Brandel shifted on the chair, taking a reflective draw from the mug, glad for the pitcher of ale he found waiting for him on the room's small table. Peculiar family to welcome a stranger so readily. Fitting, he, supposed that the house would also be odd.

His gaze remained on the light flickering across the polished walls. The dancing reflection was not the strangeness. A subtle magic apart from that of the residents flowed through this structure. It thrummed faintly along his nerves, carrying the vague suggestion of music. He could detect neither melody nor words. Just a rhythm. One, two, three, four, five, six, seven. One, two, three. One, two, three. Common enough.

Rising, he strolled across to where his jerkin and shirt lay on the hearth in front of the fire. Still soggy. He kicked his boots closer to the table to allow room to pace between it and the bed. The subtle thrum of the rhythm persisted. He noticed it first when he returned from the stable. In the darkened silence of the house, the faint beat was more a pressure against his mind than something heard. For a while it roused his curiosity. Now, it was becoming an annoyance.

His pace carried him to the bed, back to the table, and round again. At length, he paused to lay a hand against the wall. The pulse gave the impression that the rock lived. The thought prompted an unsettled shake of his head and he withdrew his hand. What purpose did this magic serve – beyond annoying him? He might believe the one called Shadow cast it precisely for that reason, save the spell was not of her making. After experiencing her gift in the grove, her signature was now recognizable. And it did not mark this enchantment. In truth, the magic held no discernable signature. Another peculiarity. Every spell and enchantment retained the signature of the one who cast it.

Returning to the table, Brandel dropped onto the chair, draining his mug. Strange people. Strange house. Very strange magic. The repetitive rhythm seeped through his muscles, numbed his mind. His eyes closed.

Blood across the plains. Banners bearing the crescent of the red moon flap in the wind. Half human, half bear-like creatures track those who flee. Darkness runs ahead. Withered corpses lie in its wake, the emblems of the Soldiers of Damsa Dana crumbling over them.

Brandel jerked awake and to his feet, his insides twisted with guilt. What was he doing, sheltering in warmth and safety, a hot meal filling his stomach and good ale within his grasp while his men fought and died? How many were lost in his absence? How far had the Red Moon Warriors advanced? He attempted to clear his head of its fog; to concentrate; to stretch his mind outward, seeking for any among his men. There was nothing. Had been nothing since he crossed the border into Knife Point. Not even Strongbow responded to note Brandel's reports.

"Rest. You can do nothing for your men, now." The sending was Serenity's. He recognized the tone.

"Stay out of my head!"

"Your dream drifted to me, not I to it. Your mind is unguarded." Brandel stiffened. Ale, warmth, and comfort made him careless. His growl rumbled, *"I should not be here. I must leave. Tell me how to reach Knife Point Keep. The sooner I deliver the Lord of Brightwater's request, the sooner I can return to fight with my men."*

"You cannot find your way without us. And we will not go out in this storm. Sleep. We will leave the moment the tempest abates."

He pounded a fist on the table. *"Breag Nemhain's forces are advancing across Brightwater. The Soldiers of Damsa Dana and my people are being slaughtered. By what right do I eat and sleep instead of fight?"* And how could anyone sleep with that infernal rhythm hammering along his nerves?

"You fight for your people by coming here. We will see that you reach Knife Point Keep. The journey will be quicker if we start out well rested."

Slumping back to the chair, Brandel drained his mug and poured another. The woman was right. He needed their help, at least until he could get his bearings. Damn this land with its suffocating forests and its tempests. In the lowlands, travel was still possible in such conditions, though admittedly hazardous with so much lightning. At least the plains did not threaten to drop trees one's head. Again, he drained the mug. Go to Knife Point Keep. Demand to meet with the lord of the land and deliver Strongbow's urgent request. That was the command laid on him. His fingers drummed on the table. That and find the one called Grandmother.

His finger drumming was replaced with a snarl. The Lord of Brightwater and the High Priestess of Damsa Dana pinned their last hopes on this Grandmother. A great Seer. A most powerful Witch. Believable enough. But a woman from the time of the returning of the Goddesses? No Witch lived beyond five, perhaps six hundred years. There may be some among the Alainn who could claim lives of two thousand years or more. But a human Witch? Impossible! The woman was a myth.

Sagging, his head dropped to his folded arms. Memories stirred of the tales his mother once told. Of Grandmother. Vague images of an antiquated woman drifted through his mind. A woman wrinkled beyond recognition, gray hair so thin her scalp could be seen, and whose slits for eyes barely contained the spark of life. Her features were skeletal, her smile grim. Her chuckle rattled an eerie screech.

The sound came again. This time as a sharp and piercing shriek, nearly jolting Brandel from the chair to the floor. A string of expletives accompanied his attempt to gather his wits. Another shriek sent him tripping over his boots in his race for the door. The lights in the corridor flickered on as Serenity charged from a room further down the hall, disappearing into the adjacent room, her anxious cry of, "Whisper!" echoing in her wake. Several more calls carried on the echoes of her former cries before the shrieking died away, replaced by sobbing.

Brandel reached the doorway seconds behind Serenity. The woman sat on the edge of a bed, hugging the small girl close and rocking with her. The other girl stood just inside the door, pale and shaking.

"Nightmare." Shadow's simple statement rang with her apprehension. "She has them. A lot. They are…"

Serenity hushed her with a hiss, the woman's attention remaining on the child wrapped in her arms. "Whisper, what did you see? Can you tell me?"

The little redhead's trembling shook her mercilessly, her long hair trailing across her near ghost-white face, her distress mirrored in her eyes as her darting glances found him. "You." The word was so faint Brandel was not sure whether she spoke it or sent it to his mind. In the same hush, she continued with, "You must find her. Grandmother will need you. They are coming. You are not safe, here. We are not safe. They must not find us."

"How soon?" Serenity pressed. "How soon are they coming?"

The girl's gaze remained on Brandel, her murmur of, "Before the night is out," edging ice along his nerves.

"Both of you," the woman ordered. "Dress yourselves. I will prepare." Rising, she brushed Whisper's hair from her face. "Breathe, child. Deeply. Calm yourself. You did well. Be ready to leave as soon as you collect your packs."

Pushing past Brandel, she gestured for him to follow. "You will find no safe harbor, here, after all, I fear. They traveled faster than I anticipated."

"Who?"

"The Red Moon Warriors. Or at least some of their scouts."

Brandel froze. He saw them. Marching across the plains toward the foothills. In his dream.

"Come!" Serenity was urging. "Collect your things and go to the stable. Wait for us. We will meet you there." With that, she disappeared into the kitchen, rattling and banging as she collected items.

Brandel returned to his room, donning his shirt, jerkin, and boots. He snatched his coat, quiver, and bow and was out the door while Serenity was still stuffing a large pack. The wind was as fearsome as before, bending him against it in his rush to the stable. Noble stamped, his snort accompanied by agitated head tossing, the animal's eyes and nostrils flaring wide. Whether the horse's alarm was due to the weather or to approaching warriors, however, Brandel could not say. He took little time to locate the saddlebags and the few items rolled up within the bundle that served as his tent. Thankfully, the girls were thorough when they emptied his camp and delivered his belongings here. His check for missing items during his first trip to the stable found everything neatly stowed.

With Noble saddled and the saddlebags and roll secured, he led the animal to wait just inside the stable door. Traveling would be faster on his own, of course. But he would not leave the woman and girls at the mercy of the Red Moon, be it scouts or warriors. Breag Nemhain's ilk were incapable of mercy.

His wait was brief. Three hunched figures darted from the house, Shadow and Whisper clinging desperately to their coats, their hoods already blown back across the tops of their small packs. Leading Noble to meet them, Brandel gathered Whisper, hoisting her up to the saddle, then settled Shadow behind her. Serenity pointed to the other side of the white-water river.

"We cannot cross with it raging like that," he yelled over the wind.

"We can," she mouthed. "Follow.

3

Stay close," Serenity directed, ducking through the crashing waterfall. Brandel braced, biting back the expletives on his lips as the force of the water rushed the icy torrent down the inside of his coat. Sputtering, he emerged in a narrow hollow, Noble tugging against the lead in protest. Brandel tightened his grip, turning to sooth the horse. Whisper, however, was already leaning against the animal's neck, her soft words calming Noble's snorts and head jerking.

One more frigid drenching brought them out on the other side of the river. Though no sign of the Red Moon scouts was yet seen, Serenity urged haste as she led them away. Night's darkness and the dense forest shrouded them, the roar of the falls at last fading in the distance. In its place rose the howl of the winds and the creaks, moans, and cracks of the trees. Above, the forest canopy lessened the deluge on their heads to some degree, though every splinter and crash of a branch set Brandel's nerves on edge.

The gale continued, their path growing more difficult as the land began a steady climb. Muscles accustomed to traveling the flatlands and undulating hills of Brightwater strained at the increasing grade through mud and tangles of undergrowth. Dawn crawled through the darkness in wet grays and vague yellows when Serenity at last halted in a small clearing. Brandel followed her glance back toward the valley and her home. Black smoke billowed above the forest, there. The woman remained for several seconds, her hair trailing streams of water down her face, her dark eyes revealing her sorrow. She said nothing to the girls who sat hunched on Noble's back, their hoods pulled up and sagging around their faces under the weight of their soaking.

At last, the woman turned and nodded toward a massive boulder part way up the steeper rise to their left. Brandel attempted to wave her off. The area was too open. They would be easy prey if they rested on the slope. Moreover, the rain was gushing a flood of mud and debris from the top of the hill down over the rock, cutting gullies where it rushed. Serenity ignored him, climbing with confidence. Still, he held his ground until the woman disappeared behind the massive stone.

He hesitated a moment longer, a hand to his knife hilt as he opened his senses to the fluctuations in the ambient magic. The disturbances, sadly, gave no clue as to whether the enemy remained at the burning house or were pursuing their small company. Swiping the water from his face and shooting a disgruntled glance at the path Serenity had taken, Brandel followed, picking his way up the slope through the gushing sludge. Behind him, Noble struggled with the loose footing and the slurries of muck, once again snorting his disapproval before they reached their destination. It was a snug fit, coaxing the beast with the girls astride through the narrow space between boulder and hillside. Once inside, however, the hidden cave proved spacious enough.

"We can rest here through the day. We will leave at nightfall," Serenity advised, dropping her pack to the ground. Brandel nodded, lifting the girls from Noble's back. Pale and shivering, each looked about to collapse. With her feet to the dirt, however, Shadow dispensed with her pack and moved to the cave's opening, ready to slip out, despite her lips being blue and her hands shaking. "I will kkkkkeep wwwatch."

Serenity motioned her back. "No need. We are safe enough, for now. Even if the warriors happen to guess the direction we have come, the muddied ground and the wind torn woods will make us near impossible to track."

Shadow cast one last glance at the opening before turning to join Serenity and Whisper. "I sssuppose it would be too mmmmuch to expect to build a ffire."

"Everything is wet enough to produce a lot of smoke, and there is nowhere to vent except through the opening," Serenity agreed. "We should get out of our clothes, though." Pulling open her pack, she withdrew several soggy, parchment wrapped items before retrieving shirts and leggings for the three, along with a heavy woolen shirt she extended to Brandel. "I am sorry I cannot offer you dry pants, as well. Nothing we possess would fit you. The shirt should do well enough to cut the chill a little, though."

Brandel accepted it with cocked brow.

"Belongs to a friend who sometimes stays with us." she replied.

More than a friend, he suspected based on the reactions of the girls who shot Serenity amused glances.

Serenity ignored them, pulling a blanket from her pack and using it to shield Whisper and Shadow as they changed.

Brandel turned his back to them, anyway, removing Noble's saddle, bags, and roll before wiping the horse down with the wet saddle blanket.

"You will find a rope line," Serenity indicated. "A few paces further back. Should be long enough to hold our wet things."

Squinting into the shadows, Brandel spotted it. "You know this cave."

"The foothills and mountains are laced with many. I know a fair few of them. This one is often used by a local hunter when he needs to seek refuge from the weather." Worry edged her tone. "Though it appears he has not been here in a good while."

Brandel kept his back to the threesome while wringing his shirt and jerkin and draping them over the rope. "What makes you say so?"

"No recent fire, and no scent of any recent kill."

Brandel sensed there was something more the woman might say, though she refrained.

Noble moved up behind him as Brandel pulled on the wool shirt Serenity had provided. "Sorry, my friend," he said in response to the horse's head butt. A quick rub to the animal's muzzle accompanied, "No grains for you, today. I hope you ate well while you had the opportunity." When he returned his attention to his companions, he discovered that Serenity had also changed from her drenched garments. In addition to the wool shirts and leggings, Serenity and Shadow bore sheaths on their belts, the hilt of a long knife showing from each. Despite their drier clothes, however, all three continued to shiver.

Serenity returned to her pack to pull a small bundle from an outer pocket. "We may not dare a fire," she said, gently peeling layers of the parcel open. Several wrappings of cloth, a layer of damp leaves, then of wet rags all covered a final wrap of copper. Within the copper were five glowing pieces of coal. This, she laid on the ground, carefully folding out the edges of the copper and leaving the coals at its center. Shadow helped her gather stones, using them to build a dome over the small source of heat. A murmured spell and a flicker of sparks from Serenity's fingertips concluded the efforts. Beneath the dome, the coals grew hotter. As the stones heated, a faint haze of fog lifted around them.

"This will last us for a while," she sighed. "If we stay tucked close, we will feel the warmth better."

Brandel stepped closer, eyeing the construct.

"We are not helpless, Master Journeyson," Shadow snipped.

"I did not believe you were, or you would not be living alone in the middle of nowhere. I have just never seen coals carried or used in such a manner."

"You do not march or fight in winter?"

"Aye. But the land is open, and we do not hide. Our forward scouts give ample warning should our fires draw attention. If those attracted are friend, we share our meal. If foe, we fight."

The girl studied him with unconcealed scorn as she made her way closer to the warmth of the stones. "We know how to defend ourselves, too."

"I dare say." Brandel's gaze skimmed to the little redhead. Whisper sat mute next to Serenity, the blue gradually fading from her lips, though she still shook from the cold. Prescient, this one. A Seer. A true one, he judged, given that the warning in her dream proved accurate. Prescience, while often claimed, was actually a rare gift and seldom manifest as more than fleeting images of the immediate future, though he suspected Whisper's attribute held greater potential. Shadow's gift was far more unusual. In truth, Brandel knew of no other Witch who could wrap themselves in strands of fog and shadow and disappear.

"I possess other talents, as well," Shadow huffed. "Just as Whisper and Serenity... and you. Shall I tell you what your strongest attribute is?"

Brandel shrugged, biting back his anger at failing to shield his thoughts, again.

"Your mind can join with animals," the girl proclaimed. "Perhaps not all, but certainly a fair number. Yet you do not use this magic."

"Try hunting an animal for food when you can feel its fear in the hunt and its pain in death. One must eat, however. So, no I do not call upon that ability."

"Speaking of food," Serenity put in, reaching for the parchment wrapped parcels next to her pack. The bread she took from one was soggy, but the cheese and jerky from another were dry enough. "I had little time to collect things, but this should get us by for a day or two. After that, Master Journeyson, we shall look for opportunities to hunt. As you said, we must eat."

Brandel seated himself on the opposite side of the heated stones from the others. "Perhaps we should split and go our own ways once night falls. You know the area well and can find places to hide. I can move faster alone. Once I reach Knife Point Keep, I can send help to you."

"You will never make it to the keep without us." Serenity glanced at her niece. "And Whisper indicated that you must find Grandmother. We will take you to her if she allows it."

This was the second time they suggested the woman they referred to as 'grandmother' might wish to remain hidden. The High Priestess Danu said something to that effect, as well. "Why does this grandmother hide?"

"Shhh!" Whisper hissed, gesturing for their conversation to cease, her gaze darting to the cave entrance. From outside came the sounds of thrashing through the wooded underbrush accompanied by voices barely discernable beneath the bluster and rain.

"We found no indication they escaped to this side of the river," snapped a man, straining to yell above the wind.

"We cannot leave any possibility unchecked," rumbled another. "Confound this bloody storm! If they came to this side, their trail is washed away. I will see if I can pick up some track further on. You go back. See if the hounds found them on the cottage side. Send news to me if Coyote holds them."

"I will not risk that river again. Your arrow securing the rope to that tree scarcely held us for the crossing the first time. Contact Coyote from here."

"You will do as you are told, or Aifa will know of it. I will not waste energy on a sending. You scoped the lay of the area near the cottage. Deplete your own reserves and teleport back if you wish. If nothing has been found, then lead the others here. You can retrace our steps to search for anything we may have missed while you catch up to me."

The roar of the wind is all that held for the span of several seconds. Then came the charge of a teleportation spell. At least one man was gone. But how many remained? Bellowed cursing seemed to come from only one, though the amount of thrashing indicated more. It was not worth sticking his nose out from behind the concealing boulder, however, to ascertain their numbers.

Shadow moved toward the entrance once more, Serenity frantically waving her back. The girl ignored the gesturing, drawing fog and shadows around her as she slipped out. Many long and anxious minutes elapsed before Brandel grabbed his bow and quiver, ready to go after her. He almost ran her over as she stole back into the cave, wisps like the tatters of a moonless dark still trailing.

"At least a dozen men remain" she sent, side stepping and darting a disgruntled glance at Brandel. *"They have a single rider accompanied by a brood of trackers sniffing for our trail. Thanks be to Ciuin Rose for the storm. The rain and the mud are making their task difficult. And…"* Shadow's lips pinched, her gaze shifting back toward the cave's entrance. *"And, judging from the high agitation of the trackers, something else is out there. It has them spooked."*

Brandel tensed. *"What would spook trackers?"*

Shadow responded with an uneasy shrug.

"How many of the creatures?" he pressed.

"At least six. Hunched beasts that seem half human, half bear."

"I have seen them. I know what they are. I did not know their numbers had increased to such an extent as to spare more than one so far from the Red Moon's primary forces."

Shadow's eyes narrowed, her irritation striking a sharp tone. *"And what makes you think it is not the Blood Moon Goddess's chief forces descending on us, here? Perhaps they are tracking you."*

Brandel's retort fell short as Whisper interjected, *"You experienced my vision, Shadow. You beheld the map in the hands of the Red Moon scouts. It marked the location of our home. Master Journeyson did not have that information. They acquired it elsewhere."*

"How do you know he did not possess it?" Shadow snapped.

"He is an honest man, whether you choose to see it or not. No lie marred his mannerisms or his words. He did not know the way. He would never have found our home had my magic not led him. And the…"

Serenity's face was contorted in surprise and fury that finally erupted in, *"You saw the enemy with a map to us? When? Why did you not mention this before?"*

Whisper paled, sinking in on herself, leaving Shadow to answer. *"It was her nightmare just before we left in the night. So strong was the image that it flooded from her mind to mine. There was no way to tell how long ago the scouts crossed the valley, or even if they had done so at the time of Whisper's vision. It revealed only that they would do so. The glimpse of the map in their hands was fleeting, though our home was clear enough."* Shadow hesitated, swallowing. *"And then our home was ablaze. In the vision. You acted so swiftly after her nightmare that we had no time to tell you its details."*

Outside, the sounds of the hunt soon faded, leaving only the drumming rain and howling tempest. Still, the day wore on with little more conversation. Brandel's thoughts swung between the trackers and Whisper's vision. Why would the Red Moon bring so many of the creatures, and what might spook such vile beasts? As for the girl's nightmare… He doubted the cottage appeared on any map save the one revealed in her seeing. Judging from what he learned of his great grandmother's gift of Sight, minor as it was, the map was likely no more than the image presented by Whisper's gift to warn her of the danger descending on them.

For their part, the trio of females kept to themselves, Whisper curled in a blanket next to her aunt, who slept most of the day. Shadow paced the enclosure, frequently stopping to listen. Thrice he watched her tense at some sound beyond the boulder. Each was short-lived, however, returning her to her pacing.

Day at last crept toward dusk. Beyond the cave, the rains continued to fall, water running a curtain between the boulder and the cave entrance and spreading a pool just inside. At least the howl of the winds had died. As darkness deepened, Brandel pushed to his feet, stretching to work out the kinks from sitting too long braced against the damp earthen wall. A quick check of his shirt and jerkin found both cold and wet, still. He tucked them into his saddlebags before undoing the ties around the roll that served as his tent. Setting aside the cooking pot, a pair of spoons, and two small jars, one with salt and the other with pepper, that were rolled within, he spread the thick hemp fabric on the ground. Long knife in hand, he cut a strip to wrap around his cooking items, tying the bundle with a length of rope cut from the line used to hang their clothes. Better to save the rope he carried, lest it be needed for other purposes. The remainder of the fabric he cut into quarters.

Shadow's brow pinched in disapproval. "You are destroying your shelter. We might need it."

"It will serve us better this way. Keep us drier." He tossed a section to her. "The cloth is treated with oil. It is gummy to the touch. But that is what will keep the rain off. Had there been more time before we fled, I might have thought of this sooner."

Serenity nodded her appreciation as he handed a quarter to her and another to Whisper. Pulling her knife, the woman cut the remainder of the rope line into four lengths. With the oiled cloth draped over their heads and packs and leaving enough free for some degree of movement of their arms, the girls used the rope to secure the cloth around their waists. Shadow then assisted Serenity with collecting and delicately repacking the copper-wrapped lumps of coal. With everything stowed in her pack, once more, Serenity wrapped herself and her pack in her quarter of cloth.

Brandel proceeded to saddle Noble, securing the saddlebags and the bundle, then donned his coat and pack, tossing the last piece of fabric around his shoulders. Given that its length barely extended to his waist, he secured it with the rope tied around his pack and chest. At last ready, he once again lifted the girls to the saddle.

Whisper reached a hand to the horse's neck, patting him. "You are a beautiful boy, and very strong." Her quiet comment drew a flick of Noble's head. What she said next, Brandel did not hear, though it prompted the horse to turn and stand waiting at the cave entrance.

"You, can join with the minds of animals?"

"Sort of," the girl acknowledged.

It was a curious reply. Either one could connect with them or they lacked the ability. Receiving no clarification, he took Noble's reins and led him out.

4

anu ignored the relic inside the case, shifting, instead, to the proper angle for studying her reflection in the glass top, smiling at how closely she resembled her Goddess. The white hair was natural, given her age of three hundred years. The magic to retain her fine features and lapis eyes, however, required considerable effort. Worth it, though, as she looked the very image of the statues and paintings. Satisfied, she turned to provide her striking profile for Strongbow, Lord of Brightwater to behold as he stepped from the shadows. She sensed his presence, of course, the moment he entered the compound; felt his anger along her nerves when he slipped into the chapel. Fool! By what right was he angry with her, High Priestess to the Goddess Damsa Dana? He should look on her and be grateful she granted him this meeting. "I warned you."

"You warn." Strongbow's tone was knife edged. "But your warnings are vague, or come too late, or provide no indication of the ultimate consequences of actions taken. You said we should attack the Red Moon raiders on the shores of Turbulence. You did not speak of the horror they brought with them."

Danu spun to face him squarely, her white robes billowing at the sudden motion. "I tell you what the Goddess Damsa Dana, Dancer of Magic, Mother of Light tells me. You were told to wait and strike at first light. You called for the strike at night."

"First light would have put the sun behind our foe and in our eyes. Striking at night gave us the advantage. Or should have done, were it not for those beasts of death, about which you said nothing. Why did the Goddess not tell you of those? Or did you simply fail to mention them? And was it the Goddess who told you that I should send my best soldier on the same fool's errand that already cost me seven other men?"

"The Goddess of the Blood Moon, Breag Nemhain continues to gain strength, as she has done since the deaths of the great heroes. For centuries before you, the Soldiers of Damsa Dana and the Guardians of Ciuin Rose fought to maintain control of the Isle of the Sisters of Sorrow. Your predecessors withdrew and the guardians would not fight alone, so the Red Moon took the isle.

For centuries more the Soldiers of Damsa Dana and the Guardians of Ciuin Rose continued to fight to hold the Fire Islands. Your predecessors withdrew and the guardians would not fight alone, so the Red Moon took them."

"Do not dodge my questions, and do not school me in our history. I know it well. History also teaches that our predecessors believed the followers of Breag Nemhain would be content with taking the Sisters of Sorrow Isle and go no further, therefore saw no reason to continue to waste the lives of our soldiers. They believed the same regarding the Fire Islands. I am not to blame for the short-sighted beliefs of our ancestors or their actions. Still, after each of those withdrawals, Brightwater did see generations of relative peace with only the occasional skirmishes along our coasts. We needed no help from Knife Point. Even when the raids increased, we defended our lands. Have defended Knife Point's border, as well. The warning's offered by your predecessor always granted us ample time to mount our defenses, as did yours, in the beginning."

One hand swiped his graying hair from his eyes. Danu noted how he fought to keep his snarl from his lips.

"You offered no warning to indicate the Red Moon would grow bolder, or that we would not continue to defeat them," Strongbow accused. "You offered belated warnings regarding the assaults on our northern coasts. And you gave no warning of this new menace they bring with them."

"I told you over a year ago this day would come. Begged you to send emissaries to Knife Point asking for their aid in our battles."

"You told me mere days before the Red Moon arrived in numbers far greater than we had ever seen. Only as their warriors overtook our leading forces did you declare that we should send to Knife Point for assistance. What you did not say, what the Goddess apparently failed to tell you, is that men sent to request their aid would not return. The Guardians of Ciuin Rose leave us to continue to defend our lands and theirs alone."

"They did not come because your messengers were too weak or too traitorous to deliver your request. And now the numbers of Damsa Dana's soldiers diminish with each invasion."

The Lord of Brightwater erupted. "We might yet be winning if you had not insisted that I send my best lieutenant off to play messenger. I need him here.

The more so with it plain that the Guardians of Ciuin Rose will sit in the quiet comfort of their lands while we are destroyed."

"They hold no trust in us," Danu hissed. "But your lieutenant can convince them we will not abandon them this time. We fight on our lands. There is nowhere for us to retreat. If we lose, Knife Point will face the Red Moon in their lands and will face them alone."

"They will likely murder the lieutenant, just as they did those who went before him."

"The Guardians of Ciuin Rose murdered no one," Danu growled.

"And you would know this?"

"Do you not think Damsa Dana understands the soul of Her sister? Ciuin Rose would never permit innocent lives to be taken. Far more likely your messengers grew weary of your stupidity and refused to obey your command."

"Careful, Priestess. You tread a thin line."

Danu edged her tone in ice. "High Priestess. Of the Goddess Damsa Dana, Dancer of Magic, Mother of…"

"Do not lecture me on the name of the Goddess, either. I have served Her all the days of my life."

"But it is not to you She speaks. Yes, it was She who told me the lieutenant must travel to Knife Point. If he cannot enlist the guardians, then he must find the Grandmother and bring her to us."

"A myth," Strongbow seethed. "I was a fool to listen to you. There is no such woman. The weapon you seek is a story. It is by our own hands, by our own blood that we must defeat Breag Nemhain's warriors."

"The Soldiers of Damsa Dana are losing."

"Because you fail the Goddess and us. You no longer hold the ability to hear Her voice."

Danu's increasing fury choked through her words. "Do not doubt my abilities, Lord of Brightwater. You are losing because the Soldiers of Damsa Dana lose faith in you and in themselves."

Strongbow's outrage matched her own, the air sparking at the clash of the two. "Do not insult Damsa Dana's soldiers. They fight with courage. You offer late warnings with too little information and no direction."

The High Priestess Danu flared crimson; threat clear in her tight response. "You forget whom you address. I am the…"

"I forget nothing. I remember the numbers of soldiers who have died because of your failure to give us timely and appropriate warnings. Either our Goddess has forsaken us, or you no longer hear Her voice. In your vanity, it is your own desires you hear."

The priestess stiffened, her eyes narrowing to slits as her long strides set her no more than a hand's breadth from the Lord of Brightwater's face. "Now it is you who treads a thin line. Your words are blasphemous. The Goddess Damsa Dana would replace me should She believe me incapable of hearing Her voice or serving Her."

"Would She replace you? Perhaps Damsa Dana is weakened. Perhaps the Goddess of the Blood Moon devoured Her."

Hatred smoldered in Danu's bearing. "Careful, my lord," she grated, venom thick in her words. "Lest your blasphemy bring Her hand down on you where you stand."

"I do not fear the Goddess I serve. Nor am I deaf to the murmurs among our people. They are not blind. Their discontent in you grows. You do not serve the White Moon Goddess, they say. You serve only yourself. Perhaps your days as High Priestess are numbered, and it is you upon whom the Goddess' hand will fall."

The tension igniting the air redoubled as Danu drew on her magic, building a spell to strike him down. Strongbow did not waiver. "I have long anticipated your turning on me and am well prepared to deflect and counter whatever magic you call upon. Test me and I guarantee that you will be the one to suffer. If you should survive, you will be arrested and thrown into the abyss for treason."

The charge of her spell held steady for half a heartbeat before dissolving, Danu's fury still sparking around her.

"Better. Now, High Priestess, I suggest you remain here on the grounds of the temple or in your quarters. The guards are aware of your shortcomings and are loyal to me. Their orders are to kill should you try to leave. They will obey without question. Worship the White Moon Goddess or yourself. I care not which. Should Damsa Danu send you premonitions of some foul event, send word by way of one of the temple priestesses. I am done with you."

Danu fought to control her rage, her hands twitching with the urge to charge a kill spell at Strongbow's back as he strode from the chapel. His warning, however, held truth. The magic of his shielding was too strong. Her strike might well rebound. Chanting words of calm, Danu marched back to the glass case, her gaze, this time, on the relic - a fine silver chain. Legend held that the chain and its missing amulet each held tremendous power; that united, they formed a weapon superior to any the Red Moon might wield; held that only the one called Grandmother possessed the magic to reunite the two. The lieutenant must find this Grandmother. Bring her and the amulet back to Brightwater. Let the old woman mend the weapon. That was the word spoken by Damsa Dana to Danu's mind. And Danu would see it done, even if it meant arranging for Strongbow's demise.

Strongbow strode across the temple grounds without fear. Danu valued her life too highly to attempt his murder on this night. Still, he held no doubt that she would seek some means of eliminating him. *"Damsa Dana,"* he prayed. *"Dancer of Magic, Goddess of the White Moon and Mother of Light, guide me. If this woman remains Your servant, send her visions that will bring us victory. If she serves only herself, take her. Bless another with her position."* Passing through the gate, he absently returned the guard's salute. "Lock her in," he commanded. "The priestesses may come and go. Just be certain the High Priestess does not attempt to disguise herself as one of them."

The guard offered no comment, though his expression suggested he would welcome the opportunity to sink his sword into the woman's heart. This was not the only guard to hold that opinion. There were others, however, who were in the woman's thrall. How many was uncertain. The possibility of split loyalties troubled him. Still, so long as he kept his disputes with Danu out of the public eye, he could count on every soldier following his command.

Unthreading his horse's reins from the hitching post, he led the animal along the dark cobblestone, glancing at each building as they passed. The ground floor shops were closed and darkened, the lamps within the merchants' homes above casting twitchy patches of light through the windows to dance in the warm autumn night shadows. These were his people.

Craftsmen's quarters lay in another part of the town. Those, too, were his people. His manor house lay within Brightwater's primary keep, which stretched between the merchants' and craftsmen's quarters. He spent precious little time at his manor house, of late, his teleportations taking him across the length and breadth of Brightwater to meet with officers and encourage soldiers. The Red Moon Warriors were striking fishing and shipping villages along the full length of the coast, now, and were attacking the farms further inland, depriving his people - those who survived - of food and of goods. The warriors would launch an assault on the capital soon. If Riversong fell…if Riversong Keep fell… the whole of Brightwater would fall.

His jaw tightened. The High Priestess could be thanked for that. He might almost believe that Danu delayed her warnings, limited her information on purpose. "Damsa Dana," he rumbled. "If she serves You no longer, if she is failing our people for her own purposes, You would know this, would You not? I must believe that Your High Priestess harbors no malice toward our people. For me, however, she displays only hatred and contempt. Is it Your wish to replace me? Why would it be so? Always I have served You; served our people in Your name. Why do you pit us, Danu and me, against one another?" His questions went unanswered, for his was not the gift to hear the voice of his Goddess.

At last, he mounted and set his horse in a gallop toward the keep. He would see to reinforcements there, and then set extra guards at Riversong's gates. If Journeyson returns with Guardians of Ciuin Rose, let it be soon. It did not bode well, however, that he could not telepath with the lieutenant. It had been so since Journeyson crossed the border into Knife Point.

5

Brandel squinted against the needling rain, dependent on his shadow sight to track Serenity as he silently cursed the conditions. The dense cloud cover blotted out any possibility of moons or stars confirming his sense that they traveled northwest. Nor did the silhouettes of the surrounding trees offer any suggestion in that regard. His dislike of the woodlands grew with every passing minute. They concealed too much; might, even now, be concealing an ambush.

"You worry over much," drifted delicately through his mind. Whisper's sending.

"What would you know of my worries?"

"Your constant glances to the sky suggest you are concerned about our heading, and your tension indicates you fear enemies in the shadows."

"And you are not worried?"

If there was such a thing as a mental shrug, it came from the girl. *"Nothing hides, here, that does not belong, Master Journeyson. I would know, were it otherwise. As would you unless your senses are too dulled by your worries. To further ease your mind, our journey is taking us to the northwest. The path of the scouts and trackers led due north. With others likely to follow them, it is better that we stay with this path."*

So, his sense of direction had returned. That much was a relief, though the choice of routes was not. *"If my memory of Strongbow's maps is correct, Knife Point Keep lies slightly north and a little east of your home. Our route has already taken us too far afield. It will add time if we continue on this north-westward path. I need to reach the keep as quickly as possible."*

"It will add less time than if we are captured."

"We should separate." This, he directed at Serenity, as well as the girls. *"I can travel faster alone."*

"You suggested as much before," Serenity returned. *"You are wrong. Refusing assistance in reaching the keep is likely why none of the previous messengers ever arrived, Master Journeyson."*

"Those were, as you said, messengers. I am a soldier."

"A soldier of the lowlands. The mountains are treacherous. You cannot ride a straight line to get through them. Which passes will you take? Will you recognize the ice conditions and know when it is safe to cross a frozen slope or body of water? Can you detect the conditions ripe for an avalanche? Do you know where upon the glacial fields the crevasses lie? If you wish to reach your destination, your chances are far greater with us."

"Then I will take one of you with me. The other two should do as I suggested."

Shadow's, *"It is all of us or none,"* hummed a sour note in his mind.

"Fine," he snapped. *"We will do it your way. Just do what you can to shorten the time required."*

The silence that fell wore on him, as did the steady uphill grade of the forest floor, the difficult footing in the soggy vegetation, and the ever-present gnarl of tree roots. Aside from the occasional cry of a wolf in the distance, the only sound was the steady rain through the canopy and the slosh and crackle of their footfalls. Late in the night, a foreboding found a hold in his soul. Something followed, though he detected no real sense of a presence other than that of his companions.

Serenity at last signaled a halt, retracing her steps to speak aloud. "There is a clearing ahead. We skirt it to the left and turn toward the steeper grade. Sunrise will come too soon, and we need to be across the ridge of this hill and well into the valley on the other side before we seek shelter for the day."

Brandel acknowledged with a grunt, though daylight seemed a vague possibility beneath the shroud of forest, cloud, and rain. Mud caked his boots, making each foot rise and fall a weighty prospect and leaving him to marvel at the woman's steady pace. Noble, as well, proved equal to the task. Hard to tell how the two riders fared, huddled as they were within their coats and oiled cloth coverings.

Darkness and rain continued interminably, feeding Brandel's sense of foreboding and prompting many a backward glance. At what hour they finally rounded the crest and picked their way down the other side, he could not guess. Down proved more treacherous than up with the slimy footing of moss, lichen, and rotting vegetation. Even Serenity started showing signs of fatigue, grabbing at passing branches or undergrowth when her feet threatened to slide out from under her. As the pre-dawn light fought to break through, Brandel noted the stoop of the woman's shoulders and the drag of her feet. He was no better. The bite of the moisture laden air mixed with his bone weariness. His joints ached from the climb and the constant twist and shuffle to clear the tangle and watery holes on the forest floor. Nor did reaching the valley provide any respite. The ground was a mire that threatened to strip his boots from his feet, adding to the trial of each step.

"The river is near," Serenity commented when she stopped to survey the ground. "It overtopped its banks, recently." Pointing, she remarked, "There. Another cave lies on that hill. Whisper, can you seek aid in locating it?"

Whisper slid from Noble's back, Shadow immediately behind her. Closing her eyes, the smaller girl stood rock still for several long seconds. When she opened them, she pointed to a nighthawk that circled above them. It swooped and settled briefly on a tangle of vines roughly two-thirds of the way up the slope. Serenity eyed the area in silence, then set out again following a deer trail until it veered off in the wrong direction. From there, she worked her way through fireweed and nettles to reach the vines. Whisper and Shadow followed close behind her while Brandel coaxed Noble up the steep grade. More than once he feared the horse might stumble and break a leg. Sunrise was well past, morning struggling to break through the murk of clouds and fog and mist when he and Noble joined the waiting threesome.

"Hurry," Whisper urged. "The chatter of the birds suggests others are closing the distance behind us."

Serenity held the vines back while they ducked through the low entrance. The ground inside proved much drier than outside. Gently nudging Noble away from the entrance, the woman drew the snarl of vines back into place. "Let us move further back. There is a bend a short distance in. Beyond it, we can light a small fire."

Even with the shadow sight, Brandel found it difficult to make his way without tripping over rocks or scrapping against jagged outcrops along the cave's wall. By his account, the distance was near a kilometer before they rounded the bend. There, Serenity dispensed with the oiled cloth and shrugged out of her pack, digging in its exterior pocket for the precious coals.

"Over there," she indicated, gesturing further in. "There is a store of wood. Bring some if you would, please."

Brandel led Noble back with him, leaving the horse in the alcove where he found chopped and neatly stacked quarters of wood. He deposited an armload on the ground beside the woman even as Whisper delivered kindling from some other darkened nook. It took only minutes for Serenity to ignite a small flame, and scant minutes more for a reasonable blaze to arise.

"We dare no greater flame than this," she said, dropping from her knees to her backside. "It should warm the space enough to provide some comfort, though. And the light is a blessing." Rubbing her temples, she mumbled, "The shadow sight wears on me after a while. Did not used to be so."

Whisper settled next to her aunt, laying a hand on the woman's arm. "You neglect yourself too much, Auntie. Take some time, here, and rest. We can handle the watch. Shadow and I. Master Journeyson needs to rest, as well. He is unaccustomed to foothills and forests. He will need his energy the more once we reach the mountain slopes."

Though the girl made no effort to look across at him, he knew she was keenly aware of his slumped posture. Straightening, he proclaimed, "I am no worse for the wear than anyone else," as he moved toward the entrance. "I will stand the first watch."

Serenity motioned him nearer the fire. "We can neither be seen nor heard from here. And old spells protect the entrance."

"Old spells." Brandel emphasized the age. "Like the one rooted to your home? If that was one of protection, it failed."

Shadow turned a mix of surprise and hostility on him, but anything she might say was cut off by Serenity's raised hand. "Peace, my dear." Meeting Brandel's disgruntled gaze, she said, "The spells worked in and around that house are more than two thousand years old. The home was built and the magic set by Amhranai Fearalite to protect his wife and newborn child - Shadow's and my ancestors."

Brandel's brow shot up. "And the remnants of his spells are still felt in this age?"

Serenity nodded. "His protection remains."

"But your home burned."

"So it would seem. But that which is important remains protected." Her eyes narrowed as she cocked her head. "How is it that you know of the presence of the enchantments?"

"How could I not know of them? The constant drumming of the rhythm is enough to drive one to distraction."

Shadow regarded him with renewed curiosity. "Never before has it been detected by any but those who descended from Amhranai and Emer's line."

Serenity spread her blanket on the ground, her lips pursed in thought. "You have an unexpected gift, Master Journeyson. To detect the carefully concealed spells of Amhranai Fearalite. Perhaps you carry some of his blood?" Before he could deny her conjecture, she curled up on the blanket and closed her eyes. "We all need a bit of sleep. I will leave my mind open to Grandmother."

"Do not bother for a while, yet," Whisper sighed. "There remains at least another night's travel before reaching the flanks of the first peaks. Grandmother will send no indication of where we might find her until we are through the first pass. And then, only if she wishes to be found."

Agitated, Shadow reached for Serenity's pack, rooting through it to retrieve a soggy loaf of bread and a block of cheese. "Here," she offered, eyeing Brandel, again as she broke off pieces and handed them out. "We need to eat. Perhaps we can venture a hunt just before dusk. A little meat would be good."

"No," Brandel objected. "We may be well hidden, here, but the cooking meat would draw the attention of anyone or anything with a sense of smell."

Shadow opened her mouth to protest but was again cut off. "Master Journeyson is right," Serenity agreed. "We will make do with what we have and with foraging, for now."

The girl continued to look as though she might mutiny, at last sucking in on her lower lip and muttering as she shuffled to the wall and sank to the ground. Whisper gave her aunt's arm a gentle squeeze before joining her cousin. Snuggled together, the two wrapped themselves in softly murmured conversation, leaving Brandel to consider returning to the front of the cave.

"I spoke truth," the woman said without rolling from where she lay to face him. "We are safely concealed, here."

"What of the smoke?"

"The draft through the cave carries it to the back, where it vents from the side of the cliff that drops to a lake. As I said before, I am familiar with a good many caves. I chose this one for our rest because it offers certain advantages."

He hesitated a moment more, then headed to the back to remove the saddle and saddlebags from Noble. When he returned to the fire, Serenity was sleeping. The warmth soon had him nodding off, as well, his dreams replaying every weary step of the night, complete with the complaints of his muscles and joints. Whisper's sharp intake startled him awake.

Serenity was on her feet and at the girl's side before Brandel even registered the woman's movement. "What is it, child? What do you see?"

Hushed as it was, tension rang through the girl's voice. "Red Moon scouts. Closing on us. They are moving fast. With them are dark creatures, small and quick, with keen senses."

For several seconds, Serenity stood, her attention not wavering from Whisper. "How far?"

"They are but a short distance askew of our trail."

Serenity's voice tightened. "They have not come so close to discovering the girls since the time of the massacre. I am working a spell to permeate the forest with the scent of smoke and another to spread fear of fire among the animals. May the rush of fleeing creatures turn the beasts about in panic."

Brandel rose and headed for Noble to retrieve his bow and quiver. "Do not go seeking trouble," Serenity warned. "I do not believe they will find us, here. If the spells at the entrance fail and they discover the cave, however, we stand a better chance of killing them by keeping them confined by the narrow bend."

Brandel collected his bow and quiver, none the less, though he returned only so far as the fire, squatting with his eyes fixed on the bend. "What massacre?"

"What?"

"What massacre?" he repeated.

Serenity drew a slow breath, glancing back at the two girls. Returning to the fire, she joined Brandel, settling where she could see both the bend and her two charges. "The first strike came in the Brightwater village where my son and daughter-in-law had traveled. Sudden and deadly— like so many of their attacks. One moment I was standing in my gardens, the next I was overwhelmed with the sense of my son's panic, the flash of murder and bloodshed charging my mind, his infant daughter, Shadow appearing in my arms. Days later, another attack took place, this one in the village where Whisper's family lived. Whisper's mother managed to teleport her newborn daughter to a hiding place and sent to Lord Tine where to find her. He was the one who asked that I care for her, as well." The woman paused, watching the two girls who huddled together, struggling to stay alert, though slumber threatened to overtake them both. "They have been inseparable since; closer than sisters. They look out for one another; confide in each other."

Brandel shot a glance back at the pair. Snuggled together, the two sat with backs propped against the cave wall, their eyes closed, though the tension in their bodies suggested sleep was failing them. "I am sorry Shadow lost her family in our lands. Which village was it? And Whisper's family?"

"The village where Whisper's family lived was called Cradle. It sat in a valley surrounded on three sides by the Song Mountains. I do not know what became of the lowland village. Golden, it was called. But Whisper's village was annihilated."

"Golden." Brandel eyed Serenity with doubt. "That village was wiped out some twenty years or so ago." Perhaps he was off in his reckoning. Or Serenity could be mistaken regarding the name of the Brightwater village. Twenty years was too long ago for either girl to have been a baby at the time of that raid and slaughter. "You say the two villages were attacked within days of each other?"

"Aye."

"We were unaware that Knife Point suffered from Red Moon intrusions. We believed your southern coast too treacherous for their ships."

"They did not come from our coast, but from Brightwater's, crossing the southern border and moving into the mountains from there."

Brandel wished he could doubt her words but knew she spoke truth. So much for the High Priestess Danu's claim that the Soldiers of Damsa Dana protected Knife Point. "Were the attacks coordinated, I wonder. I mean, given the tremendous distance separating the two villages, that they would fall under attack in such close succession."

He was unsurprised by Serenity's lack of response. She could not, after all, know the plans of the enemy. More likely, the timing was coincidence.

"The girls are fortunate you took them in and sheltered them in so remote an area. I am sorry I led the Red Moon to your doorstep. That was never my intention." Brandel's gaze drifted to the girls, once more. "They are fortunate, as well, that their abilities include a magic for each that grants some degree of concealment." He wondered what other gifts they held, or if they were still too young for other attributes to manifest.

"Do not be fooled, Master Journeyson. Young, they may be, but not so much as you think. Each is past her twentieth year. And I was not mistaken in the name of the village. Golden, it was." The woman exhaled in a weary huff. "Keeping them hidden has prevented them from growing sophisticated in the way of other young women who grow up within the social settings of family and village. That and their beginning has left them less than trusting of others. Or at least Shadow is. Whisper reads people with more clarity. If she did not trust you, she would not have convinced Shadow to allow you into our home."

"Her trust was misplaced," he snorted. "I drew the hounds into the woods."

"Perhaps. They were coming, in any event. Was only a matter of time. It is no curiosity that the attacks on the two villages occurred in such a close time frame. It is the girls the Red Moon wants."

"Do not tell him more." Shadow's mumble rippled as she shot a bleary-eyed glare across to her grandmother. "It is not his business."

"That one still does not trust me," Brandel snorted.

Serenity cocked her head. "As you still do not trust us. Not entirely."

"Shall we share more about ourselves in an effort to achieve greater trust?" The hint of sarcasm carried in Brandel's tone, though he admitted privately that knowledge was always a good thing. Still, he was not inclined to speak about himself.

"No need," Serenity replied, stretching and laying back. "You come from the plains and are a Soldier of Damsa Dana. We are a family from the foothills of Knife Point. That is sufficient for now. And I must take more sleep. If you insist on keeping an eye to the entrance, Master Journeyson, do it from where you are. You would be better served, however, to sleep, as well. Whisper will warn us if any approach the cave."

6

Brandel's restless slumber delivered dreams with no images, just voices challenging one another. Whose voices and what their argument involved was unclear, but the tension and hostility troubled him. Serenity woke him perhaps an hour past dusk, the impression of heated animosity still clinging to his nerves as he scanned the darkness. The fire was extinguished, the cave grown cold, again. The girls sat astride Noble, their oiled clothes draped over their heads and packs. Guilt replaced the edge to his nerves as he noted his belongings were stowed, as well, the saddlebags and the bundle secured, his piece of oiled cloth on the ground next to him.

Scrambling to his feet, he snatched his coat and pack, tugging the cloth around his pack and shoulders once more. "Why did you not wake me earlier?"

"Do not begrudge yourself rest when you need it," Serenity admonished, handing Noble's reins to him as she moved past.

The night carried a sharper sting than the previous ones. Stars glistened faintly in the clear sky, their light muted by the three moons, each in some aspect of waning. Highest, the light of Breag Nemhain's moon filtered through the breaks in the trees, grotesquely coloring the thin fog. The Red Moon Warriors often attacked encampments of the Soldiers of Damsa Dana on nights like this. Brandel turned to face east. His men were out there - somewhere - fighting. He should be with them, not here on foreign soil, sneaking through the nights in the company of three civilian females.

"It will be difficult," Serenity was saying.

The encroachment of her voice on the still air jerked Brandel's attention around to seek for her in the darkness. She stood on a small rise, pointing through the trees at a ridge washed by the bloody moon. Difficult? Difficult is following his lord's command against his better judgment, the more so given his suspicion that assigning this task to him was Danu's doing. Still, the order came from Strongbow. He was duty and honor bound to see it through.

"We must climb," Serenity said. "But the way is hidden beneath the brambles and is soft with the rotting leaf litter. Mind neither Noble nor you catch an ankle in the snarl or break one stepping in a hole. Once we reach the top, we descend to the west to cross the valley between this rise and the last of the foothills. Our climb will begin in earnest, then." She considered for a moment, eyeing the sky. "The temperature is dropping. I fear we will encounter snow, soon. A trader's abode lies along our route. We will rest there. Perhaps he will allow us to obtain more appropriate clothing and supplies before we push deeper into the mountains."

Brandel silently cursed himself for an idiot. His intention at the outset of this mission was to cross the border and penetrate only so far as the oak forest shown on Strongbow's map. Patrols of guardians were said to pass through there frequently. He would intercept one and request of the guardians that they teleport him to Knife Point Keep, or at least to outside its gates. There, he would, as an emissary from the Lord of Brightwater, request an audience with the Lord of Knife Point, would deliver Strongbow's call for aid, and teleport himself back to the barracks in Riversong. Strongbow's information, however, proved inaccurate. According to the girls, no patrol of guardians had passed through that area in a fair while.

So. Here he was, in the cold and rain with snow in the offing, and his winter clothes back in Brightwater. He was a soldier. An officer. He knew better than to count on initial plans succeeding. What got into his head to leave him so ill prepared? As if to emphasize his lack of forethought, the wind picked up, the moons disappearing behind a rushing layer of clouds. The frigid bite sliced against his exposed face and stung his hands while the wet from their long, soggy march seeped through his boots, bathing his feet in an icy soak. Progress was plodding, the grade ever steepening, his back and legs protesting the strain of leaning into the climb. Why anyone should choose to live in such a land was a mystery. Even Brightwater's rocky coast offered less challenge and less rain than this interminable upward, wet slog.

Brandel's disgust rumbled in a low growl. Perhaps the Soldiers of Damsa Dana should cease patrolling the border. Let more warriors cross into Knife Point. Let weather and the terrain take their toll and the Guardians of Ciuin Rose defeat what was left.

Shame and guilt immediately singed his mind. That was not the way of the Soldiers of Damsa Dana. They fought to protect their land and Knife Point. He regarded the matter as atonement for their ancient predecessors' abandoning the guardians, first in the war for the Isle of the Sisters of Sorrow, and a couple of centuries later, in the war for the Fire Islands. It further shamed him to learn that warriors were crossing Brightwater's border into Knife Point, despite the High Priestess Danu's assurances to the contrary. While the numbers of warriors might be small, for now, if the guardians refused to join them in this war, Brightwater would not be able to hold back the tide. The Red Moon troops would pour into Knife Point. Then it would be more than a scattered village or two coming under attack. Cradle was a tragic but small price they paid for their inattentiveness. The new assaults would be far more horrendous.

"They are not inattentive, Master Journeyson," Serenity declared, turning on him. "Nor have the Guardians of Ciuin Rose ever been so. Our border with Brightwater is long, our southern coast exposed, the terrain, as you have noticed, is difficult, and our guardians stretched thin. And before you curse me for reading your thoughts, your shielding has dropped, again. Exhaustion and lack of oxygen can do that."

"Not to me. I have fought many a long battle without…"

"This is a different kind of battle. One with which you are unfamiliar. You are out of your element, here, and not in control of the path you take. Guilt gnaws at you for leaving your men. You question the reasons you were chosen to come here. The cold and wet bites through your flesh. Your muscles cry out, unaccustomed as they are to the rigors of hill and mountain." Her dark eyes fixed him with a stare that dared him to debate the matter as she finished with, "You do not think clearly, Master Journeyson, because, in addition to fatigue, your lungs and brain struggle for oxygen as we climb."

Brandel resented the woman's assessment, though he could not argue with her findings. Her quiet harrumph grated on him, as well, until he noted and followed her shifted gaze. The crest was, at last, only a few more meters above them. There was, however, no relief in reaching it. Once arrived, they caught the full force of the bitter wind. Moreover, the open terrain left their silhouettes against the night sky exposed to searching eyes. Serenity quickened their pace, scrubs and wet grasses catching at her pant legs, then slapping back against Brandel's. He was surprisingly grateful when they descended the high ridge to re-enter the woods.

Descending, Serenity, too, was again showing signs of fatigue, her pace slowing, her shoulders stooped beneath her pack.

Halfway down, a vision of darkness so intense and filled with such terror froze Brandel mid step. Noble screeched, jerking back and stripping the reins from his grasp. He grabbed for them, his free hand going to his knife hilt. A few paces lower, Serenity stood rooted, staring anxiously back up the hill at the girls. Whisper sat rigid in the saddle; her unblinking gaze fixed on the empty air.

"What is it?" Shadow sent.

Serenity, too, waited for an answer. When none came, the woman gestured toward the forest canopy. Shadow nodded her understanding and slid from Noble's back, then shinnied up the nearest tree trunk, disappearing among the shadows and branches. Whisper remained mounted, now trembling, her gaze still locked on the ether.

"What do you see?" Serenity pressed.

"Darkness that does not belong," came the response. Whisper's eyes refocused, her expression fearful. *"Perhaps Shadow can tell more from above."*

The woman considered with pursed lips, *"We should move on. Shadow will have no difficulty following us."*

Brandel's nerves remained on edge. Though he sensed no presence other than that of his small company, the feel of malevolence weighed on him. He could not fault Noble's reluctance to move. Standing about, however, was not likely to be any safer. Fingers wrapped through Noble's bridle, Brandel urged the animal forward.

Less than another hundred meters ahead of them, Shadow slipped from the canopy, shooting a glance over her shoulder before approaching the others. "Whatever was here is gone, now."

"Do you know what or who it was?" Serenity asked.

A shiver took the girl as she shook her head. "I cannot say what they were. Their magic is alien to me. Viler, even, than a tracker. I think perhaps there are two or three of them, though."

Brandel's hand tightened on the hilt of his knife. "The magic is too strong for them to have gone. Perhaps they are using a spell to conceal themselves."

"It was dark magic they used." The music in Shadow's voice reflected her unease, her tone weighing on each word. "Where they passed, the woods shriveled. I saw the remains of squirrels, a rabbit, and two does, withered and ashen on the path they left." She leveled her midnight eyes on Brandel. "They are not here, though. Judging from their trail, they are moving toward the pass. We should turn back. Find another route."

Serenity took a measured breath. "It may not be safe for us to proceed, but I do not believe it is safe to go back, either."

"I am going on," Brandel declared. "You three should seek shelter with a friend, if you know any in this area."

Serenity grasped his arm to prevent his lifting Whisper from Noble's back. "We travel together, Master Journeyson. Those sent before you failed to complete this journey. Grandmother asked that we see you reach Knife Point Keep."

"Sketch a map showing the route from this location. I will follow it."

"If you do not fall off a cliff or freeze to death," Shadow sniffed. "Or get swept away in an avalanche. And you will never find Grandmother without us."

Brandel scowled, shooting glances into the surrounding darkness. Arguing was likely to get him nowhere. And he might well need their help in reaching the keep. "Fine. We go on together. Shadow, can you watch for signs of the creatures from above? That should allow us to avoid them."

Shadow gave an indignant harrumph. "Of course, I can!"

Serenity eyed the girl with concern. "Are you certain you are up to traveling in the trees to guide us?"

"Better in the treetops than down here." With that, she was lost to the night, once more. Even straining his shadow sight, Brandel caught no glimpse of her, nor any movement among the branches so long as she did not speak.

"None can find her," Whisper said. "Not if she wishes to remain hidden within the shadows. It has always been so. It is how she came by her name."

"And yours?" Brandel returned. "Why do you speak so softly?"

The girl did not answer. Instead, Serenity gestured them on saying, "Shadow will send to us if we need to alter our direction. As it is, we may eventually need to cross where the creatures passed. She says their magic is fading. May it dissipate entirely before we arrive."

"I can go into the trees to help watch for signs of them, too," Whisper offered. Her fretful expression, however, indicated she preferred staying with Noble.

Serenity shook her head. "You need to keep your mind open to any warnings that Shadow may not be able to detect. Better if you do not have to split your attention between that and working your way through the canopy."

The relief in the girl's features was obvious. Laying her hand gently along the side of his Noble's neck, she murmured, "Let us do this together, then, shall we?"

SLIEVGALLION: THE GODDESS WARS

The flicking of Noble's ears settled to perked forward, the horse allowing Brandel to lead him, once again.

As they climbed toward a saddle between two rounded crests, the snarl of roots and forest litter lessened. On the back side of the saddle, the way dropped perhaps a hundred meters, then began climbing again. The forest through which they traveled changed from a mix of deciduous and evergreen to mostly evergreen, the grade now necessitating a switch-backing route. In addition to the steep grade and the forest detritus, pockets of mud once again sucked at their feet, marking an increased number of trickling streams that cut rivulets through the decomposing vegetation. Now and again came the rush and roar of a waterfall or the drone and splash of a nearby river. Serenity kept their march parallel to one such watercourse for a fair distance, finally breaking from the woods to stand at the edge of an embankment that dropped several meters to raging water. Through the night-shrouded trees, Brandel made out the outline of a bridge some distance upslope.

Again, Noble balked, jerking the reins from Brandel's hand. Ears once more flicking back and forth and with lip curled, the horse snorted several times. Brandel retrieved the reins, turning to study the dark landscape.

"There," Serenity indicated, with a nod in the direction of the bridge.

A sliver of red moonlight broke through the cloud cover long enough for him to see it - a strip of trail darker than the surroundings that ran from the woods onto the bridge. Gripping the reins, Brandel urged the horse forward, Noble's snorts increasing.

"Ssshhhh," Whisper encouraged, though even she had difficulty calming the animal. Little more than ten meters from the path leading to the bridge, Noble screeched, pulling backwards, his tail curled tight against his backside.

"This is close enough," Brandel said. For as far along the path as could be seen, everything once living now lay withered and dead.

"Shadow!" Serenity sent. *"What do you make of this magic? Can we risk taking the bridge?"*

"I cannot say what risk lies on it."

Brandel glanced from the river to the opposite bank. *"Are the creatures near?"*

"No. As I said before, they are gone. I am worried about their direction of travel, though."

Serenity's agreement showed in her tightened lips.

"I will not take Noble across that bridge," Brandel determined. "Can we backtrack to find another way across?"

SLIEVGALLION: THE GODDESS WARS
42

"Not for many leagues," Serenity said. "And we are going to require heavier clothing sooner rather than later, I think. We need to seek shelter at the trader's home."

Running a hand over his mouth in thought, Brandel eyed the water and the opposing bank once more, catching glimpses of fish splashes as they darted through the water beneath the bridge. "Then I will cross Noble through the river. I can lead him under the bridge and come up on the other side of the trail the creatures left."

Serenity grasped his arm. "We cannot tell how deeply the dark magic extends. Perhaps it carries down to the river. And the waters are too dangerous, in any event. Deep, frigid, and swift. Join with your animal. Use your will to calm him. Better to stay on dry land and cross the bridge quickly."

"No." Brandel's refusal was absolute. "Send Whisper into the trees to see if she and Shadow can find a way to cross through them. Join them if you can. Or tread the bridge if you wish. Noble and I will take to the water."

"I am not leaving Noble." The strength of Whisper's declaration was almost enough to grant normal volume to her words. Almost.

Serenity looked about to protest further but swallowed it. "I will cross the river with you, then. I have not the youth, agility, nor the proper attributes to take to the trees. Nor do I like the darkness of this magic any more than your horse. If you are so adamant about keeping him from the bridge, then I will follow your lead."

The path down to the water's edge proved daunting. The slope was both unstable and slimy. Any concern Brandel might have had about leaving clear tracks in the mud, however, began to wash away with the return of the rain.

"Hold," he called. Feet planted at the water's edge, he surveyed the river and the opposite bank. The crash of a waterfall could be heard some distance downslope, though it was impossible to tell how far. If any lost their footing, they would be swept away and over the falls. Squinting into the rising fog, Brandel located a large tree on the bank diagonally across from them. Handing the reins to Serenity, he rummaged in one of Noble's saddlebags until he found his coil of rope. Again, he eyed his chosen target, measuring out a length from the coil and cutting it. Retrieving an arrow from where his quiver was attached to the other bag, he knotted one end of the rope to the shaft, working a silent spell to prevent it releasing. Taking his bow from its attachment, he aimed and shot. The distant sound of the thunk told him his aim was true and that the arrow was well sunk in the wood. Still, he tested its hold, tightening the line before securing it to a massive root that wound its way down the bank.

"Here." Brandel exchanged the remaining length of rope for Noble's reins. "Loop this end over the anchor line, then fasten it around your waist." He handed the reins up to Whisper, then knotted a section of the rope to Noble's saddle before securing the remainder to himself.

Raising a concerned glance to Whisper as he replaced his bow on the saddlebag and tightened the binding to it and to his quiver, he urged, "Wrap the reins around your wrists and tie them tight to the saddle horn. Then hang on with all your might. Do not let go until we are safely on land, again. Understand?"

Whisper gave a dismissive sniff. "Of course, I understand. I will be fine." The subtle waiver in her soft assurance, however, betrayed her attempt at confidence.

Before Brandel could offer any further advise, Serenity plunged into the water, losing her footing with the first step. Slammed backward into Brandel and then Noble, she fought for balance, at last setting her feet beneath her and using her grasp of the anchor line to drag herself forward.

Brandel marveled at the woman's strength and determination. The effort to remain upright, pulling himself along while periodically catching and supporting Serenity and urging his frantic horse forward wore on him, further straining already fatigued muscles. Whisper, too, struggled, the rush and weight of the water beating against her legs threatening to tear her from her perch. Thrice, he grabbed at the girl's ankle and tugged her back. It seemed hours before they reached the far side. Brandel untied the rope from his waist and dropped to the bank, his energy spent, his body shivering uncontrollably.

"We nnneed to rreach the traders abbbode," Serenity stammered. *"Shadow? Are you with us, still?"*

Several uneasy seconds passed before the reply came, thin and exhausted. *"No thanks to the distance I had to travel to find a narrow enough section of river for tree branches from each side to come close to meeting. The jump was frightening. And then I had to locate living trees on either side of the dead path that were close enough for another jump. Equally frightening. But yes. I am here. Drier than you, but not by much, I would guess. Damn this rain! The oil cloth kept slipping from my head and I very nearly lost my hold and footing to end up in the river without any anchor."*

"I had every faith in you., my dear. And do not curse the elements. It is not their fault that we are caught out here."

"*Well,*" Shadow grumbled. "*I am not going to offer them praise unless they relent and give us a little dryness and warmth.*"

"*We must look elsewhere for that.*"

"And that would be?" Brandel managed from where he lay on the muddy bank.

"With the trader."

Brandel's experience with traders was minimal, at best, and he preferred to keep it that way. The ones that visited the lowlands with their pelts and leathers rarely charged a reasonable price for their goods, and always offered too little for the supplies they purchased. The merchants of Riversong cursed them, though they bought the furs and hides, anyway. The idea of seeking shelter from a man of such questionable character did not sit well. The more so, given the hint of doubt in the woman's words. Still, what choice did they have? If they continued with soaked clothing and the winds rising once more, the girls, at least, might not survive.

Shadow's low growl running through his mind suggested he left his thoughts unguarded, again. Fatigue was making him careless. Pushing to his feet, he ran his hand over Noble's neck, noting for the first time since clearing the river that Whisper still sat astride the horse, huddled close and shivering fiercely. "I hope this trader friend of yours has a fire burning and a barn with feed."

Serenity shrugged. "I cannot ssay what he has, these days. We shall fffind what we shall fffind. We just cannot sstay where we are."

"Agreed." Straightening Brandel reached to untie the reins from the saddle horn and unwind them from Whisper's wrists. Her attempted smile of thanks proved little more than a quiver. Turning to Serenity, he waved her on.

The woman's estimation of distance seemed to fall far short of reality, their slow and trudging march dragging on into the wee hours of morning. Moreover, Brandel would have missed the cabin altogether had it not been for Serenity's signal to hold. The small stone structure nestled beneath the trees was all but lost in the thickening gloom.

"Wait here," the woman instructed.

"*Let me,*" Shadow sent from somewhere.

"*If Bear still uses this place, he will likely not remember you. He saw you only twice, the last time at least seven years ago. He will remember me, though.*" Squaring her shoulders, Serenity strode toward the cabin without caution, making herself as conspicuous as possible. No sound or stir came from the structure. Nor was there any indication of light in the windows. The woman did not hesitate when reaching the door, knocking as she entered. For a moment she was gone from sight, then reappeared, gesturing them forward, her eyes scanning their surroundings.

Brandel halted Noble next to the short front stoop and lifted Whisper from the saddle, setting her on unsteady legs on the steps. "Let me take care of your horse." Shadow's voice suddenly at this back startled Brandel, spinning him around, his hand to his knife. The girl took him in with mocking amusement. "You do not sense or recognize my presence, Master Journeyson? Your abilities are feeble."

"Shadow!" her grandmother reprimanded. "Mind your manners. You know better." Glancing at Brandel, she suggested, "Let her take the horse. She knows where to hide him and can tend to him." With that, she turned and led the way inside. Whisper remained on the steps, trembling so severely her knees threatened to give way. Brandel handed the reins to Shadow, then scooped Whisper up and carried her inside, kicking the door shut. The cottage consisted of a single room. A small table and one chair occupied its center, with a cupboard standing along one wall. Everything was covered in a thick layer of dust. Tattered curtains hung in the two windows, one on each side of the room.

"It appears your friend has not been here for some time."

"Perhaps," Serenity responded as she headed to the back, murmuring a few words and running a hand over the wall. A moment later, a panel slipped back to reveal a tight and empty closet. Stepping into the space, Serenity dropped to her knees, extending a hand close to the dirt floor, a thin light glowing from her fingertips. "Reveal and yield," she stated.

The dirt floor trembled as a latch raised from beneath it. Serenity brushed the dirt away, then struggled to lift the heavy cover to which it was attached. Brandel set Whisper down next to the wall and squeezed into the closet. "Let me."

The woman nodded, rising to move aside. "Just lift as quietly as possible. I do not wish to alarm the woodland creatures who might give warning of our presence."

"Give warning to whom?"

"Whomever may be near enough to hear."

Brandel huffed at the stupidity of his question, then leaned into raising the hatch. The muffled grate of metal on metal filled the little cubicle, despite his efforts at silence. Relieved when the sound ceased, he straightened to regard the black hole before him.

S erenity nudged Brandel to one side. "I will go down, first, and deal with Bear if he is home."

Muffled by dust, her footfalls faded as she descended into the pitch abyss. The long minutes of waiting with no sound other than his and Whisper's breathing had Brandel's hand to the hilt of his knife. At last, some distance below, a light flickered, giving pale definition to the outline of the woman standing at the base of the steep stairs. Gesturing for them to join her, she disappeared once more.

Brandel ushered Whisper down ahead of him. "Slide the wall panel back into place," Serenity called back. "And close the hatch as you come down." With one final glance around the small cabin from inside the cubical, he slid the wall panel back until it caught with a click, then carefully lowered the metal cover as he descended the steps.

"You can bolt it from this side, as well," Serenity advised, the light in the underground room growing.

"What of Shadow?"

"She knows another entrance."

With the bolt secured, Brandel completed his descent, the smell of damp earth and mold heavy in the air. "What is this place?"

"Bear's home. It seems you were correct, though." She swept a hand over the dusty table where a large oil lamp now burned brightly. "He has not been here in a good while. Perhaps he left for one final hunt in the mountains before winter. I do not like making myself at home or using his stores in his absence. He is not a particularly sharing sort of individual. But we need a safe place to dry our clothes and warm ourselves before we seek a friend near the pass."

"I would not worry about making use of anything of Bear's," Shadow sang in an edgy undertone from deep within the darkness at the back of the underground abode. "I found his blackened and withered body along with that of his mule not far from the entrance to his storehouse and stable. He was returning from a hunt, I think. The mule was laden with furs. None of them are fit for use, now." Stepping into the light, the girl shed both the oiled cloth and her coat, shaking them out and hanging them from a peg on the stone wall. "The entrance remains hidden, though. And none of the stores appear to have been disturbed. Nor do I detect any magic about the place beyond the faint remnants of Bear's. I brushed Noble down, gave him a blanket and some feed and water. He is warm and safe. I dare say more warmth, here, would be nice."

Serenity handed her wrap and coat over to the girl stating, "Working on it," before heading to a crib piled with wood. "And Spirit?" she asked, layering kindling and a few chopped quarters in a large, flattopped stove set against the wall behind the table.

"No sign of her." Shadow sucked at her lip, her brow curled down as she eyed Brandel.

"Why are you looking to me?" he asked, searching out another peg on which to hang his dripping oiled cloth and coat. "I know no one by that name. They probably fled in terror." He turned to Serenity with a second question. "Are you sure about setting a fire? The smoke could draw some unwanted attention."

"Spirit would never flee in terror," Shadow snipped. "And she is not a person. She is a wolf. A beautiful white one. And fearless. My bet is that she is hunting those foul creatures. I thought you might reach out. Try to connect with a wolf from a local pack to see if..." Her voice trailed off, dying in a flat tone. Heaving a sigh, she said, "Never mind. You refuse to use your magic, and I doubt Spirit will align with any pack. At least, not for a while."

Her grandmother straightened to watch the flames ignited by the sparks from her fingertips catch in the kindling and the wood's splintered surfaces. "Let us hope Spirit is not chasing those creatures, or she may suffer the same fate as Bear. As for the smoke, Master Journeyson..."

"Brandel. Just Brandel."

"Master Brandel," Serenity corrected. "Bear constructed the venting to carry smoke and its scent far from here. While the Red Moon Warriors have not set foot in this part of our lands for many years, their scouts have been sighted many times. They have never discovered this place." The slump of the woman's shoulders came with her weary sigh. "Had not. The warriors had not set foot. But they are here, now. I mourn the loss of Bear. But I am grateful for his vigilance in maintaining this place."

"This place." Whisper's tone reflected her sorrow. Glancing around, Brandel found the little redhead holding out a clean shirt, pants, and thick socks, her eyes downturned. "Bear will not be needing these." As Brandel took the items, she slipped around him to stand next to her aunt, adding, "You are not likely a modest sort, Master Journeyson, but I would prefer you change further back in the passage, please."

"The passage. The one Shadow just came in through? It leads to where Noble is tucked away, I take it."

"Aye."

Brandel draped the dry clothing over an arm and headed back along the drafty tunnel, regretting almost at once leaving the growing warmth and light of the living quarters. The way was long, winding, and narrow enough in places to prevent two people walking abreast. When he finally wandered out into the stable, Noble greeted him with a nervous whinny, butting his head against Brandel's shoulder.

"Glad to see you, too," Brandel returned, giving Noble's nose a gentle rub. His quick assessment assured him for a second time that Shadow was thorough in her care of the animal. Not only was he brushed and draped with a dry wool blanket, the feed and water troughs were filled, and fresh straw from a stack of bales was spread in his stall. Satisfied, Brandel at last changed from his soaked clothes. Being a fairsized man, himself, he was surprised at the more than ample fit. Bear's name, it seemed, was aptly applied.

Stuffing the shirt inside the loose pants, he cinched his belt to take up the excess, then sat to pull his socks and boots back on. The shock and charge of the horse's sudden mental connection tossed him over backward, the sense of the animal's hyper-alertness and fear rippling across Brandel's nerves, the scent of a predator thick in his nostrils.

Brandel was back on his feet in less than a heartbeat, eyes narrowed and mind focused as he scanned the stable. The small structure appeared to be dug into the earth, wooden beams bracing the dirt walls and ceiling. His saddlebags were draped over the railing of a second stall, too far for a sprint to gather his bow and quiver while maintaining a focus on the steep, ramped incline that led up to a thick snarl of blackberry vines at the timbered entrance. Why was everything underground with these people?

Noble's rising panic struck him another painful jolt. Predator! Close. Squaring himself with the entrance, his feet braced, Brandel grasped the hilt of his long knife. As the tip cleared its sheath, the massive head of a white wolf poked in through the tangle of vines. The wolf bared its teeth, its growl a low rumble. Clearing the entrance, it moved deliberately, its head lowered, body tensed for a lunge, fur bristling, blue-gray eyes like a brewing storm fixed on him.

White wolf. The one belonging to Bear? The one Shadow referred to as Spirit? The wolf's ears pricked back, uncertainty infecting the tension in her shoulders. Had she detected his thoughts? How could she? He had not opened his mind to her, though he realized it remained open to Noble.

"Spirit," he said aloud. Another rumbling growl accompanied her poised tension, the wolf still eyeing him, now with almost as much nervous anxiety as menace. Perhaps she looked for Bear.

The images slammed him. A huge man with a barrel chest and massive arms, his skin and thick hair dark as night. With the images came a perception of commitment, of trust. Uncertainty again shivered through Brandel's senses emanating from the wolf's consciousness. Aware that he was now wearing the dead man's clothes, Brandel steeled himself, holding his ground as the wolf ventured a cautious approach, her eyes never leaving him. Sniffing the shirt and pants from a good pace away, she gave a mournful howl, then spun and bolted back up the ramp and out.

Brandel remained frozen, not daring to turn away and only just daring to breathe. Where had she gone? Would she return? If she ran with a pack... Sucking a deep breath and letting it out slowly, Brandel forced his mind to open beyond the connection with his horse, setting his feet against the shock and cacophony of the feral 'voices' that assaulted him. Birds. Fox. Rodents of all varieties. Deer. Elk. Bear. Wolverine. Cougar. Bobcat. Anything that walked or crawled within a dozen kilometers of him rushed and scorched along his senses. On and on, each creature as startled as he by the sudden presence they felt; each darting away as they shut him out until...

The charge slammed him again. The white wolf. She, however, did not start at his intrusion. Nor did she shut him out or flee. With a wary tolerance, she observed, feeling him out as he probed her awareness. Brandel's jaw clenched. The wolf was aware of the entrance to the stable. She likely knew her way around the trader's underground abode, as well. Not a comforting thought.

Another consciousness edged along the joining, charging his nerves with searing pain that carried the horrific impact of a dark malevolence. Brandel's joining jarred shut, his senses still on fire. Noble's screech accompanied the animal's rearing panic, his hooves driving down on the stall's railing and shattering it. Staggered, Brandel grabbed for the bridle, barely snaring it in his fist and jerking the animal's head toward him. "Sssshhh! Quiet! Noble!"

The effort to calm himself was almost more than he could muster but was necessary before he could soothe his horse. It seemed an eternity before both were sufficiently under control for Brandel to experience more than Noble's snorting breath or the roar of his own blood in his ears. At last, the crashing of his heart gave way to a steadier pulse and the ability to listen for other sounds; feel for other presences. There was nothing. Only an unsettling and deep stillness. Swallowing, Brandel took time to pull on his second boot before collecting his saddle and saddlebags. These, he tossed loosely over Noble's back along with his wet clothes. Snatching his bundle that stood propped against the wall, and with nerves still raw from his joining with horse and wolf…and whatever that other thing had been… he led Noble as stealthily as possible through the tunnel to Bear's living quarters.

8

Shadow met him halfway along the tunnel, wild-eyed and frantic, the discord in her voice raking Brandel's frayed nerves. "What was that! What did you do?"

Brandel shot a hasty glance back over his shoulder. "Can we block off this passage? Is there another way to escape?"

The girl's dark eyes narrowed as she planted herself in front of him. "For us, yes. The same way you got in. With your horse? No. Nor is there any way to seal this off short of bringing it down on top of us." Fists clenched, she hissed, "What did you do?"

"The white wolf. Our minds…" Brandel pushed past her. "We joined. For a moment. She found the way into the stable."

Shadow rounded on him. "Spirit? Of course, she did. She is…" Disbelief rang through the girl's words. "She was Bear's companion and…and protector. She would never! Spirit would never join with you. Only Bear. No one else. Ever."

"The wolf joined with me," he declared, side stepping her. "Briefly. Until…"

Dodging back around, Shadow set her feet again, her fists jabbed to her hips. "Until what?"

"Until…until something else pressed in."

"Pressed in?"

Again, he pushed her aside. "I broke the joining. Now, tell me how we can leave. That wolf may come back."

"What pressed in?" Shadow persisted chasing after his lengthening stride.

"I do not know." In truth, he had a dark suspicion.

The warmth and light from the living quarters met him as he cleared the last bend. Serenity sat on the edge of a cot, a hand grasping Whisper's. The little redhead lay unmoving, her color ghostly, her eyes fixed in an unblinking stare at the earthen ceiling. Brandel thrust Noble's reins backward at Shadow, though he did not wait to verify whether she took them. "What happened? What is wrong with her?"

Serenity rose, turning on him. "You tell me, Master Journeyson."

"He says…" Shadow left Noble where he stood to place herself between Brandel and her grandmother. "He says he joined with Spirit. And something else joined with them."

Serenity stood motionless, her features unreadable. "Spirit would never permit a joining with another human. Only with Bear. Why would she let you in?"

"Maybe because she scents her master on me now that I wear his clothes. What does it matter? We need to gather whatever supplies we can carry and get away from here. The wolf knows the way in, and she may be less curious and hungrier the next time. Can the girl be moved?"

"I can move myself," came the soft murmur. Whisper ventured a slow, shaky breath, then pushed to an unsteady elbow. At least her color was returning.

Serenity tried to ease her back. Whisper resisted. "Master Journeyson is right. We need to leave. But not because of Spirit. The creatures have doubled back in search of us. They will find us if we stay."

Swinging her legs to dangle over the cot's edge, she studied Brandel, her lips pinched, her brow drawn down. At length, she stood, teetering a little, but batting Serenity's hands away as the woman tried to push her back. "I am fine. Just give my head a minute to put the world right, again."

To Brandel's mind drifted her delicate, "*I do not understand you, sir. You say you do not like using your gift but apply it at perhaps the worst possible of times.*"

"What would you know of the appropriate times for joining?" he barked.

The girl sighed. "I can join with a few creatures. Birds, mostly. Still, I seem to have an empathic connection to Spirit. She is a friend. I was able to sense the power of your connection with her. Never has she allowed anyone other than Bear to do that. There is more than Bear's clothing that draws her to you, I think. Something about yourself." A shudder swept her. "I also felt her panic when another energy touched your mind. A dark and dangerous energy. You connected with the vile creatures that killed Bear, did you not? Why would you do that?"

"I do not know what it was that connected with us. It was certainly not by my initiation."

A soft rumble found its way from the girl's throat as she turned from him. "But you left your mind open for it."

Serenity stepped back, allowing Whisper to pass, headed for two long tables at the back of the space. Furs were stacked on each table. Behind them, tools of a tanner and fur trader hung on the wall. For several minutes, Whisper fingered through the furs on the first table, at last sending, *"Animals cannot initiate the joining."*

"Nor are animals capable of possessing magic. Yet your cousin stated that the creatures out there worked a dark magic. So, what are they?"

Whisper's emerald eyes settled on him, the fear reflected in them chasing a chill through Brandel. *"I do not know the creature's nature, Master Journeyson. But…"* She left the thought unfinished as she tossed a fur toward him. Gathering three others, she headed toward a set of cabinets where Serenity and Shadow were scrounging what they could.

"Not much here," Shadow muttered. "Bear must have taken most of his supplies with him for his hunt. If he still had any on his return, they would do us no good, now."

"I believe we have all that is worth taking. Help me pack them in those satchels I found." Gesturing toward Noble, Serenity added, "I suggest you properly secure the horse's saddle and your bags and roll. We will need to attach the satchels, as well. If there is anything here that you would find useful, take it."

Whisper laid the three furs she chose for herself, her cousin, and her aunt across a chair. "I've selected the four thickest furs I could find. They should do as well as the oiled cloth to keep the rain out and will provide better warmth." Her small face creased in a weary and grief filled frown. "They still smell of Bear."

Musk, pine sap, soured beer, and sweat were the primary odors, with a whiff of salt and borax. They permeated the fur in Brandel's hands. Setting it aside, he fastened the saddle and secured everything before taking up his pack and draping the fur over it and around his shoulders. A very faint tingle suggested Bear also used magic to assist in his curing process. For a moment, Brandel stood staring at his hands. It would require both to hang onto this thing, and he might have need of at least one hand for other things. The wall of tools provided his solution. "Here," he said, returning to the others. "These tail splitting guides can be used as pins to hold the furs closed around our shoulders. Just make a couple of small slits on each side of the fur and lace the guides through them."

Serenity followed his instructions, securing the furs around Shadow and Whisper before fastening her own. When all was ready and the girls back astride

Noble, she rested a hand on Whisper's leg. "Does your sight show you anything of the creatures?"

"I cannot see their appearance; only what they leave in their passing. I sense them, though. They are not near." She hesitated, her voice taking on a tremor. "I think they have gone after Spirit."

Brandel's realization that he, too, was concerned for the wolf came as a surprise. Serenity's smile suggested she caught the thought. The next surprise was the simplicity with which they left the stable. Shadow's, "Let us pass," had the thorny vines folding back on themselves, clearing the way, though Brandel guessed it had more to do with the music of the girl's voice than the words.

Outside, the narrow trail led down the hill from which they just emerged. Brandel hugged the uphill side, as the other boasted a steep drop over a tumble of rock and through trees. How far it descended was difficult to tell in the dark shadows despite the thin suggestion of a glow announcing the coming dawn. Brandel tried to figure how much time they spent in Bear's hideaway. Did they enter the cabin at night, or was it early morning? Had they been within for an hour or two, or for a whole day? Awareness of such matters was second nature to him. Or at least it used to be. His senses kept getting knocked askew by strain, fatigue, and unexpected connections. He needed time for everything to resync. Frustratingly, it was not likely to happen any time soon.

As they approached a leveling out, the path turned away from the hill. Serenity paused at the edge of the woods, staring out across an open meadow. Brandel joined her. "Keep to the left," she advised. "Stay close to the tree line. When we reach the other side, look for a creek."

A quick check of the far side indicated a thinner woodland with more undergrowth. By the time they reached it, snow was falling in large, wet flakes, accumulating as slush beneath their feet. Morning was well upon them when the first burble of the creek was heard.

"Too much," Serenity groaned at their approach. "It runs more like a river. Better that we cross there, where it narrows. We do not need another soaking."

Brandel scouted the narrowing, relieved that the water was not so deep as to overtop several boulders and a thick broken tree branch. He and Serenity balanced their way across without incident, Noble carrying the girls across the water. For a while, the snow turned to rain, then yielded to afternoon sunshine. The woods, here, were sparse, the trees more stunted and twisted as they climbed. Near dusk, the sun disappeared behind gold-lined clouds and the snow returned in earnest.

Then the trees gave out altogether, leaving them on a boulder strewn scree slope. Brandel liked it no more than Noble, with the slick footing on shifting rock. They caught up to Serenity on a level shelf, a ridge rising some ten meters above them.

"What is it? Why have you stopped?"

"There is nothing, so far as I am aware," Serenity returned. "And I prefer to keep it that way. I want to see what lies on the other side before we cross the ridge line." Dropping to her hands and knees, she crawled the final distance to the top, then crept onto it, sending, *"Leave the horse and the girls and come."*

Brandel turned the reins over to Whisper, casting her a worried glance.

Whisper stared down at him, indignant. "We have survived these woods and mountains without you for the whole of our lives, Master Journeyson. I believe we can manage a few minutes more without you."

Chagrinned, he crawled to the ridge top and scooted out to join Serenity, who lay flat on a jutting boulder, gazing across the valley.

"There," she pointed. On the other side, another slope rose, much steeper and higher than the one they just conquered. Near its top, the mountain split into two peaks, a narrow saddle separating them. "My friend lives on the far side, just below that saddle. The climb will be difficult, whether by day or night. By day, however, given the lack of trees for cover, we are more likely to be spotted. If we can get to the valley, we can shelter within the forest tonight and set out again at daybreak. That will allow us to reach and cross above the tree line at nightfall."

Brandel considered, searching for any indication of a trail of blackened and dead vegetation. The surrounding slopes and stunted woods bore no such marks. Behind him, he heard Noble's nicker as the horse and riders cleared the ridge, Whisper smiling. "I told you we could survive without you."

"I thought you were to remain below."

"Aunt Serenity sent to us that we should come. Noble is quite good at picking his way." Her smile shifted to a grin. "Especially when he is not having to walk in your footsteps."

"Traitor," Brandel grumbled, shaking his head at the horse. "Fine. You keep his reins." Scooting from the boulder, he extended a hand to Serenity to help her to her feet. The wind was fierce, standing at the crest. Brandel's fur threatened to take flight, despite its pinning.

"This way," Serenity called, moving downslope across another scree field. "The snow is getting heavier. We need to make our way past the loose rock before full night descends."

It was more than the openness of the expanses of loose rock that troubled Brandel. The grade on this side of the ridge was steeper than the one they ascended, and he was nowhere near as surefooted as Serenity. Looking down into the diminishing light was not encouraging. There was little choice, however, but to continue. Setting his jaw, he once again followed as Serenity picked her way, switch-backing down and into a primarily evergreen forest, the scent of fir and cedar thick on the air.

Despite the evergreen canopy along the valley floor, enough snow filtered through to conceal roots and rocks. Beneath them, the marshy ground again sucked at his boots. Well into night, Serenity at last signaled a halt. Shadow slipped down from Noble's back, offering a silent nod to her grandmother before disappearing, almost before Brandel's eyes. Several uneasy minutes passed, the stillness that lay around them increasing his wariness. The girl's abrupt reappearance startled him nearly to a yelp. Her glances of amusement and annoyance were beginning to get on his nerves, as well.

"No sign of any unnatural creatures," the girl reported tightly. "There are bear in the area, though."

"Whisper, do you…" Serenity's question fell short at the sight of the girl hunched against Nobel's neck, the reins loose in her hand as she slept. "I will take that as an indication that she senses no immediate danger," the woman huffed. She took a moment, standing quite still, listening. "There," she announced. "The creek lies there." Brandel slipped the reins from Whisper's hand as Serenity set off, again. Her path paralleled the water for at least a hundred meters before she turned aside, climbing a steep cut in the creek bank to a small landing beneath a massive overhang. "We dare no fire, but this should keep the snow off our heads. We can rest here till morning."

Settling Noble near the back, Brandel recovered his piece of oiled cloth from one of his saddlebags and spread it in the driest location he could find, then gently pulled Whisper from the horse. Shadow slipped her cousin's pack from the girl's shoulders, laying it beside the cloth as Brandel laid Whisper down and rearranged her fur to better cover her.

"Shall I unsaddle Noble for you?" Shadow asked.

"No. Leave him. We may need to make a hasty escape."

She looked about to argue, then nodded, dropping wearily to the ground beside the animal.

Brandel joined Serenity at the outer edge of the landing. The woman sat with her legs hanging over the edge, her dark eyes studying the shadows. "She is weak." Brandel gestured toward Whisper. "Is she ill?"

"It is not weakness. It is the strain of the visions, I think. She has never had so many in such quick succession."

Brandel sensed there was more to it than that but refrained from pressing the issue.

"You asked how Whisper got her name," Serenity said. "Before hiding her, Whisper's mother cast a spell to keep the baby's cries from drawing attention. The spell should have broken when Tine found her. But some piece of it yet clings to her. Or perhaps Whisper refuses to let it go. The spell is all that remains of her mother."

"A rough beginning for the little one. For both girls, in truth. When did Whisper's visions begin to manifest?"

"Who is to say? I only knew of them when she was old enough to say what her mind saw. I suspect they troubled her from the beginning."

"And your granddaughter?"

"Shadow." Serenity drew a deep breath, letting it out slowly. "Her gift manifest at birth. My son sent to me of her extraordinary ability. Startled into a world of light after the darkness and warmth of the womb, the babe promptly wrapped herself in strands of gray. She was but a few days old when he sent again that he observed her playing with the strands, darkening them, lightening them, coiling them round her." Another brief silence was followed by, "It was shortly thereafter that the babe was sent straight into my arms, a tiny bundle of darkness. Took her hours before she released the shroud of shadows."

Brandel darted another backward glance. Shadow still sat where she dropped, her knees bent, her arms and head resting on them. "You have done well by them, keeping them safe."

Serenity smiled. "They are much stronger than you think, Master Journeyson."

"Brandel," he corrected. "I recognize that more and more. Your granddaughter in particular. She is very…" Words failed him.

Serenity snorted her amusement. "Tough? Headstrong? She is like her father. Has a mind of her own and generally chooses to listen to no one else's views on any given matter, save, perhaps, Whisper's."

"I can hear you!" Shadow snapped. Moaning as she pushed to her feet, she shuffled around to sit on the other side of her grandmother, reaching in a pocket before extending a hand across to Brandel. "Biscuits and jerky," she said. Brandel accepted with a grateful nod. Reaching in her pocket, again, the girl withdrew another couple of biscuits and some jerky and offered them to Serenity. "So," the girl ventured. "What is it that worries you, Master Journeyson?"

"What makes you think I am worried?"

"Oh, please! Your features could not possibly crevice any deeper. Something is on your mind."

Brandel considered retorting with his surprise that the girl had not simply read his thoughts, but bit the words back, exchanging them for, "Aside from the likelihood of being pursued?"

"It is about Whisper and me, is it not?"

Brandel chewed his lip for a moment. "You, I am not concerned about. You do not like me. That is fair enough. I understand your reluctance to accept strangers at face value. You offer no threat to me. And I give you my word, I offer none to you."

"So, it is Whisper. You like her. You worry for her."

True enough, though he was not going to admit as much aloud. "It is indirectly about her."

"Indirectly?"

He shrugged. "Your grandmother worries about her. And it is not just about her visions."

Serenity made no reply for several seconds. "It is unlike Whisper to sink so deeply into slumber," she confessed, at last. "Something more than her visions wears on her. Wearing her down. She is blocking something from me." The woman's sharp scrutiny turned to Shadow. "If you know what it is, tell me."

Shadow flinched. "I told you all she shared with me."

"And the vision that was so strong that you were drawn into her seeing?"

"There was no more to it than what we told you. Honest." The girl fell silent, her fidgeting a clear indication that something else gnawed at her.

"Spit it out, dear," Serenity said.

"She is…she is hiding something from me, as well. I can feel it. But when I try to press her about it…she…she shuts me out entirely."

Serenity pressed no further, and soon she and both girls were sleeping.

For Brandel, sleep did not come easily. Every small sound jerked him awake. He gave up as the first hint of morning peaked with a faint coral glow through the boughs. Serenity and Shadow were curled around Whisper, none of them stirring, yet, though Whisper's features were creased, her lips moving silently in some dream. Shoving to his feet, Brandel stifled his groan at the protest of his joints. His movements were greeted by Noble's nicker. A soft 'ssst' and a scratch along the animal's jaw soothed him back to silence. The nearby creek drew them both out from the overhang for a drink. The shock of the frigid water ached all the way down Brandel's throat and rushed an intense pain to his head. Still, it was fresh and quenching.

Scooped hands part way to his mouth for another drink, an itch along his nerves froze him. Something was near. Something watched. It gave no sense of threat, but its presence was disturbing. Straightening, Brandel scanned the area, but found nothing. With Noble's reins in hand, he made his way back to the others, gingerly nudging Serenity. "We should leave."

The woman rolled to her back and opened one bleary eye. Recognition of him and their situation seemed to dawn grudgingly. At last, she sat up, yawning. "It is not fully light, yet."

"Something watches us."

Stiffening, she darted glances around. "Who?"

"Animal, I think. I felt its presence. It offered no sense of threat. Still…"

The woman was on her feet, waking the girls and repacking the satchels and her pack. The satchels were handed across to Brandel, who promptly fastened them across his saddlebags once more. As he worked, he sensed the watchful presence fade. Whether it had gone, or whether it realized he had detected it and was now shielding itself he could not discern. He prayed it was the former.

Moving in silence, the small party finished collecting their few items. Brandel lifted each girl into place on Noble's back. "Take the horse into the stream," he directed Whisper. "And wait for me." As Whisper complied, Brandel located and uprooted a small scrub, using it to wipe out any trace of their sheltering beneath the overhang. Before joining the others, he carried the scrub downstream several meters, then discarded it in a snarl of blackberries.

"Where lies the saddle between the peaks from here?" he asked Serenity as he rejoined the others.

"North and a little east."

"Then we shall travel in the creek for now. Look for a bank that is rocky like this one rather than muddy. That is where we will move back into the woods."

Daylight broke in earnest when, at last, the slushy mud banks gave way to rock. The effort to climb from the creek, however, proved more problematic than

Brandel had hoped. The bank was steep and the rocks covered in a layer of slush. That they managed without a spill was both a surprise and a relief to each of them. Tucked well into a more promising forest once more, Brandel caught glimpses of the rose and coral-gray of the autumn sun glow through the clouds. For a time, it stretched splotchy, thin shadows between the trees. As the morning wore on, the clouds thickened. He sensed nothing more of the presence he detected earlier, however, and though the snow began to fall, again, they made fair time until the ground began yet another climb, the grade steeper, even, than it appeared from the ridge. Once more, switch-backing was necessitated.

Well into late afternoon, they stopped to rest within a now dwindling cover of trees where stiffer breezes stung Brandel's face. The girls remained huddled together on Noble's back, sipping at the water Serenity offered them. Brandel drank from the water skin he kept in his saddlebag, refilling it with snow before he took the time to assess the last of their climb. There were few trees at this altitude to block the view, and it was daunting. The twin peaks towered like malevolent sentinels above them. Between the two was the narrow gap, the route to it appearing a near vertical ascent.

"It is not so bad as it appears," Serenity told him. "There is a trail."

"One that cuts back and forth across the face, no doubt."

Serenity chuckled at the distress in Brandel's voice. "Better that than having to climb straight up. We will rest here until nightfall. When we start, stay close behind me and hug the uphill side. The trail is firm enough, but it is also quite narrow."

Night came all too soon for Brandel's liking. He dreaded the exposure on the barren upper slope and the narrow trail. Finishing off his ration of jerky, he struggled to his feet with a quick glance at Whisper. Neither she nor Shadow had eaten anything.

Whisper exchanged his glance with a cock of her head. "Do not worry over us. Noble is the one doing all the work. And do not worry over Noble. Let me keep his reins. I will see that he follows true and without issue."

Brandel no longer doubted the girl's skill with the horse. Nor did he doubt her knowledge of the mountain trails. With a nod, he fell in behind Serenity, increasingly grateful for solid ground beneath his feet. Though there was now some ten centimeters of fresh snow covering the way, the footing beneath was firm. How long it took to achieve the saddle, he could not say. Long enough for weary aches to wear on his patience. He bit back his complaints. When Serenity gestured a halt, he settled against the side of the nearest rising peak to stare out at the vast array of other white pinnacles surrounding them, hardly noticing the woman's silence for several minutes.

He found her across the saddle from him, her back braced against the side of the opposing peak, her eyes closed, her face creased with concentration. Brandel feared she may have injured herself in the climb, or that she was, perhaps, coming down with some illness, when she finally straightened, her dark eyes troubled. "My friend's home is there," she said, pointing to a gray splotch against the white snow some distance down from their perch. He says he is on the west peak above. He has watched our progress since our descent into the valley. He welcomes us to take shelter in his abode."

"But?"

"But something does not feel right."

"Do we have another choice?"

Serenity shrugged. "Not if we wish to survive the night. Whisper sent to me that another storm is building. We need to be indoors."

"Then lead on."

The woman hesitated a moment more, lifting her eyes to the peak where her friend kept watch. Its top was lost, now, in the accumulation of low and menacing clouds that hid the remaining moonlight. Turning, she began the trek downslope, edging in the direction of the distant splotch. As with their ascent to the saddle, the footing was firm. The distance, however, proved deceptive. For a long while, the dark spot on the snowfield never appeared to get any closer. Dismay was taking hold when, at last, Brandel could make out the shape of at least three wooden structures set on a shelf that jutted out from the slope. Braced against the mountainside some twenty meters above the buildings and further supported by enormous wooden beams, was a construct that formed a downward sloping roof.

"Snow-shed," Serenity explained. "Heavy snowfall and avalanches from above slide off it to the slope below the shelf, thereby protecting the buildings. Gray enhanced the shed with magic to prevent its collapse."

A level path picked up to carry them the remaining distance to the buildings. The first of the two proved to be a storehouse and stable. Shadow and Whisper both slid from Noble's back, Whisper handing the reins to Shadow. "I will see that your horse is again cared for," the older girl sang. "Gray's animals tend not to take kindly to strangers." From inside the stable came the growls and hostile barks of at least two large dogs, perhaps more.

At Brandel's startled reach for the reins, Shadow gave a weary sniff. "The dogs will not harm Noble. I promise you. It is humans they distrust."

Though still wary, Brandel left his horse in Shadow's care and headed toward the house before she opened the stable doors. Serenity and Whisper were already within when he arrived, the woman tending a fire in the massive fireplace while the girl moved about the kitchen. Brandel stomped his boots several times, knocking off snow before he entered. Light from the fire scarcely filled the surprisingly ample space. Soon, however, Serenity had lamps lit in nearly every nook and corner.

The living quarters boasted a pair of large sofas, two fat, overstuffed chairs, a wooden rocker, a couple of tables, and a wall full of bookshelves. Near the kitchen stood a long table that might seat upwards of a dozen or more people. Cabinets lined the kitchen walls with a huge, flattopped woodstove occupying one corner of the room. A sink with a pump was situated in a counter beneath a shuttered window and near a back door.

The fireplace that now blazed gloriously, giving off a most welcome warmth, was flanked by a pair of openings to hallways. Serenity drew his attention with a gesture toward a door leading from the kitchen to the outside. "You will find an outbuilding a short distance from the house with a latrine on one side and a shower on the other. Neither are heated, though Gray managed to install a means of delivering hot water for the shower." Eyeing Brandel, she submitted, "You may want to avail yourself of the shower after dinner. Gray will likely have some fresh clothes for you."

"What is this place?" Brandel asked.

"A watchpoint and a way station. Gray can survey the lands for signs of trouble for many kilometers in any direction from his perch on either of the peaks. Travelers whom Gray determines pose no threat are welcome to take shelter here for a night or two in exchange for information."

"And if he deems them a threat?"

"He brings an avalanche from the peaks down to block their way."

9

The stomping of boots and a rattling cough from outside announced Gray's arrival. A man of short stature and muscular build with a thick, dark, grizzled beard and full head of curly black hair entered with another round of barking and wheezing.

Serenity spun, her fists on her hips. "My gracious heavens, man! How long have you been suffering that?"

He gave a good-natured shrug. "Less than a fortnight, I think. 'Tis nothing, my dear. Nothing." His face lit up at the sight of stew, bread, and dried fruits laid out on the table.

"Nothing indeed!" Serenity exclaimed.

Whisper, too, was concerned, darting to help her aunt strip the man from his coat and layers of sweaters, then ushering him to one of the chairs. Shadow had a hot drink in his hand almost before he was situated, while Whisper was away, again, returned to the kitchen and rustling around in the cabinets.

"I am out, little one," the man rasped. The flush of his face and glaze of his brown eyes indicated he suffered from more than a cough. "Have not had an opportunity to look for more. This good meal will do me wonders."

Shadow headed for the wall pegs where their furs and coats were hung. "Do not bother to look for any of the herbs tonight, child," Gray called after her. "The weather is too forbidding and risky. It can wait." His sudden eruption of coughing suggested otherwise. Still, he waved her off. "Seeing you three, again, having my meal prepared, that is medicine enough, for now." Turning his dark eyes to Brandel, he wheezed, "So, my dears. Who is our friend, here?"

"Master Brandel Journeyson," Whisper said, anxiety still rippling through her soft words. "Please. Let Shadow and me look for..."

"Nonsense! I will not have you out in the cold and dark with the snow getting heavier. I will take the dogs out tomorrow to sniff some out for me. So, from whence does Master Brandel Journeyson hale?"

"He is a soldier from the lowlands."

Gray's brow cocked with greater interest. "Indeed? Well, now. What would bring a soldier of the White Goddess to the mountains of the Rose Goddess?"

"He seeks Grandmother," Shadow put in.

The man chuckled. "And can he not speak for himself?"

Brandel cleared his throat, striding across to offer a hand. "I can. At least two of these three, however, are quicker at the tongue than I."

Gray's chuckle rolled into a laugh, triggering his cough, again, as he accepted Brandel's hand and shook it. "That they are." Setting the mug Shadow had given him on a near table, he pushed to his feet. "I need to clean up for dinner," he said. "Then I wish to hear this man's tale."

Whisper made to protest his heading toward the outhouse, but Serenity motioned her quiet. "Let Gray do as he wishes in his own home, my sweet."

The little redhead held her tongue until Gray left. "But he is sick," she objected. "He needs to stay inside and warm."

"Be that as it may, we are his guests."

"Whisper and I are his guests," Shadow corrected. "You…"

Serenity's sharp look silenced the girl. "Besides," the woman continued. "He has weathered many an illness; has been doing so since generations before you two were born. I will look in his cupboards to see what might be helpful to add to his tea while you warm it again."

Brandel hung back, watching the three scuttling about, Whisper warming the tea while Serenity and Shadow searched the cupboards.

"Wait!" Shadow proclaimed, stopping mid-stride between cabinets. Spinning, she dashed for the back door and out into the dark, leaving Serenity and Whisper with perplexed stares. A few minutes later, Shadow darted back in the front door, carrying a small vial, announcing, "The medicine he keeps for his animals!"

"Well done!" Serenity acknowledged. "I will have to dilute it. Maybe mix it with just a little…"

"Angelica and horse heal," Whisper finished for her as she set about pulling a couple of jars from one of the cabinets. "He does not have much of either. In truth," she murmured, pulling out several empty jars and a few with only a thin layer of crumbled vegetation in the bottom. "He does not have much of any of his herbal supplies left. The lungwort is gone. So is the plantain, wild cherry bark, ginger, and lobelia."

"Some of those are quite expensive," Brandel whistled.

"Some," Serenity agreed. "Gray has the means. He chooses, however, to spend on his animals and takes too little time to search out local herbs for himself."

Whisper unscrewed the lid for the angelica and started to hand it off to Serenity, her motion jerking the jar back for a sniff. "No." Sucking in on her lower lip, she ventured another sniff. "This is not... I mean, it is. But...but something is not right with it."

Serenity took it from her, taking a whiff, her face paling. Shoving it back to the girl, she opened the vial Shadow brought in from the stable, smelling it, as well. "This is good. What about the...?"

Whisper passed over the jar containing the remains of the horse heal. Serenity opened and smelled, instantly recoiling. "Take out everything! Every herb, every spice, every ingredient in his kitchen. We need to check them all. Now!"

Gray walked back into his kitchen stunned by the sight of the woman and girls emptying his cupboards of jars and bags and other containers, Serenity carefully sniffing each of them. Some she set to one side and the others as far from her as she could push them on the counter.

"What the! What insanity is this?" he demanded.

"Someone is trying to poison you," Serenity shot back, pointing to the containers that were shoved aside.

"You are out of your mind, woman! No one who has been in my company would dare such an act!"

Serenity slammed the jar she was holding onto the counter, stuffing her fists to her hips again. "Someone dared it!" Pointing, she indicated each of the containers that either held the last remnants or were emptied of the medicinal herbs. "Each of those was tainted. Did the stench tell you nothing?"

The man stared, aghast. "I can smell nothing," he admitted. "Head's been stopped up for weeks."

Serenity drew a steadying breath. "Girls, take these out. See if you can dig a deep hole and bury them, jars, bags and all." Striding across to Gray, she gripped his arm and led him back to his chair, shoving him onto it. "Did you collect those yourself, or did you purchase them?"

"Purchased," he sputtered.

"From whom?"

"The village apothecary. Same as always."

"How long ago for these?"

"A month. When I went down to pick up my food supplies." He swallowed, blinking at the rage in the woman's face. "I planned to return last week. Heard from a passing traveler, though, that the apothecary had died. Quite unexpectedly."

"Girls!" Serenity shouted as the two started for the back door, their arms full of the contaminated herbs. "As soon as you finish, go to the outhouse. Strip from your clothes and leave them outside for burning, then shower. Thoroughly! Master Brandel!"

He jumped at the woman's bellow of his name. "Through the doorway on the near side of the fireplace, you will find a series of rooms. Go to the third one down. You will find clean clothes for Shadow, Whisper, and me. Kindly take some to the shower room for us. While you are at it, the fourth room down should have clothing to fit you. Take what you need with you and leave everything just inside the door. I will take to the shower, first. As soon as you bring the clothing, I will return to do what I can to rewarm our dinner. Thank Ciuin Rose that the foods and spices were not tampered with."

There was nothing for it but to do what the woman dictated. Judging from her countenance, she was not about to suffer any contradiction or refusal. Brandel had never been cowed by any person, before. But this woman… Shaking himself, he set about doing as he was told. Gray shot him an apologetic and anxious glance as Brandel passed the man on his way to the kitchen and out the door carrying an armload of clothing. Outside, the girls were struggling to dig the hole, the rocks and frozen ground resisting their every effort. Striding past them, he knocked at the shower door.

"Just inside the door, as I mentioned" was Serenity's response. Again, he did as directed, depositing the pile inside the door.

Returning to the girls, he took the shovel from them and motioned them to the shower. They acknowledged with grateful nods, careful to strip of their clothes around the corner where Brandel could not see them. Exhausted and full of questions, Brandel stared at the hard ground, wondering if he would be any more successful than the girls.

"Let the shovel strike, and the stone shall yield. Feed then into the maw, the deadly toxins, to be devoured and spit unto Hell. So, too, feed in the clothing contaminated at Her instruction. Let She who sent this death taste of it and know Her failure."

Startled, Brandel spun in place to stare into every shadow. The voice was distant, the touch of it on his mind carrying the sense of great antiquity. "Who are you? Show yourself!"

"Do as I bid. And your clothes, as well. They have touched the others."

So imposing was the command that he did as instructed, this time muttering under his breath. It was one thing to take orders from Lord of Brightwater or an officer of higher rank. But from civilians and a voice in his head… His strike of the shovel point on the ground carried the force of his agitation, the ring of the blade on rock jarring through him. Shaking himself, he prepared for another attempt to break ground, pulling the shovel up short as a small opening, dark as pitch, gaped at his feet. Brandel edged back, eyeing it. When it ceased to grow, he collected each of the containers, tossing them in, waiting to hear them strike bottom or crunch against one another. The sound never came.

Serenity and the girls stepped out of the shower house as Brandel was headed back to the hole with their discarded clothes. The sight of the gaping pit left them exchanging impressed glances and again nodding their thanks before they darted past, wet hair wrapped in towels, barefoot, and shivering. Brandel set to tossing the garments into the abyss, then removed his own. It pained him to toss his boots in, as well. But he would take no chances with whatever the toxin was. Last, he threw the lighted torch he took from the outside wall of the outbuilding. As it tumbled in after the clothing, the ground trembled beneath his feet, belching smoke, the hole sealing itself. For several seconds, he stood with his gaze fixed on the spot where the pit had been, shivering from shock as much as from the cold on his exposed flesh.

At last, he minced his way to the small, square building that stood near the back of the large house, relieved to find the room steamy and pleasantly warm from the showers previously taken. The clothing he delivered for himself now lay neatly folded on a bench next to a stack of towels. A copper pipe dropped to just above head height in one corner. Mounted on a stone wall behind the pipe were two faucets. How the whole arrangement was plumbed and what source heated the water he had no way of knowing. Nor did he particularly care, at this moment. All that mattered was the bar of soap left on a low stand and the fact that the water that ran from the copper pipe was hot. Clean and dried, he donned the fresh clothes and braced himself for the barefoot race across to the house.

Whisper greeted him at the door with stockings and boots. "Gray says these should fit. They were left by a traveler."

At his arrival, Serenity set about dishing the bowls of stew from the pot to which she had returned it. Gray was asleep in his chair, snoring faintly, an empty bowl and a plate of breadcrumbs sitting on the table beside him. Whisper rejoined Shadow at the table. Both girls looked about to nod off where they sat. The clatter of the bowls as they were laid in front of each roused them.

"May the White and the Rose bless us," Serenity prayed.

Brandel had not realized how hungry he was until the first bite passed his lips. No conversation was exchanged, each person intent on the hot stew, the bread, and the fresh water at hand. Whisper finished first, watching him with the flutter of a smile. As he finished, she took the bowl and replenished it. There was no hint of refusal from him, bringing a brighter smile to the girl.

Gray was the one who finally disturbed the silence, his cough announcing his waking. It was still an unhealthy series of barks, though the rattling had eased. "What the hell did you slip into my meal?" he roared, searching out Serenity. "I feel like I have been drinking for a month without end."

"A much-diluted version of what you reserve for your horse and dogs. Be thankful I did not give you a full concentration. You might have slept eternally."

Straightening, he fumbled at the arm of his chair, then slumped back. "Think I will just stay here a while longer. Seems your efforts are little better than the poison you claim was in my herbs."

"Had I not given you the medicine, you would likely be dead within another day," she harrumphed. "How long had you been taking those herbs?"

Gray's face contorted as he tried to think. "Most of this past month. What was in them?"

"I do not know. Whatever it was, it seems, was designed to work slowly. Weaken you. Make it look as though you fell ill and died from a disease of the lungs. If the apothecary had been mixing the poison into his herbals, he likely died of exposure to them."

"Michaelmas would never have knowingly mixed such a concoction. We have been friends since we were children. He was a good man. Someone else is responsible for this. And when I learn who, they will pay for it dearly."

He closed his eyes. Brandel thought the man had fallen asleep again, until Gray offered, "There is ale in the storehouse next to the stable. And wine, as well. Serenity, would you please check its safety, and then offer some to our guest? Take the girls. They can help you carry in a keg of each. I would offer my assistance, but do not think my legs will support such an endeavor. Your fault, my girl," he concluded with a snort.

Serenity cocked a questioning brow at him, but followed his request, ushering the girls with her. Brandel moved to join them, but she waved him back. Once they were gone, Gray turned an inquisitive scrutiny on him. "Serenity tells me you helped get them here safely."

"More like she helped me."

Gray half coughed an amused acknowledgment. "More like. Shadow is a little leery of you. Whisper, however, trusts you. Why would that be?"

"I have no answer for either part, save that I suspect Shadow trusts very few and Whisper far more."

That produced an outright laugh from the man. "A keen observation, I would say. So. You seek Grandmother. May I ask why?"

"There are rumors. Hints that this woman once knew those who brought the Goddesses home to our world."

Gray's brow creased. "And you have questions you think only she can answer. Perhaps she can. Perhaps she will." He sighed. "Perhaps she will not. She is not easy to find, you know. Values her privacy. She may not want to be found."

"So it has been said."

"And still, you seek her."

Brandel vented a weary sigh. "I have my doubts as to the sanity of such a search. Surely, there are none still living who once knew those who returned the Goddesses. There is no one else, however, of whom I can ask my questions." He was silent for a moment. "Is it true? Is this woman as ancient as they say?"

Gray shrugged. "She is the oldest human any here have ever known."

Brandel straightened, striding across the room to sit on the sofa facing the man. "You have met her?"

"A very long while ago. I know Grandmother's guardian better."

"Her guardian."

Gray shifted on his chair, seeking a more comfortable position. "There are those who have sought her for centuries," he rasped. "Including some from among the Red Moon Warriors. They claim she has a weapon of great power."

"What kind of weapon?"

"I would not know. I never asked Grandmother." Gray chuckled. "It is above my pay grade."

Serenity returned with the girls, the woman balancing a keg on her shoulder, the girls carrying another between them. Serenity turned a questioning glance on the men. Gray merely smiled back at her. Scooting forward, he made to rise. "I believe I will leave your company, now, and find my bed." His arms appeared unwilling to take his weight to push him from the chair, however. Grumbling, he settled back once more. "On second thought, perhaps I will just sleep here for tonight. Enjoy your visit. Help yourselves to whatever food and drink you wish... and that my saintly Healer deems is untainted. If you are still here in the morning, I will visit with you more." Within seconds, he was snoring again.

"Girls," Serenity called toward the kitchen where the two had been cleaning the dishes. "You should find your beds. You know your way."

"I am not tired," Shadow returned, belligerence crossing her face.

"Is that why you looked as though you would fall asleep with your face in your dinner?" her grandmother pressed. "I cannot say how long it will be safe to remain here; whether we are still being pursued or whether some other danger lurks. What I do know is that we have the coming of an early winter to consider. We may be able to rest here for a day or two. Make certain that Gray is on the mend. But we can stay no longer. Sleep in comfort while you can, my dears."

Shadow continued to stand her ground, her look of defiance undiminished until Whisper strolled to her, taking her hand and urging her toward the room where Brandel found clothes for them.

10

Mug of ale in hand, Brandel scanned Gray's cases of books for several minutes. Most were histories. Some passed for history, though Brandel suspected much of their content was the consequence of embellishment over time.

"What part of the histories do you doubt?"

He glanced around at Serenity who stood regarding him, a freshly filled glass of wine in her hand. "I need to be more cautious," he muttered. "It is becoming a bad habit, leaving my thoughts unshielded." Serenity merely waited for his answer. With a shrug, he offered, "I believe the Goddesses were involved in a great battle when They returned, and that They cried out for mortals to help in the fight. Those who responded, however, came from this world, not some other."

"How do you explain that none among the Witches, Tanai, or creatures who took up the fight had ever been seen on this world before that day?"

"Could simply be the author's enhancement of the tale. Even if true, Slievgall'ion is large. Plenty of remote places to live without being found." Taking his mug to a chair, he nodded toward Gray. "So, who is he?"

Serenity cast the man an anxious gaze on her way to a corner of one of the sofas. "A Guardian of Ciuin Rose."

"A guardian. Here?"

"Why not here?"

"I thought they traveled in companies, constantly patrolling the land."

"Most do so."

"I never encountered any patrols when I crossed the border. Nor, I dare say, did the Red Moon Warriors who now pursue us."

Serenity stared into her glass, gently swirling the wine. "Their numbers have never been so great as the Soldiers of Damsa Dana. Nor has our overall population ever been so numerous as Brightwater's." A brow lifted as she raised her eyes to

SLIEVGALLION: THE GODDESS WARS

meet Brandel's. "And we lost a great many of our people in the wars that followed the return of the Goddesses."

Brandel flinched under her stare. "As did we."

"Your people left us to fight alone."

"That was not my doing."

"No," Serenity agreed softly. "It was not. It was well before your time." She took a moment to sip her drink. "We never fully recovered from those losses. Life here is harder than in the lowlands, and the life of a guardian is perhaps the most difficult. Few are willing to take up the mantle when their families need them to work the farms or to keep the family businesses alive."

Her lips pinched as she studied her glass, again. "Our patrols ride hard over great distances to guard our border with Brightwater. The terrain is difficult, even in the foothills. It takes several days for a company to complete a circuit of their assigned section, leaving great swatches of the border unprotected at any given time. When trouble crosses into our foothills, the guardians rely on those who live in the area to send word. Given the remoteness, however, enemy scouts and warriors may go unnoticed for days or weeks. If they strike before their movements have been noted, we may not learn of it until much later, when a patrol manages to pass through the destroyed village or farm." She paused, her glance going to Gray. "The mountains, of course, are even less populated than the foothills along the border and even more difficult to patrol. Thankfully, the terrain and weather tend to take care of much of the matter for us. Still, there are two passes that are accessible. This one and one to the north of Knife Point Keep. Each has a single sentry assigned. This one is Gray's responsibility. By day he observes from one or the other of the twin peaks above this station."

"And by night?"

"The night creatures alert him to any person or persons within fifteen kilometers of the saddle. He knew of our coming as we descended the crest of the last slope and passed through the woodlands below."

Worry was clear in the crease of her brow. "Should Gray die, this passage would be unprotected. His falcon would get word to the others, of course. But it could take days for another guardian to reach this place to investigate and take command. Someone tried to kill him. To leave this pass open, is my guess."

Brandel suspected the woman's concern was for more than leaving a pass unprotected, though he refrained from saying as much. It was none of his business.

"The Red Moon Warriors are undoubtedly behind the attempt on Gray's life," he growled. "You say they come across from the south of Brightwater?"

"Do not blame your soldiers. Neither should you be surprised, however, that scouts and warriors make it through. The Soldiers of Damsa Dana cannot possibly guard the entire length of the border. Not when you also have an expansive coastline."

Brandel's jaw tightened. She was right, of course. There were not enough soldiers to maintain a constant vigil over every stretch of the border. Nor did Strongbow invest in many patrols in the south, deeming them unnecessary. He relied on the High Priestess Danu to alert him of incursions that were about to take place. For more than a century the High Priestess assured Strongbow that none from the Red Moon were infiltrating the southern coastal region between the Rose River basin and the border. The coastal cliffs prevented it, she said. His flesh crawled. Damsa Dana would not turn on Her people. She would send warning; would protect them…if She could. Either Brightwater's Goddess was weak, or She was dead. There was no other explanation for Danu's unpunished failures and lies. And the magnitude of them was only now becoming apparent.

"How long?" he asked. "The Red Moon started breaking through how long ago?"

"Waves of invasions come. It has been so since the return of the Goddesses. The enemy strikes, wiping out a village here and another there, then disappears. Sometimes their attacks come in quick succession. Sometimes they strike once and do not return for a year or two, or even for decades."

"And they always cross the southern border?

"It is uncertain. That is why the guardians patrol its length. Though, as I have said, their numbers are too few to cover the distances efficiently."

Brandel slumped forward, his elbows braced on his thighs, his head in his hands. "I need to send to Strongbow. He is unaware that the Red Moon are getting through. But I cannot reach him. Not since I passed into Knife Point. The guardians need to stop blocking my sendings, need to let my messages get through."

"There is no such block from our side. More likely, the Lord of Brightwater fails to respond because his mind is bent on the battles there. And what do you think he might accomplish if you do get word to him? You came here seeking our help in your lands. Had you the numbers to search out every potential entry point, to search the whole of your lands for those who slip through, you would not need our help." Her lips pinched as she stared into her now empty glass. "Still, this is the first assault this far inland since…since Cradle. I thank the Goddess for Whisper's vision, or we would not be sitting here, now. I sent to the Lord of Knife Point of the attack on our home and that we are pursued. If he can send aid, he will do so. We must assume, however, that we are on our own until we reach the keep. We must also assume that more warriors may be crossing where our pursuers did."

Serenity looked to Gray, once more, almost smiling at his snoring. Venting another sigh, she said, "The warriors are not our only concern. There are others willing to do Breag Nemhain's and her High Priestess' bidding. A Witch here and there, quietly sewing discord, pitting family against family, race against race. The Alainn do not listen to the devious ones. But among the creature races and Witches, it is easy to encourage jealousies and hatred."

Brandel grimaced. Rising, he retrieved his empty mug from the end table and headed for the kitchen to wash it. "There are always malcontents and those who incite trouble. That is true enough. Nor do I doubt some of our people offer support to Breag Nemhain's ilk if there was something in it for them. We discovered a core of smugglers bringing warriors into our ports and harboring them in their homes. The traitors were arrested and are now in prison."

"If one core was found, do you not think others exist?"

"If you think we are unaware of such a likelihood, you are wrong." Turning from Serenity, he headed to the pegs where the coats hung.

"Where do you think you are going?"

"I am tired. I need to sleep."

Serenity leaned back in her chair with a shake of her head. "In the stable? Do not be a fool. Your horse is well. You may not be, however, if Gray's dogs take a dislike to you. Better that you remain in the house. You will find the first room in the hallway to the right of the fireplace prepared for you. Your belongings are there. Shadow brought them in while you showered."

Brandel glanced toward the door. He had forgotten about the dogs. "Very well. But I leave at dawn. I suggest you and the girls remain here where you will be safe."

"You will lose your way and freeze in the mountains without us."

Brandel stood for a moment, staring at the floor, his exhaustion and irritation apparent in his snapped, "You have too little faith in me."

"And you have too little trust in us. If Gray is better in the morning, we will leave with you. If not… You would do well to wait with us."

Brandel turned toward the designated hallway without further comment. Grating as it was, the woman was right – again. He did not know the mountains. He could easily meet the same fate as the messengers who came before him, whether it was falling prey to wolves or falling from a cliff or ridgeline or losing their way in a whiteout and freezing to death. No one from Brightwater was equipped for the conditions, here. Strongbow followed the way of his predecessors since their retreat from the war in the Fire Islands, keeping their people isolated. The Lord of Brightwater was ignorant of the challenges of this land. Those he sent were ill prepared.

Brandel's dark thoughts were not much uplifted upon his entry into the designated room. The small blaze in the squat stove occupying one corner provided scant light and the warmth eased none of the chill of his brooding reassessments of Brightwater, its lord, the High Priestess, or his Goddess. For a moment, he stood with his back to the closed door, eyeing his saddlebags and bundle where they lay on the floor at the foot of the bed. His quiver and bow were slung over the back of the room's single chair. His heart demanded he take them, face the dogs to retrieve his horse, and set out on his own. His head, however, understood the truth of Serenity's words. His chances of making it to Knife Point Keep were unrealistic without her.

Trudging to the chair, he dropped onto it to tug off his boots. Still in his clothes, he tossed the blankets down enough to crawl into bed. Sleep took him almost before his head found the pillow.

Blackness. Everywhere across the land. Withered vegetation, gray and crumbling animal corpses strewn over forest and field. A faint light shimmers beneath, green struggling to rise through the wasted landscape. Laughter mixes with cries of mourning.

The flash of a face with jewel-green eyes superimposed on the silhouette of a white wolf. Behind shimmers a desolate white peak dotted with blasted and blackened boulders. Steam rises from the steepest part of the upper slope. Below the vent, a crevice breaks open. The roll of thunder accompanies the churning of a great turbulence of rushing, roaring snow and ice that sweeps away all before it.

The scent of smoke choked Brandel awake, a tension of voices vaguely registering from somewhere beyond his closed door. Rolling to his side, he closed his eyes attempting to ignore the distant conversation, only to blink them open again at the persistent smell. Chilled and struggling to sit, he turned a fuzzy scrutiny to the room's wood stove.

Only a few glowing embers remained.

"Brandel Journeyson!" The rap at the door was urgent.

"A moment," he returned, rubbing his temples. He made his way with a yawn, opening it to Gray's troubled countenance.

"I am sorry to disturb your sleep, but the little one had a premonition."

"Whisper," Brandel sighed.

Gray nodded. "Death comes this way. It is not yet so close as the crest of the slopes beyond the valley you crossed, or the night creatures would have sent warning to me. Still, the girl believes you should all be away before dawn. There are coats more fitting for the mountains and thick snow boots awaiting you. The snows will get worse as you progress toward Knife Point Keep. Here." He thrust a bundle into Brandel's hands. "These will serve you well enough. Pack what you wear, now. You will need the lighter clothes once you are safely within the keep."

"What of you? Will you be coming with us? If what the girl saw is the same creature…or creatures that left death along our trail, you will not be safe, here, either."

"I cannot leave my post. I will free my animals to seek what shelter they can. Then I will climb one of the peaks and send word to the Lord of Knife Point of how many come through the pass. I will be out of harm's way in the heights." With that, the man strode back toward the living area, turning to add, "You should consider allowing your horse its freedom, as well. Sturdy as the beast is, he will not fare well where you are going. Let him seek safety elsewhere."

Gray's words dug into Brandel's mind as he sorted through the items from the bundle he was given. Where they were going. Not safe for the horse. Judging from the clothes, it was not likely safe for any creature, be it horse, human, or otherwise. If a thick undershirt, two heavy wool shirts, fur-lined pants, and heavy, fur-lined boots were necessary, it was little wonder none of the messengers made it to their destination. Whatever the case, he was not abandoning Noble.

His hands stopped short of pulling on the second wool shirt, noting the pale rose embroidered on the standing collar. The symbol of the Guardians of Ciuin Rose. Bristling, he almost tossed it back to the bed in disgust. He was a Soldier of Damsa Dana. He was honor bound to bear Her symbol. His clothes, however, now lay burned and buried, the ones he just peeled out of those of some stranger.

"Forgive me," he muttered, donning the shirt bearing the rose. "Please know that I do not dishonor You, Goddess." In a second thought, he added, "Nor do I mean any dishonor to your Sister, Ciuin Rose in my balking."

Dressed and with his repacked saddlebags slung over a shoulder, his bundle under an arm, and his bow and quiver in hand, he made his way to the living quarters where Serenity once again hovered over a pale and trembling Whisper. Shadow sat next to the smaller girl, holding her hand. Each was attired as he was - fur-lined pants and thick wool shirts. Even the knee-high boots Gray offered were fur-lined with lacings up the front.

Their host eyed the saddlebags with a shake of his head. "That will never do." The man disappeared outside, returning minutes later with a large pack, banging it on the floor to dislodge the layer of snow. "This will suit your travels better. Leave your bags here. You can retrieve them if you pass this way again."

Brandel thought to argue, but Whisper's faint warning edged through his mind. *"Gray knows these mountains better than anyone, sir. You would be wise not to question his judgment."*

Anger smoldered in his, *"I suppose you also agree that Noble should be set free."*

"If you wish your horse to survive, yes. Please, Master Brandel. Trust what Gray says."

Snorting his disapproval, Brandel closed his mind to the girl. For the next few minutes, he transferred the items from his saddlebags to the pack, attaching his quiver to a side lacing. The bow would ride his shoulder over the pack's strap. Glancing at the bundle, he pushed it aside, then turned and gave a disgruntled nod.

"There." Gray pointed to a pile of coats on the kitchen table. Each was hooded and fur-lined, like the pants and boots. Thick mittens were also provided. A second pack, much like the one Brandel now carried, stood on the floor next to the table. Gray lifted it to Serenity's shoulders as she finished fastening the coat.

Brandel set aside his gear and lumbered into the remaining coat, tucking the mittens in the pockets. "All of this is really necessary?"

Gray cocked a brow at him. "Very, lowlander. The mountains are brutal." The man took his own coat from a wall peg and pulled it on, snatching a lantern and lighting it with a flash from his fingertips as he led the way out to the stable. The sound of hounds barking turned to menacing growls as the group approach.

"Quiet," Gray commanded, opening the door. "You know all but one of these friends. Treat him well. He intends no harm to our sweet ladies or to me."

The dogs obeyed, though they eyed Brandel warily. Seeing the girls, both animals lunged at them, tails wagging, and nearly knocking Whisper to the ground.

"Please!" she giggled, getting her face washed with a pair of large tongues. Shadow giggled, too, reaching for the nearest. Both dogs instantly turned their wagging and licking to her.

Hanging the lantern from a hook, Gray called, "Crusher! Seeker! Heel!" The dogs left the girls reluctantly, trotting to him to sit at his feet. Gray gave each a thorough head scratch. "You must go," he said. "Find safety." Closing his eyes, he pressed his head between the dogs. The animals whined briefly, turning anxious glances to Serenity and the girls. "No. You must seek safety on your own. Go. Head further into the mountains. Find high places. Perhaps you will be safe, there." Releasing them, he watched as they shot out across the shelf, disappearing around the curve of the slope.

Gray repeated his farewell with his horse, a magnificent Persheron that made Noble seem a pony. Brandel opened the stall for his friend and grudgingly pulled the bridle free. Stroking the horse's neck, he once again opened his mind, reaching to join with Noble's. *"Follow after the other,"* he sent. *"Stay safe. Stay alive. If I survive, I will return for you."* A slap to Noble's rump sent the horse charging after Gray's.

Whisper's meek, *"Thank you,"* brushed through Brandel's head. *"He at least stands a chance, this way. Gray's animals will watch over him."*

The faintest hint of pale gold girdled the lower mountain crests to the east. "It is almost daybreak," Gray noted. "You had best away. Without snowshoes, traveling will be difficult. But I have none to spare. The boots should at least keep your feet warm." Striding to Serenity, he studied her in silence for a long minute, then turned her face up to his and kissed her soundly. "Follow the trails whenever possible and you will not miss the snowshoes so much. Stay safe. Stay alive."

She shuddered slightly. "You, as well. We will return when we can." Spinning on her heels, she set out across the shelf, the back of her mitten brushing her cheeks. Brandel averted his gaze from the unexpected event, watching Shadow and Whisper move to fall in behind the woman. Belatedly, he turned to offer his thanks to Gray, but the man was already stalking back toward the small stoop at the front of the house. There was nothing left for it but to follow the threesome.

11

The struggle through calf-deep snow slowed their descent, wearing on each of them. Roughly midway down the slope from Gray's outpost, the trail leveled, rounded a small rise, then descended once more. By noon, they trampled through slush in a forested valley. Tatters and lace-veined skeletons of leaves clung to a few scattered deciduous trees. Fir and hemlock and spruce dripped icy water on their heads. Whisper sent to Brandel the names of lingonberry, chokecherry, holly, snowberry, and dozens of other plants as they passed. Some he knew, though he let her go on uninterrupted. Now and again, they discovered remnants of the summer's wild blueberries and blackberries. While the berries were well past the height of their sweetness, Brandel still relished the finds.

The skies never broke their overcast and the chill frosted their breaths, yet the closeness of the forest and the day's efforts left Brandel sweating and wondering when Serenity might call for a rest.

"Not for a while. We will climb again, soon," Whisper sent.

"You know where we are going?"

"To Knife Point Keep, of course. But it lies deep in the mountains and the same route is not always accessible. Which path we take and how long the journey requires depends on the weather."

Knife Point Keep. A dangerous place, according to rumors. The way in was said to be treacherous. If it were any more treacherous than their journey thus far, he had little doubt that each of the messengers sent before him had perished. His arriving alive, however, could only be considered successful if the Lord of Knife Point granted him audience and agreed to send aid to the Soldiers of Damsa Dana. Each conversation with Serenity left him more doubtful.

If the Lord of Knife Point refused, would Serenity follow through and take him to this Grandmother? The old woman may refuse him, as well, and remain hidden. Perhaps that would be for the best. The more he thought on it, the less inclined he was to return any information about the woman or whatever weapon she might possess, knowing news would reach the High Priestess Danu. His duty was to report to Lord Strongbow, of course. But could Strongbow keep such a weapon safe from Danu's hands if the High Priestess decided to turn on him? Their animosity toward one another was well known, despite Strongbow's attempts to keep it quiet. And Brandel trusted the High Priestess less and less. Outright battle between Danu and Strongbow could tear Brightwater apart, though, and at a time when they needed all to fight the Red Moon threat.

Such disturbing thoughts turned his attention to the trio ahead of him, suspicion growing at the back of his mind. *All this distance in such harsh conditions. They know this land well. Why not teleport from one safe location to another?* He supposed that Knife Point Keep might, itself, be protected against outsiders gaining entry in such a manner, but…

"You are falling behind, Master Brandel. That is not wise. Clear whatever thoughts trouble your mind and focus on keeping pace."

Brandel stumbled at Serenity's unexpected sending, noticing that he had, indeed, fallen behind. Lengthening his stride, he quickly caught up. *"Why do we risk ourselves in this manner? Why not teleport as near to the keep as possible?"*

"We cannot guarantee any location is safe. How many Red Moon Warriors crossed our border at the same location you did? Did others cross before you? Are they crossing in other places? Where are they? Even if we are not concerned with emerging in their midst, there is the possibility of emerging in the middle of some roaming pack of wolves. Moreover, the landscape here is ever changing, especially in winter. The lowlands may remain the same over time. But here, trees fall, avalanches occur, boulders and rock falls litter areas previously clear, flooding rivers take out paths, waterways sometimes change course. It would be impossible to travel often enough to know every change that has occurred."

"Some things change," he acknowledged. *"But a farmer's field or orchard will look much the same, year after year. A building might burn to the ground or have an addition taking up space where once there was a garden or a walkway. Teleporting to fields within sight of a particular landmark works well, regardless of the season."*

The permanence of most of Brightwater's features never struck Brandel as a liability until now. If Red Moon spies knew the lay of the land, they could count on the information remaining unchanged over time. With such information, they could teleport full companies of warriors to Brightwater's vast unpopulated areas. It would require tremendous energy, of course. And Brandel could think of no one with sufficient capacity to accomplish such a feat all the way from the Red Moon stronghold of Rift to Brightwater's plains. But taking it piece-meal…teleporting a handful of warriors at a time, say from the northern coast of the Sisters of Sorrow Isle to the southern plains of Brightwater… That might be possible for someone with the strength of a High Priestess. Would Aifa use her power in such a manner? Would it weaken her, and by how much for how long?

It was one disturbing thought too many. Brandel shoved it aside. Only in myth did any Witch, High Priestess or otherwise, have the strength and power required to teleport anyone over such a distance.

"There was a time when Witches could teleport between worlds," drifted through his mind, carried with sorrow and a flicker of hope. The voice was not that of any of his companions, though its delicate gentility reminded him of Whisper.

"Careful of your footing," Shadow called over her shoulder. "You will do yourself no good if you fall and break a leg or disappear over a cliff."

Brandel suddenly back-stepped, barely missing a deep hole between entwined roots. A broken leg, indeed! No more speculations. No more imaginary voices in his head. Suffering the sendings from his three companions was quite enough. Keep his mind on the business at hand – that being a black and white world of clouds and snow and eternal climbing. Morning bled into afternoon and afternoon into evening. The drop in temperature as night fell ate through all the layers of Brandel's clothing and made breathing more difficult, despite tugging his hood tightly around his face and fastening the flap that covered his mouth and nose.

"Over here."

Brandel squinted into the deepening shadows to find Serenity gesturing to him from a boulder-strewn clearing to his left. Within it stood the remains of what might once have been a stronghold of some sort. Its ramparts now stood crumbling, its outer walls marred with gaping holes framed in black-scorched timbers and stone. The woman strode to one such opening, her penetrating gaze taking in the nightscape around them before motioning for them to pass through. Shadow went first, followed by Whisper. Serenity waited for Brandel. A subtle nudge at the back of his mind kept him hovering just outside. The sharp twinge along his nerves told him someone was trying to connect with him. Not… He sucked in. Not someone. Something.

Animal. It was probing. Testing. Curious. And then it was gone.

"Keep moving," Serenity urged. *"Shadow and Whisper know the way."*

The girls darted this way and that around piles of fallen stone and broken statues, Whisper on Shadow's heels. At last, they came to an opening with hinges but no door. Within could be seen more crumbling walls. Further back lurked darkness. Brandel hesitated.

"Stay out here and freeze, if you prefer," Serenity chided. *"Personally, I will welcome a warm meal and a comfortable bed for the next few hours."*

"Why do we waste our time? We should keep moving."

"It is no waste of time to eat and rest. The terrain gets more difficult as we go. Better to take it properly nourished, well rested, and alert. You already wobble where you stand, Master Journeyson. You have come this far. I have no desire to lose you over a ledge or down a crevasse because your legs cannot support you."

Brandel set his jaw. His legs did wobble, no mistake. And he had no more desire to die than she had to 'lose him'. Exhaling a snort, he scrambled over the doorway's threshold and through an area that looked much the same as the ruins they had just navigated, save this space was enclosed beneath a high, cracked ceiling, and it angled downward. Well into the chamber, what little light lay at the entrance dwindled, turning to a blackness so intense that it sucked his breath from him. His footsteps faltered, and he stood, squinting, trying to make his shadow sight sort out the vague images that rose around him as he listened for the sound of the others. Somewhere behind him came a swoosh, a rush of air, and the feel of a powerful spell. Light erupted all around, revealing a high, broad passage. A second doorway he had passed through without notice closed tight, sealing out the icy draft. Images he was unable to make out, before, proved to be pillars rising some five meters high to support a solid stone ceiling. A fading trinity knot was painted at its center.

"This way," Serenity called from halfway down the long passage.

At the far end of the corridor, another door opened for them and sealed behind them. Here lay yet another passage, this one narrow. It twisted more precipitously downward than the chamber above, taking them through a maze of turns, passing at least a dozen closed doors, the air growing steadily warmer as they traveled. Serenity stopped at a wall that blocked any further progress. Laying her hand to it, she closed her eyes, her lips moving in silent invocation.

A faint seam appeared, the stone wall parting along it. Once more, as they passed through, the way closed behind them. The seam disappeared, leaving no trace of the opening. Only then did Serenity relax, dropping her hood. Brandel glanced around at what appeared to be a dining hall designed for a great army of people. Tables filled the room, arranged in long rows, benches tucked in around them. Perhaps a meter out from the back and side walls stood a series of enormous braziers. Between them rose stone pillars upon which were mounted burning torches. The light from the accumulation of flames glistened from the polished marble of floor and high ceiling. Muting the glare were tapestries that draped the walls, their woven art depicting stories Brandel knew from childhood; stories that told the account of a battle fought on a different world just before the Goddesses returned to Slievgall'ion. He always thought the world depicted in such works looked amazingly like this one, though he had never seen anything like the round, white stone structure with earthen top that stood prominently atop a hill.

Clanging of something dropped rang from an adjoining room, followed by running footsteps, spinning Brandel around, his hand grasping the hilt of his long knife. A tall, round woman dashed into the hall, wisps of gray hair peaking from beneath a white cap, a worried scowl etched across her brow until she spotted the visitors. "My Sweets!" she exclaimed, charging toward them, her arms outstretched and her apron flapping against her long pants. Hugging the two girls first and then wrapping Serenity in a warm welcome she stepped back to regard them with an even, hazel-eyed scrutiny. "You look worn to a fare-thee-well. Come. Sit. Whisper sent to me of your coming. I have hot meats and bread preparing." Ushering the party to one of the long tables near the door through which she had come, she waited for them to sit, then turned her scrutiny to Brandel.

"Your lowlander friend, Master Journeyson, I take it." Studying him more closely, she concluded, "A Soldier of the White Goddess. An officer if I am not mistaken."

Brandel shot an accusatory glance at Whisper. "Ah, my son. The child did not tell me more than your name. The fact that you are a lowlander is suggested by the fact that you wear borrowed clothes to suit this climate. That you are built like a fortress and carry yourself like a soldier and man of authority says the rest." A click of her fingers produced a large flagon of ale, a pot of steaming tea, and four mugs atop the table. "Take your ease. I will return with dinner shortly. And then I want a full accounting of what has prompted this visit."

The woman scuttled back through the doorway, leaving Brandel to stare after her. Serenity chuckled, standing long enough to dispense with her pack and her coat. Brandel did likewise.

"Juniper never seems to realize that her guests may need to take care of other matters before being seated. Here." Serenity extended her arms to collect the girl's and Brandel's coats. Once gathered, they, along with the packs, disappeared.

Brandel waited for an explanation of this place and how Serenity knew of it, but none came. Instead, Serenity and the girls seated themselves, the girls pouring mugs of hot tea for one another while Serenity poured ale for Brandel and herself.

"So. Where are we?"

Serenity took a long breath, letting it out slowly before tasting the ale. "She remembered. Juniper always remembers. This is my favorite. A stout from your part of the world."

Brandel's brow cocked, and he ventured a taste, appreciation spreading across his features. "It is, indeed. From the fields and breweries of Singer Hollow." Granting himself a more fulsome sampling, he shifted sideways, straddling the bench and propping one arm on the table. "And this place?" he prompted for a second time. "What is it?"

"Once a temple," Serenity stated.

"For the Rose Priestesses." Shadow's statement held tremendous pride. "My mother was a priestess here. My father was one of the Guardians of Ciuin Rose."

"Once a temple," Brandel repeated. "Judging from the ruins above, I take it holds that purpose no longer."

Shadow shook her head, her eyes downcast. "This was the first temple built in honor of Ciuin Rose. Constructed during one of Her many visits from another world in a time long before the Great War, it is said. Then the souls of the Goddesses returned to us, bringing their war with them. When Breag Nemhain was defeated and those who fought for her were driven from the mountains of Knife Point and the plains and coasts of Brightwater, none believed the remnants of her armies would strike so far from the land they settled. And for some time, they remained in Rift. The remnants of her armies became the first of the Red Moon Warriors. Even when they began raiding the coasts of Brightwater, we still did not fear them; nor when they began to venture inland, sending scouting parties across the Brightwater border into Knife Point. What the Soldiers of Damsa Dana did not defeat, the Guardians of Ciuin Rose did. Or so we thought. A little more than three decades ago, a contingent of their warriors slipped unnoticed through the forests. They raided no villages. Their sole purpose, it seems, was to strike at the very heart of those who worship Ciuin Rose. To destroy her first and most prominent temple."

"The priestesses had only the warning from their Seer," Serenity put in. "But the vision came to the Sister too late. They stood no chance. Less than a handful escaped the slaughter."

Brandel shot a sympathetic glance at Shadow. "Her mother did not die, here," Serenity said. "My daughter-in-law was one of the few to escape, carrying word of the massacre to the guardians. She and her husband died on a different battlefield."

"Golden," Brandel recalled. Serenity nodded.

"After the attack," Shadow put in, "my mother and two other priestesses returned here. They worked their magic, repaired what they could, strengthened what remained of the complex; hid it with strong and carefully woven spells, undetectable by any but the scant few remaining priestesses. Unless you know this place, you will not sense the magic here as anything more than the last vestiges of long-ago days. Nor will you be able to locate the way in without proper guidance from…"

Serenity shushed her. Brandel turned an appraising eye to the woman. "You are one of the Rose Priestesses."

"No more," she sighed. "The order died with the death of my son's wife. She was the High Priestess. She removed me from my position in the order to prevent my joining when she and a small contingent of guardians traveled to Golden to meet with Sisters of the White Goddess. I have always wondered whether she foresaw the attack that was to come, and that is why she sent me from our temple. So that I would be free to take her child. But if she saw, why did she lead them all to their deaths?"

Whisper turned and laid her small hand on her aunt's arm. "You know the Sight rarely encompasses all that is to come. Perhaps she saw enough to cause her to take precautions, but not enough to call off such an important meeting."

Brandel regarded the girl. He found it curious that Whisper was the one possessing a Seer's attributes while Shadow, the daughter of the High Priestess, did not. Serenity turned a faint smile to Whisper. If she intended to say anything further, however, her words were silenced by the sounds of Juniper's scuttle back into the hall, followed by a line of three young girls and three young boys, each attired in warm pants, black boots, and belted tunics of dusty rose. The girls wore their hair pulled back in a single braid with a ribbon of the same color as their shirts tied in a bow at the base of their neck. The boys each had shortcropped hair. None looked to be older than perhaps ten. Among them, they carried some part of the meal, from plates and bowls and utensils to a platter of meat, a handled cauldron of soup, a basket of bread, and a bowl of dried berries. The children silently set about their duties, laying out the place settings in proper order and setting the food to the table, their smiles broad, their eyes eagerly taking in their guests. Serenity returned their smile, though she and Whisper and Shadow all refrained from addressing any of them. When the children finished with their tasks, Juniper led them back to the kitchens.

Brandel raised a curious brow.

"Lovely, are they not," Serenity said. "They are orphans from the villages and farms. Life, here, is harsh. Not all possess a sufficient degree of the magic for self-healing when injuries and illness are prevalent. The children who have no other family are taken in by the guardians and placed here to keep them safe. Here, they are given duties and training. Those who show promise will either be accepted into the Guard or sent to the Sisters of the White Goddess to learn what it is to be a priestess. Perhaps, in time, the Order of the Priestesses of the Rose Goddess may be reborn. Those children who seem unlikely to fit well as either guardian or priestess will return to the villages with skills to help them survive."

The meal proceeded in silence, everyone tucked into their own thoughts. Brandel wondered how many orphans existed in this land and whether all were taken in or only a few. If a few, how were they selected and what became of the rest? In Brightwater, at least some of the orphaned girls were taken into the Sisterhood to be trained as priestesses, the boys taken in by the soldiers.

"What happened to those who destroyed the temple?"

Serenity's voice tightened. "The guardians pursued them all the way to the border with Brightwater and beyond. They gave no mercy. Not a single warrior survived."

The rest of the meal was finished in silence. Brandel turned to lean his back against the table, a full mug of stout in his hands, his gaze taking in the hall. The numbers of the Priestesses of the Goddess Ciuin Rose must have been impressive for the temple to accommodate so many for meals. Perhaps it was the orphans who now filled this hall.

"You need your rest, Master Brandel." Serenity's statement cut through his thoughts, the more so when he realized she was now standing at the end of the table. A glance around indicated that Shadow and Whisper were missing. "If you will follow me," the woman added, "I will show you to your quarters. We will remain here for the night and through tomorrow's day. We leave again at dusk."

12

The sleeping quarters were laid out barracks-style, though only the bed nearest the door was prepared with sheets and blanket. Serenity nodded toward his backpack propped against the wall next to the bed. His coat hung from a peg just above the pack. "Showers and toilets are through the arch at the end of the room," she indicated. "Sleep well, Master Journeyson. The breakfast bell rings early."

"Brandel," he said as she turned to walk away. "Either Lt. Journeyson or just Brandel."

She glanced back with a smile. "One more thing, before I forget. Do you possess the magic of flame, Master Brandel?"

A slump of his shoulders and a roll of his eyes at the persistent 'Master' accompanied his simple, "No."

"Ah. Well, then, I will have someone check the spells on the torches to make sure they light for you at your need. Shadow sight may not be sufficient in the darkness, here."

Left alone, Brandel wasted little time in digging through his pack for the lighter clothes, dismayed when their stench preceded their extraction. Gathering them, he made his way to the bath. He would scrub them and hang them over the short walls of the shower stall after his own thorough soak. Dumping his arm load in the middle of the floor, he located a bar of soap and a fresh towel on a shelf over one of the many sinks and set to his own scrubbing in the comfort of the steaming shower water.

When he at last stepped out, he found his pile of dirty laundry gone. Pinned to the same shelf from which he had taken the soap and towel was a note indicating his belongings would be returned to him on the morrow. Upon his return to the sleeping quarters, he found a new set of clothes neatly folded on the trunk at the end of the bed. Brandel eyed them briefly before giving in to the allure of the mattress, pillow, and blankets. He had no idea of the hour but was sure Serenity was right. The breakfast bell would ring all too early.

For a while, his sleep was deep and untroubled. Somewhere in the dark of night, however, he awakened with the sense of someone nudging him. Sitting brought the nearer torches to light, revealing no one. Blearyeyed, Brandel fell back, drawing the covers around him again as the torch went out. On the verge of sleep, the nudging began, again.

His mind unwilling to wake, "What?" scraped past a snore.

Sunrise lifts above a pale blue-white wash of jagged peaks, a strange coloration of gray to faint yellow edging them. Shadows move. Stealth sets a smooth motion of muscles, each paw placement cautious and silent, senses alert to danger. A foul scent raises hackles, the body hunching low against the snow, watchful. Creatures woven of darkness and hunger creep. Where they pass, the snow freezes in a black crystalline mass. Any living thing caught within the path withers to ashen death. The creatures stop, empty eyes seeking.

Brandel shot upright, nearly falling from bed, his heart leaping at the clanging of the bell. A warning! A… Hand to his chest, he cast about, the sound of the bell clattering to a close. Aromas from the dining hall wafted in. With a steadying breath, Brandel tried to shake the lingering impressions of the dream from his head. His stomach rumbled.

"Fine way to wake a man," he growled, rising and dressing in the clothes left for him.

Serenity and Whisper sat facing one of the dozen braziers at the far end of the room. The light playing across their features indicated a tense discussion. At the sound of his footfalls, Serenity glanced around and nodded acknowledgment of his presence. Whisper's focus remained on the flames from the brazier. He started to offer a 'good morning,' but Serenity waved him silent. Instead, he strolled to the table where their previous meal was served, helping himself to a glass of juice from the pitcher that awaited them.

Juniper swept in and past him without a glance as she rushed down the length of the hall to Serenity. The women exchanged a few brief words before Juniper spun and headed back to the kitchens. Serenity and the little redhead remained a few seconds more, then rose and joined Brandel at the table. His creased brow must have spoken his question for him.

"Shadow is out. She will return soon," Serenity provided, taking a seat on the bench across from him. Whisper sat next to her, still appearing distracted.

"Juice?" he asked, glancing between the two.

Whisper's startled blink and shy smile preceded her soft, "Yes, please," while Serenity responded with a nod.

He poured, handing glasses across. "Is the girl...uhm... Shadow. Is she..."

"She is safe," Whisper said. "Though it is more challenging for her to hide in the light of day and the white of snow and with few trees, she manages."

"Hide?"

The little redhead ignored his question, asking one of her own. "You dreamed? Before waking this morning?"

Her query surprised him, drawing a scowl. "I dreamed. I often dream." Finishing his juice, he considered a second glass when the children filed in with breakfast, setting it out in the same manner as before. A loud rumble of his stomach prompted a giggle from two of the little girls. Their duties complete, they filed back out, once more. Brandel eyed the platter of eggs and the one with slabs of bacon. Next to those stood a basket piled with fresh biscuits, a bowl of butter balanced on top.

A large pot of tea materialized near Serenity's plate, stirring an appreciative smile. "Help yourself, Master Brandel," she said, pouring a mug and handing the pot to Whisper. He needed no second encouragement, making short work of the meal.

Shadow strolled in from the kitchens as he finished. She carried a biscuit in one hand and a slab of bacon in the other. "Do not worry about me," she snipped at his sudden guilty glance at the empty platters on the table. "I ate with Juniper before I left. Just snacking, now."

Straddling the bench next to her grandmother, she finished the bacon, then the biscuit, licking her fingers to get the last bit of butter. "Whisper was correct," she said, at last. "The creatures were outside the ruins. They have moved off to the east, now. If we keep to the north, tonight, we should be safe."

"To the east," Brandel repeated. "What lies to the east?"

Shadow cocked her head, considering. "Depends on how far they go. Two valleys over is a village. There are a few farmsteads near it. I had Juniper send word to the villagers. Perhaps some will evacuate to the sanctuary at Mt. Wisdom."

"Only some?"

"Only some," Shadow confirmed. "They will try to send their children, of course. But the depth of the early snows makes the passes dangerous. Guardians will come to meet and escort those wishing to leave their homes. Still, many will refuse to go. Their homes are their homes. Their winter stores and their livestock are there. They will try to protect them if they can."

"They cannot. Not from such creatures."

"Do not underestimate us, sir," Whisper declared.

"I am sorry, little one. But I do not see how…"

She dismissed him again, reaching for the last biscuit. "Will you come with me, Shadow?" she asked, swiveling around to stand. "I want to visit the classrooms."

Shadow disentangled herself from the bench to join her cousin.

The two disappeared through the kitchen, leaving Brandel and Serenity. "Classrooms?"

"Indeed. Do you think we would take in the children and not offer them schooling in something more than work in the kitchens?"

Serenity shook her head in amusement. "You look surprised, Master Brandel."

"Just Brandel," he grumbled. "Just Brandel."

"Very well. Brandel, then, come with me."

Their trek through the first of what turned out to be two kitchens found Juniper, another woman, and a man hard at work preparing the next meal. The adjoining kitchen contained a much larger oven than the first. Fresh bread baked within it, triggering another stomach rumble from Brandel, despite his fill from breakfast. The area also boasted several small tables and short benches, all cleaned and empty.

"This is where the children eat," Serenity stated. "They are fed first, then sent to their chores before going to their classes. Rotations are taken with respect to the chores, each group of children spending time in the different areas of our sanctuary. The ones you have seen are on their last week of duty in the kitchen. They will go next to the laundry, then to the barns and stables."

Leading him on, they traveled down a long corridor with open doors on either side. "These are the laundries and sewing rooms. The children learn not only to clean garments of various textiles and of leather, but to make and mend them." The end of the corridor bore a single door. The woman pushed it open to bright sunlight and sharp, cold air. A quick backward glance as Brandel stepped out revealed they had just come out from a wall of rock that towered well above them with a broad plateau stretching out before them. Here were housed a series of barns and stables. The stables appeared empty, but cattle, pigs, and goats filled the barns, with a variety of fowl clucking and crowing and squabbling about the grounds. At the end of the row of barns stood a storehouse.

"How do you get the animals up here? Surely, you do not parade them through the building."

"There," Serenity said, pointing. At the edge of the plateau was a wide path leading down. Brandel strode to the edge, shielding his eyes against the glisten of sun off patches of snow. The path followed a switch-backing route, disappearing in a stand of stunted evergreens partway down.

"It follows the line of the river below."

"How do you protect this area from enemies?'

"The route along the river is long, the only crossing about thirtyfive kilometers to the southeast. This side of the crossing is rocky, giving no indication of the trail that weaves between boulders until it squeezes around a sharp bend. To any who make the crossing, it appears that the only thing to the north is a sheer rock face, while an obvious trail leads further south to a mill that sets next to a waterfall. Even at the time of the attack on the temple, none among the warriors found the path that would bring them up here."

Their ability to use terrain to camouflage or hide critical areas was impressive. Equally impressive was the joy that existed, here. Though he lacked his coat, Brandel strolled the plateau, returning smiles. Laughter was common among the adults and children alike. The cold quickly took its toll, however, forcing Brandel to climb the stone steps up to join Serenity, who waited for him near another door.

"I ask for quiet, here," she said, allowing Brandel to enter first. A series of doors on each side lined the long corridor, each one closed. Serenity motioned for him to peer in through the small leaded windows to view the children and teachers in the classrooms. Judging from the writings on the wall-mounted boards, one class provided instruction in reading, another in mathematics, a third in languages, a fourth in geography with maps of Slievgall'ion covering the walls, and a fifth in herblore. The sixth and seventh dealt with the various aspects of magic, while the tenth and eleventh concerned the magic specific to healing. A twelfth room was empty.

"This one is heavily shielded," Serenity explained. "The children can practice their spells, charms, and enchantments within."

Past the classrooms, the hallway wound through the mountain, dropping downward a few steps before leveling off and revealing two more doors. "The one on the left is the girl's quarters. The one on the right is the boy's."

Beyond those doors was a wide arch. Brandel stepped through and into a magnificent open space. Marble floors and the polished granite ceiling reflected the light of dozens of wall torches and a center candlefilled chandelier, the combination providing a bright atmosphere. Cases of books lined half of one wall, with seating areas of comfortable chairs in front of each. There were also tables holding paper with styluses and small bottles of ink. In another part of the room tables were set with a variety of board games. A few art easels occupied a far corner. In between the torches, bright tapestries covered the walls, each depicting some region of Slievgall'ion or showing historical events or stories from myth and legend. One of the long walls held an enormous fireplace, a warm blaze dancing within. Along part of another stood a piano and harp, behind which were shelves filled with other musical instruments.

"These are fortunate children."

"Not so much. Most witnessed the slaughter of their families or saw them die of diseases beyond the capacity of magic or our medicines to cure. If we can bring some happiness into their young lives, then they are more likely to grow in the light of the Ciuin Rose and not sink into darkness."

Brandel ran a hand through his hair, then darted after Serenity, who was moving into yet another hallway. "Impressive. But why are there no guardians here, to protect this place?"

"It is believed by all but the guardians and the few who dwell here that this temple was utterly destroyed. No enemy dares trespass within the haunted ruins above where so many innocent priestesses died. With the protection of extra layers of cautiously woven magic, we remain safe. Guardians who pass this way will sometimes use it as a way station, but even their visits have grown fewer and further between as the time spent on their patrols grows longer."

"Are there other way stations, then?"

"Gray's, another at the other pass that I mentioned before, and a smaller one that lies on the other side of the mountains near our border with the Alainn outpost lands. Those are not hidden. Thus, they house no children."

"And if you run out of room to house more?"

"The mountains, of course, support only a small and scattered population. While the numbers of orphans vary, we have never had so many that we could not accommodate them, here."

"And if war comes to you the way it has to us? Will you still have sufficient accommodations for all the orphans?"

Serenity shuddered. "The war is here. And worse is coming. We will provide for as many children as need be, though they are likely to be the first to die. If not from exposure as they flee their homes, or from starvation as they wander, then by the hands of the assailants. Check the numbers of the parentless children among your own people, if you think I am wrong. Any who refuse to turn their backs on Damsa Dana and Ciuin Rose and worship only Breag Nemhain the Dark Heart, will see their children slaughtered before following them into death."

The truth of her words stung deep. Brandel saw too many ruined farmsteads and villages where the occupants lay slaughtered. The young were the hardest to look upon. Perhaps he never considered the fate of Brightwater's orphans beyond sending them to become soldiers or priestesses because he encountered so few. It would be no different for these people. That, alone, should provide ample reason for the Guardians of Ciuin Rose to join the Soldiers of Damsa Dana. Yet he feared it would be too little. Was his best hope to seek for a myth of an antiquated woman with the prayer that there was some truth of a weapon?

Ice bit into his marrow. And if this Grandmother is no more than a myth, or some delusional old woman, or perhaps someone too senile to remember anything about the earlier times or any weapon?

Realizing that Serenity had crossed the kitchen where bread was being taken from the ovens and was halfway across the one where a pot of soup for the midday meal was cooking, Brandel lengthened his stride to catch up to her. He said nothing about his thoughts, however.

"I will leave you to do as you choose, for now," Serenity said as they returned to the dining hall. "I advise against going outside the confines of the temple, though. And recommend in favor of your taking your rest. Juniper will send a light meal to you and will provide a more substantial early evening meal for us so that we may depart as the night approaches."

Brandel ignored Serenity's recommendation, taking up residence on a bench near the fire where Serenity and Whisper conversed, earlier. A mug, a keg, a plate with a small loaf of bread fresh from the ovens, and a block of cheese appeared on the table next to his resting elbows. The stout, especially, was a welcome offering, his desire being to drown his unwelcome visions of dead children and his doubts about the Grandmother. The doubts remained. No Witch could be as old as was claimed of this woman. The few who survived into their fifth or sixth hundred years often lost themselves, either in too many memories or in the inability to recall anything at all. Eventually, all died.

Death is a natural condition, his mother once told him. One from which none are fully exempt. Not even the Alainn. She spoke of many things, his mother did. It was from her he first heard of the ancient one. His mother believed in Grandmother; believed that the one so named was once a companion to the Goddesses and the people who returned them to this world. His head drifted to his folded arms. His mother believed, and as a child, he did, as well. Now…

A twitch. A charge along his nerves. A white landscape stretched out, seen from low to the ground; keen senses detect the scent of prey. There. In the shadow of a boulder. Eyes and mind focus. Head lowers with nose skimming above the icy white crust. Muscles tense, holding taught, moving in silence. A powerful lunge. Teeth bite deep into soft fur, tearing into flesh and warm blood. The edge of hunger eases but does not abate.

13

Brandel awoke with a half-completed snore, catching the chuckle from a man sweeping the floor near him. A few tables away, a woman busied herself wiping them down. The bread and cheese plates from earlier were gone, his mug empty, though the keg on the table still held ample drink. He drew a refill, then swung his legs out from beneath the table, the nearer torches sparking to life at his motion. Across the hall, more lit as Whisper wandered in. Even from this distance, Brandel detected her faint smile.

Pushing to his feet, he ambled across, stretching out kinked muscles on his way to join her at their now customary choice of tables. Her smile broadened, the deep jewel green of her eyes shining in the flickering illumination of the hall as she gracefully settled on the end of the bench. "I am sorry, Master Brandel. I did not mean to interrupt your nap. You might have been more comfortable, though, had you sought your bed."

"It was not my intention to nap at all," he yawned.

"You are the better for it, I am sure. It will be a difficult night of travel. We must climb to another ridge line. Following it will shorten our distance since it will keep us above the valley. We hoped Ciuin Rose would bless us with an overcast night to hide the moons. But it is not to be. We will be more exposed in their light, fading though it is. Still, it is better than in the light of day."

Brandel's head cocked, his curiosity about the child renewed. "You foresee the weather?"

Whisper's sigh accompanied her swipe of a strand of red hair back from her face as she watched him sit across from her. "I will thank you to stop thinking of us as children, sir. Shadow and I have both seen our twenty-first birthday. To answer your question, though – about foreseeing the weather – sometimes." Her gaze dropped for a moment before returning to him. "What is it that you see, Master Brandel?"

"I have not that gift," he returned. "If I did, perhaps I would know where to find this Grandmother. And for the love of the heavens, will you please stop reading my thoughts and stop calling me 'Master'? It is just Brandel."

"If you stop thinking of Shadow and me as children," she chided. "As for knowing what the Sight might show you if you had the attribute, no Seer knows what their gift may reveal or when. That it would grant you knowledge of Grandmother's whereabouts is most unlikely, though. So, I ask again, what have you seen?"

Shadow's arrival spared him the effort of convincing Whisper that he held no Seer's gift. Anything that entered his mind was either woven from dreams or came straight from what his eyes took in.

Shadow plopped onto the bench beside her cousin. "Which book did you finish, this time?" she asked, poking a teasing finger at Whisper. "or should I ask how many books you finished?"

"More than you," Whisper sniffed. "Among them, the first volume of The Origin of the Goddesses."

"You have read that one a dozen times, already."

"And I might read it a dozen more."

"What does it matter, their origins? All we need know is that they are at war."

Whisper chewed at her lip, exasperation in her questions. "Why? Why are they warring? They are sisters. Sisters should stand together."

Shadow heaved a sigh and shook her head. "Not all do. We cannot change that."

"But we should try to understand why Breag Nemhain betrayed her sisters. Maybe then we could understand how to stop the war."

Brandel leaned forward to rest an elbow on the table. "It is part of the human condition."

Shadow shot a glance across at him as if only now recognizing that he was there. "What?"

"Nothing. Only something my mother used to say. About practically everything. Part of the human condition, she would say."

"And what does your mother say about your leaving your people to come here?"

"Nothing. She is long dead."

Shadow winced, the belligerence so frequent in her expression softening. "I am sorry. I..."

"There is no need for your apology. It was not by your hands. And it was a long while ago." Brandel straightened, pushing back from the table. "It is my apology that needs offering since I interrupted your conversation. I will just find my way back to my belongings and get them repacked."

"You may as well remain where you are." Serenity's voice carried from the archway that led to the sleeping quarters. "There will be time to prepare for our departure after our meal. Juniper says the children will be serving it shortly."

Even before Serenity reached the table, the children filed in, a pair of youngsters lingering after the food was laid out. Brandel was enjoying a mouthful of roast pork when one of the little girls crept nervously to his side, leaning to whisper, "What is it like, sir? In Brightwater?"

His glance brought crimson to the child's face, and she started to back away. "Give me a moment," he managed, swallowing. She still looked ready to flee. Brandel motioned her closer. "Brightwater," he confided, "is beautiful, especially in autumn. The low, rolling hills that approach our border with Knife Point are covered in trees with bright leaves of orange, red, copper, and gold. The grasses across the prairie are golden, and the grains grown in the lowlands are being harvested."

"The lowlands. Are they truly flat as a tabletop? And the coast, sir? I have never seen an ocean. What is it like?"

"Not so flat as a tabletop," he laughed. "But near enough. As for the coast, it is wild, rocky, and windy. Water stretches out for further than the eye can see. Some days you cannot tell where ocean leaves off and sky begins. Storms often sweep in, churning the gray waters and slamming the rugged coastline with white spray that showers taller than the trees of your forests."

Eyes wide and only half believing, the little girl backed to her companion, the two dipping curtsies before scurrying off to join the other children. The one who asked the questions paused in the doorway, turning to cast him one last glance over her shoulder.

Serenity chuckled. "She will talk about you for an age, now."

"Why is that?"

"You are a man from a world entirely different from her experiences. And you shared a glimpse of it with her. Be careful. She and her friend are likely to tell the others. You may well find a chorus of young voices pleading for more information."

"I would show them, if I could."

"Would you?" Shadow's murmur sounded dubious.

"I would. I would show you and Whisper and Serenity, as well once this war is won and we can travel in peace."

Shadow regarded him, finally flashing a brief smile as she rose. "I have seen the bright colors of autumn in our foothills but would love to see your prairies and coast. For now, however, I must see to my own repacking."

Brandel excused himself, as well, aware that nightfall was approaching. His heavy travel clothes he found freshly laundered and laying on the bed next to the coat and mittens Gray had given him. The clothes he left on the floor of the bath the night before were also laundered and tucked at the bottom of his pack. The rest of his belongings along with two clean blankets were arranged in a neat pile next his coat. On the trunk lay a new rope, a small axe, and several bundles of dried meats, dried fruits and berries, some cheese, two loaves of bread, and a thick skin of water. Whether he had Serenity and the girls to thank or Juniper and the children, he hoped to discover before leaving.

"Say nothing," came Shadow's fierce sending as Brandel strolled back into the dining hall, the pack hanging over one shoulder. The girl sat on the corner of the table where they had taken their meals, her features devoid of expression, though grief reflected in her dark eyes. Whisper hovered next to her, the girl's eyes red, tear tracks still fresh on her cheeks. Both girls already wore their coats and packs, as did Serenity who stood facing Juniper. The latter fidgeted with her apron. Serenity was ashen faced, her eyes downturned. The conversation exchanged by the two women was too quiet for Brandel to make out. He heeded Shadow's warning, however, and remained silent.

Serenity hugged Juniper, then stiffened, striding toward the passage that led back out to the ruins and the night. Brandel quickly fastened his coat and slid the second strap of his pack over his shoulder, securing his bow across the strap. As they reached the edge of the tumbled and crumbling outer walls, he had a clear view of the diminishing red moon framed prominently between the two distant mountain spires that rose above Gray's way station. His glance darted back for a second scrutiny. Was that smoke rising from the saddle between the peaks?

The sharp crunch of Serenity's footfalls was joined by those of Shadow and Whisper. Setting his back to the visage, Brandel fastened the pack's chest strap, and joined them. No one spoke.

They kept to the edge of the site, hugging the shadows of crumbling remains for as long as possible, covering an area of at least a kilometer of rising terrain. At last setting the ruins to their backs, they cut downslope along a narrow ledge, then climbed again. With the rose moon now in its dark stage, the light from the sliver of the blue-white moon vied with that of the crescent red moon to mute the stars. Beneath the anemic red wash, they crested the ridge Whisper had mentioned. Brandel regarded the narrow path that ran along its top with an anxious eye. Rising and falling, it skirted ice-covered boulders, stretching from a near peak and scooping out across the night to end atop another, somewhat lower mountain crest. The distance was impossible to judge. It would be a treacherous stroll, though, given the rising wind. One severe gust, a trip, or a slip could sweep any one of them from their high perch, dropping them to their deaths far below.

Ahead of him, the threesome made slow progress as they eased past boulders and struggled through snow or over packed ice, the wind increasingly battering them. "Wait!" Dropping his pack, Brandel dug into it, retrieving the new rope. *"Wait!"* he sent.

As one, the three turned. Serenity understood at once what he intended and gestured them back to where he stood. Taking one end of the rope, she tied a length first around Shadow and then Whisper before securing the end around her own waist. Brandel tied the trailing end around himself. Another moment was spent untying the axe he had been given from the supporting loops on the outside of his pack. If someone slipped, he might just be able to anchor them all with it.

Without another word, they set off once more, Brandel praying to both Damsa Dana and Ciuin Rose that Serenity knew what she was doing, marching them along the narrow ridge. Time and effort could be saved by teleporting. Did the landscape, even here in this treeless and frozen void, change so much as to pose a greater risk for teleportation than what they faced under the current conditions?

His legs wobbled mercilessly long before they trundled up the last rise. Serenity pointed to a shelf at least ten meters below where they stood. "We shelter there while we rest."

"And we get down to it...how?" So cold was he that Brandel's lips could barely form the words around his shouted question. And having done so, the wind threatened to carry them away before they could reach Serenity's ears.

Without response, Serenity untied herself from his rope, drew a knife from beneath her coat and dropped to her knees, digging and slicing into the ice. Though he refused to untie his connection to the girls, Brandel managed to slip past the shivering pair to kneel beside the woman, drawing his knife, as well. *"Tell me what you are looking for and let me dig for it."*

"There is a ladder anchored, here. It extends down to the shelf. Just be careful not to cut it."

The heavy mittens made competent use of the knife impossible. Pulling them off, Brandel shoved them into a pocket, then began hacking, chopping, and scooping at the ice. Several centimeters down, he finally discovered a metal U-bolt, a thick knot of hemp secured to it.

"To your left about fifty centimeters you will find the other bolt."

Brandel nodded, laying his knife aside briefly while he rubbed his numbing hands together. Taking up the task once more, he leveraged his blade into the ice as near the uncovered anchor as he could gauge, shoving and lifting to break free the top layer of frozen ground. The sharp edges of shattered ice sliced through his skin, leaving red smears as he worked. At length, Serenity laid her hands on his.

"You have done the hard part. Let me take over, now."

Rocking back, he brushed his bloodied hands along the top layer of snow before returning his knife to the sheath beneath his coat and fetching his mittens, fumbling to pull them back on. Serenity, in the meantime, removed hers to grasp both ends of the hemp, her eyes closed in concentration. Ice trickled to a melted stream running the length of the ladder, the heat the woman was calling into play following exactly along the hemp. After several minutes, she drew the ladder free and slung its end over the edge, watching as it fell into place. Brandel considered that she might have saved him the cuts and abrasions by using that gift to melt the area around the anchors in the first place.

"I will go first."

Before Brandel could protest or at least suggest she anchor herself to the rest of the group, again, Serenity was over the side and climbing down. Once on the shelf, she glanced around, sending, *"Wait a moment."*

For several minutes, her hands swept back and forth in an area near the face of the cliff. Beneath them the snow gradually melted to reveal the surface of the rock ledge, the water running toward the shelf's edge to refreeze next to the remaining snow. At last, she stood looking up at him. *"The rope tying you together is not long enough. Untie Shadow first and send her down. Then you can readjust the rope to help Whisper. I do not think she has the strength left to climb down without assistance."*

Brandel obeyed without question, nervously observing Shadow's progress down the ladder. Only when Serenity had a safe hold on her granddaughter, ushering her to the side, did he turn his attention to the little redhead. To his dismay, the girl was slumped on the ground, her shivering worse than before. Settling to his knees behind her, he untied himself and lifted her, snugging her tight against him before securing the rope, once more. *"Can you stand?"*

Whisper failed to respond. Bracing himself, he edged her to the ladder and again removed his mittens stashing them in his pockets. It was a delicate maneuver, rotating around with the girl tied to his front and then easing over until his boot found the first rung. With Whisper between him and the rock face, he worked his way down. The bite of cold and pain in his hands made grasping the hemp worrisome, yet he held on, taking one rung, then the next, then the next. The measure of his relief when he felt Serenity's grip on the backs of his legs expressed itself in a long, exhaled moan. Feet firmly set on the shelf, he worked the knot in the rope loose to release the girl, lifting her into his arms and depositing her near her cousin.

Serenity was out of her backpack in an instant, pulling free a blanket and wrapping it around the two. In the next moment, she was calling small twigs and branches to her from areas of the slope adjacent to their shelf. For several moments, they hovered as she encircled a small space with rocks. Letting the sticks and twigs fall, she arranged them, then withdrew the familiar pouch from a pocket on the side of her pack. Protected therein lay her folded copper with the lumps of glowing coals. At first, the best their heat could provide was sizzling smoke. Over several minutes, and assisting with the heat from her hands, however, Serenity coaxed a small blaze to burn.

"That is bound to attract attention," Brandel warned.

"I hope so." Serenity called more branches to her from the sedge and brush covered lower slopes. These she stacked near the wall, holding the fogging heat from her hands over them to dry them as much as was possible.

"You hope so," Brandel grunted. "Well, let us just hope it is not the attention from whatever has been stalking us."

"It is a risk we must take. This is harder on Whisper than I had expected. We have made this trek before, but never on the heels of so many of her visions. If the Guardians of Ciuin Rose spot our flame, they will come to check us out."

"And if it is something else that spots it?"

Serenity sat back with a heavy sigh. "I do not think those creatures have come round to this side. There has been no sign of them crossing our paths. Nor has Whisper had any indication that they are currently on our heels." Gaining her feet, she retrieved her pack, digging in it, once more. "Here," she murmured, withdrawing a bundle and unwrapping a jar and some strips of cloth. "Let me see your hands."

Brandel blinked at her for a moment before the burning sting registered in his mind. Once more removing his mittens, he held his hands out, only mildly surprised by the amount of blood on them. "I can work the healing, myself," he muttered.

"I am sure you can, Master Brandel. But I prefer to take no chances."

He had no time for further argument, as the woman was already rubbing snow over the wounds to clean them. That done, she gently dried them with the warmth from her hands, then spread ointment from the jar across them, finally wrapping strips of cloth around the sliced flesh. "They should not be stuffed inside your mittens for a while, yet. Come sit by the fire."

In truth, Brandel was glad not to have to pour energy into healing. He was not sure he was that much better off than Whisper. Shadow, on the other hand, observed her aunt in silence, her gaze flicking now and again to him when it appeared she did not think he was looking. The girl…young woman…made no move to leave her cousin's side, however, keeping the blanket pulled tight around them, Whisper's head on Shadow's lap.

Seeing the direction of Brandel's attention, one corner of Serenity's mouth curled in a faint smile. "They are close."

"So you said before."

He felt the useless fool, sitting next to the fire while Serenity continued to buzz about, taking food from his pack and distributing a little around. Shadow cast a worried glance at Whisper.

"She will eat when she wakes," Serenity assured her. "I just pray she has no more visions for a while. Her mind needs to rest as much as her body."

Brandel nibbled at the bread Serenity offered, shooting a glance back up to the top of the cliff. "Why did you not use your magic to melt the ice up there."

"Ice is much harder to thaw than snow. And there was the snow to clear from the shelf before I could make a fire. I dare not leave myself too exhausted to function. Nor should you. Sleep, if you can." Scooting to brace his back against the cliff, Brandel stared out at the shadowy landscape and the surrounding mountain peaks. To his left, the red moon had set, the thinnest sliver of a newly waxing rose moon all but lost in the last bit of light from the waning white moon and the pale glow of a coming sunrise. Brandel disliked the notion of sitting exposed on the ledge in the light of day. It was unlikely, however, that Whisper could recover enough, either to climb back to the top or to scale down the rest of the slope before nightfall.

14

Agentle shake of his shoulders brought Brandel grudgingly awake, his hand going to his eyes to shield them from the late morning sun. Groaning, he unwrapped from his blanket and pushed to his feet, shaking out his stiff and aching limbs. "Are we leaving? Is Whisper up to it?"

"There," Serenity said, gesturing across the frozen landscape at a glint of metal. Brandel tensed, turning to reach for the bow and quiver attached to his pack.

"No need for that. Those are guardians."

Squinting, Brandel found it impossible to tell more than the fact that an encampment stood within a stand of trees in the distance and a good deal lower than their perch. "How can you be certain?"

"I spoke with them." Serenity pointed, again, this time at a series of broken branches partially buried in the snow about a hundred meters down slope of where they stood. "I need a larger fire. Are you capable of teleporting a couple of those branches?"

"A fire? We have a fire."

"Not large enough."

Brandel had no idea what the woman had in mind. Their current fire was putting out enough smoke to let the guardians, and anyone else who happened to be in the area, identify their precise location. Shrugging, he leaned to peer down at the branches, considering. It was impossible to figure just how deep the snow was, much less how large the limbs might be. Assuming they were not snagged under boulders or larger pieces of broken tree, he could teleport one or two of them, but... Straightening, he took the measure of the shelf they were on. "This is not large enough to hold such a blaze. Are you sure..."

"The shelf will hold it. Just get me a couple of those branches as soon as I clear more snow from the edges."

Heaving a sigh, Brandel studied the exposed portion of the tree limbs, again.

"Are you sure you want me to try this?" The thin quaver of Shadow's question created a warble to the music that ran through it. Brandel glanced back to find the girl standing near the current blaze, her troubled stare fixed on it.

"The tents are too close together, the only open space holding their large fire. Teleporting outside of their camp risks sinking us in a snowy mire or locking us in the middle of a tree trunk or some other equally unhealthy predicament. And I will not waste their time asking for any among the guardians to search for a clear area and send the image to me." Serenity set her focus on the small burning brand she held, sweeping it back and forth to clear the remaining snow faster than the use of her hands had earlier achieved. "Plus, I have not the strength left to teleport us along with our packs."

"I can teleport us."

Serenity shook her head. "The same reasons I will not attempt it hold for you, my dear. With the assistance of their mage, you can work the passage."

The tension in Shadow's voice now produced a subtle shrill ring. "But how do you know there is someone who can…"

Serenity drew a deep breath, exhaling it in a frustrated huff. "I spoke with Lt. Starn. He is preparing to receive us."

Brandel caught Shadow's surprised inhale. "Uncle Singer is with them?" With an agitated toss of her head, she responded to Brandel's unspoken question with, "You need not look so stunned that I should have an uncle who is a Guardian of Ciuin Rose." Her eyes flicked back toward her aunt. "Though I do not know him. He…" her voice trailed off.

The unexpected dulling of Shadow's usual self-assuredness settled a vague unease over Brandel. "What is this business about him being ready to receive us?"

Instead of answering, Serenity gestured downslope. "Master Brandel, if you please…"

"What?"

"The branches."

"Brandel," he snorted, glaring down the slope. "Just bloody Brandel!" Applying a bit of magical heft, he tested what could be seen of the broken limb, noting the weight against his level of energy. It was doable so long as it was not wedged beneath something larger. The branch rose clumsily from beneath the snow, trailing brown vines and mud. Having the measure of it, Brandel delivered it with a wet thunk to the middle of the shelf. The second piece of wood proved either too heavy or lodged beneath something, forcing Brandel to search out another.

He found a section of log jutting from the snow a little further down. Again, he tested, carefully lifting it free. It proved smaller than the piece already delivered, but would hopefully meet with Serenity's approval, whatever her purpose.

The woman enhanced the flame in the bits of wood spread beneath the first branch. Eyeing the second piece dubiously, she grumbled, "Will have to make this do, I suppose." With the blaze steadily growing, she turned and made her way to Whisper. The girl was awake, though Brandel had no idea how long she had been so. Laying within the folds of the blanket, she watched the fire without comment.

"How are you, my dear?" Serenity asked, kneeling beside her. "Can you stand?"

"Of course, I can," Whisper sniffed. "I slept well. I am ready whenever you are." Her voice was even quieter than normal, however, and she still shivered. It appeared a struggle for her to gain her feet, but she refused her aunt's offer of a hand, casting a sidelong glance at Shadow, instead. Whisper's cousin stood apart from them, her hood thrown back, her black hair whipping in the gusts stirred by the rising heat as it mixed with the sharp air. Her midnight eyes were fixed on the flames, her features set in concentration. "I hear," she murmured. "I see your pattern and will match it."

Whisper inhaled; let it out in a rush with, "I have never done this."

"Just do as you are told when you are told," Shadow encouraged, her gaze never leaving the blaze that was now eating steadily along the lengths of the branches.

Brandel twitched, his unease intensifying. "Never done what?"

"Over here, if you please, Ma…Brandel. Stand next to Shadow." The gesturing of Serenity's hands orchestrated the movement of the wood, shifting it to allow the flames to spread as evenly as possible.

Brandel edged around the fire, Serenity grabbing his arm as he neared her, positioning him so close to Shadow that their arms brushed. She directed Whisper to stand next to him before taking her own position on the other side of her niece. "Do not budge until I say so."

Brandel was liking this less and less. "And then what?"

She shot him a smile. "And then we step into the flames."

"We do wha…?!"

"Hush," Shadow snapped. "I need to concentrate. Do exactly as you are told if you wish to survive."

Horrified, Brandel, realized what they were asking him to do. Impossible! He was no Fire Mage. He even lacked the ability to ignite so much as a spark with his fingers. This was… He swallowed. Many tales told of those who had tried and failed to pass through the flames. Tales of their screams as they burned alive. His near backstep was halted by Whisper's hand on his. *You will be safe. Shadow will let no harm come to you. Just do as you are instructed.* The calm quiet of the girl's voice in his head brought a steadiness to his nerves.

A song arose, almost as soft as Whisper's words as it touched his mind. A melody only, intense for all its softness, driving in a rhythm of sevens and threes. That common rhythm. The same as the one woven into Serenity's and the girls' home. Dances were also set to it, many in honor of the Soul Bearer who, at least according to legend, returned the souls of the Goddesses to Slievgall'ion all those centuries ago. There was no dancing, here, though, save for that of the flames. His brow creased as he shot a glance at Shadow, knowing the song came from her. She was weaving a dance within the fire; a pattern. Barely detectable, but… Around them rose a faint haze. It started at their feet, tendrils stretching out, curling around, slowly encompassing them.

"Now!" Serenity charged. "Step into the flames, now!"

So firm was the command that he followed it before realizing he had done so. He flinched automatically as the fire leaped around him, scarlet and yellow tongues flicking at the protective haze. But the heat never touched him, even as the blaze erupted in a blinding blue-white flash. A moment later, the flames dropped back, revealing the curious faces of men and women surrounding them. Shadow's song continued as Serenity commanded they step from the blaze. Once clear, the sweet beauty of Shadow's voice faded, the music gone. The girl swayed. Without thinking, Brandel spun and caught her, lifting her from her feet. For a moment, a fiery flicker in her dark eyes warned that she would strike him for his effrontery. But it died instantly, Shadow falling limp in his arms, her head resting against his shoulder, her breathing shallow and unsteady.

"Here!" a voice called. A burly man waived their group in his direction. Serenity stayed near Whisper, motioning for Brandel to be careful to avoid the man who still stood with an unblinking gaze on the dying flames. As they approached the guardian who had called to them, the man turned to lead them toward a large tent. Others parted before their small party, allowing them to pass, their watchful silence a weight against Brandel's back as he moved through them.

Their guide halted long enough to hold a tent flap open for them, barking over his shoulder, "Another cot and three more chairs."

The enclosure was even more spacious than it appeared from the outside. At its center, fire burned on a massive brassier, its warmth a welcome greeting. To one side stood a small desk and chair. Close to that was a long table holding a map, its corners held in place by stones. On the opposite side of the tent was a single cot piled with several blankets.

"Lay her there," the man indicated.

Brandel deposited Shadow gently, pulling the blankets from beneath her and draping several across her. When he turned, he found the original man gone and the one whose attention was fixed on the flames standing just inside the tent flap. Tall, with hair and eyes as dark as Shadow's the man regarded Serenity hesitantly, the woman's features gradually giving way to a relieved smile.

"Singer." The word was almost a sigh.

"Mother," he grinned. "It has been so long. So long. You look tired."

Serenity could hold back no longer, throwing her embrace around him. "Until you responded to my sending, I was not certain you would be among this company. I feared… I feared…"

Singer gave her a tight hug that lifted her from her feet. Releasing her, he stepped back, with a chuckle. "I still live. My men protect me well. I, on the other hand, feared for you. No one had word of you for ages. No one save Gray, perhaps. But he says nothing. As my men do for me, he protects you."

Serenity's face darkened. "What word did he send and when?"

"Gray sent to us that foul creatures crossed our borders and moved into our lands. He spotted them at the saddle and was planning to set fire to them. We have heard nothing since. I was taking a company to check on his outpost; see if he succeeded in destroying them."

"He would report his success," Serenity ventured. "If he…"

Singer reached for his mother's hands. "Perhaps he was forced to flee the flames and simply has not had an opportunity to send again."

Serenity swallowed. "Nothing would prevent his reporting. Nothing except…"

"Do not count him dead, yet. Your husband is the wiliest guardsman around. More so, even than father was."

"Lieutenant," called from just outside.

Turning to the flap, Lt. Singer pushed it aside, allowing entry for a man carting a cot and three others bearing chairs. With a gesture, the lieutenant indicated where to place them. The men did so, snapped a salute, and left. "Now," Singer directed, pointing Whisper to the cot and his mother to the chair that had been placed nearest him. "Let me guess," he said, nodding at the girl who plopped wearily onto the edge of the just provided bed. "You must be Whisper. You are as diminutive and lovely as your mother, and you have your father's red hair." Whisper flashed a timid smile.

"And this," he continued, turning his attention to the girl lying on the cot, her face pale and her eyes closed. "This must be Shadow. She resembles her father, though she is far prettier."

A faint huff issued from the girl, her eyes fluttering open, her head turning to regard him, her brow creasing. "Uncle Singer," came out in a long exhale. "I remember almost nothing of papa. But you... you look just like the pictures of him."

Singer ran a hand through his hair, his lips pinched. "Indeed." Shifting his attention to Brandel, he gestured to one of the empty chairs. "Sit. Please. We received word of the attack on my mother's home. I feared for each of you until Juniper reached out to say you were at the temple. Tell me what your journey has revealed. We need as much intel as we can get."

"The creatures are in pursuit of me, I fear," Brandel muttered, making his way to the chair and sinking onto it.

Serenity shook her head. "I would not be so sure. At least, I do not believe they are solely in pursuit of you."

"The little one?" Singer asked, regarding Whisper as he pulled the chair from his desk around to join the group. "She inherited her mother's gift of Sight?"

"Stronger than her mother's," Serenity agreed, her tone tight. "She has had visions for at least as long as she has been able to speak of them. I suspect they have always visited her. But they come with increasing frequency and intensity, of late. Their meaning is not always clear, save that they come as a warning. She foresaw Master Brandel's arrival days before he entered the woods. Saw scouts from the Red Moon coming with deadly intent. She insisted that she and Shadow find Master Brandel and bring him to me before the scouts happened across him. She also foresaw the dark creatures Gray tried to kill. Whisper believes they seek for her."

Shadow sat so suddenly that the returning color washed again from her face, leaving her weaving. "She...she what?!" Gripping her head in her hands, Shadow took several deep breaths before turning an accusatory glare at her cousin. "You did not tell me! Why did you not tell me?"

"I was not, at first, entirely certain. I saw only that these creatures seemed apart from the scouts who came behind Master Brandel. But I sensed..." A shudder ran through Whisper. "They know me. They try to reach into my mind through my visions. But I have blocked them."

"By Ciuin Rose and Damsa Dana, child!" Serenity swore. "That much you failed to tell me! It is no wonder you are getting weaker. How much energy must you expend to weave your shielding so tightly as to keep those things out of your head?"

"It is not so bad," Whisper mumbled.

Serenity sputtered, "Not so bad? Not so bad? You should have said! I could help to strengthen your shielding."

"But..."

"But nothing! We will sit you down this very night, and I will build a stronger spell around you." The woman was shaking with her shock and obvious terror for Whisper. Shadow was still simmering, perched on the side of the cot, angry tears glistening on her cheeks.

"It would appear," Singer put in, his voice calm as he passed a reappraisal over Whisper. "That you do well enough on your own. Still. Mother is correct. Let her help." Before Whisper could respond, the lieutenant shifted his attention to Brandel.

"So, Master Brandel, what is your story?"

Brandel heaved an agitated sigh. "Will everyone kindly stop with the Master. My name is Brandel Journeyson. I am a Soldier of the Goddess Damsa Dana. My rank is Lieutenant. Strongbow, Lord of Brightwater sent me to achieve what his messengers could not. I was unaware I was being pursued by the Red Moon Warriors much less that I would end up leading them to these ladies."

The lieutenant steepled his fingers. "And to what purpose did Strongbow send you?"

"To speak with the Lord of Knife Point and ask for aid in our battles with the Red Moon Warriors."

"And he seeks Grandmother," Shadow snarled.

"He must find her," Whisper put in. It was the first time Brandel could recall hearing an edge to the smaller girl's voice or seeing a confrontational set to her jaw.

Shadow opened her mouth. Closed it. Sucked in on her lower lip, blinking at her cousin.

Singer's glance skimmed from one girl to the next before he returned a steady scrutiny to Brandel. "I see. I do not know that we can help with that. However, there may be someone who can. You must suffer a few days with us as we wait for our scouts to check Gray's outpost. When they return, we will take you to Knife Point Keep. I will attempt to contact Grandmother's guardian when we arrive."

Brandel pursed his lips, then nodded. "Perhaps I could accompany your scouts. I owe Gray much for the clothing he provided. I would not have lasted long without it."

"The scouts left this morning. They should return by evening two days hence. Take your rest, here, while you can. Our trek to Knife Point Keep is long and difficult." Rising, he headed for the tent flap, stopping long enough to add, "Tents are being prepared for you near mine. We will post guards to protect you." His glance skimmed first to Shadow and then to Whisper. "You will alert me to any visions?"

Whisper's faint smile accompanied her short nod of agreement.

15

The ladies disappeared into a tent to one side of Lt. Starn's. Brandel assisted with the setup of the tent designated for his use on the opposite side, grateful for the cot, chair, and small brazier provided for him. Once his pack was deposited, however, he meandered the encampment, anxiously eyeing the jagged peaks all around. On maps, the inked band of the Knife Point and Song Mountain ranges were impressive but far from imposing to his inexperienced eye. It was a different matter, standing in their midst beneath the shockingly intense blue of a cloudless sky. On the plains, he could see to the far horizon. Here, great mountains rose to the heavens all around, each streaked with blue-gray shadows and gleaming crystalline snow. He missed seeing the horizon.

The thought of home circled him round to his men and the other companies of Soldiers of Damsa Dana. Where were they? How many Red Moon Warriors now warred across Brightwater, and how far had they pressed? Were they, even now, flooding into Knife Point and the mountains? How many were hidden among these massive slopes? He turned an anxious eye to the encampment. Would the warriors make it to Knife Point Keep before he did?

By early evening, clouds moved in, once more, the bitter cold conspiring with the thin, sharp air to prevent Brandel's taking a full breath. Pulling the flap on his hood across his nose and mouth to warm his inhales, he set himself to a study of those in the camp. The guardians who were off duty at any given time invited him to sit with them around the central fire, where they talked of past battles and shared their meals. Only the older ones, including some of the women, had seen much in the way of major battles, one woman declaring recollections of fighting on the Sisters of Sorrow and the Fire Islands. Brandel refrained from expressing his doubts, unless, of course, she was the one calling herself Grandmother. He doubted that, as well, though he could not say why. Easier to believe were those who spoke of the slaughter of the priestesses at the Temple of Ciuin Rose and their pursuit of the warriors, leaving none of the enemy alive. The youngest of the guardians had, for the most part, experienced only skirmishes here and there when the occasional cluster of scouts or a small raiding party infiltrated their lands.

Brandel offered up his own tales of wars up and down the coast and into the farmsteads and towns of the lowlands. Lt. Singer Starn was chief among those who listened, often prompting Brandel with questions about tactics and weapons. The man's expression remained unreadable throughout. After such exchanges, he wandered out into the night to take his time at watch.

On the second night, Lt. Starn approached Brandel from the camp's outer perimeter. "The cold is hard on you," he observed. "Join me in my tent. You can warm yourself while we talk."

"I do not wish to impose myself more than is necessary."

"It is no imposition, Lt. Journeyson, I assure you."

Brandel fell into step with Starn, ducking into the tent behind him. He was surprised to see Serenity and the girls seated in chairs placed around the large brasier. The three had not ventured out since their arrival. Though they each looked better rested, they also appeared apprehensive, starting at the sound of the men's entrance. Serenity cocked an expectant brow at Lt. Starn.

"Still no word," he responded. "If the scouts do not return by daybreak, we must leave without them and learn their report when they join us at Knife Point Keep. Serenity slumped back, Whisper's hand going to her aunt's arm. Starn nodded toward an empty chair next to Whisper while he moved his around from his desk. Brandel settled, uneasy under Starn's scrutiny.

"You know what it is to lose fellow soldiers," Starn said, pouring mugs of ale and handing them round before he took his seat. "Aye. Too many to count."

"Yet I hear no grief in your voice. Not upon your arrival, nor when talking with my men."

"I mourned for them when they fell. I cannot afford to carry grief with me. It devours the soul, leaving only an empty shell."

"So, you do not seek vengeance?"

"Oh, I do, indeed. When it comes, each time it comes, I revisit my sorrow and exact my revenge in great measure."

"Why did you leave the service of the Soldiers of Damsa Dana?"

Brandel tilted his head, eyeing the lieutenant in confusion. "As I told you before, I did not leave the service of the soldiers. My mission on behalf of Lord Strongbow is to obtain an audience with the Lord of Knife Point."

"Whisper tells me you are an honest man. A man to be trusted. But your skills are better served on the battlefield. Why would Strongbow send you?"

"Others were sent before me. None ever returned. Strongbow indicated that our High Priestess Danu believes they took the opportunity to flee the war and have gone into hiding."

"What do you believe?"

"That none turned coward. Your lands are unlike ours. Harsher. Treacherous beyond anything I have known. The others were likely as ill prepared as I. It is my belief that each perished in their attempt to reach Knife Point Keep."

Starn ran a hand over his chin in thought. "No one from Brightwater has ventured deeper than our foothills in many centuries. Your people have forgotten the mountains. I believe as you do. Unfamiliar with the wilds and without a guide, they likely perished. That still does not answer my question. Why would you leave your men for this mission?"

"I did not choose this mission. I follow Lord Strongbow's orders."

"If your lord wishes to send a heartier person than his messengers, why not send a military man of lesser rank?"

Brandel was certain the decision was Danu's, though he had less answer for why she would choose him than he had for Strongbow's doing so. "I cannot say. I do not question my lord's decisions. I carry out his orders."

"It is the duty of Lord Strongbow and the Soldiers of Damsa Dana to battle the Red Moon Warriors in your lands. Our experience in joining the soldiers in previous battles does not foster faith that they will remain to fight if we step in. Still, the Lord of Knife Point will determine whether it is to our benefit to send guardians back to Brightwater with you." Lt. Starn rose and strolled to his desk, refilling his mug. "Did Lord Strongbow also send you to seek Grandmother, or do you do so of your own accord?"

"That mission, too, came from the Lord of Brightwater, though I suspect it was the High Priestess Danu who prompted it." Brandel knew any lie would be detected but dared not speak of his doubts regarding Danu or of the hostility between the priestess and Strongbow. Nor did he dare speak of his concern about delivering any weapon this Grandmother possessed into Danu's hands, adding only, "Were it left to me I would not be here. Given the circumstances, however, I do not deny my wish to learn if the stories are true. Did this woman, this Grandmother live at the time of the Goddesses' return? Perhaps she possesses some…insight; something that might help us defeat the warriors of Breag Nemhain."

Starn settled his gaze on the flames that danced upon the brazier.

"And if Grandmother refuses to be found or to answer your questions?"

Brandel pushed to his feet, his jaw set. "Then I must ask why it is she hides. What are the secrets she keeps?"

A low growl ushered from Shadow. "Do not level accusations of secrecy against Grandmother when you are full of your own."

"What would you know of my secrets?" Brandel thundered, fists clenching.

"Peace!" Starn's voice rose sufficiently to draw the attention of the guard posted outside, the man's head and the point of his drawn blade poking in from the flap.

The lieutenant waved him off, the man casting a dubious glance at Brandel before returning to his position. Starn drew a deep breath followed by a long, reflective exhale. "Our guest has answered my questions with no indication of lie in his words." Starn's knotted brow, however, warned Brandel that he understood things were left unsaid. "We will allow Grandmother's guardian to determine if Lt. Journeyson is worthy of finding her." Rising, he concluded with, "Take what sleep you can, for now. As I said earlier, we shall leave at daybreak, regardless of…"

His words were cut short by a commotion just outside the tent. A heartbeat later, a voice called, "Lt. Starn, the scouts are returned."

"Enter!" Starn barked.

A disheveled and soot covered guardian stepped through and snapped his attention. "Sir. The way station is destroyed. The fires left nothing but cinders and ash. We found no sign of Gray, sir. No sign of his living or his dying. But there is indication that the creatures he warned of escaped. The trail of withered death stretches away to the south for some distance. We lost them at the falls below Grave's Peak."

Striding to the table bearing the large map Brandel had seen the first day of their arrival, Starn ran a finger south from the Knife Point range to the Song Mountains. "South. Why south?"

"We cannot say sir. They will find little enough in that wilderness."

"Thank you, Hawk. You and the others need to eat and rest. We will allow a couple of hours. We must not wait for daybreak. Pass the word. We set out for the keep in two hours."

"Aye, sir." The guardian saluted once more, turned on his heel, and marched out.

"I am sorry," Starn said, addressing the women. "I do not trust that those creatures will continue to push to the south. If they follow the river from the falls, they will come to Healer's Gap. They could make their way through the valley forests and return northward, back into the Knife Point range and head for the keep. We will leave tonight. That should enable us to stay well ahead of them, should that be their plan."

Serenity, still ashen from the lack of good news, nodded, gesturing for Shadow and Whisper to follow as she rose and headed across to the entry. "We shall be ready," she sighed, passing the lieutenant. Shadow turned a glower on Brandel as she stalked past. Whisper, however, managed her familiar shy smile.

"I can go south," Brandel offered, striding across to look at the map. "I can check for signs of them at the river; track them, perhaps."

A furrow worried across Starn's forehead, his hand running over his hair. "Thank you, lieutenant. But I prefer you remain with us. The information you possess concerning recent battles with the Red Moon along with your request for the assistance of the Guardians of Ciuin Rose must reach our lord as quickly as possible."

Brandel turned to go but was stopped by Starn's hand to his shoulder. "Lieutenant, Shadow is correct. You hold secrets. The little one, Whisper, trusts you, though. Do not betray that trust."

16

Serenity settled on a log next to Brandel to attach snowshoes to her boots while Brandel scanned the campsite in amazement. Every tent, every brazier and other large items had disappeared well before the two hours had passed. "They have safe storehouses secreted throughout the mountains," she provided. "Items too bulky or heavy to pack in and out without horses are teleported as needed."

"Why not eliminate the need for packs and teleport everything?"

Serenity cocked a brow. "Say you need your bow right now, to save your life. Will you have time to complete a teleportation to retrieve it and then nock and draw your arrow? Moreover, how much magical energy are you willing to expend when you may have greater need of your reserves for other matters? The physical exertion of carting packs around is far less a strain than magically manipulating every necessary item from one location to another. Or do the Soldiers of Damsa Dana possess such magical strength as to rely solely on teleportation to establish their camps?"

Brandel's exhaustion was becoming obvious. As Serenity pointed out before, he was not thinking clearly or he would never have asked such a ridiculous question. Serenity patted him on the shoulder as she rose and strode away, calling back, "You will have time to recover and regain a clear head when we reach the keep. In the meantime, I would look to those lacings on your snowshoes."

Brandel stared at the shoes. He had no idea how to attach the contraptions. With a roll of her eyes, Shadow came to his aid. "Do you not have snowshoes in the lowlands?"

"I have never seen them."

"You do get snow, though."

"Yes. Quite a lot." Shooting a glance around, he amended his statement. "Quite a lot less than here. Rarely do we have more than our horses can manage. I understand, now, why you insisted I leave Noble behind."

"Gray and Whisper insisted."

"You disagreed?"

"Of course not!" she sniffed. "There. The shoes are secure. It will require some practice for you to walk in them without tripping yourself."

He started to thank her, but she had turned from him and was on her way to join her grandmother and her cousin. She was correct, though. Walking in the bloody things amounted to an entirely new challenge. He almost preferred sinking in the snow up to his thighs.

A thickening layer of clouds blotted out whatever moonlight there might be, making the landscape a wash of grays as they set out. Brandel struggled to keep pace without falling over his feet. After several long and aggravating minutes of stumbling about and a couple of near face plants, he at last worked out the motion and a rhythm, though he was once again introduced to a new set of muscles, the existence of which he was hither to unaware. Late in the night the company was divided and roped together in teams of six or seven. Brandel was placed in the middle, with three guardians in front and three behind.

"*Another storm approaches,*" drifted softly through is mind. "*The guardians have markers to guide them, but do not want to risk us or the newer members among them becoming disoriented and wandering off a cliff.*"

"*So, you can get lost out here, too.*"

A sigh rippled through Whisper's reply. "*In weather like what is coming, Master Brandel, anyone can become lost. That is why they use markers.*"

"*I see none.*"

"*Rods are hammered into the earth. They do not show above ground. Each one, though, bears an enchantment. Guardians wear amulets that alert them of the location of each rod.*"

"*What happens if the enemy gets their hands on these amulets? Will the rods lead them straight to the keep?*"

"*Each amulet is attuned to its bearer at the time of their initiation into the service of the Guardians of Ciuin Rose. One person's amulet will not work for another.*"

Silence followed as concentration was required in the fog that rolled up from who knew where. So thick did it become that Brandel could not see the person in front or behind him. And still they climbed...and descended... and climbed again, Brandel led by nothing more than the tension on the rope. By morning's light the fog lifted, the wind picked up, and the snow returned, increasing over the course of the day until further travel became impossible, even for the guardians. Only then did Starn call a halt, collecting everyone in a cluster. No one untied their rope or removed their pack. No one attempted to strike a fire. Instead, they sat huddled together, everyone facing in. Brandel opened the flap across his nose and mouth long enough to snap ice loose from it, then promptly refastened it. Tucking his mittened hands under his armpits, he ducked his head down to keep the blowing snow out of his eyes. In the distance, he thought he heard a wolf call rise on the gale, dismissing it when no one else seemed to notice.

Trotting footfalls. Nose testing the air. Eyes taking in the monochrome world. Urgency pressed the need to keep moving.

"Time to go." The delicate music of Shadow's voice cut through, her hands, however, were less gentle with their shaking. "Wake up. We are moving, again."

Brandel blinked and pried himself from the ground. "Not asleep."

Her harrumph was notably dubious. "Right."

With the wind diminished and the snow now a gentle flutter, they continued through the remainder of the day and through the night. Brandel's mind became as numb as his nose and limbs. He lost track of how many rests they took, whether he pulled any of his rations from his pack to eat, or the number of times he drained his water skin, repacked it with snow, and tucked it between his coat and his heavy clothes to allow it to melt as he climbed.

Clouds remained through the next morning and into the afternoon, scrubbing the world of all color. At last, they thinned enough to reveal the jagged spire of the tallest mountain Brandel had yet seen. Near the top jutted a massive black structure, sun sporadically glinting off its surface when clouds permitted. Brandel's expectation that they neared the end of their march dissolved in dismay as the spire seemed never to get any closer. One moment, it loomed above them. The next, the path led them downslope, sight of their destination lost behind neighboring peaks. When it reappeared, it was as distant as before. Exhaustion weighed on him. And the desire to sleep. Yet he knew well the fate that awaited should he give in.

"You are strong. That is good"

Brandel stumbled, gathered himself, darted glances around. The words were spoken with a woman's voice, though not that of any he knew.

"When twilight begins to choke off the pale hint of day, you will clear your last crest and stand below the keep."

He straightened, his eyes to the sky. Twilight was upon them. Dragging his feet up to the ridge that formed the crest of the latest slope, he stopped. Looming above was a great, black octagon, torches blazing from its ramparts, the white-shrouded peak of the mountain that backed it barely visible from their angle. A narrow ledge carried them down to a broad lake whose waters lay hidden beneath a crackle of ice. Skirting it, they began the long crawl up a precipitous switchback to a set of black iron gates that rose four meters above the level of the trail. The gate to the rising side of the slope was anchored in the steep rock face, the outer one in the bedrock beneath it. The edge of the outer gate needed no wall to keep the unwanted out, as the ground beyond it fell in a breathtaking sheer drop of at least a hundred meters.

A blare of trumpets heralded their arrival. The returning guardians maintained a cautious distance as the outside gate plowed open, knocking a small avalanche from the path to cascade down the steep drop. Single file, they marched through, arriving at a wide shelf with a series of benches. At last freed of the rope team, Brandel joined the others in sitting long enough to unlace the snowshoes, handing them off to a minor company of children.

Another interminable climb took them up several flights of stairs that zigzagged toward a wall and another gate. Inside the gate lay a flat courtyard, another wall and gate, and yet another set of stairs. Around him, the guardians began to wander off in various directions. Serenity and the girls were greeted by two women who whisked them away, leaving Brandel standing alone mid-courtyard.

"This way," Lt. Starn called to him, striding toward the last gate and the long stairs that spanned the full distance between the two front turrets, the steps climbing up the front of the massive structure. The whole of of the octagon rose as an unbroken piece of polished obsidian faintly swirled with greens and browns. The turrets that rounded outward from the points appeared to be made of the same material. Nowhere did Brandel see any indication of seams or joins.

At the top, they passed through an enormous set of double doors carved with a single rose beneath a crescent moon. Starn led a puffing Brandel into the warmth of a high-ceilinged space. A broad, spiral staircase stood just beyond the doors.

Brandel bit back his moan and followed as Starn mounted the stairs. Several steps up, he stopped briefly, his gaze drawn to the grand interior. Here, only five equal sides could be accounted for, with a sixth, longer wall, running straight across the back. Large braziers burned near the outer walls. Between each was an archway opening onto the turrets. At the very center of the space stood a marble statue Brandel took to be the Goddess Ciuin Rose, her head mere centimeters from the ceiling. The cut and curve of her robes and the way her waist-length hair swept gently behind her gave the impression of a Goddess in motion. The features of the face were delicate, the cast of her gaze gentle. Curiously, she bore a striking resemblance to Whisper.

"Beautiful, is she not?" Starn remarked over his shoulder. "Our Goddess. You may take your time to admire her tomorrow. For now, please come along."

Their climb wound to a landing on a second level, where Starn exited the stairs, though it continued upward. Brandel followed the lieutenant into what appeared to be the keep's dining hall. Within, the space was not only foreshortened across the back, but down one side, as well. A floor-to-ceiling window stood on the western wall and another on the wall facing northwest. Through them, Brandel could make out the shapes of three turrets, though no open arches led to them on this level.

Brandel was sweating before they made it to the first row of long tables and benches, the braziers flanking each window and spaced around the perimeter of the hall providing ample warmth and light. Still, he followed Starn, noting the raised dais at the far end of the hall. The single table of at least eight meters in length and the ornately carved high-backed chairs were the most elaborate Brandel had ever seen. He was unsurprised, however, by the great tapestry draping the wall behind. Lord Strongbow had a similar work in his manor house. Both depicted the familiar pitched battle on a mountain top. This one, though, was more elaborately done, with silver metallic threads creating streaks of lightning across a clear sky and glistening blue knots indicating flashes of magic all around. In Strongbow's tapestry, the Goddesses were each depicted as eyes set within their corresponding moon, Damsa Dana's being most prominent. Here, they appeared as delicately shaded ghostly images that seemed to be fleeing a central figure – a child with flowing auburn hair.

The thud of Lt Starn's pack on a table snapped Brandel's attention back to the man. The lieutenant suggested with a gesture that Brandel should relieve himself of his pack, as well. "Leave it and your coat here, lieutenant. They will be taken to the quarters that are being prepared for you. In the meantime, I wish you to make the acquaintance of the chamberlain to Knife Point's lord. He awaits us in his library. If you will follow me, there is yet another set of stairs for you to climb, I fear."

Again, Brandel swallowed his weary moan, keeping pace with Starn. A doorway in the northeast wall took them into the kitchens where several men and women worked. The kitchens bent around the northeast and east sides. There, another door opened onto a narrow stair well. Two flights up brought them out in front of an east facing floor-to-ceiling window. Brandel gave only a passing glance to the outside. Instead, his attention was drawn to the large, rectangular room filled with cases and shelves and several long tables.

"This is our archives," Starn said. "The history of our people is here, as are records going back many thousands of years to the first coming of the Goddesses to Slievgall'ion."

Moving on, he led Brandel through a large, open archway to a brighter room. The spiral staircase rose through the front of this level, as well. At the center of the room stood a single large brazier, its warmth and light augmenting the light from three chandeliers bearing many multiples of candles. Again, floor-to-ceiling windows occupied the space between outside turrets on the northwest and northeast walls. All other wall space was filled with bookcases bearing tomes of every size. A long table covered with paper, quills, and maps stood near the center brazier. A dark-skinned man with long white hair pulled back in a braid quickly rose from his chair and desk in front of the northwest window. His impressive height was tempered by a slight stoop, his steady and shockingly ice-blue gaze acknowledging the two men.

"Chamberlain Fairchild," Starn addressed the man. "Our lord wishes you to make the acquaintance of Lt. Brandel Journeyson. He will be our guest for a while."

"Welcome to Knife Point Keep and Fortress," the man said, his voice deep and resonant.

Brandel made to bow, not knowing how one was supposed to greet or address a chamberlain. Strongbow was counseled by the High Priestess Danu.

The chamberlain waved him up with a snort. "No need to humble yourself, Lt. Journeyson. I am not the lord of the realm. Merely his advisor. You look tired. It is a long and difficult passage from the lowlands to this place. Please." He gestured toward the chair by the desk. "Rest yourself."

"Thank you, chamberlain, but I am fine. I will take my rest shortly."

"Indeed," the man affirmed. "I will not keep you long. A hot meal is being taken to your quarters. I understand, however, that you bear a message from Strongbow, Lord of Brightwater."

Brandel's eyes skimmed between the chamberlain and Starn. "It is a simple message. A request for aid," he stated. "The Soldiers of Damsa Dana fight to keep the Red Moon Warriors from your borders. But our numbers are diminishing. We can no longer stand alone. I had not known, until coming here, that a horrific battle has occurred within recent memories in your lands, and that ongoing skirmishes arise. I am sorry for the loss of the temple and of so many of your priestesses, and for the death and destruction that continues. If more such losses are to be avoided, however, we need the Guardians of Ciuin Rose to fight with us."

"A simple request," the chamberlain sighed, repeating Brandel's claim. "Not so simple, I fear. Knife Point is a harsh land. We have few villages and fewer towns. Farms are widely separated. There is challenge enough, patrolling our mountains and foothills to protect our people. To send aid to another realm would leave us even more vulnerable. It has only been by the grace and strength of Ciuin Rose that the wars are not fully at our doors, even now. If we leave our land, the warriors will surely come, and in greater numbers." The chamberlain stopped the slow pace he traced around the room and ran a hand over his white hair, Brandel noting for the first time the delicate point of the man's ears. An Alainn!

A smile flicked across the chamberlain's face. "Not all Alainn removed to the west of the mountains to remain apart from humans. Some of us refuse to turn our backs on our friends." He drew a long and thoughtful breath, his lips pinched. "Lieutenant, kindly show our guest to his quarters. Let him eat and rest. I will discuss this matter with our lord."

"There is one other matter, chamberlain," Starn put in.

"Ah yes. The matter of seeking Grandmother. At present, she prefers not to be found. Still, I sent word to her guardian asking that he come. It is my understanding that he will be arriving tomorrow. You may discuss with him your reasons for wishing to find this woman. Perhaps you can convince him of your need. Perhaps not." The chamberlain strolled to his table of papers and maps, dismissing the men with a flick of his hand.

Starn turned and motioned Brandel to once again follow, leading him to the back stairs and down one level. This time the stairwell offered two doors. Starn headed for the one at the back of the landing. Brandel was ushered into a chamber that was something of a trapezoid in shape. A raised stone hearth in the back outside corner glowed with a small blaze which warmed the room nicely. Starn nodded toward the canopied and curtained bed in the center of the room. At its foot stood a long, low chest, Brandel's pack setting on the floor, propped against it.

"There are blankets in the chest, should you need more for your bed," Starn offered. "Your coat is there." Brandel followed the direction of Starn's gesture to find the coat hanging on a peg next to yet another door.

"I hope you find your accommodations comfortable, lieutenant. There are other ways of traversing the levels of the fortress, though the stairwell we just took is the quickest. You will find a private bath behind the curtained opening, should you wish to clean up before breakfast." Again, Brandel glanced in the direction indicated, noting the curtained arch in the back wall. "I will send someone to escort you back to the dining hall for breakfast and will arrange for a tour of the fortress and full keep afterward. Both of the doors to your chamber have bolts that can be dropped into place, should you wish to do so, though it is unlikely you will be disturbed." Nodding to a long, satin rope that hung at the side of the bed, Starn said, "Should you desire anything, all you need do is pull the bell."

Alone, at last, Brandel trudged to the chair that stood askew of a writing desk. Sagging onto it, he relieved his feet of their boots and socks, then sat for several minutes staring at the darkness through the window that backed the desk. The aroma of the food that awaited him on small table finally captured his attention. Peeling himself from the chair and dragging it with him, he settled, lifting the silver covers from the plates to find a whole roasted chicken, potatoes and carrots baked with garlic and covered in a rich gravy, bread still warm from the oven, a small bowl of butter, and two baked apples. Two pitchers occupied the center of the table. One held water, the other ale.

His stomach full and the weight and strain taken from his muscles, he lounged near the window, a filled mug in hand. From somewhere beyond his room drifted a gentle song on Shadow's rich voice. The song spoke of a quiet glen at the foot of a mountain, a soft summer breeze lifting the fragrance of wildflowers beneath a warm sun.

17

The sound of knocking at his door dragged Brandel from sleep. His mind still foggy, he teetered on the edge of the chair, grabbing at the table to keep from falling off. The rapping came again. With a disgruntled glance toward the undisturbed bed, he called, "Come," yawning as he pushed to his feet. The stiffness of his muscles demanded stretching, the chill in the air an admonishment for his failure to stoke the hearth before succumbing to his fatigue. The hearth stood, now, cold and dark, the thin morning light through the windows casting weak shadows about the room.

A young boy dressed in acolyte's robes edged the door to, peering in, his gaze first skimming to the dead coals in the fireplace. "Sir," he said upon spotting Brandel. "It is cold, sir. Would you like for me to build up the fire for you before I take you to breakfast?"

"Thank you, but that will not be necessary. Clearing last night's dishes your doing?" he asked, gesturing toward the table that now stood empty.

The boy shook his head. "No sir. One of the kitchen boys gathered them. Said you slept like the dead." The boy's brow furrowed. "Did you not find the bed comfortable, sir?"

"More like I did not find the bed at all," Brandel admitted. "I cannot even recall how much of the dinner I finished before I fell asleep." Catching a whiff of himself, he grimaced. "Is there time for me to wash? If so, point me in the proper direction."

The boy's gray eyes studied him briefly. "One moment, sir," he said, though he made no motion to leave. A few seconds later, another boy appeared carrying a pile of fresh clothing and disappearing through the curtained opening with them.

The first boy grinned, a hand flipping straw-blond hair from his eyes before pulling a block of sweet-smelling soap from a pocket on his robes and a cloth from another. "I thought you might wish as much," he said, leading the way through the curtains. "So, I came for you a little early."

Brandel stopped short, staring at the large tub that the second boy was filling with hot water from faucets set in the wall.

"Plumbing, sir," the first boy grinned. "Lt. Starn's great ancestor designed the keep and the fortress and included some very nice amenities. All living quarters are supplied with hot and cold running water and working toilets, sir. A great benefit when the alternative would be jogging down cold, dark stairs and out to experience the snowy bite in the dead of night."

"Indeed! My thanks, uh…"

"Jerkin," the boy said. "On account of that is all I wore when I was found. This here…" He nodded to his companion, "This is Owl, 'cause his eyes seem always to be wide open takin' in everything. He never says much, though."

Brandel smiled his acknowledgement, a brow ticking up at the second boy's appearance. Though smaller than the first, his compact frame was well-muscled, judging from the bare arms showing beneath rolled-up sleeves. It was the boy's coloring, however, that captured Brandel's attention. Skin, not quite the wash of yellow of those claiming an ancient Azan ancestry, nor as dark brown as the Affers people, the boy looked almost golden. The short clip of his dark hair failed to eliminate its tight curl. And his large, round, brown eyes did, indeed, appear to be taking in everything. Realizing he was staring, Brandel cleared his throat and turned back to the first boy. "My thanks to you both, Jerkin, Owl."

Jerkin gestured in the direction of a counter on which the stack of clothes now lay. "We had to guess at your size, sir. Owl is better at that sort of thing than I am."

"Had help," Owl confessed. "The Lady Serenity told me what to choose for you."

Jerkin grabbed his companion, hauling him back through the curtains, calling over his shoulder. "We will leave you to your bath, sir. Will wait for you in here. Just call us if you should need anything." Brandel bathed quickly, despite the temptation to soak in the hot water. He would not insult his hosts by being late to breakfast. Dressed in the clothes Owl provided, he took a moment to stand before the long mirror attached to the wall. Above the left breast pocket of the white linen shirt were embroidered two moons. The larger was blue-white, the impression of pale blue eyes set within it. Overlapping its edge was a small, rose-tinted moon, the suggestion of emerald eyes stitched in silvered green threads. He now bore the emblems of both the Goddess Damsa Dana and the Goddess Ciuin Rose. Black wool pants tucked into polished black boots set off the white shirt. Swiping his hair back from his eyes, Brandel scowled. He had lost weight. And he needed a shave.

"On the back of the sink," Jerkin shouted to him. "I would be happy to do the honor, sir."

"I can manage."

"Oh. And sir, leave your traveling clothes on the floor. They will be collected and laundered."

Both boys looked quite smug when Brandel returned to the outer chamber. Running a hand over the emblem on the shirt, he began, "Where did you…"

Owl glanced at his feet sheepishly. "Was the Lady Whisper who asked to embroider it for you last night when I approached our lady guests about providing fresh clothes. Lady Serenity suggested the size you might require."

"Lady Serenity has a good eye for fit." Brandel fingered the sleeves. "And the magic woven into the shirt to warm it?"

Jerkin flushed. "My idea, sir. Seein' as how you are not accustomed to our lands. We saw you at the sanctuary beneath the temple ruins. Saw how you disliked the cold. I feared you might find it difficult to keep from the chill, here, given that it is colder, still. I can remove the spell if you prefer."

"No, no. Your thoughtfulness will not be forgotten. You have my sincere gratitude. So. You were at the sanctuary."

"Aye, sir. It is where we live, generally speakin'. Juniper sends us here when there is need to help with extra guests."

Brandel nodded. "Juniper is a good judge of good people."

The boys beamed. "Now, sir, if you are ready." Jerkin strode to the door that opened to the center of the fortress. "We can show you to breakfast."

Their route was not by way of the back stairs, this time, but along a wide, inside corridor that bent around toward the front of the fortress to a great arch that opened to the spiral stairs. On the wall opposite the arch was a closed door.

"Those are the officers' quarters, sir" Jerkin advised, leading him out to the staircase. "And this," he gestured to the wide chamber that curved away from the spiral stairs on both sides and was filled with racks of weapons. "This is the armory."

Brandel would have liked a closer look but the boys led on. It was only one level down to the dining hall where breakfast was already underway. The quiet assemblage of less than a hundred men stunned Brandel. Those present turned upon his entrance and rose, offering a salute in welcome. Brandel returned it, his glance skimming the room for an appropriate place to sit.

"Here, sir," called to him from a table near one of the two windows. The guardian beckoning him was one of the men from the encampment. The one who delivered news of Gray's way station if he remembered correctly. The man was probably half again Brandel's age, sported a short, graying beard and crisp green eyes. Brandel strode to the table, nodding his gratitude. The man welcomed him with a hearty handshake. "Name's Hawk," he said. "Rank is Sergeant." A glance at Brandel's shirt lifted a brow.

Brandel's hand brushed the emblem, a glance searching out the two boys, neither of whom was anywhere to be found. "Owl...I believe that is what he said his name is...said that it was the Lady Whisper's handiwork."

For a long moment, Sergeant Hawk's eyes studied him. Nodding, at last, the man gestured toward the bench. "Join us. Please."

A plate appeared before Brandel as he sat, the fare a grand offering of fresh poached eggs, slabs of ham, a stack of hotcakes, and a great mound of potatoes. "Butter and syrup are there," Hawk indicated with a gesture toward a plate and a small pitcher that matched a series of others situated down the length of the table. A steaming mug appeared next to his plate. The smell was wonderful, though Brandel did not recognize it.

"Coffee. We trade for it with merchants from the south of the Alainn's outpost lands."

"The Fire Islands?"

"Aye, sir. The Red Moon's hold there is not as strong as they would wish. Two of the islands have underground resistance. They finance their efforts with their coffee trade. It has been a little more difficult to obtain, of late. Our last order arrived late and was half of what we expected. So, it is served only every other morning. The kitchen staff prepare it with a dash of cream. If you prefer, I can send for a mug without."

"This is fine." Following his first sip, he amended his statement to, "Excellent, in fact. Coffee, you say."

The two fell silent for several minutes, each enjoying their meal. At last, Brandel gave a satisfied sigh, patting his stomach. "The fortress employs fine cooks."

"Overworked cooks," Hawk chuckled. "Though on this morning, life is not so bad for them. Given the limited staff, here, Lt Starn sent for the two boys to attend you. Juniper always recommends the pair, though I hear she also groans about losing each of them to the keep. Still, she sends the best suited among her young students when there are more in residence, here."

Brandel turned enough to glance out over the few filled tables where guardians sat chatting as they ate. "There are more of you, then."

"More, aye. Though nowhere near enough. Nor do the guardians all gather at once. Better to maintain a rotation of patrols. We expect one rotation to be returning by nightfall."

Brandel regarded the few guardians in the room, noting as he did at the encampment, the number of women among them. All wore the same uniforms comprised of white pants and shirts with the rose insignia embroidered on the left side below a rose tented moon bearing green eyes. "Women serve in your fighting ranks."

Brandel's comment seemed to surprise Hawk. "Aye. Do they not serve with the Soldiers of Damsa Dana?"

"They serve as priestesses of the Goddess, not as fighters."

"Strange," Hawk murmured.

"I understand there are no longer any priestesses here," Brandel put in, as though that explained the situation.

"True. But that makes no difference. Even when we had our priestesses, we had women guardians. Some served as both."

Brandel considered, wondering why they would risk their women. His people believed in protecting them.

"Protecting them from what?"

Startled, he spun to find Shadow staring at him indignantly.

"Do not read my thoughts," he snapped.

"I do not have to. Your face says it all. We can fight as well as any man."

"You should not have to."

"Why? Do you think we lack the right to protect our homes and our families?"

"It is not a matter of right. It is a matter of…"

The musicality of Shadow's voice soured even more. "The strong protecting the weak?"

"Seems to me you and Whisper benefit from a fair degree of protection."

Hawk rose and clapped Brandel on the shoulder with an amused snort at Shadow's bristling. "Do not get this one started, my friend. She is a fearsome little fiend. Fights as well as any man, as she said. Never has appreciated being hidden away."

"Sometimes it is a necessity to hide," Serenity put in, strolling up behind Shadow.

The girl glanced around. "Where is Whisper?"

"We received word that the Lady of Knife Point returned in the night."

Shadow's face contorted between dismay and delight. "And Whisper did not send to me that she was going to see the lady? 'Scuse me!" With that, the girl darted off, disappearing on the spiral staircase, her footfalls echoing as she rounded them upward in a run.

Hawk offered a bow to Serenity, gesturing for her to join the small group at his table, his expression carefully composed. "I was unaware of our lady's return. No one was summoned to prepare for her."

Sitting, Serenity shrugged. "Perhaps she wanted no preparations. We learned only when Lt. Starn sent word to me that she wished to see Whisper and Shadow."

"What of the Lord of Knife Point?" Brandel asked. "Is he in residence, as well?"

Hawk shook his head. "Who is to say? He does not always make his presence known. The Lord of Knife Point has many duties, seeing to the needs of our people and staying informed as to the skirmishes and such. When he is in residence, he often spends many a day in the library or the archives studying maps or seeking information. The guardians have their duties, as well. Lt. Starn sees to their needs and oversees the fulfilment of their obligations when our lord is unavailable."

Brandel returned a scrutiny to Serenity. "Your son."

The faint flicker of a smile passed across the woman's lips. "My son."

"He carries a heavy burden. Where is his Captain?"

"Murdered," Hawk replied. "A new Captain has yet to be named. We await the Lord of Knife Point's decision in this." Offering another bow to Serenity, the sergeant bid her a good day. "Lt. Journeyson, would you care for a tour of the fortress and keep? Lt. Starn says he promised you such." Brandel stood, following Hawk's example, granting Serenity a bow, then fell into step with the man.

The tour was an eye-opener. The Soldiers of Damsa Dana maintained no fortress so great as Knife Point's. Everywhere, men and women worked together, sharing in duties. Small fields dotted the area within the gates, most showing signs of a harvest, a few with winter crops beginning to show their tops.

Though it seemed unlikely, Brandel still had to ask. "You grow enough to feed everyone within the keep?"

"Hardly, sir. Knife Point's farmers contribute ten percent of their crops. Never more. The fields, here, help to make up for lean years, providing for us and our people when their yields are lean. We also keep livestock and boast some of the most skilled practitioners of animal husbandry."

The tour carried them through the smithies where the necessities for horses and mounted guardians along with armaments were made. From there, they went to the training fields where guardians learned and practiced their combat skills, be it magic, sword play, archery, or hand-to-hand. Families who worked within the keep and its grounds lived in structures below the fortress but within the second set of gates. The children received schooling, here, and helped with the lesser duties. As with every other aspect of life, men and women shared equally in tending the children.

"The keep provides for horses," Brandel commented, glancing back in the direction of the stables.

"Aye," Hawk acknowledged. "Though more are kept in locations scattered throughout the foothills. Patrols are mounted year around, there. We ride in the mountains, too, when winter is not upon us or when the snows are tightly compacted. I understand you released your animal before coming here. It was a wise decision. These animals are accustomed to the altitude and the cold. A lowland horse may not handle the higher elevations as well. The slopes near Gray's way station are much safer for your beast."

By the end of the tour, the day was fading to late afternoon, and Brandel's mind was spinning from his attempt to keep names and duties straight for each person met. The only part of the keep not included in the tour were the lord's and lady's quarters at the pinnacle of the fortress. While Brandel was unsurprised by the exclusion, Hawk's comments about the lord and lady stunned him. They shared a common room, he was told, but not sleeping quarters, as they were not husband and wife. How could a woman rise to the position of Lady of Knife Point if not married to the lord?

Hawk was chuckling as he led Brandel back to the fortress.

"What?"

"You are surprised that men and women are equal in all things, here."

"Including the rule of your land, if I understand correctly."

"The lord and lady do not rule. They govern. They oversee. They guide. They do this jointly, always taking counsel from and with one another as well as from the chamberlain and from the people." Hawk cocked a brow. "Though

I think perhaps your intrigue comes more from hearing that they do not share a marriage bed."

Brandel flinched, drawing another chuckle from the sergeant.

"They are close, our lord and lady. But no. They are not wed. It is said that each lost their love in one of their many battles and neither wishes to wed, again." Hawk hesitated for a moment. "I hear that men and women lead separate lives in your lands, even when married. Seems an odd way to live, to me."

"Not separate," Brandel objected.

"No?"

"Of course not. They live together, eat together, enjoy one another's company."

"But they do not work side by side."

"Some things are too difficult for women."

"Ah. Your women are weaker than ours. I am sorry for them."

Before Brandel could stumble through some clarification a great bell rang out.

"Dinner," Hawk declared. "Come. Perhaps the Lady of Knife Point will grace us with her presence, this evening."

Brandel was struggling to hide his shortness of breath when they began the climb up the spiral stairs back to the level of the dining hall. Hawk took the climb in easy stride, with Brandel huffing along behind him. At last stopping on the landing at the head of the dining hall, the sergeant turned and clapped Brandel on the shoulders, making no attempt to contain his laughter. "Your women may be weak, but you are a mighty man! Trotting up and down the fortress and keep without a word of complaint. The few outsiders who once came here often attempted to teleport between levels once they were acquainted with the logistics."

"Attempted." Brandel had assumed there would be measures in place to block any effort to teleport into the keep from the outside. But not allowing teleportation from within?

Hawk nodded. "Attempted. It is forbidden, here. Ancient spells prevent it. Any who tried found themselves abruptly tossed into an icy horse trough in the stables. And that goes for guardians. Those who are not fit enough to manage the rigors of using their own muscles are no longer fit to serve in our ranks. Jobs are found for them elsewhere."

Brandel's scowl added to the sergeant's mirth. "And you gave them no warning?"

"No more than we gave you, my friend. The shock of their dunking tends to stay with them as a reminder far longer than a mere warning would accomplish."

"So, why tell me, now? I might have opted to try at some point."

Hawk shook his head. "Not if I am any judge of character. I do not see that you would insult your hosts in such a manner. I understand, now, why the cousins approve of you."

"One cousin, perhaps," Brandel huffed.

"Do not let the Lady Shadow put you off. She has a hard exterior, but she trusts the Lady Whispers assessment. Now. Shall we eat?"

18

Т

he guardians' numbers were more than double the count from breakfast. Still, most tables remained empty. Hawk strolled to the table they occupied for the morning's meal.

"Just in time," he announced to Brandel, nodding to a piper who stepped from between braziers at the back of the raised dais. Filling his bag with air and pumping a few preliminary discords, he set to a full-throated and regal harmonic pronouncement, bringing everyone to their feet.

As the noise of shuffling to stand died away, a panel in the short side wall of the dais slid open. Lt. Starn strode out in full dress uniform of black pants and black dress jacket with silver trim over a crisp white shirt. The bars of his rank shimmered in silvered rose threads on the upper left jacket sleeve, while a single rose overlapping a rose-colored moon set with striking green eyes adorned the left corner of this shirt collar.

Behind Starn and on the arm of the tallest and darkest man Brandel had ever seen came what he would have taken as a child, save for her white hair. The man she was with was an Alainn, judging by the point of his ears and the turquois trimmed in silver waist coat he wore. His appearance was the more striking with his piercing blue eyes. The similarity between this man and the chamberlain left Brandel wondering if the two were related.

The woman, on the other hand, was so diminutive that Whisper, by comparison, might be considered tall. Burnished red streaked the temples of the woman's white hair, which fell in a long braid down her back. Faint creases were visible at the corners of her eyes. Yet her fair skin shown with a flush of youth, highlighting her delicate features. The easy grace of her movement carried into the flowing lines of her velvet pants and simple velvet tunic, both of a deep green and unadorned with any trim.

Hawk elbowed him. "Our lady's guardian is Lord Tine On Stoirm. It is rumored that his mother was a human Witch of remarkable dark beauty."

"Was?"

"Aye. She died in a battle many ages ago. Or so the tale goes."

"And the woman? What is her origin?"

"Little is known about the Lady of Knife Point, though some believe she is one of the Priestesses of Ciuin Rose who escaped the slaughter and the destruction of the temple. She does not speak of her past. Stunning, is she not?"

Brandel nodded his assent, though his gaze now turned to Whisper, Shadow, and Serenity as they entered. Whisper moved tentatively. Her sapphire brocade gown with a floral pattern woven through in silver threads set off the timid flush of her face and the red of her hair. Her eyes met his for a moment, triggering a delicate blush and her shy smile. There was nothing shy about Shadow, only a suggestion of discomfort. The rich amber of her brocade gown, woven with leaves in gold threads, accented her fair skin. Her blue-black hair fell in soft waves to brush her shoulders as her midnight eyes flashed in his direction, daring him to think anything negative about how she was attired. Serenity, too, wore a brocade gown, hers aqua with ripples in both silver and gold, her hair braided in a circlet atop her head.

"Are they related?"

Hawk leaned closer. "Are who related?"

"The Ladies Serenity, Shadow, and Whisper to the Lord or Lady of Knife Point?"

Hawk shrugged. "Not to anyone's knowledge. The three you speak of, however, have long been under the special protection of our lord and lady. The two girls are sought by the Red Moon, though none will say for what purpose."

Tine On Stoirm seated the Lady of Knife Point while guardians stepped out from the back wall to seat the other ladies. Tine then took his place between the lady and Serenity. Lt. Starn remained standing. At last, the piper wound down his tune, allowing Starn to raise his voice in welcome, bidding everyone eat in good cheer. His pronouncements complete, the lieutenant took his place in the second chair to the right of the Lady of Knife Point, the empty chair presumably indicating the absence of Knife Point's lord.

With the brief pomp of the evening dispensed, the hall came alive with talk and laughter and eating.

"Where does she reside?" Brandel asked.

Hawk glanced at him, downing a bite of the roasted meat.

"What?"

"You said the Lady of Knife Point does not stay here."

"She maintains a small, private keep deeper in the mountains, though she does not stay there much either, I am told. She travels."

"Travels?"

Hawk shrugged. "They say she goes from village to village, farmstead to farmstead. She talks with people. Tells stories, sometimes. Often shares dances she knows. There are some who say she is a little mad."

Brandel rounded a stunned gaze on him. "Is she?"

"None here believe it. Judge for yourself, should you meet her."

"With her travels, perhaps she has learned of the whereabouts of the one called Grandmother."

"Not likely. But the one with her…he would be the one to ask. Not that I expect he will give you an answer."

"The dark Alainn, you mean."

"Aye. Tine. They say he is at least as old as Grandmother. He is her guardian."

"Why is he here, then?"

Hawk shrugged again. "The Lady of Knife Point enjoys his company, so he often turns up here when she arrives."

Brandel ate in silence for a good while before venturing. "When might I meet this Lord Chinee Owen Stoirm?"

"I am betting it will be soon. Every person here knows of your interest in locating Grandmother."

The evening gradually concluded, the Lady of Knife Point and her companions having departed a good hour earlier. Brandel stayed, even after the last guardian wandered off, a half empty mug of ale on the table before him, the vision of the woman still fresh in his mind. He was certain she studied him as she ate, though he never caught her eyes on him. Nor did she appear to converse much with any around her. Who was this Lady of Knife Point? How did she come by her position?

There was no doubt that the guardians revered her.

"You think too much."

Brandel jumped, bumping the table as he shot to his feet.

"For pity sake, relax," Serenity huffed. "You should know by now that I do not bite."

"You just startled me. I thought everyone had gone to their beds."

"Only those among the guardians who are not standing watch." She eyed him for a moment. "I expected you to be preparing for bed, given the rigors of our recent travels and your long day touring the grounds."

Brandel shrugged. "My mind is too busy trying to make sense of this place and the people. What of Whisper and Shadow? The journey was hard on them, as well."

"They are in our quarters, but they are far from asleep. Given their excitement over being summoned by the Lady of Knife Point, earlier, and being seated with her at dinner, the two are wound up enough to chatter all night."

Brandel chuckled. "Is that why you are about? Too much chatter?"

"I was sent to fetch you."

"Fetch me? By whom?"

"Just come with me. Leave your drink. You will be offered fresh."

She did not lead him back to the spiral stairs, as he expected. Rather, she took him to the sliding panel through which those who sat at the high table had arrived and departed. Behind it was a narrow passage at the end of which was another set of stairs. Two flights up and they emerged in the chamberlain's archives. Serenity led him through the room and through the library to the spiral staircase, Brandel wondering why they had not simply taken that route in the first place.

"Too many eyes," Serenity said. "Some meetings are better kept in silence."

From the library, Serenity led the way up the last flight. They emerged in a brightly lit chamber, the light coming from a series of overhead chandeliers as well as a large brazier in the center of the room. Dark green velvet curtains masked the two great windows on the northeast and northwest walls, though the window that rose behind the spiral stair held no coverings. Cushioned chairs were spaced around one side of the open room, while on the other stood a grouping of settees, smaller chairs, and small tables.

The Lady of Knife Point sat in one of the cushioned chairs next to a table, her casual manner surprising. She sat with her feet tucked under her in the way children often perched, her hair undone from its braid, a few strands cascading over the front of her shoulders. Lt. Starn sat in the chair on the other side of the table, sipping a glass of wine, while Tine On Stoirm strolled between bookcases that flanked each of the windows and filled much of the back wall.

The strange emerald glow within the Lady of Knife Point's eyes made Brandel edgy as she watched the pair approach. Serenity dipped a curtsy, prompting him to offer a deep bow. The woman waved them both up. "There will be none of that. I do not stand for such obeisance. You know this, Serenity. Why do you persist?"

Serenity smiled. "It is because of my respect and love for you."

"Then come and give me a hug."

Serenity obeyed, then dismissed herself to one of the settees, accepting a glass of wine from Tine.

"Come," the Lady of Knife Point offered, gesturing to a chair across from her. "Sit with me, Master Journeyson. I understand you seem to prefer ale over wine." A mug appeared on a table next to the offered chair.

Brandel hesitated.

"Oh, come," she sniffed "We are all friends, here." She raised a brow "Are we not?"

Brandel managed a nod, starting to bow again. He caught himself.

"My lady," he ventured, hovering in front of the chair. "I am honored."

"Then for pity sake, honor my request and sit. You will strain my neck having to stare up at you."

He sat. The lady shifted slightly, her arms resting on her lap as she regarded him more closely. A faint smile curled the corners of her mouth. "You remind me of them."

"Excuse me?"

"Never mind," she sighed, brushing off the comment with a flip of her hand. "Just the mumblings of an old woman. So, Master Journeyson, I understand I have you to thank for keeping Serenity and the girls safe in their trek to the keep."

"In truth, it was more the other way around, my lady."

The woman gave an amused huff. "No doubt. Still, you earned the respect of the girls. Not an easy accomplishment with Shadow. Am I right, Serenity?"

The woman acknowledged with a simple nod. The Lady of Knife Point shot her a sympathetic glance. "You are worried, my dear. Still no word from Gray?"

"None, Lady S…" Her response was cut short by the clanging of a bell. Both Serenity and the Lady of Knife Point stiffened, their features frozen as they listened for the number and pattern of the clangs. "He is here," Serenity dared in an exhale, shooting out of the settee. "Gray is here!"

The lady gestured her back. "Stay, my dear. I just sent word that he is to be brought here at once."

Several long minutes drug by in silence as they waited, Starn making his way to the stair landing along with Tine. When scuffing footsteps sounded from below, the two men darted down the stairs, returning with Gray supported between them. The man looked far worse, even, than Brandel's first encounter with him. More grizzled if that was possible. He also bore the remnants of a massive burn down the length of his right arm and across the right side of his face. Serenity's horrified inhale mirrored Brandel's shock, the woman rushing to Gray and nudging Tine aside to take his place.

Gray managed a bemused sidelong glance at her. "I look worse than I am, my dear."

The Lady of Knife Point was also on her feet, which, much to Brandel's surprise, proved to be bare. Gesturing to the longest of the settees, she declared. "There. Let him lie there. I have sent for the keep's Healers."

Gray tried to push Serenity and Starn away as they settled him where the lady indicated. "I do not need to lie down. I tended to my wounds days ago. I am weary, but not much the worse for the wear."

The Lady of Knife Point, huffed. "Let the Healers be the judge of that. Your skills for rejuvenation appear to be woefully inadequate or greatly overstretched. How many wounds did you suffer?"'

Gray's eyes darted to the lady, seemingly noting her presence for the first time. He made to rise, but Serenity and Starn held him back. "Stay put!" Serenity commanded. "Or I will add to your collection."

The man flinched, reluctantly dropping back. "Fine. But I am not laying down. I may be slow in mending, but I am mending." His grimace filled his features when the Lady of Knife Point knelt before him. "My lady. Please! Do not expend your energies on the likes of me."

"Hush!" she rumbled. "The likes of you keep the likes of the rest of us safe. Now let me look."

Brandel closed the distance enough to watch in awe as the lady's hands examined Gray's arm and face, then deftly swept over the rest of him, her face growing more anxious as she worked. The grizzled appearance eased from the man, the creases of pain that lined his face lifting, the brown of his eyes brightening. "You did well for yourself," the lady said, straightening as her hand patted his. "But the burns are magic in nature. Your skills are no match for them."

A clamor from the stairs produced two women and a man, each dressed in the green of the Healers, the three rushing from the landing to Gray. The Lady of Knife Point's stern gaze warned Gray against objecting to their examination and ministrations. The elder of the women at last turned to the Lady, her question written on her face. The Lady of Knife Point nodded. "I have dealt with the dark magic. I leave the rest to you."

When the other two completed their work, applying a thick salve and dressing Gray's arm in bandages, they administered the same salve to his face. Once done, the two younger healers left without a word. The elder Healer remained, obviously in telepathic communication with both the lady and Serenity. At length, she, too, departed.

The lady returned to stand over Gray. "Tell me, my friend. How did you come by these burns? Not from the fires you set at your outpost, surely."

Gray looked entirely relaxed, now, sunken back on the settee, his eyes closing from his fatigue and the relief from his pain. "No," he said, his voice barely audible. "Was from the creatures, my lady."

"The creatures. Tell me of them."

"Where they tread, all withers, blackens, and dies. I could see their approach by the trail of death they left. It is why I set the blazes, hoping to stop them; kill them by fire. Fire is nothing against them. When they passed through and out to sniff the trail Serenity and the girls had taken, I followed, watching, waiting for some indication of how I might destroy them. I do not understand the dark magic about them, but it seems akin to ancient stories I heard as a child. About how the Goddesses come from a world where souls of the dead, in ravenous hunger for the comfort of living flesh to house them, seek and take on the bodies of fresh corpses. The magic of these beasts had that feel. The feel of hunger for wrapping themselves in the living. It is, I think, what occurs at their touch. They suck the life from any living thing in their path, the power of their hunger leaving behind toxic and burned remains. It brought to mind other ancient tales. Tales of spells used to banish souls so that they could not return."

Ice ran along Brandel's nerves, and he noted that the lady shivered, as well, though her face remained impassive.

"I do not know of any such spells," Gray continued. "But I tried to conjure one. It was difficult. And painful. Like driving spikes into my own soul. When I caught up to the creatures at the ledge where you had camped, I cast the spell. Two of the creatures I hit squarely. Their remains still lie on that ledge. The other took a glancing blow, the back flash catching me on the right side. I know I wounded the beast. Its scream near split my head. And then it vanished, the charge of a teleportation left hanging on the air."

With his last statement, Gray sagged, snoring as his head drooped to his chest. "Take him to the lord's chambers," the lady directed, gesturing to Starn and Tine. "Let him sleep there for the night. Serenity, stay with him. Let me know if he wakes and needs anything."

With a flick of Starn's hand, Gray's sleeping form disappeared, Starn and the Alainn striding through a curtained archway on the right side of the chamber's back wall. Serenity nodded her thanks as she followed them.

"Sit with me a moment more, if you will, Lt. Journeyson."

Turning, he caught the lady's penetrating gaze fixed on him, the deep emerald glow unnerving. Never had he seen eyes that held such a burning radiance. The lady quickly lowered her gaze, gesturing to the chair he had previously occupied. With a hesitant nod, he returned to it, taking up the mug of ale and downing a stiff swig. The lady seated herself across from him, once more.

"The glow," she said quietly. "It is a sign of who I am. None outside of this chamber have witnessed it. In my concern over Gray's report and his condition, I failed to hide it. She now raised soft, earthen green eyes to him. Promise me that you will not speak of it to any."

"Who are you? Why did you send for me?"

"You will receive the answer to your first question soon enough, I think. For now, it is a story too long to tell. I summoned you because I need information from you. I learned of these creatures before Gray's account. Have you seen them?"

Brandel downed another swig of his drink. "Seen them? No. Seen the consequences of their passing, yes." He took a deep breath. "It is possible that the Lady Shadow saw them."

The Lady of Knife Point considered in silence for several seconds. "If this is so, it was a grave mistake for her to get so close to these... things. They seek for both Shadow and for Whisper, though I do not think they would approach either close enough to harm them. They would undoubtedly send word, though."

"Send word. To whom? To the Red Moon Warriors."

"To their mistress," the lady stated. "The girls are a treasure long sought after."

"Why?"

"Because they could lead our enemies to a greater treasure."

Before Brandel could ask more, the lady rose, dismissing him with, "Can you find your way back to your quarters, lieutenant? Or shall I call for Starn to guide you?"

Brandel finished his ale in a single gulp, rising. "I can find my way."

"Good. I will speak with the Lord of Knife Point upon his arrival. We must make a determination regarding the request for assistance from your Lord Strongbow. Perhaps we can reach a decision for you by tomorrow. Sleep well."

As Brandel reached the landing for the stairs, the lady's words drifted to his mind. *"If you still wish to meet Grandmother, be ready to leave by tomorrow evening."* Turning, he saw the curtain across the arch on the left side of the backwall flutter, the Lady of Knife Point disappearing behind it.

19

Brandel dragged himself from the tub, still bleary from a restless night. His nightmares hung in his mind – visions of the trail of death left by the creatures; images of Gray's burns; uneasy reflections on the man's descriptions of the dark spell needed to destroy the creatures. The combination raised a deep foreboding. Wrapped in a towel, he shuffled back to the bedroom to find Jerkin and Owl waiting for him.

"There you are, m' lord," Jerkin grinned. "We brought fresh clothes for you."

Draped across the properly made bed were black trousers, another white linen shirt, and a garnet jacket trimmed in bronze braid with the same symbol as had been embroidered on his previous shirt now adorning the left breast pocket of the jacket. Brandel eyed the jacket. The color suggested he was recognized, here, for his ability to communicate with animals, despite his profound distaste for the 'gift'. But why the bronze trim?

"They are a gift from the Lady of Knife Point, sir. Though the Lady Whisper once more insisted on doing the embroidery on the pocket."

The boys stood to the side, looking eager for some indication that they might assist Brandel in dressing. In the end, he motioned them forward to help with the buttons on the double-breasted jacket, then allowed them grinning inspection as they turned him round to dust imaginary flecks from the jacket and pants.

"Quite regal, you are, m' lord," Jerkin declared, getting an affirming nod from Owl.

"My thanks," Brandel returned. "But I am no one's lord. If Brandel, is not sufficient then lieutenant or Lt. Journeyson will do." The two boys conferred briefly, Jerkin responding, "Lt. Journeyson, then. Lt. Journeyson, breakfast is being served. We can take you to the dining hall if you wish."

"Again, my thanks. But I can find my way."

Knife Point was more alive on this morning than it had been previously. Guards were posted outside every door Brandel passed, including his own. They were posted, as well, on every landing of the great spiral stairs. The dining hall, while still far from being filled, also boasted a greater number than before, conversation among the guardians a constant buzz through the hall. Brandel found his way to the table where Hawk sat, the man listening intently to those nearest him. He acknowledged Brandel's approach with a gesture to take a seat on the bench next to him.

Piling his plate with boiled eggs, slabs of bacon, biscuits, and dried fruit, Brandel, too, sat listening. Everyone, it seemed, knew of Gray's arrival. Moreover, the Lord of Knife Point also arrived in the night. Brandel shot a glance to the head table, but it remained empty.

"The lord and lady are taking their morning meal in their common room," Hawk provided. "Rumor is it that they will make an announcement at lunch."

"Announcement," Brandel repeated. "About?"

Hawk shrugged. "Some think it will be a decision to send troops to join the Soldiers of Damsa Dana. Others believe we will be sent to strengthen our own borders. In either case, we are preparing for war." Hawk ate a few bites before adding, "I know which you prefer, lieutenant. And I agree. We need to send troops to the aid Brightwater. Better to stop the Red Moon Warriors before their full force reaches our lands."

If it is not already too late for that, Brandel worried. The creature that survived Gray's attack likely teleported straight back to its masters with news of the girls. If Shadow and Whisper were the treasures the Lady of Knife Point suggested, then the warriors could be pouring across those borders, even now.

"I fear, however," Hawk was continuing, "that the lord and lady may not agree to your request."

"Why do you say that?"

"Their focus, as always, is the protection of Knife Point and Grandmother." Hawk leaned in close to Brandel, whispering, "That old woman should have been commanded to attend our lord and lady many an age ago to offer up whatever information or weapon she possesses." Straightening, his brow creased. "There is something else, as well. Something that they may take as an omen of the need to pull all troops back to guard this keep. The white wolf known as Spirit has been sighted outside our gates. We can only surmise that her wandering so far from her home means that her companion is dead. But why come here? She looks half-starved yet refuses to eat the food we leave for her. Nor will she leave the gates. None among the guardians dare approach her. She howls and she waits. Many fear that she came here, fleeing from the death beasts; that the beasts may well be coming this way."

Brandel shifted uneasily. The wolf looked for Whisper, perhaps. She said they had a connection. "Is the Lady Whisper aware of the wolf's presence?"

Hawk cocked a brow. "No. Is there a reason she should be?"

"Uhm. Not particularly," Brandel hedged. Maybe Whisper did not want her affinity for the wolf known. "She just seems to be good with animals. Perhaps she could calm the wolf; ascertain the reason for its coming to the gates of Knife Point Keep."

"Aye. Whisper possesses a way with animals. Spirit is a special creature, though. Only Bear dares approach her. And he never comes to Knife Point. What the wolf is doing here is a worrisome puzzle. My guess is the old trader is dead, and the wolf is lost without him. I do not expect she will survive much longer."

Brandel chewed his lip. "I would like to get a look at the animal. Do I need permission to travel down to the outer gate?"

Hawk studied the man, his eyes settling on Brandel's jacket. "Your color tells me one of your attributes is the ability to connect with animals. But if you expect to connect with Spirit..." His voice trailed off. After a moment's thought, he added, "It is your skin if you attempt to get close to the wolf. I will take you down, though. Let me send to Jerkin that you will need your coat."

Mere minutes later, Jerkin trotted into the hall carrying the heavy, fur-lined coat and mittens, Owl following purposefully behind, already dressed for the frigid temperatures outside.

"What is this?" Hawk asked, eyeing the boy.

"I wish to attend Lt. Journeyson, sir. In case he has need of something that I might fetch for him."

"Do you?" Hawk chuckled. "Well, Journeyson, it appears you have attracted a loyal follower. What do you say? Does the boy go with us?"

Brandel could hardly decline, given Owl's hopeful expression. "If you wish it. Were I you, however, I would choose to stay where it is warm."

"The cold is no bother to me, sir."

The bright and clear day with fresh snow on the surrounding peaks glistening jewel-like in the morning sunshine was marred suddenly as a deep crevasse high on the nearest neighboring slope rumbled and split. The roar of a dense and broiling white cloud caused the ground, even where they stood, to tremble at the crash and sweep of the massive avalanche. Brandel stood tensed and in awe when minutes later, white puffs could still be seen tumbling from above the split to spill the remnants of the great wave of snow and ice into the maw.

"That," said Hawk, "is why Bear chose never to venture to these heights."

Brandel lengthened his stride to walk beside the sergeant. "Does that happen often? And does it happen on this mountain?"

"Happens on every mountain. Our troops are always mindful of the signs and the risk."

Brandel's shiver had nothing to do with the cold. Traveling on in silence, he gave thanks once again for having been born in the lowlands, his gaze repeatedly darting upslope. Hawk and Owl, however, seemed unconcerned.

Their path narrowed as they neared the lower gate, the way bordered on each side by the piles of snow that had been cleared from it. On the outside of the gate, at least a meter of fresh snow covered the hard pack of earlier snowfalls , as none ventured where the lean and ragged white wolf could be seen pacing. At Brandel's approach, she stilled, her stormy blue-gray eyes turned to him. There was a weak nudge at the back of his mind, the signature clearly that of Spirit. She was trying to connect with him. Bracing for the impact, Brandel opened his mind, reaching for the sense of her. The contact was not as severe a jolt as he expected, perhaps because of the animal's weakened state. Still, the images came sharp and clear. Those vile death creatures - easily a dozen of them - leading Red Moon Warriors through the woods to the stables that had once been Bear's.

"How long?" he called.

"Sir?" responded one of the guards.

"The wolf. How long since she arrived?"

"Only hours after you did, sir."

"Has there been any indication of anyone or anything following her?"

"Not according to our scouts, sir."

That much, at least, was a relief. Still, there was the wolf to worry about. She was not in good shape. Turning to Owl, Brandel declared, "Meat! I need meat for her!"

"Sir?" Several stunned guards gaped at him. "We tried to feed her, but she refuses."

"She may take it from me. Where is the meat you offered?"

"Out there. In the snow where we tossed it."

"Let me through."

Two guards barred his way. "Sir, we cannot. That wolf is a threat to any who get near her, even as starved as she is. Perhaps more so, given her hunger."

"Let me through," Brandel persisted.

The guards' quick glance at Hawk brought a reluctant nod from him. "Let him through."

It required no small amount of effort to push the gate open enough for him to squeeze out. The wolf backed up several paces, head down, eyes focused, and hackles raised as the pile of snow was pushed out. Pounding heart in his throat, Brandel climbed over the mound plowed by the gates. The wolf held her ground. "Where?" he called back over his shoulder.

"There, sir. To your right about two meters up on the slope."

Brandel spotted the indentation where something large had been tossed and climbed far enough dig it out. With the hind quarter of a sheep's carcass in hand, he slid back down the slope, holding it before him. Would she come? And would it be for the sheep's carcass or his? How could he get her to understand his offering? Could she understand words? *"Spirit,"* he sent. The wolf stirred from her tensed and guarded position, her eyes still on him. *"I will not harm you. I thank you for your warning. Now, you must eat. You must survive. Whisper will want you to survive."*

At Whisper's name, the wolf relaxed a little, though she still followed Brandel's every move. So, how to convince the animal to eat? Lifting the carcass, Brandel made to take a mouthful, then lowered it, holding it out for the wolf once again. *"Eat. Spirit, you must survive. For Whisper."* The animal approached warily, her attention now wavering between Brandel and the meat. At last, she stopped, scarcely a nose length from the offering. Brandel laid it to the ground and backed away. Spirit's first bite was tentative, still watchful. Then, she tore into it, ripping and swallowing it in great mouthfuls. Brandel backed his way to the gate and through, turning to Owl. "Can you get more? She needs more. If you can bring it, I will take it out to her."

Owl's eyes were as wide as his namesake's. "Aye, sir! Right away!" Spinning and dashing back up the path toward the courtyard and fortress, the boy cried out, "He did it! Lt. Journeyson! He fed the shewolf! She took the food from him! He needs more!"

Within minutes, guardians and citizens alike crowded the path, passing chunks of meat down and watching in awe as Brandel took each piece through the gate and laid it before Spirit, who continued to eat her fill. Sated, at last, she trotted straight to Brandel, freezing him where he stood. Instead of the attack he feared, she turned and sat at his feet, eyeing the gathering on the other side of the gate. Pressing through the crowd came two small, heavily cloaked figures Brandel at first took as children. He quickly determined from the subtle spring in the graceful gait of the taller one, however, that it was Whisper. The movements of the one with her were equally as graceful, though as a glide without the spring. It was not until she tossed back her hood that he recognized the Lady of Knife Point. Behind them trailed Tine, Serenity and Shadow.

Whisper and the lady passed through the gate to stand a respectful distance from Brandel and the wolf. The lady eyed him with mild amusement. "Whisper said you had it in you to connect with Spirit. I must admit, I did not dare to believe it, fearing the wolf would perish in grief for her companion. The animal is not a cat, but you are, without a doubt, Fedel'ma's descendant. Has the wolf shown you why she is here?"

"Yes, my lady. She…"

The lady raised her hand to stop him. "Not here. Come to me in my common room in an hour. We will speak, then."

Whisper was all smiles as she returned up the slope with the Lady of Knife Point, this time with the lady on Tine's arm as he assisted her on the steeper sections. Serenity and Shadow lingered for a few seconds, staring between Brandel and the wolf. Before turning to go, Serenity shot him a nod of approval while Shadow fixed him with a mix of curiosity and respect.

Brandel stared down at the wolf. *"I must go,"* he sent. *"Again, I thank you for your warning. You are free, now. Go and live as you please."*

Spirit made no move to leave. *"Stay, then. I will see that you are given food."* As he took a step toward the gate, Spirit rose and stepped with him. Brandel stopped, mouth pinched. *"You cannot go within. You must remain here. I will return for you."* Still, as he moved, so moved the animal.

"You have connected with the beast," Hawk called, tension in his tone. "Where you go, she will insist on going. It was her way with Bear."

"Then, how am I to return? The lady said I must meet with her."

Hawk drew a measured breath, motioning the guards back from the gate. "So I heard. We will allow Spirit to pass through with you. I pray she stays at your side as loyally as she did Bear's. While none could approach her, none feared her so long as she was in his presence."

Walking the grounds with a great wolf at his side was not Brandel's idea of a healthy experience for anyone. But he had no idea how to alter her sudden attachment to him. Glancing down at her, he sighed, *"Really? Is this the way it is going to be? Would you not prefer be free?"* As he moved forward, however, she paced him. *"You know this is going to be very awkward."* The wolf cast a brief glance up at him, but maintained her pace at his side, scattering the onlookers in a wider arch around them.

20

Guardians stared and gave wide berth as Brandel and the wolf made their way up the long stairs toward the fortress. An armed company marching for the gates abruptly halted, clearing the path, gaping at the pair. Workers securing structures ceased their efforts, gathering just close enough to catch a glimpse of the wolf and the lieutenant. The pair of guards stationed at the massive fortress doors kept as much distance as possible as they drew the doors open.

Trailing a safe distance behind, Hawk called, "Take the spiral stairs. It is faster than trailing through the back halls."

"Anyone near the stairs will know where we are going."

"Believe me, they know, already."

Guardians cleared the stairs at each landing, their stunned expressions focused on the wolf as they saluted Brandel. He could sense their lingering gazes before the sound of their boots once again echoed behind him. Hawk left them at the landing on the third level. Uncertain whether he was early, late, or on time, Brandel hesitated at the top of the fourth level in front of Chamberlain Fairchild's library, glancing around for a clock. Not that he had any idea of the time when the lady spoke with him below.

"*You are on time,*" Shadow sent, the music of her voice edgy. "*You are a strange one, Master Journeyson. Companion to a wild wolf no one thought would join with any but Bear.*"

"*I will thank you to stay out of my head,*" he returned, more annoyed than irritated. "*And the connection with Spirit was not at my instigation.*"

"*Which makes you all the stranger.*"

His final assent to the lord and lady's common room was made with less breathlessness than previously. Whether that could be accounted for by his slow return up the mountain path or because he was adjusting to the current altitude and the rigors hardly mattered, so long as he could present himself with an air of steady composure.

"My lady," he said, snapping to attention as he spotted her standing before one of the great windows. At her side was another Alainn, this one just as tall as Tine On Stoirm, though the man's skin was pale as alabaster, his hair short-cropped and white. The icy topaz gaze the man turned to him sent a chill through Brandel's veins. The Alainn's smile was warm, though. "Lt. Journeyson, I assume. And Spirit. I was told she attached herself to you. Most curious. And most welcome. I feared for her survival since word came of Bear's death." A graceful sweep of his hand directed Brandel to a chair situated with enough space next to it for the wolf, "Please. Make yourself comfortable."

Brandel obliged, Spirit circling the chair once before laying down beside it. Lt. Starn, Serenity, Shadow, Whisper, and Gray were seated at a small grouping of chairs. Tine crossed the room and offered Brandel a warm mug of coffee while the fair skinned Alainn escorted the lady to the same chair she occupied the night before, then took the last chair, saying simply, "I am Stoirm."

"The Lord of Knife Point," the lady put in.

Stoirm waved her off. "My title matters not. What matters is you, lieutenant. You and the wolf beside you. Swan tells me that Spirit bears a message."

A perplexed crease knotted Brandel's brow. "Swan?"

The lady sighed. "That would be me. One of several names acquired over the years."

Brandel started to ask how many several equated to but thought better of it.

"More than I care for, lieutenant." Her comment drew a resigned sigh from him. Lady Swan's smile was fleeting, but none the less charming. "I did not intrude upon your thoughts if that is what disturbs you. As I was once told I often did, you wear your questions on your face." For a moment, the gathering sat in silence, Swan's gaze on the wolf. Spirit appeared unconcerned, her head resting on her forepaws, her ears flicking.

"So," Lord Stoirm said, at last. "Why is the animal here?"

Brandel glanced down, automatically reaching a hand to Spirit's head to scratch behind her ears, hesitating, then completing the act with satisfaction. "She brings a warning. Or so I believe." With a glance in the direction of Serenity and the girls, he explained, "She showed me the vision of Red Moon Warriors in the vicinity of Bear's dwelling."

"A late warning," Shadow grumbled.

"I believe this is a new group. A larger force. They follow behind at least a dozen of those foul creatures Gray encountered. The creatures led them to the stable entrance to Bear's abode." The sudden itch running through Brandel's nerves told him the tension in the room jumped sharply.

Gray sucked in. "A dozen! I barely dealt with two. Had it not been for that dark spell, I would not have accomplished that much. The act caused as much pain to my mind as the burning from the spell's rebound did to my body. How many others will be willing to attempt the conjuring of such a spell?"

"Do not attempt it, again," the Lord of Knife Point warned. "Leave it to those who understand it."

Shocked countenances fixed on him. "Who, in this world, aside from the Red Moon demons, would find cause to learn such magic?" Whisper's murmured question reflected Brandel's thoughts. Lord Stoirm ran a weary hand over his face. "Since the death of her mother, only their current High Priestess Aifa knows the spell. She sought and destroyed those of her mother's followers who knew it and forbids all else to learn it. She fears some among them may attempt to turn it on her. There are, however, a few among us who know it."

Brandel swallowed. "Like you, my lord?"

"Like me."

"And me," Tine acknowledged.

"And me," came Chamberlain Fairchild's voice as he stepped from the stairs onto the landing.

The Lady Swan shuddered. "And me."

Lt. Starn gave a tense shake of his head. "When my thrice great grandfather asked me to learn the spell, I never believed I would find reason to use it. But the spell is in my power, as well."

Serenity's features paled, her dark eyes darting between each of those confessing to possess the magic. "A dark spell, indeed, if it caused Gray such pain and injury. How can you wield such a magic? Can you use it against a dozen of these creatures and survive?"

"There are more of the beasts." The fear in the Lady Swan's eyes belied the calm with which she spoke. "They are, even now, passing through the lowlands heading for our realm."

Brandel sprang to his feet, Spirit's senses snapping to high alert as she rose with him. "I need to get back! I need to stand with my men!"

"There is little you can do to help them, now, lieutenant." Lord Stoirm rose and strode to the brazier at the center of the room, staring into it. "There was treachery within. Someone allowed the Red Moon Warriors access to the gates of Riversong. Your lord is dead, the Soldiers of Damsa Dana either dead or scattered. It appears that we are the last to stand against this foe. We must drive the current forces back and fight them at our borders. If they take our realm…"

Sinking back onto his chair, Brandel stared at the Lord of Knife Point. "You know this about Brightwater? How?"

"I saw it in my vision two nights ago," Whisper confessed.

"And you said nothing of it to me?"

"What would be the point, Master Journeyson? To allow you to charge back to your death?"

"Better to die with my people than to hide myself, here."

Lady Swan leveled her gaze on him. "You are not in hiding. You are here on a mission."

"A failed one." Brandel dropped his head to his hands. "I came for the support of the guardians. Now, you tell me there is nothing left to support."

"None has said that." Lady Swan rose and crossed to stand before him. "There are the remnants of your troops to gather and bring here. And there is Grandmother's advice to seek."

Brandel raised his head, his eyes narrowing. "You will take me to her?"

"You will meet her."

"And what of my people? If the scattered troops are gathered and brought here, who will be left to protect the people of Brightwater?"

"We are sending messengers into the nearer villages to bring those who are willing and able to the mountains. Those who do not come will spread the word. We must take our stand, here, to protect what is left of those who worship the White and the Rose Goddesses."

"I must leave," Brandel persisted, his fists clinched at his sides. "I must be the one to collect and organize what remains of our troops."

Lady Swan took a deep breath, exhaling a slow and weary sigh. "Will you know who among them to trust? As Lord Stoirm stated, there was treachery within the ranks of the soldiers." Her glance settled briefly on Shadow. "There is one among us who can sense the nature and degree of magic in others. She will be able to tell if there is darkness in them. We will gather those we can find and take them to her." Swan's brow ticked up a notch as she faced Brandel. "You believe Shadow does not trust you. She read the truth and honesty in you from the beginning. Her uncertainty is about herself." The lady shifted her gaze back to Shadow. "A failing you must overcome, child. You hold your ancestor's gift. Believe in it."

"What of Whisper, Gray, and myself?" Serenity put in. "What task do you assign us?"

"Serenity, you must return to the sanctuary beneath the temple ruins with Shadow," Lady Swan directed. "Identify among the girls and young women who come to you, those with the greatest capacity to learn the spells of the sisterhood. Call upon the few priestesses within the temple to help you. Train the girls and young women in the magic they will need for battle. Pray that at least one among them holds the power to hear the words of Ciuin Rose and that the Goddess provides guidance."

Turning, Lady Swan regarded Gray with concern. "We need for you to return to your outpost to keep watch if you are up to doing so. That is the most likely pass for the creatures and the Red Moon Warriors to take, assuming they believe you dead. Do not attempt to fight them. Send word to Lt. Starn the moment you see any approach the saddle."

"Aye, my lady. I am up for anything you need of me."

"And me?" came Whisper's quiet inquiry.

"You must remain here, child."

"But..."

"You would be the greatest prize for Aifa to take."

"As would Shadow."

"Shadow has the greater skill to hide herself from them. You are the most vulnerable."

"I will never give up Grandmother's secrets."

"Not willingly. But Breag Nemhain's High Priestess would take them from you, anyway. You must stay at Knife Point. Stay safe. If visions come to you regarding any threats to yourself, send to Chamberlain Fairchild at once."

Whisper's eyes teared, her features crestfallen as she glanced at Shadow. Shadow stared back, torment clear in her expression. Serenity said the girls were inseparable. Brandel realized what a tremendous sacrifice Lady Swan was asking of them.

The lady joined Lord Stoirm at the brazier, linking her arm through his. "Sacrifice is needed of us all." For a moment, she stood staring in silence at the icy world beyond the window. "That my long life would lead to yet another battle…" Her voice trailed off. Shaking her head, she lamented, "I did not ask for long life, nor for the powers I hold, nor for the battles I have fought. But I will fight them as long as I am able. Ciuin Rose and Damsa Dana depend on the strength and resolve of each of us to defeat Breag Nemhain. It seems we must do it, here, in the realm of the gentle Ciuin Rose, though she ever sought for peace." Her exhale was long and weary. "Go, now. Those who are to leave must make themselves ready. Chamberlain Fairchild is arranging for you to be teleported as near to the sanctuary as possible. Lord Stoirm and I must announce to the others that we are preparing for the war to come to us. Lt. Journeyson, gather your belongings and return here within the hour."

21

Jerkin and Owl were waiting for Brandel when he returned to his quarters. Eyes wide, they constantly sidestepped the wolf as she made a nervous prowl of the chamber. Jerkin gave the animal much wider berth than Owl, who allowed Spirit the space to go where she pleased but seemed more curious than fearful.

"Do not get too near her," Brandel cautioned. "She may tolerate Whisper and me, but she remains a wild creature who could decide she prefers gnawing on our bones to putting up with us."

Owl's lips pinched as he stepped a bit further from the animal.

"Wise decision," Brandel nodded. "I see the two of you kept busy," he remarked with a glance toward the bed where his pack lay open next to an array of items.

Both boys shrugged, Jerkin offering, "'Tis our duty, sir, to see that you have all you might need."

"It is a mark of a good soldier," Brandel affirmed as he changed into the heavy traveling clothes. "Knowing your duty and taking care to do it well."

Next to him, the boys folded the items he removed, tucking them near the bottom of his pack. At his cocked brow, Jerkin said, "Lady Swan suggested you may have need of them, later." A final glance at the pack caught the embroidered symbols Whisper designed for him. His fingers brushed across the white moon with its clear blue eyes gazing out. Was the Goddess Damsa Dana dying or dead, that she did not protect his home and his people? It had always been said that she was the strongest of the three; that Ciuin Rose was the quiet, gentle one who avoided war. How could this peaceful Goddess protect any of them?

Shaking such thoughts from his head, he completed his preparations, lacing the pack shut and attaching the axe, his bow, and his quiver to its outside. Spirit matched his stride as he hooked the pack over a shoulder and grabbed his coat from its peg near the door. The two boys trotted along behind him. Stopping, he turned on them. "Where do you think you are going?"

"With you," Jerkin replied.

"No! You two are to stay here. I doubt the Lady Swan would permit your traveling with us, in any event."

"She sent to us that we could, sir," Owl returned meekly. "Our packs are waiting for us."

Brandel stood, for a moment, stunned. "Fine!" he snapped. "Keep up."

"Uhm…." Owl cleared his throat. "Might I suggest, sir, that we take the back stairs to the archives? The attendants to our lord and lady were sent to the temple on the first level to receive instructions for their new duties, so that way should be clear. Guardians and staff have been gathering at the landings, waiting for another glimpse of you and your wolf. And…" He eyed the wolf with a mix of concern and doubt. "And we would not want her to decide to gnaw on anyone's bones, should anyone spook her."

Brandel gave a huff of amusement. "First, she is not my wolf. Spirit belongs to no one. Your point, however, is well taken." Spirit moved with him as if she were part of him, turning to head for the back passage and stairs. The boys kept pace at a cautious distance. Their arrival in the lord and lady's commons found the chamber empty, though much commotion could be heard from the two quarters at the back. Shortly, three young women darted out from the Lady Swan's chambers, their rush promptly brought to a standstill with three unified screeches at the sight of Spirit. Lady Swan brushed the curtain aside to peer out.

"For pity sake, girls. The wolf will not harm you. Join the others in the temple below. The lead girl nodded, dabbing tears from her eyes. Still, she and her companions gave ample space as they rounded past Brandel and Spirit, then dashed down the spiral stairs out of sight. The lady shook her head, tsking. "They would not last a day, where we are headed. Far better for them to remain here, despite their tearful pleading." Glancing at the boys, she gestured to the curtained arch to the right of her quarters. "If you are still intent on this path, you will find your packs in Lord Stoirm's rooms. Grab them and let Stoirm know we are ready."

The boys disappeared into the lord's quarters, returning with their packs draped over a shoulder and their coats in hand. Behind them came Lord Stoirm, Tine, and Lt. Starn, each dressed in heavy coats, their packs strapped to their backs.

"Sgt. Hawk now has command," Starn was saying. "He understands his orders for where the troops are to be dispersed and will see it done. I am coming with you, and I will have no argument."

Tine looked amused, though Lord Stoirm's features read agitation.

"You think we cannot fight, should the need arise?"

"Of course, you can fight," Starn huffed. "Given what stalks you, however, do you not think it wise for another who can cast the dark spell to accompany you?"

Lady Swan glanced between the men, a hand rubbing her temples. "They do not know to look for us. They seek the girls. It is unlikely the warriors will think to hunt for them near the temple ruins. And even if they do, the sense of death etched into the site by the ancient slaughter hides all indication of anything living further within. Shadow will be safe, there. The Soldiers of Damsa Dana will be taken to her in secret for her to assess. And Whisper is much safer here, with the fortress and its guards to protect her."

"The fiends maybe be searching for the girls," Tine agreed. "But if they catch scent of us, do not think they will not know you, Swan. You are the true prize they seek."

The lady fell silent, her small frame sagging against the wall. "After so many ages, that they should still be able to recognize me…"

Lord Stoirm moved to her side, taking her hand. "Maura saw to it that every beast bred to aid her mother's line would know you. Keeping to these mountains is all that protected you. May it protect you, still."

"That protection is shaky, at best," Starn put in. "Now that some of the Red Moon Warriors and their creatures are past Gray's outpost, with more on the way."

"We waste time," Stoirm pointed out, patting Swan's hand before releasing it. "Let us be away from here. It is a difficult journey that lies ahead."

The starkness of Lady Swan's quarters surprised Brandel as she led them through. A fire burned low on a raised hearth in a back corner, casting shadows across a canopied bed and a small writing table and chair. Heavy velvet curtains of silvered gray shot through with strands of amethyst draped the massive window, sealing out the world of ice and snow beyond. An open curtain in the arch to a partitioned section in the other back corner showed it to be the lady's bath. Swan strode past, heading for the back wall. For a moment, she stood in silence, her hand flat against the smooth surface. A whisper from her produced a fine seam that ran from ceiling to floor. Another whisper and a panel slid open. Once they were through and the panel snapped shut, torches sparked to life.

The sudden light left Brandel blinking for several seconds. As his vision settled, a narrow chamber was revealed, running the length behind both Lady Swan's and Lord Stoirm's chambers. At the center of the space stood a long table draped in a rose silk cloth with white edging. Arranged on it were three ancient paintings - each a picture of a different young girl dressed in a long gown, their likenesses vague resemblances of the three goddesses. Lady Swan stepped to the obsidian wall that backed the room and began a murmured incantation, Lord Stoirm quietly stopping at a corner of the table where he withdrew and pocketed a strange charm from a small silver box. Brandel's glimpse of the item was brief, but he noted the trinity knot set with a dull red stone at its heart.

As Swan's incantation finished, the obsidian face of the mountain opened in the same manner as the wall at the back of her quarters. Brandel squinted, his shadow sight struggling to adjust to the black tunnel through which a frigid draft whistled. Those who were yet carrying their coats hastily donned them, then shouldered their packs.

"Allow me." Starn stepped to the front and into the tunnel to lead the way. "Watch your steps. Torches do no good, here. Wind and magic prevent them from holding their flame. Once the passage seals behind us, we will grant a moment for our shadow sight to adjust. Even that, however, will be of limited use. Keep a hand to the wall, if necessary. The way twists downward."

Spirit snarled at the darkness as the opening ground to a close. Brandel felt the wolf against his leg and feared she might trip him. Instead, she set her tread to parallel him, her warmth still notable, though without interfering with his movements. Starn spoke truly regarding the minimal use of their shadow sight. Brandel made out only vague delineations of jagged wall and ceiling. Failure to pay strict attention often resulted in knocking his head against a low-hanging protrusion of rock or scraping against a sharp outcrop. The whistle of icy air numbed Brandel's nose, and the steepness of the downward grade left his legs and hips protesting in short order. All that prevented any of them from slipping and sliding the full way was the roughness of the ground beneath their feet.

There was no way to know how long they spent in the dark descent from the top of the fortress, but it seemed an eternity. When at last, the way made a sharp curve to the right and widened into a cave, the pale light from the cave's opening suggested the lateness of the day.

"Wait here," Starn urged, moving cautiously out. Minutes later, he returned, motioning them to join him. The group emerged in a narrow and ice-coated

SLIEVGALLION: THE GODDESS WARS

chasm between two cliff walls, daylight nearly gone. The path between cliffs meandered for a good distance, its slick treachery mitigated at least in part by the protrusion of rock through the ice. At last, it emptied near the edge of a lake. The air, here, lacked the chill that blew through the tunnel, the warmth seeming to come from the steam rising from the water. Much to Brandel's and Spirit's dismay, it also carried the choking stench of sulfur.

"We need to reach the woods on the other side of the lake," Starn indicated, pointing across. "The way winds and is marshy. Just stay clear of the lake water."

For the first time since Spirit had taken up with him, the wolf moved from Brandel's side, making her way just ahead of him, periodically shaking her head in agitation. Likely, it was the odor she disliked. Brandel agreed, pulling the flap from his hood across his nose and mouth.

"The wolf has the sense of it," Owl declared. "She is finding the way for us."

"Aye," Starn acknowledged. "It would appear so. Follow Lt. Journeyson. Be careful to stay where he treads."

The way was rocky and slow, the woods much further than Brandel had guessed. Worse, the sulfur was raising a headache. Spirit kept a steady pace, halting only when Brandel fell too far behind. Night fully cloaked them when the wolf turned and trotted away from the lake and well into the forest. Not until the sulfurous fumes at last diminished, did Starn call a stop.

"We can rest here until daylight, though we dare risk nothing more than a small fire beneath stones for warmth."

Lady Swan stripped her pack from her shoulders, settling to the ground and digging a pair of packages from it. One contained bread, the other dried meat, both of which she shared around. Turning to the wolf, she leveled her gaze on the animal. "I cannot speak to you in the way of Master Journeyson, my friend. But perhaps you will understand my words. You seemed always to understand Bear's, whether he spoke within your head or aloud. We could not pack meat for you, Spirit. You must hunt on your own."

Spirit sat at Brandel's feet, her head cocked, her eyes on the lady. For a moment, the wolf hesitated, venturing a quick glance up at Brandel. Then she rose, turned, and sprinted into the woods. Brandel's mind instantly filled with the image of hunting and the sense of a promise to return.

Jerkin and Owl both gaped, first at the Lady Swan, and then in the direction the wolf had gone. "She understood," Jerkin managed. "The wolf. She understood what you said to her."

Swan shrugged. "Perhaps. More likely, she sensed that her companion would be safe in our company and determined for herself that she must eat."

"Companion," Owl murmured. "You and Master Journeyson both have referred to the connection as companionship, and not as that of a master and a beast."

"It is a mistake," the lady sighed, "to think that any human is the master of any animal. If we are fortunate enough, they may grant us the blessing of their companionship. Maybe even their friendship. But we do not...cannot...own them. To attempt to do so risks either their turning on us, or our breaking their spirits and their souls, destroying them."

Brandel regarded her for several seconds. "You seem to possess a remarkable understanding for someone who claims to hold no ability to join with them."

"Once upon a time," Swan said softly, "I had a very dear friend whose closest companion was a cat. Both taught me a great deal."

Tine, was busy digging a small pit when Brandel dropped his pack from his shoulders, setting it against a tree trunk. Starn was collecting twigs and branches from the ground, snapping them to fit well within the pit. Stoirm, in the meantime, was collecting stones and building a ring of them around the pit to support a large, flat rock. Even with magic, it took Starn a few attempts at igniting a blaze in the wet wood. The boys hung back, looking uncertain.

"If you are waiting for me to warm myself, I will do so from here," Brandel grunted, slumping down beside his pack and extending his feet toward the heating rocks. "Go ahead. Get as close as you need."

"It is not that, sir." Jerkin shifted from one foot to the other, one hand fidgeting with the edge of a sleeve. "It is...well...Owl and me... we are here to see to your needs, sir. What would you have us do?"

Leaning back, Brandel closed his eyes, crossing his arms and tucking his mittened hands in his armpits. "Stop calling me sir, to start with. And I would have you back at Knife Point, safe and warm." He opened an eye enough to see the boys shoot a glance at Lady Swan in entreaty.

The lady shrugged. "Do not look to me. The man can obviously see to his own needs. Make yourselves as cozy as is possible and get some sleep. Tomorrow we cross through Hollows Pass, drop down to the valley, and then start a steep climb."

22

Whisper jerked awake in a cold sweat, her nerves charged with foreboding, her vision clinging to her mind. The first of its kind, this vision. Not washed in the colors of the world but formed in monochrome, which somehow lent a more disturbing quality to its sense of urgency. Yet, it provided nothing specific to explain the warning. A woman was involved, her face shrouded in shadow. Judging from her clothing, Whisper assumed her to be a priestess, though with nothing more than grays to color her robes, she could not determine which goddess the woman served. What message did the vision wish to reveal regarding this priestess?

The fast rapping on her door so startled Whisper, she nearly fell out of bed. Hand pressed against her thundering heart, she rasped, "Who are you? What do you want at this hour?"

The rapping came again, this time more insistent. Swinging her legs around, she snatched the robe from the foot of her bed and made her way to the door. "Who are you?"

"My lady! I am Sgt. Hawk. You must come with me!"

Fumbling with the latch, she edged the door open and peered out. "Why?"

"You are in grave danger, my lady."

"Here?" Whisper shot a glance down the hall. "In the fortress? How so?"

"I can explain as we go. Please, my lady. You recognize me, do you not? Faithful Guardian of Ciuin Rose. I have served Knife Point and our Goddess since a boy."

She studied his face, briefly, nodding. "Yes. I know who you are. You are Lt. Starn's right hand. I ask again, how am I in danger, here?"

"The creatures that bring death where they pass. They are close. We are doing our best to hold the Red Moon and their creatures from the gates, but we may not be able to do so for long. Dress quickly, my lady. We must get you away from here. We will take a path that avoids the gates. It is risky, especially at this hour, since we must avoid using torches to light the way There is no choice, though. Please, my lady. Hurry."

Her vision's foreboding coupled with Spirit's warning of the beasts seared through her. Danger lay at the gates. Why had the sight not warned her sooner? And why did it show her a woman and not these demon creatures? Behind her questions and the terror that took her, a small doubt niggled at her mind. Something was not right about Hawk's words. They did not suggest a lie so much as an omission of some part of the truth. "A moment." Shutting and latching the door, she leaned against it. What did he conceal? Had the creatures already broken through? Was he trying to keep her calm by not saying as much?

"My lady!" Sgt. Hawk's plea came low and tense. "Please hurry. In Lt. Starn's and our lord and lady's absence, your safety is entrusted to me."

She found no hint of deception in that statement. Scrambling from her robe and nightgown, Whisper donned her heavy traveling clothes, then searched her wardrobe for the heavy coat and mittens the guardians provided for her. The white fur would provide better camouflage on the snowy slopes than the brown one she arrived wearing. Last, she snatched her pack from beneath the bed. She would need to get word to Shadow, Serenity, and Swan as soon as she knew more; knew if the priestess in her vision was responsible for these death beasts; knew where Hawk intended to take her.

As Whisper raced back to the door, Hawk breathed a cautious, shush. "Quietly, my lady. We cannot allow any but the few of my men who wait for us to know you have gone or in which direction. If the Red Moon Warriors take the fortress, those here will be tortured for information."

Whisper gave a trembling nod, easing herself through the door and closing it again. Two of Lt. Starn's men waited in the corridor with the sergeant. "How many others?" she asked.

"A dozen of us, in all, each willing and eager to assist in keeping you hidden and safe."

Hawk was about to protest Whisper's hesitation when she gestured toward her room. "Summon each of them here. I can show you another way out of the fortress."

It was the sergeant's turn to hesitate, at last nodding. "Very well. I will send for them. It will take them some minutes to get here from where they are posted. Let us wait for them in your chambers rather than risk being seen where we stand."

Whisper eased her door open motioning for Hawk and the other men to join her. Inside, she stood for a moment, her hands fussing with the fur on her coat. Anxious and impatient, she headed for her window, thinking to catch a glimpse of the battle below.

"It looks out on the wrong side to see the gates, my lady. Still, I caution you to stay clear. We would not want any beast who might break through to catch sight of you."

Whispers lips pinched at her foolishness as she fell back from the window to stand in shaky silence at the center of the room. Several minutes passed before the last of Hawk's chosen guardians joined them.

"Where to, my lady?"

"The private stairs."

The guardians shot her perplexed glances but followed without question, moving in single file through the tight passage adjacent to her chamber's bath and up the equally narrow stairwell. The first flight up took them to a landing between the quarters for the Lord of Knife Point's attendants and the chamberlain's archives. She doubted any of the attendants remained. They were likely sent to the temple on the first level earlier in the day to receive new orders. Still, she proceeded in silence. The second flight up delivered them to the Lord of Knife Point's chambers.

"Curious," Hawk remarked, stepping into a room filled with bookcases and a writing table, the lord's bed shoved off in a corner. "Odd place for a lady's private stairs to empty."

"They are not my private stairs. Lord Stoirm says the fortress is riddled with such secret ways. I cannot say why this set leads to his chamber. I know only that Shadow and I discovered it when we were children, ducking in and out of closets and hallways. It was a game, and it delighted us to find a way into Lord Stoirm's rooms. We never risked doing so when he was within the keep. But it amused Lady Swan to see us popping out of his rooms when she was here." Whisper allowed the torches to come to life as they passed from Lord Stoirm's chambers through to the commons, then into Lady Swan's quarters. No one came or went when neither the lord nor lady were in residence. The empty stillness and isolation weighed on Whisper. Swallowing, she bit back the threat of tears. She could commune with Swan at any time, of course, though this was not the time to do so. Nor did speaking telepathically fill the ache of missing the woman. It was a familiar ache; one that often gnawed at her. Why she should be so attached to the Lady of Knife Point was their secret. And she shared it with no one. Not even Shadow or Serenity. Her ache for Swan's presence was exasperated, now, by the absence of Shadow, as well.

Shoving her thoughts and her sorrow aside, Whisper made her way to the back of Lady Swan's chambers, staring at the wall and struggling to recall the incantation needed to open it. She and Shadow were shown this exit several times over the years; had even been escorted out and back in through it twice to familiarize them with it. The last time they had done so, however, was... Whisper frowned. She could not recall, exactly. Four...five years ago?

The words came to her in a flash, her hand flicking almost imperceptibly, her lips moving in silent recitation. A panel slid open. The group passed into Swan's small, private temple where ancient paintings of the three Goddesses adorned a table. Whisper had difficulty imagining the Goddesses in physical form, much less as the young sisters in the paintings. They cared for each other once upon a time. Or so the ancient legends told. Why did the one turn so vile and hateful?

The wall panel snapped closed, torches flicking to life. Setting her hand to the obsidian wall that backed the private temple, she repeated the silent recitation. Again, a panel slid open, the icy draft intensifying the unease that gnawed along her nerves. She was leaving with a handful of guardians who should be holding their posts to protect the fortress and their fellows. Yet, Sgt. Hawk's primary assignment was apparently to protect her above all else. Again, she swallowed past her constricting throat and the threat of tears. In protecting her, these men placed others at greater risk. *"Do not think on that, now!"* she insisted. *"The creatures and the warriors must not take me. They must never learn Grandmother's secrets, or our world is lost."*

Forcing a steadying breath, she cautioned, "The way spirals steeply down and is without light. Our shadow sight will be of little help. Keep a hand to the wall to guide you and keep your senses alert to overhangs and sharp protrusions."

Hawk nodded. "Let me take the lead, my lady. If you should take a misstep, I can catch you."

"I will not misstep, sergeant. The way is familiar. And most of the protrusions are well above my head. I will lead. You mind your skull and protect your shoulders and shins."

23

Brandel jumped from sleeping to sharp attention at the sound of Lt. Starn's shouted, "What?!" Next to him, Spirit leaped from sleeping to a low crouch, teeth bared, her growl a low rumble. Without thinking, Brandel laid a hand to her head. The wolf's growl died, though she remained tense. Tine and the lord and lady were on their feet, as well, the two boys only beginning to stir at the commotion. Starn's countenance was pale and agitated as he turned to Lady Swan.

Swan stood trembling, her features graying. "Something is amiss. I feel it, though the sight shows me nothing." Her hand reached for Starn's arm. "What is it? What news did you just receive?"

Starn drew an unsteady breath. "Whisper is missing. So are Lt. Hawk and eleven other guardians."

"Missing?" Lord Stoirm exhaled in a stunned hiss. "How can they be missing? Is Knife Point under attack?"

Starn spun to his belongings, repacking his partially emptied pack. "No. All is quiet, according to the chamberlain. He was notified when Hawk and some of the guardians failed to report to their respective watches. A search within the fortress and the grounds of the keep found that Whisper is missing, as well. No one saw them leave the fortress, though two among the guardians reported seeing a man or two slip around toward Whisper's quarters. We must go back to find the girl."

Lady Swan was as still as marble for several seconds. "Whisper refuses to connect with me. I sense no immediate threat or harm to her, but I cannot tell where she has gone or with whom."

"That makes no sense," Starn rumbled. "Why would they leave the fortress? And how in the name of Ciuin Rose did they leave without being seen?"

Stoirm squared on his lieutenant. "You are sure the keep is not under attack? That the creatures did not slip in?"

"I am certain. Fairchild says the keep is quiet and all accounted for except Hawk, the eleven, and Whisper."

Swan backed to the nearest tree, bracing against it, doubt vying with hope in her words. "Perhaps the child had a vision. Foresaw the coming of the creatures and warned Sgt. Hawk. There is a…"

"Possibly," Starn agreed, though his troubled expression suggested he believed otherwise. For several moments, he stood, his unfocused gaze indicating a telepathic discussion taking place. Finally, with a shake of his head, the lieutenant reported, "The chamberlain is increasing the guards at the gates. Scouts are, even now, searching the routes in and out from Knife Point."

Swan fell silent for several seconds, her eyes closed. Opening them, she shook her head. "I would breathe easier if Whisper would open her mind to me. But…"

"She will do so if she has need of you." Stoirm's tone was reassuring despite the crease of his brow. "The girl is stronger than many believe."

Rubbing her temples, Swan cast a weary glance at the hot stones and then at the pale light filtering through the trees. "We slept longer than I intended. Day will break, soon. We must be on our way."

"We are returning, then," Starn acknowledged.

"No, lieutenant. You may return if you wish. We continue. Lt. Journeyson needs to consult with Grandmother. And Grandmother needs to learn what she may."

Starn's eyes narrowed, his breathing tense as he stared in the direction of the fortress. "I stay with you," came in a leaden exhale. "Fairchild will choose another man to take command until I return. As for Hawk, he will answer to me the moment he is found. In the meantime, may he and those with him guard Whisper well. If any harm comes to her…"

Lt. Starn's unfinished threat hung in the air as Tine roused the two boys. Brandel worked with Stoirm to hide all trace of their camp before they set off, once more. For a long while, Brandel stewed over the missing girl. He liked Hawk. Thought the man trustworthy. He must have had good reason for stealing away in the night with Whisper. Likely, Lady Swan was correct. One of Whisper's visions gave warning and she turned to Hawk for help.

Thoughts of the girl faded as their trek wore on. The woods were close and muggy, not to mention buggy. Whether it was better to wear his coat and suffer from dampness inside his clothing from so much sweating as well as outside from the snow, or to stuff it over the top of his pack and endure the bites and stings of periodic swarms of insects was a question that had no answer. For her part, Spirit appeared unconcerned, trotting just ahead of him. When at last the trees thinned, the way became steeper and rockier. As they climbed, the snow deepened and mixed with layers of ice. Here, even the wolf had her struggles over the slippery and uneven surfaces. A dense layer of cloud settled to dull the daylight, making the bite of the wind sharper and removing any further thoughts of dispensing with his coat.

For the better part of the day they climbed, the increasing depth of the snow necessitating Starn's teleporting snowshoes for them from who knew where. They reached Hollows Pass in early evening. Once through the narrow gap between two opposing mountain peaks, the way was precipitously down. Snowshoes were tied to packs as rope and anchors were required to drop to the valley floor. Spirit disappeared from Brandel's side, no doubt concluding that her companionship had extended as far as she cared for it to. He lost sight of her white fur against the snow and turned his concerns to the boys and himself. He feared for their lives more times than he cared to acknowledge as he watched first Jerkin, then Owl repel from one anchor point down to the next. Feared for his own life when the rope squealed from the strain of the weight it bore. So relieved was he to reach the bottom, he might have set permanent roots where his feet landed, save for Lord Stoirm's insistence that they keep moving.

Their camp was set in yet another cold and wet wooded valley. With daylight, Lord Stoirm dropped behind, covering their tracks with simple spells to set the snow in gentle swirls, erasing signs of their passing. Brandel caught Lady Swan's darted backward glance and soft chuckle. When she noted his watching her, she sent, *"As a child I thought learning such spells was nothing more than my aunt's attempt to keep me occupied while she tended to more important magic."*

Her smile charmed him. It was a rare moment that the lady was anything other than serious. Her mention of her childhood prompted the question of her age. Her features suggested perhaps one hundred fiftyish; her white hair potentially upwards of that. It was the haunting depth of her eyes, however, that hinted at years well beyond a Witch's normal span of four or five hundred. Certain comments previously made by her, or by Tine and Stoirm suggested as much, as well. Tales spoke of Witches who had, at one time, lived for many thousands of years. Brandel's ancestor, the distant grandmother from whom part of his name derived, was said to have been one such individual. He long ago dismissed such myths. They involved dark concepts of souls moving from one body to another to survive through centuries without end.

"*Do not be so quick to dismiss the ancient tales, or to judge.*" The lady's sending carried more sorrow and weariness than Brandel's mind could fully grasp. Turning from him, she picked up her pace, calling back over her shoulder, "You do wear your thoughts on your face, you know." One more brief chuckle followed her pronouncement, though it held little amusement. Moments later, she gestured toward the twisted trees to one side. "It appears Spirit has decided to rejoin us."

Brandel followed the direction of her gaze, spotting the animal closing the distance to them. Judging from the blood still staining her muzzle, she must have found a fair meal. As if in response to his thought came the image of a crippled deer and Spirit's smug satisfaction at a completed hunt. The sending left Brandel's stomach rumbling.

Late in the afternoon, after a day filled with too much bright sun reflecting blindingly off the ermine landscape, as cloud shadows gathered on the horizon, he caught a distant glimpse of pale gray stones marring the glistening white. The Lady Swan paused, her arms hanging at her sides, her gaze fixed on the ledge upon which the stones stood. "I hear," she murmured, her features weighted with fleeting mixes of joy and grief. "Do not overwhelm me. Not here. Not now. Let me reach the hall. Let me rest."

Tine was at her side, his arm around her. "You should rest before going further."

She refused with an almost imperceptible shake of her head. "I will rest in the valley, but not here. We can use one of the ruins in the village to shelter for the night."

Shrugging out from under Tine's protective arm, she began picking her way down the slope toward yet another wooded valley. In the fading daylight, Brandel caught the gleam of a small lake on the far side of the woods. Frigid cold, dark holes in the ground, icy waters, trees, and wind-blasted mountainsides. That seemed the sum of Knife Point. He longed to be back in Brightwater relishing the autumn harvests, sharing ale with his fellow soldiers, or fighting with them and understanding his purpose as leader of his men in battle. What purpose had he, here?

His chest tightened. What purpose had he at all? If Brightwater was overrun, its lord dead, the soldiers dead, defeated, or traitorous... Why had Strongbow not called for the aid of Knife Point long before now? It made no difference, at this point, that the Guardians of Ciuin Rose would not return with him. Even if he found this Grandmother, what use was she when he had no home left for him to defend?

"You have a home to reclaim. Fight with us. It has never been you who needed us, but us who need you."

Brandel stiffened at the Lady of Knife Point's gentle voice, realization finally settling. It was she whose voice came to him even before they met. Jerkin and Owl caught up to him, waiting at his side as he stood staring. Lt. Starn allowed the lady to pick the path of their descent, Tine hovering near to assist her at the slightest stumble. She stumbled often, always pushing Tine away; always gaining her feet and trudging on.

"Is there something amiss, sir?" Jerkin asked.

Brandel shook himself. "Hmm? No... Maybe." A sideways glance at the worry crossing Jerkin's and Owl's faces prompted, "No," as he moved on.

By nightfall they reached the leading edge of the woods. Lady Swan seemed to draw strength, here, her stride steadying. Brandel almost welcomed the lesser snowpack beneath the fir, hemlock, and cedar, save for for the moss and mold found everywhere. Surely, some of that mold had taken hold on his feet, as his boots no longer held out the damp.

Swan maneuvered through the undergrowth, slipping past bogs and over fallen trees. Brandel was near concluding that the woods were magical and had no end, when she at last stopped, her weighted sigh of relief indicating the degree of her weariness. A short distance ahead stood the remains of an abandoned village. Stoirm took the lead, now, moving with stealth through the shadows, halting frequently. Brandel's senses shifted to a higher degree of alert. Near the far end of the village, their company stopped, again. On a more isolated strip of ground stood a solitary building. The graying and splintered wood of the structure peeked between layers of brown moss and lichen. Its small front stoop was overgrown with wild rose and nettle. Still, the door and windows appeared to be intact.

Swan started to move around Stoirm, Starn snatching her back at Stoirm's gesture for all to wait while he made cautious entry. Minutes later, he gestured their party inside.

"I could have told you it was safe," Lady Swan sniffed with indignation. "My spells protect it."

"Perhaps," Stoirm snorted. "But I prefer to guarantee your safety for myself."

"You will find wood in the box near the fireplace," Swan continued, ignoring him. "Any smoke that rises, tonight, will blend with the heavy mist and fog that is settling in. And there are ancient spells that will give warning if any but the normal woodland creatures approach."

Tine and Jerkin were already busy laying a fire, Owl gathering packs and setting them near the door. Stoirm did a final check of the grounds as he waited for Spirit to follow Brandel inside. Instead, the wolf side-stepped the door, laying down at the edge of the stoop. "Suit yourself," Stoirm huffed, closing the door. Starn worked his way around the small room, shuttering the windows and, for extra measure, pulling ragged curtains closed over them. "You need to sleep," he said, pointing the Lady Swan toward the single bed that occupied one corner of the room.

"So do we all," she returned, though she shuffled toward the bed, dropping onto it. Pulling her mittens off, she lay in silence, one hand massaging her right temple.

With a fire now burning, Tine stripped from his coat, dropping it to the floor, and went to her. "Are they still trying to talk to you?" he asked, lifting her enough to slide her coat off, then sitting on the edge of the bed and taking her hand.

"They argue. There is great tension and anxiety in them, though they are not speaking it to me." Closing her eyes, she repeated, "They argue," and was then asleep.

Stoirm pulled his coat off and collected Tine's and Swan's, hanging them on pegs near the door. "This is not a good place for her," Tine grumbled.

"It is not good for any of us," Stoirm replied. "Too many voices. But it is necessary."

Starn paced another circle around the room before pounding the dust off a chair and settling on it. "They will get worse. At the compound. The magic is too strong."

"But necessary," Stoirm repeated, strolling to the door and cracking it enough to peer out, then closing it again. "I will take the first watch. You and Tine and Lt. Journeyson get some sleep. I will wake one of you in two hours." Giving Lady Swan's hand a final pat, Tine retrieved his coat and stretched it out on the floor to lay on it.

Brandel tossed his coat near the fire and laid down but got little sleep despite his exhaustion. Every crackle of the fire, every night noise from outside woke him with a start. At last giving up, he pushed himself to an elbow, realizing that it was Tine who now moved about the room checking windows and occasionally cracking the door open to glance outside.

"You are very fond of the lady," Brandel whispered, indicating Swan with a jerk of his head.

Tine turned and cocked a brow. "Awake again, lieutenant?"

Brandel shrugged. How the others could sleep was a mystery, given their circumstances and what hunted them.

Tine shot a glance at Lady Swan. "Aye. I am very fond of her. She has sacrificed much. More than any other, I think. She still sacrifices, though few are aware of the depth of it."

"She knows where we are going." It was not a question, particularly, though Brandel waited for some reply.

"Aye."

"Then why do we not teleport? Or is the place like the sanctuary beneath the ruins and Knife Point Keep, spelled to prevent such intrusion?"

"The Healers complex holds no spells against teleporting. But we cannot be sure it is safe. It was destroyed during the first age of the Goddess Wars here on this world, before the days of the rise of the Red Moon Warriors. Breag Nemhain's daughter, Maura hated those who came to the aid of Soul Bearer and her companions and took revenge in great measure, slaughtering all. For centuries, she kept a watchful eye on the place, guaranteeing that none would inhabit it again. With Maura's death, her daughter Aifa the Red lost interest in the old ruins. Still, she sometimes teleports a small contingent of her Red Moon Warriors to see that it remains a place of the dead. We shall have to approach with great care."

"Why go there at all? Why would this Grandmother wish to draw us to such a place to meet with her?"

Tine drew a long, slow breath, a fleeting glance darted again to Lady Swan. Turning from Brandel to make another check of the windows, he muttered, "Because it is necessary."

24

How temperatures could get any colder was a dismaying mystery to Brandel, yet the new day did so. Or, perhaps it was his bone weariness that robbed him of warmth more than the teeth of the wind. Within the woods, the trees swayed, moaned, and cracked, but also blocked enough to keep each within their party upright instead of bent against the blow. As they climbed yet another steep and exposed slope, however, the battering threatened to tear them away and throw them back to the valley far below.

"*Only a little way further,*" murmured through his skull.

"And just how far is only a little further?" he grated.

Lt. Starn, who had chosen to bring up the rear, lengthened his stride to catch up to Brandel. "Did you say something?"

"Only responding to Lady Swan's sending that the distance is not much further."

Starn's lips tightened in a thin line, his brow cocked as he eyed Brandel. He said nothing, though, as he dropped back a few paces, his eyes ever skimming the surroundings. At least magic was not necessary to cover their trail. The winds were handling the task without assistance.

Brandel set his attention once more to the climb still before him. This was impossible and insane. No battle ever presented a greater threat. He should never have left the lowlands. Should be with his men.

"*You would be dead.*" The voice came as a subtle moan. As before, it seemed a woman's voice, though now he thought about it, the texture of it did not quite match the Lady Swan's. Nonsense! They had no other lady in their party. Grumbling with each step, he forced numb feet and aching knees and hips up the last of the rise to a narrow path protected by a rock overhang. The overhang extended only a few meters. The path continued for perhaps a kilometer before it rounded onto the wide ledge holding the complex of gray stone buildings. Most were crumbling, though some few appeared intact. The air, here, was still, as if the mountain held its breath. Still and silent…and empty. Nowhere did smoke rise to indicate fires that might warm inhabitants.

Brandel rubbed his arms at the charged and expectant feel of the place. Even Spirit was uneasy. Brandel could sense her raised hackles and the tension in her body.

"This way," Lady Swan indicated, leading them toward the handful of buildings that seemed most intact. Among them stood a structure that backed against the mountain. Stoirm forced the door to for her. "I am here," Swan exhaled wearily. "Please let me be. We need shelter and rest."

Brandel opened his mouth, his question left hanging as Tine drew up beside him. "The spirits speak to her, here. It often proves overwhelming, pulling ancient memories to the fore. You will begin to understand, I think. Once you are rested."

Gesturing Brandel to follow, Tine closed in behind the Lady Swan, asking, "Will you let me help?" Her sag was answer enough for him as he caught her and held her upright. "Together, then." She nodded, the two of them making their way to granite wall at the back of the room.

The undertone of their chant raised every hair on Brandel's body and set Spirit to a mournful whine. What words they were speaking was lost in a dizzying spin of buzzing air. Dirt, debris, and snow shook loose as the ground rumbled and made a slow rise and fall, a split forming in the wall. Lady Swan disappeared into the darkness, Tine still at her side. Brandel followed, with Spirit hugging his legs. Behind him were the footfalls of the others. And then came the snap as the split in the mountain wall sealed itself, leaving them in blackness so deep that no amount of shadow sight could penetrate it.

"Do not move," Stoirm directed, his voice booming in the abyss. "Wait for the light."

A faint thrum rose through the stone beneath Brandel's feet, the subtle hum lifting in the stillness. In the distance, a glow ignited, held, and spread toward them. At last, a length of narrow corridor was awash with light. Brandel gaped at the fixtures mounted on the walls on both sides. No candles, these. Nor were they torches or small braziers or oil lamps.

"Electricity," Brandel breathed.

Stoirm edged past him and the wolf. "Powered by generators deep within the mountain. Once upon a time, they provided light and heat to the entire complex. Now, they remain hidden, providing energy only to this sanctuary."

Starn pushed past, as well. "Are you planning to stay here gaping, or will you come and make yourself more comfortable?"

Jerkin muttered something about comfort being an agreeable thing, trotting past Brandel with Owl on his heels. Brandel reached for Spirit's head, finding more comfort in the touch than in this unexpected place as he trailed after the others. The corridor soon opened out on a bright chamber furnished with a few chairs and small tables. Bookshelves stood along two short walls. A long shelf with a series of hooks was mounted on the wall near where they entered. Lady Swan set her pack on the floor beneath it, then slipped from her coat and hung it on one of the hooks, depositing her mittens on the shelf above.

"Please," she said. "Do make yourself comfortable. You will find the room warming nicely, now. We can take a few moments, here, before wandering further."

Brandel dropped his pack next to Swan's, the warmth of the air gradually thawing the cold bite that had numbed his face. His puzzled glance around as he removed mittens and coat prompted an amused snort from Stoirm. "You will find no fireplace nor brazier, here. Sadly, though the technology is old, it remains implemented in very few locations on Slievgall'ion. The world lacks the appropriate infrastructure for supporting wide use. Much of the machinery needed to implement such measures have long been banned. Amhranai Fearalite saw to it, however, that the technology was provided to the Healer's complex after the return of the sisters to Slievgall'ion. His gift to the Healers for..." He hesitated briefly before finishing with, "For their great efforts and skill in saving so many lives."

"Technology," Brandel repeated.

"And fairly primitive, at that," Lady Swan sighed, plopping onto one of the chairs to remove her boots. "It was only possible because of a massive underground river cutting its way down and out in a great waterfall somewhat higher on the slope. Perhaps you will see it. Later." Standing, she headed for a single door at the back of the room. "Rather than staying here, I believe we could all stand to eat. Come. The kitchen and dining areas are this way. Perhaps we can scrounge something from the cupboards. Tine has always maintained a food cache, here."

The aromas of cooking food greeted them as they passed through the door into a short hallway, and then into a dining room where a few chairs stood in small groupings at one end, a table large enough to seat perhaps two dozen people filling the other. The table was set for their number. Rattling noises carried from the adjacent room. Lady Swan shot a stunned glance at Tine, who offered a guilty shrug.

"She insisted. The moment she learned we were leaving the fortress. She can make herself a most annoying, irritating mental presence. Turned her persistence on the chamberlain and on Father, as well. There was nothing for it but to arrange a fire passage for her. Father agreed to Chamberlain Fairchild's request to teleport to the village ruins in the valley below Knife Point Keep right after we left. In the ruins, he laid the fire, brought Juniper and two others to him, and then provided them passage into the mountain before he teleported back to the fortress."

Brandel's brow lifted. "I thought teleporting into and out of the fortress was prevented by spells."

Lt. Starn shrugged. "A few possess…extra privileges."

"Then why did we not save ourselves all the trouble and teleport here?"

Starn shook his head. "Lord Stoirm, Lady Swan, and Tine could. But not without some risk. The rest of us lack that…privilege. Even the chamberlain cannot teleport others to him at the keep or teleport them or even use the fire passage to get them from the keep. It is why he went to the valley."

Brandel considered asking what risk was faced by those who held this 'privilege' but closed his mouth at the sight of Swan's accusatory glare at both Stoirm and Tine.

"I knew we could not use the fire passage for you to enter this place," Stoirm grumbled. "Not without disturbing the spirits more than your mere presence does. But I deemed it safe enough for her and a minor cadre of staff."

"For…her who?" Swan sputtered. "What staff?"

The tall, rounded woman who burst through the door from the kitchen, large tray in hand, broke into a huge grin at the sight of the Lady Swan. "There you are, my dear! I feared we started dinner too early and that it might be cold by the time you arrived. Lt. Starn had it figured just right, though."

"You!" Swan snapped, spinning on the man. "Why would you risk her life bringing her here?"

"She said she would set out with her entourage to try and find you without our help if we did not bring them," Tine answered for the lieutenant.

"And you believed her?"

"Of course, they believed me," Juniper snipped back. "I meant what I said. As soon as I knew you were leaving the keep, I knew you would be headed someplace even more remote and inhospitable."

"And just how would you, at the temple ruins, learn of what was transpiring at Knife Point Fortress?"

"Do you think I do not keep my ear tuned to everything pertaining to you?" Juniper harrumphed. "Shadow's arrival, and without Whisper, was a dead giveaway that something was afoot. Was not hard to guess what."

The normally composed Lord Stoirm fidgeted under the Lady Swan's continued dark scrutiny of those in on the act. "She learned nothing from us."

"Of course not! You and your son and Lt. Starn are as closed as a tomb. Nor could I get a word out of Shadow. That, too, said you were up to something that probably involved your leaving the fortress. Did not know where you might be headed, but I knew it was apt to be someplace dark and dank, and that the travel would be a trial for you. I was not going to allow you to arrive in some deep hiding hole and go without proper meals.

"It was too great a risk. What if you had encountered the enemy in the valley below the keep, or…"

"It was a risk worth taking. And we encountered no one. Do not worry your head about the children in the sanctuary, either. They are in good hands." Setting the tray of mugs and pitcher to the table, she turned to Owl and Jerkin. "You two. Make yourselves useful. Come help get the meal laid. Then you can take your places at the table."

The boys jumped to do as they were bid, dashing into the kitchen. Juniper remained long enough to eye Spirit. "That one," she said, brow cocked and hands on her hips. "I am told she follows Master Journeyson. She will not eat anyone, will she?"

Swan's stunned and irritated countenance dissolved into a halfthreatening glare. "Perhaps." At Juniper's shudder, she relented. "Spirit will harm no one so long as she is allowed to hunt."

"I will not be stopping her! Does she wish to hunt, now?"

Brandel glanced down at the wolf that stood next to him, his mind open to her. "Soon, I think. The smell of meat is exciting her."

"Aye. Well. Like I said, I will not be stopping her, unless it is me or one of mine that she is after." With that, the woman disappeared back into the kitchen.

"Do you recall the lay of the ruins through which we entered the mountain well enough to lead Spirt back out?" Stoirm asked. "Once she has hunted, ask her to return to that spot and reach out to you. You can go back for her and bring her inside."

"I assume the passages will allow me out. But how will I get back in?"

"Send to me when you are ready. I will open the way for you to return."

Sensing the increasing eagerness for a hunt in Spirit, Brandel nodded, fetching his coat as he passed back through and headed for the passages. Outside, the world stood in silence, the lengthening shadows of afternoon spreading eerily through the remains of the complex. Spirit's hunger and desire to hunt cut a clear impression in his mind, the animal darting away. For several minutes, Brandel remained connected with the wolf, stunned that it happened without a jolt, exhilarated by the sense of the ground racing beneath her feet, the scent of prey heavy in her nostrils.

A crackle as of feet on loose stone drew him out of the trance, his own senses suddenly hyper-alert, seeking the source of the crack. It came again. Spinning, he discovered it to be nothing more than a section of a nearby broken window frame crumbling under the weight of snow. For another moment, he stretched his senses outward. No presence pressed in on him. Alone, standing on a shelf beneath surrounding mountain peaks, an orange sunset casting its last glints, he was overwhelmed by a beauty he had taken little time to see, before.

Breathing deeply, he lowered his gaze to the ruins scattered around him. A Healers' complex, Stoirm called this place. Peering through shattered windows and broken walls he found rooms strewn with longrusted scraps of metal and shards of glass, vegetation winding through. It was impossible to guess from the remnants that this might once have been a place of healing. Long minutes, he spent, wandering the perimeter, studying the lay of the grounds. What at first he took to be a series of buildings, he now understood to be the remains of one great stone structure surrounding an inner courtyard with the remains of a garden that was now a tangle of brown weeds and broken benches and statuary.

His continued exploration took him past the complex to the edge of the shelf. Darkness created by the mountain peaks crept across the valley below. Twilight now hung where moments before the orange glow of the setting sun edged the western peaks. In the fading light, he made out the outline of a strange plateau standing between the shelf and the opposing peak. He could tell little about it beyond the fact that a stone wall stood prominent on this side. He found no way to cross to it, however, save by teleportation. Not a risk he was willing to take, given that he had no idea what was to be found there. He could well end up materializing in the middle of a boulder, or face to face with some wild creature.

As the light diminished and the cold intensified, Brandel headed back toward the section of the complex set against the rockface of the cliff. Pausing, he reached out mentally for the connection to Spirit. If her hunt was complete and her feasting done, he could take her back in with him, now. The faint brush of connection was focused intently on stalking some prey. Better to leave her alone, for now.

Lord Stoirm was true to his word, opening the passage for Brandel at his sending. Once safely back within the mountain, he found his way to the room that served as both dining and sitting room. Stoirm, Starn, and Tine were relaxing in the sitting area in quiet discussion. Lady Swan sat alone at the far end of the area, an open book on her lap, her eyes closed.

"Your connection with the wolf is surprising," she said softly, though her eyes remained closed. "Spirit would never before allow anyone other than Bear to accomplish what you have done. You are very blessed."

"Am I?" Though making the connections with the animal was becoming easier, it still left Brandel with a minor headache and a hollow in his stomach.

"You will see," Swan assured him, her eyes finally opening to settle a gentle scrutiny on him.

Tine moved across the room to take a chair close to her. "How are you feeling?"

"I am fine," she huffed. "Just tired. Too many voices." Returning a glance to Brandel, she offered a faint smile. "Did you enjoy your stroll around the site?"

"Was I gone so long as to make my explorations obvious?"

"Not so long as I expected," she admitted. "But then, I forget that you are not accustomed to the mountains. The cold here is quite unlike that of winters in the lowlands." Glancing absently at the book on her lap, she closed it and laid it on the table next to her chair, her brow creased as though she was listening to something.

Jerkin appeared from the kitchen, grinning broadly as he licked a bit of gravy from his lips. "Dinner is being set out."

Tine offered a hand to Lady Swan. Her expression shifted to one of annoyance. "I can stand on my own, young man. I am merely tired, not incapacitated."

Tine shot Brandel a bemused glance but made no reply as he stepped back, allowing Swan to lead the way. In truth, the lady's grace in motion was as fluid as any woman Brandel could recall seeing, betraying none of her exhaustion.

At the table, he noted the benches had been replaced by chairs. Swan sought out the shortest of them, settling on it with a sigh as she eyed the table. "I like that my feet touch the floor but would appreciate several centimeters being removed from the height of the table. Eating with my chin resting on it is...is...."

Stoirm snorted his laughter as he and Tine found their way to chairs. "There was a time, my lady, when you took such annoyances in silence."

Brandel was grateful the woman's piercing gaze was fixed on the Lord of Knife Point and not on him as she commented, "I do believe that at my age, I have earned the right to speak my mind."

Now it was Starn who erupted in laughter. "Speaking your mind, my lady, is something you do well. I would love to hear Stoirm's tales of you in quieter years."

Swan shot a daring glance to the Lord of Knife Point. "You are to keep your tales of me to yourself!"

Stoirm's features became serious, though his eyes gave away his mirth. "Of course, my lady. And I shall see what might be done to amend the issue of the table before our next meal."

Brandel held back, uncertain which seat would be appropriate for him to take. Starn clapped him on the back as he passed, taking the chair across from Swan. "Take the seat beside me, lieutenant."

A platter bearing slabs of beef surrounded by potatoes, bowls of steaming vegetables, another of dark gravy, and a tray of hot bread with small bowls of butter filled the table. Juniper appeared in the doorway from the kitchen, directing Owl to set a large bowl of steaming soup at the table's end, where she could ladle it into bowls for Jerkin to set around. Behind them came a young girl of perhaps fifteen, carrying a tray of mugs filled with water, while another somewhat older girl followed her with mugs of ale.

Once all was laid out, Juniper nodded to the last two empty place settings, one next to Brandel, the other next to Starn. "Thank you, my young men. You may take your seats, now, and enjoy your meal."

Both boys looked reluctant to sit at the table with such royal personages. Stoirm motioned them forward. "You need not be shy. You are part of our company and welcome."

Still, it took a moment before either of the pair moved, Jerkin being the first to edge his way around to sit next to Lt. Starn. Owl chewed his lip as he made his way over to sit next to Brandel. As the others started filling their plates, however, the boys' reticence vanished.

The meal was completed, the discussion turned to the technology employed in the site when Lady Swan pushed to her feet, a mix of weariness and anxiety working across her features. Excusing herself, she disappeared through an arch on the west side of the room. Each of the others rose with her, Stoirm waiting until she was gone before stating, "We could all stand to shed our traveling clothes. We will meet, again, later, in the library." Without turning, he addressed the boys. "Jerkin, Owl, you are welcome to join us, as well. You may find the education worthwhile."

Brandel and the boys followed Stoirm through another arch in the west wall and down a short hall. To their immediate right was a door that stood open. Stoirm paused, nodding to the barracks-style sleeping quarters. "Lt. Starn, I hope you will not mind sharing these quarters with my son, Lt. Journeyson, and the boys. The doorway at the back leads to the toilets and showers. There is work I need to do in my quarters before I go to the library. You may go and browse whenever you are ready." With that, he strode to a door further down the hall, leaving the others to tend to their own business.

Each of them found their packs in the sleeping quarters, propped at the ends of beds. Jerkin and Owl poked about the room, testing the beds, gaping at the pictures that covered the walls. Brandel glanced about. "Who was this… sanctuary…meant for?"

Starn and Tine exchanged brief glances, Tine shrugging. It was Starn who answered. "For those Healers whose gifts were sufficient to the teachings of Grandmother."

The statement took Brandel entirely by surprise. "Grandmother! The woman was a Healer? I thought she was a Seer,"

"Is," Tine corrected. "Arguably the greatest in both categories."

"Is this where she hides? Or is she secreted in some deeper, darker place?"

Getting nothing more from Starn or Tine, Brandel gathered his lighter pants and shirt from his pack and headed for the bath. He was in one of the shower stalls when the boys ventured back, their exclamations reflecting his own impressions. Plumbing. Electricity that both lighted and heated the rooms. Primitive technology, Lady Swan called it. If this was primitive, what would a greater technology be?

Cleaned and dressed, Brandel strolled back to the anteroom they first entered to sit for a while. A search for the library could wait. He woke sometime later, disturbed by his own snoring. Or perhaps it was the nudge at the back of his mind. Spirit had returned to the ruins. Bracing himself with a deep breath, Brandel rose and made his way out, not bothering to fetch his coat. The world outside was dark and it was snowing, again. Did it do nothing but snow, here, the whole of autumn and winter? His muttered question still hung in his mind when he felt the wolf's presence and spotted her threading her way through the rubble toward him. Brandel wasted no time in sending to Lord Stoirm and was greatly relieved to return to the warmth of the sanctuary. The wolf's appearance at his side brought a startled gasp from Owl, who had just entered the anteroom and now stood mid-step, the wolf quietly eyeing him.

"She will not bother you," Brandel offered. "She has eaten her fill." In truth, the wolf would harm none in this company unless someone posed a threat to him...or to the Lady Swan, he realized. The lady may not share the same sort of connection he had with Spirit, but the wolf was still somehow bound to the woman, just as Spirit seemed bound to Whisper. It was an intriguing relationship they had.

Owl hesitated another heartbeat or two, then made his way around Spirit, heading toward a chair next to a small table. Brandel returned to the one he occupied before going to fetch his companion, wondering aloud, "Where are the others? Starn and Tine were not in our sleeping quarters when I returned from the shower."

"They are in the library, I think," Owl returned, still eyeing the wolf with mix of concern and curiosity. "Jerkin is still amusing himself with the water in the showers. Lord Stoirm, I think, is still in his quarters. Cannot speak to the Lady Swan's whereabouts. I came out a little while ago and spent a bit of time in the kitchen talking with Juniper and Phoenix."

"Phoenix?"

Owl flushed. "Aye. One of Juniper's staff. One of the girls who helped serve dinner."

Brandel nodded. "The one with the red hair? Pretty girl."

"Pretty quiet. And..."

"And?"

Owl's brow pinched as he turned his gaze to his shoes. "Nothing, sir."

Brandel stifled a chuckle. "When it comes to girls, the issue is never 'nothing'. Come. Let us go find this library."

Owl's features lifted. "Me, sir?"

"Indeed," Stoirm replied from the doorway that led from the anteroom. Owl nodded, giving ample distance between himself and the wolf as he followed the Lord of Knife Point and Brandel back to the sitting/dining area and through an arch in the back wall that opened on a short corridor. For a minute, the boy stood in silent rapture. "The library must be enormous! I can smell the paper and ink from here."

Stoirm laughed. "Tis a keen nose you possess. Lead on. I will join you shortly."

Grinning, the boy strode purposefully down the corridor that cut to the right, stopping at a massive wooden door. Before he could knock, the door opened of its own accord, the sight of the chamber drawing a stunned gasp from both Owl and Brandel. Brandel slipped past the boy who was now oblivious to Spirit's proximity as he stood gaping. Brandel was no less dumbstruck. Brightwater held no library so large as the one at Knife Point Fortress. Yet the whole of that one would fill less than a corner of this space. Only the very center was devoid of the shelves and their tomes, containing, instead, several groupings of chairs and reading tables and a single long table upon which lay an enormous map. Starn and Tine stood over it in solemn discourse.

"Take a look around if you like," Tine called, looking up.

Owl shuffled further in, mouth still hanging open as he began wandering the aisles, a grin broadening enough to swallow his face. Brandel considered the metal labels attached to the ends of each row of shelves. Literature, Mythology, Biographies, History, Mathematics, Sciences, Classics. Magic had a several rows dedicated to it. The sciences had nearly as many. Meandering the rows, he stopped at one indicating the latter. Many of the shelves bore an additional tag etched with 'Technologies'. The first book he pulled, a large, leather bound tome, was filled with pictures of machines it claimed could fly. "Filed wrong," he muttered. "Belongs in mythology."

"It is appropriately filed." Lady Swan stood at the end of the row, watching him. "Nothing in this section is myth."

"Machines cannot fly," Brandel persisted.

"They can, and they do. Or at least they did. They could fly people across their world. Could fly them to the stars, too."

Brandel replaced the book, stalking away from her. The lady was obviously delusional.

"She speaks the truth," Tine put in.

Turning, Brandel shot a dubious glance at the Alainn who now stood at Lady Swan's side. "Where do I find such a machine?"

"Not on Slievgall'ion. Such technologies are forbidden, here. Forbidden so as to protect this world."

"Protect it from what?"

Swan was still watching him, though it was Tine who continued to speak. "Technology comes with a dark side. Like magic misused, it can cause great harm."

"Good that it was banned, then. Why would anyone wish such machines, anyway?"

"To cover great distances."

"Teleportation can accomplish that. Or the fire magic, assuming one wishes to chance traveling that way."

"Those can only deliver you to a place you know, or to a place with a Watcher to bring you through. You can use your own feet, of course, to travel areas between where you are and the places unfamiliar to you. Machines can carry you faster across the ground or in the air."

"Horses can do the same...on the ground, of course. This..." He swept a hand toward the books. "Just wild stories."

"Not so wild," Lord Stoirm put in, striding into the room. "Some of those machines now exist, here."

His words brought the conversation to a startled silence. Following Tine and Swan back to the center of the library, Brandel eyed the Lord of Knife Point. It was Lady Swan, however, who murmured, "Where?"

"In the lowlands. They were used in the attack that killed Lord Strongbow and in pursuing and slaughtering the Soldiers of Damsa Dana. Chamberlain Fairchild learned of it from some refugees, and just sent to me of their reports."

Swan crumpled onto the nearest chair. "She has broken the magic of the ban. We did not believe she had the strength to do that. Nor did we believe she had the materials or the knowledge necessary to build the machines."

Brandel spun and headed for the door. "Where are you going?" Stoirm shouted after him.

"To return to my home. Find however many of my men still live and fight. If such things are real...."

"Did you not head my words days ago, lieutenant? It is too late for you to provide any assistance to your men. Guardians of Ciuin Rose are seeking for survivors and will see that they are well tended. Your mission now lies along a different path."

Brandel turned an icy glare to the Lord of Knife Point. "And yet I see no means of accomplishing it. Where is this Grandmother? What possible need have I of anything some old woman might offer?"

Lady Swan's weary sigh carried a mourning that sank into the depths of Brandel's morrow. "Grandmother is here."

"Then take me to her!"

"Wow!" came Jerkin's exclamation as he strolled into the room "What a pla…" The rest died as Tine shushed him. Lady Swan seemed not to notice the boy, nor anyone else, at the moment. One hand swiped vaguely at the air, her voice weighted with sorrow and anxiety as her features subtly shifted, creases adding to her face as though she aged multiples of years in a matter of seconds. The burnished red at her temples faded to match the stark white of the rest of her hair. "I am here. Speak to me, now, if you will. I will try to listen and understand."

25

Tears glistened on Swan's cheeks. "Too much! It is too much! The memories! I cannot tell which are mine and which are not. Take the memories! Keep them! Show me only what I must do."

"Who is she talk…"

Tine promptly silenced Brandel's question with a glance. "Listen and learn," he whispered. "And you had best sit down."

The voices came first. Three of them, if Brandel's grasp of the shifting tones was accurate. They seemed distant and discordant, at first. As their volume grew, the discord proved to be from the chaos of the three attempting to speak simultaneously through one mouth. Then came the visions - so powerful that Brandel staggered backward into a chair, dropping onto it with a thump.

Three little girls at play. A fourth appeared…disappeared… reappeared. The three faded. The remaining child wrote with a finger on a dirt floor. Blood erupted. A decapitated head. More blood. Flames burst from a massive pyre. Screams. A curse is cast to the winds.

A young woman sits in a capsule…a machine… skimming above the ground. Ruins and toxic waters flash by below.

Three young girls living among the Alainn.

A young woman talks to a cat. And the cat talks back with human voice.

Blood and fire. A necklace glows around a youthful neck. A fine silver chain adorned with a single charm - a trinity knot with a blood red stone at its center.

A battle. Dark and stormy, lightning igniting all around, a gale carrying the crackle and bang of weapons and explosions of magic and the stench of blood and death. An instant of searing pain in his chest. Blinding light. Snow. Deep. Bitter cold. Hands that lift. Words that sooth.

Brandel lumbered to his feet, bent over, grasping at a bookcase, his head spinning, his chest pounding. The images kept coming – three sisters with a fourth girl or young woman often superimposed on them; a tall, dark-haired young man with a voice woven of music; a collage of faces and places, fire and bloodshed – all running with a tangle of emotions. Intense passion. Terror. Hope, fragmented and fragile. Hatred. So vile the hatred! Desperation mingled with a sense of grief so profound it threatened to stop his heart. So much chaos could pull his mind and his soul apart.

And then they ceased, leaving his mind blind and numb. Struggling for his breath, he managed to clear the sudden void in his head enough to cast about for the others. The two boys were nearest him, both sprawled on the floor, pale and shaking. Lt. Starn and Lord Stoirm leaned against the long table, watching him. Tine stood beside the Lady Swan's chair, a hand resting gently on her shoulder.

The Lady Swan. Brandel forced his still blurry vision to focus on her. Paler than before, she remained still as stone. Her eyes were closed, her cheeks wet with her tears. Her hands gripped the arms of her chair while her breathing settled from ragged gasps to soft sobs. "I need no reminders of the past," came as a choked plea. "I need guidance. You told me that you would send a Soldier of Damsa Dana. What do you wish of me now that he is here? Or what do you wish of him?"

The lady's voice changed, taking on a strained and stretched tone. "My soldier arrives too late. This is her work. She arranged for messengers to be sent first. Too weak to survive. Sent this one only when she wished to remove his leadership from his men. We can offer no help to the Lord of Brightwater, who lies dead, his soul banished by Aifa that it can add no strength to our cause. My soldier can provider no help to his lands or his people. He must remain with you. He must keep you safe. Together, you must fight."

Swan's voice became her own. "How can I allow another to stand with me? All who do so die. How can we fight? The Guardians of Ciuin Rose are too few. Most are not fully battle hardened. Aifa has called upon dark magic to create beasts of death. And now we learn that the followers of Breag Nemhain are calling upon the ancient technologies. They come with machines that roll across the land and fly above it. They come with weapons Slievgall'ion has never before experienced. Weapons they can use while they we remain too far removed for us to apply our magic. Her kind are uncovering the secrets we long tried to keep buried. All of this they now possess. Aifa will have no more need of me if she takes this world."

Swan's voice changed, again, coming, now, in a quiet, weary tone. "You know what she wants of you. The granddaughter of Nemhain uses Danu as her puppet to lure Whisper to her. If she takes the girl, she will take from Whisper your secrets. Yet, she will lack, still, the last piece to accomplish her desire. No longer are either of you safe within the realm of Knife Point. Whisper must find her strength and escape. You must flee. My sister's soldier can help to protect you. Seek the aid of others."

Swan's grip of the chair tightened, her hands going white from the tension. "There are no others!"

The faintest stir of air brushed Brandel's face. The soft voice saying, "You forget the Alainn, Caer."

Swan sucked in, a cracked moan breathing out, "Caer. Caer died many ages ago. She walks this world no more."

"She lives." The words fell gently. "Caer is strong. She carried our souls, fought for us, won us into this world to save another. Her strength remains. Her courage remains. Know her, again, little one. Take the Soldier of Damsa Dana with you. Seek out the Alainn. They will not turn away Caer DaDhrga."

"And what of my descendant? I cannot leave her to the Red Moon Warriors."

"You must let others seek for her. You must go to the Alainn with Damsa Dana's soldier."

Brandel's fists clenched, his eyes fixed on the Lady Swan. "Go to the Alainn, yourself. I must return to Brightwater. Save whom I can. I will search for Whisper, as well, and get her to safety."

The strained voice hissed him to silence. "You can do nothing for your people. The temples of Damsa Dana are burning. My priestesses have either turned to Breag Nemhain, are destroyed, or are fleeing. My High Priestess has been stolen from me, though she knows it not. You must take Caer DaDhrga and your knowledge of the battles you have fought to the Alainn. They will need that knowledge if they are to seek out the granddaughter of Nemhain and stop her."

"You make no sense!" Brandel bellowed. "Who is Caer DaDhrga? What is this great secret she carries? And where is this Grandm…" His question dribbled to silence, his stunned gaze leveling on Swan. This was the woman he sought. Stoirm and Tine had each said as much, had he listened.

"They are gone." Lady Swan's words were only just audible. Brandel continued to stare, open-mouthed, at her slumped and trembling body. "If they say this is what we must do, then it is so."

Starn straightened, his features set, barely suppressed rage in his tone. "Hawk has led the child into peril. I will seek them out and bring Whisper back to you, Grandmother. And Hawk will pay dearly for his treachery."

Stoirm considered in silence for several seconds before nodding. "Juniper and the girls must be sent back to the temple sanctuary. I can teleport them to the nearest farmstead and send guardians to escort them from there. I will send you back to Knife Point through the flames. Collect only a handful of guardians and go in haste. The longer you wait, the more difficult it will be to find their trail. I will travel with Tine, Caer, and Lt. Journeyson. Hopefully, my presence will make it easier to obtain a meeting with Lady Grian Geal."

"Wait!" Brandel barked. "Who the hell is Grian Geal? And... and..." Pointing a finger at Lady Swan, he continued, "And what the hell are you?"

"Lady Grian Geal," Tine put in, "or Lady Sunrise, in your language, is the queen of the Alainn on Slievgall'ion. She fought with us at the battle that brought us here. And she fought with us for many an age, until we thought we had defeated the followers of Nemhain. Weary of battle and of humans, who yet hold mistrust of my people, she led the remaining Alainn into the wilderness to live in peace, leaving only a handful in the outpost lands west of Knife Point. As for Grandmother," Tine laid his hand on Lady Swan's shoulder. "She is Caer DaDhrga, the soul bearer who returned the ancient sisters - those you call Goddesses - to this world."

The startled intake of breath from the two boys matched Brandel's. For several long seconds, Brandel stood silent, finally rumbling, "That is not possible! That Caer...she would be...what... two...three thousand years old, now? Still young enough for an Alainn, I am told. But humans cannot live that long."

"Some can," Tine noted. "The forebearer of Lt. Starn certainly did so. As did others."

"That..." Lady Swan rocked back against the chair, wiping her wet cheeks with the backs of her hands, her voice still cracked from her earlier sobs. "That was cheating," she managed. "It was the ancient curse that allowed their souls to live through so many lifetimes."

"And yet," Stoirm said, "they continued to live here for another thousand-plus years after the curse no longer applied. Long enough to see a time of peace before the Red Moon Warriors reemerged."

Swan shook her head. "For me, it is a cheat, as well. The souls of Dana and Roisin constantly work to rejuvenate me. They possess the strength to hold their secrets from Nemhain, even in death. Should I die, my memories would be absorbed with my soul into Slievgall'ion. I lack the power to hold her out. Nemhain would be able to find what she seeks and would speak it to her granddaughter."

"What, precisely, does she seek?" Brandel pressed.

"The way to recreate the gateway that would allow Nemhain's passage back the worlds we left behind. Back to the realm where the curse was first spoken. Back where her soul might once again live in flesh."

"Fine. Good riddance! If the Goddess Breag Nemhain returns to this other…world…this place of the origin of the Goddesses, then let her. And let her granddaughter and the Red Moon Warriors go with her. We would be rid of them all."

"Not if Nemhain is capable of opening and closing the gateway at will. She could rain bloodshed over two realms. Assuming, of course, that anything remains of the realm we left behind." The depth of sorrow that edged Lady Swan's last statement dug into Brandel's mind, raising a vision of a desolate world suddenly bursting with life - so quickly that the force of it tore the world apart.

"We need to move," Stoirm declared. "We can discuss these matters later." Glancing at the boys, he gestured toward the door. "You will need your belongings. You will be traveling with Lt. Journeyson. Cannot risk your sharing what you have just witnessed with anyone outside of this company."

Jerkin looked pleased. Owl, however, darted a glance in the general direction of the kitchen.

Stoirm snorted. "If all goes well, Phoenix will still be at the temple sanctuary with Juniper when you return. I will send Juniper and her staff back as soon as I return Lt. Starn to Knife Point."

Owl nodded, trailing Jerkin out the door. Stoirm followed, with Starn close behind. Tine hovered near Lady Swan, waiting for some indication that she was ready to return to her quarters to prepare for their journey. Brandel stared from one to the other, at last muttering, "This is a dream. A nightmare."

Drawing a long, ragged breath, Lady Swan pushed from her chair. "So thought I, many an age ago, in a different set of worlds. Nightmares." Turning, she said, "Tine."

"Yes, Swan."

She sighed, her features once again shifting to the ones Brandel knew as Lady Swan's…and then shifting more, softening to a youthfulness, her white hair darkening to a honeyed auburn." If I am to act as Caer DaDhrga once more, then let me return to that name. Perhaps the sound of it will dig out the strength and courage Roisin believes lies within me, still." A strand of her hair fell forward. She lifted it, her brow creasing as she studied the change of its color, the smolder set deep within her green eyes sparking to an emerald glow.

Tine's features shifted from concern to the softness of a smile. "With great pleasure, Caer."

Glancing from Tine to the empty air, she demanded, "And you stop! I do not need to return to an appearance I lost long ago. I can seek whatever remains of Caer DaDhrga without it!" Once more, her features and coloring shifted back to that of Lady Swan, the strand of hair in her hand becoming white. "Better. Now," she rumbled, at Tine. "Tell me, what preparations must we make before setting out for the lands of Sunrise?"

"We can make use of the fire passage to deliver us to a way house. That will grant a sizeable distance between us and our pursuers. It will also allow us to provision for the remainder of the journey."

Brandel held his ground, staring dully at the diminutive woman. With a slight cock of her head and a slowly steadying voice, Lady Swan…or Grandmother…or Caer DaDhrga…or whomever she truly was, asked, "You have more questions?"

"More confusion," he snarled.

"That, I do not doubt. Anything I can resolve for you at this moment?"

"Why so many identities?"

"To stay hidden." Great sorrow weighted her words. "Long ago, when my husband and two of our children, along with my dearest of friends, were slaughtered in battle, I escaped only because Stoirm came to me and whisked me away. I was severely wounded and wished to die and to be buried with the ones I loved. But Dana and Roisin refused to allow it because of the memories I carry. Their memories. Still, we allowed the world to believe that Caer DaDhrga had died in that battle. Nemhain stirred the souls of the dead in search of me for several centuries before concluding that I still lived. In that time, I came to be called Grandmother by the handful of people who knew the truth of my identity. Grandmother because of my years. For use among others, Stoirm chose Lady Swan in honor of an ancient Celtic tale told him by Lt. Starn's ancestor, Adrian Starn. Amhranai Fearalite to the Alainn. The name Caer derives from the name of a young maiden who, in this myth, turned into a swan. Anything else I can answer for you?"

"You mentioned another name. Belonging to one of the voices that spoke through you, I think. Roysheen?"

Caer shrugged. "Roisin. The people of this world know her has Ciuin Rose."

"So, it was two of the Goddesses who spoke to you... through you."

A faint huff escaped Caer. "Goddesses! Nonsense! Not that there was ever any convincing the people of Slievgall'ion of that." With a deeper harrumph, she turned and left, Tine at her side. Moments later, she sent, *"I have learned far less than I had hoped by coming here. But it is all that Dana and Roisin will share. My path is still uncertain. For now, I choose to follow Roisin's advice. I will go to the Alainn. Roisin also seems adamant that you should remain with me. I leave that choice to you, Brandel Journeyson. Whatever you decide, you must be ready to leave once Stoirm has seen Singer returned to the fortress and Juniper and those with her to the temple ruins and their sanctuary.*

26

Stepping into a blaze went against Brandel's every instinct. That he survived the first fire passage did not mean he was guaranteed a second success. Moreover, Spirit was not with him before. Jerkin and Owl were no less anxious. Between the anxiety-ridden tension in the three humans and the mere fact of the rising flames, Spirit exuded such terror as to nearly incapacitate Brandel. Thrice, Tine demanded he calm the beast before Brandel seized control of both himself and the wolf sufficiently to hold her in check. The struggle took its toll. The moment their party was clear of the flames, Brandel collapsed in a shaking heap, Spirit streaking off through the woods.

Jerkin and Owl were at Brandel's side, helping him to his feet, each boy shaking almost as severely as he. Still, they collected themselves and took stock of their newest surroundings, Brandel attempting to hide his shakes by brushing mud and damp leaves from his pants. "These people and their caves and their fires," he snarled, the remaining tremor in his voice giving away the state of his nerves.

The Lady Swan and Tine dowsed the flames as soon as the Fire Mage who brought them through released the pattern within them.

"Our thanks, Ember," Stoirm offered.

"At your service, as always, my lord," the woman returned.

Tine buried the coals and ashes to make as quick an end to the smoke as possible while Brandel attempted to collect his composure under the scrutiny of the mage. An Alainn, her height fell just shy of Tine's, her skin as fair as Lord Stoirm's, her eyes as emerald as Swan's when the magic took them, though Ember's lacked the unsettling glow. A flip of the Alainn's hand sent her golden-red braid back over her shoulders, its length falling past her hips.

Tine straightened, nodding his thanks, as well. "Forgive us, for pulling you away from your duties."

"My service to you and Lord Stoirm are part of my duty, Lord Tine. A service I requested long ago. I will escort you to the inn, then must return to my post."

Without further words, she led the way out of the cave and down a steep slope to a riverbank. Brandel kept Jerkin and Owl in front of him, worried that the sense of their edgy nerves coupled with his was working to keep Spirit from rejoining him. A glimpse over his shoulder for some sight of the wolf found only Stoirm trailing a short distance behind him.

At what point Stoirm disappeared into the woods, Brandel could not say. He was aware of the absence sometime into their company's trudge through thickets of brambles. The Lord of Knife Point's return at least an hour later was announced with his quiet, "Your companion follows, though she seems loath to come to your side, again. I believe she should be willing to alert you to any pursuers closing ranks behind us, though."

Brandel darted another backward glance. "You expect those demon creatures to catch up to us?"

"No. I discovered no sign of them from the ridge we passed. But neither am I willing to take any chances. Other enemies lurk. Spies willing to track us, perhaps."

"And where is it we are going?"

"To speak with Grian Geal, ultimately. In the short term, we will find shelter for the night in a local inn."

"How safe can a public inn be?"

"As safe as any other location, at this point. Tine and Caer are friends with the proprietress and trust the woman. A word of caution, however. Caer is known here only as Lady Swan."

Stoirm moved past him, passing Swan and the boys, as well. Catching up to Tine and Ember at the front, the three exchanged a brief and hushed conversation. Several minutes later, Stoirm called a halt near a clearing, gesturing for the group to stay quiet and to stay put. Tine ventured out alone, striding toward a lone two-story brick structure. The afternoon sun glinted off the windows of the upper floor and raised steam from the slate roof, despite the cold in the air.

Tine's rap at the door produced a boy of about the same age as Jerkin and Owl. He greeted Tine with an instant smile and a grasp of the Alainn's hand, urging him inside. Tine stripped out of his snowshoes, then followed the boy. A few moments later, he returned to the front stoop, waiving the others forward.

Inside, Jerkin and Owl hung back near the door, their eyes wide at the unexpected find. The interior gleamed with clean, whitewashed walls, polished ceiling beams, and wooden floor. Brandel sidestepped the pair, Ember edging around the three of them to join Stoirm, Tine, and Swan…Caer, Brandel corrected. It was difficult to get his mind around her other identities. Swan, Lady of Knife Point, he could grasp. But Grandmother…the Soul Bearer once known as Caer DaDhrga… A Witch whose life had spanned so many centuries remained too great a leap of faith for him to easily accept.

The proprietress, a bronze-skinned woman, swept out from behind the counter, leaning to hug the Lady of Knife Point, then wrapped her arms around each of the three Alainn in turn. Standing off to one side was the boy who responded to Tine's knock, Caer's coat draped over his arm, his curious gaze fixed on Jerkin and Owl.

"Come, come," the proprietress declared, gesturing to all. "The cooks are putting soup on for you. You all look weary and chilled. Step, please take their packs and their coats for them."

The boy nodded, collecting the items from each and setting them near a broad set of stairs. "Hi," he ventured, approaching Jerkin and Owl last. "Name's Step."

"Hi. Jerkin. That would be me. This here is Owl."

"Welcome to River House."

Jerkin shot a glance toward the door. "River?"

"Aye. It cuts through the woods at the back of the house. Runs a bit low at this time of the year when the waters from the mountains are beginning to freeze over. Cannot miss the roar in the spring, though. Still, she runs deep and swift enough autumn through winter, to provide all the fresh water we need. Even got plumbing, here. Got hot showers, warm rooms, and good food."

Brandel left the boys to their discussions, following the others as they moved into a large dining hall. Most of the tables were small, seating no more than three or four. A larger table with seating for ten occupied the space near a blazing fireplace. Brandel was relieved that, for the moment, at least, there was no indication of other guests.

"Thank you, Hawthorne," Tine smiled, offering the woman a second hug. "Your hospitality never fails."

"Not for friends," she returned, her dark eyes narrowing.

Stoirm ventured a glance over his shoulder toward the front counter. "There are others, here?"

"Not at this time. Booted the rowdies out three nights ago after they cast dispersions on the Alainn, declared the Guardians of Ciuin Rose as weak-minded fools, and claimed that the Goddess was dead and gone. I will not tolerate anyone speaking ill of our guardians or the Alainn, and certainly will not stand for them blaspheming our Goddess."

"Did you know these rowdies," Stoirm pressed.

"A couple of them, aye. Hunters from south of Hollow's Pass. Cannot say what they were doing this far north at this time of year. Generally, do not see the likes of them 'cept for maybe every other year in the spring when they bring pelts this way for the traders. The other men with them were strangers. Eight of them. They do not dress nor act like they belong in the mountains."

"Where did they go?"

Hawthorne shrugged. "Did not ask. Nor do I care, none, either, so long as they stay far from my place. Hard enough to get customers when so many are worried about traveling, what with winter settin' in so early. Do not need their sort spookin' folks away. Now, no more talk of that ilk. Let me see that rooms are made ready for you. You just make yourselves comfortable here. Mead will be brought round momentarily. Soup should be ready shortly."

"Not for me, my friend," the Alainn woman proclaimed, saluting as she took a step back from them. "I must return to my duties." Turning to Stoirm, she said, "I will meet you at the border." The subtle pop of her teleportation surprised Brandel, leaving him staring at the empty air.

Hawthorne stared at the space where the Alainn had been, then gave a sad shake of her head before returning to her own duties. "Would have liked a nice chat with Ember."

"Can you believe this place?" Jerkin asked, trailing Owl into the room. He settled with a plop on the chair next to Brandel. "Right here, in the middle of nowhere. All clean and sparkling and well-stocked."

Stoirm huffed his amusement. "And where would you say Knife Point Keep is, if not the middle of nowhere. It is no less clean and well-stocked."

"Aye sir! But that is different! The keep and fortress take care of the guardians. This…well…it seems more a large house than an inn. Step says three are all that work in the kitchen, and three more tend to the rooms. Step does the running of errands and assisting the kitchen staff when they need to harvest things from the gardens in back. He also hunts for their meat. We warned him about the white wolf. Told him not to dare shoot her."

"I suspect," Brandel put in, "that Spirit can take care of herself. Still, thanks for warning the boy. Would not want him panicked, should she turn up on the doorstep, here."

Both boys finished their meal in minutes, asking to be excused to see how they might assist Step. Relieved that they were occupied with something other than fussing over him, Brandel took his time with the dinner, only half listening to Tine and Stoirm discuss the next leg of their journey. The warmth of the dining room, a full belly, and several glasses of mead once again accented his fatigue. Perhaps it would be less noticeable if he avoided such comforts.

Owl's gentle tug at him brought him alert enough to catch the boy's grin and to realize the others were gone. "Rooms are ready, sir. They offered Jerkin and me a room next to yours, but we could not accept. So, they put us in with Step, downstairs."

Brandel struggled to his feet with a yawn and a cocked brow, chagrined that he was left dozing in the dining room. When Owl's comment finally registered, his brow hiked. "Why could you not accept?"

Owl led him out of the dining room and up the stairs to the top landing. "Because, sir. You are a lieutenant. A great soldier. And Tine is guardian to the Lady Swan. And Lord Stoirm and the Lady Swan are Lord and Lady of Knife Point. Maybe, someday, Jerkin and me…maybe we will earn the right to become guardians or earn a title of some sort. But for now, we are just…well…just Jerkin and Owl."

Brandel burst into laughter. "There is absolutely nothing 'just' about either of you. You have as much right to rooms up here as any. Still, if you are more comfortable bunking with Step, that is fine, too."

"Thank you, sir. And this is it. First door on your left. Lord Stoirm is down the hall some. Lady Swan is around that corner, last door on the right, and Tine is in the room just this side of hers. Just thought you should know. If you do not need me for anything else, I will go back down and help Jerkin and Step bring in more firewood. After that, Mistress Hawthorne said she would have hot chocolate and biscuits for us. Hot chocolate! Can you imagine, sir? Said the Alainn provide it for her. Said they grow it in the valleys of southern Sunrise."

"Well, enjoy the hot chocolate and biscuits. Maybe I can sample some at breakfast."

"You never tasted it either, then?"

"Once. Long ago. When I was a child. I have forgotten the taste, though fond memories of how much I enjoyed it linger. Go on. Go tend to the firewood and enjoy the evening with Step."

Brandel found his room spacious and comfortably furnished. A fire burned brightly in the corner fireplace, welcoming him with warmth and light. At the back of the room stood an open door leading to the bath with the amenities he was fast coming to expect. At the center of a small table beneath the room's window stood a vase with sprigs of jasmine, though where the proprietress might come by the flowers at this time of year was a mystery. The whole of the suite smelled faintly of the scent, which, he suddenly realized, reminded him of Lady Swan…Lady Caer… He heaved a sigh of exasperation. It would take a while before he could make himself come to terms with this woman.

Showered and refreshed, he returned to the room proper to discover a steaming mug of hot chocolate and a plate of biscuits on a table. A padded chair stood askew, waiting for him. Owl's doing, no doubt. He chuckled, easing himself onto the chair to enjoy the treat and the view. At the edge of the clearing, tucked just within the woods, he caught a glimpse of white. Spirit. Opening his mind, he reached out for her. Her return brush was filled with resentment. The wolf remained angry with him for the indignity and terror of the fire passage. That she allowed him to note her presence and connect with her, however, indicated she did not intend to shut him out. He filled his thoughts with those of a successful hunt and a comfortable rest - his way of sending his wishes to her. For a while, she offered no response. At last, just as he was pulling the shutters closed, the images came to him. She had, indeed, completed a successful hunt and was now settling in a hollow at the base of a tree where she could keep watch on the house. He had no way of knowing if she would understand his 'thank you', but sent it, anyway. In return, he detected a sense of satisfaction.

Windows shuttered, he sat before the fire for a while, worrying over his men -whomever were left among them; worrying over the people of Brightwater; silently mourning the loss of the realm's lord; wondering who had betrayed him. When his eyes would remain open no longer, he prepared himself for bed and fell into a troubled sleep.

27

Tension and doubt traced an icy trail along Whisper's nerves. Scurrying to keep pace with Hawk, she demanded, "Where are we going?"

"We must get you to safety, little one. Away from Knife Point. Out of the mountains. The creatures are focusing their hunt for you, here."

"Where are we going?" she repeated, her quiet voice reflecting the chill that gnawed at her nerves.

"To the coast."

Whisper stopped, planting her feet. "No."

"It is the only place safe enough for you. I have received word that the High Priestess of Damsa Dana has retreated with a handful of priestesses and soldiers to a hidden sanctuary where they are regrouping. The Red Moon Warriors and their Priestess will never think to look for you in Brightwater. Not when they are convinced you are in Knife Point Keep."

"Why would they be so convinced of that?"

"We are wasting time, Lady Whisper. The longer we linger, the greater the danger."

"I will not be that far removed from Shadow. I must send to her. Let her join us."

"Later. When you are safe. For now, the two of you are better off with distance between you. Too risky for you to be traveling together."

"I must send word to her, at least."

"Not here. Not now. Someone might be able to break through your shielding and learn of your destination. Please, Lady Whisper. Let us protect you, as we have been charged. Lady Shadow is safe where she is, for now. Few are aware that the two of you are apart. They will expect to find you both at the keep."

"If they break through the lower gates, they will learn of our absence soon enough."

"All the more reason for us to hasten away."

Whisper stood her ground, glancing back at the distant black gleam of the fortress against the white-cloaked mountain peak. How far had the Red Moon Warriors pressed upward? Were they through the lower gates? Had they breached the upper gates? Her terror for those left behind cut through to her marrow. How could she leave them? She should stay and fight. Yet... Biting at her lip, she turned and nodded, motioning Hawk to lead on. She could not risk being captured and having her knowledge forced from her.

For a night, a day, and a second night, they worked their way up and over two ridgelines and through a saddle between two major peaks. The route took them out and around the mountain on which the keep and fortress stood, Hawk explaining the object was to come out far behind the warriors who threatened the gates. They were descending another slope when they encountered the tracks of a contingent of mounted warriors leading in the direction of the keep. So, too, they saw the remains of withered plants and animals that happened to be in the path of the foul creatures of death. To Whisper's eye, the tracks did not look numerous nor old enough to deliver hordes to the gates of the fortress. Moreover, the warriors could not have continued much further on horses. The animals would never survive the combination of altitude, deep snow, and below freezing temperatures. Or...perhaps they were aware of the impractical use of horses further in and planned to rely on whatever means of travel left the strange marks in the snow. Wide bands of sharp lines cut deep. Where once stunted scrubs had grown, now lay crushed and splintered timber mixed in the snow. More curious, still, the marks looked as though someone had set them on the ground and then lifted them straight up, again. She could find no indication of their traveling over land. Nor did she see signs of their leaving. How could something so large have come straight down and lift straight up, again, leaving no other trails? The chill that gnawed at her became a foreboding so powerful that it almost dropped Whisper to the ground.

Hawk, ever watchful, rushed to her. "What is it, little one? Are you injured? If you are tired, I will have one of my men carry you for a while."

"What hunts us?" she managed. "More than the warriors and the demons. What beast so large that it crushes small trees can come to sit on the ground and lift again? Only birds can do that. But I know of no bird so great, nor with feet so strange as what left the tracks I saw."

"I hoped to save you the worry over that," Hawk sighed. "Not a beast, but a machine. The one who sent me word of the sanctuary where we must take you also told me of the machines. An ancient and long-forgotten technology, she said. The priestesses and warriors of Breag Nemhain discovered the writings and have built devices that roll and crawl upon the ground and some that fly in the air."

"You lie!" Whisper hissed. Yet Hawk's statement carried no hint of falsehood.

"You know I do not, my lady."

"This individual. The one who has sent you the warnings. She sent word to the others at Knife Point Keep; sent word to Grandmother and to Lord Storm and Tine, as well?"

"I can only presume so. Assuming she was able to reach out to them."

Whisper turned back. "The Lady Swan and her party. They went silent the moment they left. We must find a way to catch up to them. We must warn them."

Hawk grabbed her shoulder, spinning her around. "They cannot be found, Lady Whisper. You know that. And do not think the Lady Swan will answer your sendings. Neither of you can afford to give anything away regarding your locations. Our only hope lies in getting you to the sanctuary on the coast. We will return to collect Shadow so that she may join you when we know you are safe."

The trembling that started with the first chill in her nerves now threatened to shake Whisper apart.

"You are too cold." Hawk gestured to one of the others. The guardian responded promptly. A man of lesser rank than Hawk, though Whisper had never paid much heed to the various titles. Fairchild, she thought was his name. Like the chamberlain. A relative, perhaps.

"Do you have a blanket to spare?" Hawk asked.

The man nodded, pulling his pack from his shoulders and digging into it. Handing the requested item across, he readjusted the contents and shouldered the pack once more.

"Thank you, Private. Is there a place we might rest for a time?

"I will scout ahead. I believe I know a place." The man saluted and trotted away. Hawk wrapped the blanket around Whisper's shoulders, then picked her up in his arms.

"I…I can walk."

"You need to rest," he huffed. "So do you…and the others."

"When Private Fairchild sends to us that he has secured an appropriate location."

Whisper considered arguing; insisting that he put her down and let her travel under her own power. But the foreboding, the cold, and her sense of loss as the distance from Shadow increased, left her too shaken and drained. Instead, she ducked her head within the folds of the blanket, tears trickling into the wool, adding to the cold against her cheeks.

Day was breaking when Private Fairchild returned. Whisper had twice been transferred from one man's arms to another. None offered protest. Ashamed, she wriggled to free an arm and to pull the blanket from her face. "Enough," she murmured. "Let me stand. I need to walk."

Her current bearer shook his head. "Not until Lt. Hawk states that you are rested and warm enough to continue on your own."

Lips pinched, she glanced from the man carrying her to Hawk, whose stride had carried him some distance from them. "Sgt. Hawk," she corrected.

"Aye. He was Sgt Hawk, until Lt. Starn left him in charge of your safety, my lady. Promoted him to lieutenant."

"Well," she sniffed. "Sergeant or lieutenant makes no difference. He has no right to prevent me from…"

"From what, little one," Hawk asked as he strode back. Whisper fixed him with a rebellious glare, prompting a hint of a chuckle. "Very well. You can put her down, now, sergeant. Fairchild has found a burned-out homestead where we can shelter. Sections of the house still smolder, so if we start a small fire for warmth, it will likely be regarded as remnants of the destruction. This way."

Whisper's legs at first failed to hold her steady. When the lieutenant reached for her, again, she pushed him away. "Just give me time to get the circulation back in my limbs." He refused to leave her side, however, waiting patiently as she stretched out the kinks and flexed her knees and ankles. Feeling stable, at last, she followed in the direction Hawk had gone. The farmstead proved less than a kilometer away. The barn was, indeed, still smoldering. Mercifully, no stench of death hung about the area. Whisper prayed the inhabitants were able to flee well before their home was attacked.

Hawk investigated the remains of the house, gesturing the small company into the back of what had once been the kitchen. Part of the roof remained, offering some protection from the light snow that was beginning. The cooking hearth still held wood, which one of the other men ignited with a flick of his fingers. The blaze was kept small, the warmth limited, but it was enough to give some degree of comfort. Hawk had Whisper settle closest to it, pulling a blanket from his own pack to add to the one wrapped round her. Two of the men made a circuit of the kitchen's debris, digging out a few jars of preserved vegetables and a couple of pouches of jerky to share around.

Whisper had little appetite and gnawed on a jerky strip only to satisfy Hawk, her eyes closed, her soul aching. She had no idea how much she would miss Serenity and Shadow. Mostly Shadow. They had not been parted since they were babes. The lack of her cousin's presence was like missing a piece of herself. Were it not for Hawk's persistent warnings - that somehow, someone might break through her shielding - she would contact Shadow. Until recently, she did not believe anyone capable of accomplishing what Hawk suggested. But the struggle to hold some unfamiliar, intruding consciousness from her mind was proof enough that the possibility existed. Had she needed further convincing of the power held by some among Breag Nemhain's dark forces, she need only consider the demons of death and the resurrection of ancient and lost technologies. Such workings made breaking her shielding seem too simple a thing.

28

Shadow meandered the halls of the sanctuary, muttering. What sense did it make, sending her here and leaving Whisper at the keep? If the sanctuary was safe enough for everyone, here, it remained safe enough for Whisper, as well. She looked out for her cousin, protected her for the whole of their lives. She missed Whisper far more than she ever dreamed possible. And there was little to do, here, to keep her mind occupied. At least thus far, few Soldiers of Damsa Dana found their way into the protection of the Guardians of Ciuin Rose, leaving her with too much time on her hands. Even her assignment to work with the young children, testing them for some degree of aptitude in shadow magic failed to lift her spirits. For none among them demonstrated any aptitude at all. So far as Shadow was able to determine, she, alone, possessed the attribute.

Often, she tried to imagine what Whisper might be doing. Was her cousin bored and lonely, too, or did Lady Swan keep her busy? Shadow's lips pinched. No. Swan was traveling to some other ancient site. How Juniper learned of it was anybody's guess, but the woman raised such a fuss that she was finally granted permission to take some of the children there to prepare for Swan's arrival. She, of course, was not allowed to go.

So. Swan was wherever Juniper had gone. Whisper was at Knife Point Keep. And here she was, wondering why it felt so achingly like the distance separating her from Whisper kept changing.

Oceana pulled Shadow from her frustrated thoughts with a gentle clearing of her throat. "I am sorry to disturb you, Lady Shadow. Lady Juniper, Phoenix and I have returned, and Lady Juniper asked to speak with you. Lady Serenity is with her, now."

Shadow straightened, tensing as she eyed the nervous girl. Eighteen, maybe, and so thin she looked skeletal, despite getting decent and regular meals since being taken in. Shadow could not imagine how Oceana and her sister, Phoenix, managed to survive their flight from Brightwater with nothing but rags on their backs and eating only scraps or whatever they might forage. The anxiety on the girl's face prompted, "Is something wrong?"

"It is not for me to say, Lady Shadow." The girl's gray eyes darted about, refusing to make contact with Shadow's, Oceana's fidgety hands fussing with strands of brown hair that had worked out of her braid. "I am to fetch you, m'lady. And to return with you. That is all."

"Very well," Shadow agreed. "But please stop calling me your lady or addressing me as Lady Shadow. We are family, here. You are as a sister to me. Remember?" Shadow struggled to keep her voice soft and even, given the number of times she repeated this to the girl and to her biological sister. She wondered what sort of background they came from that they did not understand the concept of a sisterhood. While there was no longer an active temple of priestesses in Knife Point, the few who yet survived remained sisters and welcomed those who lived beneath the temple ruins as sisters and brothers. The Guardians of Ciuin Rose also accepted all in the same manner, treating one another as sisters and brothers. Serenity strived to teach this to each child who came to them. Within these confines, no one was above or below another. All learned the same lessons. All shared in the food and the warmth. Their attire reflected whichever tasks they were assigned at any given time. Even Juniper, however, sometimes reverted to using the titles that both Serenity and Grandmother wished to erase.

Old habits die hard is what Grandmother frequently told them, though she would add that it did not excuse them from continuing to try to break the old ways.

"Are you coming, my…Shadow?"

"What? Oh. Yes, of course."

The girl fell in several paces behind Shadow as they made their way to the dining hall. When Shadow stopped, Oceana whispered, "Not here. In Lady Serenity's classroom."

Shadow sighed at the girl's use of title, again, but moved on, curious as to the reason for Oceana's nervous tension and the need for privacy. Serenity rarely used the classroom, given how infrequent their visits to the sanctuary had become in the last several months. Moreover, it was the one reserved for the children's practice with their magic, hence, it was the most secure.

Juniper and Serenity stood at the front of the room, waiting. Phoenix, at least three or four years younger than Oceana, sat alone at the back of the room, pale and shaking. As soon as Shadow and Oceana entered, Serenity waived the door shut, the lock clicking into place. That simple action rushed a wave of alarm through Shadow. No room, no closet, no cabinet, here, was ever locked.

"What has happened?" she blurted. "What…"

"Hush," Serenity commanded. "Juniper, tell her what you told me."

The woman nodded, her grave features strained with worry. "It is what Oceana and Phoenix told me." Juniper took a deep breath and pushed the words out all in a rush. "Whisper is missing from Knife Point Keep, along with some of the guardians. Sgt. Hawk appears to have taken her away."

Shadow paled, slumping onto one of the desk chairs. "To where? Why? Whisper would never sneak away with him if she sensed anything wrong."

"Oceana, Phoenix." Serenity motioned the sisters to stand together. "I understand this is difficult for you, but please understand, we do not accuse you of anything, nor hold you to blame for the actions of others."

Phoenix rose slowly, shuffling her way to her sister, her head bowed, her face streaked with tears. "Go ahead," Serenity coaxed. "Repeat what you told Juniper."

Oceana took her sister's hand, holding it tightly. "We overheard. Accidentally. The High Priestess in Brightwater summoned us, and we were instructed to wait in the antechamber. High Priestess Danu was in a temper. She was yelling at one of the priestesses. She said the Goddess Damsa Dana spoke to her and demanded that the two whom Grandmother most treasured must be brought to her. Lord Strongbow refused, she said. She called him treacherous. Called him blasphemous and a heretic. She said the Goddess would see to his removal from his office."

The girl took a deep breath, then continued. "High Priestess Danu told the priestess she sent word to one she trusted among the Guardians of the Goddess Ciuin Rose; a man who is her kin. Said that he recognized the need. He would bring at least one of the treasures to her if he could."

As Oceana took a breath, Phoenix shot a tearful glance from Serenity to Shadow. "We did not know," she moaned. "We had no way of knowing who the trusted guardian might be. Had no way of knowing what treasure she spoke of. We were outsiders, even in our own land. Cast out because our parents were murdered, and we were too poor to buy our way into the temple to serve as priestesses. When High Priestess Danu summoned us to the temple, we thought…we hoped she had changed her mind. She had not. Instead, she called us a drain on the stores of Brightwater. Told us we had a choice – to starve or to flee to the realm of Knife Point. So, we fled. Guardians found us at the border and brought us here."

"Then…" Phoenix studied her feet. "Then Juniper took us to the place to prepare for Lady Swan to arrive. While we were there, a boy named Owl told me they had received word of Whisper missing from Knife Point Keep. He said she was taken by a guardian named Hawk. The Lord of Knife Point promptly returned us, here. That is when Oceana and I put the pieces together and realized this must be the doing of the High Priestess."

Shadow sat stunned for several long minutes. "Why would Sgt. Hawk not tell Lt. Starn that the High Priestess of Damsa Dana asked him to take us to her? Why would he steal Whisper away? The matter should have been taken to Lord Stoirm. He and Lady Swan would have arranged for safe passage of the both of us to Brightwater."

Serenity folded her arms, scowling. "They would never agree to such an arrangement. Nor would I. High Priestess or no, her demands are too risky. Whisper should have remained at Knife Point Fortress. And you," she added, fixing a stern scrutiny on Shadow. "You will remain here. Do you understand? Whisper will be found and returned to us." Turning to Juniper, she stated, "Please gather my pack for me."

"And where are you going?" Shadow demanded.

"To Brightwater. To have a few words with the High Priestess." She glanced back at Oceana and Phoenix. "On a few counts, not the least being that one does not charge a fee to become a priestess or turn young girls away. And one especially does not tell them to starve or flee."

"No!" Oceana and Phoenix chorused. "You must not!"

"Why?"

Oceana swallowed. "We do not trust that woman. She is foul. One of the younger priestesses whispered to us that Danu teaches dark magic."

Serenity stumbled back a step. "She would not. Not as High Priestess of Damsa Dana. The Goddess would not stand for it."

"The priestess said some of their elders are learning about the spell to banish souls. To destroy a person's soul…to prevent them from joining with…"

Juniper's gape shifted to a working of her mouth before the words finally came out. "Why did you not mention this before?"

"We were afraid," Phoenix sobbed. "We are new, here. We are not familiar with your ways. There are no priestesses, here, who practice the rites or who teach the ways of the sisterhood. No one to speak with the Goddess Ciuin Rose. No one to guide the teaching of magic to keep it from the darkness. We thought, perhaps, you also taught such dark spells."

Serenity and Juniper both wrapped the girls in their arms. "You will find no such magic, here," Juniper assured them. "And while none among us, here, speaks with the Goddess Ciuin Rose, there is one who does."

"Grandmother?" Oceana ventured hesitantly.

"Yes," Serenity said. "How did you know?"

"We heard rumors that the one called Grandmother spoke with your Goddess. That Grandmother also holds many secrets. Why else would the High Priestess Danu wish to take what Grandmother treasures most and draw the ancient one to her? We cannot say to what end Danu wishes to learn those secrets, but we fear her and fear what she may intend."

Juniper spun on her heels, wailing, "Ciuin Rose protect us!" Rushing from the room, she called back, "I will prepare your pack, Lady Serenity. You must take some among the guardians with you. I will summon..."

"I suspect my son is hunting for Hawk and Whisper, even now. I will seek him, first. Once we safely return Whisper, Singer and I will travel together to Brightwater."

29

Shadow slipped silently through the ruins, wrapping herself in wisps of gray and black, blending with the monochrome of the night. Her grandmother left less than an hour earlier after reaching out to Singer. He agreed she should join him, though she would have to manage a couple of teleportations to do so. It was good that the two would join their efforts. Serenity had, after all, experienced many years of war, fighting many a battle at the sides of her husband and children. She was skilled, strong, and determined. She would stop at nothing to get Whisper back. Still, Serenity did not share the same connection with Whisper that Shadow held. Shadow's jaw set. They should have taken her with them, as well.

"I will find you!" she declared in an undertone, her eyes scanning every shadow, every motion set about by the breezes or by creatures scurrying about their business, or by the magic of the music in her own voice. She tried to reach out to Whisper. Repeatedly. To no avail. "You are alive," she breathed. "You must be. Why do you not answer me?"

Once away from the temple ruins, the trees became her highway, allowing her to move with ease while keeping her senses tuned to any indication of others who might be near. The woods remained empty save for the creatures that belonged therein. Yet, the faint sense of something foul ran along her nerves. Whether to seek it out or avoid it posed a dilemma. To seek it risked putting her life in danger and jeopardizing Grandmother. She had long considered, however, that Grandmother's identity must already be known, or at least suspected by the enemy. Why else would they wish to take either her or her cousin but to lure Grandmother to them. So, the risk was to her own life, really. And to avoid seeking this foul thing could mean missing some sign of Whisper. So. Seek it out, then. She would follow in the direction of the foulness.

Her pursuit took her through the night, leaving her blurry eyed from lack of sleep as the first thin light of a cloudy morning lifted over the surrounding foothills to creep through the forest. Only a few meters beyond, the trees gave way to eroding earth and boulders along a stretch where frequent rockfalls crushed anything that attempted to grow. Better to rest within the cover of the forest. Finding a comfortable fork in a massive fir, Shadow pulled her cloak around her, weaving her spell of concealment and shielding, careful to blend it with the ambient magic of the woods. And there she slept.

Waking came in late afternoon - much later than she intended. It also came with the sounds of voices. Red Moon Warriors rested below her perch. The flame and red crescent moon insignia on their coats marked them. One sat with his back against her tree, two others a couple of meters from him. Another nine or so rested at the base of the rockfall slope. The three below her complained among themselves.

"We need tanks to push through the woods and carry us up into the mountains. Or better, the aircraft to carry us over them. Drop us into the heart of Knife Point Keep," grumbled from the man leaning against the tree.

"Tanks are too dangerous in the passes and too heavy to risk on the ice fields. And the aircraft cannot fly high enough to reach the keep. Or so I am told," supplied a woman hunched over a small container on which a pot of water boiled.

"You have read the books," the man against the tree countered. "There are ways to make aircraft go higher. They once flew among the stars."

"Do not believe everything in those old tomes," snorted a second man who sat next to the woman. "True enough, the High Priestess Aifa has managed to get a few machines in the air. That does not mean any of those sorts ever flew beyond the sky. Even if it were true, she lacks the minds of the ancients who wrote those books. Lacks the resources they possessed. If, indeed, they had such resources as to pull off such feats. More like myth than truth, in my estimation. Truth, after all, is that those bloody things can barely stay in the air."

"Does not matter what Aifa has or what she lacks," the first man grunted. "All we have is our feet. And it is time we use them again. Fix your tea and drink it, Milla. We need to be on our way. Those soldiers are still a few hours ahead of us. Need to stop them before they can connect up with any of the guardians."

The woman muttered under her breath but poured the liquid into a mug, letting the herbs within steep briefly, then drank it straight down, leaving Shadow to wonder how she managed not to scorch everything from her throat to her stomach. "So," the woman growled. "Which way do you intend to go?"

"To the old temple ruins."

The woman stiffened. "No."

The man leaning against the tree straightened. "What do you mean, 'no'?"

"Just what I said. No. The ruins are said to be cursed, and not by our High Priestess. The souls of the long dead priestesses do not rest easy. They ensnare the unwary. Haul them into the ground to die."

"Foolish garbage. The souls of those slain priestesses are banished. They are no part of Slievgall'ion. If those souls still exist, it is not in this realm."

"Not all are banished," put in the second man as he stood and brushed the leaves, snow, and mud from his pants. "I agree with Milla. I have been to the temple ruins. Lost half our company, there. Witnessed men screaming as wraiths pulled them beneath the earth."

An uneasy silence settled before the first man shook his head, declaring, "More like you were ambushed by guardians. Aifa will be interested to learn that you fear facing them again."

"An ambush by the living does not draw people into the ground," the other man persisted. "I do not fear the living. It is the dead I fear."

"Fine. Walk back and tell Aifa, yourself. We are going to the temple ruins. That is the direction the scouts said those soldiers were headed. So, that is where we go."

Shadow held to her branch, watching as the three joined the other nine. The man who had leaned against her tree signaled for the rest to gather their gear and head out. For several more minutes, she remained, fighting the urge to follow them. All her life, she had heard the stories of the dead souls. But she never saw any evidence of them. She and Whisper and her grandmother always passed within the ruins in safety. It might be educational to learn if the stories were true. Following this group, of course, would not get her any closer to Whisper. Still, she should send warning of the warriors.

Weaving her shielding with extra care, she reached out for Juniper. At length came an irritated, *"Where the bloody demons are you? We have been looking for you for a day and a night!"*

"I am going for Whisper," Shadow returned.

"Serenity is going to be furious."

"It will not be the first time grandmother is angry with me. I need to warn you, though. There are twelve Red Moon Warriors heading to the ruins. They are apparently tracking some Soldiers of Damsa Dana. Keep everyone inside and set an extra guard."

"We will need to send someone out to meet the soldiers and get them inside with us."

"Too risky. Keep the children safe."

An exasperated huff attached to Juniper's, *"You are a fine one to caution me about risk! Follow behind the warriors. Stay hidden. But get yourself back here!"*

"Not until I find Whisper."

"Shadow! You…"

Shadow broke the contact, fists stuffed to her hips. Juniper was as bad as her grandmother. Just her luck to have two such women eternally fretting over her. Her exasperated huff accompanied her climb to a higher bough to gain an overview of the area. Unless she misjudged her route, the temple ruins were perhaps thirteen or fourteen kilometers south east of her. A farmstead lay another seven or eight kilometers almost due north. Seeing it, however, even from this height, was impossible, given the rise and fall of the forested slopes. Slipping a hand into her pocket, Shadow jangled the small pouch. The family who owned the farmstead were acquaintances. They would welcome the coin she offered for a few supplies. And perhaps they had news of Hawk; had seen his company pass through the area.

Dropping back through the branches to her previous perch, her shoulders slumped, doubt creeping in. She was so sure of herself when she left the sanctuary. Certain that she knew which route Hawk had taken. She had, after all, considered the possibilities long and hard. The shortest distance to Brightwater lay southeast from the keep where they could make the border crossing still northeast of Gray's Way Station. Shortest it may be, but it was also one of the most dangerous. Shadow did not believe Hawk would risk Whisper's life taking her through that stretch. She was equally certain he would avoid the pass above Gray's way station, knowing Gray had returned to keep watch from the heights. She was convinced he would go south to Healer's Gap. The valley was easier to travers and would allow them to cross a shorter spur of the mountains, coming out just west of where the Hope River branches off the Singer River. Her goal was to reach the river ahead of them. Lay in wait. Seek the right opportunity to steal in and rescue Whisper. But what if she was wrong? What if he was chancing the northern route?

Shadow buried her face in her hands, fighting back the threat of tears. Why would he do this? Brightwater was under siege, its lord dead. According to Oceana and Phoenix, Hawk was in communication with Danu, so he must know where she hides. Still, he risked the Red Moon Warriors finding and capturing them the moment they cross the border. The very thought of such treachery from a Guardian of Ciuin Rose nearly shook her from her perch. Grabbing a branch to steady herself, Shadow made another attempt to reach out to her cousin, using as much care to shield her sending as she had done with Juniper. There came a vague sense of motion and great drowsiness, and… Shadow held her breath. And a sense that the distance between herself and her cousin had diminished.

Shadow prayed it was true – that the distance was closing. At least she confirmed Whisper was alive. But was her cousin unharmed? The lack of any indication of pain seemed a good sign, though Whisper might be blocking it the way she was blocking her thoughts. Why would her cousin shut her out like this? They never shut each other out. Shadow's lips pinched, her insides hollowing at the sharp pang of betrayal. Whisper did keep things from her. She never told Shadow of the struggle to keep some dark force at bay. What other secrets had her cousin kept?

"Does not matter!" she sniffed, working her way lower in the tree. The thud of her drop to the ground reflected the weight of Shadow's lingering anger and resentment, though she tried to cover it by repeating, "Does not matter," as her gaze skimmed the forest shadows and the rockfall beyond. "I will find you, anyway. Will get you back." Squaring her shoulders, she turned in the direction of the farmstead. She needed supplies and it was her closest option.

She made good time, skirting the edge of the rockfall, steadily working her way north. Time and again Shadow attempted to reach out. Time and again she swore at Whisper's failure to connect with her; then swore at herself for setting out without thinking this through. Had she done so, she would have taken the time to pilfer more supplies from Juniper's stores and not need this side trek.

The farmstead lay in a clearing a couple of valleys beyond where she overheard those heading for the temple ruins. If the weather held, she could cover the distance in another day, allowing time to rest. Shadow dared not push too hard; leave herself too exhausted. No telling what sort of rescue she might need to execute, once she finds Whisper. Sgt. Hawk was smart and cautious. He would hold Whisper under close guard. How many guardians were with him? Oceana and Phoenix failed to say. "You failed to ask!" she shouted in disgust.

The echo of her frustration faded to utter silence, the rustle of leaves ceasing almost instantly. Nor were there any bird calls or animal sounds of any sort, she realized. Dread raised her flesh, sending her from the lower branches back up into the canopy. Who…or what…had her outburst attracted? Crouching in a crook high above, she focused on the forest floor, searching in every direction. There, in the distance, she saw the line of withering gray stretching in a trail from a distant ridge. It was advancing toward her. In its approach, ancient trees - living and healthy moments before, now crumbled in death. The creatures. But how many?

A strange noise rose from the direction of the ridge. A sort of combined whir and whoop, whoop, whoop. Squinting into the dusk, Shadow froze as a machine lifted above a neighboring slope, rising up… and up…and up. A wheel of some sort topped the machine, its rapid spin a blur. Once well above the treetops, the thing moved forward, paralleling the trail of death which continued to move toward her.

Curling tight against the branches, Shadow wrapped the gray strands of darkness around her, waiting. Whipped air beat at her as the impossible machine approached, then stopped and hovered. Below, the death beasts darted through the woods, stopping at the base of her tree. Each the size of a small fox, the creatures looked more like a cross between a wolverine, a cougar, and a rat. Gleaming eyes turned upward, though whether they searched for her or watched the machine mattered little, given that her tree was suddenly dying from beneath her. If she remained, the sickness would surely take her, as well. Yet she dared not move until the machine and the creatures passed.

The gray withering drew less than two meters from her feet when the foul beasts turned and continued their deadly trek, the machine adjusting to fly south instead of continuing to parallel their trail. Shaken, Shadow edged downward far enough to make a jump to the next tree. The sickness crept up it, as well. Again, she jumped, almost missing the branch of another tree. Her coat sleeve caught with a rip as her hands raked along a branch. Her grab at cedar fronds and twigs, hanging on as they bent and snapped under her weight, dropped her onto a lower branch. Shadow clutched it, her breath ragged, her body trembling. Did she judge right? Did her swing carry her out beyond the reach of death? Gradually, the sense of life in the tree flowed through her. Life, not sickness and death. Steadying her breath, Shadow climbed down to a stronger branch, and then another, until she crouched next to the trunk, high enough from the ground to see what lay around her. In the dimming light, she stared out through the cedar boughs, realizing that the creatures' path of destruction cut her off from the direction she intended to follow. Worse, it ran in the same direction as the party of Red Moon Warriors she saw earlier. Once again, she would need to warn Juniper.

30

The view from the window was once soothing, the waters of the White Moon River glistening in its dance over the rocks and splash across boulders. It was the reason Caer always requested this room when she stayed at River House. Today, the river offered no comfort, running cold and gray beneath the overcast sky. Still, Caer sat by the window, staring out. *"Please, Roisin. I need to know more. Guide me."* She knew her plea was in vain. The voices of Roisin and Dana were weaker here than at the Healer's complex. Perhaps she should have stayed longer at the hidden sanctuary where she was protected by Adrian's ancient spells.

Adrian. The thought of his name rushed other names from her lips. Dylan. Emer. Fedel'ma. Brandon. Jenna. Sidra. With them came the rush of tears.

"We are ever with you," murmured faintly through her mind. *"We rest. We wait."*

Caer swiped at her eyes. "I hear your voice and dare to believe. Foolishness, of course. Only the souls of the sisters can speak to me. Still, I know you lie in the bosom of Slievgall'ion. And I wish to join you. I am tired. Why can I not rest with the eternal sleep granted to you?"

"You are not, yet, done," came to her, carried on Dana's faint and strained tone. *"We must come full circle. Remember the beginning. There lies hope."*

"The beginning," she groaned. "I was at the beginning. I saw no hope."

"There is always hope. There must be."

Caer looked up, startled. When did Lt. Journeyson come to stand in the open doorway?

"You seemed as hopeless as I not more than a few hours ago, lieutenant."

"Aye." He agreed, strolling to Caer's table to help himself to a chunk of bread and retreat to the wall, there sliding to the floor to eat.

Rubbing her arms, Caer regarded him. "You are so much like him. Like them. I try not to see it. But it continues to stare me in the face."

"What?"

"You remind me of those for whom you are named." Caer gestured to the chair across from her. "Come. Sit. The chair is more comfortable than the floor. And here, there is a view."

Brandel rose, his brow ticked up. "I remind you of... You cannot mean my great, great, great...whatever...grandparents?" He pulled out the chair and sat, casting a blank glance to the window before turning his attention back to her. "Are you saying you knew them?"

The ghost of a smile teased the corners of Caer's mouth. "I did. Your distant grandfather was a friend before I met your distant grandmother. He lost his first love, my best friend, because of me." Sighing, she raised her mug of tea, sipping at it, curling her lip and setting it aside. "Cold. Where are Tine or Stoirm with their touch of fire to warm it for me?" With a minor shrug, she set the cup to her palm, drawing heat to her hand until steam lifted from the cup's contents, then sipped again.

Brandel continued to eye her, looking dubious. "You truly are the one myth refers to as Caer DaDhrga, the Soul Bearer?"

"Caer is sufficient," she sighed. "Perhaps Dana and Roisin are correct; that by taking back my name I can find the old courage. Find what it is I must do to bring to fruition the little bit of hope that remains."

"Tell me about them," Brandel prompted.

"Hmmm?"

"My...distant grandparents. Fedel'ma still lived when my great grandfather was young. Or so I was told." He regarded the woman who bore so many identities, his head cocked. "If I may be so bold, just how old are you?"

"Long past too old." A faint smile returned. "You look a lot like Brandon. Built like him, too. Solid as granite. When you sat against the wall, you became his very image - slumped in silent agitation, munching. He did not much like your grandmother at the time of their meeting. Did not trust her. For a while, his trust in me hung by a thread. He was strong. Strong and stubborn and loyal to me to a fault, despite the blame. Del was his match in strength and bullheadedness and trusted Brandon no more than he trusted her. Did you know that, where we come from, Witches possess the ability to live many lives? Their souls transmigrate. When I first met Del, she looked to be about sixty by the Tanai span of age."

"Tanai. The ancient term for humans who lack magic?"

"It means 'the shallow'. They were named so, both for their lack of magic and because they lacked the ability for their souls to return after death to inhabit another host."

"I think I would prefer to be a Tanai than for my soul to take over someone else's body."

"It is not quite like that. At least, not by the time of my birth. The soul of a deceased Witch seeks for the fresh corpse of a Tanai to inhabit. When Del was murdered, she knew she needed to return to us right away, and instead of taking the time to look for a suitable human body, she inhabited the living body of her cat, Merripen."

Brandel gaped. "You joke."

"Not in the least."

"My distant grandmother's soul moved into a cat's body?"

"Indeed. It came as quite a shock and fright to me. At the time, you see, I knew nothing of Witches. Was unaware I was one."

Brandel's gape became more pronounced. "How could you not know?"

"A long story. Too long for this telling. To return to the matter of your great grandmother, she did not remain in her cat for long. Though her next transmigration was even more startling. She came back in the body of a woman who had, only hours before, died in your grandfather's arms."

"His first love."

"No. Another woman. When he saw she had come back to life, Del feared he would expire from the shock. When he realized that it was not the woman he thought, but was, in fact, Fedel'ma, he threatened to murder both Fedel'ma and her niece Emer, on the spot."

Brandel leaned back, shaking his head. "None of this was passed down to me."

"No," Caer sighed. "Few who came through with us knew the tale. Those who wrote the histories were from this world and copied them from oral repetitions of the stories told by Adrian and Stoirm. The chroniclers, of course, desired to create heroes. The private lives of those heroes held little interest for them. Better to weave the legends from the battles fought. Very much like the ancient bards of our world's early histories."

Brandel's brow took a dubious twitch. "So, the heroes did come from the world of the Goddesses' origin."

Exasperation came out in a loud groan. "They are not goddesses. They are Witches. Extraordinarily powerful ones, to be sure. But Witches, all the same."

Brandel sprang to his feet, backing away from her.

"Do not go telling me that my words are blasphemous, lieutenant. I carried one or more of their souls for many years before coming here. Their memories often become so entangled with mine that I struggle to distinguish which belongs to whom. The sisters are no deities."

"But they created this world," Brandel insisted.

"No. They discovered a way to open the gateway between worlds and then proceeded, over much time and with help from a great many others, to bring Earth's life here."

"I do not see how that is any different. They drew life from the ground, thus they created it."

"They drew nothing from the ground of this world. Earth is the name of the world of their origin."

Brandel blinked at her. "Earth. Their world is named for dirt."

"Named for the world upon which humans dwelled, as opposed to the heavens above or what the people of the time believed to be the underworld beneath."

"And this world is the origin of my distant grandmother and grandfather?"

"Your grandmother. Your grandfather was born on a far distant planet in another solar system, though his ancestors were from Earth. The technology which you find so difficult to accept as other than magic included great ships that traveled between the stars."

"And you. Where was your origin?"

"Yet a different world from your grandmother's and grandfather's. In truth, I was born on one of those ships that carried people to the stars."

Brandel swept his gaze upward, staring hard at the plaster ceiling as if he might bore holes through it to see the sky. "So much distance, and yet the three of you found one another."

"So much distance," Caer nodded. "And even more to bring us here."

"You wish to return to those other worlds?"

Caer dropped her eyes to a silent study of her lap for several long seconds, at last conceding. "I wish to learn the fate of those worlds. I need to learn Earth's fate, at the very least. Opening the gateway, holding it open for as long as Nemhain forced caused a tremendous explosion of magic from Slievgall'ion through to Earth. Whether it allowed for a rebirth of an abundance of life on that world or whether it wiped all from the face of it…that is what I wish to discover."

Caer rose, moving quietly around the chamber, her fingers running over furniture and walls. The thrum of magic that permeated River House was not as great as that in the secret place at the Healers' complex yet remained sufficient to be an annoyance. It also provided the very strength that allowed the souls of Dana and Roisin to speak with her, even if faintly. Caer feared these were the last of the places where she might yet hear their voices. They were silent almost everywhere else, now.

"We struggle."

"Why? Against what?"

"The souls taken into the heart of Slievgall'ion are less and less those of our followers and more of Nemhain's. Her followers murder. And while Aifa forbids their learning the use of the banishing, the torture imposed before death leaves souls too damaged to survive for long after. Our followers kill in battle but leave the souls intact. The heart of Slievgall'ion is no longer filled with light. The magic grows vile. Think of the creatures created by Nemhain's granddaughter."

"The creatures of death. Aifa used the poisoning of Slievgall'ion's magic to create the creatures of death?"

"Creatures of death," drifted in a weary whisper. *"And more will come. Stop her."*

"How? How do we stop such abominations?"

"Remember the beginning."

"The beginning. But I stood at the beginning. I do not understand."

"Find the beginning." That last statement started thin and faded to emptiness.

"You were speaking to them?"

Caer spun to find Brandel watching her. How quickly she forgot his presence.

"What did they say?"

"To remember the beginning. To find the beginning."

"The beginning of what?"

"The time that we delivered the sisters and the war to Slievgall'ion, I thought. Now I am not certain. The beginning of the war between the sisters? The beginning of Witches?"

"Why is finding the beginning so important?"

"The magic of this world is being poisoned. We must find a way to stop Aifa. To stop the Red Moon Warriors. To… Roisin urges me to find the Alainn and go to the beginning. Dana tells me to find the beginning. Somehow, the beginning holds the key to ending this." She swept a hand at her surroundings. "We are at the beginning. Very near it, anyway. Were closer at the Healer's complex. That is where we arrived all those long ages ago."

"In the Healers' complex?"

"Aye. No. I died while inside the gateway. My soul returned to my own body because it was not destroyed. But I remember nothing until I awoke at the complex."

"Then you arrived somewhere else."

"I... Maybe."

"The legends suggest Mt. Sorrow as the location for that first dark war."

Caer shuddered. "And do you know where Mt. Sorrow stands?" Brandel shook his head.

"Nor do I. It is marked on no map."

"Who would know?"

"Stoirm. Tine."

"If that is the beginning you must find, then they should take us to that place."

Caer chewed her lip for a moment. "Meaning no offense to Dana, it is Roisin whose advice I most trust. She urges me to seek the aid of the Alainn. That is where we go, first. We leave in the morning."

31

Whisper jerked awake in a cold sweat, her scream caught in her throat. Sucking in, she darted a glance around before nervously propping herself up on an elbow. Darkness was thinning. She was on the floor in the remains of a farmhouse, guardians moving about nearby. It was a dream that woke her. A nightmare that urged the scream. But the scream refused to come. She dropped back, pulling the blankets up around her head, unable to stop her shaking. No sound. In the nightmare. No matter how desperate her attempts, no matter how many times she tried, her scream passed in silence. While her speaking voice lacked volume, screaming was never an issue. Her night terrors, her visions often produced such a wail as to wake the dead. Yet in this…

She fought the return of the vision, but it came, anyway. A woman. Shrouded and standing in darkness, a silhouette against the white light that surrounded her. The vision shimmered as the woman tossed back her hood. The white light faded, revealing a pale face twisted with malice. White hair writhed around it as blue eyes filled with rage fixed on her. Blood dripped from long fingers to fall on the bodies at the woman's feet. Bodies that mostly lacked faces. Two, however, turned blank eyes to Whisper. That was when she screamed, seeing the dead eyes of Shadow and herself staring up at her. But her scream produced only silence.

"It is time, little one," Lt. Hawk declared, his hand on her shoulder. "We must move on."

Whisper drew herself into fetal position, pulling her blankets tighter around her, the vision still clear in her mind. What did it mean? Did it foretell hers and Shadow's deaths? Would the Red Moon Warriors capture and torture them? Would Aifa take Grandmother's secrets from her?

Lt. Hawk knelt next to her, gently rolling her to face him. "Are you ill, Lady Whisper? We can find Healers for you later. For now, though, we must leave."

Forcing her limbs to move, Whisper sat, drawing her blankets with her, a waiver in her voice. "Take me back."

"We cannot do that, little one. We keep going. Keep moving you to safety."

Whisper shook her head. "I need to find Shadow. To warn her."

"Warn her of what?"

"If they capture us, we will die."

"That is precisely why we go on. We will go back and search for Shadow, I promise you. But not until we get you to the coast."

The vision gradually settled out, leaving Whisper's clear eyes to focus on Hawk. "Where on the coast of Brightwater are you taking me?"

"The High Priestess Damsa Dana is sending soldiers to escort us. You will be safe under her protection."

"She...sent word to you of this?"

"Not telepathically. I do not understand the reason, but our sendings are unable to go beyond the border with Brightwater. Danu sent one of her birds to me. A falcon. You know of the High Priestess' birds?"

Whisper nodded. Everyone knew of Danu and her birds. She favored them over telepathy, even when sendings worked.

"One of her falcons came to Knife Point Keep on the same day you arrived."

"Why did you not mention this to Lt. Starn or to Lord Stoirm?"

"I did."

"Yet, they told me to remain at Knife Point Keep."

"They did not believe the journey would be safe, despite Danu's assurances. Unfortunately, it proved less safe for you to remain at the keep than to make this journey. With no means of getting word to either our lord and lady or to Lt. Starn, I had no choice but to rush you away."

Once again, Whisper detected the subtle hint of a falsehood somewhere in Hawk's statement. What part was the lie? Why would he lie to her about any of it?

"I am going back," she persisted.

"I cannot let you do that, little one. My oath is to protect you."

"Your oath is to protect Knife Point and our people."

"And for now, the way to do that is to see that you remain safe."

"Then take me to the sanctuary below the temple ruins."

Hawk's lips pinched to a tight line as he regarded her. "Let us get you warm and we will discuss it further. I will return shortly with something for you to drink. When you are more awake, we will discuss the matter again."

Whisper snuggled back in the blankets as she watched him go. Her head throbbed as the vision attempted to reassert itself. A warm drink. Let her head clear. Perhaps she could then make a reasoned argument to the man.

When he returned, the aroma of the black tea drifted on the steam from the mug in his hands. Good. That should shake the last of her nightmare from her. Her first sip, however, tasted not of the tea, but of…of…

The pain in Whisper's skull exploded with such force she lost what little food was in her stomach. And then came blackness. At some point, she felt her head was banging against a boulder. When the fog at last began to lift from her mind, she realized that, in truth, her head was bumping against the back of a guardian. The slow and unpleasant business of gathering her wits brought back the nausea. She tried to bend to one side, only to discover her mobility limited by the rope that bound her to the man. It was no easy matter to control the roll of her stomach. When it finally subsided, the ache in her back impressed itself on her, as did the realization that her legs had gone numb from dangling astride the horse. Horse. When and where did they obtain horses? And why would Hawk betray her like this?

"Lt. Hawk!"

"He is riding ahead, my lady."

"Do not 'my lady' me with me tied to your back lieutenant… sergeant… Whomever you are!"

"Corporal, my lady. Name is Weatherstone. Sorry for the insult and indignity. We dared not risk you raising a fuss and trying to run off. We will be out of mountains and into the foothills by nightfall. Need to make it east along the upper fork of Singer River. We will camp there."

"I demand to speak to Lt. Hawk, this instant! Untie me and put me down!"

"Sorry," the corporal repeated. "You remain where you are. Lieutenant's orders. You can chew him out all you wish once we make camp. Not that it will do you much good. My suggestion is that you trust him. He is doing what must be done to protect you."

"Kidnappers are not worthy of trust," Whisper snapped, though the heat of her anger failed to carry in the softness of her outburst. Just once! Just once in her life, she would love to bellow her words loud enough for the whole world to hear.

"I cannot feel my legs," she grumbled. "And my back is killing me. So is my head, no thanks to whatever ugliness that kidnapper Hawk put in my tea."

"He did it for your own good," Weatherstone insisted. "I will send ahead, though. See if we can find a spot to rest a while. Give you a chance to get down and stretch your limbs."

Seconds later, Weatherstone added a third and genuinely more apologetic, "Sorry, my lady. Lt. Hawk says we are not stopping until we reach the river."

Everything ached from her confinement. Worse, Whisper's throbbing head made her vision fuzzy. If passing out was on the agenda, she wished for it to happen sooner rather than later. But it was not unconsciousness that took her.

A woman in darkness. Blood dripped from her fingers and ran from bodies piled at her feet. The woman reached for Whisper. She tried to jerk away; was held fast, her heart slamming her ribs. "You will help me. You can summon the ancient one. She will come for you."

"No! This is wrong!"

The corporal drew reins, barking, "Stop wriggling, my lady. Look down. There is a drop to the side. You will make the horse nervous. Neither of us want to take a tumble down that embankment with a horse on top of us."

"I will not! Not until you stop and we turn around! We are endangering Grandmother."

Getting no further response, Whisper struggled again.

"Do not force us to knock you out, again. Lady Whisper."

Whisper's growl rumbled in her throat, but she stopped moving. They had not, yet, reached the border with Brightwater, though the proximity to the border grew ever more worrisome. She had to find a way to escape before they crossed it. If Shadow were here, she would know what to do; would have a plan. Shadow always had a plan. Emptiness ate into Whisper's soul. She was alone. Never had she been so alone.

Closing her eyes against the continued throb in her temples and the threat of tears, she sensed, for the first time since setting out on this insanity, the life that surrounded her. Animals. Watchful. Wary. A stag looked on from somewhere upslope. A pair of wolves hid in the underbrush not far below him. Raccoon, squirrels, snakes, birds... But no sense of Shadow or of Grandmother. She reached out, again, seeking for a bird. If she found a suitable one, she might be able to join with it and... What? In the absence of her soul, Hawk would likely think her body dead. Might bury her alive.

Shuddering, she opened her eyes and noted that their path now bent away from the drop-off. Jaw set, she twisted, ready to slide from the horse and run, only to be reminded of the rope binding her to the corporal.

"Last warning, my lady. Try anything more, and I will dose you with more of that knock-out juice."

"Try it," she snarled. "And I will bite your hand off!"

Full night was on them when they at last left the mountain slopes behind and worked their way through the wooded foothills, making steady progress south by southeast. By midnight they reached the the Singer River somewhere just north of the fork, stopping to make camp beneath an overhanging boulder upslope of the river's banks. Lt. Hawk strode back to them to assist with untying her and lifting her down from behind Weatherstone.

"This is a mistake," she hissed, her legs giving out.

Hawk caught her. "The mistake was waiting this long to lure the old woman down from the mountains," he rumbled, picking her up. "With the weapon Grandmother possesses, perhaps Brightwater could have defeated the Red Moon Warriors, preventing them from ever setting foot in Knife Point's lands. The Lord and Lady of Knife Point refused to listen to reason. And Lt. Starn listens only to their counsel."

Setting Whisper to a blanket one of the other guardians laid out for her, he motioned yet another of his men over. "See that she is kept warm and that she has something to eat and drink."

The man nodded, striding off to where the horses were tethered and returning with a couple of packs slung over his shoulders. From one he pulled a heavy fur, wrapping it around Whisper's coat and tucking its length around her legs. From another he pulled a flask of water, handing it to her. "Drink a little while I get a fire going. Jasper has some rabbits he caught this afternoon. A hot meal will make you feel better."

Whisper turned her back to him, fighting back the sting of tears as she curled up on the blanket and pulled the fur over her head, her mind and stomach both tumbling at the the ugly recognition of Hawk's lies. Why didn't she heed her misgivings before they ever left Knife Point Keep? This was never about protecting her. It was only about Grandmother. Perhaps there had been no attack on the fortress and keep. Dismay at her stupidity and fury at herself and the traitorous Hawk roiled within as she lifted the blanket enough to peer out at the guardians moving about just beyond the overhang.

"How long do you think it took before the owner of these animals noticed them missing?" asked one of the men brushing down the horses.

"Hardly matters," snorted the second. "Did not look like the owner had the means to launch a pursuit. Hawk will see that the man is well compensated, though."

So. They not only kidnapped her, they stole the horses, as well. These were not honorable men. They did not deserve to wear the insignia of Ciuin Rose. May the Goddess strike them down for their treachery!

The original speaker shot a glance in Whisper's direction. "I pray the lieutenant is correct. That we are doing the right thing. Dragging the girl out here."

"Lt. Hawk is correct in one thing. Had the Lord and Lady of Knife Point ordered the old woman to come out from her hiding place and share the weapon she possesses with us and with Brightwater, this would not have been necessary."

"Will taking Lady Whisper truly draw the woman out?"

"They say the ancient one loves the two - Lady Whisper and Lady Shadow - more than she loves life. She will come."

"The lord and lady and Lt. Starn love the girls, as well. If any harm comes to Whisper…"

"It is our job to see that does not happen."

"You will endanger Grandmother's life and all of Slievgall'ion!" Whisper choked. "For a weapon? There is no weapon!" Either her voice failed to carry, or the men were ignoring her.

Rolling to her other side, she stared across at the now blazing fire. Skewered rabbits roasted above it, the aroma making her dizzy from hunger. The guardian in charge of the meal, however, stood several meters away, talking with Hawk. Three others were stretched out on the ground not far from the fire, already taking their turn at sleep. Considering the two tending the horses and the man posted near the river to keep watch, that left four unaccounted for. Stationed around the camp's perimeter, no doubt. Once more she felt Shadow's absence as a crushing emptiness. Why could she not think clearly without her cousin near at hand? Why could she not formulate her own plan of…

A yell went out, the guardian near the water's edge gesturing at the woods across the river. Whisper propped herself up, squinting into the distance where the silhouettes of riders could be seen approaching. A brief wash of moonlight through a momentary cloud break caught the crest of the Soldiers of Damsa Dana on the banner they carried. Again, foreboding raced along her nerves. She would stand no chance, at all, of convincing the soldiers to return her to Knife Point.

And with the number of those guarding her increased, what chance did she have of escaping? Chewing her lip, she skimmed a hasty glance around. Hawk and the cook were heading down the slope. The men who had been sleeping were on their feet and moving out from under the overhang, while the two who tended the horses were now focused on the soldiers on the opposite bank. This was her chance. She had to escape now! A quick check found her pack against the wall of the overhang.

Her dash resulted in a heart-stopping stumble. Righting herself, she snatched the pack and darted for the forest shadows. She may not possess the ability to wrap herself in wisps of darkness, but she was fast, and she knew how to hide in the trees. Staying low, she raced up the hillside and into the dense undergrowth. There, she shouldered her pack and looked for the guardians posted in the woods. Her heart stopped again when she spotted the nearest hunched next to a boulder not six meters from her. Thankfully, he, too, watched the activity at the river. Slipping past him, she was well up the hill before she left the underbrush in favor of climbing a black cottonwood. From there, she worked her way, branch by branch, tree by tree, toward a cluster of hemlock higher on the slope. The needles would provide better cover than the near leafless deciduous trees.

High in the top, she settled into a significant crook to wait and observe. As soon as the guardians discovered her missing, they would begin their search. Let them think she fled as far and as fast as possible. She would see what directions they took as they expanded their hunt, then determine the safest route past them.

Her anxious gaze was drawn back to the overhang, which prompted a round of silent, angry expletives. In her haste, she left a trail in the damp and slushy earth. But what could she do about it, now? If ever she needed Spirit's help, this was the time. But Spirit was too far away. Besides, she was unable to connect with wolf the way Journeyson did. The closest she could come to such a connection was with birds.

Her lips pinched. True enough, she had never been successful in connecting with other animals. But the last time she attempted to do so she was quite young. And there was Spirit. She managed at least an emotional bonding with the wolf. Accomplished that when she first met the animal. She was twelve at the time. Perhaps her assumptions were wrong. Perhaps she did have the ability to connect with creatures other than birds…and the wolf.

Jaw set, she took a deep breath and reached out. Detecting the sense of their presence was easy. Animals were everywhere around her. Small ones. Large ones.

Closing her eyes, she made the more difficult jump, seeking for the mind of a willing creature…any creature. Most shut tight against her. Some…some seemed curious. So, how to communicate with those?

Her efforts were interrupted by movement across the river, where at least twenty men dressed in the white of the Goddess Damsa Dana watched as Sgt. Hawk gestured to the south of their camp. From her perch, Whisper could just make out the bridge. As the riders disappeared, the guardians began making their way back toward the overhang. Her tracks were sure to be spotted.

Desperate, Whisper reached out, again, her mind racing to work out how Journeyson communicated with Spirit. It had to be akin to telepathing with humans but couching the message in a manner that creatures understood. It occurred to her, as well, how her aunt succeeded in stampeding animals when the Red Moon Warriors were too near the cave where they hid. Eyes closed, she concentrated, filling her mind with the vision of flames and the sense of terror; picturing animals running. Not running. Charging. From everywhere around - all racing for the overhang. The strain of extending the image and the terror outward set her temples afire, but she held it. And then it happened. Animals of every sort darted out of their shadowed recesses, charging down the hillside, flapping, running, galloping, hopping, crawling across the ground, trampling her trail; trampling the fire beneath the overhang and everything else that lay in their way. Some dashed back into the woods on the other side of the encampment, others charged into the river to disappear in the woods on the far side. Guardians scattered, many falling into the river, themselves, in their scramble to get out of the way. As quickly as it began, the stampede of creatures ended. Sprawled men gathered themselves from the ground and dredged themselves from the water.

"Lady Whisper!" Hawk shouted, racing up to where he left her. The blanket and fur lay in tattered shreds. The sergeant picked up pieces, paling as he cast frantic glances around. "She has escaped! Find her!"

Instantly, the men sprang into action, dashing in all directions to search for her. "Look to the trees!" Hawk demanded. "She likes the trees!"

Whisper's heart took another plunge as she realized how the stark white of her coat stood out against the greens and browns of the hemlock. Stripping from it, she pulled it wrong side out, leaving it open as she drew it on and praying the subtle tan of the fur lining and the mottled greens of her travel clothing would provide reasonable camouflage. Adding one more strain to her reserve of energy, she cautiously wove her spell of concealment, blurring the edges her form might set against the backdrop of the tree. For the remainder of the night, guardians and Soldiers of Damsa Dana, alike, searched the grounds. Whisper remained huddled close against the tree's crook as they passed beneath, too exhausted from her effort to stampede the animals and to weave her spell to move, and not daring to breathe when those searching for her made squinting scans of the branches above them. At one point, a heated argument erupted between Hawk and the ranking officer of the soldiers. Their words were impossible to make out, but their anger was clear enough.

For the whole of the next day, she kept to her perch as the search continued. Toward dusk, most returned to the camp. Whisper considered leaving her crook until Hawk and two of the soldiers turned in her direction, again eyeing the slope. Her chest tightened as they started the climb once more. Hugging the branches, she curled as small as she could make herself, fearing Hawk's scan of the boughs. The soldiers, on the other hand, kept their eyes on the ground, searching for any sign of her trail. Blood rushed her ears at her heart's race when they stopped beneath her. Hawk, however, was pointing toward the mountains.

"...far from here," he was saying. "The girl is likely headed back toward the old temple ruins."

"Why there?" growled one of the soldiers.

Hawk hesitated, at last offering, "Because she believes Lady Shadow is... near there."

A momentary silence was followed by, "Lady Shadow, you say."

"Aye."

"This may not prove to be the disaster it appears. If the girl is correct, and if we can reach the ruins ahead of her, we can lay a trap. Capture both girls. It would be a great good omen to be able to take the pair to High Priestess Danu. Double the likelihood of the old woman coming down from the mountains."

No. She had to find Shadow first. Still, she dared not move from her tree until the soldiers and the guardians pulled up camp and moved out. Nor did she dare attempt to telepath her cousin. Not while her energy remained low and while others were so near. By nightfall, the guardians and soldiers were gone, their path obviously aimed for the temple ruins. In the silence and darkness, Whisper descended, hitting the forest floor in a run. Without a horse, she could not travel as fast, but she must get to Shadow before they did.

32

Fire. Blood. Death. Dancing. One, two three, four, five, six, seven. One, two, three. One, two, three.

Caer woke, the lingering image of pools of blood, of bodies, of fire flickering to the rhythm of the dance still clear in her mind. "Are you trying to speak to me?" she whispered. "Please. Roisin. If you have a warning…news…a vision… Make it clear." There was nothing.

Shivering, she slipped from the bed and dressed, grateful for the clothes Hawthorne had laid out for her. The fleece lined pants, linenlined wool shirt, and wool over-jacket eased the chill while she stoked the fire on the raised hearth. Light was just beginning to creep in between the window's wooden shutter slats. Caer warmed herself near the rekindled flames, rubbing her hands for a few minutes before wandering to the window and opening one of the shutters to gaze out and down on the garden and the river. The garden lay empty, buried in the layer of snow that fell in the night. So much snow so early in the season. Did Aifa have weather workers among her priestesses? Were they responsible? Or was Slievgall'ion showing her disfavor for the violence that covered her lands?

A world aware of itself. Caer huffed. The magic in this world was strong, but not strong enough to make a planet self-aware. The souls trapped within the world's confines, however… Perhaps they were aware, at least on some level. The increasing number of dark souls likely had a hand in matters. It was a profoundly unsettling thought, the returned chill it raised sending her back to the fire.

A gentle knock at the door preceded, "My lady."

"Come. The door is not locked."

"That may be well and good, here," Hawthorne stated, pushing the door too. "With the present company. But I pray you are more cautious elsewhere."

"Hawthorne!" Caer exclaimed, eyeing the tray laden with a bowl of hot oatmeal, slices of toasted bread smeared with freshly melted butter, a plate of

SLIEVGALLION: THE GODDESS WARS

scrambled eggs, fried potatoes, and thick slices of bacon, along with a mug of steaming tea. "You have outdone yourself!"

The woman grinned. "Lord Tine sent to me that he heard you stirring. Lord Stoirm told me, last night, that you would be leaving early. Breakfast is being delivered to the others, as well. And the supplies Lord Stoirm requested are packed and waiting behind the registration counter." Setting the tray to the room's table she turned to go, hesitating at the door. "Lord Stoirm did not say where you are going. I wish you would return to Knife Point Keep. You will be safe in the fortress. I do not trust the strangers that are making their way into the mountains. It is rumored that Red Moon Warriors have crossed into our lands, as well. I do not like the thought of you wandering about."

Caer crossed to the woman, hugging her. "Thank you, my friend. But I am in excellent company."

Hawthorne nodded. "Aye. But three men and two boys against the likes of the Red Moon Warriors, my lady?"

"It is our intention not to run afoul of any such threats. We will be cautious. Now I have a warning for you. Do not open your doors to strangers, any longer. Should you sense the presence of someone you cannot readily identify, use your magic. Conceal River House and remain within until they are gone."

Hawthorne's already worried countenance deepened. "If you say so, my lady." As she turned to go, Caer caught her by the arm.

"One more thing, my friend. Foul creatures have moved into the mountains. Creatures whose very passage causes death. If you sense doom approaching, work your concealments and take yourself and all others within to the deepest part of your cellars. Wait there for at least a day before returning to these halls. If, upon returning, you still sense that presence, go back to the depths. Do not emerge until you sense it no more. Do you understand?"

Her bronzed skin paling, Hawthorne's brown eyes darted a glance toward the window. "Then the rumors are true? Such beasts are walking our lands?"

Caer nodded, giving Hawthorne a final hug. "They are true. The creatures, however, are not likely to find their way here. Still. Use the same caution you urge on me. Stay safe."

Hawthorne slipped through the door, pulling it closed, her anxious footfalls scurrying down the hall. Caer stood next to the room's small table, eyeing the breakfast laid out for her. Thanks to her own dire words, food now held little appeal. Past battles and trials, however, taught her that eating was critical, as there was no telling when the next meal might come. Still, half of the eggs and potatoes and a single slice of toast remained on her plate when she set about to retrieve her pack from the closet. A brow shot up as she hefted it. The pack was heavier than she remembered. With a leaden sigh, she dragged it to the bed and unpacked it, laying out three changes of clothes, a bedroll, two water skins, rope, an array of knives, the carefully wrapped package she always carried with her, some cooking items along with jerky, biscuits, cheese, dried fruit, herbs and ointments, strips of cloth, and a small stone bowl with pestle. Her eyes rolled. The clothes, half the knives, the cooking supplies, the food, and most of the herbs and ointments were Hawthorne's doing, no doubt. How the woman managed to get it all in the pack, however, was a marvel. Caer sorted, setting aside everything but the rope, the blanket from the bedroll, a couple of the knives, her wrapped package, and some of the food and herbs.

"If Hawthorne put food in your pack," Tine sent, *"leave it. She has plenty in some additional supply packs down here. How close are you to being ready?"*

Caer set aside the food. *"Give me but a few minutes more."*

"Make it as few as possible. Father says another storm is building. We need to be away from here and into the protection of Singer's Hold before it hits."

Singer's Hold. Adrian's Hold. Like the sanctuary beneath the temple ruins, like Knife Point Keep, the magic that protected the Hold, was by his hand. His spells still held, even all these centuries after his death. The age-old ache of grief rose once again. Adrian gone. Her beloved Dylan gone. Emer, Del, Brandon. Her daughters Rose and Summer, and her son Hugh. All gone. Gone, too, was an aunt she loved so many ages ago on a far distant world; gone were the friends she once knew in that other set of worlds.

Forcing back the grief, Caer returned her focus to the task at hand. She would not need the clothes Hawthorne selected but would likely have use for something light and formal, assuming Grian Geal agreed to entertain their presence. Rummaging in the closet produced what she desired, along with a few extra under garments. With those tucked to the bottom, she picked through the knives, choosing two - a compact blade that she slipped into the side of her right boot, and a kris knife with its sheath.

The last remaining item was the wrapped package. Caer dropped onto the bed beside it. Why did she carry this thing? She should have destroyed it ages ago. It went against the ancient ban on such items. According to Slievgall'ion's histories, the ban was put in place after the sisters delivered the third wave of people to this world. Never was any such weapon to pass from Earth to Slievgall'ion. That ban was now broken, thanks to Aifa. Yet, Caer was still loath to handle the item.

Hesitating, she at last stripped away the cloth from the package, her fingers curling around the handle of the small handgun - the gun Brandon used to kill her. Remaining on the opened cloth were a few rounds of ammunition. These passed through the gateway with Brandon when the opening blasted them to this side. Adrian advised him to keep it, but also to keep it well hidden. After Brandon's death, one of his and Fedel'ma's granddaughters delivered a locked box to Caer. The woman had no idea what was within; only that instruction had been passed to each of Bran's and Del's children and grandchildren that, upon his death, the item was to go to Caer. She would know the spell to unlock it. For many years, the box remained locked, Caer unable to call to mind any spell Brandon may have passed to her. In the end, it turned out to be a single word - the name of his sister, who was murdered on a far distant world many centuries ago. The path of Brandon's life was set with that murder and the annihilation of the colony known as Ahira.

Caer studied the gun with a mix of distaste and grief, then slipped it and the ammunition into an inside pocket on her jacket, donned her coat, shouldered her pack, and left the room, casting a guilty backward glance at its disheveled state and the remains of the breakfast left for Hawthorne to clean up.

Tine was the first to greet her. "There you are. Thought I might have to go back upstairs to look for you."

Caer ignored him, pointing at the two supply packs, propped against the wall. "Which of those do I carry?"

"None," Stoirm declared.

Caer glanced around at the others. Tine, Brandel, and Owl had each attached their personal packs to the top of a supply pack. "I am as capable as any of you to..."

"You are more capable than any of us at seeing visions of what is to come," Stoirm returned. "Often startling, frightening visions. I will not have you falling off a cliff because you are heavily weighted when a vision comes."

"I am equally capable of keeping my footing."

Stoirm turned his back on her, gesturing to the snowshoes that had been left on the front stoop upon their arrival. Taking up a supply pack, he handed the last one over to Jerkin. Face twisted in agitation, Caer pulled her pack from her shoulders long enough to slide her boots onto the smallest of the snowshoes and fasten them. As she readjusted her pack across her back once more, she caught sight of Hawthorne standing in the doorway between the kitchen and dining room, anguish etched in her features. Straightening, Caer shot her a smile, sending, *"Be well. Be safe. I will return for another visit, soon."* The woman gave a short nod and disappeared into the kitchen, dabbing at her eyes.

Outside, the sun was already above the eastern mountain peaks, the clear air sharp. Caer tugged the hood of her coat closer about her face, squinting in the light that reflected off the snow. At least half a meter had fallen in the night, adding to the calf deep layer that covered the ground before. It was nothing like what they had traversed when they left Knife Point Fortress. Nor was it anything like what they would face in the mountains bordering the outpost lands belonging to Sunrise. The valley, here, lay between the Knife Point and the Sunrise Mountain Ranges, protecting it from the most severe of weather. The protection, however, would not last as they climbed.

"Make haste," Stoirm called over his shoulder, setting out for the woods. "We are later than I had hoped for starting. We need to make Singer's Hold before the system building in the north blows down."

"How soon do you expect that to be?" asked Jerkin, trotting after the Alainn.

"Two days if we are lucky."

"Two…!" Jerkin strangled out. "How can you tell a system that far out is building?"

"My weather station."

"Your weather… Your what?"

Tine strode up next to the boy. "My father is not named Stoirm for nothing. His name actually means storm."

Jerkin's mouth formed around a silent and confused, "Oh."

Caer stifled her giggle as she caught up to Owl, who trudged behind Jerkin and Tine. "He does not cause storms, except to stir his enemies into storming rages." To her knowledge, Stoirm possessed no ability to predict weather, either. More like he had a contact living along Knife Point's northern coast who telepathed him the warning. His 'weather station'.

They cleared the valley and began the climb into the Sunrise mountains well into the afternoon. Stoirm insisted they continue into the night, despite the deeper snow and the frigid winds. Only when they crossed through the first pass did he search out an outcrop beneath which they might shelter. Caer dumped her pack, collapsing next to it. She was getting far too old for journeys such as this.

Her muscles ached. Her joints ached. Her bones ached. Taking the blanket from her pack, she wrapped it around herself and closed her eyes, summoning a minor healing spell; letting it ease some of her discomfort. She would not waste energy on anything more. Guilt already ate at her, knowing that Tine stood guard while the two boys divided some of the rations from Owl's pack for the night's meal. From somewhere, Brandel's and Stoirm's voices took up a quiet discussion, though their words were muffled and indistinct. She could sense Brandel's tension, however, and was aware that he searched the snowy darkness for a sign of Spirit. So much like Brandon, he was! Strong. Determined. Bull-headed. Loyal. As always with the old memories, her throat constricted, the familiar tears threatening. Snuffling, she curled up and drifted to sleep.

At some point, Spirit wandered into their camp. The wolf stopped long enough to brush Caer with a cold nose before trotting over to where Brandel and Tine sat talking. The boys rattled pots and the smell of dinner lifted on the air. She could sense Stoirm's presence. Knew he was close. Soothed by the proximity of her friends, she slept, again.

Fire. Blood. Dancing. One, two, three, four, five, six, seven. One, two, three. One, two, three. Remember the beginning. Find the beginning.

33

Moving was a struggle. Caer could scarcely feel her extremities and her brain insisted she forget about rising. Just go back to sleep.

Unable to focus long enough for her muscles to receive the proper mental command, her attempt to bat at the hands that shook her produced only a twitch.

"We have to go!" roared in her ear. "Caer! The storm is building faster than anticipated. We must move! Now!" Stoirm's hands gripped her upper arms and hauled her to her feet while Tine grabbed her blankets and stuffed them into her pack. Still foggy, she wobbled, barely aware of Stoirm rubbing her arms and legs to warm them. "Can you walk?"

The question took a moment to register. Owl shoved a mug to her lips. "Here, my lady. Drink this. Hawthorne packed it for us." Hot, bitter liquid flowed into her mouth and down her throat before she could reject it, triggering a round of choking and spitting. The clearing in her head was instant, however, as was the pain in her legs and arms as they registered the teeth of the frigid temperature.

"I am up!" she grumbled, still choking and shoving Owl's hand aside. "You trying to scald me or drown me?"

Owl flinched. "Neither my lady. Only trying to get you awake and moving." He cocked a brow at the mug and its steaming liquid. "Worked, too. Here. Better drink a little more, though. Just to be…"

Caer edged back. "You drink it! Where is my pack. If we need to leave, then let us do so."

Brandel already had her pack tied to one side of his. Stoirm turned her in the direction they needed to go. "You just concentrate on keeping your feet moving forward. Follow Spirit's tracks. Lt. Journeyson convinced her to find safe passage for us."

Caer followed orders, noting with sudden dismay the thundering roar and crash of an avalanche somewhere in the distance. Tine stayed close on her heels, the boys and Stoirm behind him. Her backward glance, however, found Brandel was missing.

"Where is…?"

"Checking out something Spirit detected. He will join us soon."

"We should not leave him behind. He lacks knowledge of the mountains and their dangers."

"Stop worrying," Tine sent. *"The man is far more capable than you think. And he is not far behind. He will catch up to us before we reach the ridge ahead."*

Caer looked up, squinting against the blowing snow. The ridge looked impossibly high in the current conditions. Protruding from it was a massive cornice of snow and ice that could easily break loose at any moment. There was little alternative, though. To either side, buried beneath the swirling white lay a series of crevasses. This was one of the very few times she wished Adrian's spells might not hold; might allow them to teleport straight to Singer's Hold.

"Have faith," whispered through the back of her mind.

"In what?" she snapped, uncertain of the source of the comment. Tine, most likely. It was a phrase he was fond of using. Still, the tone was not quite right.

Stoirm's, "Keep moving!" was all but lost on the winds.

The climb was excruciating, bent against the gale. Barely able to see from behind the fur-lined hood and the blizzard, Spirit's trail was becoming harder to distinguish. As if hearing her thoughts, the wolf appeared in front of her, then turned and moved back up the slope once more, staying within Caer's line of sight. Near frozen and shaking, Caer at last cleared the ridge line, gazing down the other side, then ducking flat on the ground. *"Red Moon!"* she shot, grabbing the scruff of Spirit's fur and yanking the animal down next to her. The wolf's low growl prompted an immediate release and, a hoarsely whispered, "Sorry. But we cannot let them see us. Please. Be still."

To her surprise, the wolf silenced, snugging in closer to Caer's side, though Spirit's ears remained pricked and her hackles raised.

Tine, then Stoirm crept up on the other side of her, Stoirm motioning for the boys to remain just downslope of them. Last, Brandel crawled up to crouch beside Spirit, breathing hard. "I found their tracks several meters below the outcrop. That they failed to spot us is a sheer miracle. Looks like they climbed the ridge at its lowest point and crossed down. Are they headed to Singer's Hold?"

"They appear to be headed that direction," Stoirm affirmed. "Will not be able to find the Hold but they could certainly prevent us from getting to it."

Brandel slipped back a little, easing the strain of his crouch. "Is there any way for us to reach it before they do?"

"Not without slowing them down."

"Can we scatter them?" Caer asked.

Stoirm cocked a brow. "How do you mean?"

"You know what covers these slopes. They seem to be aware of the risk, as well. They march single file with a couple of leads testing the ground with poles. No ropes, though. Scatter them and some are bound to end up in a crevasse."

Brandel considered. "I may be able to help with that. Give me a minute." For several long seconds, he sat with eyes closed, one hand laying lightly on Spirit's back. The wolf rose, turned, and bolted down the slope, initially retracing their path. Halfway back to the outcrop, however, she veered and shot further downslope, lifting a howl on the winds. Two… three more howls answered from the distant wooded valley.

"I think," Brandel began, moving back up to the top of the ridge and gazing down on the forty or so Red Moon Warriors trudging across below them. "I think we should ease ourselves off of this ridge on the side we need to descend."

"They will see us," Jerkin called from his perch a couple of meters below Caer. She doubted he could see the warriors, but he had obviously been paying attention to the dialogue, despite the wind's roar.

Caer squinted at the line of men moving cautiously across the ice field. In addition to the leads with their poles, some used their axe handles to tap out the stability in front of their feet. "Maybe not. Their attention is on their footing. If we are cautious, we can slip across and down to a shelf off to our left."

"I see it," Brandel confirmed after raising enough to peer over the ridge.

Caer grabbed for his hand as he started to move. "Better to take this slowly. If we knock enough snow loose, they will certainly take note."

Nodding, Brandel eased himself from the ridge, slipping down and edging to his left. Caer followed, with Tine and the boys coming single file after her. Stoirm was the last to make it to the shelf. "Now what, lieutenant?" he asked, squeezing in with the others.

"Wait for it," Brandel smiled.

Minutes later, Spirit shot up and over the lower section of the ridge, howling in unison with a wolf pack at her heels. Red Moon Warriors spun, glancing at the pack driving toward them. A few held their ground, screaming for others to do so even as they struggled to free weapons from their coats. Others scattered. Within minutes, the hungry wolves were on them. In the chaos of charging animals, loud pops, and a rending crack with clouds of snow, several men and animals fell, screaming, into a great rift.

"What the?" Brandel gasped, watching in horror as pop after pop echoed around them dropping wolves in pools of blood. Spirit wheeled and darted away, racing for the lower point of the ridge and disappearing from sight. "What magic is this?"

Caer slumped. "Not magic. Technology. Firearms."

"I thought the Red Moon's weapons were huge machines that could strike from such a distance that magic could not reach them."

Caer stared at the carnage below. Men and wolves dead and dying. Some had fallen into crevasses. Survivors among the men struggled to regroup. "Firearms come in all manner of sizes, lieutenant. Most of which can kill from distances too great for our magic to counter." Turning, she searched the terrain for some hint of the white wolf, but there was no sight of her.

Bitterness sharpened Brandel's accusing hiss. "Had you told me of this, I would never have asked Spirit to bring the pack."

"I had no way of knowing these warriors possessed guns. No one knows to what extent Aifa has produced such weapons." Tears stung her eyes. She would not have wished this on the wolves, either. Stiffening, she slipped cautiously from the shelf.

"Where are you going?" Stoirm demanded.

"They are still distracted. And the clouds preceding the storm are moving in. We should be able to move without their noticing if we do so quickly. We need to get to Singer's Hold. Need to reach the Sunrise outposts. We need the Alainn's help to stop Aifa."

There was no more discussion. Stoirm pushed past her, crawling low, testing the ground beneath his hands. Their progress across the upper slope was cumbersome, but they made it to the bend and another rise that would take them up to a saddle between two minor peaks. At last able to stand, they traveled on, climbing the slope and clearing the saddle to descend on the other side. Brandel still scanned the surroundings, as did Caer, searching for Spirit.

"She will never trust me, again," Brandel groaned, trudging downslope.

Caer felt his anger as an itch running along her nerves. *"She may surprise you. She has bonded with you. If she understands what you ask is for your protection, she will accept the consequences of acting."*

Brandel's glare pierced her. *"But I will not. I will not again ask her to act without knowing the risks to her. And I will not put my life above hers."*

"She will act to protect you, nonetheless."

His next sending exuded sarcasm. *"You seem to know a lot about animals and bonding for someone who claims no ability to accomplish it."*

"I had a lot of time to observe and learn."

The wind was picking up and the sky darkening. Large flakes began falling. The leading edge of the storm was well upon them. Caer forced her attention back to their destination - another four or five kilometers away, yet.

Jerkin struggled to catch up to her, his hood pulled so close around his face that only his eyes could be seen. She shook her head, pointing at her ears in response to his attempt to say something, the combination of the covering over his mouth and the wail of the wind garbling his words. Fumbling with mittened hands, he pulled his hood back enough to yell, "How much longer?"

Caer's shrug was lost within the depths of her coat. *"I cannot say,"* she sent. *"Depends on how much worse the weather gets. I hoped to make it before nightfall. I doubt we will be able to do so, though."*

Dismay creasing his face, Jerkin fell back with Owl. Caer's backward glance found the boys both struggling to stay on their feet. If they did not reach Singer's Hold soon, Jerkin and Owl might not be able to make it.

"Can we teleport?" she directed to Stoirm. *"Not to the hold, but close enough to shorten the journey."*

It took several long minutes before Stoirm replied. *"We can try for the shoreline at the creek bend. It should be frozen sufficiently to prevent our soaking, should we miss by a few meters. That would put us less than half an hour from the hold. Let us pray that no enemy is camped there. I will wait for everyone to gather, here, then share the sight of the location. Those with the strength can help to teleport those who struggle."*

Raising her hand against the blowing snow, Caer squinted ahead, spotting Stoirm somewhat downslope near a massive broken tree stump and praying she could make it that far without slipping or stumbling over unseen rocks or roots and breaking an ankle or worse. Several minutes later, her boots hit a patch of ice, sending her headlong toward the stump. Stoirm's quick sidestep and catch landed her in his arms.

"I have changed my mind," he declared, righting her. We cannot go on like this. We need to teleport closer to Singer's Hold than the creek bend."

"The ledge," Caer breathed, her insides hollowing. "But it is so narrow."

"It is wide enough if we stand close together."

"Can you fix on the surroundings well enough for others of us to assist with the teleportation, and can we get everyone there without dropping us off the edge?"

"We will find out soon enough."

Tine was the next to join them, followed by the two boys and Brandel. It was obvious from their cautious avoidance of the ice patch Caer hit that they witnessed her near catastrophe.

"We are going to make a jump," Stoirm announced. "Teleport to an area that should be clear of any potential enemies. It will be tricky, and we will need to stay close together. Very close. Caer, you and the boys stand in a huddle. Tine and Lt. Journeyson and I will stand just outside of you. Keep tight and do not move away from one another until I say so."

Owl and Jerkin looked too weary to be concerned. Caer put her arms around them as they snuggled in close to her. Once all were in place, Stoirm wasted no time asking for or expecting assistance from anyone. The sudden disorientation left Caer as light-headed as always, making her grateful that Stoirm placed her on the inside of their small circle. Though exhausted, it was Owl and Jerkin who prevented her dropping to her knees, her irritation expressed in a muttered, "Damn it!"

The boys jerked back, Owl bumping up against Tine.

"Careful, son. There is not much ground for us to stand on, here."

"Sorry, sir!" Owl yelped, glancing from Caer to Tine to the abrupt drop-off less than a meter behind where Tine stood. The boy swallowed hard, his gaze darting back to Caer.

She rested unsteady hands on the boys' shoulders, drawing them back to her. "You have no need to apologize, Owl."

"Should not have touched you, my lady! Not my place!"

"Oh, for pity…! I am not your lady, nor anyone else's. You kept me from falling on my face, or worse."

Brandel was backed up against the cliff, his attention fixed on the empty space beyond their narrow shelf. "What is it about you people with dark holes in the ground, and narrow ledges on steep cliffs? How is this any safer than running into Red Moon Warriors?"

Stoirm gave a short huff. "At least the cliff face shelters us from the wind. And we are not under attack, which we likely would be, had we teleported to the creek's bend."

Caer followed the direction of Stoirm's gaze, tracing the pale blue line of the ice-covered creek to its bend some distance to their north. It would have been difficult to pick out the white tents lining the snowy bank except for the red crescent moon, flames rising from the scoop of its cup, emblazoned on the tops. Caer counted at least a dozen of the Red Moon crests.

Now, it was Jerkin backing against the cliff. "Can they see us?"

Stoirm shrugged. "Depends."

Jerkin mustered a weak, "On?"

"Whether any of their scouts happen to look this way. So, try not to do anything that would draw their attention. Like triggering an avalanche while climbing."

Brandel paled as much as the boys as he stared up the sheer cliff face. "Are you insane?"

Caer sucked in, her exhale ragged. It was a struggle to steady her voice. "There are steps and handholds cut into the rock face. Stoirm will go first, clearing them." Sitting, she unstrapped and removed her snowshoes, shoving them to the back of the ledge next to the ones Stoirm and Tine had just removed. Brandel, Jerkin, and Owl reluctantly followed suit, Owl's gaze constantly darting from the cliff to the long drop.

"It will be fine," Caer assured him, nodding to where Stoirm waited, rope in hand. She prayed her voice was more reassuring than she felt. She disliked this climb in the best of times, though she forced herself to make it often enough. It was the most direct and the most protected way into Singer's Hold. "We will be lashed together. And…" "And?" Brandel prompted.

"Nothing. It will be fine."

Stoirm lined them up, securing a length of the rope to each of them. Caer protested when he placed her second. "The boys should be right behind you. They are inexperienced and…"

"And will need more assistance when we reach the top."

She might have persisted but knew Tine would be in full support of his father's decision. In the end, the lieutenant was secured behind her, followed by Owl, then Jerkin, and finally Tine.

"Each step is only deep enough to support from the toe to the arch of your boot," Stoirm warned. "Set your foot in it squarely and carry your weight forward over your toes. The hand holds are carved as handles you can wrap your fingers through. I will set the pace. We need to clear the top before we lose the last of the daylight. Stay focused on a solid placement of your feet and a solid grip of each handhold."

Caer followed Stoirm, setting her feet in the notched steps, grateful that, for her, at least, the depth was enough to hold most of her foot. The downside was that it required a little more motion to free each foot before moving up to the next step. It would be a grueling climb for all. Taking a firm grip of the first handhold, she closed her eyes. *"Ciuin Rose. Please,"* she sent. *"Provide what courage and strength you can, especially for the two boys."*

Whether Dana or Roisin would hear her…whether they would or could answer her plea, Caer had no way of knowing. But she could hope.

"Are you alright?" Stoirm shouted down to her.

"Sorry. Aye. I am coming."

Handhold after handhold, step after step, she climbed, sometimes feeling Stoirm's tug on the rope urging her on, other times feeling the tug of those behind as someone among them faltered or hesitated. Legs and arms cramped and ached, finger joints often locked from the strain. Yet, she managed, grateful beyond measure when Stoirm at last reached a hand to her and hauled her up over the lip of the cliff. Turning, she watched Stoirm pull the lieutenant up and extend his hand to Owl. That was when she heard the sing of the arrow; felt Owl's solid shove as he raised up and dove at her, knocking her backwards to the ground. His cry as he fell on top of her was muffled by the thickness of her coat. Behind him, Jerkin scrambled over the lip, Tine tight on his heels, grabbing the boy and yanking him to the ground as another arrow swished just above their heads.

"Back!" Stoirm yelled, pulling Owl from Caer and dragging him by the armpits. More arrows arched up over them, thunking into tree trunks or skimming through snow. "Away from the edge. Stay low."

A snarl alerted them to a new threat. Caer grabbed at Stoirm's hand before he could pull his knife from its sheath, her gaze fixed on a beast crouched in the lengthening shadows of a massive boulder. Tine, however, had his knife to hand, the motion of his throw nearly completed when Caer yelled for him to stop. Jerking his arm back, his throw went wide, sending the knife to glance off the rock. The beast snarled again, then whimpered, creeping from the shadows.

Spirit, her white stained with blood from a wound in her side, collapsed in front of Brandel. Her sending slashed her pain through Caer's mind. Brandel's sharp gasp told her he was likely the intended recipient. Kneeling next to the wolf, he examined the small, round wound. "What did this?"

Caer could not meet his outraged glare, saying only, "I will explain later. First, to safety." Glancing toward a cluster of stunted and twisted trees, she pointed. "There."

"Those offer no cover," Brandel growled.

Caer locked her arms around the wolf just below the animal's forelegs. Scooting backwards through the snow, she dragged the wolf with her until Brandel scooped Spirit into his arms. Crouching in his run, he followed Caer as she also kept low, darting for the area she had indicated. Behind them came Stoirm, carrying Owl, with Jerkin and Tine watching the rear. With everyone gathered, Caer whispered her invocation of the spell. "Amhranai Fearalite, hear me. Singer, know me and open the way that our party may enter."

The instant charge to the air and the sudden change in pressure and temperature left Caer's ears ringing and her head spinning. The solid slam of a hard, dry floor beneath her crumpled her to her knees, though it also told her the spell delivered them. Moments later, the circular chamber was ablaze with the light of fifty braziers equally spaced around its circumference. Though the air remained chill, the frigid bite of the world above made the space feel uncomfortably warm beneath her wraps. Dispensing with her coat, Caer shot to her feet, setting her head spinning again. It took another moment to steady herself and get her bearings. At the center of the chamber stood the fire pit, now cold and gray with ash. Her glance went to the three arches set in the wall that encircled the space, the markings etched above each telling which held stores of food, healers' supplies and blankets, which led to a latrine, and which to an underground stream.

Gesturing to Jerkin, she directed, "Come with me!" The boy hesitated, glancing anxiously at his friend.

"If you wish to help Owl and Spirit, then come! Journeyson, help Tine build up a fire in the pit. Stoirm, can you from here erase the signs of our presence beneath those trees?"

"Already done. I will help Tine. Let Lt. Journeyson stay with the wolf."

Torches ignited along the wall as Caer led the way through a short tunnel, taking a quick measure of the food stores in the first room. In the second, she took mere seconds to locate the necessary herbs, ointments, bandages, and other necessities, loading Jerkin's arms before her own. Upon their return to the chamber, she sent Jerkin to the tunnel leading to the stream. "There are buckets at the water's edge. Fill two of them and bring them."

By the time the boy returned, the pit burned with a low flame. It was one of Adrian's specialties, creating a magic that would allow a fire with minimal fuel. In this case, a shallow layer of well-dried wood. The supply, like the food and medicinals were frequently replenished by the guardian responsible for patrolling this area. The braziers that lined the chamber and the wall-mounted torches, on the other hand, burned with what seemed a perpetually renewed film of oil. Caer choked a silent prayer of thanks for her long-dead friend's magic. *"We are ever with you,"* whispered back, her tears running freely at the memory of the pure music of his voice.

Stoirm and Tine joined her as she tended, first to Owl, removing the broken arrow tip, bathing the wound in fresh water, working the spells of healing as she administered herbs, washed the wound again, and applied ointment and bandages. By the time she finished, the boy was feverish but sleeping.

When she turned to Spirit, her heart sank. It was difficult to tell the severity of such a wound, and it took several anguished minutes to remove the bullet before working the healing spells for any internal bleeding, then bathe and dress the wound.

Brandel snatched the small metal piece that Caer had dropped after removing it from Spirit's wound. Turning it over in his hand, he demanded, "What is this?"

"A projectile from a weapon. A bullet fired from a gun." He met her explanation with a blank stare. "A firearm," she said. "There are any number of types of them. And they can shoot varying sizes and types of bullets. Spirit is lucky. This one came from a small caliber gun."

"You are speaking gibberish, Lady Swan. I do not know the words you use."

"It is Caer, if you please," she sighed. "And I apologize. You would not understand. These weapons, like much of the technology from our original worlds, are part of what has long been forbidden, here. Firearms are weapons that use an explosive to propel projectiles at unimaginable speed over great distances."

Jerkin paled. "This is what the Red Moon Warriors used on that ice field against the wolves? And they have machines that can roll over the land and fly above it? How are we to fight against such things?"

Brandel dropped from his knees to his backside, stroking Spirit's head, his brow caverned. "If they have such weapons, why was that last group using bows and arrows when they fired upon us?"

Caer shrugged. "I can offer only a guess or two. Perhaps they do not have an ample supply of the guns or the ammunition. More likely, they feared using them below the cliff."

"Why?" Brandel pressed.

"The noise firearms are capable of making might trigger an avalanche. They attacked us from below a slope heavily laden with snow. If the sound echoed around and jarred loose the cornice, they would be buried. They likely used the guns against the wolves out of sheer instinct to protect themselves, without giving much thought in that moment to the potential for further disaster."

Exhausted, Caer, too, settled from her knees to her backside, shifting enough to study Owl, once more. "Spirit will mend well enough. But the boy… The arrow carried a toxin. I lack the herbs, here, to treat it properly. He needs to return to the sanctuary beneath the ruins. Juniper will know how to care for him." Raising her eyes to Jerkin, she said, "You should return with him."

Jerkin stared at his friend for a long moment, then shook his head. "He will be in good hands with Lady Juniper. I will stay with Master Journeyson…and with you, my lady. It is what Owl would do."

Caer managed a weary smile. "If that is your wish. Stoirm. Will the magic, here, permit you to use the fire to send the boy back?"

"If there is a Watcher at the temple who can match the pattern of the flames."

"If you deem it safe, see if you can find whom you need and let them receive Owl."

34

Owl shifted his position, slightly achy from fever, his nightmares still fresh in his mind, though the comfort of his bed and the smells of the evening meal wafting in from the kitchens helped to push them aside. What horrid sickness had taken him that should prompt such terrible dreams? Rolling to his right side, sharp pain shot from his shoulder down his arm and into his back, sparking a cry. The nightmares returned, clear and all-the-more frightening as he recognized their reality.

"Are you alright, my boy?"

Owl eased himself to his back, grimacing, Juniper suddenly hovering over him, anxiety creasing her face.

"I…fine. I just…" He cast a slow and confused glance around. "How did I get back here?"

"Lord Stoirm. He alerted a Fire Mage at Knife Point Keep, who teleported to the edge of the ruins and sent to us his need of our assistance. They brought you home through the flames. You gave me quite a scare, young man. The note that came attached to you stated that the arrow that struck you carried a toxin. Thankfully, they sent the arrow tip with you, else I may not have been able to identify it and apply the antidote in time. You are quite lucky to be alive."

"I do not feel very lucky," he moaned. "Where is Jerkin?"

Juniper hesitated. "He… remained with the Lady Swan and Lt. Journeyson."

Owl started to sit, was hit with a spinning room, and dropped back, muttering, "Then I need to go back to them."

"You need do no such thing. What you need is to stay put and recover. I dare say, the others are no longer where you last saw them, anyway. The Fire Mage said they are on the move, though he failed to mention their destination. Likely, he does not know."

"I know where they are going."

"Then keep it to yourself, Owl. Let no one else know. You can serve them best by remaining here, healing, and keeping your silence."

Owl closed his eyes. This was not right. He pledged his service to Master Journeyson. Needed to help the Lady Swan...Grandmother... Caer...whomever she truly was. Jerkin was with them. Jerkin could not do everything on his own. Sensing that Juniper was about to leave, he reached for her arm, "The Lady Shadow. I would like to speak with her if she will come."

Juniper's mouth pinched and she looked away. "Lady Shadow. She..." Juniper swallowed. "She is not here. She has been missing for several days."

Owl popped up, setting the room to spinning once more. Gritting his teeth against the dizziness and the pain, he choked, "She has gone to find Whisper."

Juniper's brow creased, the tension in her voice matching that of the air. "Aye. Do not let me lose you, too, Owl. Stay. Rest. Heal. I have need of you, here."

Slumping back on the bed, Owl drew the covers over his head, his breathing labored against the pain in his shoulder, arm, and back. Once the throbbing subsided, he pushed the covers off his face, grumbling, "Think! Think! What can I do? Where would Shadow go? Where would that traitor Hawk be taking Whisper? The harder he tried to think, the more he ached, until, at last, he wailed, "Useless! I am utterly useless!", the exhaustion of his hopelessness sinking him in sleep once more.

His second waking brought him less pain. It also brought him breakfast. He no more than stirred when one of the young girls from the kitchen appeared. Phoenix! The girl's smile was timid, her eyes averted as she set her tray on the table near the bed. "Lady Juniper says you like eggs and potatoes and plenty of toast with butter."

Owl sat up, wincing at the brief slash of pain. His eyeing of the laden tray accompanied, "I do!"

"Good. Then eat. And rest again. I will come for the tray when you have finished."

"Can you stay? I should like some company."

Phoenix darted a glance toward the door. "A few minutes, perhaps. My chores are caught up in the kitchen, and I am not due to report to the dining hall for classes until this afternoon."

Phoenix pushed the small table nearer the bed, Owl setting to the food with a hunger that suggested he had not eaten in a good, long while. Noting Phoenix' nervous smoothing of her apron, he gestured to a chair that stood between his bed and the one Jerkin generally occupied. "Please. Sit. Talk with me."

Phoenix obliged, sitting forward as if she might take flight at any moment. "About what?"

Owl paused, his fork halfway to his mouth. "The dining hall."

Phoenix giggled. "That is an odd topic."

"No. I mean…" For the first time, Owl realized his bedroom held more than just his and Jerkin's beds. At least five more were crammed into the space. "Why are you reporting to the dining hall for classes, and…." He gestured at the room in general. "And why are there so many beds in here?"

Phoenix dropped her gaze again, her face paling beyond her fair complexion. "The beasts." A streak of tears glistened on her cheeks.

"What beasts?"

"The ones that bring death. They came."

Owl's heart sank to the hollow left in his gut. "Here? In the sanctuary?"

Phoenix gave a small shake of her head. "In the ruins. Close enough, though. Whatever evil dwells in their magic penetrated the outer halls. Had we not received warning…" The girl managed a shuddered breath before continuing. "Lady Juniper gathered us, sealed us in the dining hall with her spells. How long we waited, sitting in silence… in the darkness…" She drew another long, ragged breath. "It seemed an eternity. Even there, deep within the rock, with Lady Juniper's spells protecting us, we could sense their presence; knew they were extending their dark powers outward; seeking to kill anything that fell within their range."

"But you survived."

The girl's hesitation preceded a tremulous, "Most of us. My sister… Oceana…she and two others hid in the classrooms, too afraid to move for fear their motion would be sensed. The classrooms are too close to the exterior. Too close to the plateau where we keep… kept our gardens and livestock. They lacked Lady Juniper's spells, though she tried to expand them. When the beasts had gone, when we sensed their darkness no longer, we found Oceana and the other two girls. Withered. Gray. Crumbling to dust. Just like all that lay on the open plateau. Since that time, we have kept to the dining hall, the common room, the kitchens, and this room. We fear the creatures may return. Or…or more may come."

Owl sucked in. "And the Ladies Whisper and Shadow?" The girl shrugged, misery etched in her eyes.

Swinging his legs over the edge of the bed, Owl steadied himself to stand. Phoenix was on her feet and at his side, forcing him back. "Stop! You will undo the good Lady Juniper has done before your wound heals."

"I can heal it myself," Owl rumbled. "You will need food, here. I can hunt."

"We have food. Knife Point Keep sent a supply as soon as they learned of our crisis. The Fire Mage who brought you said he would arrange for more to be sent in a few days."

"The Fire Mage," Owl repeated. "Who from Knife Point would have such a gift?"

"An old man. The one they call Chamberlain Fairchild."

"The chamberlain?"

"It is said he is a descendent of the Singer who once loved the Goddess Ciuin Rose and later loved the warrior Emer." Phoenix scooted the table closer to Owl. "We have had enough talk, now. Lady Juniper will not be pleased if I allow you to neglect your breakfast. Eat. Please. Someone will return to check on you later."

"You."

"What?"

"You return. If it pleases you," Owl added sheepishly. "I would talk with you more. Until then..." He took a deep breath, letting it out slowly. "Until then, I just want to say that I am sorry. Sorry for all you have been through. Sorry for the loss of your sister."

Phoenix blinked at him, then turned and left, her footfalls becoming a run as soon as she was out of the room.

Owl stared after her for several seconds before settling his attention on the last of his breakfast - now cold. His fault. Lady Jumpier and Phoenix were correct, though. He needed to eat. Needed to regain his strength. He also needed an ally if he was to leave, again. And leave, he must. Whether to go in search of Lt. Journeyson and Lady Swan, or to go in search of Lady Whisper or Lady Shadow, sadly, he could not decide."

35

Whisper blinked into the early morning light, grateful for the glow of a sunrise and the subtle warmth that penetrated the shadows of the few remaining leaves on the boughs that supported her. Easing herself from branches that served as a bed for the night, she climbed higher to assess the lay of the land. Below, she could hear the rushing water of the Singer River. From the top of the forest canopy, she picked out the nearest mountain peaks. Grave's Peak to the northwest was just discernable beneath the cloud cover. The twin peaks that stood above Gray's way station, as well as Knife Point Keep were both impossible to see. Hawk's company covered a lot of ground in a very short time, making it almost to the border with Brightwater. But then, he had horses, at least for a fair portion of the journey. Probably employed a teleportation or two, as well. What disturbed her most was the fact that the Soldiers of Damsa Dana crossed the border to join Hawk and his men. Crossed the border to remove her from Knife Point against her will. Well, they failed. She was still in Knife Point.

She shot a dismal glance at her surroundings, unable to discern through the density of the woods the precise location from which she had escaped. Still, her senses told her that her home lay somewhere to the northwest, the temple ruins further northwest, still. With no horse, she would have to rely on her own feet until she recovered enough to attempt a teleportation. Once she was close enough to trust her shielding to hold, she cold telepath a warning to Shadow. Then she would make for Knife Point Fortress.

A shudder wracked her. She could not travel that distance without supplies. And even supposing she completed the long trek without incident, what would she find? Hawk claimed Knife Point Fortress and Keep were under attack when they left. Maybe that was the lie she detected when he came to her, that night. Or maybe the guardians beat the enemy back. Or… Her insides knotted at the possibility that the enemy may have taken the keep. Whatever the case,

Grandmother was no longer there. And it was she who must be warned about the treachery of some among the Guardians of Ciuin Rose and their ties to the White Moon Goddess. *"Where have you gone, Grandmother? Can you open your mind to me? Please open your mind to me!"*

The faint suggestion of laughter fluttered in the fringes of her mind. Sucking in, Whisper gripped the branch, slamming shut her outreach and doubling her shielding. The malicious tone was not Grandmother's. Had her initial shielding been so weak that her sending was detected by someone else? A scan of the area found the woods empty, the only sound that of her rumbling stomach. A heated wave of dizziness and shakes rolled over her. Her desperate need to eat was making her delirious as well as shaky. And she had not so much as a crumb in her pack. Their sudden evacuation from the keep gave her no time to collect anything in the way of food. She had relied on Hawk and his men for that.

Working her way down, she made another quick scan, then dropped the last two meters to the slushy forest floor to scavenge for berries, mushrooms, lichen, and rosehips. The berries were dry, the rest either tasteless or bitter. A couple of scoops of slush washed down the fare. Above her, a stiff breeze snapped a branch. Another gust hinted at the rising humidity and carried the scent of ozone. A storm brewed. *"Now? Ciuin Rose, why now?"* Darting a nervous glance up at the increasing sway of boughs, Whisper climbed again. Better to stay above the ground, making her way among the sturdiest branches, than to have the weaker ones dropping on her head.

She balanced precariously as she made her through the trees. Compounding the difficulty of navigating the swaying and creaking boughs was her near constant survey of the ground below. She doubted she would stumble across Hawk and company. They were well ahead of her. It was the possibility of encountering a company of Red Moon Warriors that she feared. By nightfall, exhausted and shaking, Whisper located a massive cedar and snuggled into the branching of two stout limbs. The persistent wind, the constant rock of her perch, and the moans and cracks of wood all around did little to encourage sleep, yet it won out, in the end.

She snapped awake as voices rose from below. Arguing. A glimpse of the Red Moon insignia on the back of a warrior's cloak raised her flesh and froze her in place. Another warrior stood nose-to-nose with the first, the second man's face crimson with his outrage, though the subject of their disagreement was indiscernible, their words tangled in the wind and muffled by her hood.

The arguing hushed when two more warriors appeared, dragging a man between them. Whisper clapped her hands over her mouth, stifling her threatened gasp. Tattered and beaten, Hawk turned his face up to his captors. For a moment, they appeared unfocused. One of his captors grasped his hair, jerking his head further back. Hawk's eyes cleared, shock registering.

"My lady! You should not be here! I am sorry! I never meant to lead you into harm. Withdraw! Hide!"

Stunned that he spotted her so easily and angry at her carelessness, Whisper scrambled higher, edging away from the scene, seeking cover seven trees further removed while re-establishing a spell of concealment. Protecting her sending with an additional layer of shielding, she sought for the lieutenant's mind. *"Where are the others?"*

For several long seconds Hawk made no reply. When it came, anguish wrapped it. *"Dead. We were betrayed. The Red Moon Warriors knew that Danu waited for us to bring you to her. They set an ambush. Slaughtered everyone save me. They will torture me to learn where you are. Leave. Now! Go as far and as fast as you can. Give me no glimpse of your direct..."* Hawk's scream rose above the winds, excruciating heat scorching Whisper's mind. Her hands tightened on the branches as she struggled to hold to her perch.

The connection vanished with Hawk's unconsciousness. Unconsciousness. Whatever wrong Hawk did, he never harmed her. There was always truth in his words when he claimed his desire was to protect her. He did not deserve torture and death at the hands of the Red Moon. She had to help him but could not afford to let the warriors find her. Capturing her would provide everything Aifa desired.

Fighting to keep her trembling in check, she climbed from tree to tree, moving further from the scene, traveling in a broken pattern through the boughs, her mind grasping at the beginning of an idea. A risky idea, to be sure. She needed a safe place to hide, though. And the nearest possibility was.... Closing her eyes, she pictured the giant oak that stood at the edge of the sacred grove near their home. From its top, the clearing in the wild woods where their house stood would be visible. *"Ciuin Rose, protect me. Let no Red Moon Warrior mar your sacred grove with their presence."* Holding the image of her favorite oak in her mind, she teleported.

The branch snapped, sending Whisper in a heart stopping drop to another one a few meters below. Ash and smoke rose thick in her nostrils. Heat scorched her hands as she grasped a thick bough. Yelping, she teleported herself straight to the ground, surrounded by the silhouettes of blackened and scorched trees, many broken and laying in ash and dust. Others smoldered from within. Next to her, the branch on which she emerged lay in pieces in the debris. Embers still glowed from inside the trunk of her chosen oak. Heat also rose through the soles of her boots. Struggling through smoldering fumes and thick ash, choked with her tears, Whisper stumbled through the remains of her beloved grove, at last making her way to the wild woods that stretched between the oaks and the cottage.

The wild woods, too, lay in ruin, though their burning appeared to be older. Here, where the ash was cold, a greater horror greeted her. A trail of animals, withered and crumbling, spoke of the death creatures' passage. Their desecration cut through the woods from somewhere south of the grove, disappearing in the darkness as it wound north. The sight of so much death rushed a new flood of tears. Hiccupping a breath, she trudged on toward her house, shaken with grief.

Even before she emerged from the burned woods, her tear blurred vision caught the rest of the destruction. The cottage, the stable and gardens - all blackened and trampled. Somewhere in her head, she knew it would be so. Confirmation sickened her to her core. For a long while, Whisper wandered aimlessly among the tumbled stone and burned timbers. What power could be so great as to break the magic of the ancient oak grove; what hatred so strong as to leave so much death and destruction in its wake?

The weight of her grief and hopelessness dropped Whisper to her knees next to the pile of debris that had once been the entrance to their home. Nothing remained to provide a place for her to hide. Nothing remained to provision her.

"*Dig!*"

Though faint, the urgent command echoed in Whisper's head. Tears still stinging her eyes, and without any understanding of why she complied, she waded into the debris and started digging, tossing aside broken timbers, chunks of wall, and the remainder of their kitchen's furnishings. Weary, her body aching, trembling with misery and hunger, and her mind at war with itself over the insanity of her efforts and the compelling urge to continue, she reached the cliff face that had served as the back wall of their cottage, a blacker patch in the darkness indicating an opening. The entrance to their hallway. The cottage was destroyed, but the warriors could not bring down the solid rock from which the back of their home was carved. She tried to dig more, to widen the way, but the beams were too heavy, and she dared not waste her magic. Every dram of energy would be required to find and save Hawk and to send warning to Shadow.

Removing her pack and her coat, she tossed them through, then slid into the blackness, dropping to the floor with a muffled splat.

A foul itch raised her flesh. Magic. But not the magic that once protected their home. Faint traces of the ancient spells flitted in tatters across her nerves, chased by her shock at the realization that the music within the walls had gone silent. Rooted in ankle deep water, Whisper waited for her shadow sight to break through the darkness. When she at last spotted them, she pulled on her wet coat and lifted her dripping pack from the floor to retrieve a candle from one of its exterior pockets. A faint spark from her trembling fingers lit it.

With her pack draped over one shoulder, she continued down the corridor, her despair growing with each room she peered into. All lay in ruins. Nothing of the furniture remained whole. Bits of shredded clothing were strewn everywhere. Broken pieces of stone and pipes littered the bathroom, water spouting from a ragged-edged pipe. The amount of power required to do...all of this... was beyond anything Whisper could imagine. The ability to break the ancient spells and the hatred that drove so much desecration!

No spell can last forever. Serenity said that often. Still, Whisper never conceived of the possibility that the magic of the grove could be broken. Believed whatever force lay behind it...believed that Singer's magic, too, would prove her aunt wrong; that such spells would stand for eternity. The grove, after all, was ancient beyond all reconning. And this... This was the home Singer constructed for his warrior bride, Emer, and their children and their children's children. It is how the home came into the hands of Serenity, who descended from his line. His spells were intended to protect them all. He even went so far as... so far as...

Whisper sucked in. The secret room. At the end of the hall. Both Whisper and Shadow believed it a myth, though Serenity spoke of it as reality. She even taught them the song to open it, warning that it would only respond in the direst of circumstances. Whisper and Shadow, of course, tried the song on multiple occasions, to no avail.

Whisper's sudden giddiness almost made her laugh. Their circumstances as children were never dire, despite their belief to the contrary. Punishment for bad behavior did not qualify. But this... Breath held, Whisper waded down the hall, her senses tuned to even the slightest hint of the ancient enchantments. There was only the vile magic that continued to raise her flesh. Each step added to the weight of her despair, until... Only two paces from the back wall, a faint tingle trickled along her nerves carrying that wonderful, familiar thrum of sevens and threes. The Singer's magic remained. Subtle. Faint. She feared it might be too seriously weakened by the Witch who broke the other spells to respond to the song of opening. Yet, a step closer, her sense of the magic strengthened. Testing, she stepped back a pace. It weakened. Another pace back and it was once again lost in the foul magic. She closed the distance to the wall, again, and braced a hand against it. Eyes closed, she opened her mouth to sing.

The words evaded her. Her mind chased through spell after spell. Shaking with frustration, she cried out, "Ciuin Rose, if this is not a most dire circumstance, I cannot imagine what would be. It is not my dire need, but Hawk's. If he yet lives, I must help him. But I must hide so that I may do so. If a room lies behind this wall, it may be Hawk's salvation."

Closing her eyes again, she pried through her memories, seeking the song. And it came. Whisper's murmur lacked the depth of Shadow's, or even Serenity's magnificently musical voices. Yet she sang, "In darkness am I, my world upturned. Desperate, I cry, my need to be heard. I trust the Rose to know my word."

No opening appeared. Whisper crumpled to the wet floor, sobbing. She had it right, did she not? Those were the words. Still, she ran them back through her mind, struggling to discern where she may have gone wrong. Those were the words, but…but the melody and rhythm were wrong! If not the familiar cadence of sevens and threes that had come to mind, then what? For aching minutes, she struggled to remember. But the melody and rhythm remained hidden. Despair deepened, her tears trailing a rivulet down her face. The stories had to be true. She needed that secret room. Time was running out for Hawk. It might already be too late.

"I need the song! Sweet Ciuin Rose, what is the music?" As she rocked and cried, a bittersweet sound drifted in the dark recesses of her mind. A haunting lamentation. A memory jarred, rising with terrifying clarity and crushing her anew with grief. Her mother's eyes when the baby she held close started to cry. She cast a spell, hushing the baby. A song of sorrow lifted on her father's voice, filling her mind. His song blinked to silence and her mother's face vanished, replaced by cold, dark emptiness.

This. This was the place her mother sent her. To this hidden space. She remembered the damp smells; remembered the comforting sense of its magic - the Singer's magic. This is where Tine found her and delivered her into Serenity's arms.

Whisper shoved to her knees, pressing her hand to the wall once more, calling forth her father's song of sorrow. Soft and low, the lament carried the rise and fall, as of keening on a dying breeze. Holding to it, she repeated, "In darkness am I, my world upturned. Desperate, I cry, my need to be heard. I trust the Rose to know my word." New words joined in her mind, and she sang them. "For the circle turns, dance all the way, though once returned we cannot stay. Ever round and begin again, moving on, there is no end. The circle turns while the drum does sound and dancing feet do tread the ground." The song had to work. Was she not niece to Serenity and cousin to Shadow? Did she not sense Singer's magic? She was of his line, distant as that connection might be. His magic would respond. She sang, again.

The creak was subtle. Whisper dared not stop; sang, again. The creak repeated, the opening revealing itself as a patch of black set against the darkness of the wall. Though it widened, it was barely enough for Whisper to pass through. She extended a hand, first, frigid air stinging her fingers. Rising, she turned sideways to squeeze through, dragging her pack after her and disappearing into the void. Behind her, the creak sounded once more, this time sealing the way closed. Only then did a faint light ignite – a glimmer on the opposing wall. Pushing to her feet, Whisper made her way to the lamp set in a niche, the light slowly growing as she moved toward it. With the light, warmth crept into the space.

Jagged edges of jutting rock and hollowed out sections of the walls left Whisper gaping. Within the hollows were carved shelves, some containing empty jars and baskets and bowls. A quiet spring trickled through, seeping from beneath the wall on one side and cutting its way beneath the back wall. As her turn carried her gaze around, her feet tangled in something on the floor. A startled glance down found a bundle of faded blankets, a tiny object glistening from their folds. Kneeling, she recognized it as a baby's ring. Her breath caught. Her ring. It still carried the dual signatures of her mother's magic and the magic inherent within her.

Whisper's knees gave out, dumping her onto the floor, the ring clutched in her hand, another memory struggling to the fore. Her mother did not place this ring on her tiny finger. She wrapped it in the blanket with her baby, just before teleporting her away. Wrapped it, saying, "From our ancestors this has been passed down, spelled with hope. You must survive, my child, and carry that hope forward."

Whisper clutched the ring tighter. Hope had come through with her. She survived the horrendous murder of her parents. She survived the lonely darkness of this place until she was found. She survived the destruction of her home and her separation from the only family she has left. She survived being kidnapped, and her poorly planned escape.

If she could survive all of that, she would survive what she must do to help Hawk and would still get warning to Shadow in time.

Situating her pack against the wall and snugging into her coat, she and laid down. Eyes closed, Whisper focused, stretching her mind out in search of the nearest creatures. She needed one that could help her locate Hawk, praying that he was not far from where she last saw him.

"Please, Ciuin Rose, hear my plea. Let me find him, again. Let me save him!"

Her prayer stretched out on the strands of her search until she found what she sought. The release came as a ragged and unnerving rending, her soul lifting upwards. It hovered for a moment, the vision of her body lying below. Then came the sharp snap as she settled in and became one with the creature she chose.

36

"N o!" Shadow sucked in, biting down on her lip, her frantic grasp of a branch preventing her stunned fall from the tree. Breath held, she shot anxious glances around, fearing her yelp may have drawn unwanted attention. There was no one. Shaking, she braced herself in a substantial crook of the burned-out maple, turning her attention to the sensation that had alarmed her so.

"You did not do this!" she growled. "Whisper! Reach out to me. Tell me it is not true!" The vision flashed again - the ground passing far beneath her, the wind currents lifting her.

"By all that is holy, why would you do this? Slipping your soul from your body almost killed you, before. You swore you would never do it, again!" Shadow willed her mind to stretch further, expending extra energy to shield it from any intrusion but that of her cousin. *"Return! Go back to your body! Or at least let me know where it hides so that I can protect it!"* But the vision was gone.

Hot tears filled her eyes as Shadow sat hunched in the branches, her blurred gaze darting in every direction. Where would Whisper go to hide? Why would she set her soul free to join some... some bird? Was her body injured? Was this her only means of escape from the traitorous Hawk? Was it her only means of seeking help?

"I will come! Just tell me where! Please!"

Whisper remained silent. Frightened, angry, and dismayed, Shadow sagged between the branches, her head falling back against the one supporting her back. "How can I help you if I cannot find you?" she demanded of the air. "Do not dare die on me, Whisper! Do you understand? If you die...if you die...I will..will murder you!" A humorless huff at the insanity of her own statement escaped her.

The cold of night added to her trembling, and hunger gnawed beyond her stomach to her backbone. She attempted to ignore both. The farmstead stood as a dark silhouette a third of a kilometer from where she sat astride the maple's blackened boughs. The orchard, fields, and the buildings lay in ashen ruins, faint embers still glistening from parts of the house and barn. The smell of death came on a gust of wind. She would find no help, no food, here. The items she filched when she left the sanctuary could not be stretched to cover more than another day. She would be no help if she died of hunger or froze to death before she could find her cousin. What an idiot to leave without thinking through a real plan and acquiring more rations.

"So, what are you going to do?" Shadow growled. "Just sit here?"

Slipping to lower branches, she dropped to the fresh layer of crusty snow. Her fingers required flexing to work out their stiffness before she could pull her knife from its sheath. With a murmured, "Ciuin Rose, assist me in my hunt," she set out, her footfalls laid with great care and silence.

Across the burned fields and orchard, she crept, staying low, her shadow sight studying every twitch of dried grass, every shift of gray upon gray as she moved. There, beneath a twist of crushed and blackened wheat stocks, she spotted the rabbit; was on it before it registered her approach. Her blade struck quick and clean, giving the animal no moment for pain. Satisfied, she continued her creep toward the barn. Here, where the smoke would mix with that of the smoldering wood, a small blaze to cook her prize might go unnoticed.

With her senses tuned to any hint of others in the area, Shadow searched out a small clearing next to one of the areas where embers still burned. Broken and splintered wood provided the makings for a spit. As she worked to clean the rabbit she sang quietly. "I know not what little family I have robbed of their kin with this deed. I ask their forgiveness for my need. I ask your forgiveness for depriving you of your life for the sake that I may feed." The cadence shifted as she moved to the ending, the lack of rhyme underscoring the words. "May you nourish my mind and soul as you nourish my body. May I take to myself your cunning and speed and skills of quiet, allowing me to honor you by using them for good. May your soul slumber in peace."

Her meal finished and the signs of her small cooking fire extinguished and scattered, Shadow sought shelter, locating a shattered window on the far side of the barn. The window frame was partially driven into the earth by the collapse of the loft. Behind it, the broken walls formed a triangular space in a section that no longer smoldered. Breaking out the remaining shards of glass and brushing away as much as possible, Shadow removed her pack and tossed it inside, crawling through after it. Curled within her coat, she drifted to sleep, praying that slumber would unite her mind with Whisper's and show her where she must go. But her dreams held only images of home.

She awoke with a revelation. That was it! Home! If Whisper escaped, she would try to make her way home. Where better to hide. Uncurling, she sent, *"Please, Whisper! Talk to me!"* Still no response. With a quick scan outside, Shadow crawled from her shelter. Though she sensed no threat, she dashed back through the orchard and fields to the edge of the woods. The remains of trees were too widely spaced to allow her to travel through their canopy, so she raced within their thinning ground shadows, constantly repeating, *"Please! Return to your body! Let me find you! Let me take you back to the temple sanctuary!"*

Wherever the woods were sufficiently dense, Shadow took to the trees. Where they gave way to clearings or burns, she ran. Twice, over the next two days, she was forced to seek cover in thickets as troops of Red Moon Warriors passed, urgency growing within her as she noted their numbers. The third day took her along a creek she hoped to use to reach the next tree line. The sides of the creek bank, however, proved too steep for her to climb, forcing her back into the water and down to another stretch of blackberries. Every moment weighed on her. Her heart told her Whisper's body lay in hiding at home, her cousin's soul not yet returned to it. The body required nourishment. If Whisper's body died...

Shadow dismissed the thought, forcing her focus back to the blackberry vines. So intense was her drive to clear them to reach the nearest trees that she almost missed the sense of others approaching. The distant roar brought her to an abrupt halt in the middle of the thicket. Dropping down, breath held, she listened. The roar continued, getting closer. Within minutes, the machine, much like the one she saw before, lumbered overhead, moving south and west. Following behind it marched yet another a large contingent of warriors.

Raising up, Shadow peered above the snarl of vines to observe their passage as they trampled a muddy swath paralleling the creek less than ten meters from where she crouched. When a warrior turned an uneasy scan her way, she ducked from sight once more. She had no idea how long she squatted there, wrapped in her shadows, breathing in shallow spurts before the splashing of the last to cross the creek died away. Even when the ground shaking and noise of their passing ceased, she remained, grateful for the instinct that kept her there. Minutes after the troops had gone, mounted riders - at least six of them - galloped by, charging into the creek and up the other side, racing in the direction of the marchers. And still, Shadow hunched within the blackberries, fearing to creep out until the last of the thin daylight vanished, deriding herself for her fear of teleporting. Yet, with so many warriors, she dared not risk emerging within one of their camps and being captured.

At last, in darkness, she picked her way through the remainder of the thicket to the trees, then turned south, relieved when the terrain once again fed into the more densely forested slopes. The deciduous trees no longer held their leaves, providing less cover for her. Still, it was safer to make her way from tree to tree than to travel along the ground. Working with the wisps of mist and the deepening grays, keeping the magic of her shielding tightly confined around her, Shadow continued through the night, her senses alert for any indication of more of the enemy. More than once, she reconsidered teleporting to the edge of the woods near their home. Each time, her lack of knowledge of where the enemy might be camped prevented it.

Weariness forced her to stop as morning light fought its way through the night's fog. At least the evergreens were more prevalent, here. Climbing the tallest, she settled against the trunk, running one hand across the needles to shed water onto her other palm. It was a bitter draught, sharp with the taste of the fir. Wrinkling her nose, she repeated the measure with another clump of needles. Did so, again, until her thirst quieted. She needed to rest. Would take just a few minutes.

Dawn had progressed to mid-morning when another image jolted her – that of a huge eagle dropping from the sky. Frozen in terror, Shadow gripped the branches, her mind reeling. Had some hunter taken down the great bird bearing Whisper's soul? No more delays! No matter the risk, she had to teleport.

Exhausted, Shadow found it difficult to focus. The tree she wished to draw to mind remained a haze. Only one thing stood clear in her mind. The bedroom she shared with Whisper. May it be uninhabited by the enemy!

Pain stabbed her right calf. Her hands clapped over her mouth to stifle her cry. When her shadow sight finally settled, the ruin that lay around her sucked her breath away. Instead of teleporting into the open space of her bedroom, she landed atop the mangle of broken furniture, a jagged piece of wood from her bedframe slicing into her leg.

"Idiot!" she hissed, lifting her leg away from the splintered wood. "You knew the house would be in ruins!"

A reach for her pack found it missing from her shoulders, prompting another hiss of, "Idiot! What did you do with it?" She did not recall the last time she laid it aside, much less the last time she retrieved it. Jerking her mittens off, she braced a hand against the wound, scanning the area for anything she might use to bind it. Her hobble made it difficult to navigate the debris. Several painful seconds later, she reached the remains of one of the mattresses, tearing free a strip of sheet to tie around her leg. Her muttered beginning of a healing spell fell short at the sounds of horses outside. Swearing under her breath, Shadow limped to the broken bedroom door, leaning into the shambles of the hallway to listen.

"Must be here, somewhere. The lost pack and the tatters from a coat indicated the owner headed this way."

"Maybe," snorted another voice. "Or maybe the individual fell into the river and drown."

"And maybe you will end up on the end of my sword," rumbled the first. "Dismount. Everyone search the area."

Panic overwhelmed the pain. Shadow dared not let them find her. Biting her lip at the effort of moving, she hobbled into the hall, working her way to the back, avoiding as much of the debris as possible. If Serenity's stories were true…if the old spells still worked… if she remembered the incantation… In truth, she had no idea what might be revealed, assuming the right words came to her. At least the haunting melody lifted effortlessly to mind. But would she find a secret room, or would the magic draw the enemy straight to her?

Her heart raged against her ribs as she noted the lack of Singer's ancient spells within the ruins. Relief was near overwhelming when she detected its faint thrum a mere pace from the hall's end. Setting her hand to the wall, she was further relieved to find the the words coming easily, the lamentation of the song lifting in a murmur from her lips. "In darkness am I, my world upturned. Desperate, I cry my need to be heard. I trust the Rose to know my word. The circle turns, dance all the way, though once returned we cannot stay. Ever round and begin again, moving on, there is no end. The circle turns while the drum does sound and dancing feet to tread the ground."

Subtle as the creak was, the sound echoed in Shadow's mind like a thunder burst. *Please, Ciuin Rose! Let them not hear!* Hesitating only long enough to glance back down the still empty hall, she slipped through the narrow opening, the way sealing itself behind her. Tears of pain and fear streamed her face. If Whisper came home, where was she? Buried in one of the other rooms? Would the Warriors find her body? Shaking, she backed toward the wall, swiping at the tears as her shadow sight adjusted to the dim glow that lit the space. Shadow's heel snagged, tripping her, her fall softened by…

The sound of people on the other side of the wall instantly silenced her startled gasp. Her heart, however, thundered all the louder in her ears as she stared down at Whisper. Or, at least at Whisper's body. Her cousin's breathing was so shallow, the pulse so weak… Still, the body lived. Exhausted, relieved, still hurting, and angry that her cousin's soul remained missing, Shadow sank down beside the body and cried.

37

Their brief respite at Singer's Hold was both torment and relief. With Owl returned to the temple sanctuary, Caer focused her healing on Spirit. Mending a wild creature was not like mending a human. Caer had no knowledge of which spells might work best for a wolf. Still, Spirit improved. The effort, however, was a drain on Caer. Stoirm at last put a stop to her ministrations, insisting she see to her own needs and sleep.

Sleep proved futile. The sisters vied for her attention, their voices, though distant, retained their vehemence. Breag Nemhain often overpowered Dana and Roisin, taunting Caer, hinting that she would soon have in her possession those that Caer loved most. Dana and Roisin fought to the fore, blocking Nemhain as they urged Caer to remember the beginning, but argued about the path Caer must take. Dana shouted for her to return to the Healer's complex and from there to work her way to the mountain slope that the gateway blasted them onto all those centuries ago. Roisin insisted Caer follow through with her plans to seek the aid of the Alainn. Singer's Hold lay much closer to the border with the Sunrise outpost lands than to the Healer's complex. And, of the two, Roisin's was the voice Caer most trusted. Agreement from Stoirm and Tine came without argument, as Caer expected it would.

The voices of the sisters silenced once the company left the hold, though Nemhain's mocking laughter sometimes filtered through. It was a distraction Caer could ill afford, the terrain between the hold and the border being the most rugged the mountains had to offer. Glacier fields and crevasses abounded, the crack and roar of avalanches a frequent menace. Time after time, they trudged across the ice fields, climbed to various passes, descended, climbed again, sheltering in caves to rest or to seek relief from a whiteout. The fourth night out, Caer groaned from the strain. Every part of her ached from the combination of frigid temperatures and exertion. She fought to stay awake. But for what? Freezing to death would be a blessing. She begged Roisin to release her, to allow death to find her. She had done so since the battle that took Dylan from her an age ago. But Roisin and Dana kept her alive. Now, Roisin insisted she go to the Alainn. To what end? What if they refused to speak with her? What if they chose to remain separate from the Goddess Wars?

Caer stifled her humorless chuckle. Goddess Wars. A title given the ancient battle by those who believed in the mythologies that evolved through the centuries. She long ago gave up her attempts to enlighten the masses. They would believe what they would believe. Her eyes closed in weary dismay of their foolishness.

"Caer!"

She stumbled, teetered, her eyes flicking open. Tine's arms were around her, steadying her, his anxious gaze on the crevasse millimeters from Caer's feet.

"She cannot go on like this," he called to his father.

Stoirm nodded. "We cannot stop here, though. We continue until we find suitable shelter." He finally called a halt when he discovered a cave with a steam vent.

Unpleasant as the venting gas was, the warmth was welcome. Spirit discovered a series of marmot dens not far from its mouth and ate her fill. Tine located and excavated another den. It seemed a sin to slaughter the poor animals as they hibernated. Still, Caer silently expressed her gratitude to the small creatures whose deaths would now contribute to their lives.

The sulfur in the vent's fumes raised a throbbing headache. Guilt gnawed at her as she dug in her pack for her blanket, wrapped it over her coat, and staggered to a section of wall as far removed from the steam opening as possible. She should assist Jerkin in preparing the meal. But the pain in her head and her soul forced her retreat.

Jerkin muttered his thanks to the animals as he worked, prompting Caer to repeat her gratitude as she lay beneath her wraps. Her lips pinched as she tried to remember when she first started the practice of thanking animals for their nourishment. Sometime after her arrival on Slievgall'ion, she supposed. She had no memory of doing so as a child. But then, as a child, if her memories held true, she and her aunt grew most of their food in their small garden. What they did not grow came to the colony in shipments from other colonies. Caer exhaled a long and dismal sigh. Such a long time ago! Such memories seemed a dream from someone else's life.

Jerkin's continued preparations drew her attention back to him. He deserved at least as much gratitude as the animals he prepared. It was by his hand that the fire was laid and the marmots cleaned. And now he cooked them. She had been skeptical of the boy's ability to survive this journey; remained skeptical. She should never have agreed to their coming; regretted her decision most with respect to Owl. The boy saved her life, but at grave risk to his. She prayed he was mending, and that Jerkin would not meet a similar fate – or worse.

"Is there something wrong, m'lady?"

The boy's puzzled expression and question prompted a blush as she realized she had rolled to her side and lay staring at him. "Only that you do not deserve such a fate as has led you here. You deserve a comfortable life, safe at the sanctuary or within the keep, or wherever else you may choose to go."

"None of us deserve to be here, m'lady. We did not start the bloody war. We did not ask to be caught up in it. But someone must fight to protect everyone. If we can find a way to stop the killing, is that not worth our efforts? That is what we are doing, is it not? Looking for a way to end the bloodshed?"

Caer breathed a weary sigh, nodding.

"Then I do not wish to be anywhere else. Now…" Pouring water from his leather water skin into a cup, he handed it across to her. Drink."

"I have my own water skin."

"I saw you empty it not an hour ago. I have refilled it, but the snow is not yet melted. So. Drink."

"On one condition."

Jerkin cocked a brow. "And what would that be, m'lady?"

"That you stop addressing me as royalty. I am no different from you."

"But you are the Lady of Knife Point."

"As are all ladies of our realm. As you are a young man of Knife Point. We both work to serve those who suffer under the encroaching dark magic of Breag Nemhain."

"But…"

Caer sat up, folding her arms and fixing him with a stern scrutiny. "No more m'lady or I will not drink another drop of water."

Jerkin blinked at her several times, his mouth working to form another protest, though he seemed unable to find appropriate words. "Fine," he sputtered, at last. "So, how do I address you, m'…?"

"As Caer. That is my name. The name I was given at birth. It is who I must be, again."

After several more seconds of indecision, Jerkin ventured, "Caer DaDhrga, if I remember what you said correctly." She nodded.

"Fine. Mistress DaDhrga, then. Now, will you please drink?"

A distant memory flashed to the fore - a young and handsome Dylan sitting across his desk from her, his insistence that she drop his title of 'Doctor' and the 'sir' when addressing him. He went by the name of Hugh Jorn at the time. The closest she could bring herself to agreeing was to call him Jorn. The memory prompted a giggle as she responded to Jerkin with, "That will have to do for now, I suppose." Those having been Dylan's exact words brought another chuckle.

"Good," he said, setting a dish of meat in front of her. "You should eat, too."

Tine and Brandel rose from their quiet discussion as Stoirm ducked back into the cave from his watch, brushing snow from his coat. "My watch," Brandel said, snatching his coat from the ground.

Stoirm motioned him back. "The blizzard is severe enough to prevent any man or beast from venturing about."

"Still, I would feel better having a set of eyes outside.

"As you wish. Just stay close to the entrance. In the whiteout you may lose your way."

Brandel agreed, fastening his coat and pulling up his hood as he stepped out into the night, Spirit at his side. It troubled Caer that the wolf still moved with a slight favoring of the injured side.

Stoirm discarded his coat near the entrance, taking up a bowl and some of the of the meat as he plopped down across the fire from Caer. "Tine tells me you have not slept."

Caer shot Tine a disgruntled glance. "Nor has he. And he can mind his own business."

"You are my business," Tine shot back.

"Not by my choice!"

"By the promises given to those who loved you, Caer. And I will not go back on them."

Caer's gaze dropped to her lap, her voice catching. "And for how many more centuries do you intend to stick to those promises? Surely, they were not meant to last for eternity."

"My oath came with no completion or expiration date. Hence, eternity it is."

Moaning, Caer pushed to her feet and shuffled around the small space, stretching, at last returning to her place away from the vent. Perhaps she might catch a bit of sleep. Tine joined her, spreading his blanket on the ground and chuckling at the resigned glance she turned to him.

Though the meal was meager enough, her stomach no longer rumbled. And the warmth of the cave was adding to her fatigue, despite the headache from the fumes. Stretched out on the blanket, she covered herself with her coat and blanket, her eyes closed as she listened to the muffled voices of conversation.

Faces. Jumbled. Overlapping. Blood. Fire. Two young women lay on the ground. Both pale and unmoving. Whisper and Shadow. Still as death. More faces overshadow the two. More blood and fire. Voices twist in competing demands - Come to me and I will spare those you love... You must go to the mountainside... You must go to the Alainn.

Tortured cries. Battles. So many battles, all tangled together; the air filled with the screams of souls as they are banished; the stench of death everywhere. We are ever with you. We are...

Caer woke with the familiar startled jerk, darting a glance around to verify she remained within the warmth of cave. Stoirm, Brandel, and Jerkin lay sleeping. Tine was close. Just outside the entrance, she assumed. Spirit was missing. Outside, the wind howled. In the first pale suggestion of light, she could see the snow blowing sideways.

Sliding out from under her coat, she pushed to her feet and headed for the metal pot that sat atop the fire. The water had boiled dry. Snatching one of her mittens, she lifted it away, thinking to take it to the entrance to fill it with snow to melt. Tine ducked back inside in front of her. "You do not want to be out there," he said, taking the mitten and the pot from her. "The gale will pick you up and throw you off the mountain. Seems we are going to be here for a while." He disappeared with it for only a few seconds, returning with it packed with snow already melting from the pot's remaining heat. "Here. When it is hot, take some tea from my pack."

Caer cocked a brow at him as she took the pot back to the fire.

"Was not my doing," Tine sighed. "Hawthorne stuffed several small bags of it in without my knowing."

"Where is Spirit?" Caer asked.

"Downslope a few meters, tucked into a hollow. I do not think she likes the fumes in here."

"Nor do I," Caer agreed. "They have given me a headache and nightmares."

Now, it was Tine whose brow cocked as he leaned against the wall next to the opening. "Nightmares or visions?"

Caer shrugged. "Nightmares…I hope." With the pot back on the fire, she looked away, rubbing her temples, her voice taking on a tremor. "The girls are in trouble, I think. Maybe. I…" Turning back to face him again, she fought the fear that tightened her throat. "I cannot say for certain. I no longer know anything. The voices argue, each demanding something different of me. I saw…I saw Whisper and Shadow lying in darkness, pale and…I…"

Tine crossed to her, wrapping her in his arms, his hug dwarfing her against his height and the thickness of his coat. "You would be aware if something happened to them. Your connection, particularly to Whisper, is strong. As for the voices, stop listening to them. Listen to your own voice. What does it tell you?"

She pulled away, her head bent as she shuffled to her blanket, dropping onto it and tucking her legs beneath her. "How can I trust my own voice when I cannot tell which voice it is? How can I trust listening to it when it is what got us here, in the first place?"

Tine dispensed with his coat and wandered across to sit next to her. "When are you going to stop blaming yourself? The war started long before you existed. And you certainly did not ask to be the only remaining descendent of all three. You are in this mess because, by accident of birth, you are the only hope of stopping Nemhain."

"But I did not stop her, did I? I just moved the war to a new place, endangering the people of Slievgall'ion, and likely destroying the whole of Earth, and who knows what else, in the process."

"Or you saved the Earth and all else with it. You also granted us centuries to try to work out how to hold the Dark Heart at bay."

Caer gave an irritated grumble. "Look where that got us. We are no closer to stopping her now, than we were when we first arrived. In the meantime, her descendent defies the laws, creating an arsenal of long banned weapons. Her kin and warriors torture and murder, leaving souls too damaged to survive while we have steadfastly refused to ban the souls of the vile. Those now lying in the bosom of Slievgall'ion are growing ever darker and more tormented. They are drowning the voices of Dana and Roisin. They whisper in the winds and across flowing waters, making all believe that there is no hope."

"If there was no hope, those souls would not need to work so hard to convince the living."

Caer opened her mouth to ask what hope Tine believed existed, then closed it without speaking. If he held to hope, she would not be the one to destroy it. In her silence, she realized there was another awake. Raising her eyes, she saw Jerkin sitting on his blanket, his curious gaze fixed on her. Sighing, she asked, "How long have you been listening?"

Jerkin shrugged. "A bit, m'la… Mistress DaDhrga." For several seconds, he chewed at his lip. "Is it true?"

"What?"

"That you are a descendant of the Goddesses?"

Caer's second sigh was even heavier than the first. "They are not, nor have they ever been Goddesses. They are Witches, just as we are. You and me. Even Tine is part Witch."

Tine chimed in with, "The more attractive part."

That prompted a laugh from Jerkin and a giggle from Caer. "Still," Jerkin pressed. "They are far more powerful than any Witch before or since. They created this world. That makes Them Goddesses, does it not?"

"We have been through this before," Caer moaned. "They did not create this or any other world. They merely found a gateway between worlds. The combination of science with the magic of a great many Witches over the centuries allowed life from Earth to be brought here and for it to flourish."

Jerkin remained unconvinced. "The souls of the Three reside in the fastness of this world. Their voices still speak to some. How is that not Goddess-like?"

"I do not pretend to understand the mechanism by which this happens, but it does not make any of them deities."

"The voices speak to you." The statement was both question and conviction. Caer nodded.

"Do They listen when you speak back to Them?"

"Perhaps." Caer rubbed her arms and stood, returning to the pot where the water now boiled. "No more questions, Jerkin. My head aches and I need to think."

Tine rose with her, strolling to his pack and selecting a small packet, sniffing it. "Here." He poured a few tea leaves into a mesh bag pulled from the same packet and delivered it to Caer. "This should help with the headache."

Caer retrieved her mitten, setting the bag in a cup and pouring water over it. The delicate aroma of jasmine and chamomile lifted, easing the smell of the fumes. Cup in hand, she returned to her blanket, her back propped against the wall as she sat with her eyes closed. Listen to her own voice, Tine said. What voice did she have? What could it possibly tell her? She straightened. That the girls are alive. He was right. Their deaths would strike her a vengeful blow. Still, that they were in trouble, she had no doubt. Anger flooded her. They were in trouble because Dana urged the High Priestess Danu to kidnap Whisper! Why? If Dana wished to take either Whisper or Shadow for their safety, why not speak directly to her?

Caer's jaw set. Because she would never have agreed. Dana had no right to demand it. Was Dana even to be trusted, any longer? Perhaps her soul was corrupted by the overwhelming numbers of vile souls now joined to the world? And if Dana's…then…then perhaps Roisin's, as well. The possibility was terrifying.

Listen to her own voice. Listen…

Stoirm's sudden leap to his feet startled Caer, her tea splattering over her hands, burning them. Tine's hands over hers instantly relieving the pain, though he and Caer both shot an anxious scrutiny to Tine's father.

"Build up the fire!" Stoirm barked. "We have to leave. We are being summoned."

Caer blinked at him. "Summoned? By whom?"

"Queen Grian Geal."

That brought Jerkin and Brandel to their feet, Jerkin stammering, "Wh… who the d…devil is Queen…Queen…?"

"Queen of the Alainn, in this world," Tine replied, heading to his pack and gathering the items he had taken from it. "Call Spirit back."

Brandel hesitated. "I do not believe she will go through the fire with us, again."

"If she chooses to remain, so be it. But we must go," Stoirm declared.

Caer finished tucking everything back into her pack. Donning her coat, she slipped the pack over her shoulders and headed toward the fire, casting about the cave for bits and pieces of wood that might be used to increase the flames. "There is precious little fuel, here."

"I think I may be able to provide more," Jerkin suggested. Before she could question him, he closed his eyes in concentration, then collapsed in a heap as a pile of splintered wood appeared at his side. His glance at it brought instant dismay to his face.

"This is not right! This should be a pile of split wood from Hawthorne's stores. She showed me where it is. Told me that I should memorize its surroundings; that if the need arose, I should take as much as I could manage. These…these are splinters; broken pieces of…of wood frame. These…"

"We cannot worry about that, now," Tine put in. "We will send others to search for Hawthorne and her people when we can. She provided us with a means of doing what must be done. Let us pray we can thank her. Later."

Brandel, in the meantime, was into his coat and pack and standing in the cave's opening. "She will not come," he sighed, rubbing his temples. "She fears the flames and is not yet trusting of us after the injury she suffered."

"Let her stay," Caer urged. "She can take care of herself."

Brandel tensed, then nodded, closing his eyes, perhaps to send one last goodbye. He and Spirit bonded such a short time ago, and yet their connection was strong. Leaving the wolf behind was not easy for him to accept. The pain of it showed in the furrows tracked across his brow.

Stoirm, Tine, and Jerkin set to building up the flames. As the blaze rose, Tine gestured for Caer, Jerkin, and Brandel to stand between he and his father. Then, the two Alainn lifted their song. After a few fitful seconds, the flames settled into a steady pattern and the faint haze of the magic shielding grew around the group.

Tine continued the song when Stoirm spoke the word, indicating time to step from the flames. They emerged in a meadow nestled in a bowl surrounded by unfamiliar mountains. Tine still held to the song, maintaining the pattern of the flames until the Watcher who brought them through signaled the release. Perhaps three dozen Alainn ringed them, each facing out, the dark hoods of their cloaks shoved back from their heads, their swords in hand as they kept silent vigil. As the bonfire fell back to a minor blaze, the Watcher turned amber eyes to the new arrivals. Tall and golden skinned, flaming red strands of hair fell loose from her long braid to frame her delicate features. Her elegant silver cloak flapped out in the stiff breeze, revealing a warrior woman's build, both beautifully feminine and solid as granite. If ever there was a Goddess, Caer thought, this would be Her.

"My queen." Stoirm and Tine bowed before the woman. Brandel and Jerkin immediately followed suit while Caer dipped a low and reverent curtsey.

The woman waived them up. "Queen no longer. Rise. Come with me. We must kill the flames and depart before the sun is fully risen."

Stoirm and Tine exchanged stunned glances as they helped the others dowse the fire. With the flames out, their small party fell in with the Alainn, the golden-skinned woman leading the way with long, quick strides that Caer had difficulty matching. Tine snatched her into his arms, keeping pace with ease. No one spoke and no one stopped until the woman called a halt several minutes later next to a boulder fall at the foot of a steep rise. The woman stood listening intently for but a few seconds, then swept a hand in front of the largest stone. It rolled to the side, revealing a dark tunnel into which the woman disappeared. Once all had gathered within, the woman's stern voice stated, "Conceal." The boulder rolled back into place, leaving them in blackness too deep for their shadow sight to penetrate. "Light," the woman spoke. Along the length of the downward sloping tunnel, torches sparked to life. "The way is long, but we are well-hidden, here. Still, I prefer to reach the first rest station before we break for food and water."

"Put me down," Caer complained, wriggling in Tine's arms.

"You cannot keep up."

The woman turned to regard them. "Welcome, Caer DaDhrga. I wish our meeting again was under different circumstances."

Indeed. Centuries it had been since Caer last met Grian Geal. She was not queen at that time, but a princess whose beauty seemed at odds with her warrior's body. The two aspects melded in striking elegance, now. Caer opened her mouth to reply, but Grian Geal waved her off.

"Save your breath, little one." To Tine she said, "Let her walk. We can keep the pace slower, here."

Reluctantly, Tine set Caer to her feet, keeping close behind her as they set out. The way was, indeed, long. And cold. The more so after the relative warmth of the cave. Caer was beginning to regret walking on her own when they at last reached a rounded and level landing. There, the stone walls held carved stone benches. Interspersed with the benches were smaller niches within which bubbled pools of water fed by underground springs.

Grian Geal motioned for Caer to sit. "We will rest here. Drink. We will share food around." With that, the woman turned to her people, speaking in the language of the Alainn. Caer understood little, picking up only bits of a discussion concerning their destination. As soon as Tine was certain of her comfort, he joined his father and the others.

Brandel and Jerkin wandered over to sit with her, Jerkin staring wide-eyed at the Alainn clustered around Grian Geal.

"You look like Owl," Caer teased. "Try not to stare."

"Sorry, m…Mistress DaDhrga. I just…I have never seen more than a handful of Alainn in my whole life. How many do they number, altogether, do you think?"

Caer shrugged. "Perhaps they cannot even say, at this point."

Brandel gestured at their surroundings. "Do those of you who live in the mountains always spend so much time underground? First it was the…"

Caer shushed him with a glance. "The locations are known to only a few. Best to keep it that way. As to your question, we prefer, of course, to be above ground. But dark times require dark places to hide. I only wish I knew what Grian Geal meant when she said she is queen no longer."

Silence held among the three for the next several minutes, Caer wishing she might hear more of the discussion among the Alainn. It did not bode well, if Grian Geal was no longer ruling their realm. At length, Stoirm and Tine returned, Stoirm's countenance clearly troubled. Though Caer was eager to learn the news, she did not press him. Two others approached, as well, each offering bread and strips of jerky. It was all but impossible to guess the age of an Alainn, and these two were no exception. The men were obviously battle hardened, judging from the number of scars across their faces and hands. Only dark magic could have caused wounds that would leave such marks on a people so skilled in healing.

"We will be moving on in a few minutes," Stoirm advised. "There is a chamber where we will stop to take counsel and spend the night. But it is about four hours from here. The first hour will be downhill. The second and third will climb again. Somewhere into the fourth hour, the way will level off. It will be a hard push, but Grian Geal is anxious to meet with others, there." Caer nodded, glancing at Jerkin.

"Do not worry about me," the boy sniffed. "I am good to go."

"My concern," Stoirm put in, eyeing Caer, "is you. You look as though you might collapse."

"Looks are deceiving," she huffed. Not entirely true. She was exhausted. Too many difficult days and nights with too little sleep.

"*Close your mind to us.*"

Caer stiffened, recognizing the murmur as Roisin's. "*I cannot. I will not shut you out. I have need of the visions you send.*"

"We send no visions. The visions are your own. You waste energy, keeping your mind open to us; straining to hear what we might offer over the voice of Nemhain. My voice grows weaker. Dana's..."

Whatever else Roisin wished to pass along was lost in a long sob, followed only by the faintest, *"Close your mind. Listen for us no more."*

"What is it, Caer?" Tine's hand was on hers, the sense of his proximity filled with tension.

Caer blinked at him, realizing that she was shaking, all warmth drained from her. In the beginning, after their arrival on Slievgall'ion, she believed Roisin's and Dana's voices were forever gone from her. Voices that had been with her since... since... She could not remember a time when at least Roisin's gentle soul did not commune with her. The emptiness left by the departure of their souls was frightening. So, she sought for them - for Roisin and Dana. And their voices returned. Over time, Nemhain discovered a means of breaking through. Now, the Dark Heart's threats and demands tended to drown out her sisters. Still, Caer listened; strained to pull the two from the menace of the one. They gave her strength; guided her; provided a measure of hope. How would she learn what must be done when her head was empty of all but her own voice? Caer's hands clapped over her ears, her head bent almost to her lap at the terrifying laughter that filled her head. With a snap, she willed her mind to slam shut against it. The instant silence sucked her breath from her, redoubling her shaking. She was, for the first time in more than an age, alone.

38

"**S**he pushes herself too hard."

"Let her rest longer. Someone can stay with her. The rest must come with us."

"I will stay."

Caer squinted into the dim light, trying to identify the voices around her. The first was Tine's. The last...

"Stay put." Tine shoved her shoulders back until she was lying on the bench again.

She tried to push him aside. "Let me up. I can..."

"You can be still for a while." This voice was not Tine's. A woman's face hovered over her. Grian Geal. "You are not as young as you once were." The Alainn's words came with a gentle smile, her amber eyes taking in Caer with concern. "And you have not yet learned to look after yourself. Too much worry for others."

The Alainn's cool hand brushed Caer's cheek. "You will stay here for a little longer. I am leaving more food and water for you. Tine will remain. Two of my people, also. They can see that you get proper rest along the way. Join us when you are able."

Caer tried to sit, again. "I am perfectly able..."

Grian Geal's smile broadened as she forced Caer back. "You are able to run yourself to a ragged shadow. Though our paths have not crossed in more than an age, you are precious to me, little one. Stoirm and Lt. Journeyson and the young man with them will go with us. But you are in good hands." Leaning close, she added softly, "Do not be afraid to be alone in your head. You will find that you think with greater clarity, that way." Again, she brushed Caer's cheek, then rose from the edge of the bench and returned to those who awaited her.

Caer considered pressing her protest, but a sharp glance from Tine cut off anything else she might say. Once the others were away, Tine offered his hand, helping her to sit. "Here," he said, motioning one of the remaining Alainn forward. The woman thrust a mug into Caer's hands. "Drink. It is hot and it will help warm you."

Caer sipped at it, the steam rising around her face. Tea. How did they manage hot tea? The Alainn chuckled, a small flame dancing on her palm. "You question how a Fire Mage manages heat, little one? You are not that feeble of mind, yet, I dare say."

Brow creased, Caer studied the woman. Grian Geal's daughter, Everbloom. The first time Caer saw her, she was standing at her mother's side in the battle that delivered them to this world. All she knew of Everbloom at that moment was the silver armor she wore. Caer did not learn her name until meeting her following Adrian's death. The Alainn held a beautiful ceremony honoring Amhranai Fearalite – the name by which they knew him. Grian Geal had just become queen. And that only because Stoirm declined the kingship.

Everbloom was as strikingly beautiful as her mother - red hair flowing in long curls, pale skin accented with high cheekbones, yellowbrown eyes that had not yet achieved the amber of Grian Geal's. The daughter fell short of her mother's height by very little, was shy of Tine's by a head. Behind the woman hovered another, this one almost matching Tine's height. Caer was unfamiliar with this Alainn, who watched her with profound curiosity.

"This is Morningglow," Everbloom said, sweeping a gesture in the direction of her companion.

Caer returned Morningglow's scrutiny with equal curiosity. Both Alainn women were attired for battle - tall leather boots fitted snugly over heavy woolen pants, silver chainmail showing beneath their cloaks, silver gauntlets on their arms, swords at their sides, and bows and quivers over their shoulders. "You have been fighting! Has the Red Moon come to you, as well?"

Everbloom nodded with a sigh. "They came on us from the west. We had no knowledge of their ability to navigate the Wilder Seas with vessels large enough to carry such a host. Their vessels approached our shores from beneath the surface and rose in the dark of night with fog as their cover. They carried weapons and beasts with them, many of which we have not seen since before we were swept to this world, others, even more terrifying we have never before known. The weapons are explosive and outmatch the distance of our magic. The beasts..." Everbloom paused, shaking her head.

"They leave death in their wake," Caer provided.

Everbloom nodded. "You have seen them, then."

"No. But we have seen their paths. How many such beasts came ashore? And how did they manage to transport such creatures without killing everyone on the vessels?"

"I cannot say how many. Perhaps a dozen. Large numbers are not necessary when the mere passing of these demon creatures kills everything within two meters of them, and when our magic is powerless against them. How they transported them, again, I cannot say. Perhaps they employ a special dark magic to protect those who accompany the creatures. The invaders attacked our coastal villages near the mouths of the West Swan River with their explosives, first, then sent the beasts in. We received the first sending about the attack in the early hours of morning eight days ago. By the time we arrived with soldiers, we found nothing but death and ruin. We followed their trail until we were sure of their destination. Adni."

Caer sucked in. "Your capital!"

Again, Everbloom nodded. "We teleported to her gates and sent for more soldiers. We arrived barely an hour before the assault began. Mother led a small contingent of us through underground tunnels to come up behind the Red Moon to attack them while their weapons were pointed toward Adni. But they greatly outnumbered us, and their magic was vile, burning us as an acid would do. We feared they would set their demon beasts on us, as well. We did not know the beasts were already ravaging Adni. Outnumbered and with our people falling to their dark spells within the city, we were forced to retreat. Those of our people caught inside Adni surrendered, denouncing Mother as queen and calling for her immediate capture and execution. We had little choice but to vanish, taking refuge in Deep Hall."

Caer was trembling, again. "How could your generals surrender to such monsters?" At Everbloom's defensive stiffening, Caer managed, "I am sorry, my sweet. I understand that they did what was necessary to save as many of your people as possible. Still..." She took a moment to settle the quake in her voice. "How safe is Deep Hall?"

"The location remains the queen's secret. Only she can take people there. Once we join her in the lower chamber, she will deliver us to the Hall. There, we can..." Everbloom's voice trailed off.

Can do what? Stay hidden for the rest of their days? Caer shook her head. No. Grian Geal would not hide. She would fight. But how many would follow her?

"You worry that we are too few," Everbloom said. "It is our worry, too. Our lands are vast, though. And Mother sent word to those she most trusts. We shall see who and how many respond."

Caer lowered her head to her hands, unable to stop the tears. "Always, we battle. There was a time when I thought…when I believed we were victorious and the wars were over. A brief span of a century when Nemhain's High Priestess and the Red Moon Warriors retreated to Rift beyond the Isle of The Sisters' of Sorrow. Even when the skirmishes began, again, along the coast, I believed we would prevail once more. It has not proven to be so. And now…"

Everbloom sat beside her, taking Caer's hands from her face. "Do not lose hope, Little Swan. You are our greatest treasure. You know the Sisters like no other. Somewhere, deep within your memories… within their memories…you will find the answers we need to defeat Nemhain and the darkness she spreads. For now, you must close your mind to your fears; you must eat; and then we must take the next leg of our trek to the lower chambers."

39

Descending, again. The steep, spiraling steps were bad enough. That they were hemmed in on both sides by solid rock drew Brandel's groan. Why could these people not stay above ground? He longed for the open sky and clear air of the lowlands, not this frozen world with its dark, secret ways. For all he knew, they were descending into hell. The only thing that argued otherwise was the cold.

Torches lit their way, flickering to life at their approach and blinking out after the last person passed. In that brief light, the stone shimmered with veins of deep blue and crystalline white before returning to the blackness. From somewhere behind him came Jerkin's sharp inhale at the dazzling sight. It was not the blue or white of gems Brandel desired. It was that of sky and clouds.

A quiet chuckle from the nearest Alainn drew Brandel's attention to the fact that his frustrations had been expressed in his audible muttering. Clamping his mouth shut, he concentrated on tempering the length of his stride. If he overstepped the narrow tread, catching a boot heel on the back of a riser, his tumble would likely cause a cascade of bodies and produce some serious injuries, assuming any survived the rolling fall into the abyss.

"You do not care for our choice of pathways down the mountain?" the Alainn asked.

"I dislike the constant darkness and stone all around. Feels like a coffin."

"You would prefer the ice and snow, the crevasses and blowing wind and wild creatures and Red Moon Warriors," the Alainn laughed.

Brandel flinched. "When you put it that way, this seems a fraction less bleak."

"Indeed. At least you do not grumble about the descent, itself. Perhaps you are becoming accustomed to mountain life, lowlander."

"More like grudgingly accepting."

Again, the man laughed. "I must confess, I prefer the rolling hills and the pastures and fields of Sunrise, myself. My name is Bavol."

Brandel nodded. "My name is…"

"Brandel Journeyson. Your reputation as a fierce soldier and battle leader precedes you."

Brandel shook his head. "If rumor is true, the soldiers are dead or scattered, leaving no one to lead in battle, any longer. My home is overtaken. I overheard some of your people saying that our capital of Riversong no longer stands."

"This is our understanding. Word came to us from my sister's daughter who fled Riversong with her husband and child. I am sorry, Brandel Journeyson. I know the pain of losing so many good people to such a ruthless enemy."

Brandel stumbled in his surprise. "Are the outposts of Sunrise under assault, as well?"

"Worse. The attacks have reached the southern and western coasts of Sunrise, itself, and the Red Moon forces are driving inland."

Brandel stopped, a hand braced against the wall as he stared at Bavol in disbelief. "They sailed the Wilder Ocean? How? When?"

"All will be explained when we reach Deep Hall."

The two continued in silence, Brandel lost in dismay over the news. If the Red Moon could navigate the South Wilder Ocean to reach the western shores of Sunrise, the entire coastline of Brightwater was vulnerable. With the Lord of Brightwater dead, Riversong destroyed, and the Soldiers of Damsa Dana dead, captured, or fleeing, all hope was lost. Unless… "The forbidden technology."

Bavol nodded. "I fear we also need to employ the ancient technology if we are to survive. We need to fight under equal conditions."

"How can we achieve such a goal? We lack their weapons. We do not even hold the knowledge of the necessary resources or the means of making them."

"The technology was forbidden. It was not lost."

Again, Brandel stopped, his brow pinched. The books. His assessment of them as fantasy was fast dissolving.

"I am told that the Little Swan possesses a vast store of the ancient writings and pictures. The information may be in those. Swan may also be able to locate individuals with the skills to build the weapons and machines."

"I have seen such books."

"At Knife Point Keep," Bavol said with a nod. "Those scarcely scratch the surface of what was once known in other worlds."

"I also…" Brandel hesitated. Likely, the library at the sanctuary within the Healers' complex was something Swan… Caer…wished to keep secret.

Bavol's eyes widened, his stunned voice hushed. "The Healer's library. You were given access to it. Few are granted that privilege. What did you learn from it?"

"I had no opportunity do more than browse before we left. In truth…" Brandel inhaled, letting it out in an agitated huff. "In truth, I thought the books contained little more than myth. Now…" He shook his head.

"Perhaps," Bavol ventured. "Perhaps when the council at Deep Hall is done, you can return to the library. Learn what must be done to create for ourselves weapons to match the Red Moon's."

Once more, the pair continued in silence, Brandel chewing at the side of his mouth. Given the destructive ability of the weapons that the Red Moon now had in their possession, it was little wonder that such knowledge was locked away and forbidden. Still, no other way to defeat their enemy presented itself. He was not the one to try and glean from the books all that was necessary, however. And there was the matter of time required to learn, to acquire the resources, and to make what was needed. He shot a glance back and upward. The Lady Swan, Grandmother, Caer DaDhrga - or whatever name she chose to use – was said to possess a great weapon. Perhaps it was one from the forbidden ancient technology. If so, why does she not use it? How many lives might have been saved if…

Running. Snow crunching beneath wide paws. Urgency driving the race through the night. Leaping over a fallen tree. Cutting this way and that through the forest. Seeking for…

Brandel missed a step, Bavol's quick grab of his arm preventing him from falling headlong into the rock wall and possibly tumbling down into those below.

"Careful, my friend."

Bavol's words barely registered. Bracing himself against the passage wall, Brandel darted a glance around, half expecting to find the open world around him, once more. Half expecting…

Bavol fixed a worried scrutiny on him. "What is it? What did you see?"

What, indeed! He held no doubt that the connection originated from the wolf. Where was she going? Why the urgency? He believed she sought for something…or someone. Not for him. Spirit could track him by way of their mental connection. Even if she remained unable to reach him, she would seek a place to wait for him. But she was running through forest, not along mountain slopes. She had descended from the heights and was looking for…for…

The flash of the scent of evergreen boughs and a glimpse of a face struck him. A face pale as death with eyes closed. "Whisper!" he breathed.

Bavol moved closer to him, motioning for those who had backed up behind them to move on down. "The lowlander needs a moment's rest. Go on ahead."

Once the soft roll of chuckles had passed, Bavol pressed, "What did you say? Whisper? What about the girl?"

Brandel tried to shake the image of running and the sense of urgency from his head. "I…I am not certain. Something from Spirit."

"The white wolf? You are the one who bonded with her? How? What did she send to you?"

"Only a vision of running. In the forest. And the scent and image of the one she urgently seeks."

Bavol stiffened. "The girl must be in trouble." He was silent a moment, then motioned for Brandel to follow. "I sent word to Grian Geal. She wants us to join her as quickly as possible. Are you up to continuing?"

With Brandel's nod, the Alainn charged down the steps, calling out, "Coming through! Clear the way! Coming through!"

The extent of Brandel's shaking only became apparent when he straightened from his lean against the wall. Steeling himself, he set off on the heels of Bavol - downward; ever downward. All moved aside as they descended. Past wider areas set with benches for resting. Past trickling springs that cut their way through stone to cross the passage and disappear beneath stone once again. Bavol stopped at only a few, allowing some rest, then descending again. And then they climbed. And climbed. At last, the way leveled. Legs burning from the rush and strain, knees threatening to turn to jelly, Brandel pushed on, the sense of near panic driving him. Somewhere, in the blur of the passage and the burn and pain of muscles and joints, he at last stumbled into an enormous cavern, the light of myriad torches glistening off crystalline formations, damp walls, and a pool of water at the cavern's heart. On the far side of the pool stood Grian Geal with Stoirm, their anxious gazes now fixed on Brandel as he worked his way through the unexpected number of those who were gathered.

"The wolf connected with you?" Grian Geal's question came even before he reached her.

Legs spent, Brandel dropped to his knees, managing little more than a nod.

Grian Geal knelt before him. "Take a breath, Brandel Journeyson. Then tell me. It was about Whisper? You are sure? Did the wolf show you the girl?"

Brandel licked his lips and sucked a steadying breath. "My connection showed the ground moving fast beneath Spirit's feet. She was running in snow. Through the forest. Not in the mountains. The trees were those of the foothills. Spirit navigated over downed and burned trees. I felt the wolf's fear; caught her scent of Whisper. Saw Whisper's face, white and with closed eyes. If the girl is not dead, the wolf fears she may soon be."

"We can do nothing from here," Grian Geal said. "Let us hope the wolf reaches her in time to protect her. Come. I will take you along with Stoirm and Bavol." Rising, she made a quick scan of others within the cavern, gesturing to seven more to follow her. "These people, I will also take. And the young man who risked breaking his neck trying to keep pace with you, Master Journeyson. The rest I will return for."

The queen motioned to yet another Alainn. "Car'Adawc, I leave you in charge. Let all eat and rest. Keep your mind open for any others of our people who need to be rescued from the outpost lands. Contact me that I may bring them here. I will take counsel from you once everyone is delivered to Deep Hall."

The man saluted, watching as his queen wrapped herself and those nearest her in the ripple of teleportation.

Brandel was dismayed to discover he was still on his knees when the teleportation deposited them. With force of will, he pushed to his feet, wide-eyed at what lay around him. The immense hall was filled with light and with people - with Alainn, to be more precise. Men, women, children, gathered in various groups, some at tables, some standing, some seated on the floor. Everywhere could be heard the buzz of tense discussions rising and falling. The language had a certain musicality and rhythm to it, the words not only unfamiliar but with sounds near impossible for Brandel to duplicate.

At the appearance of their queen, a hush fell across the hall. Grian Geal granted a quick nod to the assembled, motioning her small entourage to continue with her. Brandel struggled to keep pace with Stoirm, thankful that they negotiated no more stairs. The way was level across the high polish of the stone floor. Behind him, he could hear the rapid patter of Jerkin's footfalls as he followed. The room remained silent as Grian Geal led the way through the clustered groups to a set of heavy wooden doors at the back...or perhaps it was the front of the hall. They opened at a subtle murmur from the queen and closed with a thud once they were through.

"Please, Master Journeyson.," Grian Geal said, gesturing past a large table at the center of the room to several comfortable chairs scattered around the room's edge. "Sit. Take a moment to catch your breath." At a small flourish of her hand, another Alainn was at Brandel's side, helping to relieve him of his pack and coat.

Stoirm had already dispensed with his, and was settling on one of the chairs, his head in his hands, his eyes closed. Bavol and the others Grian Geal brought with her likewise rid themselves of coats, cloaks, and packs, and were talking among themselves as the queen crossed to the far wall. Another soft murmur, and the stone wall shimmered to transparency, revealing the thin light of a late autumn afternoon. Brandel's brow cocked. Were they not underground?

"Come see for yourself," Grian Geal offered, casting him a faint smile as she added. "I did not muddle in your head to know your mind. Your thoughts are carried in your expression and in your eyes, as once was the case with our Little Swan."

Brandel hesitated, dreading the push from the chair. Stifling his moan, he gained his feet and crossed the room to stand slightly behind the woman.

"You owe me no particular courtesies beyond what you would offer to any other person. Do not be afraid to come stand at my side."

He hesitated, again, then stepped up to join her, his downward gaze skimming across the view of an immense and turbulent body of water.

"This is the last and greatest of the Westerly Outpost Mountains. What you view from here, few others have ever glimpsed. Of those within this room, Stoirm is the only one who is familiar with the sight, knows the location of Deep Hall, and is not under an enchantment that wipes it from his memory when he leaves this room. It is information we can ill afford to have wrenched from the minds of any who may be captured. We are built well beneath the crest of mountains, yet still high above its roots. This room looks out on the Kuheeoo-nu - the Protection Ocean. It looks toward our home, the continent of Ga Gréine - Sunrise to you."

Brandel stared down at the cresting, foamy waves that thundered against the jagged shoreline far below. "I am honored that you share this with me, even if its memory is erased." His gaze traced the line of the last of the rocky and boulder-strewn surf outward to the expanse of whitecapped blue-gray extending to the horizon. He knew the tales of the continent the Alainn called home; knew that it lay between the Wilder and Protection Oceans. It was said that the whole of their realm was larger than Brightwater, Knife Point, and the Outpost lands combined.

As Sunrise had long been protected by the two great oceans, the Outpost lands were protected by its rugged coast on the west and the border with Knife Point on the east. "How did the Red Moon Warriors manage to attack your outpost lands? I hear tell that the entire coastline is as formidable as…" His scrutiny dropped to the white crests and foam that slammed the against the bottom of the cliff. "As what lies below."

"Most of the coastline is rugged. A stretch that lies just north of where the White Moon River meets the ocean, however, holds shallows calm enough for small boats to come ashore." Grian Geal fell silent for a few moments, at last adding, "Over the centuries, many ships sailed from Rift to the Fire Islands, and from the islands to the deep waters just off that strip of coast. Anchored, they launched their smaller boats to make their assaults from the shallows. Always, we were able to repel them. Now, they come in greater numbers and with heavier ships carrying weapons that keep them well out of the range of our magic. These new ships also travel the waters further north. Some even travel beneath the ocean surface. They attack more of the coastline by sending warriors across in flying vessels that rain fire down before settling to ground."

Her voice tightened. "Now, they also attack Ga Gréine. In doing so, they have divided the minds of our people. Many who lived in the outpost lands now wish to take a stand on our home shores. Others say that we must remain here and fight with the kin of Amhranai Fearalite and with that of our little Swan. It is why I am gathering all I can to Deep Hall where a determination must be made."

"And what will you say?"

Grian Geal made no answer for a long while, her gaze on the crashing waves. "I am no longer queen of my people," she said, at last. "Many in Ga Gréine surrendered to the Red Moon and now fight for the Dark Heart. Only a few still follow me. I would return to Ga Gréine and fight to take back our lands. But I would also honor our oath to Amhranai Fearalite and to Swan. What I fear is that, divided, we can win neither war."

Brandel's shoulders slumped, his fatigue weighing more heavily upon him. Turning his back to the ocean, he shuffled back toward the chairs. "Then we are without hope."

"Hope remains, though I do not think it lies with armies. It lies in the hands of Swan."

Dropping onto the nearest chair, Brandel raised his gaze back to the once queen. "If armies cannot win, how can one woman do so?"

"I have no answer for that; only trust that she will find a way to defeat the Dark Heart. She must be protected. And to protect her, we must also protect Whisper and Shadow."

40

Hawk lay far below, crumpled in a heap near the edge of the encampment, injured and left to die. The eagle's strength was great, but not so great as to carry a man. Whisper would have difficulty finding any woodland beast strong enough to handle someone of Hawk's size. Those that might carry him lacked the ability to lift him. Time to reassess her plan. But first, she must rest, again.

Wrenching her soul free of the bird was even more painful than entering it, even with the creature's acceptance. With a cry, Whisper felt the great eagle drop. She spent the last of her energy uttering her spell as her soul slipped once more back into her own body. "Gentle winds lift the wings. Settle this creature with care. Deliver it with kindness to the ground that it may once again take to the air."

She awoke shivering and with a ravenous hunger. For several painful moments, she lay in darkness, her shadow sight slow in returning. Her extremities ached from the chill of the ground and from however long it had been that her body had lain unmoving. Only as her senses crept back to her did she become aware of another lying beside her. Her gasp brought Shadow instantly awake.

"Whisper! Are you insane?" Shadow croaked, the music of her voice stretched thin. "How dare you depart your body! Where did you go? It was foolish and dangerous! What if you lacked the strength to return? You nearly killed yourself when you tried this, before."

"I was a child, then. I have greater strength and control now. And I am back," Whisper pointed out, her voice rasping in her dry throat. "All safe and sound. And starving."

"Fine! You are back in your body, now. But your body might have died, had I not found you, blanketed you and fed you droplets of water. Thank Ciuin Rose for the spring that runs through here."

Whisper attempted to brush her cousin's hands from her shoulders, but her arms refused to obey, dropping limp to her sides. "I had no choice. I had to find him. I have to save him if I can. Is there anything to eat? And my throat needs a drink."

"Find who? Save who?" Shadow demanded.

"I need to eat. Perhaps we can find something left in the remains of our house."

"The warriors left nothing," Shadow huffed. "I did manage to sneak out after I found you. Gathered a few last berries and caught a small rabbit. I think I can get a fire started if we dare it. Is this space vented? Where might the smoke go?"

For a few seconds, she rummaged in a pile of cloth at her side - remnants of some clothing and bedding. At last, she pulled free a small bag filled with autumn's last offering of wild blueberries, blackberries, chokecherries, and even a couple of shriveled apples. "Here," she said, thrusting them at Whisper. "I will figure out where best to build a fire. Then I will retrieve the rabbit. I stashed it in the snow, outside."

"Leave the rabbit, for now," Whisper managed, at last sitting. It took a moment for her head to stop spinning; another for her hands to stop shaking enough to stuff berries in her mouth and take a few bites of apple. "Show me where you found these. I can make do with a few more. Is there a cup for some water? Then I must find another creature to host me."

"You will do nothing of the sort! You are too weak to make your way around, outside. Red Moon Warriors stalk the area. They would catch you in a heartbeat."

Whisper blinked in dismay. "They are still here?"

"Not here, specifically. They set watchers in the woods. I think they expect us to come home."

"I cannot leave him to die."

"Leave who?"

"Hawk."

Shadow stiffened. "The traitor who kidnapped you? Of course, you can leave him! Let him rot!"

Whisper ignored her, struggling to her feet. "Let me concentrate. If I can just find a willing animal…"

Shadow grabbed her arms, pulling her back down. "You *are* insane! Your soul cannot leave your body, again, so soon. You will kill yourself! And for what? For a traitor?"

Whisper yanked away. "He is not a traitor. He believed he was doing the right thing. Believed he was protecting me. I did not understand the true depth of his belief until after I escaped. During his search for me, the Red Moon captured and tortured him. He knew exactly where I was, at that moment, and he refused to give me up. He is seriously injured, and I know where he is. He needs my help, Shadow. And I cannot do it as I am, now. I…" Her lips pinched, her eyes narrowing. There was a way, if…if… Is it day or night, outside?"

Shadow blinked at her. "What? I cannot tell from in here. I do not recall how long ago it was that I went out to collect the berries and such. Hours, I think. It was dusk, then. Perhaps it is night, now. Or maybe morning. Makes no difference. I am not letting you leave this room."

"But I am still hungry." As if to emphasize the point, Whisper's stomach rumbled loudly.

"Fine. I will go find something more for you. But only if you promise not to do anything stupid. No leaving. Not physically or letting your soul run amuck."

"I could not leave my body again, right now, if I tried. Not without something more to eat. I promise to stay put if you promise to hurry back. If you are gone too long, I will come looking for you."

Shadow's exasperation blew out in a heavy groan. "It is cold in here," she grumbled, snatching what was left of a couple of blankets. Wrapping both around Whisper's small frame, she stated, "Stay snugged up and sleep if you can. I will return soon with whatever edibles I can find."

Whisper nodded, spreading one of the blankets as she watched her cousin listen at the wall, sing the spell, and slip out. The wall closed seamlessly behind her. For several moments, Whisper sat shivering, her legs drawn to her chest. The small confinement seemed to close in on her, now that she was alone, again. Setting her jaw, she turned her focus on another matter, stretching her mind; searching; feeling for the sense of…

Spirit connected with her almost immediately, the jolt rocking Whisper over backward. Visions swept her mind. A series of caves or tunnels or…Whisper could not discern what the darkened ways might be. A vision of flames, people shimmering within them. It was accompanied by anxious, grief-stricken howling. Then came deep snow on a high bluff and Spirit's desperate attempt to track Journeyson, the wolf's despair at the distance he had gone. Another desperation slammed her. Spirit had somehow detected Whisper's need and abruptly changed course. Now, the wolf was running through snowy woods, racing…racing… coming to…to her.

Stunned, Whisper scooted to brace her back against the wall. Always, with other creatures, the connection provided her the ability to view the world through their eyes and to override their will. This was different. She was seeing through Spirit's eyes, yes. But Spirit remained acting of her own accord. The pain of the wolf's loneliness and grief were near overwhelming. After Bear and now Journeyson, Whisper was the only other human with whom the wolf held any connection. Never before had it extended beyond an empathetic sharing of emotions. Now…now they shared a sense of one another's fears and needs.

"To me," Whisper sent, filling her mind, first with a vision of their home as it had been, then another as it lay in ruin. She sensed the animal ceasing its run. It stood, confused by the conflicting imagery. How could she clarify? *"I need you,"* she sent, this time with a vision of the waterfall and the surrounding burned woods. If Spirit would come to the waterfall, surely the wolf would pick up her scent. The vision from Spirit moved again, uncertainly at first. Then the connection was gone. *"Run!"* she sent. *"As fast as you can!"*

Whisper slumped back as she sorted through the images Spirit had shared. There was a fire passage, and Spirit refused to go into the flames. Bereft of her close companionship with Journeyson and her inability to reach him, the wolf detected Whisper's desperation and made a choice. She was coming. The thought was both reassuring and troubling. Why would Grandmother and the others need a fire passage? To where? That Journeyson would leave the wolf was extraordinary, considering the strength of their bonding. Only some dire circumstance would cause the two to separate in such a manner. Whisper feared for Grandmother and the others. Still, the circumstance freed the wolf to come to her. To come to her. Curling within the blankets, Whisper lay back, her eyes closing. Spirit was coming.

The feel of a chill breeze, the smell of smoky air, and the aroma of cooking meat woke her. The wall sealing off their hiding space stood cracked open just enough for her to see Shadow moving about in the hallway on the other side. Judging from the light that seeped through at the far end, it must be early morning. Whisper's stiff joints protested as she struggled to sit, and then to stand. Light-headedness dropped her against the wall.

"Stay where you are," Shadow sang softly. "The warriors are leaving the woods, but not all are gone, yet. At least that is what is suggested by the order in which the woodland creatures are creeping out from hiding and moving about freely, once more."

"To go where?"

Shadow shrugged. "How should I know? I cannot get into the minds of the animals."

Whisper tossed her hands up in exasperation. "The warriors. Where are they going?"

"Oh," Shadow sniffed. "Again, how should I know? Perhaps they think we slipped past them and they are moving their search elsewhere. Or they may be marching toward Knife Point Keep. I fear others may be lurking about, though. So, we should stay close to our hideaway. When you are stronger, we will decide our next move."

Whisper already knew her next move, and Shadow was not going to like it. Not that she would allow her cousin to stop her. This, however, was probably not the best time to test her ability to go against Shadow. "I want to come out, at least for a while. I do not much care for sitting in this space alone."

"Very well. Just keep close to the wall. I will have meat for us, soon."

Edging through the narrow opening, Whisper scrambled over debris to a broken piece of door frame and sat, eyeing the small fire on the damp stone floor. A rabbit slowly roasted on a spit between two forked branches wedged between cracks in the stone.

Shadow gestured toward a couple of leather bags next to her. "The warriors appeared to be in a hurry when they left. I found these at a one of their posts inside the burned-out woods. Flat bread and cheese are in one, dried fruit in the other. Not the tastiest of fare. They lack Serenity's skill with preparing food for travel. Still, food is food."

A few minutes more and Shadow removed the spit with the rabbit, cutting chunks for each of them and handing across pieces of bread, cheese, and a dried pear. They were part way through their meal when the sounds in the woods went utterly silent. The girls darted back into the secret space, the wall sealing shut behind them. For several long minutes, all remained still. At length, sounds of rummaging and muttering could be heard.

"Our trap worked. At least two were here," one man gloated.

"The two we seek?" called a woman, her voice echoing down the length of the hallway.

The man's tone flattened. "Perhaps."

"Where are they?" asked yet another man. "They could not have slipped past our perimeter."

The woman's voice hardened. "They are not within the ruins?"

"No. They must have heard us coming and bolted."

"Then come out of there and look to the trees. It is said they are most adept in the heights. Light the torches. Search every still standing trunk and stump. Burn the woods again if you must. We need those two."

"We need the one called Grandmother," the first voice snarled.

"She will come to us if we take the girls."

Sounds of scuffling and muttering indicated people moving away. Shadow opened her mouth to speak, but Whisper silenced her with a hand tight to her arm. *"Someone remains close. I can feel the strength of their magic. The woman, I think."*

"Can she detect the magic of this place...or our magic?"

Whisper considered. *"I could only detect the Singer's ancient magic when I was less than a meter from it."*

"Same for me," Shadow acknowledged.

"So, if the woman remains further away, perhaps the concealment will hold."

Again, no sound of movement drifted to them. After several minutes, though, a woman raged, "They cannot simply disappear unless they teleported. And there is no remnant of such a spell. Think, Danu. Where might they hide?"

Both girls blinked in horror at one another. *"Danu!"* Whisper sent. *"The High Priestess of the Goddess Damsa Dana?"*

Outraged rants rang down the corridor, along with sounds of pieces of debris being tossed about. A momentary silence was followed by a resolute, "No. They have not gone to the trees. They are here, still. Somewhere." Another silence. Finally, "You cannot fool me. You are here, little birds. Hiding someplace close. My soldiers can camp here for as long as it takes to starve you out of your secret hole. The remains of your rabbit, by the way, is very tasty."

Whisper sank to her knees. Danu. Her soldiers, the priestess said. Her soldiers, not the Goddess Damsa Dana's. But Shadow said it was the Red Moon Warriors in the woods. Whisper's questioning glance at Shadow brought a nod.

"Red Moon Warriors. The insignia is on their cloaks."

"She joined with the Red Moon," Whisper returned. *"The High Priestess has betrayed her Goddess and her people. Why would Damsa Dana permit such betrayal? Why would she not strike Danu down and replace her with another?"*

"Perhaps this one is no longer High Priestess and has been exiled." Shadow sank down beside her cousin. *"Or perhaps Damsa Dana did not strike down Her traitorous High Priestess because She lacks the strength to do so."* Shadow's trembling hand reached for Whisper's. *"Danu is right. They can remain camped outside until we freeze or starve, in here."*

Whisper managed a steadying breath, then lay down, closing her eyes.

"What are you doing?" Shadow demanded.

"I have found help. I will return for you."

"Whisper! This is too risky! Too soon after your first soul migration! You cannot!"

"What other choice do we have?"

41

Brandel's nerves itched, alerting him to Grian Geal's return with more of her people. He also recognized from the subtle ripple in Deep Hall's ambient magic and that of the teleportation spell, that Caer DaDhrga was with her. He could recognize her by the signature of her magic, of course. But this was different. It was a disturbing realization, the fact that wherever Caer went, the magic of the area was disturbed by her presence - as though her own magic was great enough to create ripples like a stone dropped into a pond. So subtle was the effect, though, that it had taken him a long time to recognize and identify the phenomena. Now, he watched as the council chamber fell silent, all eyes turned expectantly to the door.

Caer DaDhrga entered on Tine's arm, her bearing erect, her face flushing at the adoring and singing chants of "Soul Bearer" that followed her from the outer chamber. Her exhaustion was apparent, however, in the tightness of her features and the strained lines around her eyes. Eyes that currently held that strange glow from deep within, making them shimmer like emeralds.

The moment her foot crossed the threshold, every person in the room bowed or curtsied, bringing a brighter flush to her cheeks.

"Please. Rise. All of you. How many times must I tell you, you owe me no obeisance, no honor. It is I who owe you." Her voice carried, strong and clear, despite her obvious fatigue. Everyone did as she bid, taking up the singing chant of "Soul Bearer" once more. Caer's weary sigh accompanied a small shake of her head. Her shoulders sagged with relief as she passed into the council chamber. Tine motioned for Brandel to join them. In closer observation, Brandel worried that Caer appeared older than when he left her in the tunnel mere hours ago. The few strands of red at her temples had faded to white and her skin held a grayish tinge. Or perhaps it was the reflection of the gray skies filtering through the great window.

Tine escorted her to a chair at the end of the table in the center of the chamber, making certain she was comfortably seated before moving to stand behind the chair to her left. Three other Alainn, all unfamiliar to Brandel, also strode to the table. Others from the room joined them, though none sat. At length, Grian Geal strode in and moved to the place at the end of the table opposite Caer.

"Master Journeyson," the queen, stated. "Please sit with us." There was but one chair remaining, roughly mid-table to the queen's right. As he took his place, Grian Geal declared, "There is much to be discussed, this night. Before we begin, introductions are in order." Nodding, first to those on her left, she provided, "I believe all here know Stoirm, Lord of Knife Point. Beside him is Amhranai Neal, then Everbloom, Brightflower, Meadowbrook, and Car'Adawc. Our Little Swan needs no introduction. Nor, do I believe, does Lord Tine. Next, is Deahlan, Morningglow, Master Brandel Journeyson of the Soldiers of Damsa Dana, Samhradh, Riverfall, and Dochas, father of Knife Point's Chamberlain Fairchild. Welcome to all. Please be seated. Dinner will be served as we confer."

Only when Grian Geal had taken her seat did any others move to do so. Immediately, servers rushed in, delivering place settings, platters and bowls of food, and offering ale or wine to each. To Caer was delivered a mug of fragrant warm mead, bringing an appreciative smile to her lips. Brandel opted for ale, allowing the server to fill his plate with steaming meat and vegetables alongside a bowl of stew and a thick slice of warm bread. As the servers retreated, Grian Geal spoke, again. "We give thanks to the creatures whose lives were sacrificed that we might be nourished. May we receive from them their strength and wisdom. May we repay their sacrifice with courage and the will to protect this world." Her words were greeted with a round of, "Aye."

"Let us learn, first from Counselor Amhranai Néal," the queen directed, then speaking his name in the common language when she addressed him. "Cloud Singer, what do you contribute to our knowledge for the sake of our discussion?"

Pushing to his feet, Cloud Singer began with, "Our homeland burns. Red Moon has set ablaze the fishing villages along the southern and western coastline. They slaughter the people and destroy the land. Even the Goddess tides that sweep upland cannot wash clean the stench of death they leave in their wake."

Grian Geal's penetrating gaze never faltered as she watched him. "How far inland from the coast have the Red Moon pushed?"

"Last word is that they are working toward where the Swan River begins her fork, my queen."

"That far," Grian Geal breathed. "They move so swiftly! Everbloom, will you report, please."

Cloud Singer sat and the woman directly across from Brandel rose. As with all Alainn, it was impossible to guess her age. Younger than Grian Geal, for certain, but beyond that, he had no clue. In appearance, she resembled the queen - golden skin and red hair. Everbloom's eyes were not quite amber and shown with less intensity. Her frame was slender, carrying less a warrior's build than the queen. A furrowed brow preceded Everbloom's pronouncement. "Adni is destroyed."

It seemed most in the room were aware of this, though shocked inhales rose from the woman seated to the left of Everbloom - the one called Meadowbrook, if Brandel remembered correctly, and from the man named Deahlan seated next to Tine.

"Our capital was attacked with the use of explosives hurled by machines before the beasts of death were sent in. Those few who survived were quick to surrender." Everbloom's voice tightened with the last statement, her eyes misting. "We have had no word from anyone in or beyond Adni since our own retreat."

Grian Geal nodded. Everbloom sat as the queen turned to the man seated to her right. "Councilor Dochas, what do you add?"

The richly black-skinned Alainn pushed slowly to his feet, his deep-set brown eyes making a purposeful scan of the gathering from beneath his bushy white eyebrows. The resemblance of this man to Knife Point's Chamberlain Fairchild was only to be found in the dark skin and white hair. Dochas was erect, his features hardened, his eyes penetrating. Fairchild walked with a slight stoop, the intensity of his shocking blue eyes reflecting a gentle kindness.

"There is word from the town of Flaxfields that the Red Moon followed the West Swan River north to where it branches into the East Swan, and south again as far as Green Water. As Everbloom stated regarding the attack on Adni, so, too, the Red Moon did to Green Water with launched explosives and followed that with the beasts of death. However, the number of explosives seems to be diminishing as they progress. They have yet to make it across the plains between the branches of the Swan, hence Flaxfields yet stands. They are, however, fearful of attack from both the east and west at any time and beg for the return of our people from our outpost regions to help defend them."

Councilor Dochas took his seat, his eyes once again scanning those gathered. Around Brandel, murmurs were growing, though they were spoken in the Alainn tongue, therefore indecipherable for him. The queen raised a hand to silence them. "Lord Stoirm, let us learn from you."

For several seconds, Stoirm remained seated, his countenance grim as he studied the faces of each person in turn. When he stood, the room fell utterly silent. "There is none here older than I. I have seen more wars than I wish to count; lost more family and friends than any among you. I know the hardships and sacrifices demanded and given. Our people fought many wars before the Dark Heart and will undoubtedly fight many more, long after she is gone. This Dark Witch, however, is the gravest foe to beset Slievgall'ion, plaguing us longer than any foe before her. Many among you mumble that we should abandon our outpost lands to protect our nation of Ga Gréine. Others rumble that we should surrender to the Dark Heart's Red Moon Warriors. I tell you this. Neither is worthy of our heritage, of our people, of those who fought in the beginnings of this war, or of our future. We would dishonor all whom we have lost and all who are yet to come. We have failed to stand forward to battle the Dark Heart except in our own Outpost lands for too many centuries. Our failure is what allowed Aifa to move against Brightwater and Knife Point and led to the attacks on our home. Would you now surrender, allowing the Red Moon Warriors to destroy all we hold dear, to slaughter our people and take this world entirely for themselves? For that is what lies before us if we do not fight. That may be our fate, even if we fight, but I will not stand by and let it happen without resistance."

The woman called Meadowbrook shook her head, raising a fist to him. "Your words are those of a soldier. Most of our people are not. And the failings of which you speak are not ours, but the Soldiers of Damsa Dana who abandoned the guardians of Ciuin Rose on the battlefield many times over."

Stoirm turned on her, his penetrating gaze causing the woman to avert her eyes. "Had we joined in the battles with Knife Point and Brightwater for the Sisters of Sorrow and Fire Islands, it is possible that Brightwater would never have retreated. As for my being a soldier, do you think I am a so by choice? I am what I am because I will not die in shame, allowing others to be murdered because I lacked the courage to stand with them. I cannot speak to the failure of the Soldiers of Damsa Dana. That is for their people to address. Our shame is that too many among us retreated to Ga Gréine refusing to take to the battlefield with the humans to stand against Breag Nemhain when her daughter first raised the Red Moon threat."

Meadowbrook's features hardened. "You bear the greatest blame for the wars with the Dark Heart. Was it not at your bidding that our people accepted the daughters of your father and protected them, allowing the vile Nemhain to grow in strength and evil?"

Stoirm leaned forward, his hands braced on the table as he fixed her with his cold scrutiny. "Did you know how any of those within your household would turn out, in the end? Did you believe that each would grow to be honorable? Or did you guess that one closest to you would turn on us? We Alainn are not exempt from producing dishonorable people. It is so among all people. Will you deny that one who came from your care turned vile? That your own son turned traitor, selling his knowledge and powers to Nemhain's daughter for his own gain?"

Meadowbrook's eyes widened, her face paling, even as a stunned inhale swept the room. Stammering, Meadowbrook at last hissed, "How dare you!"

"How dare I what? How dare I make public what you have hidden for centuries, that your son did not die in battle, as you claimed, but turned from your home and joined with Maura? That Aifa, daughter of Maura and granddaughter of Nemhain - Aifa is also the daughter of your son?"

"You...you...do not know..."

"Oh, but I do, though sadly, I only learned of it recently," Stoirm rumbled. "And you cannot, in honesty, deny it."

Grian Geal tensed, her erect posture stiffening, though she kept her voice even. "Your words bite into my soul with their truth, Lord Stoirm." Shifting her attention to Meadowbrook, the queen asked, "Why did you never bring this to the Council? Why did you keep it tucked in silence?"

Meadowbrook paled further, shriveling where she sat. "I dared not, my queen. My village would ostracize me; make me an outcast."

"You do not know that. Others of our people have been shamed by some within their family, yet they spoke honestly of it; stood by their oaths to our people and to me, serving both. They are treated honorably by all."

Tears spilled down Meadowbrook's face. "My shame in raising such a son was too great. Better that he be dead than that I claim a traitor as my offspring."

"Your shame is not in your son's deeds, but in your silence. Your words of council in this matter no longer hold weight. If you wish to continue serving, here, you will sit in support of whatever this council decides and will take up whatever task is assigned to you."

Meadowbrook's weak nod was accompanied with, "Yes, my queen. I will obey."

"Are there any other among my councilors who would speak?" Grian Geal asked. None responded. "Then it is time to learn what Master Journeyson, lieutenant of the Soldiers of Damsa Dana, might say."

Brandel blanched. What words could he speak? Rising, he darted glances around. "It seems my lands are already lost, the Lord Strongbow murdered. I cannot say how many among the Soldiers of Damsa Dana remain, or where they might be. My mission is broken. There is no longer reason to ask the Guardians of Ciuin Rose for help in fighting to save Brightwater. Yet, I will ask this. I ask that Alainn and guardians fight with whomever among us yet lives. We will fight to protect your lands if you will fight to help us take back ours. Splintered and separate, we give the granddaughter of Nemhain Dark Heart too much advantage. Together, perhaps we have a chance to defeat her. We must face Aifa and the Red Moon Warriors. If what she seeks…" He hesitated, glancing nervously at the small woman whose emerald eyes studied him. "If what she seeks that she might complete her ultimate victory is held by the one known as Grandmother, then we must protect her, even as we turn to her for aid. Perhaps she possesses some piece of knowledge… some…item that can help us." With that, he sat.

Caer did not stir, though her face appeared even more worn than when she arrived. "I hold no weapon, Master Journeyson. What I hold lies in memories."

The man next to Dochas, Riverfall, Brandel thought he was called, leaned forward, his eyes narrow but gleaming, his voice gentle. "Then it is your memories we must investigate, Little Swan. Are you willing?"

"They are twisted and entwined. I have struggled for centuries to pull them apart." For a moment, the room was silent. At last, she nodded. "But I will try. For I, too, believe that something within those memories is the thing Aifa seeks, something Nemhain Dark Heart desires above all else. Roisin whispered that I must come to the Alainn. Roisin and Dana both insist that I find and return to the beginning. Perhaps here is where I discover which beginning is required."

Riverfall sat back, his brow deeply furrowed as he considered. "And what are the possibilities for beginnings?"

Caer closed her eyes, her sigh deep and filled with the weariness of her soul. "I thought it to be the place of our arrival on Slievgall'ion, where we first brought the Goddess Wars to this world. But a whisper in my mind tells me there are other possibilities that yet lie hidden. Perhaps that is why Roisin sent me to you. Perhaps, among you, memories might rise and separate, allowing me to learn from them; to know what must be done."

42

The turmoil in Caer's head prevented sleep. The sisters no longer whispered to her. Rather, the twisting and churning of their ancient memories along with her own, were an increasing torment. So many flashes - childhoods, tortures, loves, losses, hopes, pains - all interwoven. But which memories belonged to whom? She needed her journals; needed to look back over what she wrote in the years following her arrival, here. Perhaps they would help her disentangle the chaos. She destroyed those journals, though, for she feared that someone among Nemhain's clan might discover them. The more knowledge they gained of Roisin and Dana, the greater the possibility that the souls of the two sisters might be destroyed.

"What you need," spoke a gentle voice just inside her door. "Is a spell, Little Swan."

Caer was vaguely aware that Grian Geal had slipped within her room only moments ago. Rolling on her bed, she blinked at the silhouetted figure backlit by the dim light of the hallway. "What spell is there that could help? I have tried so many. They only add to the confusion."

"An enchantment, perhaps, would be a better term."

"It makes no difference what it is called. Magic seems not to be the answer."

"Perhaps not. Still…" Grian Geal motioned to Caer. "Will you come with me?"

Curious, Caer swung her legs around, reaching for the robe that lay over the end of the bed.

"Better to dress. It is a cold trek."

Caer made no attempt to bring up the lights the way she once did, long ago, on a different world, though the whole of Deep Hall was equipped with the technology. Instead, relying on her shadow sight, she found her way to a small wardrobe, choosing a pair of linen-lined wool pants, a fleece shirt and wool overshirt, then digging for a pair of heavy stockings. Grian Geal waited patiently.

"Take the hooded cloak, as well," the queen suggested. "It will add warmth. You will not need your boots, however. Shoes will do."

Caer pulled the cloak on and raised the hood, at last noting that the queen held her cloak draped over her arm. "You knew I would come."

"I hoped," Grian Geal smiled, tossing her cloak over her shoulders. "Let us go while the others sleep. We must not be disturbed."

Together, the women walked in silence through the long hall, past the council chamber and the commons to what Caer determined must be Grian Geal's own quarters. The queen's bed was crisply made, though the desk that occupied a space along the opposing wall stood in disarray, piled with papers, charts, and maps. Grian Geal passed a hand before a bookcase next to the desk and stood back as it slid sideways along the wall to reveal a narrow passage.

"Is your shadow sight sufficient to navigate the descent on the spiral stairs, Little Swan?"

Caer hesitated a moment, staring into the darkness until she could make out the first curl of the stairs. "It is sufficient."

Grian Geal nodded, making a sweep of her hand to draw the bookcase back into place, sealing the entrance behind them. "Use caution. The way is long and steep. Time is a factor, however. We must not stop to rest."

Lips pinched, Caer summoned strength to her weary legs, following behind the queen. Steep seemed an understatement. Grian Geal's long legs allowed for a graceful glide down the steps, while Caer silently bemoaned the fact that so many people failed to recognize the challenges such deep risers posed for those of shorter stature. But then, she supposed this secret place was never intended for anyone other than the ranking elite of the Alainn. At least the queen had the good grace to suggest the warm clothing, as a biting draught cut up from below.

Painful minutes drug by before they reached a landing that opened into a great domed cavern. Large braziers were mounted around the circular wall, with an even greater one standing in the middle of a pool at the center of the space. Grian Geal murmured words in the Alainn tongue - something about bright and holy - and the braziers each flared to life, their light dancing in spectrums of dazzling color off myriad diamonds set in the floor. The pattern of the gems created three equally spaced tendrils that swept out from the bottom of the pool, across the floor, and up the walls. Where the domed ceiling met the walls, each tendril connected to one of the three points of a massive trinity knot. High overhead, at the heart of the knot, gleamed a giant ruby.

Caer's hand automatically went to the hollow beneath her throat, though she had not worn the necklace in many a century. Not since her arrival on Slievgall'ion when the life and magic of it died. Life pulsed in a faint flutter in the one above.

"You feel it," the queen said, one brow lifted in mild surprise.

Caer nodded. "Whatever life it possesses struggles."

"It is weak. I only pray that it retains enough strength to assist us in this working. I fear the air may yet be uncomfortably cold for you, but we must dispense with our clothing, here."

Only now, did Caer realize that the cavern was growing warmer since the braziers came to life. "Our clothes," she repeated.

"All of them," Grian Geal acknowledged, removing hers.

Caer began stripping of her cloak and clothing, relieved to find the temperature bearable, though there was still enough chill to raise goose flesh. With her clothes folded and stacked on the boulder next to the queen's, she turned to find the woman wading out into the pool.

"This," Grain Geal said, "is not so warm. But this is the way of it." Holding out her hands, she waited for Caer to join her and take them.

The shock of the cold water sent an instant ache through the whole of Caer's body and prompted her sharp inhale. The moment her hands touched the queen's, however, the ache abated, though the cold did not.

"Hold to my hands and do not let go. Do you understand?" Once again, Caer nodded.

"Good. I will let nothing happen to you. Just do exactly as I say."

A song rose in Caer's mind, gentle, delicate as a whisper, at first, the melody scarcely discernable. The words, when they came, were in the Alainn tongue. Not their adopted language from the time Tar On Tine used the Fire Passage to journey to Earth, there to wed the human Witch, Samhradh, but their own, far more ancient native language. Caer understood none of it. And while her ear could detect the subtlest nuances in the sounds, her mouth was incapable of duplicating the lilting musicality of it. Their speech reminded her a little of Adrian's magically musical voice, though his was a rich tenure, and this was high and sweet, like a bird's song.

"Close your eyes, Little Swan. Do not worry over the words Their translation to human languages is near impossible Listen only to the melody and the flowing rhythm. Let it fill your mind."

Gradually, Caer's eyes drifted shut, the soft, haunting music overtaking any suggestion of words. She dreamed she was floating in the wide ocean illuminated by the three moons, each overlapping the other ever so slightly. Dana's moon was highest, huge and brightly bluewhite. Catching the lower edge of Dana's was Roisin's - the smallest of the three - the delicate rose nearly washed out by the greater moon. Last was the Red Moon, just clipping the upper edge of Roisin's and the eastern edge of Dana's. The Red Moon's light spilled a bloody glow out across the waters. Around her, the ocean began to heave and toss, waves growing, cresting in wild, reddened foam, sweeping over her. From beneath, something snared her legs, pulling her down. Down beyond the reach of air. Down through the blood. Down into darkness. Down with her lungs burning in their demand for her to breathe. Breathing would drown her.

Heart crashing against her ribs, Caer struggled to break free; fought to reach the surface...until, with one great gasp, her lungs filled with the ocean. She expected great pain. Felt only a spasm or two. Then peace. She was no longer in the ocean. She was the ocean. A collage of distant shores appeared to her, as though she could see every shore at once. Creatures swam around and through her. Within it all, she felt a malignancy growing, strangling all that it touched. Shorelines erupted in flames. Creatures ceased their swim, their bodies washing against her. The waters turned red, spreading a creeping darkness. Again, she struggled, no longer one with the ocean but crushed by its weight, the darkness closing in until... Caer sucked in, sputtering, coughing, her head buzzing.

"Be still, Little Swan!"

Hands tightened on her hers, keeping her in place, cold, damp sand moving beneath her as she struggled to sit.

"Be still," came again, the voice soft and soothing.

She calmed, blinking into the dancing shadows of the great cavern, shivering in the cold. "What..."

"The ocean washes away the webs in which we trap ourselves. Gives our minds the freedom to see what lies hidden from us. I cannot say what you saw or felt. The vision was your own. My enchantment still holds, however. May it guide the waters within your mind to find the stream you must take from here. Now, let us get you dressed and back to your quarters. We must do so quickly, as the Goddess tide is moving in and will soon fill the cavern. In your quarters, you will sleep. Do not fear whatever dreams come to you. Accept them. May you find within them this beginning that you seek."

Caer was of little use, her shivering making it impossible for her to accomplish the simplest of tasks. Grian Geal seemed unconcerned as she dressed Caer. At last, snug in her clothes and wrapped in the hooded cloak, once more, Caer was directed to sit on the boulder while the queen donned her apparel. Properly attired, Grian Geal reached a hand to Caer. "Can you stand?"

The feat was not an easy one, her legs and knees feeling as stable as wet sponge beneath her. "Take my arm, little one. I have called for assistance, but it will be several moments before he arrives, and we need to get higher."

Muttering beneath her breath, Caer swore at her weaknesses, willing her legs to firm and her feet to take each step up the spiral stair.

"You are not weak, Little Swan. You are worn from your journeys and from this enchantment that now sits upon you. You will feel better after a good sleep and a hot meal. Just keep climbing."

How long she struggled to hold to Grian Geal's arm; how long she dragged each foot from one step to the next, Caer did not know. Often, blackness took her between steps. Below, she could hear the rush of water. An attempted glimpse back was denied by the queen, who continued to press her to gain another step, and then another.

Somewhere, in the muddle of her darkening thoughts, another voice was heard.

"Delicately," the queen urged. "She is in a fragile state, right now."

Arms lifted her from her feet. Her head found a solid shoulder to rest against. And all was darkness.

43

Whisper could not guess the distance Spirit traveled to reach her. The depth of the animal's exhaustion and disorientation ached along Whisper's nerves. The wolf's bond with Journeyson constantly urged her to return to the mountains, there to track and rejoin him. It was cruel to keep her from doing so.

"Forgive me, my friend," Whisper sent as she settled her soul with Spirit's. She felt the hackles raise and the deep rumble of the wolf's growl. *"Please. Let me stay for just a little while."* The wolf paced in agitation, the growl still vibrating through Whisper's soul. *"I mean you no harm, my friend. I do not know why you left Master Journeyson, but I could use your help."*

The animal continued to pace, the tension of her muscles and the anxiety of another presence sharing her body shifted Spirit's growl to a whine. Whisper envisioned Journeyson's face, hoping that might calm the wolf. Instead, a flood of anguish swept her soul. Images of flames and humans disappearing repeatedly flashed to mind, intermingled with an even briefer flash that suggested Spirit endured a fire passage. That brief image invoked panic. An image of flames with Journeyson vanishing invoked both terror and panic. The wolf went into the flames once but could not override her terror to do so a second time.

"Calm," Whisper sent. *"There is no fire, here. And you and your companion will be reunited. Soon, I think. He will not like being parted from you any more than you from him. For now, I thank you for coming to me. And I ask your forgiveness for my intrusion and for what I must ask of you."*

Spirit ceased her pacing to crouch in the brambles at the edge of the woods, the ruins of Whisper's home visible through the tangle, the disturbing scent of ash and burned wood thick in her nostrils. Little wonder that it raised the memory of the fire passage for the wolf. *"I am so sorry, Spirit. The fires are gone, though. They burn no longer."* Spirit remained tense, the faint scent of…of Shadow and

Whisper carrying through the ash and dust. Shadow waited within the ruins, fearful and agitated as she watched over Whisper's body. *"Ciuin Rose, prevent her doing anything stupid! She must not come out of hiding!"*

Other scents were more prevalent and drew the wolf's attention. Pacing outside of the remains of the cottage was a woman, her white cloak muddied and stained with ash. Her hood was thrown back, revealing a long white braid. This was not one of the Red Moon. Her cloak, instead, bore a white moon on the left side – or at least a moon that was once white before the whole of the cloak was covered in so much grime. The two men who stood watch near the woman wore once white coats that were equally muddied and stained. Beneath the open front of one coat could be seen the red moon emblazoned on an armored breastplate, while Dana's moon yet stood out on the back of the second man's coat. These were soldiers, not warriors. And the woman could only be the High Priestess Danu. Whisper had never met the woman but knew well the descriptions told by others. Once a woman of fine figure, some said. Grown soft and rounded in the comforts of the temple. Yet she retained the sharpness of her blue eyes, and the white hair gave an impression of ice about her.

Had she been in her own body, Whisper was sure her heart would have faltered at the rush of her own panic. Danu and Soldiers of Damsa Dana in league with the Red Moon! How could this be? Why would the Goddess allow such a traitorous priestess to live? How could she allow her soldiers to wear the emblems of Breaug Nemhain? A deeper panic seized her. Had the Dark Heart, at long last, destroyed the souls of her sisters? Were the Goddesses Damsa Dana and Ciuin Rose dead?

A low snarl lifted from Spirit. Whisper instantly hushed it, forcing her thoughts back to her immediate circumstances, which now seemed far more dire. Spirit apparently understood her need. For a moment, the wolf dropped and rolled in the ash, then began moving stealthily through the remains of underbrush, stalking from blackened tree to blackened tree, locating at least a dozen soldiers about a hundred meters out from the house, their watch set to the areas beyond. Likely, there were others even further afield who searched for her and for Shadow. Would they truly burn the woods a second time to find them? What could she and one lone wolf do against them?

Spirit, she realized, was creeping low, staying within the undergrowth where possible, moving deeper into the woods. Whisper's first thought was to stop the animal, turn her back. Instead, she trusted Spirit, allowing the wolf to move where she wished. Quietly, they made their way to a rounded knoll. The smell of smoke drifted to them, and out across the way they could see that whatever was yet burnable in a section of the forest had, indeed, been set ablaze, again. And then another. It appeared that the soldiers were igniting a massive arch, trapping the remains of their home between the river and the newly spreading flames.

Spirit bristled, her growl guttural. There was another flash of imagery – the impression of a howl that drew other wolves; a charge over snow and ice; bright flashes followed by the echo of loud bangs; wolves falling all around; blood on the snow; a sharp and searing pain. Spirit shook herself, growled again, and then lifted her howl in earnest – long and loud. The answering howls were close; and then they were closing. Aggression replaced fear as Spirit joined their rush of the woods, dancing past catching flames, scenting the smell of humans. The soldiers were caught unprepared as wolves broke for them, teeth catching and ripping at flesh.

Apart from the pack, Spirit made straight for the ruins, surrounded by the screams that rose on the winds. Two enormous males charged from pack's hunt to accompany her, then split off to lunge at the two guards who had remained with Danu. Spirit's focus was on the woman. Before the wolf could launch, however, Danu vanished, her hiss of, "How dare the creatures of this world attack the High Priestess of the Goddess Damsa Dana!" rising with the screams on the air.

Once Whisper was convinced by Spirit's prowl that the area was cleared of the enemy, she released her soul as gently as possible, though she knew from her own pain that Spirit suffered, as well. Settled, once more, within her human body, she pushed herself to sit, her moan spinning Shadow around to glare down at her with a start. "You have to stop doing that!" she snapped. "You are going to be the death of me!"

"Right now," Whisper murmured, moaning again as she struggled to her feet. "Right now, I am the life of you. Well, Spirit and I are the life of you."

"What?!"

Whisper waved her cousin silent. "We need to leave. The woods are burning. We need to find Hawk. And we need to get word to Grandmother that the High Priestess Danu is working with the Red Moon Warriors."

A shiver twitched Shadow. "I heard her cry. Was it really her? Has she truly become traitor?"

Whisper fought a similar shivering twitch that threatened to crumple her to the floor. "Her appearance fits the descriptions we have heard. And her cloak bore the white moon."

Shadow quickly steadied her cousin. "You are in no condition to do anything. I will send to Juniper. See if the way is clear for us to teleport to the temple ruins. Once we are safely inside, we can deliver our message and you can rest."

"Not without Hawk."

Shadow's countenance darkened. "Why do you waste your time on that traitor? He is…"

Whisper pushed Shadow's steadying hands away. "I told you. He did what he believed was right. He thought he was protecting me and protecting Knife Point. I know where he is. We can teleport to him and then return to the temple, assuming the grounds outside are safe. Spirit may join us or return to the mountains to seek Master Journeyson, as she chooses."

"Spirit!" Shadow's voice was dumbfounded.

Singing the spell and flicking her hand, Whisper opened the portal to the chamber and staggered out, Shadow close behind her. Spirit watched as they emerged, her stormy eyes fixed on Whisper, who went immediately to the wolf. "Thank you, my friend," she sighed, hugging the animal. "We must leave, now. Will you travel with us, or will you go to find your companion?"

The wolf rose, pacing before Whisper briefly, turned her head toward the distant mountains with a whine, and then moved to brush Whisper's side. "Very well. Just so you know, we will be teleporting." The animal responded with another whine but remained as she was.

The itch and shimmer of the teleportation delivered the threesome beneath a large, partially burned-out oak. Several charred and fallen trunks lay in a jumble nearby. Shadow froze, her anguished gaze skimming the surroundings. "I thought this a bad dream. Their burning broke the magic. They have desecrated our sacred grove!"

"Hush!" Whisper snapped. "For all we know, there may yet be warriors or soldiers near at hand. Over here."

Shadow followed as Whisper made her way to a hollow beneath several other burned-out trunks. There, she found Hawk, just as she had seen from the eagle's eyes. "He is not dead!" she breathed. "But he needs more attention than either of us can provide. I will do what little I can for him. You do your sending to Juniper. Shield it well, though." She knew Shadow was frowning; heard her anxious, deep breath.

"I am told we need to wait for nightfall," Shadow said, at last.

Whisper glanced up with a scowl, trying to hide her trembling. "He needs help, now."

"Too risky. Juniper says Red Moon warriors prowl the area by day but are too afraid to remain there at night. We must wait. It is only a couple of hours from now. Get some sleep. Spirit and I will keep watch."

Resigned, Whisper nodded, dropping to her backside next to the comatose Hawk. Fear that they might lose him before they could get him to the sanctuary overrode any hope of sleep, though. As darkness fell, only the red moon bathed the world. Whisper was grateful when clouds moved in, blocking the sight, though the cold mist added to her shivering.

"It is time," Shadow declared, offering a hand.

Whisper accepted, pulling to her feet. With the two gathered on either side of Hawk and the wolf at Whisper's side, they teleported once again, arriving at the outskirts of the temple ruins. Whisper took Spirit's calm as an indication that all was clear. They no sooner arrived than a Healer and two of the Guardians of Ciuin Rose appeared. Whisper gestured to the man lying between her and Shadow. The men froze, stunned.

"The traitor!" one snarled.

"He looked after me," Whisper replied. "He protected me. See that he is treated well."

Juniper and Owl greeted them in the dining hall, both jittery with their mix of worry and relief. Juniper promptly wrapped Shadow and Whisper in warm hugs. "You have worried me out of several years of life, I will have you know!" she scolded. The guardians carrying Hawk edged past, disappearing into the hall that led to a portion of the classrooms that had become the men's quarters. Juniper's glower followed them.

"Him!" Owl snorted. "I am glad he is caught! Hope they lock him up for…"

"Do not be so quick to judge," Whisper sighed. "Please, Juniper. See that Hawk receives the best of care."

The woman's brow cocked, but she nodded, gesturing to the two cousins. "Come. Sit. Hot soup is being dished up for you." Her gaze fell on Spirit before darting back toward the wall where the entrance now lay hidden, again.

"Master Journeyson is not with us," Whisper said. "I do not know the circumstances, but judging from Spirit's mind, he has taken a fire passage that the wolf would not travel. She is anxious and edgy, though. Let her stay close to me, for now."

Once more, Juniper nodded, motioning, this time, to Owl. "See if we have some meat we might offer the animal."

Whisper shook her head. "I do not think she will eat. I will set her back to the outside world as soon as I feel it is safe to do so."

Shadow was already sitting straddle of one of the benches, her eyes glancing toward the kitchens. "Where is my grandmother?"

Juniper did not answer for several long seconds, her features creased with renewed worry. "We do not know. She has not returned from her journey to find Singer or to meet with the High Priestess Danu. We have had no word from her since she left."

Whisper's features darkened as she collapsed onto the bench beside Shadow. "Why would she go to the High Priestess?"

"To confront her," Shadow grumbled. "To demand that you be returned safely to her."

Whisper's glower swept the faces of the others. "People need to stop fretting over me. I am no child! I was fine!"

"Fine!" Shadow snorted. "You were not fine! You were…"

"Fine!" Whisper repeated with as much volume as she could muster. "I managed my own escape, thank you very much. And Hawk protected me when he might have revealed where I was, despite their torture of him. And it was Spirit and I who drove off the High Priestess and her minions in order that we could return, here."

"Aifa?" Juniper spat. "She is here? In the realm of Knife Point?"

"Not Aifa," Shadow put in. "Not only have some among the Soldiers of Damsa Dana fallen in with the Red Moon Warriors, so has the High Priestess Danu. The soldiers wear the Red Moon along with the emblems of Damsa Dana. Or so Whisper tells me."

Two young boys appeared from the kitchen, neither of which were familiar to Whisper. Each carried a large bowl of steaming soup, setting them on the table. Bowing and flashing curious glances at the two bedraggled cousins, they trotted quickly back to the kitchens. Another two youngsters, a boy and a girl, this time, entered the hall, one with utensils and the other with a tray of mugs and a steaming pot of tea. Like the first pair, they bowed and curtsied, casting curious glances as they returned to their work.

Whisper's gaze followed them. "They are new, here."

"Aye," Juniper nodded. "Owl found them, along with a dozen others, half starved; some suffering from burns and other injuries."

"Found them? Where?"

Owl flushed, studying his feet under Juniper's stern glance. "He snuck out a few nights ago. Went to look for you two. He found the waifs, lost and frightened, in the woods near the river. Thankfully, he had the good sense to return here with them. Two of the girls and four of the boys are still being tended by Healers. Only four of the fourteen are from villages or farmsteads of Knife Point. The others managed to find their way here from the plains of Brightwater."

Whisper's perturbed study of Owl softened. "I wish to see them. Each of them. The injured and those who are not."

"Of course, my dear," Juniper sighed. "But you need to eat and rest, first."

"I need to find a way of getting word to Grandmother before all else," she returned. "They must know of the treachery of the High Priestess Danu."

"I know of no way to accomplish that. They are beyond our reach, my dear. And we have other concerns, here. Not only have we taken in these children, we have Soldiers of Damsa Dana sheltered in caves not far from the ruins. We dared not take any in until Shadow returned."

Juniper's lips pinched as she turned her scrutiny to Shadow. "You must see each of them. If you find them honest and worthy, we will have them brought here. Those who are not…The guardians will deal with them."

"I would prefer to go out again and look for my grandmother. But…" Heaving a weighty sigh, Shadow gave a short nod. "But I will see each of those men, first. Tomorrow. I need to clear my own head before I apply my gift." She finished her soup and shoved to her feet, shuffling off in the direction of the commons.

Whisper was left sitting in silence, one hand absently stroking Spirit's head. Juniper continued to hover near at hand, Owl shifting anxiously from foot to foot behind her. "Please," she sighed. "Go on about whatever needs doing. I will rest here for a while. Is there any mead? I think I would like some warmed."

Juniper flicked a hand at Owl, sending him off at a trot to the kitchens. When he was out of earshot, the woman sat across from Whisper. "You do not know all that has transpired," she sighed. "Troops of Red Moon Warriors passed through this way, climbing over and defiling even the ruins above. They had with them some of the death beasts. Shadow's warning came to us in time for most of us to seek refuge deep within. Some few, however, did not make it away from the classrooms. They were too close to the outside and perished. The presence of the creatures also destroyed our livestock and gardens. We now rely on supplies sent to us by the guardians. And they are having trouble finding farmsteads that are not burned to the ground."

Whisper slumped further. "Forget the mead," she murmured. "Forget worrying over me."

"Nonsense! The warmed mead will do you good. Will help you sleep. I will have Owl bring the drink to your quarters. And do not attempt to send to Grandmother. Wherever she has gone, the distance is too great for a well-shielded sending to reach her. Tomorrow, we will think of some other means to get word to her."

Juniper was right, of course. Reluctantly, Whisper rose and made her way from the dining hall to the commons and down the hall to the quarters she shared with Shadow and Serenity. Serenity. Tears welled up. Where was she? Was she alive? Had she been injured or captured?

Shadow was not in their quarters, for which Whisper was grateful. In the silence and emptiness, she gave herself over to her sobs that were cut short by a soft wrap at the door.

"My lady?" came Owl's voice.

"A moment," Whisper managed, searching for a kerchief to blot her eyes and blow her nose. "Come," she said, at last.

The boy pushed the door to, peering in at its edge. "Your mead, Lady Whisper."

She motioned him forward, regarding him as he set the tray and mug on the room's table, then retreated toward the door.

"Stay a minute, if you would," Whisper sighed.

Owl stopped, cocking his head at her. "Do you need something more?"

"No. Nothing. Only... Only to know what happened here when... when the..."

Nodding, Owl finished for her. "When the death beasts came. I was not here at that time. Phoenix told me of it. Her sister was one of those who perished in the classrooms."

"Oh." Whisper plopped onto the side of her bed, her gaze downcast. "I am sorry. Please tell Phoenix that I am so very sorry."

Owl retrieved the mug from the table, taking it to her. "Here. You should drink it while it is still warm, my lady."

Whisper accepted the mug with, "Stop. Please."

"Stop what?"

"Do not refer to me as 'my lady' or 'Lady Whisper'. I am simply Whisper. Nothing more."

"Not so. There is much more to you!"

Whisper slowly raised her eyes to meet his. "Like?"

Shrugging, Owl ticked off, "Like your gentleness. Like your kindness. Like your manner of bringing calm to those who need it. That is why you wish to talk with the children who were found, is it not?"

"That you found," Whisper murmured. "Because you set out to look for me. Why would you do that?" Her brow creased. "And what brought you back here, to begin with? I thought you and Jerkin were with Master Journeyson."

"It is something of a long tale, my…Whisper."

"Condense it, if you can."

Owl was silent for several moments, obviously puzzling over what to say. Finally, shrugging again, he said, "I was injured. Took an arrow from a Red Moon Warrior that apparently carried a toxin. Lady Swan did what she could for me before having Lord Stoirm send me, along with the arrow tip, here to Juniper. That was when I learned about the appearance of the death beasts, here. And…"

"And?"

"And when I learned that you were still missing and that Lady Serenity, and then Lady Shadow went to search for you. I could not return to Master Journeyson. They had moved on, you see. And I have no way of knowing where or how to join them. Jerkin remains with them, though. I could not simply sit here in the safety of the temple while everyone else was risking their lives and while you were in grave danger at the hands of the traitor Hawk. So…."

A smile gave a soft curl to the corners of Whisper's mouth. "So, you set out to find me and found the children, instead. Thank you for your attempt, Owl. And thank you for bringing the children to safety."

Blushing, Owl nodded. "I would have gone looking for you, again, but Juniper kept a much closer eye on me, and set a new enchantment about the place. One that prevented my going out, again."

The last comment made Whisper giggle. "I can imagine. I must thank Juniper for protecting my would-be-rescuer. As for Hawk, he was never a threat to me, misguided as his intentions may have been. And I am fully capable of taking care of myself."

Owl blushed again. "Aye. That is a certainty. But no one knew what Hawk's intentions were, or how you were faring. And with Lord Stoirm and Lady Swan and the others off on their own major business, someone needed to see that you were not harmed. Phoenix agreed. She was as worried as the rest of us. Had she not distracted Juniper the first time, I would never have made it out of the temple. Not much Phoenix could do to help, though, once Juniper set the enchantment."

"Indeed." Whisper considered briefly. "Does that spell still hold? The one Juniper set to prevent your leaving?"

Owl shook his head. "No. It dissipated the moment you and Lady Shadow returned.

"Good," Whisper nodded, taking the warm mead and drinking it nearly straight down.

Owl gaped at her. "That should give you a whirling in your head the moment you stand!"

Pushing to her feet, Whisper smiled. "I am well accustomed to drinking mead. I do not recall it ever having any effect on me other than calming my nerves. Now, my friend. I believe there are some children I should see. Would you be so kind as to take me to them? And afterward, I would like very much to talk with Phoenix. To offer her my thanks for her support of your endeavor."

Straightening, Owl nodded. "Yes, yes. Of course. Just follow me, my... uhm. Just follow me."

44

Caer woke beneath the warmth and weight of several layers of blankets. She had no recollection of how she made it to bed. Scarcely recalled meeting with Grian Geal. There was something about a spell. And there was water. Lots of frigid water. Beyond that, there was no memory until this waking.

A knock at the door was followed by Tine's voice. "Are you up?" When she failed to answer promptly, he poked his head in. "Ah. Still trying to warm yourself, I see. It was quite the drenching you took, last night."

She blinked at him, struggling to push up despite her desire to remain beneath the comfort of the blankets.

Tine gestured toward the chest that stood at the bed's foot. "Fresh clothes have been laid out for you. Breakfast will be provided in the council chamber."

Caer groaned. She desired to meet with no one. Her head was a muddle and she wished to clear it; perhaps to remember the reason for her dunking.

"You will be left to your thoughts, Little Swan. No one will trouble you. The queen understands your need to think. There are decisions that only you can make."

Everbloom and Morningglow pushed their way past him, Everbloom giving him a playful shove. "You have served as wakeup call. You can leave, now. Let us get our Little Swan dressed."

He shot her a fleeting grin and bowed out, closing the door behind him.

"I need no help," Caer muttered, swinging her legs over the bed's edge, thankful that the room was almost as warm as the covers. "I know how to dress myself."

"Indeed," Everbloom huffed. "But it will go much faster with assistance. You never did care for the gowns with all their lacings."

Another groan escaped Caer. She did, in truth, hate the long gowns with their entwined lacings down the back. Why could they not just let her wear a pair of long pants and a shirt? She bit at her lip, a swell of grief washing over her. Emer never liked the gowns, either, though Del loved them.

"You have an image to maintain," Everbloom put in.

"Stay out of my thoughts."

"Not in them. Do not have to be."

Gathering up the garments, Everbloom laid them out on the bed next to Caer while Morningglow assisted in removing her nightgown. Though she refused to admit it, the feel of the linen undergarments followed by the warmth of the deep green velvet brocade over dress was pleasant. Morningglow set to lacing up the back while Everbloom fluffed the white satin that was gathered and bunched in the slits of the long sleeves. With the lacing completed, Morningglow edged Caer back onto the bed. "Your foot, m'lady."

Caer scowled but raised first one bare foot and then the other, allowing the young woman to slip long stockings and soft velvet shoes onto them. "There," she said, drawing Caer from the bed once more and turning her around. "Quite elegant."

"And quite unnecessary," Caer grumbled. "Especially if I am to be left alone to think."

Everbloom chuckled. "Ah, but you will be passing through the commons to get there. Our people need to see their Little Swan is in good health and well treated. Rest has done you good. Some of the red has returned to your hair. You might wish to dowse the glow within your eyes, however. Let them shimmer with their natural green."

Caer shrugged. "I had not realized that the glow was unshielded."

"It seems to come more frequently since last you spent time with us." Everbloom headed toward the door, Tine returning before she reached it. "Prompt as ever," she stated.

"Always."

Caer watched their admiring glances and stifled a grin. How often she had pressed Tine to leave his obsessive watch over her and return to the queen's service. His retort was always the same. He was in the queen's service, attending to Caer. Yet, she knew he desired to spend more time close to Grian Geal's daughter.

Her gaze returned to him. How magnificent he looked in his black pants and boots and silver waistcoat. Everbloom's gown was, of course, the topaz of the House of the Alainn, its trim a shimmering silver braiding. Morningglow's attire was a muted topaz, the trim a soft russet. Tine awaited Caer, his arm at the ready. Everbloom blocked the way, shooting him a withering glance.

"You are not fully attired, sir."

Tine looked about to protest. Instead, he merely sighed, the jacket appearing in his hand from wherever it had been stashed. Black like his pants and boots, it bore the insignia of the Royal House of the Alainn, a topaz horizon emblazoned with golden rising sun. It also bore topaz and silver braiding at the shoulders. Everbloom straightened and buttoned it, then led the way, with Tine and Caer a pace behind her and Morningglow following. Their little procession wound through the corridors past a compact dining hall and through the commons. All present bowed and curtsied as the group passed, making Caer fidgety. Tine's free hand closed on hers where it lay on his arm. She knew he was smiling at her discomfort.

"After so many centuries, I would think you would be accustomed to being treated as royalty."

"Never!" she sent back. *"And you are a fair one to talk. You distance yourself from royalty and its trappings every chance you get. All save the lovely Everbloom, that is."* From in front of her she caught Everbloom's soft chuckle. Caer's sending to Tine was intentionally left open for Everbloom to note.

The door to the council chamber swung in with a wave of Everbloom's hand. Tine escorted Caer inside, leaving her with, "Should you need anything, just send to me."

Caer nodded and watched he and Everbloom leave, pulling the great door shut behind them. Alone, she stood for several long minutes, her scan of the room much sharper than before. Compliments of a decent night's sleep, no doubt. The massive window revealed the gray skies and heavy rain that pounded the waters below. The roar of the surf was only barely noticeable from this height. The crash of it against the rugged shore, however, could be felt as a subtle rumble beneath her feet. A glance at the council table found piles of papers and uncurled maps strewn across it. Grian Geal did not lightly leave such things lying about. What was it the queen expected her to do with them?

A tray appeared on the end of the table, the pleasant aroma of bacon, eggs and toast greeting her and ushering a low growl from her stomach. Caer sat, sipping at the mug of hot tea and munching as she regarded the materials that covered most of the rest of the table's surface. If she was meant to dig through all of this, where was she supposed to begin?

A random selection of one of the papers nearest her produced a map she felt should be familiar, yet it made little sense. Markings were superimposed on other markings, all of which were faded from time and use, making them impossible to decipher. Her breakfast finished, she rose and strolled around the table, eyeing other maps. Yet, her eyes continued to be drawn to the one she initially picked up. Why should it seem so familiar when it was so unreadable?

Dismissing it again, Caer meandered to another part of the table where other papers were stacked. A closer scrutiny of the top sheet brought a gasp. It was the first page of a compilation of memories – the memories of Dana. Several pages down, and the memories continued. Deeper in the pile they became the memories of Roisin, and deeper still, those of Nemhain – all in her own flowing script. This was the journal she wrote in the first two centuries after arriving on Slievgall'ion. The memories of each of the sisters were painstakingly pulled from their twistings in her mind; were sorted to determine whose memories were which. The effort was exhausting. And she was never sure she had each memory properly assigned.

Caer flipped through page after page. This was not possible. How could they be here? An urgent foreboding long ago prompted her to set her work ablaze. Nemhain must never discover all the memories of her sisters. Never. So, Caer watched these pages burn until there was naught but ash left. Yet... Yet here they were.

Her hands shook as she made her way to the desk and chair next to the great window. Morning was long gone and the evening well established when she at last looked up from reading. So much work to unravel memories, and she never completed the task. Somehow, she was now expected to find a particular beginning within them. That was Damsa Dana's repeated urging. Find the beginning. But so many were intimated in those ancient memories. Was the beginning the time she took from her mother the fluttering soul of Roisin? Or the time she called Dana's soul to her, knowing she could not rescue that of her beloved aunt? Or was it when the sisters and Adrian established the gateway between the two worlds? Or the time of their arrival on this one?

Her anxious gaze shifted to the view of the endless roil of ocean that stretched out below, the black of the night waters only discernable from the black of sky by the white crests that rose and crashed. "Find the beginning," she moaned. "I am no closer to understanding what that is supposed to mean than I was before."

Wearily, Caer allowed the last page in her hand to slip to the floor, her eyes closing. It was too much. How was she to sort it out?

Water. So much water. Frigid. Rising around her. Rising. Needles of pain from the cold gradually giving way to numbing. Still rising. She would surely drown if she did not move. The thought held no fear.

Submerged. And yet, she breathed. Massive waves crashed overhead, sounding as Nature's war with itself – beating, thundering. All of it far above her. Calm remained around her. No creature disturbed her, though they swam around and through her.

Flames erupt in the distance. The water carries her toward it; holds her near enough to see the battle. Weapons once known on another world hurl death and destruction at a village. Fields and vineyards burn. Buildings ignite. The beasts of death prowl the outskirts. Another inferno erupts in the distance. Again, she is carried toward it. Again and again. Village and farmstead and keep after village and farmstead and keep.

A stain of red grows, spreading until the very water is as blood, darkening until all was black. Within it is carried the stench of rotting corpses. Her lungs burn. Her head throbs. Her body cries out for air. She is drowning!

Panic. Thrashing. A fleeting glimpse of a pale pinprick of light. A murmur. Seek the beginning. The far distant light flicks out.

Gasping, choking, Caer flailed awake, tangling herself in layers of blankets. Hands pull them away. A cool, gentle touch brushes her cheek.

"Calm. It was but a dream. Calm."

Still gasping, Caer blinked into the light of her quarters, blankets and pillows strewn around her on the massive bed. Tine and Everbloom stood next to it, Tine's hand stroking her cheek once more. "Time for you to wake."

"Aye," Everbloom agreed. "It is midday, already. You have missed breakfast and lunch."

"I had…" Caer blinked again at her surroundings. "I was… How did I get back from the council chamber? And…" A glance down revealed she was dressed in her nightgown. "And who undressed me and put me back in bed?"

"I undressed you," Everbloom replied. "Last night when Lord Stoirm brought you up, drenched to the bone."

"You…you and Morningglow dressed me this morning, You and Tine escorted me to the council chamber. I had breakfast there while I…"

Tine shook his head. "You have not left this room since Father delivered you here, last night, Little Swan. On my word."

Everbloom eyed Caer, curiosity in her eyes. "Mother said you would likely have dreams; see visions. Tine, will you please fetch Morningglow for me? We will get our Little Swan dressed and have a meal brought to her, here. She seems hardly in a state to go wandering about in search of the dining hall."

With a nod, Tine turned and made his exit, Morningglow passing him at the door. "No need to fetch me," she smiled. Our queen sent to me that Swan is awake." She pulled the door shut behind her and headed to the large wardrobe that occupied one corner of the room.

"What shall we dress you in? One of the fine gowns or…"

"Pants," Caer muttered. "And a warm shirt."

Morningglow and Everbloom both chuckled. "Pants," they chimed in unison.

"It has long been said that you favor pants over beautiful gowns," Morningglow declared with a shake of her head. "Though I cannot understand why that should be. We have no pants to fit you, my lady. I hope black leggings will do." Morningglow retrieved a pair, along with a linen undershirt, a deep green and white silk damask shirt, and a furlined green wool vest. "If it is a chill you wish to avoid, the long boots over the leggings should help to keep you warm."

Caer protested that she could dress herself, to little avail. The two young women appeared to enjoy fussing over her, taking their time to cinch in the long damask shirt with a narrow white belt and fastening the vest over it with a round silver broach set with a single, multifaceted emerald. By the time they finished combing out and braiding Caer's long hair, a knock at her door announced the arrival of the meal she was promised. Caer was surprised to find Stoirm delivering it.

Leaving the tray on the room's table, he turned to greet her with a cocked brow. "How are you feeling?"

Caer shrugged. "Confused. What happened, last night?"

"What do you remember?"

"Very little," she sighed, making her way to the table. Storm held the chair for her, gently pushing it to once she was seated. "I remember going with Grian Geal down a long, spiral stair. After that, I remember something about water, but nothing more."

"The queen performed a cleansing spell. It washes away ties and bindings that prevent one from seeing what needs seeing."

"I did not need to see myself drowning," Caer harrumphed before setting to the food.

"Is that what you saw, last night?"

"It is what I dreamed just before waking."

"What else did you see?"

She considered as she ate. Stoirm did not press further, but waited, his back propped against the wall as he watched her.

"I thought…" She pursed her lips, her mind mulling back through what seemed so real, until now. "I thought I awoke and was taken to the council chamber to sit alone and rummage through papers and maps and such."

"And?"

"I found a map that seemed familiar, though I could not read it. And among the papers were writings I made long ago. The writings in which I tried to sort through and separate the memories of the sisters. I burned them, though. More than an age ago. Yet, they were on the table in the council chamber. Every page. I read through them. And then I fell asleep. That was when I dreamed of the water; dreamed it carried me to the sites of villages and strongholds that were under attack. So many. All destroyed. The waters turned to blood and blackened, the last tiny hope of light extinguished. And that was when I dreamed I was drowning."

Stoirm remained silent for several long minutes, then pushed from the wall. Strolling to her, he placed a gentle kiss on the top of her head, then departed, calling over his shoulder. "Tell Tine of any further dreams."

Everbloom followed him to the door, closing it as he left, then settled against it to regard Caer. Morningglow hung back near the bed, her brow knotted in confusion. "The queen has not performed such magic in many an age. It is said…" Everbloom silenced her with a glance.

"What is said?" Caer pressed.

"As Lord Stoirm pointed out, the enchantment clears one's mind to see what they need to see. Sometimes, the dreams and visions that come are too much for the individual. They cannot cope with the truth. You, Little Swan, are not one of those individuals. No matter what truth arises, you will know how to deal with it."

A shiver ran through Caer. "So, I am guessing there will be more dreams and visions. No surprise in that, I suppose. Still, I have learned that the Seer's gift does not always show the whole of what needs to be known. Is it to be different, now?"

Everbloom shrugged. "The gift has never been mine. I cannot say what will come of your ability now that the cleansing has been performed. Perhaps it will make things clearer for you. Perhaps it will simply show you more from which you must decipher the truth."

Caer felt a headache coming on. "Wonderful," she muttered. "So. What is next on my agenda for today? Another icy drowning?"

"No more cold water," Everbloom chuckled. "You may wander where you will. Take your meals with us or in the privacy of your chambers. In time, you will know what next needs doing."

Caer sighed. "I simply wait for more visions or dreams before I know what I am to do. Is that it?" Her lips pinched, the map in her dream flashing to the fore, a portion of it coming into focus. Mt. Sorrow. She could not see its precise location, only the name of the mountain. "No. That is not quite right. I think I must return to the mountainside where the ancient battle delivered us to this world. Perhaps more will become clear, there." Raising her gaze to Everbloom, she added, "But I do not know the way there. When I awoke on this world, I was among the Healers."

Everbloom nodded while Morningglow paled. "We have a rough idea of the location. If that is where you must travel, then we will see it done." Casting a glance at Morningglow, Everbloom directed, "Tell Lord Stoirm and Lord Tine. We will need to keep our party small. Tine will undoubtedly go. Master Journeyson will make his own determination whether to go or to stay with the queen or to return to Knife Point to help gather what remains of the Soldiers of Damsa Dana. The one called Jerkin will also have to decide where his path lies. I will stay with you Little Swan. Beyond that, we will leave it to Lord Stoirm to determine how many others should accompany us."

"I will go, as well," Morningglow put in, though her eyes were filled with dread.

"You need to stay with Queen Grian Geal."

The woman shook her head. "Please. Though I fear that place like no other, I wish to stay with Lady Swan."

45

Unease pricked the nerves at the back of Whisper's neck, keeping her from the slumber she wished. She remained beneath the blankets, rolling to her side, trying to dismiss the apprehension as physical discomfort. It remained. Shifting to her back, once more, she held her breath, listening for any sounds or indications of intruders. Only Shadow's soft breathing disturbed the stillness. From the floor beside her bed, Spirit raised up, the wolf's eyes reflecting Whisper's anxiety. Perhaps therein lay the source of it. The wolf needed her freedom.

Rising, she dressed, collecting her coat and mittens before slipping from the room, Spirit padding softly beside her. The hour was early - perhaps about five of the morning, given that Juniper's door stood open and the room empty. The woman was, no doubt, in the kitchen preparing the morning's meal. The fare was growing more meager, despite the guardians' efforts to replenish the sanctuary's stores. Often, Whisper heard murmuring among them regarding increasing numbers of Red Moon Warriors crossing the border with Brightwater, destroying every farmstead they encountered. Juniper did her best to feed everyone with what was available. They needed the ability to grow their own food, once more, but even with the plateau cleared of the death brought by the beasts, it would be spring before the ground thawed enough for planting. Assuming the dark magic had not left the ground permanently barren. The thought added to her anxiety.

The rattling from the kitchens brought Whisper to a stop long enough to peer around the edge of the open archway. Juniper scuttled about, just out of sight. If the woman caught her trying to slip out, Whisper would likely be set upon with a spell to adhere her feet to the floor. But Sprit needed her freedom, and Whisper could not bear to take their parting within the darkened passage. With Juniper still out of sight, Whisper darted past the kitchens and across the dining hall, the wolf on her heels.

Falling snow greeted them as they left the passages and crept across the ruins. The accumulating depths gave broken rock and walls eerie shapes in the shadows. Above, clouds hid the moons, assuming there was anything to see of them. Whisper no longer recalled what day it was, much less which moon was in what stage. Spirit kept close to her legs, alert for any danger. The night was quiet, however, Whisper's only sense of others coming from the handful of guardians who maintained a constant vigil in the surrounding woods. More guardians were posted at the cave where they held the Soldiers of Damsa Dana. But the cave was tucked deeper in the forest, too distant to arouse any sense of their presence.

Whisper dared go no further than the edge of the ruins. For a moment, she stood, Spirit at her side. "It will be a long journey for you. And winter truly has come early. I do not remember an autumn being so cold or blanketed in so much snow." Kneeling, she stroked Spirit's head, her gaze lost in the beautiful gray-blue of the wolf's eyes. "But you must go, my friend. My soul is open to you that you may sense the depth of my gratitude for your help. May you find safe passage back to your companion. I am sure Master Journeyson needs you more than I. Go, now. Be cautious and be safe."

Spirit remained for several long seconds, a soft whine raising as she turned from Whisper to the encompassing shadows. At last, with a gentle nudge to Whisper's leg, the wolf shot away. The emptiness left at the animal's parting washed with unexpected grief over Whisper. If the sorrow struck such depth in her, how must Spirit and Brandel Journeyson have felt at their parting? With a hand clutched over her heart, she turned back toward the passage, renewed apprehension creeping through her. Freezing in place, she set her attention on her surroundings. All was as it had been. Still, her anxiety pressed to a foreboding. Cautiously, Whisper moved through the shadows, an eye to the sky as the deep gray fought toward dawn. Just beyond the ruins, a few winter birds welcomed the faint light with their chirruping.

Braced behind a crumbling wall, Whisper opened her mind, shielding herself from any inadvertent detection, seeking for the source of her apprehension. The vision crashed through her skull, buckling her knees and dropping her to the ground. Serenity! Bloodied and beaten. Lying in the snow. Unconscious. A dark figure crouched over the body; righted itself; moved away. As suddenly as it appeared, the vision vanished.

Whisper struggled to breathe. Serenity was unconscious, not dead. Please, let it be so! But…but where was she?

The foreboding intensified. Urgency filled the thin, *"Stay away! She survives, but only so long as the priestess fallen from grace does not know who she is."*

Tears streamed down Whisper's face as she gained her feet and raced back to the entrance and the passage to the temple sanctuary. Halfway along the passage, Shadow came running toward her, breathless and choked.

"You saw?"

Whisper nodded. "The warning. It came to you, as well?"

"It…it did. But how can we stay away? My grandmother is injured! We need to find her!"

Whisper swallowed and drew a shaky breath. "She needs to stay alive." Reaching an unsteady hand to Shadow, she said, "Let us go back inside. To think. To work out a plan."

Shadow jerked from Whisper's grasp. "There is no time!"

"You heard the warning. She will remain alive so long as her captors are unaware of her identity. If we act too hastily, if either of us is captured as well, then all is lost. Come back with me. Please. Shadow."

At last, Shadow turned back, her trudge witness to her agonized reluctance. They had only just returned to the dining hall when Juniper and Owl burst from the kitchen, each wrapped in their coats. The pair stopped short at the sight of the girls.

"What in the name of the Goddess Ciuin Rose!" Juniper barked, eyeing each of the cousins in turn. "I saw Shadow tear out of here, no coat, no scarf, no mittens. Neither of you have any business leaving. Not with the enemy potentially on our doorstep. What got into your heads?"

Whisper flinched under the woman's stern scrutiny. "I took Spirit out. Set her free to find her companion."

The comment prompted Juniper's quick but relieved glance back toward the passageway. "Aye. That is a good thing. Now. What of you, Shadow? What possessed you to dash out without proper clothing?"

Neither of the cousins had to suggest to the other that it might be best to keep the vision between the two of them. "A…a sudden… fear." Truth. She prayed Juniper would press no further.

Juniper's features relaxed further. "Awoke and found Whisper and her coat missing, did you?" She gave a weary shake of her head as she began pulling her coat off. "And you thought to go running out into the cold without coat and mittens to fetch her. What am I to do with the two of you?" With another shake of her head, she turned back toward the kitchen, muttering something about their connection to one another creating double the trouble.

Owl remained for several more seconds, his brow creased. At last, he pulled his coat off and turned to follow Juniper, shooting one last glance over his shoulder.

Whisper dropped onto one of the benches, still wearing her coat. Shadow plopped onto the bench across from her, bracing her arms on the table and leaning toward her cousin. "We are wasting time, sitting here."

"Hush! Let me think."

"About what?"

"I know who has her. I just do not know where."

"Who?" Shadow demanded.

"The priestess fallen from grace. That can only mean Danu. That Serenity is not dead suggests as much, as well. Had the Red Moon filth found her…" A shudder ended Whisper's words. Taking a measured breath, she managed, "The Red Moon would not waste time taking a prisoner unless they discovered some connection between Serenity and Grandmother. Serenity will do everything in her power to prevent them learning who she is."

"I do not see how that helps us find her."

Whisper waved her silent again, as Owl reappeared, carrying a tray with two steaming mugs of tea. "Here," he said, setting them to the table. "I thought you might need to warm yourselves." Leaning in close, he whispered, "There is more to this than your releasing the wolf, I will wager. If you have news…if something has happened to the Lady Swan…or to Master Journeyson… If you are planning something to help them, I want in on it."

Neither Whisper nor Shadow made any move to look at him, though Whisper offered, "So far as we are aware, they are both fine, Owl."

"Something is amiss," he persisted. "If there is anything I can do to help, I still want in."

Whisper raised her tea to her lips, murmuring, "It is Serenity," between sips.

Owl straightened, his face grave. "What can I do?"

"Nothing, for now. I need to figure out where she is being held. Then we need a plan for getting her out."

"Keep me informed," he stated flatly. "I mean it. I want to help. And someone else will want to help, as well."

"Not Juniper," Shadow muttered. "The less she knows, the better."

"She knows a lot more than you give her credit for, I would bet," Owl countered. "But no. Not Juniper. Her name is Phoenix."

The cousins exchanged surprised glances. Whisper dropped her gaze back to her tea. "I think Shadow and I will take our next meal in our quarters. Can you arrange for you and Phoenix to bring it to us?"

"Your meals in your quarters," Owl agreed before departing, empty tray in hand.

Shadow leveled an icy stare on her cousin. "We should not get anyone else involved."

Whisper ignored the comment as she ran the vision back through her mind, looking for any clues as to the location. It focused on Serenity, though, showing nothing of her surroundings beyond snow.

"Whisper!" Shadow hissed. "Are you listening to me?"

"What? Uhm." She glanced around, noticing that a handful of guardians and a couple of men she did not recognize - rescued Soldiers of Damsa Dana, perhaps - had filtered in. Must be time for breakfast.

"Come on. We need to get to our quarters."

"Why?"

"Our next meal. That would be breakfast. Owl and Phoenix will be bringing it to us there."

Whisper was on her feet heading for their room, leaving Shadow to scramble to catch up to her. "You did not hear a word I said, did you?"

"Shh!" Lengthening her stride, Whisper led the way through the kitchens, into the commons, and down the hall to their rooms.

Shadow slammed the door behind them, rooting herself in front of it, her fists on her hips. "Whisper! Stop! Look at me, damn it! We cannot get Owl or Phoenix involved! We…"

Whisper stopped in the center of the room, spinning to glare at her cousin. "We are going to need help. Just how much of the vision got through to you?"

"That my grandmother is injured. That she is lying in the snow."

"Did you not understand the warning?"

"Of course, I did!"

Glowering, Whisper set to pacing, muttering, "Stay away."

"Stay… I am not anywhere near you!"

Exasperated, she threw up her hands, spinning to face Shadow, again. "Not from me. That was the warning. Stay away."

"I heard what Serenity sent! So what? We cannot just leave her there!"

"It did not come from Serenity. She sent nothing. Her mind is closed. I sensed it from the vision. I think…I think she must be trying to keep her captors out of her head."

Heavy silence weighted the next few seconds. Shadow drew a ragged breath. "The Red Moon Warriors?"

Whisper shook her head. "I have no sense of any persons beyond that of the dark visage that loomed over Serenity. It was Danu. That much seems clear. But she certainly will not be alone."

Shadow's lips pinched, her brow knotting. When she spoke again, the music of her voice sounded a half-strangled note. "You said… You said the warning did not come from Serenity."

"It did not. But who spoke it…"

A knock at the door interrupted Whisper's thoughts. Hesitating, she responded to the second knock, calling, "Enter." A flip of her hand opened the door a sliver.

The girl named Phoenix carried in a tray with two covered plates. Behind her came Owl bearing another with a teapot and two mugs. Hesitating just inside the door, the pair waited for instructions, Phoenix taking in the private quarters with a surprised cock of her head.

"Something troubling you?" Shadow asked, gesturing the two toward the table set against the wall.

"Uhm… No. I just… It is…" Phoenix avoided eye contact with Shadow as she distributed the two plates, then moved aside to allow Owl to set his tray at the center of the table, filling the mugs with tea.

"Say whatever is on your mind," Shadow encouraged.

The girl glanced at Shadow, then waived at the room in general. "I expected something fitting your…your positions, my lady."

"Our…" Shadow darted a confused scrutiny around the room.

Whisper gave a half attentive huff. "She means, she expected our rooms to be more elaborate."

Shadow shook her head. "We hold no special status, Phoenix. We are no different than you."

"But you are. You come from royal lineage."

"Whose voice?"

Phoenix sucked in, venturing an apologetic curtsy to Whisper. "Mine, my lady. I am sorry if I disturbed you."

Shadow grimaced. "She was not criticizing or asking about you. Her mind is on other matters. As to the issue of lineage, trace your family back far enough and I dare say, you will find royalty, as well."

"My mind is listening," Whisper mumbled. It was a half-truth, at best. She was vaguely aware of the conversation as she puzzled over the vision.

"Oh no, my lady!" Phoenix objected. "My family does not descend from the Singer or from the Soul Bearer or any of the other heroes. We just…"

"Stop," Shadow groaned. "I do not know what the priestesses in Brightwater teach, but remember what I have told you. We may not have many priestesses to carry our teachings, any longer, but we still hold to them. We are all as sisters and brothers, here. Lord Stoirm is like a father to us all. And Lady Swan like a mother."

"Begging your pardon," Owl cut in. "But we have little time. How is it we can help you?"

"Stay away."

Startled, Owl raised a disgruntled glance to Whisper, "But I thought…"

Whisper blinked at him. "Sorry. I did not mean you."

"Never mind her," Shadow sighed. "She is thinking."

Owl and Phoenix moved back toward the door, waiting in silence once more.

Several seconds elapsed, Whisper mulling over, "Not Serenity's voice. Not Danu's. I have heard it before, though. Long ago. Long ago." Her words trailed off as she paced a circuit of the room. Midway through the second circuit, she turned to Owl and Phoenix. "We cannot do this alone. Shadow and I. But…"

Owl's eyes narrowed. "You cannot do what?"

"It will require some delicate planning. And I will need the help of…of a bird, I think."

"No!" Shadow declared with a stamp of her foot. "You are not doing that, again! It is far too dangerous."

"I need to sort out the details…"

Owl's mouth worked as if to ask another question. Phoenix put her hand on his arm. "Let Lady Whisper work it out in her mind, first. She will explain when it is clearer to her." Shadow cocked a brow at the girl. Phoenix dropped her gaze to her shoes. "My sister is…was much like this," she explained. "She tended to think aloud. No one could talk to her until her thoughts were well ordered."

"My thoughts refuse to order themselves," Whisper complained, rubbing her temples. "They keep spinning with snippets of visions and hints at possibilities. Nothing will settle."

Phoenix offered a faint smile. "Then speak your thoughts. All of them. Perhaps they will order themselves in the telling."

Whisper shuffled around to the chair on the further side of the table, pulling it out and dropping onto it with a thump. "Serenity is captured."

Owl straightened, tensing. His, "So you hinted at be..." again cut off by Phoenix' hand to his arm.

"I believe she is held by the High Priestess Danu. My earlier vision suggested as much. And it felt like her presence."

Shadow clinched her fists "Then they must be somewhere near the remains of our home. That is where the traitorous woman was, the last we knew. A good enough place to begin our search."

Whisper's lips pinched. It was a good place to start, but... "They are not there, now. When Spirit threatened Danu, when the High Priestess vanished, she teleported far enough that I could no longer sense her. I need to search for her camp."

Shadow started for the door. "I will alert the guardians. They can send out..."

"No. If Danu becomes aware of the search, she will guess that her captive is someone important. Right now, she does not realize Serenity's value."

"What makes you so certain?"

Whisper drew a slow, agitated breath. "Because Serenity sealed off her mind. Danu may suspect she holds someone of...interest. But she can tell nothing for certain. For all she knows, she may only hold a farm woman who perhaps escaped the Red Moon Warriors so traumatized that her mind was broken."

Shadow shuddered. "Are you sure her mind is not...?"

Rubbing her arms to ward off her own shudder, Whisper submitted, "I know the feel of a dead mind."

Silence held for several long seconds. Whisper knew Shadow waited for an explanation. She was not going to oblige. It was a pain too deep to share—the song of her father when she was teleported away from her mother's arms; the loving connection with her mother that suddenly broke, the ghostly remnants of her mother's mind going cold and empty.

"So." Shadow eyed Whisper but did not persist, returning, instead, to the issue of Serenity. "If my grandmother's mind is sealed, how did she manage to warn us to stay away?"

Whisper turned with a long moan. "I told you. The warning did not come from Serenity."

Growing more exasperated by the moment, Shadow rumbled, "Then who sent it?"

"I told you that, too. I have no idea. Just not Serenity. And not Danu. That is all I can say for certain. That and the fact that I have heard the voice before. If I could just remember when…remember where."

"Never mind, then. Never mind," Shadow growled. "We need to determine how to find my grandmother."

"I told you that, as well, if you would just listen. And do not tell me I cannot do it, again. I see no other possibility."

Owl could take it no longer, blurting, "So, how are we to help?"

"I am still not sure," Whisper admitted. "Depends on what the circumstances are when I find her. For now, just stay alert. I will contact you both when I work out what is to be done." She paused, eyeing the two of them. "You are sure you still want to be in on this?"

"No question!" Owl snorted.

Phoenix nodded, tears leaving fine streaks on her cheeks. "Serenity was kind to us. Her grace, her gentleness, her…she is what a High Priestess should be. We cannot let the False One, or anyone else, take her from us."

46

Whisper stared at the ceiling, her fingers fidgeting with the bedcovers as she waited for Shadow's breathing to indicate she had given up her arguments and gone to sleep. It was a most wearing day, fending off Shadow's persistent prodding to sneak out immediately and start a search for her grandmother, and further battling the threats to sneak out on her own if Whisper did not wish to go. She understood her cousin's sense of urgency. But they had no idea in which direction Danu's teleportation took her. And Whisper's plan had a far greater chance of success than anything Shadow contrived.

As the tension of Shadow's breathing eased and settled in an even rhythm, Whisper closed her eyes. Her plan was risky, as well, but only to herself. This time, at least, she had the advantage of leaving her body in a comfortable place with Shadow already near at hand to look after her and to keep Juniper away. Inhaling, she let her breath out slowly, stretching her mind in search of a receptive presence.

Most of the night creatures of the woods skittered away at the slightest brush of her mind with theirs. One, however, remained calm, perhaps, even, curious. A bit of probing proved the creature to be a magnificent horned owl. A perfect choice for a night reconnaissance. The startled owl danced along its branch in nervous agitation as Whisper's soul pressed in with its own, the momentary discomfort setting the bird off in a screeching and wing flapping protest. After a few moments, however, Whisper succeeded in focusing the bird's attention. Enormous wings lifted them to flight, skimming low through the trees as they rose above the canopy.

Her success quickly turned to a battle of wills when she tried to direct the bird southeast over the lower peaks. She failed to consider that the hunting range for the owl was, at most, perhaps eight kilometers. It resented being forced from its territory. The battle to keep the great bird on task was almost as wearing as her battle of wills with Shadow. At last, the foothills were beneath them, and then the ruins of their home. It was, as Shadow suggested, a good place to start. The sight of the remains of the house, the stable, the woods and the oak grove beyond, once again crushed in on Whisper, dropping the bird several meters before she shook free of the grief, shifting it to fury. Danu was no High Priestess. For no one possessing the blessings of either Damsa Dana or Ciuin Rose would ever permit such wonton destruction.

Again, she forced the owl aloft, sweeping outward from the blackened debris in expanding circles as the faint suggestion of day crept over the mountain crests. Against the backdrop of the still shadowed slopes, Whisper caught sight of the glow of a campfire about midway up one of the foothills to the northeast of their home. With the owl becoming more difficult to manage, she urged it down to the trees and again stretched her mind outward, finding an inquisitive raven. Her departure from the owl and joining with the raven proved remarkably smooth, with almost no discomfort for her or her hosts. Whisper's satisfaction trilled through the raven's frame as she congratulated herself on her improving skill.

Joined with her new host, they flew to the edge of a large encampment, lighting on a high branch of a leafless maple. Below, across a snow-covered field lay the cluster of tents where men emerged to replace those who guarded the camp through the night. At the center of the cluster stood a much larger tent bearing a once prominent bluewhite moon on its top. Now, a newly painted red moon all but covered the symbol of the Goddess Damsa Dana. Just uphill from the tents, two sentries stood outside a shambled and blackened farmhouse.

Whisper kept the raven on its perch, observing the shuffle of the guard. If Danu held Serenity… The raven's gaze went again to the crumbling farmhouse where the partially collapsed roof allowed the snow to fall within. That seemed the most likely match to the location she saw in the vision. The raven offered no resistance as Whisper urged it upwards, once more, their flight carrying them in through broken sections of the collapsed roof. Were she in her own body, she was certain the stench would leave her retching. The raven, however, sought the source of the odor. The body of a man lay buried beneath a fallen timber, that of a woman sprawled near him, her head bashed in by some great blow from behind. Whisper's relief was near overwhelming when she realized the woman was not Serenity.

Prodding was required to move the bird from feeding on the corpses to make a slow, low circle of the interior. In a snow blanketed corner beneath a gaping hole in the remains of the roof, another body lay slumped against the wall. The clothes were tattered and filthy, but Whisper recognized them, instantly. Serenity! Lighting on the ground near her aunt, she encouraged the raven nearer. Serenity's breathing was thin and ragged, her coloring pale and verging on blue. Her aunt needed warmth and medical care. But how to get her out?

Another lift and circle of the interior gave little hope. A single door near the rubble from the collapsed roof provided the only unblocked exit, and both sentries stood there. Returning to Serenity, Whisper attempted to touch her aunt's mind; to offer her hope. But it remained sealed against any intrusion.

The raven startled to flight as the door banged open. Whisper fought to calm the bird, urging it to settle on the edge of the hole in the roof to observe. One of the sentries stomped in, checking on his prisoner. For several seconds, he stood over Serenity before kicking her.

"Wake up!" he shouted, kicking her again. Serenity made no response, hanging limp in the guard's hands when he bent to shake her. Whisper expected some degree of mental response, or at the very least, a flicker of eyelids or a change in breathing. Serenity displayed nothing. Grinning, the man tore her shirt from her breasts and fondled her. His next act raised Whisper's panicked revulsion, sending the raven into a screeching and chaotic flap and swirl. Guided by Whisper's outrage, the raven dove straight for the man's face. Screaming obscenities and tripping over his partially downed trousers, the sentry darted for the door.

"You tryin' to have it with a corpse, are you?" laughed the other sentry.

"She is no corpse, yet, though that bloody bird must think she is close."

"No loss. I cannot figure why Danu insisted we hold her prisoner in the first place."

Whisper struggled to control her fury, sending the bird out across the fields to its original perch in the maple. Shielding her cry to keep it from the minds of any but her cousin, she sent her urgent, *"Shadow! Shadow!"*

"Wherethehellareyou?" returned in a molten rush.

"I found her! She is in bad shape! We need to get her out of here!"

This time, Shadow's reply rang with terror. *"Out of where?"*

"A foothill. North and east of our home. A destroyed farmhouse on the west facing slope in the shadow of Grave's Peak. The encampment is large enough for at least two hundred men, but I can only account for about a hundred. Those that are here wear both Damsa Dana's and Breag Nemhain's crests. I do not know Danu's whereabouts, or that of the rest of the men. I have no sense of their presence. Come with care but come quickly. Bring Owl and Phoenix. And..."

She knew Shadow would balk at her next demand. *"And Hawk."*

"Hawk! I would not trust that man to…"

"Please! Shadow! There is no time to argue. Tell him I need his help."

"I need to find someone to stay with your body!"

"Bring it if you can. Tell Hawk to bring it. It will make my return easier. Until then, I must remain as I am to keep watch over Serenity and to send you a proper image for your teleportation."

Whisper could sense Shadow's growing anger. Had to stifle her cousin's rebellion. *"Shadow! Hawk will do this. He will do it for me. I know it."* The sense of her cousin's fury did not ease, but at least she offered no more objections. *"Shadow,"* she pressed. *"Bring only those three. Alert no one else."*

"We should attack with a full force."

"No. There are scouts posted all around. They will see the guardians long before they are near enough to strike and are sure to call Danu and the others back. Danu's contingent holds the high ground. I do not know, yet, what weapons they possess, but I fear they may be armed with some of those longrange explosive devises. They could decimate an approaching army. We must make this as quiet and secretive as possible. I will gather all the information I can to help you make a safe teleportation. Find Owl, Phoenix, and Hawk and wait for me to send to you, again. Make no move until I do."

Whisper cut off her connection before Shadow could raise any other arguments. She needed time to flesh out her plan. A distraction would be useful. Spirit would know how to accomplish one. Why had she been so quick to send the wolf away? Nothing to be done about that, now. She would just have to devise something, herself.

Serenity remained alone when Whisper returned. Every attempt to connect with her, however, failed. *"Please,"* Whisper sent. *"Ciuin Rose! Hear me! Let my aunt live. Protect her. Touch her mind with hope. Let us take her from this place."* One more glance down, and the raven lifted into the biting chill of the day.

Her mind raced as the bird flew to settle with others of its kind. What sort of distraction could she create? Could she rouse the wolves the way Spirit did? No. Not good. Even if she could manage the feat, its similarity to the attack on Danu and the soldiers at her home would be noted. And that would likely give away the fact that she was somewhere close at hand. She needed another creature. Something large. Something that… Inspiration struck. Lifting to the air, once more, she circled the encampment again, noting the locations of the soldiers scattered through the surrounding woods, how many remained in the camp, when they took their meals. She noted, as well, that the sentries at the farmhouse took only a minute or two to check on Serenity every hour or so.

Settling back on the edge of the opening in the farmhouse roof, she memorized every detail of the surroundings and waited for one of the sentries to make his check on their captive, smugly satisfied with the worried glance he cast at the raven perched over his head. A screech and a flap of her wings sent the man on his way. Then she stretched her mind, this time seeking for the feel of her objective. The sense of the massive bull elk was so alien, she at first withdrew. She needed him, though.

The elk fought her intrusion, and she fought her repulsion. Exhausted by the endeavor, the bull sank to his knees, trembling. The strain on Whisper was as bad. Her withdrawal from the raven was simple enough but joining with the elk proved far more difficult than she expected. Her accumulating time away from her body coupled with so many soul migrations in close succession was far beyond anything she could ever have imagined attempting - the more so given the battle the bull put up. She had no time to waste, though.

"*Shadow!*"

The response came immediately. "*I am here.*"

"*Do you have the others with you?*"

A momentary hesitation preceded the sense of Shadow's resigned sigh. "*They are here.*"

"*Hawk, as well.*"

"*Aye. Hawk as well.*"

Fixing her mind on the lay of the darkened room where Serenity lay, praying she had missed no detail, she sent the vision to Shadow. "*Set this in your mind. I need a few minutes, but the moment I say, teleport to this spot. As soon as I sense you are there, I will rejoin with my body and we will teleport back the ruins.*"

"*Why not rejoin your body, now and we can teleport to Serenity together.*"

"*Trust me. I need the animal that currently hosts me.*"

"*What the hell are you?*"

"*A bull elk. Now stop jabbering. I have work to do.*"

"*A...*"

Whisper closed her connection to Shadow's stunned and disbelieving reaction, focusing on her mission. As the elk staggered to his feet, she detected the scent of his nearby harem. Though still exhausted, urging him toward them posed no problem. Once he was in their midst, her vision of erupting flames panicked the bull, which, likewise panicked the cows. Whisper's only remaining difficulty came in forcing the stampede straight toward the enemy's camp. At last, the bull wheeled the females and charged in the appropriate direction. Minutes later, they tore through the startled outer ring of guards. Soldiers and warriors poured out of tents, running for their lives. Trampled tents were set ablaze by knocked-over braziers, adding to the panic of the elk, some of which split off and headed for the farmhouse.

"Now!" Whisper sent.

She almost missed the sense of the teleportation in the chaos, as men scattered, taking cover and shooting at the terrified and rampaging herd. Excruciating pain sliced through her as she ripped her soul free of the bull, sending him into an even greater rage. Seconds later, she lay gasping in her own body, exhaustion shaking her mercilessly. Hawk stared into her eyes, his recognition of her return drawing a fleeting smile.

"Lady Whisper!"

"Shhh! Put me down and pick up Serenity. We need to get out of here, now!"

"You cannot even stand, m'lady."

"I can st…"

Owl cut her off. "I have the Lady Serenity. Phoenix and Shadow are managing the focus for our return teleportation."

Staggering to her feet, Whisper gasped, "I can help."

"You will do nothing of the sort!" Shadow snapped. "You have done quite enough and more than your share. Be still and let us handle this, or I will knock you in the head."

The shimmer and disorientation of the teleportation on top of her exhaustion set Whisper's head in a spin and left her nauseated.

"I told you," Shadow snipped as they emerged within the night shadows of the woods just beyond the ruins. "You have done quite en…"

"Take them!"

A mix of Soldiers of Damsa Dana and Red Moon Warriors shot from hiding, surrounding them. Danu emerged last, a gloating grin on her lips. "I told you we would eventually find someone of interest here. Freeing the hostages in the cave required more loss of life than I anticipated, but it was worth my while, I think. Too bad none thought to take the amulet from my spy. It led me straight to them." Danu cast a glance around. "So. Why were my soldiers taken captive? We fight on the same side. And what is it about this place that brings you to it?"

"On the same side!" Shadow spat. "You fight for the Red Moon. You are a traitor to Damsa Dana, Goddess of the White Moon."

Danu inhaled, letting her breath out slowly as she gazed at the crests on the coats and armor of those with her. "Yes. I can see your confusion. Infiltrating Aifa's forces was necessary for me to learn as much as possible. How else might we defeat them?"

Whisper pushed unsteadily to her feet, her hands clenched. "You lie." The softness of her words did nothing to hide her contempt and hatred.

Danu regarded her with cocked brow. "Ah. You must be the one they call Whisper. I understand the reasoning, now. I am sorry for your lack of trust. The good man with you..." She gestured toward Hawk. "A guardian of good standing, Hawk. He attempted to bring you to me for your own safety."

"Not for my safety," Whisper spat. "To try and draw Grandmother to you."

Danu shrugged. "That, too. Had I been successful, we all might have remained safe."

"Safe? You speak of safety? Is safety why you had your men beat Hawk near to death?" Whisper sank to her knees beside the motionless body of Serenity. "Is this how the High Priestess of the Goddess Damsa Dana treats people? Taking them hostage? Allowing the soldiers to kick, beat, and..." The last accusation stuck in her throat, the horror of it too great to name.

"I am sorry to learn of the treatment of both. These actions were not by any among my soldiers. I learned Hawk and his party were ambushed by Red Moon Warriors. As for this woman, I was unaware of her treatment. I will see that those responsible are punished."

"But you did take her prisoner," Whisper pressed. "You left her in a dark and crumbling building with no food, no water, nothing for warmth."

Whisper could tell Danu weighed her words before speaking. "Aye," the woman acknowledged. "I did have her taken to the building. I rescued her from the Red Moon Warriors, though. They are the ones who captured her and would have killed her had I not requested her custody. I thought she might be of some value. But her mind was gone. No doubt compliments of Aifa's interrogations. She was all but dead when she was delivered to me. What need has she for food or water or warmth?"

A low hiss escaped Shadow. Whisper reached to grab her cousin's hand, quieting her, though her own hushed words carried equal vehemence. "You made no attempt to tend to her injuries. Instead, you left her to the whims of your indecent soldiers and to the cold."

"She is a friend of yours, I assume. I am sorry for her, of course. But to my knowledge, there is no spell nor medicine that can mend a broken mind. In her state, she remains unaware of the cold or of her mistreatment."

Shadow seethed. "That excuses nothing!"

"More than a friend, I see. Mother, perhaps? Or…Grandmother?" Whisper could not grab fast enough to prevent Shadow's launch at Danu. The sword hilt of one of the soldiers against Shadow's head crumbled her to the ground before she could reach her mark. Whisper darted to catch her but was jerked clear by another soldier.

Danu's lips pursed as she studied her captives. "Take them to the cave where they held some of you. See that any wounds are well tended. Provide them with food, water, and warmth. But do not let them from your sight. I suspect we have three valuable individuals in our care but must confirm their identities. And I must know why these ruins feel so…odd."

47

Brandel fidgeted with the pommel of the sword sheathed at his side as he paced the empty council chamber. It was the first time he had worn a sword since leaving Brightwater. He had not believed it necessary or wise to enter Knife Point looking to be more than his lord's emissary. Did not believe the enemy had already crossed into the Knife Point realm. His mission no longer existed, his belief regarding the Red Moon menace proven false time and again. The whole of Slievgall'ion was now at war with Aifa and the Red Moon Warriors.

Queen Grian Geal's and Lord Stoirm's entrance brought him about, uncertain whether to bow or salute.

"Please," Grian Geal said. "Just sit. Would you care for some wine or ale?"

Stoirm closed the door and strode around to sit in what appeared to be his accustomed place, the first chair to the right of the queen's. It struck Brandel as odd that he would do so while the queen yet stood. "Nothing, thank you," he said, crossing to join them at the table, then hesitating.

"Any seat will do." Grian Geal waited patiently as Brandel took a chair near the end of the table. "You made your decision?" she asked.

Brandel offered a stiff nod. "I was lied to and betrayed. Danu is no priestess of the White Goddess. I believe she speaks for none but herself. I also believe she was behind letting the Red Moon Warriors through Riversong's gates." He met the queen's scrutiny with solid resolve. "She had the Lady Whisper kidnapped. It makes little difference that the girl is safely returned to the temple. Danu needs to answer for her treachery."

Grian Geal and Stoirm exchanged guarded glances. "What?" Brandel asked. "What new foul deed do you report?"

"The girl is taken, again," Stoirm answered, his tone steady though his features spoke of his worry. "She and Shadow and Serenity. The girls, along with three others - Owl, a girl named Phoenix, and Hawk of the guardians - set out to rescue Serenity when they learned of her capture. All were just outside of the temple ruins. They are currently held in the cave where some of the Soldiers of Damsa Dana awaited Shadow's scrutiny. The soldiers who remain loyal to Damsa Dana and the surviving guardians who held them are now captives with Whisper, Shadow, Serenity, and the others. One of the guardians was able to send to me of the attack on them, and of their capture. That was the last we heard."

"Hawk," Brandel spat. "No doubt this was, at least in part, his doing."

Stoirm shook his head. "The guardian reported that Hawk was fighting at their side, though he suffered a grievous wound at the hands of Danu."

Brandel shrugged off the news, more concerned for the ladies and Owl. "Is a rescue planned?" The lack of response to his question galled him. "How can you sit here and do nothing?" Again, getting no reply, he shoved to his feet. "Then I will go to them."

"There is naught any can do for them at this moment. And we need your help, here," Grian Geal stated. "We need to learn everything about this Witch who was High Priestess; everything about Brightwater and about the Soldiers of Damsa Dana, as well. Why would they continue to follow this woman when she is so obviously in league with Aifa and the Red Moon Goddess?"

Brandel's shoulders slumped, his eyes turning to the dull gray world beyond the window. "There were rumors that our High Priestess practiced dark magic. Many among the soldiers believed she was doing so to find a means of defeating Aifa. Some few believed that she turned traitor. A few others did not care which side she took, so long as she held them in high standing."

Stoirm leaned back, eyeing him. "And which were you?"

Shifting, Brandel fixed a cold stare squarely on the Lord of Knife Point. "While I never approved of her haughtiness, her seeming cold indifference to her sister priestesses, or her obvious disregard for Lord Strongbow, I refused to believe she would turn to dark magic. Never did it cross my mind that she would become traitor to our Goddess and our people. Not until I learned of the betrayal and death of Strongbow did I begin to suspect."

Brandel bit back his next thoughts - that for Danu to forsake her Goddess and her people with no retribution, Damsa Dana must be dead. Perhaps Ciuin Rose, as well. With a weary shake of his head, he added, "I must try and find Danu's prisoners. Save them if I can." He pointed to a stack of papers on the far corner of the table. "Knowing you would request information, I spent all of last night and into this morning sketching maps and writing descriptions of the lay of

Brightwater's lands and its strongholds, at least as it was when I left. There is also a full accounting of how our soldiers are trained and the types of weapons we use. May the information serve you well. And may you show no mercy to any among the Soldiers of Damsa Dana who chose to follow Danu."

Grian Geal nodded. "Then you will travel with Lady Swan and the Lords Stoirm and Tine. They are leaving for the mountain upon which the Goddesses were returned. Depart from their company when you feel you must. May you find those you seek while they still live."

Brandel, at last, bowed to the queen, saluted Stoirm, and strode from the room. Stoirm quickly joined him. "We will leave at nightfall," the Alainn said. "We must travel from Deep Hall to where the Dylan River crosses the Emer. The snows may not be upon the plains, yet. And there are roads to follow. Horses are being provided for us. At the crossing of the rivers, we will teleport to the head waters of the White Moon River."

"And from there?"

"To the remains of the Healer's complex and on to Mt. Sorrow. By what path, however, remains to be seen."

"Mt Sorrow." Brandel's scowl came with a troubled shake of his head. "A forsaken place, blasted and haunted by unsettled souls, if the stories are true."

"It is Caer's destination, none the less. I must leave you, now. Tine will come for you when it is time."

Brandel acknowledged with a salute, then turned for his own quarters. Jerkin was there, carefully packing Brandel's few belongings and laying out his traveling clothes, hooded coat, mittens, and thick leather boots. Jerkin's pack was resting against the wall just inside the door, so stuffed that the seams threatened to burst. There was no need for the boy to accompany him further. Jerkin should remain here, where he would be safe. Brandel knew, however, that he would never accept remaining behind.

"What did you pack?" he asked with a toss of his head in the direction of the boy's gear. "Surely not all of it is necessary. Your back will break under such weight."

"My back is quite strong, sir. It will not break. And every item packed is a necessity."

"Well, see that you leave room in mine for rations without over stuffing it."

"Aye, sir. The kitchen is preparing some for you. I will go see if they are ready."

As the boy trotted from the room, Brandel strode to the open door and leaned against the frame, staring down the empty hallway. Though his intentions to find Whisper, Shadow, and Serenity were declared, he was torn. Legend had it that an Alainn called Stoirm was an accomplished soldier. Whether Lord Stoirm was that same Alainn, Brandel could not say. Nor did he know Tine's capabilities on a battlefield. He knew his own abilities. Given the importance placed on Caer, was it not his duty to continue with her?

His jaw tightened. Caer trusted the two Alainn with her life. Had apparently done so for many a century. Whisper, Shadow, and Serenity, however, had no one protecting them. He was a fool not to have sent Spirit to find them when he and the wolf parted. Perhaps Spirit could have found Whisper in time to protect her, at least.

The day drug on, his anxieties rising in the waiting, his pacing at last replaced by a weary settling on a chair. What if he could not find the hostages? What if he was already too late and they were dead? He fought to keep such thoughts from his mind; worked to convince himself he would succeed. At length, he fell to an uneasy sleep, his mind playing out any number of grotesque images of the dead hostages.

"They live."

Brandel blinked awake, recognizing the soft touch of Caer's sending. *"They live? How can you know that?"*

"My connection to them is strong. And my visions tell me they are alive. The girls suffer at the hands of Danu. But not so severely as Serenity, who was taken by Aifa and a mix of Red Moon Warriors and later passed into Danu's hands."

"They will pay!" Brandel hissed.

"You must find them, first."

"Where do I look?"

"The visions offer only glimpses, but I believe they remain in the cave spoken of by Stoirm."

"You should come, my lady. Do not go to Mt. Sorrow. I fear you are being led into a trap."

"Do not fear for me, Master Journeyson. Roisin is with me." Brandel held back his gravest fear.

"She is not dead, my friend. Roisin's soul survives. As does Dana's. They struggle, but they remain."

"It is time, sir," Jerkin announced.

Brandel glanced around to find the boy dressed in his heavy coat and standing next to the bed. "When did…"

"Slipped in a few moments ago. Did not want to disturb your thoughts, sir."

Shaking himself, Brandel pushed up from the chair. "Right. Thanks. What of the rations you…"

Jerkin nodded to Brandel's pack. Snatching his own, the boy labored to get the straps pulled on over the coat sleeves and drawn up to his shoulders. "Finished the packing, sir. While you thought."

Brandel shoved his mittens in his coat pockets, draped his coat over his arm, and lifted one strap of his pack to a shoulder, then followed Jerkin down the long hall, past the council chamber, past the dining hall, and through the commons, meeting the others of their party in the passage that led out of the depths. The trek was another long climb through yet another dark tunnel, the confines and steep grade leaving him sweating and worrying about Jerkin beneath the weight of his pack and heavy coat. When they at last emerged through a narrow gap between boulders and into the night, the boy's face was red, his damp hair hanging in clumps across his forehead. Stoirm motioned a halt a short distance out, allowing Jerkin to drink from a small stream and rest. Minutes later, the Lord of Knife Point responded to a whistled call, striding out to greet two Alainn who appeared from behind one of the boulders leading horses.

"Are you sure about this, Lord Stoirm?" one asked. "Horses will draw more attention than a small party on foot."

"We will take it a leg at a time. If we get word that the Red Moon has infiltrated an area, I will send to you where we left the horses. For now, haste has precedence."

Brandel was relieved to have the mounts, though he worried about Everbloom's, Morningglow's, and Caer's ability to ride. His concern was unwarranted. Each of them secured their packs to the backs of saddles and were mounted in less time than he required, handling their reins with competence.

Caer met his chagrinned glance with a smile. "I have been riding since before your great grandfather was born, lieutenant. I dare say, Everbloom and Morningglow even longer."

He cast a dubious glance at Everbloom and Morningglow. He was beginning to accept Caer's age, but the other two appeared…

Everbloom cocked a brow at him. "Do not dare to ask us our ages, lieutenant."

He needed no further warning to set his mind to other matters.

Stoirm took the lead, Caer behind him with Everbloom and Morningglow flanking her. Brandel signaled Jerkin to fall in next while he and Tine took to the rear. The pace was initially cautious, the trails along the rocky slopes narrow and twisting. At last convinced of the sure-footedness of his mount, he turned his attention to the sky. The night was clear, the rose moon now the only one visible, its sliver waxing toward crescent. Though the red moon was the last to go to new moon phase, she would show again before the white moon reappeared. Unless Brandel was mistaken, all three would be full at the same time with this cycle. It was a rare occurrence and one that troubled him. Three full moons signified a strengthening of the magic of this world. It also brought the highest and most dangerous of the Goddess tides along Brightwater's coasts. If the Red Moon Warriors were now taking their ships further north, they would likely redouble their assaults before the tides threatened to dash their vessels on the rocks.

His growl rumbled in his chest. Aifa had no cause to send more ships. Brightwater was already fallen. With the warriors established across the land, more troops could be teleported to each location. The same could be said of bringing more troops into Knife Point, as well. As for the weapons… The…what was it Caer called them… the firearms? Many of those were apparently small enough for each warrior to carry several. The large machines, though. How much energy would be required to teleport those through?

"One worry at a time, lieutenant."

Brandel flinched. *"Do not tell me you could read my thoughts on my face,"* he shot back at Caer. *"You are well ahead of me and the night is not so bright as to catch much of a backward glimpse of me."*

"Your tension emanates from you in waves, my friend. And I saw you considering the sky. You worry what the upcoming triple full moon may bring. It is a worry beyond our control. As are Aifa's weapons. For now, focus on our immediate journey."

"About that. Why do we take this route from Deep Hall? Why not teleport back to Singer's Hold?"

"Singer's Hold is south of where we must go," Tine sent. *"As for teleporting elsewhere, we do not know how extensive the Red Moon incursion is in these lands. We dare not risk emerging in a location that may be overtaken. Once we reach the crossing of the Emer and Dylan Rivers, I will send to our outpost at the head waters of the White Moon River. If it is safe, we will teleport there. From there it is a short distance through the western arm of the Song Mountains. We can travel up the valley and then begin our climb back to the Knife Point Range."*

"Why not teleport from here to the outpost at the White Moon River?"

It was Stoirm who answered. *"Because, at present, there is no one manning that location. The individual stationed there should be completing her patrol and return to it by the time we reach the crossing of the rivers."*

Brandel rode on without further comment, Stoirm setting the horses at full gallop across the first valley. The terrain was drier than in Knife Point, the vegetation different, as well, though he had little opportunity to note more than the fact that the trees were largely pine, fir, and white oak, their forests also less dense than Knife Point's.

They cleared the last of the rocky slopes late the following night, resting at the side of a creek in a last stand of thin woods. Beyond lay an expanse of low, rolling hills dotted with scrubs and sedges. Stoirm once again spurred the horses to full gallop, resting them only when the cover of boulders or a rare clump of trees could be found. At midmorning they reached the road that followed the Emer River east. They encountered no one during their journey, arriving at the first outpost at dusk and just as a mix of guardians and Alainn were returning from a scouting expedition. The group eagerly shared a hot meal, the scouts indicating they found no signs of the Red Moon between the Emer River and the spur of the White Moon River. As night deepened, Caer insisted they move on.

Another night and day bled into yet another night before they reached the second outpost. Two Alainn were preparing to ride south. They reported receiving word of sightings of the warriors offshore below the bluffs north of where the White Moon River emptied into the Kuheeoo-nu Ocean. Stoirm allowed for a brief rest, then pushed on, delivering them at the end of the next day to the outpost at the crossing of the Emer and Dylan Rivers.

A single Alainn called Rain manned the post, her news bleak. Red Moon Warriors now held the whole of Brightwater, and everything from Grave's Peak to the slopes just below Knife Point Keep. A small party was also seen crossing the lesser slopes of the Song Mountains at the boundary between Knife Point and the outpost lands. A contingent of guardians had been dispatched, the battle brief. The Red Moon party proved to be scouts, most of whom were killed, though one, at least, escaped. If he succeeded in sending word to Aifa, they could expect the farmsteads and villages of the lesser mountains to be attacked by a full Red Moon force within days. The guardians were too few to hold them, for the majority of their ranks had been recalled in defense of Knife Point Keep. Rain provided a warm meal as she outlined the reports she received, urging them to return to Deep Hall, and from there to go with Grian Geal to the lands of Ga Gréine.

Caer listen without comment, her expression unreadable. When the briefing was complete, she thanked the woman, then excused herself.

Tine and Everbloom rose to accompany her as she donned her coat and set out for the door. Her glance warned them off.

"Give her some space," Stoirm advised. "She carries a great burden and needs time to consider her path."

Brandel's scowl prompted Stoirm's, "You would counsel her to do as Rain suggested. She is aware of that, lieutenant. It is the counsel we all wish to give. But the only decision that is ours is whether we continue with her, regardless of her decision. As I said, give her a little space."

Brandel responded with a short nod, pushing away from the table. There was nothing for him to do but pace, though, so he remained seated, knowing Rain's scrutiny was on him.

"A lieutenant," she said, though it seemed more a question. "A Soldier of Damsa Dana."

"Aye." Brandel cocked a brow. "Is that a problem?"

Rain shrugged. "You are trusted by Lord Stoirm and Lord Tine. And your young friend…" She swept a hand toward Jerkin, who was standing near the hearth where a small fire burned. "He appears quite dedicated to you."

Brandel huffed. "Too much so. I prefer he return to the temple sanctuary or to Deep Hall where he will be safe. Following me may well get the boy killed."

"You could command him to remain behind."

"To what end? He would likely follow me, anyway. Which would leave him traveling alone and some distance behind. At least this way I can provide some degree of protection for him."

"I can protect myself," Jerkin retorted. "Been doing it all my life."

"I have no doubt. But one…" Brandel started to say 'boy' promptly correcting it to, 'man'. "One man alone is not wise in these times." Rain's scrutiny relaxed a little, her gaze shifting to the door. "Our Little Swan trusts you, as well, else you would not be here. Do you intend to continue with her, whatever her decision?"

"For so long as our paths lie in the same direction, I will continue, and I will protect her with my life."

"But your paths. You expect them to diverge."

"Depends."

SLIEVGALLION: THE GODDESS WARS

"On?"

"On whether we happen across the ladies Serenity, Whisper and Shadow, or whether I must go looking for them."

"They are held captive, lieutenant."

"I am aware of that."

"And you intend to rescue them. One man. Alone."

"Two men," Jerkin put in.

Rain considered in silence for several seconds. "You would choose to go with the lieutenant rather than offer your protection to the Lady Swan?"

"Seems to me she is in the best hands possible. Lord Stoirm, Lord Tine, and the Ladies Everbloom and Morningglow will let nothing happen to her. As Master Journeyson said, one man alone is not wise."

Rain's smile was slow, but it came, at last, suggesting her approval. "Had I any others at my command, I would send half with the Lady Swan and half with you, Lieutenant Journeyson."

Brandel finally stood, returning her smile. "We will work with what is available." His glance shot to the door.

"If you are thinking to go in search of Lady Swan," Stoirm said. "No need. She is close. And she is safe. She will return when she is ready."

48

Kneeling at the edge of the stream between two massive oak roots anchored in the silted bank, Caer sent her plea. *"Roisin, I need your council."* Eyes closed, she waited. *"Roisin. Please! Is my path truly to Mt. Sorrow?"*

The emptiness terrified her. Was it as she feared? Was Roisin gone? And Dana, as well? Without the guidance of the two, what hope had she of accomplishing anything? Listen to her own voice, Roisin told her. But her own voice remained confused. Exhausted and shivering from the cold and from her fears, Caer curled up on the ground, and gave in to her sobs.

Frigid night. Charred and blackened stone stands above a new snowfall smeared red beneath Nemhain's moon. Tormented souls scream out their pain. So many souls! The tortured cries of the banished echo through the ether, the suffering of the souls locked within Slievgall'ion causing the ground to tremble. The stain of so many deaths forever mar the place of the beginning. The place of…

A hillside. White stone mound gleams on the hill's crest. Screams of the wounded and dying are drowned in the clash and fury of magic against weapons.

A map, hazed by time. Mt. Sorrow. Just the word stands prominent. Beneath lies a smear. Sliev…

Silence. The universe spins. Ghostly firelight flickers. Music, faint but lively. Silhouettes dancing, striking the rhythm with their feet. One, two, three, four, five, six, seven. One, two, three. One, two, three.

Laughter and song. So familiar, the voice.

Grief choked Caer to waking, a thin blanket of snow covering her. She brushed it away and struggled to her feet. Numb, she turned, her eyes skimming over the land, past the lighted windows of the outpost, at last staring toward the northeast. There lay the place where the great battle destroyed one world and marked the beginning of the slow destruction of another. She turned again, staring east. Somewhere out there, what remained of her joy suffered at the hands of Danu. Her heart longed to go in search of the three. Her gaze was drawn back to the northeast. There lay the path she was urged to take. And Roisin either could not or would not help her.

"Do not think about going to that place alone, Caer."

Jumping, she stumbled in her jerked spin. Stoirm grabbed her shoulders to steady her. "Do not sneak up on me!" she glowered.

"I did no sneaking. In fact, I made as much noise as I could manage on damp ground." Stoirm studied her for a moment, dusting snow from her shoulders and hood. "Roisin is silent," he said. Caer gave a slow nod. "But you possess her memories," he continued. "You will find the answers to your questions in those. And this may help." He extended a closed hand.

Caer held out her open palm and watched him lay a charm on it—a finely worked trinity knot with a blood-red stone at its heart. She had not worn this since the time of her arrival on this world. Had not even looked at it. Better that it lay buried and out of sight for all the pain and grief bound up with it. Dylan's face flashed to mind. And Adrian's. And all the rest. Dead. Gone. The necklace, too, was dead, the magic that once manifest within it long dark and silent. She split the necklace many an age ago; gave the charm to the High Priestess of Ciuin Rose. The fine silver chain she gave to the High Priestess of Damsa Dana. Both women were long dead. She could not say how the charm came to be in Stoirm's possession. The chain, however, now lay in the hands of an enemy.

Her palm twitched at the subtle flutter of a faint pulse from the charm. Her fingers instantly closed tight around it, her mind and soul torn between fear and hope. "Where did you find this?" she managed. "And why did you bring it?"

"It was sent into my keeping just before the temple fell. I set it in a box and placed it in your private sanctuary at the fortress. It has been within your grasp for several years."

"The silver box." Caer shook her head. "I thought it something belonging to you."

"And you never thought to look?"

She shrugged. "If it was yours and you chose to hide it away, it was not my business to snoop."

Stoirm huffed his mild amusement. "I do not suppose your lack of curiosity made much difference. Its magic seemed dead. Undisturbed, it remained quiet until I passed it upon our leaving. For the first time since that long ago battle, I sensed a faint urgency about it. Saw the briefest flicker within the stone. Magic is waking within it, Caer. I believe you are meant to carry it, once more."

Thrusting her hand back at him, she rasped, "No! It caused nothing but death and sorrow before. It led me to destroy a world and bring great threat to another. I will not take it, again."

"You do not know that the world we left was destroyed. And the blame for the threat brought here does not lie with you. Whether you will it or not, your feet carry you toward another battle. Perhaps this will provide the means for ending it once and for all."

"We believed that once before," Caer moaned, her gaze locked on her closed fist. "You see where that got us." For several long moments, they stood, her hand still outstretched. At last, she drew it back and opened her fingers. The pulse of the necklace was still faint, though she recognized that it matched her own heartbeat, just as it had always done in those long-ago days. And the stone did, indeed, hold a thin, pale glow. "It will be a short battle. We have no time for researching or creating an arsenal to match Aifa's. We do not have the numbers to match her warriors."

"True," Stoirm sighed. "But you have the charm."

"It lacks its chain."

"Perhaps the chain will be reunited before we engage Aifa. We may yet save this world."

"Save it...or lose it?" Caer shuddered as she stuffed the charm into her pocket, glancing up into Stoirm's remarkable blue eyes, their topaz glow faint but noticeable. Though she stiffened, her voice still trembled. "To Mt. Sorrow."

"If that is where you believe you must go. From here, however, we must travel by foot." Stoirm nodded toward the door of the outpost cabin. Tine appeared in the doorway and trotted toward them, his pack on his back, his father's and Caer's over his arms. Handing off his father's, Tine slipped the straps of Caer's up and over her shoulders. Caer glanced once more toward the outpost, her brow creased.

"Master Journeyson experienced a sudden sense of urgency. He and Jerkin are gone," Tine said. "They set out for the valley between the arms of the Song Mountains a few hours ago. Journeyson plans to go from there north toward the temple ruins to begin his search for Serenity and the girls. He will also seek for any Soldiers of Damsa Dana who remain loyal to the Goddess."

The news came as no surprise. Still, it offered Caer a small glimmer of hope. "May he find them and get them to safety," she murmured.

Stoirm's brow creased. "I have not yet had word from the outpost at the White Moon River. The next leg of our journey is in question."

Caer took a slow breath. "Then let us go to Elk Valley. Near the headwaters of the Emer River. There is an ancient burned-out hollow of a rowan tree in the midst of a thicket."

"Aye," Tine nodded. "I know the place. Decent enough to chance a teleportation. The thicket will give us good cover, should the enemy be lurking. Just grant a moment for Morningglow and Everbloom to join us."

Caer shook her head. "I will not take them where I go. They need to return to Grian Geal. The queen needs them.

Tine's lips pinched as he shot a glance over his shoulder. "They will not like this," he said. "But I agree. Let us be quick."

They emerged in a small open patch next to the burned rowan tree and surrounded by thorny wild roses. The silence of the startled night creatures lasted but a few seconds. Above them, the disgruntled hoot of an owl accompanied the flap of great wings as the bird took flight from one of the tree's dead branches. Caer sagged against the trunk. She hated teleporting. The momentary disorientation and the slight vertigo were no less upsetting than her first experiences with traveling via magic all those many centuries ago. Why she could not accustom herself to it after so much time was a mystery and an annoyance. When her head finally settled, Tine stood directly in front of her, poised to defend her, should the need arise.

"Naught here but what should be," Stoirm declared. "We can rest a bit before setting out."

"We set out, now," Caer objected. "I want to make it to the woodlands of the first rise on the other side of the valley before morning's light."

"As you wish," Stoirm acknowledged. "We can rest for the day near Merri Creek."

Tine took the lead, working through the brambles to an elk trail that ran mostly in the direction they intended to travel. Caer fumbled with the straps of her pack, though nothing she did lightened the weight on her shoulders. The way climbed, descended, and climbed again. Stumbling more and more, she fought to keep her eyes open. "Too many days and nights with too little sleep," she muttered. And then she was walking no longer. Whether it was Tine or Stoirm who carried her, she did not know. Did not care. Sleep was all that mattered.

Flickers of firelight. Warmth upon her face. Bright music. She dances, stamping and turning, gliding across the ground and around the great fire. Shadow and light play across smiling faces while hands clap out the cadence of pipe and fiddle and bodhran. Magic fills her. Becomes her. Flows into her dance. Music slows, the jig sedates, drifting into a ballad. The song rises. So beautiful the voice! The singer, a boy some handful of years her senior. His gaze follows her. A shadow crosses in front of him. Her sister's back is to her, attention focused on the singer. The older girl's sensual movements sway her body. A better match. Her sister is closer in age to the boy. Neither her sister nor she can be promised in marriage, though. Not until their eldest sister is promised. The boy rises, slipping to one side, his song never broken, his eyes again seeking her. Not her sister. He seeks her!

Caer uncurled and stretched, waking to the thin light of morning, the sun filtering through interwoven twigs and branches, her mind still flush with the pleasant sense of acknowledgement and interest. The singer was nowhere to be found, however. Instead, the reality of their circumstances settled as she noted Stoirm sleeping only a couple of meters from her, his hands folded over his chest, a blanket pulled up to his chin.

"Rise if you must, Caer," Tine sent. *"But let father sleep a little longer. He carried you most of the night and then stood first watch."*

Rolling from beneath her blanket, she gained her feet, slipping well past Stoirm before stretching again, this time to work out kinks and strains. The bite of the cold on her face was bitter, though tucked within her coat, hood, and mittens, the rest of her faired reasonably well. *"He need not have carried me at all. I can walk on my own."*

Tine shifted from behind a near boulder, one brow ticked up in amusement. *"You are not very adept at sleep walking."*

Caer made her way around the boulder to join him, sitting beside him in the unfiltered sunshine. Its warmth vied with the icy teeth of the breeze that rippled the long, brown meadow grasses. Shielding her eyes, she glanced around, taking in the sparse trees. The burble of a creek could be heard not too far distant to her right. The sound was interrupted by the rumble of her stomach. Tine reached for his pack and withdrew a bun and some jerky, handing them across to her.

"I will not eat your rations. I carry my own."

"When was the last time you checked your pack?' Caer's lips pinched. She could not recall.

Tine chuckled. "Your pack was never filled with rations. Father and I carry enough for you."

"I am not helpless!" Caer snorted, her brow drawn down with indignation, though she knew her strength was waning.

"Whatever it is you must do, Little Swan, you will need your reserves to accomplish."

Caer's shoulders slumped. "Why me? Why must I be the one to accomplish anything more?"

"You know the answer to that."

Again, her lips pinched as she turned an irritated study to the toes of her boots. "I did not ask to be the one to carry their souls. Did not ask for their memories to be locked with my own. What good are they to me, anyway? I cannot simply call them up at will. Even if I could, they show me nothing useful."

Tine shrugged. "How can you expect to know their usefulness until you know your purpose?"

"How am I to know my purpose when neither Roisin nor Dana speak to me?" The next several minutes were taken up with her angry gnawing on a strip of jerky and the bun. "I hate this, you know," she grumbled.

"We can look for a farmhouse along the way and hope for a better meal."

"Not what I meant. It is the not knowing. Not knowing precisely where I am supposed to go. Back to the beginning. I am assuming that means Mt. Sorrow. But what if it means something else? Not knowing my path. Not knowing my purpose once I reach my destination. Not having visions from the Sight to guide me. I may well be walking blind into a bloodbath."

"Your visions will guide you."

"If they come again and show my purpose. Even when they do come, they do not reveal what I am expected to do."

"You worry too much," Stoirm said, strolling around to face her. Caer had rarely seen the Alainn unshaven or disheveled. Stoirm's hair had always been nearly white, and until perhaps a century ago, he kept it long. It was approaching that length, again, and hung in tangles, dead leaves caught in it. His features, which always seemed so elegantly chiseled, had grown gaunt of late, faint creases creeping along his brow and edging the corners of his eyes. That and the fact that his coat was smeared with dirt and also carried a collection of dead leaves, gave him something of a feral look.

He grinned. "Do I look that bad?"

Caer cringed. Would she never learn to keep her thoughts - all her thoughts -guarded? "Of course not. You just do not look yourself."

"Lies never become you, Caer," he laughed. "And long journeys change the looks of all who undertake them. Even you, little one."

Turning, he headed in the direction of the creek, calling back over his shoulder, "If you wish to bathe, do so now and quickly. Otherwise, repack your packs. We have rested too long."

49

Jerkin's teleportation delivered them to a boulder-strewn clearing a little south and across two rises from the temple ruins. The boy's skill was remarkable, carrying them much further than Brandel had dared to hope, and depositing them squarely between the two largest stones. The irritated tones of a conversation kept them crouched low and out of sight.

Brandel muttered a quiet thank you to the Goddess Damsa Dana for placing Jerkin in his life. Then offered another to the Goddess Ciuin Rose, just for good measure.

"...there is anything within those ruins," one man was saying, "we will never find it. Those damnable spirits will not let us anywhere near."

"She suspects there is a hidden sanctuary. Part of the old temple, maybe," another said. "Even if true, the cowards within are offering no resistance to our presence. That comes solely from the spirits that haunt those grounds."

"So, why is she havin' us waste our time lookin' for a way in? Leave that accursed place, I say. We would be of more use helpin' with the assault on Knife Point Keep."

A muttering of expletives followed, accompanied by the sound of something heavy ringing off metal. "This damned thing is of no more use. Hittin' them trees broke it beyond repair. We will never get it back in the air. She will demand Gamble's head for flyin' it so low and bein' so careless at night. All that is left for us to do is scavenge what we can from it to take back to camp."

For what seemed an eternity, they listened to the two men banging and clattering about. At last, the scraping and creaking of metal on metal and the voices faded. Brandel ventured a glance and spotted them dragging pieces of a machine to the north. Their camp must be somewhere in the vicinity of the ruins. He and Jerkin continued to wait in silence for several more minutes before moving out from their cover to scan their surroundings. The remains of one of the flying machines lay crumpled at the feet of several large, broken, and splintered trees.

"Now what?" Jerkin asked. "We dare not go back to the sanctuary to resupply. Nor, from the sounds of things, do we dare to go to Knife Point Keep."

"We will not find the ladies at the keep, in any event. Can you shield your mind sufficiently to send to Juniper from here?"

"Aye. What do you want me to say?"

"Ask if she is aware of the enemy outside her door. And ask for any news of Serenity and the girls."

Jerkin nodded, his face creasing in concentration. Moments later, an uneasy twitch preceded, "They are aware of the enemy. As for the Ladies Whisper and Shadow, they, along with Hawk, Phoenix, and Owl, snuck away. Gone to look for Serenity, she believes. Thought she sensed the briefest flicker of their return, then nothing. She fears all are taken captive. I did not tell her we knew of their capture."

"Good."

The boy waited in anxious silence while Brandel considered further. "We need a means of scouting the lay of things. I wish Sp…"

Brandel's comment was cut short as his sense of the white wolf's presence filled his mind. Spinning, he found the bedraggled animal gazing warily at him from the very spot he and Jerkin had hidden only moments before. The rush of joy that swept him all but knocked Brandel from his feet. The bounding of the wolf succeeded where the rush of emotion failed. Sprawled on the ground, Spirit over him, he could almost swear the creature was smiling. "I need to get up," he laughed, pushing out from beneath her weight.

Spirit stepped from him, waiting at his side as he gained his feet and leaning into his hands in acceptance of the intense head scratching he offered.

Jerkin gave a nervous laugh. "I feared she was charging you to eat you, sir."

"Thankfully, I have yet to do anything so egregious as to push her to that point. Though, I dare say, I have come close." He gave Spirit's head a gentle nudge. "That is enough for now," he said, dropping to a knee to meet the wolf's gaze. "We need to get serious my friend. Can you find Whisper?"

An image flashed through his mind. "A cave, I think," he relayed to Jerkin.

"Can you describe it, sir?"

"Not particularly deep. Ten meters, perhaps. Low ceiling. Figures have to stoop to walk beneath it."

"Anything more?"

"One wall bears an etching. A landscape with a single moon."

"Is the etching's landscape wooded or open?"

"Open. With the impression of water."

Jerkin nodded. "I know that cave. It is as Stoirm learned. That is the place where the Soldiers of Damsa Dana awaited their meeting with Lady Shadow. It lies beyond the temple ruins. Sits in the woods at the base of a hill. Can you see it, again? Can you tell me exactly how many people are arranged and where?"

Brandel turned to Spirit. "I need to see more."

Spirit's annoyance rumbled through Brandel, though another image also rose. A small hand scratched in the dirt. "Stay away. We will be slaughtered if anyone comes for us." The hand promptly smeared dirt back over the writing, replacing it with, "Protect Grandmother," before erasing that, as well. The vision then made a slow scan. Shadow hovered over a prone and unconscious Serenity. The woman looked near death. Another woman…girl…sat on the other side of Serenity, pale and shaking, her face streaked with tears. Further to the back of the cave slumped a severely beaten Hawk, Owl next to him, the boy's features strained, his eyes closed. Not far to one side of him was a small cluster of Soldiers of Damsa Dana and Guardians of Ciuin Rose. All of them, Hawk and Owl included, had hands bound behind their backs. Only the women, it seemed, remained unshackled.

As the scan moved to the front of the cave, he counted no less than a dozen men wearing the crest of the Red Moon Warriors on their breast plates. Some, however, still wore cloaks bearing the White Moon, as well. Worse, standing in a line between the mix of warriors and soldiers and the clusters of prisoners was a row of what Brandel assumed were weapons mounted on tripods, all aimed inward at the captives. Whisper, for it had to be she who was connecting with the wolf, was correct. To attempt a rescue would mean their slaughter.

Brandel shook his head, his lips pinched. Jerkin eyed him with concern. "How bad, sir?"

"Unless you know of another way into that cave, we cannot effect a rescue without risking their deaths."

"No, sir. That cave was carved out by the undercutting of the river long ago. At some point, the river changed its course, leaving the scooped-out hillside high and dry." The boy studied his boots in silence. "Can we do nothing, sir?"

"For now. I will keep tabs on them through Spirit. She will alert us if the prisoners are moved."

Jerkin cast a confused scrutiny to the wolf. "How did you do it? How could Spirit tell you about the cave and who was in it with her standing right next to you?"

"Through Whisper."

"The Lady Whisper? I thought she was only able to connect with birds."

"She and Spirit share...I do not know, exactly." His gaze dropped to the wolf who lay at his feet. She looked as though she had traveled to hell and back. "Just how far have you roamed, I wonder," he murmured before raising his gaze again to reassess their surroundings. "We are too exposed, here. We need a place to hide while we determine what next to do."

"It is not as close as we might wish, sir. But I know a place where we will be safe," Jerkin offered, a nervous edge to his voice. "Though we may have a problem getting Spirit inside."

"One worry at a time. Lead on."

Making his own quick scan of the area, Jerkin darted into the woods, deftly avoiding the snarls of roots and the small boulders hidden beneath the snow. He stopped frequently, listening. Brandel, too, kept his senses tuned for the presence of others. Twice their way was blocked by a trail of withered and dead vegetation and littered with the carcasses of small animals. Brandel could not say how long ago the death beasts had been through the area. But the lingering dark magic burned along his nerves. Judging from Jerkin's misted eyes and strained expression, he suffered the same sensations as they crossed the paths. Spirit balked at each, her reluctant leaps across accompanied by a series of whines. By dusk, they reached the Rose River. On the far side stood a tumbled and long-ago burned-out farmhouse.

Jerkin stood for a moment, eyeing the river and the house, then pressed a little further north, stopping at the site where once a bridge spanned the waters. "The river is not running too fast," he said. "If we anchor a rope to the old support on this side and tie it to ourselves, we should be able to cross."

"And leave the rope for the enemy to find and come looking for us."

"Leave that to me, sir." Pulling a rope from his pack, Jerkin dug through the snow and into the ground around the base of the support. Tying the rope low, he continued to dig into the shore and out into the water perhaps a meter. Returning, he buried the tied end and the length that stretched out toward the water with mud and broken branches, packing them down with snow and rock. Rolling a boulder into the water, he positioned it over the section buried in the riverbed.

"Done," he said, wiping his hands on his pantlegs and looking rather pleased. "We can tie ourselves to this end for the crossing. I will hide the rope on that side, as well. We will need it for crossing back."

Brandel clapped the boy on the shoulder in approval. "Very clever." Spirit refused to cross with them, disappearing into the woods. Brandel had his own second thoughts after entering the river. Even tied to the rope and with the diminished flow, the frigid water battered against them and numbed their limbs as they slipped and slid on the mossy rocks and the slimy river bottom. In the end, they emerged at the end of the rope's length and well downstream of where they had entered. Jerkin grinned as he gestured toward the remains of the farm. He had judged the water's challenge near perfectly, putting them ashore in line with the ruins. Untied, Jerkin repeated his efforts at concealing the rope, leaving the coiled length in the water under a snag of exposed tree roots.

Brandel made his way up the small slope of the riverbank, Jerkin following. Both shivered in their soaked clothes. Jerkin glanced back, frowning at the trail they left.

"It is beginning to snow, again," Brandel consoled. "Nature will cover over our tracks. Perhaps I can convince Spirit to assist when she turns up, again."

Jerkin nodded, jogging past Brandel and heading toward the empty fields that lay before the collapsed building, then angled off, stopping just inside the tree line. There, he poked about in the snow with a stick until it struck with a hollow thunk. Dropping to his knees, he began scooping away snow and mud and a tangle of vegetation. Finally, a round metal cover was revealed. Jerkin cocked it open, removed his pack, and tossed it down a hole. "Follow me," he said as he disappeared into the darkness.

Brandel turned, looking for some sign of Spirit, then followed the boy's example, removing his pack and sending it in, first. The wolf could track him. And she could fend for herself.

A musty scent assaulted Brandel's nose as his feet hit the bottom. Jerkin nudged him aside with, "Begging your pardon, sir, but I need to close the cover." With a long, hooked rod, the boy reached up, caught a metal eye on the underside, and pulled the cover down, then uttered a quick spell. "It is locked, now, and I dumped mud and snow back on top."

For a moment, the space was so dark that Brandel's shadow sight could discern nothing. Then came the spark of a flint being struck, a small flame catching in long splinter of wood. Splinter in hand, Jerkin ignited a torch, carrying it with him to ignite others mounted on the walls. The space revealed was perhaps twelve meters square. Three sets of bunk beds stood along the back wall, a stack of dusty blankets on the two lower ones. A table and six chairs occupied the center of room. In one corner stood a standpipe and pump, a large bucket hanging from it. Another corner held a set of metal cabinets. Halfway along the wall between the pump and the back wall was a stone alcove with a raised hearth. An old pot still sat on the long cold ashes at the back of the fire box.

"What is this place?'

"It was my family's cellar, used for storing sacks of grains and other food items, along with shirts and pants my mother made and sold." Jerkin's shoulders sagged, his voice dropping. "My father's spells still linger. They've kept the place dry, at least." He shook himself, averting his eyes from Brandel's. "Twelve years ago, my father expanded and converted it to a hide-away. That was when the Red Moon Warriors' scouting parties started making regular forays into this part of the mountains. They raided and killed wherever they went. In the end, father grew weary of having to rebuild our house, so this became our home."

"Your family lived down here." Brandel scanned the space once more, shaking his head. "What happened to them?"

"Ten years ago, we were caught in the open while harvesting. I was at the edge of the fields. Father yelled for me to run. I made it here, my mother close behind me. But she did not join me. She slammed the cover. I could hear the scratching as she buried it. Then she screamed. I was scarcely six at the time. Was too afraid to come out for days. When I did..." Jerkin's voice caught. Brandel knew from the boy's haunted eyes that he was seeing the image of his slaughtered family.

"My...my mother's body lay only a few paces from the hidden hatch. I found my father's and my brother's bodies in the fields, their heads lopped off and lying some distance away. My sisters..." He swallowed. "Their mangled bodies were clustered near the still smoldering remains of the house."

"I am sorry, Jerkin. That you managed to survive..."

"I came back down the hole," the boy continued as he poked about a crate next to the raised hearth for the few remaining pieces of wood. "Stayed for several more days, too sick and terrified to eat. I only came out when I recognized one of the voices above. Came out thinking in my childish head that it was my father and one of my brothers. It was not, of course. Guardians learned of the raid and came looking for survivors. The one whose voice I recognized found me, half starved, wearing only my jerkin, and near frozen.

Took me to the temple ruins." For a minute, he stood, holding the wood he had collected in his arms, at last laying them in the firebox, then fetching one of the torches to ignite the fuel.

"A fire may not be wise," Brandel advised.

"It will be fine, sir. Father made certain to vent it a fair distance away near a bog where a fog often hugs the ground. He took great precautions to keep us warm as well as hidden. We will need more firewood, though, if we stay here for long."

"Long enough to dry our clothes and warm ourselves."

"A small fire will warm us soon enough. I would have fared better as a child had I been smart enough to venture out after finding my family slain. Collected more firewood and perhaps checked the remains of the house for food."

"Had nothing to do with how smart you were. You were a child, and a very young and frightened one, at that. Even grown men, having witnessed what you did, would likely find it difficult to emerge right away."

Relieved of his soaked clothing, Jerkin draped everything over a couple of chairs and laid his coat out on the table. Brandel did likewise. Thankfully, the extra shirt and pants and socks in their packs were dry enough to save them from the chill that had yet to be eliminated in the space. Brandel was retrieving some of the rations packed for him when a wrap on the entrance cover froze them both. The wrap came again - three quicks, pause, quick, long, long, pause, quick, long, pause, long, quick.

"Guardians!" Jerkin exclaimed.

"How can you be sure?"

"It is the code they use among themselves." Jerkin dashed to grab the long rod with which he had closed the cover. "They just spelled out swan."

"They…what?"

"The guardians say it is an ancient code. From the Goddess' birthplace." Jerkin raised the rod to the underside of the cover and tapped - two long, pause, long, quick, long, long, pause, two long, pause, three long, pause, two long. The response was immediate. Four quick, pause, three long, pause, quick, long, long, quick, pause, quick. "See? Guardians!" His hand worked a small circle as he mumbled a couple of words, then used the rod to push the cover up enough for two hands to grasp it and pull it the rest of the way.

"Jerkin! You down there?"

"Wilder! Who do ya think would be asking for the code for my mom's name?"

"Had to be sure, given the way Red Moon conducts their interrogations. Sender is with me. Can we join you? There is a wolf up here eyeing us like she is considering us for dinner."

"What color?" Brandel called.

"What?"

"The wolf. What color."

"White."

Brandel grinned, relieved that Spirit had not gone too far afield to cross the river. He remained dubious of the men, however. "Do I have your word that you have no Red Moon filth with you?"

"On our word, Lt. Journeyson. We are just the two of us. Name's Wilder. The other is Sender. Our pursuers are not far behind us, though."

Detecting no deceit in the man's words, Brandel nodded. Jerkin called up, "Come, then. And hurry."

The first man to drop down looked familiar to Brandel. Perhaps he saw him at Knife Point Keep. The second man was unknown. Jerkin pulled the cover back into place and muttered his spell.

"Thanks, lad," the first man said. "'We borrowed your technique for getting across the river. I followed your example of hiding the rope, as well. Our pursuers may still be able to track us from the river to here, though. Is there another way out?"

"No, sir, Captain Wilder."

"I took care of it," Brandel put in. "Or rather I have Spirit doing so. I asked her to cover for us. She is trampling the area. Making it look like a pack of wolves chasing down prey. Between that and the snowfall, we should be good."

Wilder studied Brandel with curiosity. "You trained her to do this?"

"Of course not. I merely sent her the image of what I wished. She returned an image of how she is accomplishing it. Now, how is it you know me?"

"From the keep, sir. Anyone who was there when you were knows who you are."

Brandel regarded the two men more closely. Bruised and bedraggled as Wilder appeared, the other man was far worse. His nose was broken, and both eyes were purple and green and swollen, one nearly shut. His right arm hung limp at his side, and his short, shallow breathing indicated possible broken ribs. "There!" Brandel decreed, pointing to one of the sets of bunks. "For the Goddess sake, get him to the bed!"

"I will mend," Sender rasped in shallow, ragged breaths. "I just need time to focus on healing."

Jerkin trotted up behind him with a chair. "Sit, sir. Please."

Sender hesitated, then collapsed on it with a heavy sigh. Behind him, Wilder was talking.

"I am sorry," Brandel returned. "What was it you said?"

"The High Priestess of your Goddess is…"

"A traitor. We are aware of that. Worse, she holds the Ladies Serenity, Shadow, and Whisper, along with a girl named Phoenix, a boy named Owl, and the traitor guardian called Hawk. She holds other guardians and soldiers, as well."

Wilder gaped. "How did…"

"Never mind that, right now. Tell me how you came to be here."

"We escaped. Whatever any of us thinks of Hawk's actions in abducting the Lady Whisper, he risked his life more than once, protecting the ladies. And he and Shadow were responsible for our success in getting away. Hawk caused a ruckus by feigning a fight with another captive guardian. Drew the attention of everyone away from the cave entrance and brought a number of guards back to break it up. That allowed Shadow to work her magic, cloaking us in gray and black as she escorted us out. We tried to get her to come with us, but she refused to leave her grandmother and her cousin. We heard the shouts when the guards realized two of their captives had gone missing. They are hunting us, even now. When we spotted the white wolf, we figured you would be close. Had no idea Jerkin was with you until we saw you both climbing out of the river."

Brandel swore under his breath. It could have been Red Moon scouts or warriors who spotted them. He was getting careless.

"The ladies." Jerkin darted a glance between the pair. "Are they alright?"

Both Wilder's and Sender's faces darkened. "Lady Serenity lives. She suffers broken ribs and more bruises than I care to think about. But no one can reach her mind. Lady Whisper is weak, though the precise reason I could not determine. Lady Shadow is the strongest and is most protective of the other two. Our captors tend to keep a fair distance from her. She packs a mighty magical blow when they get too close. Still, even she is suffering from beatings and exhaustion."

Brandel ran a hand through his hair. "Is there no way for us to launch a rescue of them?"

"No way we have discovered. And their guards will be far more vigilant now that they lost two of their prisoners. Aifa is likely to demand someone's head, as it is."

"I am surprised Danu did not do so in her stead."

"I suspect neither priestess has been made aware, yet. My fear is that once Aifa learns of our escape, she will move the prisoners and we will be unable to track them."

"Move them or execute them?"

Wilder frowned, considering. "I cannot answer that. We have yet to understand why Aifa did not kill Lady Serenity outright once she determined there was nothing to be gained from her. Judging from the conversations among the warriors, Danu was the one to suggest she be given into her hands. Perhaps the traitorous priestess suspects the Lady Serenity's identity. If she believes she holds valuable hostages, she will undoubtedly prefer to move them rather than kill them. The problem remains. We have no way of tracking them, should they be moved."

"We might. What can you tell us of their encampment? How many are they? What weapons do they hold?"

"They are not a large force. No more than thirty, I am guessing."

"About a third of them are stationed just outside the ruins during the day," Sender provided. "They fear remaining by night, however. Your priestess Danu suspects that a sanctuary is concealed within and demanded that the entrance be found. Ancient spirits block their attempts, though, dragging beneath the earth any who dare set foot on the site where the priestesses fell. Even Danu dares not step within the ruins after dark." He tilted his head, angling his one reasonably good eye at Brandel. "What about you? What news do you have? Where is the Lady Swan?"

"She is with Lord Tine and Lord Stoirm. Where that might be, I cannot say. We left them within the Alainn outpost lands." More than that, Brandel was unwilling to share.

"So, she went to the Alainn to ask for their aid," Wilder nodded. "And will they come? Will they fight with us?"

"The Red Moon has taken the war to Sunrise and now holds their capital, Adni. If any come to our aid, they will be far too few."

Sender sank lower on the chair. "Then we are lost. We cannot fight their numbers and their weapons."

"No!" Jerkin erupted. "We are not lost! Not so long as Grandmother lives."

Sender's eyes widened. "You found her? Did she say what weapon she holds?"

Brandel shot a warning glance at Jerkin, answering only, "We saw her. She did not speak of any weapon. But she will fight."

"As will we." Wilder's comment was accompanied with a sharp scrutiny of Brandel, his gaze then shifting to Jerkin. "If Grandmother has made herself known, then Lady Swan must be going to her. You still choose to follow this man instead of going with Lady Swan."

Jerkin looked surprised by the statement that was more a question. "Aye, sir." He opened his mouth to say more, shut it, glanced at Brandel, and finally confessed, "Lady Swan is in far better hands than I could provide. Master Brandel, well… He was alone and does not know the mountains. Figured I would be of better use to him."

Brandel smiled, the expression feeling strange after so long an absence to his face. "And you are."

Wilder nodded. "I trust the boy's judgement. We lack a commanding officer, Lt. Journeyson. We are at your command."

"For now, I command you both to rest. We will share our rations, though fresh meat would be a nice addition."

"It may not be wise to try hunting, right now, with warriors hunting for us."

"I may have a solution for that. In the meantime, we will need a plan for rescuing the prisoners. If either of you have any suggestions, speak up."

Neither man spoke. "Well, you might start giving it some thought. Sleep first, though. And let your mind focus on healing your injuries." Brandel watched Wilder assist Sender to one of the lower bunks. With his friend settled, Wilder turned and offered a salute to Brandel, then sought another bunk for himself, looking pleased at Brandel's return salute.

Jerkin was halfway to the area below the hatch, hooked rod and a rope attached to a small grappling hook in hand, before Brandel noticed. "Where do you think you are going?"

"You wished meat, sir. And we need more firewood. What is here will last us perhaps through the night, depending on what hour it is, now. But it will not last beyond that."

"We will worry about the wood tomorrow. As for eating, let me see what I can do."

Once again, he reached for Spirit's mind. The joining came with no more than a minor charge, the transition smooth as he saw through the wolf's eyes. Night was now on them. Everywhere, he could sense other creatures who belonged to this tiny piece of the world, identifying each through Spirit's senses. Focusing his attention, he imagined the wolf hunting, eating her fill. Then he sent the image of the wolf dragging a small buck, not to the entrance above, but a few meters away, and of his emerging from the ground to retrieve the meat. *"Can you hunt for us?"*

Mild annoyance mixed with an even milder amusement escaped the wolf in a sneeze. He withdrew from the connection certain Spirit would do as he requested.

50

They made good time, crossing up and over the ridge above the headwaters of the Emer River. Made good time working their way through the passes and over the lesser peaks of the mountains, as well. Now, the broad valley that stretched between the western arm of the Song Mountains and the southwestern edge of the Knife Point range lay before them. Caer stared out at the high plain where the trees gave way to grasses and sedges and several small lakes.

"They are mine," rang in too sweet a tone through Caer's head. *"The ones you love."*

The words echoed as from a great distance, carried on a malevolent laughter that chased through the wind. Caer's knees buckled, dropping her to the ground, her heart strangled to a racing flutter in the sudden hollow of her insides.

"Caer!" Stoirm was instantly at her side, Tine on his knees before her. "Caer!" Stoirm barked. "What is it?"

Her throat refused to allow words to pass. In her mind flashed the image of Serenity lying still as death, with a pale Whisper and a bruised and beaten Shadow bound beside her.

"They are in Blood Hall. Come and I will spare them."

Fury and hatred poured into Caer's, *"Damage them further or kill them, Nemhain, and I shall make you pay!"*

The laughter thinned, the sweetness souring. *"There is nothing you can do to harm me."* Yet there was a flicker of doubt in the tone.

Rocked with vertigo and struggling for air, Caer slammed her mind shut to the intruder.

Stoirm gripped her shoulders and pushed her back until she was lying flat on the ground. Tine pulled her mittens from her hands and began rubbing them, feeling her wrist periodically for her pulse rate. Neither Alainn spoke. For several

371

minutes, Caer could do nothing more than fight against the flood of desperation, fight for her breath, fight to settle the painful hammering in her chest. At last, she choked a ragged, "Nemhain. She has them. Serenity and the girls. Took them to Blood Hall."

Stoirm sucked in. "That is not possible. Only the Dark Heart's soul lives. She could not take…"

"She did. Or…or Aifa accomplished it for her. Makes no difference, either way." Shoving Stoirm's hands aside, she managed to sit up. "I…I have to go to them."

Stoirm tried to force her to lie back, once more. "You cannot!"

Caer wrenched free and staggered to her feet. "She will destroy them if I do not!"

"She will destroy them, regardless. You cannot go there. You will take her what she desires."

"She will have what she desires, whether she takes it from me or from them. I cannot stand aside and let her torture them."

"They are already lost. You know that."

Caer steadied herself with a deep breath, then stepped away from Stoirm and Tine. "If they are lost, then so are we all. Let me die with them."

Stoirm lunged for her too late. Tine, too, failed to reach her in time. Both were left gaping at the final shimmer in the empty air.

"Where…" Tine's question trailed off.

Stoirm silently swore at himself for not anticipating her move quickly enough. "She cannot go straight to Blood Hall. She does not know the way. And the place is too well shielded."

His gaze still locked on the emptiness, Tine managed a thinly spoken, "Perhaps she has gone to one of the coastal villages. To take a boat to the Isle of the Sisters of Sorrow and from there on to Rift."

Fists clenched, Stoirm's mind raced through any and every possibility, trying to determine the most likely course Caer would take. "This journey has been hard on her. She lacks the strength to teleport all the way to the coast. She will not be able to draw much more from her magic until she allows herself to rest."

"Which is not likely to happen any time soon."

"Granted," Stoirm grumbled. "But at least that provides us some bit of time to catch up to her, as she will have to travel by foot, no doubt seeking a route that will keep her off the primary roads."

"Which of the primary roads? To which port? And to what purpose? Once Nemhain takes what she needs from Caer, she will simply have Aifa murder them all. She may well have destroyed Serenity and the girls, already."

Stoirm shook his head. "Caer believes they still live or she..." His words cut off, his mind leaping back to those she spoke, freezing him in silence for several seconds.

Tine's countenance darkened as he watched his father. "Something more troubles you."

"What was it Caer said just before...

"If Serenity and the girls are lost, then let her die with them.

"Before that."

Tine responded with a bewildered shrug.

"What is it Nemhain seeks?"

"Her sisters' memories."

"Aye. And why has she taken Shadow and Whisper?"

"To lure Grandmother to her. Nemhain has at least guessed Grandmother's true identity. But you knew this already."

"Think, son. What was it Caer said?"

Tine eyed his father with growing concern. "Apparently something that I missed."

"She said that Nemhain would either take what she needs from the girls or from her. If all Nemhain needed from Shadow or Whisper was to lure Grandmother, out, she has certainly succeeded."

"Aye. And Caer is walking straight into her trap."

"She said that Nemhain would either take what she needs from the girls or from her," Stoirm repeated. "The girls know more than just Grandmother's identity. Whether Nemhain realizes it or not, she holds more than the bait to draw Caer to her. What is it they know, and why, by all that is sacred, would Caer ever have placed their lives at greater risk by telling them anything of import?"

Tine stared bleakly at his father. "She would not tell them. Not intentionally. She is closer to those girls than she has been to anyone in centuries. She would never place them in greater peril. Perhaps... perhaps some of her visions have spilled into their minds over time."

"Perhaps," Stoirm muttered. "Whatever the case, we have to find her and find them before Nemhain discovers she has more than she expected in her grasp."

"And we do that how?"

"We need to find Journeyson and to send word to Grian Geal."

Stoirm completed his sending to the queen almost before he completed his statement, his mind forming the message with caution as he strengthened the shielding around his thoughts, allowing only Tine to follow them. If, by some chance, his shielding did not hold, his message must not be interpreted. *"Untethered, the bird is on wing and seeks the darkness. We must unite the three paths."* Clearing his head, he refocused for his second sending. *"Journeyson, you are lost. Find me."*

Grian Geal's return was immediate. *"Come to me!"*

"When Faolchú finds its way."

"Pray it is soon."

Several long seconds later, came Journeyson's response. *"I am not lost. I know precisely where I am."*

"You are not where you believe."

Another long silence was at last followed by, *"Where should I be?"*

"Where morning blossoms met the rain."

No further sending came. Stoirm rubbed his temples. "Let us hope the lieutenant understood and joins us."

"The queen obviously understood that we wait for the wolf. So, you expect Spirit has returned to Journeyson."

"I hope."

Tine drew a slow breath. "And you expect Journeyson to decipher where the morning blossoms met the rain?"

"Again, I hope." Together, the two Alainn teleported.

Their appearance in front of the outpost building brought Rain, Morningglow, and Everbloom charging from the door. Everbloom was the first to erupt. "How dare you leave us without a word! We have a right to…" Her ire abruptly ceased. "Where is Lady Swan?"

Stoirm made no answer, instead scanning the area, waiting. He feared his message had not been understood when the air several meters from the building shimmered, delivering Brandel, Spirit, Jerkin, and two others. The wolf rumbled a snarl from her stand next to Brandel, her hackles raised. Stoirm ignored her, his relief escaping in a long exhale. "Glad you figured it out."

"Took Jerkin's help. Morningglow. Everbloom. Rain. Morning's Blossoms met the Rain." Jerkin grinned at receiving the credit. Brandel scratched his head. "So, what is this about my not being where I believed I was?"

"You looked to find Serenity and the others in the wrong place," Stoirm said. "They are being held in the cave…." Wilder began.

Morningglow pressed forward, anger resurfacing in her tone. "Who are you?"

"They are guardians," Rain cut in. "Though I cannot say where their allegiance lies, now."

"With Ciuin Rose," Wilder declared. "We were taken prisoner by the treacherous Danu and her band of traitors and held by Red Moon Warriors who are attached to her." He glanced toward Sender, who struggled to remain standing, the evidence of beatings still clear on his face, his right arm now in a sling. "We were among the guardians holding the Soldiers of Damsa Dana until Lady Shadow could confirm who was and who was not a traitor. Our numbers were too small to defend against the full company that attacked us. Once they had the cave secured, they carried the Lady Serenity and paraded the Ladies Shadow and Whisper in, dragging Lt. Hawk behind them. The ladies are still held in that cave."

Stoirm leveled a demanding glower on the man. "How long ago? When did you see the ladies last?"

"Four days ago. We escaped, hoping to take them with us. We recently received word that Hawk and three other guardians lost their lives making the diversion. Their efforts proved in vain. While Sender and I made it with Lady Shadow's help, she refused to come with us. She would not leave her grandmother and cousin. Sent us to look for help."

Stoirm inhaled, expelling it in a weary groan, his eyes closed in frustration. "That may well be what forced their hand. The ladies are no longer in the cave."

Brandel's eyes narrowed as he regarded the Lord of Knife Point.

"Where are they, then?"

"Nemhain says she holds them."

"Nemhain! How can that…"

"Never mind the how, right now."

"Then where?"

"Blood Hall."

Jerkin's grin vanished. Brandel stiffened. "You are certain?" Without waiting for an answer, Brandel extended his desire to Spirit – that she connect once more with Whisper. He sensed the wolf's attempts, felt her tension mount. But there was nothing. Perhaps she was sleeping…or unconscious. She could not be dead. Not dead.

"It is what Lady Swan was told by Nemhain," Stoirm was saying.

"She is a mistress of lies and deceit," Everbloom spat. "We cannot trust her word."

Morningglow and Rain each looked like they might collapse on the spot. Everbloom, however, stood rigid, her jaw set, her fists clenched at her sides.

"And just where is Caer?" Brandel asked, forcing his thoughts from Whisper.

Sender and Wilder exchanged bewildered glances. "Who is Caer?"

"Everbloom has a point," Stoirm acknowledged. "We have no evidence to verify the truth or lie of Nemhain's claim. Perhaps her declaration was meant only to draw Swan from us."

"Where," Brandel repeated, "is she?"

Stoirm raised a weary gaze to Journeyson. "Seeking a way to Blood Hall. She teleported away from us before we could stop her. It is not possible for her to teleport to that hell hole. So, she will look for another means of reaching Rift, and then will seek Aifa's lair. Tine believes she may have teleported to one of the coastal villages hoping to find a boat to take her to the Isle of the Sisters of Sorrow."

"And you? What do you think?"

Stoirm shook his head. "Tine is likely correct. If we can determine the correct port and arrive before she does, we may stand a chance of stopping her from attempting to exchange her life for the others'."

"She cannot do that!" Rain put in. "Regardless of where the prisoners are now held, Aifa will not make an exchange. They will all be killed."

"Agreed," Stoirm grumbled. "Which is why we must get to Grian Geal. She is more familiar with both the Isle of the Sisters of Sorrow and Rift than any among us. She can help us determine how best to begin our search."

Brandel's heated glower bore through Stoirm. "Then what are we waiting for?"

"For Grian Geal to send us her location. Will do us no good to teleport to Sunrise if we do not know where on the continent to find her." Stoirm felt the crushing weight of fatigue. Age, too many centuries of battles, and too much traveling on too little sleep could wear even an Alainn down. Bracing himself, he lifted his shielding enough for those present to follow the exchange. *How can we find you, my queen?*

Long seconds passed with nothing. *My queen?*

Grian Geal's response hung in a tremulous whisper. *I am betrayed. You cannot come.*

Alarm rang through Stoirm's, *Where?*

"Trapped. Fire Isl…" The reply disappeared.

Brandel sucked in. "Did I detect that correctly? Did she say…" Stoirm felt hope leave him in his heavy exhale. "She is trapped. Somewhere in the Fire Islands."

Everbloom now stood trembling, all color washed from her face. "We must go! We have to find her!"

"Caer is our priority," Brandel contested. "If we fail to stop her, nothing else will matter."

Wilder spun from Stoirm to Tine to Brandel. "Who is Caer?"

Brandel waved him off, fixing his glare on Stoirm. "You said we need Grian Geal to know where to start our search."

Stoirm nodded. "Yet, if we go in search of the queen, we lose precious time. There are at least fifty among the Fire Islands, and we have no idea where to begin."

"I am going!" Everbloom announced.

Stoirm shook his head. "Whoever holds your mother likely expects a rescue to be mounted. You will be marching into a trap."

"We are all marching into traps!" she shouted. "I will not abandon my mother!"

Tine moved to Everbloom's side, wrapping his arms around her. "Father is right. It will do our queen no good if her daughter is also captured."

Morningglow shook her head, the hint of tears glistening. "Lady Everbloom is correct, as well. We cannot leave our queen captive on one of those horrid islands."

"You know them?" Brandel asked.

The Alainn gave a slow shake of her head. "No. But I will go with Everbloom, anyway."

"I have been to the islands," Rain said, her voice low and tense. "And I have a fair guess as to where Grian Geal may be. Let me send word. Gather those who are willing to fight for her."

"You will need to be cautious," Stoirm advised.

Rain nodded. "There are those among the guardians and the Alainn whom I trust with my life."

"Very well. We will seek another means of locating Swan. Take these two men, as well. One needs medical attention. The other may still be able and willing to fight."

Wilder stiffened, snapping a salute to Stoirm. "I will fight, my lord."

Sender gave a brief nod, as well. "As will I. I can still wield a blade with my left hand. And magic does not care which hand casts it."

"Do you think they stand a chance?" Brandel asked as the women whisked the two men back inside the building.

"Of finding the queen? Probably. Of rescuing her?"

Stoirm's expression must have betrayed his lack of faith in the latter, as Brandel promptly demanded, "Then why are you allowing them to…"

"The women will do this, whether I will it or not." Stoirm set his dark scrutiny on the lieutenant. "What are your thoughts regarding where we four and the wolf should begin, Journeyson?"

"Does Caer know the lay of the Isle of the Sisters of Sorrow or any of the coastal villages?"

"She visited many of the coastal villages in the past, both in Brightwater and on the Sisters of Sorrow Isle. But not for more than a century. Moreover, I believe she lacks the reserves, at the moment, to teleport to any of them. She will be afoot."

Tine shrugged. "She might be capable of teleporting as far as the cottage. It lies about a hundred kilometers northwest of the coastal port of Turbulence. She could make her way to the port from there."

"I know that cottage," Brandel said. "It has been deserted for an age. All but hidden by the vegetation, the last I was in that area."

"It was the home of one of Caer's daughters. The daughter along with her husband and their daughter were slaughtered in a battle long ago. Amhranai Fearalite worked a spell around their home to preserve the structure, should Caer's son ever choose to return. If Caer goes there, she will teleport within; observe what lies outside. If the way is clear, she could leave the house unnoticed. Assuming she travels by foot and stays clear of the roads, it will take her a few days to reach Turbulence."

"I believe," Brandel began, hesitating as he considered further. "I believe I may be able to teleport us within the town. We can watch for her, there."

"You can deliver us without our being seen?" Stoirm pressed.

"I believe so. Still, it might be best if we stood shoulder to shoulder, facing out, our weapons drawn. Jerkin, your knife lacks range. Here." Jerkin blinked in disbelief as Brandel extended his long knife to the boy. "Take it," he insisted, drawing his sword. "Oh. And prepare yourselves to get wet." Shooting a glance down at Spirit, he murmured. "You are not going to like this, my friend. If you prefer to remain here, I will understand."

The wolf responded with a low rumble, but moved to stand in front of Brandel, ears back and teeth bared. Stoirm managed a vague and humorless grin. "Perhaps she is becoming accustomed to this mode of travel. Seems she is prepared to stay with you."

Brandel raised the tip of his sword as Tine and Stoirm unsheathed theirs. Jerkin gripped the weapon given him with both hands. Positioning themselves, Brandel set the image of their destination in his mind, praying the building had not collapsed since his last visit.

They emerged in hip-deep, icy water. Stone walls on two sides and a series of pillars on the two ends formed a foundation for the building above. The creaking and stomping of booted feet and the raucous laughter filtered down through the floorboards. "The Shipwreck Tavern," Brandel said, keeping his words hushed. "Dock workers are not yet off duty, so their business is sparce. That will change soon enough."

"You failed to mention you would be putting us in the middle of high tide," Tine thundered under his breath.

"I warned you we would get wet. A deserted barracks sets on the hillside above the shipping docks. We can take refuge within one of those."

"Providing they remain deserted," Tine snorted.

Struggling through the frigid water, they slipped out between pillars and ducked into the spaces behind other stone pilings that supported more buildings, staying out of sight of people scurrying along the raised walkways above. Spirit paddled close at Brandel's side, her unease and discomfort a clear and pressing irritant in his mind. With dusk well on them, the number of people on the walkways above diminished while the sounds of laughter and conversations within the dotting of taverns grew more boisterous. Brandel motioned them to wait as he poked his head out from beneath the town's mercantile. The shop was closed, its owner, a man Brandel knew to be dedicated to the Goddess Damsa Dana, likely slipped away home. That, of course, was providing he survived whatever battle was fought here. While several of the taverns and the mercantile still stood, there were signs of many buildings having collapsed in flames.

"This way," Brandel gestured, at last climbing from the water. Spirit needed no suggestion from him to find deeper shadows on dry land as the men made their way up a set of steps to a long and rickety boardwalk running up from the docks and skirting the edge of the town. Another set of steps delivered them to broader walkways, the remains of warehouses standing on each side. The wealthier part of the port was some distance higher and to the west. Those out and about, here, were primarily fishermen or wharf workers wrapped tightly in coats, hunched against the chill as they made their way home. None dared to look up long enough to take notice of their company.

Brandel stopped in the shadows of a partially standing warehouse, waiting for a group of five dock workers to scurry by, then darted into the scrub and wind-twisted trees, heading for the slope several hectares beyond. There stood the barracks. As Stoirm, Tine, and Jerkin joined him, he gestured to the few ships moored to posts a fair distance out from the docks. White crests of the rough waters pounded them, setting them to rocking in the uneasy waves that overflowed the wharfs.

Indicating with a nod and keeping his voice low, Brandel offered, "Judging from how high the ships ride, their cargo has been unloaded. They will not return to dock for loading other goods until the next high tide in daylight. Passengers will be the last to board. Only one ship sails between Turbulence and the Sisters of Sorrow." He pointed to a small vessel anchored beyond the larger ones. "She will be brought to dock last." He remained, eyeing the distant scene in silence for several seconds before adding, "Note the sails. Each bears the Red Moon crest." Completing the climb through the woods to the barracks, Brandel sought out the building furthest from the town. They skirted the building to the backside, shivering in the growing darkness as Brandel pried boards loose from the door. Once inside, he headed for a standing stove in the middle of the open space.

"No fire," Stoirm said. "It will draw attention."

"Not with the pellets." Brandel opened a metal box next to the stove, relieved to find it filled, a scoop hanging from its side. "These burn smokeless. Lord Strongbow's private stash. He never said how or where he came by them. Used them only in his manor house and here. With the windows boarded up and the other empty barracks as well as the trees between us and town, the small amount of light will likewise go unnoticed."

Jerkin nudged past Brandel. "Begging your pardon, sir. Let me tend to the fire."

Tine scowled at the box. "A full supply. Who else knows of this place?"

"Only the caretaker entrusted to look after it. He provided fresh bedding, replenished the pellets, and stocked the cabinet near the door with food and alcohol." Brandel flipped a gesture at the boxes standing at the ends of the beds. "You will find extra blankets in those. We can check the cabinet to see if the food is fresh, though I dare say the caretaker has not likely bothered to return since Lord Strongbow's death, unless to steal the alcohol."

Tine scanned the space, scowling. "To what purpose are these barracks provisioned if they are no longer used?"

Brandel hesitated. He did not like speaking ill of the Lord of Brightwater, even in the man's death. Still…. "Not all the barracks. Only this one. When they were abandoned, Lord Strongbow chose this place to conceal his frequent… liaisons. Though I trusted in his care of our realm, I did not approve so much his private life. He had a weakness for the ladies, many among them the wives of some of the wealthy merchants. Others avoid this place, believing it haunted. Strongbow had a gift for unsettling spells."

"How is it you know of it?"

Brandel shrugged. "Strongbow tended to let his guard down around me. I caught glimpses of it when he telepathed to me regarding upcoming battles or when he requested reports. I suspect he let the brief glimpses pass through intentionally. His way of allowing me to know his location, in the event he needed me."

With the fire slowly warming the space, each of them stripped of their clothes and draped the garments over the ends of beds to dry. Wrapped in blankets, they settled on the floor near the stove. Tine produced four mugs and a bottle of rum he found in the cabinet, pouring and handing the mugs around. "The food was moldy. We must depend on our own rations, for now."

A sip brought a round of coughing and a stream of tears from Jerkin, prompting a few slaps to his back from Tine. "Perhaps I should have warned you. It is a potent drink for someone unaccustomed to such pleasures."

Stoirm was not so timid, taking several swallows before raising his curious gaze to Brandel. "Why not teleport us straight here instead of dunking us in the sea?"

"I could not be sure that the barracks remained empty until we arrived. I was reasonably certain, however, that with the tide in, no one would be poking about beneath the tavern. Be thankful I selected one of the buildings that sets on high enough ground to leave us standing in water only hip deep, and not up to our armpits. I am just thankful that it was still standing." Brandel reached for his pack, digging in it for some dried fruit and biscuits. Both were soggy.

Stoirm toyed with his mug, then finished his drink. "So. What did Wilder mean?"

"Wilder?" Brandel considered. "What did he mean, when?"

"He mentioned a contingent of traitors and Red Moon Warriors, saying they were attached to Danu. Attached in what sense?"

"I had little time to ask, but my impression is that while those among the guardians and soldiers may well follow Danu, the warriors do so only under Aifa's orders. It would be my guess that Danu chafes under their constant vigilance, just as she did under Strongbow. There has always been hostility between Brightwater's lord and the High Priestess. If, as I believe, she was the one to let the warriors through the gates of Riversong, it has not proved quite so beneficial for her."

Stoirm pushed to his feet, leaving the mug on the floor as he headed to the box of blankets. Taking up a second, he dropped wearily onto the nearest bunk and covered himself to his head. "Tomorrow we will determine where best to monitor the area. For now, we need sleep. If you think it necessary, lieutenant, you may stand guard, first. Wake me for the second. Tine can take the third."

"I can take a watch, as well," Jerkin said.

Brandel likewise rose and strolled to one of the beds, his mind seeking for Spirit. The wolf lay in the darkest shadows near the door. "Spirit will alert me if anyone approaches."

51

Caer unfolded from her tight curl beneath the blankets, the slap of cold joining with the ache in her body and the rumbling of her stomach. Dragging a blanket with her, she struggled to her feet, wincing at the more vigorous protest of joints. Her ancient bones did not cope well with sleeping on the hard ground, or, in this case, the hard floor. A quick glance in the direction of the bedrooms once again staggered her with the stab of grief deep in her soul. So many memories in this house. Memories of her daughter's laughter, her son-in-law's booming voice, and the fast clip of footfalls as her granddaughter skittered everywhere to chase the chickens back outside after allowing them to shelter indoors overnight. Gone. Like so many others.

The raid that claimed them came barely two weeks after Caer's last visit. The Red Moon Warriors avoided Turbulence, their raiding party being too small to face the contingent of Soldiers of Damsa Dana stationed at the port. Instead, they attacked a handful of the most significant farmsteads outside of the town. Slaughtered the people, burned the crops. Turbulence faced starvation that winter, losing nearly half its citizenry. Only supplies brought in by the soldiers saved those who remained. Her daughter, son-in-law, and granddaughter did not suffer the hunger. They were among those who were slaughtered in the fields of their farms.

A hand to her breast, she struggled to shove the memories from her mind. She had no more tears to spare. Soon enough, she would join the souls of her loved ones. Soon enough. Pacing the kitchen and open parlor, she worked out the kinks and pain. She had done what little she could about her rumbling stomach over the past three days, using a trick Dylan once taught her, teleporting small items from the stores in her home. They were sparse, to be sure. A jar of peaches, one of plums; a package of biscuits. She asked Tine not to restock until after their journey. In truth, she never expected to return home.

Three days. That was how long she sat in this house, fighting the memories, teleporting some small bit of food when she could recall its precise location. Sat and waited for the stream of Red Moon Warriors passing along the road not far from the house to cease. If there was any food left in her pantry, she could not remember its placement. At least this house still had a workable pump for water. And she had coin, enough. Could purchase a meal at one of the inns between here and Turbulence. Could purchase provisions in town for the remainder of her journey.

Another rumble from her stomach prompted the consideration of teleporting straight to the docks. Turbulence, however, might well be overtaken by the Red Moon. She dared not risk dropping into the middle of a contingent of warriors. Would do her no good to be killed before she could make it to Blood Hall. Moreover, teleporting would drain her reserves more than the long hike. She will have greater need of her energy once she confronts Aifa. The fact that success in saving Serenity, Shadow, and Whisper was near impossible held no sway in her determination. Instead, she set to folding the blankets and laying them back in the closet where she found them, then went from window to window around the house, peering out to verify what her senses told her. The road and the area for as far as she could see was empty of people. Drawing her hood up, she shouldered her pack and made the short teleportation to the remains of the farm's orchard.

A thin layer of snow crunched beneath her feet, glistening with the sunshine streaming through the barren trees. She delighted in the warmth on her face, though the breeze still held chill enough to warrant keeping her hood up. A few somewhat shriveled apples still clung to a couple of branches. The swish of her hand dropped them, one at a time, onto her waiting palm. Three, she pocketed. The fourth she took as breakfast.

The sunshine did not last the day. A stiffer breeze bit at her as she struggled through tall grasses and marshy areas sucking at her boots. By dusk, she stumbled through a freshly harvested field. Lights gleamed from the windows of a farmhouse in the distance. Once upon a time she knew every family between her daughter's home and Turbulence.

Now…

With the cover of deepening shadows, Caer crept in a wide arch, staying clear of the house as she circled her way to the barn. One side of the structure was severely damaged by fire. Still, it appeared sound, overall. For a moment, she stood outside a burned-out hole in the damaged wall, stretching her senses.

Satisfied that the nearest individuals remained in the house, she slipped through the hole and dropped to the ground, noting that the barn held no hay, no straw, nor any other thing that would indicate a successful farm. At least the dirt floor was dry. In the morning, she would forage. She could not go to this family, asking to purchase supplies, when it was obvious they had nothing to spare.

Shivering, Caer settled into a dark corner, unwilling to pull anything from her pack given the possibility that a hasty retreat might be necessary. Rather, she pulled her arms from the coat sleeves, keeping it snugged around her shoulders as she retrieved one of the three apples from her pocket . When she finished, she dug a small hole to bury the core. She wanted no evidence to indicate anyone had been here. Her coat drawn tight around her, she curled within it. For a long while, sleep refused to visit, despite her weariness. At last, exhaustion overtook her.

Silhouettes in darkness. A woman lying on moldy hay, still as death. Another slumped next to her. A third paced, dragging fingers along a stone wall in passing. The slumped figure straightens.

"You cannot help us. You must not look for us. It is what she wants. What she expects. We will live, so long as she believes you will look for us. But if you find us, we all die."

A bleak mountainside. Snow and wind and blackened boulders. A flare of flames. A hill emerges as a hazy mirage superimposed over the mountainside. At the crest sits the impression of a massive, stone-walled mound.

"The beginning! You must not forget the beginning!"

A map. Mt. Sorrow written in bold script. Beneath… faded… Sliev…

A song on the wind. Drumming. One, two, three, four, five, six, seven. One, two, three. One, two, three. The ground shifts and cracks. Myriad ghostly images rise, dancing, feet soundlessly pounding the ground, gossamer robes whipping in the gale as the specters spin and stomp, circling the great mound, their thin song hanging in the air.

"The circle turns, dance all the way, though once returned we cannot stay. Ever round and begin again, moving on, there is no end."

Fire and blood.

"The beginning! Seek the beginning!"

Screams of tortured souls. Laughter. A woman. Beautiful. Terrible.

Caer jerked upright, heart thrashing. The last image was Nemhain returned to flesh. The visage loomed in her mind. In the darkness, it was impossible to dislodge it. Impossible, too, to shake the sound of the Witch's sickening sweet laughter. For several long, shivering minutes, Caer sat rocking, her arms pulled inside her sleeves and wrapped tightly around herself. Outside, the wind had picked up, loose boards on the damaged wall banging. She would sleep no more, this night. She needed to move; to walk off the terror; to warm the ice that ate into her soul. But where could she go? Her desire to rush to Blood Hall remained strong, but the voice inside persisted. *"The beginning. Seek the beginning."*

Voices cut through the wind. An argument. Caer struggled with her coat, working her arms back into the sleeves, then crawled to the opening to peer into the night. The voices came from near the house. A man and a woman, near as she could tell. The woman was pointing to the barn, shaking her head. The man turned from her and started toward where Caer hid. She could not let them find her. Could not chance their being aligned with the Red Moon. Sucking in, holding her breath, eyes closed, she teleported to the first image that came to mind.

She arrived with a thump and stumbled backward into a rusted bedframe. A quick scan of the room rushed a flood of relief mixed with a sickening anguish. The image led her teleportation true. But... The austere rectangular room, the low ceiling, the once well-polished wooden floor now crumbled through in places and dulled by layers of dirt in others, a dozen or so evenly spaced lamps that remained unlit. Even through the grime, the plaster walls cast a ghostly sheen in the darkness. Why had the image been of this place? Why had she delivered herself back to the ruins of the Healer's complex? This... this was the very room in which she awoke from death following the battle that first brought her to Slievgall'ion. Instinctively, she sealed her mind against any intrusion. She dared not allow Nemhain any glimpse of where she was...or where she was not, which was initially headed toward the coast; headed toward Rift and Blood Hall.

Fighting her shudder at this sudden and unexpected change in her course, she meandered the room. This was the section of the complex that suffered the least damage. Fate allowed that there were no sick or injured in the rooms in this wing at the time. The Healers were housed in the area across the courtyard. Maura did not waste energy where she detected no presence, hurling the full might of her magic where the Healers slept, leaving her devotees to pick off the few who ran, content to kill and leave the corpses to rot or to be scavenged. Since that time, few dared trespass on these sacred grounds occupied by the spirits of the slain. At the temple, where the priestesses battled against the massive assault, the spirits rose to take revenge on any enemy who intruded. Here, where Maura's warriors murdered the peaceful Healers, the spirits wandered in sorrowful silence.

Adrian saw to it that every member of the invading force was destroyed, their souls banished. Still, Maura continued to send small parties, here, to prevent the site from being cleansed and used, once more. This wing of the complex, it appeared, had served as their barracks for whatever time they remained here. Continued to be used by the parties Aifa sent until she bothered with it no longer. That likely accounted for the the bed, though rusted, still holding in one piece. Likely accounted, as well, for the small potbelly stove in the corner and a table and chair in the center of the room each appearing to be in functional condition. A ragged huff escaped Caer at the irony of the space proving serviceable, thanks to her enemies.

Any further considerations of Aifa, Maura, or Nemhain were promptly shut from her mind, lest Nemhain sense it and find a means of worming back into her head. Instead, she sought the box that once was filled with wood for the stove. The box stood empty. For a moment, Caer considered seeking shelter in the hidden sanctuary, rejecting it in the end. In her need, she returned to these ruins. Whether it was solely by her choice or by another's…

"Roisin," she mumbled. "Is it you who brought me here? In seeing that the Alainn will not come to our aid, did you set me back on the path you and Dana insist I must follow? Have I not done enough? More than enough? Always, it is my loved ones who suffer and die. Why can you not let me die and end this?"

"Your ending will not be the end. Only in the beginning can the end be found."

"The beginning. Mt. Sorrow. What do I seek at Mt. Sorrow that will bring the end?"

"The beginning. You must seek the beginning."

"The beginning," Caer repeated, her words thin and resentful. "And will it save the lives of those I love?"

No answer came. Caer sank to her knees, burdened with grief, despair, cold, exhaustion, and hunger. "I must go to the beginning to find the beginning. I do not understand. I…" A sliver of a thought chased through her mind and was gone, leaving only the feeling that it held the answer. For several moments she remained, at last struggling to her feet. If she must go to Mt. Sorrow and fight one more battle, she could not do so in her current condition.

Shivering with the weight of her task more than from the cold, she trudged from the room, down the hall, and out into the once beautiful courtyard where now stood a few ancient trees in an overgrowth of weeds. Little search was required in the darkness for Caer to collect broken branches and twigs sufficient to fill the stove and the box, though it required several trips to accomplish. By morning, the room was filled with warmth. Light was provided, not by the sun, for it hid behind thick clouds, but from lamps, the supply of oil for them plentiful enough in the long-deserted storerooms. Caer's effort for this day would be a search for food.

Whatever food stuffs once filled the stores was no more than a wistful memory all these centuries later. Rabbits were plentiful in the courtyard, though. By midday, Caer managed to snare two, offering thanks for the lives they gave in order that she live. Skinning and preparing animals of any kind always made her queasy with guilt and remorse. But she persevered, making another trip to the storerooms to locate a pot that would sit properly on the room's small stove. With the meat cooking, Caer pulled a blanket from her pack and managed an uneasy nap, waking periodically to check on her dinner.

Night was closing in when she found a bucket, hauled water from the courtyard well, scrubbed the wobbly table and chair, and sat down to eat, the sound of the winds and the sense of lost souls her only company. The emptiness weighed on her. She missed the others, especially Tine. Though he rarely traveled with her when she meandered the mountains, visiting farmsteads and small inns, or spending time with a company of guardians on patrol, he was ever present when she returned to her home. Her home. A small fortress, in truth. Adrian built it for her and Dylan, tucked in a mountainside in an area so remote that not even the guardians knew its location. It was where, over the course of her life with Dylan, she had taken refuge to bare their children. All gone. Her last son, a proud guardian of Ciuin Rose, poisoned, though by whose hand she never learned. She was told the souls of her children were banished. Most of her grandchildren met the same fate. She could not count the number of times she begged Roisin and Dana to let her die. Let her join the few souls of her family that lay in Slievgall'ion's keeping.

Her thoughts might have ushered the age-old and all too familiar rush of tears, save there were none left to spill. Still, it was difficult to choke down the last few bites of one of the rabbits. The second, she wrapped in cloth she tore from her blanket and buried in the courtyard snow to freeze. It would go into her pack, later. For now, she needed to sleep, again, if only the fates would let her drift into forgetfulness for a while. Sleep. And then journey to Mt. Sorrow. Not just because her teleportation away from the farm set her in this direction, but because understanding was creeping to the fore.

"I am sorry!" she cried, the depth of her anguish doubling her over as her thoughts returned to Whisper and Shadow and Serenity. "I am sorry! Sorry that everything I touch…everyone I love…dies!"

52

I do not like this!" Tine grumbled, his pacing making Brandel fidgety. Spirit lay at Brandel's feet, the wolf's eyes closed, though he could sense her awareness and tension. Stoirm stood in silence, peering through the window at the fog drifting through the docks below. Jerkin sat on the edge of one of the beds, keeping his silence, though Brandel could read the fear in the boy's eyes.

"Four days," Tine continued. "Two days and no sign of her on the road or in the town. Two more spent with Journeyson reaching out to a handful of trusted others in the immediate area, to no avail. We cannot get near the wharf with Red Moon guards and traitorous Brightwater soldiers posted everywhere. Not that there is much need. Every ship at anchor when we arrived remains in the harbor."

"So," Brandel snapped. "What do you propose we do?" The fact that so many soldiers were counted among the Red Moon forces disturbed him beyond reckoning, though he should have expected it. "Perhaps Caer made her way here before us but was unable to sail. Or perhaps she is still working her way through fields, avoiding the roads." Dropping a glance down at Spirit, he pushed away from his lean against the wall and headed for his supplies. "I am taking Spirt to the house you mentioned," he said, stuffing items back into his pack. "Maybe she can find some scent of Caer. Maybe we can track her and catch her before she reaches Turbulence."

"The area around the house may be filled with warriors," Stoirm argued.

"I am willing to take the risk."

Stoirm turned a hard scrutiny to Brandel, then nodded. "Shield your thoughts well but send to us what you find. As an extra precaution, send only 'missed' if you find signs that Caer was there but is now gone. If you find her and can prevent her taking off, again, send enough of an image of your location for us to come to you."

Jerkin moved forward, his jaw set. "I am going with you."

"Not this time," Brandel declared, not waiting for Jerkin to argue.

He and Spirit emerged from his teleportation, crouched in the ditch that ran beside the road, Spirit's low growl indicating her irritation at his lack of warning for the jump. He ignored her, his senses telling him they were alone. Still, Brandel rose with caution. The overgrown cottage stood near the crest of a small rise less than half a kilometer to the north of the road, the land leading to it a meadow of dead wildflower stems, thickets of brambles, and tall grasses. The sun was bright and the day warmer than nearer the coast, though the breeze still held a sting.

Whether Spirit was anticipating what he wished of her, or whether she had seen Caer's image and Brandel's desire to find her in his thoughts, the wolf was already stalking off in the direction of the old house, the suggestion of lavender rippling through Brandel's mind. Interesting that Spirit was also aware of the delicate scent that seemed as much a part of Caer as the deep, emerald glow of her eyes. The wolf was circling the house when Brandel caught up. On the second circuit, she stopped midway, then shot off. In the distance, he saw Spirit stop, again, pacing and sniffing beneath a pair of orchard trees. He caught up to her in time for the wolf to bound away, again, the scent of lavender now heavy in the wolf's sending. Hesitating, Brandel studied the ground, noting where someone stood long enough to leave muddied indentations in the ground. Around them lay several shriveled apples in varying stages of decay. He prayed Caer found enough edible ones to sustain her for a while.

Trailing Spirit, Brandel kept track of her by the images of the land as she ran. Though accustomed to fast marches across lowland fields, meadows, and marshes, he was not accustomed to trying to keep pace with a wolf. By the time the morning sun reached its zenith, he was forced to stop for rest and water. When he set out again, the pace was quick but more sustainable. At mid-afternoon, Spirit stopped, taking in the surroundings so that Brandel could get his bearings. His sudden appearance at her side caused not so much as a startled flinch, the wolf's gaze now fixed on the distant farm. Brandel knew these people. Honest. Hardworking. Perhaps they offered Caer shelter. *"Missed. Trailing. Come,"* he sent, sharing a momentary glimpse of the surrounding area. With Spirit still in the lead, he headed for the house. Awareness of the presence of the couple came as Brandel approached their damaged barn.

"Ho!" he called. "Temper! Mayjoy! Are you there?"

The man, younger than himself by a handful of years, poked a wary head out from the burned opening in the wall, his stunned expression shifting to concern.

"Lieutenant!" He ducked back inside momentarily. When he reappeared, his pregnant wife was close behind him. "Quickly, sir," Temper urged. "To the house! You do not want to be…" Temper's statement cut off as he grabbed his wife's arm, both freezing in place.

Brandel realized they had spotted the wolf. "She will not harm you."

"You are…one of them?" Temper choked, terror in his wide-eyed stare.

Brandel had no doubt of the man's meaning. That they would suspect him hit Brandel with the weight of a ship's anchor. "I am no traitor to the Goddess Damsa Dana. And Spirit is a friend of the Guardians of Ciuin Rose. Do you sense the truth of my words?"

"Hush!" Mayjoy muttered, slipping free of her husband's grasp and cautiously edging past him, though she kept a wary eye on Spirit. "Aye. I sense your truth. But keep your voice down. We do not know who or what may be listening. Please. To the house." Her dismay at Spirit's accompanying Brandel inside their home showed in the small 'o' of her mouth and her stance plastered against the cabinets as the pair passed her. She made no comment, however, nor did she attempt to turn Spirit back. Rather, with a nervous flick of her hand, she indicated Brandel should take a seat at their small table. Temper took the seat across from him, his anxious gaze continuing to flick between Brandel and the wolf.

"Why did you leave us? Why were you not here to lead the resistance against the attack on Riversong?" the man persisted. "The Red Moon might have been defeated. Lord Strongbow might still be alive. Our soldiers might still be loyal to him. And…" He chewed his lip, his nervous glance once again dropping to the wolf. "And how did you come by… by such company?"

"It was not by my wish that I left. Strongbow ordered my mission. To seek assistance from the Guardians of Ciuin Rose. How I came by Spirit is a story for another time."

Mayjoy set a pitcher and glasses to the table, shooting Temper a hopeful look. "Will they?" she asked. "Come to our aid?"

"They cannot. Knife Point is also under attack."

The woman sank onto the nearest empty chair, pale and quivering, her concern no longer on the wolf. "Then all hope is lost."

Brandel eyed the man. "Hope remains. I am looking for a woman. Small. White hair with red streaks at the temples. Eyes of earthen green but that sometimes glow like emeralds. She travels alone. I believe she came this way. Did you see her?"

"No one travels alone," Temper said. "Red Moon troops are everywhere, and people are reluctant to travel at all. A company of Red Moon passed through some four days back. Stole our harvest. What we had of it. The crops have been failing. Every year it gets worse. They torched our barn. Only by the grace of Damsa Dana were we able to put it out before it did greater damage."

"And no one else has come this way?"

Mayjoy and Temper jumped at the sound of Stoirm's voice. He and Tine stood in the doorway, Jerkin behind them. "May we enter?" Mayjoy's eyes widened, a breathless, "Alainn!" escaping.

Temper was on his feet, motioning them inside. "Please! My lords! You are most welcome, but you must not be seen. The Red Moon spies are everywhere."

The two Alainn moved further inside, though they declined Temper's and Mayjoy's offering of chairs. Stoirm asked again, "You have seen no one else?"

"No," Temper said. "But... Well, this may be nothing. But, last night Mayjoy thought she heard cries coming from the barn. Human cries. Like a woman in distress. We came out to investigate but found no one."

"Only..." Mayjoy cleared her throat, putting in a meek, "It did look as though someone had slept there. And it held the strong sense of a teleportation."

Brandel was on his feet. "In the barn, you say. May we look?"

With the couple anxiously following, Brandel quickly led the way, Spirit at his side. As the others joined them, Spirit moved off, investigating. The scent of lavender focused in Brandel's mind.

"She was here," Tine groaned.

Brandel knelt to look Spirit in the eyes. "Is she near? Can you track where she went."

Spirit investigated further, sniffing the ground and the air. Except for the direction from which Caer had approached the barn, each time Spirit moved away from the corner, Caer's scent vanished. Rising, Brandel gave a frustrated shake of his head. "She was the one who teleported. The remnants of the charge still hang in the air."

Stoirm nodded. "But to where?"

"She is important?" Mayjoy asked from just outside the burnedout hole. "This woman?"

Tine nodded. "Very. She is our only hope. We need to find her. She needs our protection."

Brandel tried to think. "We need to get back to Turbulence. If she teleported to the port…" The remainder of his comment remained unspoken, as Stoirm and Tine vanished, taking Jerkin with them.

"Thank you," Brandel acknowledged to the couple. "Do you have food enough to last you through the winter?"

Temper wrapped his arms around his wife. "Mayjoy hides some of her canning and the meats she dries. She has done so over the past several months. If we are careful to ration them, we can get by."

"Is it safe for you to go into Turbulence to buy supplies?"

"No, sir. We avoid that place at all costs."

"I will see what I can do to arrange for provisions to be sent to you."

"Our profound thanks, sir, but you need not bother. We can manage. Just find the woman. Defeat the Red Moon if you can."

"That is my intention. Stay safe."

"You, as well," Mayjoy offered.

Brandel's emergence back in the barracks with Spirit in tow found Tine pacing and Stoirm shuffling from window to window to stare out between the wooden shutter slats in dark contemplation. Only Jerkin noted his arrival, the boy's relief expelled in his, "You came back! I was afraid you had gone off on some other mission without me!"

For several minutes, no one spoke another word. At last, Brandel suggested, "If she teleported last night, and if her destination was Turbulence, then we either missed her or the Red Moon found and took her."

"She is not captured," Tine stated.

"You know this?"

Tine cocked a brow at him. "Aye."

"How?"

Stoirm drew a long, slow breath, running a hand over his hair. "It is an old spell. Similar to one Amhranai Fearalite once used on her."

"Who?"

"You are aware of the histories, surely," Stoirm huffed.

"The original bearer of the name Singer, you mean." The stunned note in Brandel's voice drew a snort from both Stoirm and Tine, Stoirm shaking his head. "You still have not accepted the facts. We stood together in that long-ago battle. Amhranai Fearalite, Tine, me, and others. Stood to protect Caer, who bore the souls of Dana and Roisin. Nemhain forced her soul upon Caer for a brief time. It is Caer who opened the gateway that blew us through to this world."

Brandel understood the truth of it in the depths of his soul. Yet his mind continually rejected the idea that any Witch could live that many centuries.

"Sadly," Tine put in, his agitation still driving his pacing. "I was never able to deduce the completeness of Amhranai's spell. I cannot, as he did, detect Caer's location. I can only sense when she is in danger. I know that she is fearful, but she is under no immediate threat."

Stoirm dropped onto the edge of the nearest bed. "Perhaps she bypassed Turbulence altogether. She might recall enough of the Sisters of Sorrow Isle to successfully teleport to one of her ports."

"What about going straight to Blood Hall?" Brandel was not thrilled with the idea, but it bore mentioning.

"I do not believe she knows the way."

"Aifa could send to her; show her."

"Aifa," Stoirm snarled, "will wish for Caer to struggle and suffer. She will place obstacles in Caer's path. If Caer dies, Aifa provides what Nemhain desires. If Caer succeeds in reaching Blood Hall, Aifa will hold what Nemhain desires."

"And if Breag Nemhain lied when she spoke to Caer? Perhaps the captives are not at Blood Hall. Perhaps Nemhain wishes only to use the lie as a lure."

"Truth or not," Tine sighed, "Caer believed it. Still..."

Stoirm looked to Tine. "Still?"

Tine's face creased with indecision. "I am closer to Caer than anyone living. Even you, Father. I know her mind almost as well as she does. I should have anticipated her first inclination to try to save the last of her family. Yet I am not certain that will be her final choice."

"Which would be," Brandel pressed.

"Mt. Sorrow."

Stoirm considered in silence. "You think she will turn back to the mountain."

"I think it possible."

"So." Brandel braced his back against the wall and slid down to sit on the floor, rubbing his forehead. "Now what?"

His question scarcely passed his lips when Spirit rose from the corner where she had settled, her eyes trained on the door, hackles raised and teeth bared. Moving silently, Brandel crawled to just below one of the windows flanking the door, raising enough to peer out. A single man approached from another of the barracks, bent low, staying to the shadows. His dark coat bore no insignia. Pulling a knife from his boot, Brandel vanished, emerging but a few paces behind the figure. Two steps and he was at the man's back, knife pressed to the throat. Another quick teleportation delivered them both back inside, Spirit crouched and ready to lunge.

"Who are you? What are you doing sneaking around out here?"

"Lt. Journeyson, sir! I am Sgt. Sands. I mean you no harm. I came looking for you."

Brandel eased his knife down. "Turn slowly."

The man did so, dropping his hood as he faced Brandel. The sergeant's face was twisted with doubt as his gaze swept from Brandel to the wolf to the two Alainn and back. "Sir," he began, again. "We saw you, sir. Day or so ago, lurking about the wharfs, staying out of sight. We feared you were dead, sir."

Brandel recognized the young man. A good and confident soldier. "We?" he asked. "How many are you?"

"Two dozen, sir. Hiding. We lost most of our company in the attack on Riversong. We tried to defend Lord Strongbow, but..." His voice trailed off as he eyed his captors, again, an anxious crease digging a deeper furrow across his brow. "You, sir. You are with... with..."

"The Red Moon? Never," Brandel spat.

Sgt. Sands relaxed some, though he maintained a serious scrutiny of Spirit. "I followed you the day we spotted you at the wharfs. Hoped you remained loyal to our Goddess Damsa Dana when I observed you avoiding the soldiers and warriors. The men agreed I should try to contact you. Make certain of your loyalties." His gaze flicked toward Stoirm and Tine. "The Alainn. How many are willing to fight with us, sir?"

Brandel stuffed the knife back in its sheath inside his boot, straightening with a weary grumble. "They are fighting a war in their outpost lands and in Sunrise. We can expect no help from them."

"And the Guardians of Ciuin Rose?"

"This." Brandel said, "is Stoirm, Lord of Knife Point and his son Tine. Knife Point is also under attack. The guardians will not come. Jerkin, there, has declared his service to me. And his service has proven invaluable." Tossing a nod in the direction of the wolf, he added, "And Spirit. She will not bother you so long as she senses no threat to me or to herself."

Sgt. Sands' eyes widened as he returned his stare to the wolf. "She protects you?" He ran a hand over his head as he eyed the men. "I am not sure I understand, sir. Neither the guardians nor the Alainn will come, but the Lord of Knife Point and his son, Alainn themselves, are with you."

"Aye. We search for our one hope."

Snapping to attention, the sergeant saluted. "We stand ready to serve under you, sir. If you will accept us."

"Two dozen, you say?" Stoirm put in.

"Aye. And we can contact a few others who managed to avoid capture. They will fight, as well. Just tell us where we are to take our stand, sir."

"It is too late for that kind of stand, I fear. But we may yet have a means of winning. We are set on an urgent mission. We seek a woman who needs our protection."

"A woman, sir. If you mean by that the High Priestess of Damsa Dana, she needs an execution, not our protection. If you were searching for her at the wharfs, she is not here. We do not know where Danu has gone. To her death, I hope. It was she who…"

"Opened the gates of Riversong to the warriors," Brandel finished. "I suspected as much when I received word of the death of Lord Strongbow and the taking of the city. She will pay for her treachery. No. She is not the one who needs our protection. The one we must find, the one we must protect is Grandmother."

Sgt. Sands gaped in stunned silence. When at last he managed to speak, he stammered, "She…she is…is real, sir? She…exists? What is the great…the great weapon she possesses? Will it help us to win?'

"She holds no weapon other than memories." Stoirm advised. "Hope for this world lies in those memories."

"Memories! What hope can they bring?"

Brandel closed his eyes and rubbed them, muttering, "Information that can be used against the Red Moon, perhaps." Opening them, he turned to face Stoirm. "Tine believes she changed course and goes to Mt. Sorrow, but is uncertain. I suggest you and Tine take half of the men Sgt. Sands spoke of and go to Blood Hall, in the chance she stayed true to her original decision. I will take the sergeant and the remaining men to Mt. Sorrow. If we find her, we will do everything in our power to protect her."

Stoirm considered briefly, then shook his head. "Take Tine and all the men. Better if I go to Blood Hall alone. One person may stand a better chance than a company of soldiers in remaining unseen and avoiding any trap laid by Aifa. Whether Caer is there or not, I will do what I can to rescue those taken captive."

Before any objection could be raised, Stoirm was gone, leaving Tine in rigid silence, staring at the empty space where his father stood less than a heartbeat ago. Taking a measured breath, he turned his attention to Brandel and the sergeant.

"Blood Hall." Sands swallowed, his eyes darting from one man to the next. "The Alainn went to Blood Hall? That is suicide. What captives are at Blood Hall that are worth such a sacrifice? And what is this about our going to Mt. Sorrow? That lies in the Knife Point realm. We…"

"Have little time," Brandel said. Calling Spirit to his side with a quick sending, he ordered, "Take us to the rest of your company."

Caer walked the courtyard grounds, an early morning snow falling. Five days, she had sheltered here. Eating and sleeping when grief permitted it. She must take the next step. Must make her way from the Healers' complex to Mt. Sorrow. Yet, she lacked the will to do so. Her heart would send her to Blood Hall, despite knowing it to be a trap. Those she loves still live. Were it otherwise, her heart would know. They would remain alive for as long as Nemhain believes her promise of their release will bring Caer to Aifa...for so long as the Dark Heart and Aifa remain ignorant of Whisper's secret.

Caer dropped to her knees, her soul torn. Aifa waited in Blood Hall for Caer. Waited in Blood Hall with her captives. Not on Mt. Sorrow. Dark realization slowly settled in. They were not so much drawing her to Blood Hall as away from Mt. Sorrow. Because... The reason eluded Caer, though her certainty remained. They did not want her there. Much as she wished to change course, once again, and go to her loved ones, the mountain was the path she must take.

Bent with the weight of the centuries, Caer forced her mind to seek for some memory that would show her the place of that beginning. None arose. No mountain. No lifeless slope. No vision at all. Adrian told her of the devastation - the blackened and blasted earth and stone, no breath of life left in the soil. Rumors said a slow, creeping death expanded outward from it. Caer never returned to see for herself.

Fists clenched, she set her mind to yet another study of her immediate surroundings. This. This place was her first memory of Slievgall'ion. Waking in warmth and comfort, stunned to realize she was alive. Alive when she had been dead. Emer was here...and Dylan, to ease her into acceptance of that truth. She remembered the kindnesses of the Healers. Remembered the beauty of the snow when first she saw it. Remembered...

She swallowed against the knot in her throat. Remembered the guilt and fear at what she had done, opening the gateway and allowing Nemhain to hold it for so long. In that one action, she may have destroyed a world. The guilt never left her. Not in all the centuries that passed. It was only magnified with the death of each friend and family member she held dear in this world. No matter the number of times she raged against the sisters, raged against her blood line, for that was why the task became hers all those long ages ago, the raging would not salvage a devastated world. Would not bring back those she lost. Would not bring back those she was about to lose. Unless…

The 'unless' remained vague – a half constructed glimmer of hope. That it hung by the thread of her finding Mt. Sorrow was clear. How was she to do that? There must be some memory buried deep within… some vision left from the minds of the sisters that would tell her. The more she tried to dig, to pry out the deepest memories, the more they evaded her. Let her go about the little activities that had become her daily routine. Let her eat and sleep and dream. Maybe… maybe within a dream the proper vision would come.

Shuddering, she shuffled back to the building and the room where she sought refuge. Her traveling clothes hung over the end of the bed and the backs of the two chairs. A towel and a bar of soap she found at the bottom of her pack now lay on the table next to an empty basin. Whether Juniper or Hawthorne or one of the young maidens who saw to her needs at Knife Point Keep placed it in with her belongings remained a mystery. She was grateful to whomever was responsible. Her gaze flicked to the empty bucket setting next to the door. She would need to haul more water if she was to bathe. Still, it was a simple ritual that helped to ease her mind for however briefly.

The fire in the stove, she noted, was dying. She stoked it, giving it time to rewarm the room before she discarded her coat and mittens. A couple of shuffling circuits of the room delivered her around and back to the table where a few dried berries, rose hips, and ground elder left from breakfast awaited her. The low-growing ground elder was quite an infestation of the once beautifully maintained courtyard gardens. Plentiful as it was, though, the plant was not enough to rebuild her strength. She would return to the courtyard, later, to see what, if any other creature, found its way into one of her snares. Eat one more decent meal. Sleep. And then she would leave.

With nothing more to do in the moment, she dropped onto the blanket she had spread over the rickety bed. Another nap. Another meal. Another night's sleep. The vision would surely come and she would leave. Must leave. She could not continue sitting here. Not when Aifa held those dear to her. Not when she had to return to the beginning and find a way to put an end to this. Not when…

White mountain slope. Blackened boulders. Blackened hill. Earth-covered stone mound on the crest. The world spinning. Dylan. Adrian. Spinning. Emer. Fedel'ma. Spinning. Green woods. Sunshine. Sobs.

"It is a time far distant that your gift shows you, Roisin." Nemhain turns away. "And there is naught we can do to change it."

Her response is quietly spoken. "Our curse condemns us to suffer when that time comes. Our descendants will suffer, too. The whole of our world will suffer."

Dana smiles. "You are our Seer, little one. If something is to be done, it will come to you. No more tears."

Nemhain fixes a glower on Dana. "And if her gift shows her nothing? We will die in the end, when the world is devoid of those for our souls to inhabit. We will die just as the Tanai have always done. Let us live the lives we may access for now and into the future and not dwell on what that distant time holds. Many things can change. Visions can change, as well." Nemhain's burning gaze shifts to her. "Is it not so?"

It is hard to meet her sister's stare, a chill tracing her spine as she does. "Aye, Nemhain. They do change. When we take a hand in altering the circumstances."

Nemhain sneers. "Then, perhaps, in time, your sight will show you a way to change this fate. Until then, I choose to go on living as I wish. So, go away and let me be. I have things to do."

Dana's countenance darkens. "Like taunting the Tanai children? Leave them alone, Nemhain."

"Why? They do not leave us alone. They threaten us. Burn our homes. Call us 'Witch', as though they mean by it that we are demons."

A deep ache fills her soul. "They fear us. And your taunting and tricks only feed their fears. Leave them alone."

"You demand that after what they did to our parents? To us? Did you forget what horrors prompted our spell, Roisin? We promised to return and take our revenge."

Dana lays her hand on Nemhain's shoulder. "And we did so. Now is a different life. These people had nothing to do with the actions of the past."

"You grow soft. Like our baby sister. These people will do the same to us if we do not make them too fearful to get near us. I am done with you."

"Nemhain! Come back!"

"Not until you come to your senses, the both of you. Not until you open your mind to the truth. The Tanai are vile and hateful. They will never allow us to live in peace."

My heart cries out. "You are speaking of yourself, Nemhain. Vile and hateful."

"Sssssssssssssssss! It is my right to hate those who do us harm. It is my right to seek vengeance upon them! Taunting is the least of that vengeance."

Spinning. Fire. Witches burning. Spinning.

Caer's screams reverberated around the room. Hiccupping sobs followed. Curled in fetal position, she drew the blankets tightly around her. And still, she shivered, the hate in Nemhain's sweet voice filling her head and raking ice through her. So much hatred. So much. For every Tanai to whom Nemhain brought suffering, at least five witches died, either by drowning or fire or some other torturous means. And many who were not Witch, but falsely accused, also died. Though they were not her own, the memories of those ancient times hung as ever-present nightmares in Caer's mind. The long days of hiding. Nights of terror. Of fleeing.

Swallowing, trying to calm her shaking, Caer sat up, shoving the nightmares to the dark recesses of her mind. Still, she shivered. The stove held only a few glowing coals, the room grown cold. Night was descending. Forcing her muscles to lift her from the bed, she stoked the fire once more, then bundled in her coat and headed for the courtyard to check her snares. Her stomach threatened to rebel at the idea of eating. Yet, she knew she must.

One snare held a small squirrel. Barely enough for a mouthful. Trembling hands freed the creature. The other held a pheasant. Once upon a time, the Healers raised pheasant. Apparently, some survived, their descendants remaining close to the complex. Caer knelt, torn between releasing it and the need for food. In the end, she released it and turned to gathering a few more berries, searching out mushrooms to add to her collection.

Making dinner amounted to no more than sitting down to munch on her meager fare, surrounded by the sounds of wood crackling in the stove and the flicker of the oil lamps. The solitude wore on her. Even the time spent alone as she meandered from one farmstead or village to another over the last couple of centuries did not prepare her for this isolation. Treks between destinations often took a week or more. But the solitude was always broken with time spent in the company of a friend and by her returns home. Tine never failed to arrive in time to greet her. Or would meet her when she chose to visit the sanctuary hidden deep behind this place.

He disliked her solo travels but never tried to stop her. When they were together, his presence comforted her. She could almost forget her sorrows.

A small smile crept over Caer's lips. Home…the hidden sanctuary here… both locations always warm and immaculately kept, thanks to Tine. Her smile faded as she considered how much of his time she took up. He had his own life to live – or should have. Everbloom waited for him. Though Tine did not speak of it, his love for Grian Geal's daughter was obvious to all. He should be spending as much time as possible with her. Alainn may possess near immortal lives under normal circumstances, but not even they were exempt from death by battle or murder. His life, however much of it remains to him, should be spent with the one he loves.

"What am I doing?" Caer demanded, dismissing her meandering thoughts. "Sitting here wasting time with little to eat and getting no stronger while I wait for a vision that may never come. I made my choice when I returned to this place. I should already be on Mt. Sorrow. Go back to the beginning. Put an end to the war of the sisters – an end to the Goddess Wars. Then, perhaps Tine, Whisper, Shadow, Serenity…all the others…perhaps they will be safe. Perhaps then I can die, allowing my soul to dwell with the souls of my family in the keeping of Slievgall'ion."

She nearly knocked everything from the table in her abrupt rise. Dropping the blanket to the floor, she collected her clothing, changing into the heaviest garments and packing the rest. "Find the beginning. Fine!" she muttered. "I have no memory of the mountain, so I cannot teleport. Nor do I know the terrain between here and there well enough to jump at least some part of the journey. But I will find it, nonetheless."

Dressed, she made a quick round of the room, extinguishing the oil lamps. The fire in the stove would die of its own accord. She wasted no further time with any final glance around. Donning her coat and mittens, Caer set out into the night. Above the light from the growing crescent of the rose moon were the crescent of the red and the sliver of the white moon. A hand went first to the base of her throat where once the trinity knot hung from its silver chain, then reached into the depths of her coat pocket, finding the charm. It was almost warm to the touch, even through her mitten. It held only the faintest suggestion of magic about it, though. It lacked its chain to complete its power. And the chain lay in the hands of the enemy, still. At least it lay in Danu's hands and not Nemhain's. That offered some small degree of comfort. Danu would not understand the power of the chain; would not recognize its need to be reunited with the charm.

54

Sgt. Sands delivered Brandel and company to the badly tilted deck of a damaged ship wedged between boulders along the rocky shoreline. Based on the cliffs that rose above them, Brandel guessed they were perhaps sixteen kilometers north of Turbulence. The ship's broken mast lay across the top of the crushed cabin, the shredded flag bearing the Red Moon crest flapping in the icy mist.

"Our only hope of escape from the slaughter in Riversong was to take to the river," Sands explained. "The swift current carried us all the way to Turbulence Strait. A massive storm sank two of our ships and most of the men in them. The remainder of us were tossed into the same rocks as trapped this ship. The Red Moon had already stripped her of all weapons and supplies before they abandoned her. Still, she offered better protection against the elements than the remains of ours."

He gestured to the crushed and splintered wreck of a boat in the distance, then shot a glance at the cliffs. "It is my guess they teleported everything from here to some predetermined encampment." He turned to face the crashing waves, once more. "Between the cliffs, the treacherous waters of the strait, and the ship resting partially on her side, we have remained hidden. Two or three of us at a time teleport into Turbulence now and again. At least two of us scout for trouble and listen for news while the other slips into shops where sympathetic owners help provision us and remain silent about it. I was on scout duty the day I spotted you."

Brandel eyed the broken deck, shaking his head. "I thought the Red Moon had better vessels than this. Ones that could maneuver through these waters to sail up the coast to the northern reaches."

"Aye, they do, sir. But not near as many as they might wish, it seems. Most of their fleet is such as this. The newer vessels carry more warriors than these, and mightier weapons." Sands' weary sigh preceded, "The older ships, like this one, however, do not fail to bring disaster to the southern coast. Anchored offshore, they batter coastal villages and towns with weapons that cause explosions. Then come smaller vessels ferrying ashore beasts that bring instant death. Last come the warriors, laying waste to anything that remains before they move inland."

"How did they take Riversong?"

"It was a strange vessel, sir. You will not believe me when I tell you, but it moved under the surface of the water, traveling into the mouth of Song River and upstream against the strong current. Rose up at the docks and belched metal and fire, shattering the outer defenses. When the warriors emerged from the belly of their machine, they made straight for the gates. Gates that were opened to them by the traitor Danu, who fled in terror of the death creatures the warriors let into the city. We hope the fates found her and demanded her life for her treachery."

"She lives," Brandel rumbled. "She fights with the Red Moon in their attacks within Knife Point." How much more should be said was uncertain, so Brandel shifted back to the matter of those remaining loyal to the Goddess Damsa Dana. "You say two dozen men are here?"

"Counting myself, aye."

"And you know the whereabouts of others of our soldiers."

"Aye, sir. They found a shoreline cave further north. The front of it is submerged at high tide. But it goes back a fair distance, the ground rising as it goes. So far, the tides are not high enough to reach that area, though the Goddess tides came close. If a serious storm strikes while the tides remain high, sending a major surge in, it could well drown the full cave. For now, the men hide within and send to us for supplies. We asked them to join us; to lay plans of attack that will grant us back our capital, at least. Thus far, they choose to wait."

"For what?"

The sergeant ran a hand through his hair, dismay in his expression. "For your return, sir. And for the guardians we prayed would come with you. They fear the Red Moon are too many and their weapons capable of taking us out before we are close enough to cause them any real damage." Casting one more wary glance at the wolf, he motioned for Brandel, Tine, and Jerkin to follow him.

It was difficult to negotiate the slanting steps down into the belly of the ship. Sands stopped at the bottom of the first level below deck, motioning for Brandel and the others to wait. "I need to let the men know who you are and that you come at my invitation before we descend to the next level. They are jumpy and someone may well strike you with a sword or a kill spell before they recognize you."

Brandel nodded, watching Sands make his way further down.

"Are you sure of their loyalties," Tine asked, his voice low and tense.

"As certain as I can be. Sands' words held no hint of deception. And they would not hide, had they joined with the Red Moon."

Minutes later, Sands called up to them. "You may descend."

Brandel went first, noting the awkward hang of sleeping hammocks and the pile of splintered debris that now rested against the lower part of the ship's hull. Strips of wood were nailed into the floor to allow somewhat greater ease for the men to maneuver without sliding downhill to join the debris.

"Cooking is done on the beach," Sands was saying. "We do so as tight against the cliff as we can manage, making any flame difficult to spot from above. Smoke is a concern, but we can do little about that. Thankfully, there is generally enough fog of a morning and evening to conceal it. And thus far, we have detected no indication of anyone traveling the area above."

As Brandel turned to face the men, they rose to salute, having reserved the honor until they were certain of his identity. Brandel waved them to ease, relieved to see familiar faces. Gesturing, he introduced Tine, Jerkin, then Spirit as she took the last several off-kilter ladder steps in a single leap, sliding toward Brandel until her feet hit the first of the installed pieces of wood. As one, the men moved backwards, hands going quickly to hilts of their swords. "Make no threat to her or to me and she will not harm you," Brandel hastily stated. "She stays with me."

Brows went up and murmurs stirred, but the men released their weapon grips. "Sir," ventured one near the front of the group, his gaze shooting toward Tine. "Sgt. Sands tells us no help is coming from the guardians, nor from the Alainn. Says we should travel with you to Knife Point. To Mt. Sorrow. For the sake of a woman calling herself Grandmother."

"Sgt. Sands spoke true."

Awe filled the man's tone. "You saw her, then. You verified she is whom she says."

"Aye. Talked and shared meals with her, as well. She is Grandmother."

"And what is the great weapon she possesses that would make her our hope?"

"Knowledge," Tine responded.

"Knowledge?" another man asked. "We cannot fight with knowledge! Cannot wield it in our hands or cast it as a spell to drop our foes."

"She can wield it."

Brandel wished he shared Tine's conviction. For a moment, he allowed his gaze to skim the faces of the men before him. "Grandmother is our hope," he said, holding his tone firm. "But she is in grave danger. She needs our protection if she is to make use of her knowledge. It will not be easy. The mountains of Knife Point are treacherous. You will find a frigid world, the weather colder than our worst winters. A fall from a mountain slope can drop you more than a hundred meters to your death. Or an ice crevasse may open and swallow you in its depths. Or a great ocean of snow may sweep down to bury you."

"This woman. This Grandmother," Sands began. "She is in these mountains? She endures these dangers?"

Tine nodded. "She endures these and much more. The Red Moon High Priestess Aifa, and the traitorous Danu hunt her. Grandmother endures, even knowing that her loved ones have been taken captive and will likely die. She understands that all may fall to the Red Moon if she does not return to Mt. Sorrow where the Goddesses first brought their war to Slievgall'ion, and there call upon her knowledge of them."

Sands stood in silence for several uneasy minutes. At last, he offered a single nod. "Aye, Lt. Journeyson. I will join you. No other plan to take back our land and our lives offers us hope. If this Grandmother has knowledge that will allow her to destroy the Red Moon, if she can endure the mountains and the cold, then I will endure, as well, and will protect her with my life."

Slowly, one by one, others rose and saluted, each adding his, "Aye." In the end, every man chose to leave their land, brave a mountainous realm they have never seen, and give their lives in the protection of a woman they did not know. Would the men in the cave do likewise?

55

The support of the men in the cave was not so easily won. They numbered more than fifty, in all; far more than Sands was led to believe during his encounters with their leader. With many injured and all malnourished, despite the supplies provided to them by Sands and his men, they looked little more than specters. Their leader, a corporal in rank and hardly old enough to qualify as a man, seemed the only one among them willing to take charge. The strain of command, of overseeing the care of the wounded who no longer had the strength to call upon their own healing powers, of preventing fights over food, of surviving in the cold, wet and dark of the cave, left the young man near mentally broken. In the end, it was Jerkin who won the corporal over, embellishing Brandel's bravery and deeds and weaving into the telling the story of Brandel's unique companionship with Spirit. Once the corporal committed to Brandel's command, the rest followed.

When, at last, all from the cave and the ship had gathered on the shore, Tine sent the vision of their destination to each, saying, "Line up, no more than three abreast. Journeyson, keep Jerkin and Spirit at your side. And all of you, fasten your coats."

Moments later, their teleportation deposited them in a narrow chasm between two massive cliffs, the faintest fading of darkness overhead suggesting that it was predawn. Tine headed for the dark cave opening. Those who came from the coastal cave balked. A glance back from Jerkin as he strode confidently at Brandel's side, however, had them moving, again.

Brandel braced himself. A few curves in from the opening, the way would become impossibly dark. After spending so much time in the cave pounded by the ocean, he sympathized with the hesitation of the soldiers to enter, here, and took pride in the fact that they came, anyway. Still… He stifled an irritated grumble. Was this as close to Mt. Sorrow as Tine dared teleport them?

"Some of those with us are unfit to travel further," Tine sent. *"And we will need some of the guardians to join us."*

Brandel's irritation increased, this time for his own repeated failures to shield his thoughts. The Alainn was likely correct, though.

A scrape against his arm reminded him to concentrate and to make periodic overhead hand sweeps to avoid knocking his head against jagged outcrops as he climbed, shouting the warning back to the others. His shadow sight struggled to make out even the slightest distinction of darker against dark, the effort raising a mild headache. He was pleased, however, to discover the strain of the steep grade and winding way less taxing than he expected, though he still resented the extra time this side trip would cost.

A muffled chant from Tine at last allowed them to pass into the small chamber that was accessed from the Lady Swan's…. Caer's private quarters. For several seconds, Tine stood with his ear to the inner wall, listening, before his murmured spell opened the way. Once all passed through, Tine spelled the wall closed once more. Around them, the quarters lay cold and dark and eerily still. So, too, the commons. The Soldiers of Damsa Dana stood gaping at the solid stone of the walls, some daring to stare from the windows. None ventured to sit on any of the furniture, choosing the floor, instead. Brandel joined a few in front of the window that looked down upon the inner gate, frowning. In the early morning light, he saw the massive fire that burned on both sides.

Tine raised a hand, warning none to draw knife or sword as rapid footfalls echoed up the spiral staircase. Chamberlain Fairchild rounded onto the landing, his eyes wide, his features drawn and ashen. "Tine! Thank the Goddess you have returned!" Passing a quick glance at Jerkin, Brandel, Spirit, and the ragged soldiers he asked, "Where is Lord Stoirm and Lady Swan?"

"In danger," Tine stated, regarding the chamberlain. "We thought you dead."

"It was not for the lack of their trying," Fairchild growled. "Knife Point Keep came under assault a week ago. 'Tis a miracle you managed to slip through the gates, a second miracle that you found your way up here unnoticed. No matter, though. No matter. I sent for someone you might wish to see."

"Tine!" Everbloom gasped, clearing the stair landing, her face flushed, her features tight with sorrow. The left side of her forehead bore a bruised but mending gash. Her darting gaze grew more troubled as she took in their company.

Tine took her hands. "What brought you here? Where is our queen?"

Everbloom's distraught shake of her head accompanied her choked, "Grian Geal is dead. Murdered by some fiend who lay in wait for us. Morningglow..." her voice caught. "Morningglow and Sender died protecting me. Rain and Wilder dragged me through a teleportation back to the White Moon outpost." For a moment, she stood silent and trembling. "Ga Gréine has fallen, Tine. With Rain and the few guardians she was able to call to her, we made our way back to the outer gates of Knife Point Keep just as they fell. We battled our way to the inner gates where the guardians within rallied and fought the way open for us to slip through. The inner gates still hold. For now. But the fires that the Red Moon ignited..."

Swallowing, she glanced once more from Tine to Brandel to Jerkin and the others, then back to Tine. "Lady Swan. What of Lady Swan? Of Lord Stoirm? What of..."

Tine shook his head. "Lady Swan teleported away from us before we could stop her." He darted a glance at the soldiers. "We believe... Grandmother is making her way to Mt. Sorrow. Father went to Blood Hall, where we believe the Ladies Serenity, Shadow, and Whisper, and possibly Owl and Phoenix are being held. Those among the company you see, here, who remain strong enough to fight will accompany us to Mt. Sorrow. I was hoping to find aid, here, for Father and for us." Everbloom's lips pinched in confusion. "The ladies are not at Blood Hall. Danu held them in the cave outside the temple ruins. One of the hostages sent to Chamberlain Fairchild. He arranged for a contingent of guardians to teleport to the cave and rescue them. They are here, Tine."

The flush of relief on Tine's face was short lived. "And Father?"

Everbloom shrugged. "No word has come from him. He is strong, Tine. He will return." Her glance toward the windows prompted a straightening of her shoulders. "Knife Point cannot survive if Aifa takes Grandmother. Slievgall'ion cannot survive. Come with me."

Brandel gave quick instruction for Jerkin and the soldiers to remain, murmuring to the boy that Healers and food were on their way and he must assist the corporal in seeing all the wounded appropriately tended. Relieved at Jerkin's nod of assent, he caught up to Everbloom and Tine, Spirit ever at his side. Chamberlain Fairchild parted from them, descending only to the level of the library, archives, and his chambers. Brandel caught a glimpse of library tables lined up, each covered with maps. Everbloom continued down the spiral stairs, being passed at the level of the dining hall by Juniper and several children as they darted up toward the lord and lady's chambers. Juniper spared Brandel a worried glance, but nothing more. He doubted not that she would look after the others.

At the bottom of the stairs, what had once been the temple to Ciuin Rose was now filled with Healers darting among wounded guardians, soldiers, farmers and people from Knife Point's small villages. He also recognized a couple of women who served as teachers for the children at the sanctuary beneath the temple ruins. Some among those present were not likely to survive, judging from what he could see of their injuries. The thick scent of medicinal herbs almost blocked the scent of death and disease. The walking wounded assisted where they could. Scuffling feet, the thudding of buckets of water, and murmured conversations filtered through the cries of the injured and dying.

Paths opened as Everbloom turned to the left to parallel the back wall, stopping only long enough to select a handful of Healers and direct them to the lord and lady's quarters. Brandel's breath caught as the door nearest him opened, allowing a Healer to exit. Before the door closed, he saw Whisper lying on a cot, Serenity on another, and a bereft Shadow, battered and bruised, pacing between the two. Another Healer within cast him a weary glance as she closed the door, once more. He hesitated when Everbloom moved on toward the furthest of the three doors, his impulse to burst into the nearer room and demand the status of the three women's injuries. Stiffening, he passed, trotting to catch up to the queen's daughter.

Three sharp raps brought this last door open enough for their party to be admitted. Gray stood at the back of the room, Wilder and Rain near the front, each bearing battle scars. Gray was almost as ashen as the chamberlain and looked as though he had aged half a century. Bavol, Car'Adawc, and Mil from Deep Hall stood at the front. Six other Alainn, a dozen Guardians of Ciuin Rose, and seven Soldiers of Damsa Dana conversed nervously in the center of the room. Though the soldiers were not from the troops who once served under his command, Brandel's relief at seeing them was near overwhelming. Sighting him, they snapped to attention, saluting. Brandel returned the salute, though there was no time for further greeting.

"Master Jerkin," Gray called out, startling the boy who tried to stay tucked out of sight. "I believe Juniper wishes your assistance if you would be so kind. You will find her in the kitchens, I think. You know the way."

"Aye. I...I do, sir," he strangled, the question of the man's identity creasing his features. "But I need a word with Master...er...Lt. Journeyson, first, if you please."

Brandel strode to him, about to press for the reason he had not remained in the upper quarters. Jerkin twitched anxiously, motioning Brandel to join him just outside of the conference room. "Chamberlain Fairchild sent me," Jerkin whispered. "Lord Stoirm is dead, sir." Brandel stood, stunned. Nodding, he gestured for Jerkin to depart.

Stepping back inside the room, a quick glance in Tine's direction told him the Alainn was aware of his father's death. Tine stared at his feet, his grief clear. General Bavol was speaking as Brandel made his way past Tine, wishing for words to comfort his friend. None came to him. That Stoirm sacrificed his life for a lie twisted Brandel's gut.

"Terrible business," Gray sent, motioning for Brandel to join him. *"No one can fill the shoes of Lord Stoirm. The whole of Knife Point mourns."* Gray took in the wolf at Brandel's side, others quickly sidestepping the animal. *"I was told she stays with you."*

"For the most part." Brandel acknowledged, turning to listen to Bavol's speech.

"...escaped Ga Gréine. I am told there are less than a hundred guardians remaining outside of the keep." The general strode to the backside of a table set near the front wall. Several maps lay stretched out across it. His fingers tapped agitatedly on the table's edge as he continued, his eyes darting over the nearest map. "They are joined by half that number of Soldiers of Damsa Dana and are fighting their way here." Lifting his gaze to those gathered, he asked, "What is the latest report from the gates?"

Rain pressed her way forward through the others. "They are holding, general. Barely. Gray and Chamberlain Fairchild killed the last of the death beasts at their forefront. And thus far, the fires keep the Red Moon and the other creatures among them at bay. For how much longer, I cannot say. The Fire Mages among us lack Lt. Singer's skill and strength with the magic. We try to keep them rotated, but they are tiring."

General Bavol nodded, his grave glance shooting briefly to Brandel before skimming the group at large. "What fuel is left? Perhaps we can build up the flames to allow longer respites for the mages."

"Precious little, general," Wilder put in. "Though we can add to it if we tear down the stables, some of the barracks, or some of the houses."

"Take the barracks first. If more is needed, take the houses. The stables are the only thing keeping the smoke from the horses sufficiently to avoid their panic. Now, what of the food stores and water?'

An Alainn woman Brandel did not recognize spoke up from near the wall. "The water is good for now, sir. The cisterns within the mountain are full. But ice is thickening on the lake that feeds them. If the lake freezes to a depth below that of the pipes and the flow to the cisterns stops…"

"How long can we get by with what is in the cisterns?"

Rain was the one to answer. "Depends, sir. I am told that, under normal circumstances, the cisterns can accommodate the keep until the spring thaw. We are many more times the numbers usually to be found, here, though. And water is needed to prevent the fires from spreading from the gate."

"Give me your best guess."

Rain hesitated, then said, "a month if we ration."

The general smiled. "That is better news than I had hoped. And the food?"

"Juniper completed teleporting the supplies from the temple sanctuary. Hawthorne was able to teleport all that she had left before…" The woman's voice broke and for a moment she struggled to speak. At last, she managed, "She was slain, sir. Before she could make her escape."

"May Ciuin Rose keep her soul in safety," Bavol offered, then pressed, "How does that put us with food?"

Rain shrugged. "With rationing, we may be able to stretch it to a month, as well."

Bavol nodded again. "Very well. You have all received your orders. Dismissed." A few filed out, others remained, moving to the back of the chamber, talking quietly among themselves. The general gestured to Tine and Brandel. Everbloom joined them as they approached. Bavol fixed Tine with an anxious stare. "What news?"

"Not good. The Lady Swan teleported away from us."

"So, she goes alone to Mt. Sorrow."

"Perhaps." Tine drew a slow breath, explaining, "When she was told that Serenity and the girls and those with them had been captured and taken to Blood Hall, she declared she was going to them and teleported before we could stop her. But…"

Bavol cocked a brow. "They were never taken to that hell hole. Who told… Never mind. You expressed doubt that Lady Swan has gone there?"

"We cannot be certain she followed through. There is reason to believe she altered her course. Without definitive evidence, Father went to Blood Hall. He…" Tine's voice trailed off. Taking a steadying breath, he said, "We now believe, however, that she is heading for Mt. Sorrow. We seek aid in going there to defend…" He glanced around the room,

"To defend our Lady Swan. Lady Swan who is Grandmother."

A stunned murmur swept the room Tine continued. "Soldiers of Damsa Dana joined us on our journey, here. They are willing to fight with us. They are currently being tended in the lord and lady's quarters. Not all the soldiers are fit for battle, though. We need some from among our people and some from among the guardians to go with us."

Bavol braced his arms on the table, his gaze fixed on the window. "Swan, Lady of Knife Point." He drew a long breath, shifting his gaze to skim the room. "Grandmother. The Alainn of her world knew her as Caer DaDhrga. She came here as the Soul Bearer. Her long life is greater than that of any other Witch. She rivals some of our own. She is weak, however. Time weighs heavily on her. Perhaps she would welcome death. Especially if we can get word to her that the captives whom she loves are here."

"Of course, she would welcome death," Tine thundered, ice cutting through his tone. "She has lost more loved ones to the wars than any other living person."

"Then let her be. Let her find her death. Lord Stoirm chose his path, as well. Those among our people who remain loyal are driven from Sunrise. Knife Point is our last remaining stronghold. We must remain here to defend the keep."

Tine stood in outraged silence for several long seconds before bellowing, "Are you mad?"

Bavol's face reddened, his hand going to the sword at his side. Everbloom darted between the two Alainn. "If you strike Tine, you will prove yourself mad. We must protect Swan at all costs." She shot a glance to Tine. "We also owe her the protection of the keep and the last of those she loves."

Tine's voice rasped with his grief and anger. "Father is dead. Serenity, Shadow, and Whisper are within these walls. We do not ask for all to travel with us. Those who remain will continue to defend the keep. But Caer DaDhrga, the Soul Bearer needs our protection, as well. Who will go with us?"

Brandel's hand moved slowly to his knife as he saw the general's hand tightening on the hilt of his sword. "Why should we protect her? Because of her, Breag Nemhain's followers have waged war on us for far too many centuries.

We cannot match the weapons the Red Moon possess. Nor do we have the time to create such an arsenal. So far as I can tell, your Little Swan possesses no great weapon to help defeat the demon warriors. And it is her death the Red Moon wishes. With Swan gone, their cause for war also ends. We will have an opportunity to parlay with them. Grant them the lands of Brightwater in addition to Rift and the Sisters of Sorrow Isle. Let them have the whole of the Fire Islands, as well. We hold Knife Point and take back the outpost lands and Ga Gréine."

"My mother would take your head for speaking thus," Everbloom roared.

"The queen was a fool. She believed in this Witch who was the Soul Bearer. Followed the edict that prevented our use of the old technologies. Our land was at peace until Caer DaDhrga brought the warring Goddesses back to us."

Brandel detected the subtle movement of Bavol's hand on his sword, delicately lifting it from its scabbard. *"Hold,"* he sent to Spirit, sensing the wolf's tension and realizing she offered a better resolution than his knife. *"Patience."*

Tine's hissed intake turned Everbloom toward him, her hand going to his arm to prevent him drawing his sword. "Bavol is not worth it, Tine. He is…" With her turned from him, Bavol swept his blade upward, aiming for Everbloom's back.

"Attack!" Brandel sent. Spirit sprang, her leap taking her straight into Bavol's chest, her teeth sinking into his wrist as the force of her lunge knocked him to the floor, his blade clattering away. Tine snatched it in the same motion that shoved Everbloom sideways, away from the struggling wolf and Alainn.

"Call her off," Tine said, the point of Bavol's blade now aimed at the general. *"Spirit! Release!"*

Spirit hesitated, then let Bavol's bleeding hand fall to the floor at his side. Returning to Brandel, she sat quietly, her smug sense of satisfaction creeping through his mind.

"I can forgive your ignorance," Tine was saying, though his rigid features and steady glare suggested otherwise. "You come from this world. And you lack sufficient centuries of experience to recognize the lie in your own words. But your disrespect for Queen Grian Geal and drawing your weapon on Everbloom are unforgiveable. Everbloom, please send to Chamberlain Fairchild regarding what has taken place. He will know what is to be done with the general. Tell him Car'Adawc should be given command."

Pale and shaking, Everbloom nodded.

Tine strode to the door, shoving it open his voice rising to demand the full attention of all present. "It is time that we enlighten you all. Lady Swan,

Grandmother, are one in the same. And they are Caer DaDhrga, who was, indeed, the Soul Bearer. My father and I stood against Breag Nemhain long ago in the war she declared on her sisters Dana and Roisin. We stood, too, with Caer DaDhrga, the Soul Bearer when, in her attempt to save her world, she and the sisters were delivered to this one. Caer's death will not return the Red Moon to their lands and allow the rest of Slievgall'ion to live in peace, as some among us seem to believe. If they capture her, they will use what they learn from Caer to continue the war, destroying everyone who stands in their way. They desire power. And they will wield that power without mercy."

The tension in Tine's voice darkened as he leveled his cold stare down at Bavol. "You are correct about one thing, general. Caer DaDhrga does not possess any weapon that could help us defeat the Red Moon. What she holds is far more valuable. She knows the sisters' memories – every memory up to the time their souls were released into this world. It is their memories that may lead us to a means of defeating Nemhain. If taken from Caer, those same memories could allow the Dark Heart to take this world and perhaps other worlds beyond. Caer will not willingly give the memories of Damsa Dana or Roisin over to Nemhain. But if Aifa takes her, they will rip those memories from her and relish the torture they put her through."

Bavol studied Tine as though considering fighting his way free. Brandel and Spirit stepped closer. Tine's eyes narrowed, his agitation rising. "There is one more thing you should know. The sisters are…"

"Tine!" Chamberlain Fairchild's voice boomed across the great temple hall.

Brandel detected a warning in the chamberlain's tone. Tine did not turn to meet the chamberlain's harsh gaze as he strode toward the doorway where Tine stood. Neither did he continue whatever it was he was about to say.

"Leave General Bavol to me," the chamberlain advised, closing the distance. "Car'Adawc is on his way. He is a good choice for command. You might consider placing Rain as second."

Tine eyed the chamberlain, still looking eager to complete his 'enlightening of the masses'. Instead, he nodded. "Agreed."

"Is there anything else you need?"

Tine glanced once more at Bavol. "Make sure his wound is well tended. Car'Adawc can hold his sword in safe keeping. He may yet prove worthy of wielding it. But he is no longer to be granted command of anything."

Chamberlain Fairchild turned back to the temple, calling out for assistance. One of the guardians responded, startled at the sight of Bavol on the ground and Tine holding his weapon. "If you would assist me, sergeant. General Bavol seems to be suffering from a bought of exceedingly poor judgement. We need to get him under guard. Send for a Healer to see to him after that."

As the chamberlain and the guardian escorted Bavol from the room, Rain stepped back in, eyes wide and brow cocked at the three.

"What…?"

Tine waved her silent. "When Car'Adawc arrives."

The Alainn joined them only moments later. He hovered uncertainly in the doorway for half a heartbeat, darting a glance back over his shoulder. "General Bavol," he began.

"Close the door, if you would, please," Tine instructed. He waited while Car'Adawc complied, then gestured him forward. "Bavol demonstrated a lack of trust in the queen and in our mission. You now stand promoted to general." He cast a quick glance at Rain, "And you are second in command. I trust you both to hold Knife Point Keep for as long as possible. Should it become impossible, evacuate as many as you can. Jerkin can show you the way."

"The boy who came with you?"

"Aye. He will lead you correctly. He does not, however, know the spell. Speak the names of the first Alainn and human to wed."

Car'Adawc's brow furrowed. "That would be your father, sir, if the stories be true and he was once wed to the daughter of Amhranai Fearalite long ages before you came to this world. But I do not know her name."

"You need to go further back in the history of our people. Chamberlain Fairchild will know the names. There is one more thing, general." Car'Adawc blanched.

"You will get used to the title," Tine said. "There is one more thing. I understand the need of every person available to help in the defense of the keep, but we go to Mt. Sorrow to protect Lady Swan. We expect the Red Moon to have forces on the slopes."

"I have been thinking," Brandel interjected. "It will be easier for us to leave unseen if we take only the strongest of those we brought here. We are told that Guardians of Ciuin Rose and Soldiers of Damsa Dana are fighting their way to the keep. If word can be sent, perhaps they would be willing to redirect their forces to us."

Car'Adawc nodded. "Aye. It is unlikely they could fight their way through the Red Moon at our gate, anyway. I will send Deahlan with you. He can arrange for you to meet with them."

"I am going as well."

Brandel saw the dismay shoot across Tine's face and turned to see Everbloom standing with her fists on her hips.

"You need not try and argue," she glowered. "And you, Lt. Journeyson. The only way you will make your escape without young Jerkin following is if we leave quickly, while Juniper keeps him busy in the kitchens and assisting with the wounded."

"We go, as well."

The music in the voice, though strained, was undeniable. Brandel spun around to find Shadow and Whisper standing in the door. Shadow stood with her head up, her shoulders thrown back, ready to take on any who objected. Whisper met his gaze, her pale features set with determination. Signs of their injuries were fading, but neither looked strong enough for the journey.

"Do not doubt us," Shadow rumbled.

"I stole something from Danu that must go to Grandmother," brushed delicately through Brandel's mind.

"Let me take it. You must remain here. I thought you and Shadow and Serenity lost, before. I…"

Tears glistened in Whisper's eyes. *"Serenity is dead. She sealed her mind so securely that she was unable to work the magic to heal her own wounds."*

"All the more reason for the two of you to…"

Whisper's voice was clear and strong, despite its lack of volume.

"We will go, Master Journeyson. With you or on our own."

Brandel sucked in. Let it out. "Then let us leave."

Tine shook his head. "We need supplies."

"Done," Everbloom declared. "Chamberlain Fairchild says they will be waiting for us in the library."

Car'Adawc bowed to Tine and Everbloom, then saluted Brandel. "Deahlan will join you in the lord and lady's commons. Safe journey. May you defend our lady. We will defend Knife Point."

Rain also bowed, her gaze falling to the wolf. "You are most fortunate, lieutenant. That one will defend you to her death."

56

The battle at the gate had ceased, at least for a time. The gale whipping the blizzard made fighting impossible. From the upper windows, Brandel could see nothing but blowing snow. Travel was going to be a nightmare. Behind him, those from the soldiers he collected at the coast who were fit for battle were being fitted with more appropriate clothing. Those who were too ill or injured to fight had been moved to the temple turned infirmary below. He was grateful to discover Jerkin and Owl were now reunited and that Juniper and Gray kept both occupied between the kitchens and the infirmary. To one side of the lord and lady's commons, Tine and the chamberlain conferred while Rain sat in a corner, stroking Spirit's head. It was unusual for the wolf to allow anyone but him or Whisper or Caer such proximity. But then, it had been unheard of for the wolf to allow anyone but Bear to get near her until Bear's death. Now, Spirit accepted Whisper, Caer, and Rain. What trait did these women possess that permitted Spirit to trust them? A quiet huff escaped as he pondered the same question regarding himself.

"She accepts the women because you trust them."

Brandel turned on his heels, looking for Caer, so certain was he that the murmur in his head was her sending, though something about it did not quite match her voice.

"Find her," brushed his mind even more faintly. *"You have one last part to play, though you will not understand."*

Heavy footfalls on the spiral stair drew everyone's attention. A young Alainn, looking to be no more than twenty in Witch years, rounded onto the landing, snowmelt dripping from his coat, his face red from the cold. Brandel recognized him from Deep Hall. Rain was on her feet and off to greet him with a hug.

"Deahlan! You look near frozen. Come, warm yourself by the brazier."

He returned her hug then stepped back, swiping wet strands of black hair from his face, his gray eyes taking in the others. "No time for warming," he said, adjusting the shoulder straps of his pack. "The storm will give us good cover for leaving, so long as we do not run into a cluster of warriors huddled together."

Tine greeted the young man with a hand clasp. "I am sorry to drag you from your duties, here. I know you wish to remain to protect Knife Point."

"I wished to remain to protect Ga Gréine, but it was not to be. Car'Adawc told me of your mission. If Lady Swan is in danger and I can help to defend her, then I go without hesitation. The chamberlain also sent word to those who remain beyond the fortress walls. Many among them will join us."

"Good. I believe you met Lt. Journeyson at Deep Hall."

Brandel and Deahlan acknowledged one another with a quick nod as Brandel donned his coat and hoisted his pack to his back.

"The storm is dowsing the flames, I fear. But the gate remains hot enough to sear flesh from bone. And the Red Moon block the other side. We will need to lower the rope ladder and descend the cliff face to a narrow ledge some ten meters below. It is treacherous going, but…"

"There is another way," Tine interrupted. Turning to the chamberlain, he said, "Should the need arise, Car'Adawc and Rain are aware that Jerkin can show the way for everyone to evacuate. They will need to learn the spell from you. It is the names of the first Alainn and human to wed. If you must, let Knife Point fall. Just save as many as you can."

The chamberlain cocked a brow. "Long have I guessed that there was another way in and out of the fortress and that the spell Swan told me was to open it. She never acknowledged its existence, however, nor hinted where such a way might be hidden."

"Aside from our lord and lady, there is always at least one person at Knife Point who holds the secret of the passage," Tine said. "Singer has held that secret for many years. Jerkin learned of it by happenstance. The boy is reliable, though."

The chamberlain acknowledged with a grim nod, turning back to the stairs. "Singer is among those who will join you once you are beyond these walls."

Tine led the way back to the secret chamber and the way out. Others followed with Brandel and Spirit last to pass through.

"And to think," Deahlan chuckled. "All these years I thought Lord Stoirm and Lady Swan had the power to override the spell against teleporting into and out of the fortress."

"They did," Tine returned. "They just chose not to waste that much energy."

Brandel harrumphed. "And the trek up and down this mountain in the dark followed by the trudge around the lake does not require energy?"

"Not as much as overriding the spells Amhranai Fearalite set upon this place."

Brandel's brow lifted. Whisper once said something about Ooran Fearaalchee having built the home she and Shadow and Serenity shared. Why had he not laid some magic about it to protect them?

"Amhranai was responsible for the construction of many places," Tine said. "Knife Point Fortress and Deep Hall among them. His magic still protects each of them. I suspect Whisper, Shadow, and Serenity would be safe, still, had they sought and remained in the secret space built into their home."

Guilt niggled into Brandel's thoughts. They left because of him. To bring him to Knife Point Fortress.

"We understood the risks," Whisper interjected. "And Grandmother sensed the importance of your roll in this. Because of you, a number of Soldiers of Damsa Dana now fight at our side."

Brandel grumbled beneath his breath over his ongoing failure to shield his thoughts. Aloud, he muttered, "Too few."

"Your thoughts are shielded." The music in the sending marked it as Shadow's. *"Just not against those of Amhranai Fearalite's or Grandmother's lines."*

"More than might be willing were you not with us," Whisper said in response to his audible remark.

"What makes you say so?"

"Murmurings in the ether."

"This Ooran...whatever..."

"Amhranai Fearalite," Tine supplied. "The name means Fair Singer. A joke, really. My grandfather, Tar On Tine, named him using the tongue of Amhranai's people, the tongue that became that of the Alainn who made themselves known to humans. Grandfather knew that Amhranai's voice far exceeded 'fair'. Never has there been another whose music rang so gloriously, though Shadow's comes close."

"Given what I have witnessed of this Fair Singer's work, he was a tremendously powerful Witch."

"Easily the equal to the sisters."

Brandel shot him a dubious glance. "That would make him a god, would it not?"

Tine coughed a laugh. "Such a title would amuse him. But he was no god." There was silence for a moment. "Just as the sisters are no goddesses." Behind him, Everbloom stumbled, her sharp inhale audible in the close confines.

"It is not blasphemy," Tine sighed. "It is simple truth, though the humans and Alainn of this world will never accept that fact. Your mother knew better, as do the elders of our people, here. The Alainn's dealings with the three is ancient. We know their beginnings. They are human. Witches, like most humans on Slievgall'ion, though their powers far exceed that of any other Witch, past or present, save for Amhranai's. I am surprised our queen did not pass this history on to you."

"Ciuin Rose, forgive him!" Everbloom exclaimed. "He is weary, grief-stricken, and delirious to make such claims."

"Her name is Roisin," Tine said. "She is the youngest of the three sisters. The eldest is Dana. She is the one here called Damsa Dana. Nemhain is Nemhain. She was not always vile, though envy and bitterness have ever been part of her nature." He sighed, again. "You were too young when the sisters were taken to our home world for their protection. Your path never crossed with theirs because your mother kept the three confined to one village, not allowing word of them to go beyond those people and the elders. You knew of them only as the souls borne by Caer when your mother was called from our home to the battle, bringing many of the best Alainn warriors with her."

Everbloom's tone held an edge as she asked, "How is it you would know so much about them?"

"Their mother was a human Witch of their world. Samhradh, she was called. She and her nephew, Amhranai Fearalite, were the first of their kind to acquire the fire magic. The sisters' father..." Tine fell silent, again, at last confessing, "Their father was my grandfather. My father is...was their half-brother."

Everbloom's abrupt halt had Deahlan running into her. His quick grab of her arm kept her from being knocked down the steps. Brandel and Spirit also stopped while Deahlan supported Everbloom until she could get her feet back under her. "How...how can I believe..." she stammered.

Tine finally realized the others no longer followed directly behind him. Turning, he peered back up the narrow path, his eyes glowing a pale topaz. "You are free to believe what you wish," he said. "Hold them as goddesses if that pleases you. I can tell you, however, that the only one of the three sisters who wished to be seen as such is Nemhain. Nor does whatever label you choose to apply to them alter the fact that they possess great power."

The remainder of the long trek down the dark tunnel continued in silence. Given that Deahlan demonstrated no surprise, Brandel assumed that the Alainn either accepted Tine's statements as truth or had known of this from the beginning. Like Everbloom, though, Brandel found it difficult. He had worshiped the White Goddess Damsa Dana, prayed to Her, revered Her, for the whole of his life. He had taken his oath as a soldier, and again as Lieutenant, standing before Her statue in the temple at Brightwater's capital of Riversong. While Damsa Dana never spoke to him, he often felt Her presence, especially when he was at prayer.

"She spoke," breathed across his mind. *"You did not listen. Yet you hear me."*

"I…"

The blast of frigid and whistling wind drove his thoughts from him, warning him they neared the end of the passage and would soon come into the cave.

Tine removed his pack, gesturing for the others to do likewise. "Everbloom, Deahlan, keep everyone here to rest for a few minutes. Lieutenant, will you come with me? We need to see what lies outside before continuing."

Brandel dispensed with his pack and joined Tine at the cave's mouth, Spirit on his heels. "We should rest here, as well," he suggested. "Let Spirit see what we face."

Tine considered. "She will show you what she sees?"

"Aye. And I will sense what she senses."

"Very well."

The two men returned to Everbloom and Deahlan to assist with building a small fire. Everbloom collected several stones, building a half-dome over the debris of sticks and twigs the winds had blown into the cave. Sheltered, the blaze finally caught, providing a little light in the heavy shadows and producing enough heat to take the bitter bite from the air. Brandel saw to it that the soldiers took some food and water before returning to the cave's opening. The narrow chasm beyond, protected by its two steep rock faces, had only a few centimeters of snow. Spirit stalked the gap, her senses alert, Brandel's connection with her coming with ease, now. As the chasm widened, the snow deepened, slowing the wolf's progress. At the edge of the lake, she halted altogether. The whiteout on this side of the mountain was as severe as at Knife Point's gate. The storm might provide cover for them, but it could also prove deadly.

"We need to stay…" Brandel's assessment was cut short by the scent Spirit detected on the frigid air. Something foul roamed near the lake.

The scent of it raised Spirit's hackles and froze Brandel where he stood.

"We need to what?" Tine prompted.

Brandel waved him silent while also sending to Spirit that she should return immediately. The wolf responded, spinning and racing back through the chasm and into the cave, where she skidded to a stop and turned to face the opening, crouching low and growling. Brandel already had his bow in hand, arrow nocked, as others retrieved their swords.

"Red Moon?" Everbloom sent.

"Worse," Tine replied. *"Wait here."* The charge of his teleportation reverberated around them. Long minutes crept by with no one moving, eyes fixed on the opening, senses keyed to anything that might move. The sound reached them as from a great distance. Brandel nearly lost his grip on his weapon, ice racing through his veins at the cry. More like screeching wails. Tortured, angry… the thing of nightmares. They rose, hung on the air interminably, at last fading to eerie silence. An image lifted in Brandel's mind, at first faint and unsteady. When it settled, he could see a hovel of a building near buried in snow. The image moved, slowly, as if the seer was struggling to reach the building's interior. Darkness. Then the gray of a lightless room seen through shadow sight.

"Fix this in your mind." Tine's voice was thin and held a waiver. *"Come to me."*

Deahlan grabbed his pack and Tine's and teleported. Everbloom followed. Brandel kicked out the small blaze, calling back to the others. "I will send to you where to join us. Be ready to teleport as soon as you hold the image in your mind." Stashing his arrow in the quiver at the side of his pack, he hung one strap over a shoulder with his bow over the other, then gripped Spirit's fur, teleporting them both.

"Watch it!" Everbloom yelped as Brandel and Spirit emerged practically on top of her. Righting herself, she waved off his apology.

"My fault. I should have vacated the spot. I just…"

"Where's Tine?"

"There," she indicated, pointing through the shadows to a corner of the room. Deahlan was kneeling beside the ashen and trembling Alainn, a cup pressed to his lips.

"What happened? What made that horrible noise?"

"Give him a minute!" Deahlan barked.

It took several before Tine could push from his hunched collapse to sit with his back braced against the wall. As Brandel waited, he stepped outside, noting the details of the near surroundings, and sending it to those who yet waited in the cave, grateful that the wind was less a howling demon, here, though the snow was as heavy as before. Within seconds, they appeared in the snowy clearing. Brandel motioned to the young corporal who had taken command in the coastal cave, saying,

"You are now a sergeant, young man. What is your name?"

"Adriane, sir" he replied, snapping a salute. "Named for one of the heroes who…"

Brandel acknowledged, "Aye. I know of the hero. What is your surname?"

"Gale, sir."

"Sergeant Gale, we will camp here until this storm blows over. Do the men carry tents?

"Aye, sir. Sturdy ones given to us at Knife Point. But even those are not likely to stand long under the weight of the accumulating snow. The Alainn among us say they know of a better way to shelter."

"Then follow their direction. See that our men are as comfortable as is possible in such conditions. Then report back to me. Two raps at the door will tell me it is you."

"Aye, sir."

Returning to the inside, Brandel found Tine still as gray as death. Struggling for his breath, Tine hissed, "I know what they are." No one pressed for anything more but waited until he could continue. "The death beast," he said, at last. "I killed it with…with a banishing…a banishing spell." Again, they waited for the clutch in his breathing to ease. "Killed them," he corrected.

Brandel's gaze darted to the boarded windows. "How many? Are there more?"

"Three. I killed them all. I sense no more. They harbored…" Tine's voice choked off, his eyes closing. Several more seconds slipped by before the Alainn's eyes opened again, the pain and sorrow in them searing through Brandel.

"Souls," Tine exhaled. "Souls of our dead. Souls hunger for living flesh. If the hunger is not sated…if the soul cannot find another vessel to inhabit…the hunger can drive it to madness. Aifa knows this. She found a way. A way to take tortured souls craving living flesh and direct them into the bodies of her beasts. Each beast holds several souls. But it is not the sort of flesh they need. It is not human or Alainn flesh. They still hunger for life. So…so, they suck the life from everything they touch, hoping to find what they crave. Locked within the beasts, they are unable to exchange the form for the life they most desire."

Everbloom dropped to her knees in sobs. "Souls of…of our dead? Our souls live on when our flesh is done?"

"It was their curse," Tine said. "Long ages ago. The three sisters witnessed the murder of their parents at the hands of the Tanai who feared them. The sisters, themselves, were burned at the stake." He swallowed and fell silent, again, allowing his breathing to settle to something resembling normal. "From the pyre, they cast their curse," he said, at last. "Declaring that they and any born of their lines would never die but would return from death to seek revenge. Their curse applied only to Witches of their blood line, plus two more. Roisin extended it to include Amhranai Fearalite, whom she loved. Not to be outdone, Nemhain included Madadh Mire."

Once more, he took time to breathe. "The curse applied to no others. But here…" He raised his eyes to Deahlan, who sat pale and horrified beside him. "Here, we did not expect the curse to hold at all. Souls do not return, here. Do not transmigrate to another body. We discovered the sisters' souls survived that great battle when it became apparent that they could speak to some among us. Over time, their voices grew fainter, until only a few could hear them. Caer is, perhaps, the last one capable of doing so. But the souls of others among the Witches…" Tine's shrug was a ragged twitch.

"Now. Now, it appears that perhaps all souls survive. Unless… unless they are banished." Tine's shaking returned. "By what means the curse allowing for the survival of souls extended to all I cannot say. Nor can I say whose souls I just banished in killing those beasts. But I know two among them were Alainn. I…"

Brandel swallowed to steady his own breathing. "You freed them from their torture."

"How?" Everbloom sobbed. "How could anyone perpetrate such dark magic as to bind souls to those creatures? It is madness."

Tine's gaze shifted to her. "Madness," he muttered. "Indeed." Forcing a slow breath, he made an unsteady push to his feet.

"You need to rest," Deahlan objected, rising with him.

Tine shook his head. "We need to be away from here. Some among the Red Moon no doubt heard the passing of the beasts; heard the pain of the tortured when I banished their souls. They will send warriors to investigate as soon as the weather abates. They will find the remains of the creatures where I left them on the northern downward slope. We need to leave abundant tracks moving from there to the east. Make them think we are fleeing into the lands of the Sunrise outposts. Need to keep them looking for us far removed from the cave and the secret way into Knife Point fortress." Tine reached for his pack that lay at Deahlan's feet. The young Alainn snatched it, first.

"The storm still rages. It will eliminate any trace of our tracks. When the winds die, I will teleport us to where we are to meet the party of guardians, soldiers, and Alainn."

57

I am a fool, crawling around, digging, and expecting to find anything useful!" Caer dropped to her backside, pounding a fist on the snow. "Nothing to eat. Not enough clothes in the whole of this universe to stay warm. No snowshoes. Roisin! Dana! Tell me I am not insane!" There would be no answer, of course. She sealed her mind against any intrusion days ago, knowing it would be only Nemhain who spoke. Or maybe it was weeks ago. She could no longer remember. She was more alone than ever in her long life.

"Let me just die," she moaned, falling back, struggling to scrape snow over herself. Her hand snagged on something. She grasped it; struggled to pull it free. A small branch lay across her palm. A branch still green enough to be pliable. Rolling to her side, she dug a little deeper. There were more branches. Yet she had not the strength to bind them into snowshoes.

"I would rather die," she muttered. "I am too tired. Too cold. Too hungry. Please. Please do not ask me to go on." Dylan's face lifted to mind. Then Adrian's. All the faces of everyone she loved paraded through her head. Last came Serenity, Shadow, and Whisper. The tears would come next, had she any left. How disappointed they would be. They fought. Most died. If Serenity, Shadow, and Whisper were not dead, they soon would be.

"I cannot," Caer whimpered. "I cannot let their deaths be for naught. Get up, fool. If I am to die, then let it be fighting to honor them."

For several long seconds, she remained lying in the snow, until, at last, she edged to an elbow and worked to sit, blinking at the branches that now lay next to her. Not enough. So, she dug for more. When she was satisfied with her collection, she pulled free of her pack, struggling to make her fingers work sufficiently to rummage through it for the coil of rope tucked down one side. Then, she sought for a knife to cut a length and set to pulling the twining apart. Several times, she stopped, each time calling on spells to warm her hands that they might function better. Little by little, she fashioned the branches, binding them with strands from the rope to make the snowshoes. She cut two more lengths of rope to fasten them to her boots. The effort took her the whole of a day. A hollow at the base of a tree served as cover through the night. There, she waged a constant battle between her desire to let sleep take her permanently and her desperation to carry her last fight to Mt. Sorrow and give her last breath to honor those who fought and died believing in her. As her mind struggled with itself, a hand went absently to her pocket, clasping the charm that once hung around her neck, feeling its faint rhythm reflecting her weary and fluttering heartbeat.

A warm breeze. A single full moon high overhead. A great stone mound shining white in the moonlight. Barefoot, she danced to the sound of the breeze, the whistle through the grasses, the call of night birds. She danced and a voice found her. Gentle. Resonant. He was there, moving through the shadows, his bodhran and bones in hand, though he had little need of them. The richness of his voice carried rhythm and melody alike. He sang to her of the world, rich with beauty; of morning sunrises and evening sunsets; of forests green and of sacred oak groves; of crisp waters running; of life all around. And he sang to her of love and longing. She danced to his songs. Danced until he joined her, his bodhran set aside that he could lift her in his arms. In the night shadows of the mound, they lay, hot against each other, hands moving over bare skin, caressing, gripping, holding, hungering, passionate in their loving.

A warm breeze. A single full moon high overhead. A great stone mound shining white in the moonlight. Barefoot, she danced to his voice. Not alone. Not alone. Dana danced. And Nemhain, as well. No freedom in the dance. Only purpose. Nemhain spoke the words. Dana chose the place. It was her part to reach a hand. Touch the white stone of the mound just where Dana had chosen. And the white exploded in blinding light, sucking them in. Into a new world. For so long as he sang, for so long as they danced, the gateway remained. If any faltered, it faded, leaving them breathless on a mountainside. The song came again, the words now depicting the mound and the hill upon which it sat. And they returned.

A warm breeze. A single full moon high overhead. A great stone mound shining white in the moonlight. Barefoot and bleeding she lay in Dana's arms. Magic flowed through her from Dana. Magic that mixed with her own. The healing she could not draw alone now began. Dana wept. And then Dana reached into the ground, her spell brooding. Silver rose to her fingers, and with magic she fashioned it. First was the fine silver chain, and then the charm - a trinity knot. Again, Dana reached into the ground and a crystal red as blood rose. This, too, she fashioned with her magic, setting it at the heart of the charm. As the charm was joined to the chain, Dana screamed to the night, demanding the words of creation from Nemhain. Mockingly, came the answer. But it was enough. For all the words were there, and Dana fed them to the necklace. In the night, Dana called to him. And he came, singing the song of opening. And this she fed to the necklace. Then she lay the necklace in her youngest sister's hands, Dana's hand closing around them. In the night Dana whispered a new location. Healed of her injuries but not of the grief that their cause had been their sister Nemhain, Roisin, spoke her magic. Within her grasp, with Dana holding fast over it, the necklace ignited, the light of a thousand suns bursting from between their fingers. She felt the two part, the charm and the chain. And then they were gone. Sent far away and in different directions. The magic to create and open the way was broken.

A warm breeze. A single full moon, high overhead. Coated in ages of grime and with portions blackened by fire, the stone mound was now marred, only bits shining white in the moonlight. In silence, she watched through the eyes of another whose feet were planted in resolute defiance, the sounds of battle and the screams of the injured and dying creating a dark song over the distant pipes and drums. Dana watched, also, through the same eyes. Yet it was neither Dana nor the one who bore them within, but he whom she sensed most. He stood near. She felt his power. Knew he loved her, still, though another had entered his heart, as well. The pang of jealousy stung. She quelled it. She would be gone, soon. If he survived, he deserved to be loved anew.

Around the neck of the one who bore their souls, the chain and charm throbbed, synchronized with the girl's pulse. The magic woven into it strengthened, easing the pain of the magic Nemhain beat down upon them. She need only wait, now. The time was upon them. She and Dana would end the insanity of their sister. They…

Caer gasped, fighting to breathe through the snow dropping down from the tree, the sounds and the smells of that long ago battle still ringing through her mind, her hand clasped around the charm. Its throb, though faint, summoned her.

"I hear. I understand." Distant, faint as a breath in the stillness of night, the words came to Caer. Breathed out by Whisper. And then it was there, lying on Caer's palm. The fine silver chain, threaded of its own accord through the charm, but also holding a tiny gold ring. Whisper's ring. Caer's hand closed on it, the ability to cry rushing her, once more. The ring was never meant to be returned to her unless… unless upon Whisper's death.

The heat from chain and charm now steamed in the icy air, the burn of it mitigated only a little by Caer's mitten. She thought to throw them from her, as she had once considered doing in that different lifetime on that different world.

This accursed piece of jewelry that swept her from the worlds she knew, likely destroying Earth in its wake; that dropped her in a world where the sisters' war ravaged new people, repeatedly taking from them and her those they loved most. Yet once again, she could not bring herself to do it. Instead, she thrust the necklace and the tiny ring into the depths of her pocket, its heat warming her leg briefly before dissipating.

Forcing stiff, cold muscles to move, she climbed out from the hollow to face the thin gray light of another morning and the beginning of yet another snowfall. For a moment, she stood, eyes closed. "You will pay! Do you hear, Nemhain? You will pay for all the death! For all the suffering! You, Dana, Roisin! All of you for what you created and for all the death and destruction it has caused!"

A cracking sounded on the air. And then a distant laughter, sickeningly sweet, cruel and mocking. Nemhain's laughter, though another seemed to be mixed in, running as a dark rumble underneath. Vaguely familiar, it raised Caer's flesh. She thought to scream. To demand to know whose vile souls stood with Nemhain's.

"*Sshhhhhh.*" The hush was almost lost in the laughter and rumble. "*Be still. Your journey is not ended.*"

Roisin, this time. Caer bit at her lip. She had released the shielding around her mind. She sealed in her thoughts once more. Nemhain wanted her at Blood Hall, not at Mt. Sorrow. Whatever her reason, she must not learn Caer's whereabouts, yet. Not yet. Caer would find her way to the mountain – to the beginning. And if a way exists to end Nemhain's and the Red Moon's reign, she would find it.

Her knees gave way as she tried to ease to the ground to reach back into the hollow. "If I am to do this," she muttered, "then for pity's sake, grant my body the strength to do so." While she expected no reply, having shut her mind to such, she hoped for some surge to run through her. There was nothing, and the stretch for the strap of her pack that still lay at the base of the tree left Caer light-headed. Seeking the nearest boulder, she dropped onto it long enough for her head to settle and to eat the last few bits of jerky she had scrounged from one of the pack's outside pockets, thankful to whatever fate placed them there. From the coat pocket that did not hold the ancient gateway key, she retrieved a handful of dried berries, then washed them down with swallows of snow. Shouldering her pack, Caer struggled to her feet, her snowshoes dragging as she trudged on.

By midday, the wind threatened to sweep her from her feet. Before seeking shelter and a rest, Caer braced herself at the top of one of the lesser peaks to stare off to the northwest. Dark clouds hovered over what she knew to be Knife

Point Keep. Turning slightly, she swept a glance across the vista that lay before her, hoping to catch a glimpse of something she might identify as Mt. Sorrow. Black and white and shades of gray washed the world around her, giving her no indication of the mountain's precise location. Was there ever a time when the world was full of color, full of joy?

Sitting, she scooted down the steep slope to where the grade was less a strain on exhausted muscles. From here, she could descend to the valley floor and follow it around the neighboring slope. Unless the wind became a gale, she might yet make it to an old trader's cabin rumored to be there. She could shelter for the night. In the morning, she would face the rugged climb up the next slope and again look for the massive, blackened mountainside. What was to come after that she could not say. No longer cared, so long as she could cause Nemhain harm.

The wind lessened as she descended, though the snow was increasing. Back within a bent and twisted forest, trees moaned, and branches snapped under the weight of their white cloaks. Her mind was as numb as her body when she at last spotted the trader's cabin in the deepening shadows. The steep angle of the roof allowed snow to slide off, only to be deposited in drifts up to the eves at the cabin's sides. A fair drift lay across the front, as well, Caer summoned what energy she could and muttered a simple spell that cleared the area nearest the door. Long unused, she battered her shoulder against it several times before the door gave way and opened with a bang against the inside wall. Shoving it closed, she dropped her pack where she stood and searched the dark shadows for some means of light, grateful that a dusty pile of wood lay in the box next to the fireplace. She did not care that the smoke might draw unwanted attention. Calling up fire, even the tiniest spark, had been one of Caer's hardest won bits of magic. Only Emer's patience and persistence allowed her to learn the spell. She fought the lump in her throat as she offered a silent thank you to her long dead friend.

She had no idea how long she simply sat on the floor in front of the fire before she felt warm enough to dispense with her mittens and her coat. Shooting a glance at the antiquated bed in one corner of the room, she dismissed the idea of making use of it, preferring her proximity to the small blaze on the hearth. Instead, she pulled a blanket from her pack and spread it on the floor, draping her coat over her, too exhausted to heed the rumbling emptiness of her stomach. There were no dreams until the voices came, soft and whispered. Then was the smell of food. Of food.

Struggling to one side, Caer fought to open an eye. A spit across the back of the hearth held cooking meat. To the front, a pot hung from a hinged hook, the sound of something boiling clattering the lid on top. In her dream, Caer closed her eye again. Waking would be cold, her joints and muscles full of aches and her stomach empty.

"You are not fooling me, Little Swan. I know you are awake."

Confusion creased her brow and she dared to open both eyes as she flopped to her back. Staring down was Tine's relieved countenance, though his features were grayer and more heavily lined than she remembered.

"We feared we might lose you when we found you last night, your fire burned down to coals and you curled in a tight ball beneath your coat." Tine extended a hand to help her rise.

Caer blinked at it several times, still not entirely certain of its reality. She took it, overwhelmed with the rush of relief as he drew her to unsteady feet. Everbloom was instantly behind her, shoving the room's only chair beneath her before her wobbly knees gave out. Brandel and the young Alainn who was named Deahlan promptly picked up the small table and moved it to her, as well. Spirit lay in a back corner, ever watchful. For a long while, she, too, watched in silence as they scuttled about, rolling up blankets and stashing them back in their packs. Everbloom pulled a mug from a dusty and cobweb infested cabinet, ladled boiling water from the pot into it, swished it, and then tossed the dirty water in a bent bucket that occupied one corner near the hearth. From her pocket, Grian Geal's daughter produced a pouch, emptying about a quarter of it in the mug and refilling it with water. The aroma of blackberry, rose, and wintergreen wafted at Caer as Everbloom set the mug in front of her.

"Here, Little Swan. Drink this. Dinner will be ready soon."

Caer's hands shook when she lifted the mug to her lips. Instead of sipping, she set the tea back to the table, her eyes searching the room. "Where…where is Stoirm? What are…are you doing here?" Her gaze settled on Tine. "Why did you not go to Blood Hall?"

Before Tine could reply, Caer clutched at her heart, what was left of warmth draining from her. "He is gone," she strangled. "And…and Whisper and Shadow and Serenity? Even Owl and the girl…Phoenix? Gone?" Why had she not sensed it?

Tine squatted in front of her. "Father went to Blood Hall to try and save them." The grief in his eyes matched the emptiness of her soul.

"Alone? You let him go alone?"

"He gave us no choice. Teleported so quickly, we could not stop him. Neither could we go after him since we did not know the way."

Tine rose, a smoldering anger heating his words. "And you have no room to criticize! You pop off indicating you were going for your family."

"But you thought otherwise?"

"Not at first. It cost us time, looking for you, believing you meant to go to Rift, there to find Blood Hall. In the end, I suspected you may change your mind. It split our company. Father going to Blood Hall, leaving us to turn to Mt. Sorrow."

Any further words stuck in Caer's throat. In all the long centuries they had known one another, Tine had never spoken in anger to her. So many times, she deserved it. This…this was the hardest to bear, for even in his anger and his pain, his love and concern for her ran through it.

Tine's shoulders sagged. "It was a lie, Caer. Nemhain lied to you.

The hostages were never taken to Blood Hall."

"Grandmother."

Caer tensed at the delicate touch of the word on the air. It could not be. She dared not attempt to stand but shifted on the chair. Framed in the doorway stood Whisper, Shadow at her side. With a ragged inhale, Caer reached a trembling hand toward the two. The girls rushed to her, Whisper dropping to her knees in front of Caer, the girl's head buried in Caer's lap, her quiet sobs trembling through her small frame. Shadow collapsed with folded legs on the floor next to Whisper, tears glistening in her eyes, as well, grief flowing in the music of her words. "Serenity is gone. Whisper blames herself."

"If I had listened to the warnings in my soul, I would still be in the keep. Serenity would be there, as well, after evacuating the sanctuary with the others," Whisper sobbed.

For several long minutes, words failed Caer. She could only run her hand over Whisper's hair. With one more ragged breath came, "No fault lies with you, child. Fault lies with the sisters for all that has led us here. Lies especially with Nemhain, whose vile hatred ignites wars. Lies with me for being the tool that brought them to this world. No fault lies on your shoulders." Lifting Whisper's chin, Caer gestured toward her coat. "Would you bring it to me?"

Snuffling, Whisper gained her feet, collecting the coat that still lay on the blanket near the fire and delivered it. Caer fumbled in a pocket to retrieve the necklace and the other tiny treasure. "Where did you find the ring? I thought it lost in the raid that…"

"I found it in the room where Mother sent me just before she died. The room where Tine knew to look for me. The secret room in our home."

"Had it not been your voice as it came into my hand, I would think Danu sent it as proof of your capture. Or your…" She choked back the last word, asking, "How did you come by the chain? Hawk took you all the way to Riversong?"

"No, Grandmother. I escaped from him. And then he saved my life. He never meant me any harm. As for the chain, Danu must have taken it from the Temple of Damsa Dana when she fled. I stole it from her."

Caer leaned back, staring at the girl. "You…stole it? How?"

"She carried it in a small velvet bag tied round her neck with a velvet cord. She told no one what the bag contained, though she slipped it out when she thought no one watched. What she understood or believed regarding it, I cannot say, though it appeared she feared to handle it. She never touched it with bare fingers, only with silk gloves.

And she would speak to it. Addressed it as the Goddess Damsa Dana."

Caer's brow creased. "And you stole it."

"Aye," Shadow put in. "Doing the very thing I keep telling her not to do."

Caer almost chuckled. "What creature did you choose?"

"A squirrel," Whisper said. "I followed her from the cave one afternoon. Followed her to the river where she bathed. She lay the bag inside her robes on the side of the bank. While she shivered and grumbled in the river water, I slipped in, replaced the chain with a small bit of twig, and carried the chain back to the cave where my body waited. When my soul returned, I knew the chain lay beneath my hand."

"The manner of its taking is almost worth having it returned to me." Caer shook her head. "But better you had buried it in that cave. Or thrown it into the river when you escaped." She cocked a brow. "By whatever manner you escaped." Laying the chain with its charm across her lap, she said, "The necklace rejoined is dangerous. It can…"

"You forget, Grandmother. I know its purpose. I know its secrets. And I do not think its use is done."

And if that use is by Aifa's hand? Caer bit back the words. It was not a worry Whisper deserved to carry. The burden she bore since that first day Caer held her was more than any child should hold. For in that first moment, Whisper

SLIEVGALLION: THE GODDESS WARS

demonstrated her unique gift of shifting her soul from her body to that of another living creature. It was to Caer, her soul moved, the experience a sudden jolt for them both. Why the baby made such a transmigration remained a mystery, for she never again did so with any other human. But in the few brief moments the baby's soul lay stunned within her, Whisper shared in all the memories harbored within Caer. No one knew. No one save she and the child. No. Caer could not speak of the fear that ate at her - that she would fail, again, allowing the gateway to be opened and Nemhain to again live within flesh. Instead, she returned the chain and charm to her coat pocket. As she did so, other items fell from a different pocket, rattling to the floor. Caer leaned to collect them, her lips pursed as her gaze went to Brandel.

"Lt. Journeyson. Brandel."

"My lady?"

A subtle foreboding weighted Caer's sigh. Still, she extended what she held. "This once belonged to your distant great grandfather. I never wished for it to be in my possession, but it was his desire upon his death. I believe he would want this passed on to you.

Brandel hesitated.

"Please," she said. "Take it."

Striding to her, he extended his open hand. Caer lay the gun and the few rounds of ammunition on his palm.

"What is…?"

"A small firearm. A gun. It is the weapon he used to kill me as the gateway stood open."

"To… What?"

"Never mind. Please. Just take it. Ask Tine to show you how to use it."

Everbloom cleared her throat, venturing a meek, "We have allowed enough time for reunion and talk. Dinner is ready and Swan needs to eat." Nudging Brandel aside, she cast a curious gaze at the items in his hand.

Tine drew a slow breath. "Aye. The path ahead is as treacherous as any yet taken. We will all will need our strength." He paused, setting his gaze on Everbloom and Caer. "You are all I have left," he said. "I will not lose you."

"We will not lose them," Brandel affirmed, pocketing the bullets and turning the gun over in his hands.

"So," Caer sighed. "Behold our defenders, Everbloom."

"I need no protection. But I will stand with them to protect you," she harrumphed. "Nor are we alone."

"But Knife Point Keep can ill afford to spare her defenders so long as she is under siege."

"Aye. True enough. That is why Deahlan and I were all that was available to join Tine and Lt. Journeyson when they came seeking aid. They, however, had collected a small company of loyal Soldiers of Damsa Dana. And we knew of a contingent of guardians, soldiers, and Alainn who were working their way toward the keep. Car'Adawc sent to them of our need, and they agreed to help." She nodded toward the cabin's single window. "They are camped outside. Some one hundred and fifty, plus the roughly sixty or so soldiers who came with Tine and Journeyson."

Caer gained her feet making a wobbly trek to the window, wiping away years of dirt with her sleeve. Outside, icy domes dotted the area, men and women moving about, some tending fires and cooking.

"They provided us with our dinner," Everbloom added. "And it is time you took some. You were scarcely enough to stand against a stiff breeze the first time I saw you, and there is even less of you, now."

Caer's lips pursed as Everbloom retrieved a few dusty and cracked plates from the same cabinet she had taken the mug, ladling hot water from the pot over each before handing them round. Caer's plate she kept, slicing a sizeable portion of elk onto it and adding flat bread and dried berries.

"How long?" Caer asked.

Everbloom cocked her head. "How long what?"

"How long did I sleep for you to make camp, hunt, and prepare a meal?"

Tine shrugged. "When did you arrive, here?"

"Last night. I think. I do not know the hour."

"We arrived in the night, as well, those with us creating the domes in which they sheltered. Once we were certain you lived, we let you sleep. The others," he gestured toward the window. "They arrived midmorning. Scouts went out shortly afterward. Returned with plenty of game to share."

Everbloom seemed to take Caer's frown as concern for the creatures killed. "The animals were properly honored, Little Swan."

"I do not doubt that. But...did the scouts...did the scouts find anything more?"

Everbloom shot a concerned glance at Tine. "They did not. But Tine did. Before we even left the cave at the bottom of the secret way out of Knife Point Fortress. Three death beasts. He…" She swallowed. "He destroyed them all. He knows what…"

Tine waved her silent. "The scouts have reported something more. Death has spread further outward, Caer. The whole of Mt. Sorrow is now blighted. Across the passes to a couple of the neighboring slopes, as well. Nothing lives. No tree, no bush, no animal."

"Even Spirit will not go there," Brandel added.

Caer's gaze settled on the wolf. "Spirit has more sense than I. But I must go there."

"Not until you eat," Everbloom insisted.

The sound of laughter rippled through Caer's mind, the tone deep and vile and expectant, the sound staggering her backward. Hands grabbed her, guiding her back to the chair. She scarcely noticed. It was the laughter that held her, raising her flesh as it had done previously. This was not the laughter of Aifa, nor of Nemhain. Its repugnance stirred splintered memories from a past long buried.

"Caer! Caer! What is it?"

The question registered at the fringe of her awareness. Her shudder broke the echo of that horrifying laugh. Her gasp filled her starved lungs. How long had she held her breath? How long had…

Tine was kneeling before her, his hands clasping one of hers. Her other hand, she realized, was gripping her necklace, its heat and frantic pulse near scorching her fingers, yet she could not release it. When had she taken it from her coat pocket?

Tine reached up, prying her fingers free. "You drew this to you, just now. What did you see, Little Swan?'

"Nothing." Her response sounded unconvincing, even to her ears.

"Nothing. No… No vision. Only…"

"Only what?"

"Laughter. Laughter I should know. I should know. But I cannot…"

Relief washed Tine's face. "Laughter with no vision is empty." Rising, he tapped the edge of her plate. "Eat. Sleep again. We will not move on Mt. Sorrow until early light, tomorrow."

58

"*A*bred. Gwynfyd. Ceugant. Struggle. Find the beginning. Return to the beginning. Purity. Know your true voice. Your clear voice. Ceugant. Forever we will suffer if you do not end it.*"

Black shapes hover in the shadows. Laughter. Angry screams. Blood rushing. Rivers of blood. Faces flash. Dylan. Adrian. Fedel'ma. Emer. Brandon. A cat. Fedel'ma. She smiles. Dylan. "We are with you. Always." Her children. Her beautiful children. All dead. All gone. Whisper. Shadow. Serenity. Spirit. The wolf turns and walks away. Walks into the darkness. Dylan. "You are stronger than you know." Whisper. Her face becomes a skull. "Return to the beginning. You will find us when you seek the beginning."

Laughter - two voices at odds. One sickly sweet. The second obscene.

Caer awoke, gasping, drenched in cold sweat, shaking. Tine pushed up on one elbow from where he lay on the floor next to the bed. She did not remember coming to the bed. He said nothing; only watched her, his face questioning.

"I am going."

"Going where?" he whispered in return.

"Returning to the beginning. It is what they said I must do. Return to the beginning."

"I know. You are not alone. We go with you. But not yet. Not until there is light. Not until we can see who we face."

"And they will see us."

"Aye. They will. Let them."

"Let them," Caer repeated, drawing the blanket around her. "Let Roisin know that I am there. Let Dana know. I will accomplish what they asked. Again." Her eyes closed, but sleep refused to return. In her mind ran the sound of the laughter she should know. The face that should go with it eluded her. Only her overwhelming sense of repulsion remained. For a time, she fought through twists and turns of memories. Roisin's. Dana's. Even Nemhain's. There were memories that came close. But none that fit the repugnance she felt for that sound.

At last, others in the cabin began to stir. Spirit was first, the wolf stretching and nudging Brandel. Brandel. She addressed him so rarely by that name. Lowering her legs over the bed's edge to sit, she held it in her mind, weighing it. A good name. A strong name. The name that reflected his ancestors. She tried to pull Fedel'ma's and Brandon's faces to the front of her memories. They shimmered but a moment, then dissolved, leaving her staring at the lieutenant who sat with his back propped against the wall.

Brandel cocked a brow at her. "Is there something you need?"

Blinking, she lowered her gaze. "No. Nothing. I was just…just remembering. I miss them. After all this time, I still miss them."

Brandel ran a hand over the stubble on his face, looking uncertain as to how he should respond.

"Do not listen to me," Caer groaned. "I am just an old woman."

Everbloom chuckled. "You are not 'just' anything." Gathering her blanket, she stood and stretched, then went to add more wood to the fire. Whisper and Shadow joined her, there, each warming themselves while the pot of water was moved back into position to heat.

Deahlan entered from outside, stomping snow from his boots. The last Caer knew, he was sleeping with his back against the wall near the door. She had no idea when he had risen. Tine pushed to his feet, stretching, then joined Deahlan in a quiet conversation. The young Alainn nodded and left.

Turning to Caer, Tine stated, "You should eat something. You hardly touched your dinner."

"Not hungry."

Everbloom shook her head. "I suspected you would say as much." Heading to the pot, she dipped a mug into the water and carried it to a table, then rummaged in her pack for her wooden box. "At least drink a little tea," she said, emptying the entire contents into the steaming water. A mix of aromas filled the room. Such an unusual blend. Chamomile and lavender were most prevalent. Whiffs of betony and bay mingled with blueberry. There were also hints of hyssop, galangal, comfrey, celery, and honey. Herbs primarily for protection and for enhancing one's magic.

"Where did you get this?"

"From mother," Everbloom smiled. "She gave it to me the night before…" Her voice trailed off, picking up again with, "Said it tastes like mud, but it is good for sustenance and good for the soul."

Caer accepted the mug, the subtle sense of magic settling over her as she sipped. It did, indeed, taste of mud. But she welcomed its warmth and the sense of strength returning. If Everbloom's enchantment could see her through this day, if it could help her face Aifa, or whomever she must face, with courage and conviction… The charm on her necklace seemed to respond to the magic, as well. Not only did its agitated pulse calm as Caer's did, the heat of the charm also diminished. Caer reached for it, her fingers curling around the charm where it rested in the hollow of her throat, the vague recollection of donning it in the night drifting through her mind.

Perhaps this was her mission. Return the necklace to the beginning. It was Dana's creation, its magic set by Dana and Roisin together. Perhaps they needed it taken to the place where Slievgall'ion's magic was strongest. Perhaps there, it would restore their strength. What an idiot she was, not to consider that possibility ages ago! How much suffering and loss might she have saved had that realization come to her centuries before now?

Tine, she realized, was standing next to her, watching her. "Do not blame yourself for all that has transpired," he soothed.

Blanching, Caer glanced around to see who else had read her thoughts.

"Guilt is written in your eyes, Little Swan. When will you stop carrying the weight of things beyond your control?"

Things might be in her control. Or at least in Roisin's and Dana's, had she not been such a blind imbecile! Setting aside the empty mug, she looked for her pack. Found it propped against the wall near where Deahlan had slept. Not that she expected to need it. If she delivered the amulet to Dana and Roisin, then perhaps they would at last let her soul rest. Why had they never simply told her it was the necklace they needed?

"Here," Tine said, handing her coat to her. As she turned to take it, he grasped her wrist. "You are no imbecile, Caer DaDhrga. Father knew you well. He believed in you. And so do I. Whatever has made you think yourself a fool is false. Trust the magic that Everbloom wove for you. Open your mind and your senses. Let the spells from Deep Hall draw the truth of your path to you. Do not accept simple measures as the solution to this. Believe in yourself."

Sucking a ragged inhale, she nodded. It was too simple a measure, returning the necklace. She knew it in her soul.

Gently turning her to the door, Tine said, "Now, take us where you must go."

The early morning sun lifted above the mountain peaks with a coral glow, lengthening shadows slowly brightening, drawing Caer's attention to the vast, empty field. The encampment was gone, the icy domes crumbled back to the snow.

"They are scouting the way ahead of us and will send word of any threat."

Lips pursed, Caer again nodded, following Tine to the side of the cabin where snowshoes leaned against the wall. Hers were among them. She did not recall putting them there. Tine must have found them inside and moved them. Repositioning her pack, she fastened the topmost button of her coat, snugged her hood around her face, and found a bench to sit on long enough to attach her snowshoes and don her mittens.

"Clever," Everbloom noted as she passed, gesturing at Caer's handiwork with the shoes. For a moment, Whisper and Shadow sat beside her, one on each side. They said nothing. But their presence and the gentle pressure of their hands on hers brought her unexpected comfort.

Together, their company set out, Spirit taking the lead. It did not take long, however, before Tine called a halt. "It will do us no good if we go blind from the glare."

Everbloom nodded, pulling several dark scarves from a pocket. Caer took the one handed to her and tied it around her eyes. Somewhere in the bottom of her pack she had one of her own, given to her ages ago by Lt. Singer. The guardians knew well the advantage of a fabric thin enough to see through and dark enough to cut the sun's blinding glare off the white landscape. Given the recent days on end of overcast and snowfall, the scarf had lain forgotten. Until now. On the day when she was likely to find death, on this day, the sun shone.

It was midday when their climb rounded a switchback that put them in full view of Mt. Sorrow. Even with heavy snow covering her slopes, the sight of jutting, blasted boulders sent a shock of foreboding through Caer. Their path would take them up the current slope to a pass that would carry them across. From where she stood, Caer could see the march of blackened scrub crawling down Mt. Sorrow's sides and into the dead trees in the valley below. It even crept across the pass, touching the upper slopes they would need to negotiate.

Brandel dropped back. "Any word?" he asked of Tine.

"All seems quiet. The others are spreading out, climbing to the ancient battle site from each direction."

Quiet, Caer acknowledged, foreboding rising like a black tide. The Red Moon Warriors lay in wait for them, somewhere. She wanted to warn her friends. Tell them it was a trap. Tell them to go back. She was the one who needed to go on. Not them. But she knew they would not listen. They would go where she went. Because... She sucked a weary and resigned breath. Because they believed in her.

Brandel and Spirit took the lead. Everbloom kept pace with Caer. Whisper and Shadow climbed side by side only a few paces behind. Tine and Deahlan followed. The exertion of the climb under the full exposure of the sun, the light reflecting off the snow soon had them dropping their hoods and loosening their coats. A tremor ran through Caer as they at last approached the first of the dead forests, this one at the pass that crossed onto the nearest neighboring slope to Mt. Sorrow. She thought she heard weeping. Was Slievgall'ion mourning? Spirit stopped cold, the animal shaking, the howl she raised echoing all around. Brandel knelt beside her.

"You need go no further, my friend. You are free. Return to the woods. Make your own life." When he stood and moved on, she held her ground, first whining, then raising a most anguished cry. And then she raced to him. The wolf would face her darkest fears with her companion.

When they at last crossed onto the slopes of Mt. Sorrow, it was to a silence deeper than any Caer had ever known. The air was still and stale. The smell of ash and dust lifted through the snow. Still, they climbed, switch-backing across the steep grade. At one point, they saw signs of those who had set out ahead of them, their tracks splitting as they separated into smaller groups. Brandel considered briefly before setting off obliquely toward the mountain's summit. With the grade lessening, Caer chose a more direct route. Brandel and Spirit doubled back to catch up to her, doubt in Brandel's eyes, though he did not question her.

The stillness of the air and the altitude threatened to strip Caer of her ability to breathe. It would be more so for Brandel, yet he stayed with her. It was evening before they finally came out on a high plateau. For a moment, the stillness held. Then the memories flooded her - the distant ring and clash of battle. In the twilight, Caer could almost see the long-ago flash of magic against magic, the clang of metal blades on metal blades, the swishing sing of arrows in flight, as well as the flash and blast of Tanai weapons of that far distant world. Through it all drifted screams and cries and a curse rising, carried on laughter.

That same, repulsive laughter from before. Almost the same. The laughter from that ancient battle held a deep, rumbling repugnance mixed with an eerie, high-pitched screech as of fingernails raking down a metal bucket. She remembered the sound. Madadh Mire and Ailill, the two souls locked in a single body, each vying for supremacy. Adrian told her of the curse they cast, that day, though she had no personal memory of it. She died in the gateway. Returned to her body just before being blasted through to Slievgall'ion where she lay, struggling to survive. Only now did she hear it echoing among the peaks.

"A curse upon your kith and kin! They will fall to us, one by one. Then we will come for you!"

The words screeched from mountaintop to mountaintop. But they were dead - Madadh Mire and Ailill. Adrian struck them down in a battle many, many years after their arrival. Had banished their souls.

The laughter burst over her, again, rolling like thunder, singeing her nerves and magnifying the repulsion she could not quiet. More memories rushed her mind. The man who stood in the shadows beneath her pod; the man who sat next to her on the shuttle; the man who fired at O-4; the man who stalked her and who tried time and again to murder her – all in that lifetime from that other world. Madadh Mire. Always it was the Mad Dog.

The others heard the laughter, too. She could see it in their startled and terrified stares into the ether. "You are dead!" she screamed. "Dead and banished. Long ago!"

The laughter roiled, the air filling with the obscenity of his voice. *"Ah, but no. My dear brother's banishing spell found Ailill. My stepson proved not so worthless, after all. His soul caught the blast and deflected enough of it that it merely seared me. To give him his due, Amhranai's spell did set me back for a few centuries. But my soul survived. Do you remember my curse, Caer DaDhrga?"*

Caer shuddered, her eyes searching for what she knew she could not see. He had no body. He was soul, only. As vile and hateful as Nemhain.

"Only soul?" His malignant laugh filled the air, once more. *"I am The Soul. I took my time. Remained in the background through centuries. Let the sisters' souls battle one another. Nemhain was able to beat Dana down, first. Turned her High Priestess without ever letting the Witch know she was not following Dana's path. Set the barrier to prevent sendings from passing between Knife Point and Brightwater. Sweet little Roisin. She took longer. Who would have thought she would be the stronger? Through it all, I had to lend a hand to my beloved wife, whispering suggestions, lending some*

of my strength to her without her knowing it was mine. All the while, I watched as she succeeded in fulfilling most of my curse, directing our daughter and then our granddaughter as they murdered your line, your friends, and much of their lines. Let me show you something."

Dark visions erupted. A woman stalked a dark cavern, her movements agitated. Mid-stride, she froze and looked up. *"Madadh!"* she hissed. Her eyes widened as she appeared to look straight at Caer. *"No! You told me she would come to me! She is supposed to be mine!"*

The force of the Witch's anger and hatred exploded, a kill spell echoing from the cavern walls. But the spell was in vain. Those she supposedly held captive were not there, and Stoirm was already dead by her hand. Aifa's impotent scream echoed around her, not fading, but growing stronger.

"Silence!" With Madadh's bellow, the scream abruptly died. The charge of a teleportation dropped Aifa not ten meters from Caer. The High Priestess crouched, much like a threatened wild creature. Her dark hair whipped around her face as her pale blue eyes darted startled glances about. *"Draw a coat to yourself,"* Madadh commanded.

Aifa cringed, then reached a hand, a heavy coat materializing in its grasp. She wasted no time in donning it, straightening and raising a palm aimed at Caer.

"Do not harm her!" The warning came on Nemhain's repugnant sweet tones.

"Was a good thought," Madadh mused. *"Send you to Aifa. Let her tear your memories from you. Watch you die a long, slow death, alone. Then banish your soul. Easy enough for me to take those memories from our weak-minded granddaughter and arrange for her death and banishment. I thought I would have no more need of her, once I hold the power your memories will provide. I have since had second thoughts, however. She will still be useful. You, of course, failed to take the bait. You did not go to her. So, now I must pull the memories from you, myself. Such a waste of my energy you cost me by coming here. And what have you gained by it?"*

Another vision flooded Caer's mind. This one of Knife Point Keep, the last gate shattered, Red Moon Warriors rampaging through the halls, guardians and Alainn and Soldiers of Damsa Dana dead. All dead. The lands of Sunrise flashed before her. Alainn lay dead at the feet of the Red Moon conquerors. Spinning, Caer searched for those who had come to this place of darkness with her. As she did so, shots rang out in the distance all around where she stood. Then they rang out nearer. Spirit fell next to Brandel's bleeding body. Everbloom lay in a pool of blood on one side of her, Tine on the other. Whisper and Shadow lay sprawled behind her. Deahlan must have attempted to reach Aifa, as his body lay a few meters to one side of her, the High Priestess' hand still aimed at him, a look of satisfaction on her face.

"Those who came here thinking to protect you are dead." Madadh gloated.

Caer fought to stay on her feet; fought to keep her pain and grief concealed. "You lie." Her words held a tremor, yet she filled them with conviction. It was a possibility. Nemhain lied. Surely, not the whole of Slievgall'ion now lay massacred. And though those nearest her lay in pools of bloodied snow, at least one still lived. Weak as it was, she sensed one living presence.

"You know I do not."

"I know you, like your wife, are full of deceit and dishonor."

"Shall I show you the vision, again?"

Shaking so hard her legs threatened to drop her, Caer held her ground. Dead. He said they were dead, not banished.

A map. Mt. Sorrow written clearly. Beneath, faded yet…yet readable. Slieve na…Slieve na Calliagh.

Was this what they expected of her? Dana and Roisin? No! She could not do this, again!

"It is the only way."

"No! It cannot be! I have come all this way to destroy her, not to… not to…"

"Madadh must be defeated, as well. It cannot be done, here. They are too strong."

Caer tried to shut their voices out. No. If Madadh and Nemhain were too strong, now, think what they could accomplish if granted physical bodies, once more. No! No. There had to be another way.

"The truth is difficult, is it not? Knowing how many have died on this day, alone?" Madadh's voice raked through her. Why could she not shut him out?

"It is not truth!" Caer cried. "The visions of death prove nothing coming from such a deceiver as you. Those who fight you at Knife Point Fortress still live. Those who fight you in Sunrise still live."

"Do you wish proof? I will grant you proof in exchange for your soul and all its memories."

"They are not a part of you. You are not of the sisters' blood. Their memories will do you no good. The magic of the opening will not work for you."

"Ah. And that is a truth that has been difficult for me. I have accepted it, though. That is why I have not twisted Nemhain's soul out of existence. She will open the gateway once more, and we will return to our world."

Caer's mind raced. If they open the way, what becomes of all the souls wrapped in this world? Was it possible for all souls flee through the gateway? Or will only those whose bodies lay within its boundaries have such a capability? Where did the souls of the dead reside And if they could flee...if they could go to the world where the sisters first set their curse, would they be able to live, again? It was a chance. A tiny one, to be sure. But...

"Even Nemhain can do nothing with those memories save to pass them on to Aifa. It takes a living Witch to work them."

"And that is why I brought my granddaughter here."

"I will not let you do this! I will seal the memories in so many webs of spells it will take you centuries more to disentangle them."

"I will twist your soul out of existence where you stand, little Witch."

"And what will that gain you? You know I speak the truth. I am already binding what you desire so tightly your soul will shrivel before you obtain what you seek."

A screech split the air, and Caer knew it was Whisper's rising through Madadh's laughter. *"I may not be able to work the magic of the gateway without a living puppet. But I do hold the power to twist other souls."* Whisper's tortured wail rose again.

"Let her be! I have set the spells around the memories. If you wish for me to give them over, you will meet my demands."

The screams of Whisper's soul ceased and Madadh's laughter faded, replaced by a thoughtful brooding. *"Now it is I who do not believe you. You have not the strength left to weave such spells of binding, Witch. And I tire of this game. Time to dispense with your weary body and simply take the memories."*

"No!" Nemhain's screech cut through.

"Silence!"

"If you kill this Witch, we lose everything," seeped in a thin, syrupy whine. *"She carries the amulet, once more. I can feel it on her. Kill her and you destroy the amulet. The memories are useless without it. Always, you refuse to listen to me. In this, you must. I am part of the means of opening the way, as are the memories from my sisters. But they tied the gateway to the key. To the amulet. Bad enough that in those other worlds killing her would cause the amulet to disappear. This Witch made it part of herself when she became the gateway and brought us to this fate. I warned you not to try to send her to Aifa to be killed. Be thankful the Witch did not take the bait. Listen to me or our souls will be sentenced to hunger for flesh and blood for all eternity."*

Caer sucked in. Was this truth? Was the amulet now a part of her? Or was this another of Nemhain's lies.

The roll of thunder boomed overhead. *"Give us the secrets to open the way, Witch! And then I will grant you what you most desire – the eternal rest you wish."*

For the briefest moment, Caer considered taking her own life. The knife was still in her boot. Kill herself and she destroys the amulet... And leaves Slievgall'ion at the mercy of the condemned and violent souls of Madadh and Nemhain for the rest of eternity. Gradually, things were becoming clear. If she dies, so dies the key, leaving this world in eternal suffering. If she opens the way, Madadh and Nemhain are free to find physical hosts once more. But...but so may be the case for other souls.

Shielding her thoughts with great care, she opened her mind for Roisin. Praying the sister would hear her and respond. *"Will you also find physical hosts? You and Dana?"*

"We are weak, but if you set the way properly, yes. We may be able to pass through before Madadh and Nemhain."

"And others?"

"If you are careful. If you set the placement correctly. Yes. Many others may pass, as well. It is our only hope. Return to Earth. Rebuild our strength in physical vessels that can again wield magic in a physical manner."

"You test my patience, Witch!" bellowed across the ether. *"Relinquish the memories!"*

"I will not! Not unless you meet my demand."

"You are in no position to bargain," Madadh snorted. *"I will twist the souls of all those you have loved who have not yet been banished."*

"Am I not? Twist the souls of the dead out of existence. The pain will end, and they will suffer no more." Reaching into her boot, Caer withdrew her knife, pressing the tip to her heart. "I will kill myself and leave you to do what you wish with my soul, afterward. I no longer care. At least the amulet will be lost to you, and you will not gain what you desire above all else. A return to a physical host."

There was a lengthy and weighted silence. At last, Madadh growled, *"Make your demand."*

"I do wish proof of the visions, as you offered before. Deliver to this mountainside the bodies of those you have slain on this day and in the days going back to your first assault on Knife Point Keep. I wish to see them...to know them all."

SLIEVGALLION: THE GODDESS WARS

"That is an impossibility!"

"Then I end my life here." The knife tip cut into her flesh.

"She thinks to take them all through the gateway with us," Nemhain whimpered.

"And what if I do?" The knife pressed deeper. "It is you who have no bargaining position. Meet my demand or lose all hope."

The repulsive laugh came again. *"Well, wife. Do you think you can close the gateway quickly enough to prevent the Witch's plan?"*

"I can," returned, though it lacked conviction.

"No matter. The souls of our warriors will also be able to pass through. We will simply seek and kill again those who have loved and supported this Witch. There will be an extra satisfaction in ending their lives once more, and this time banishing all their souls."

Suddenly, bodies rained down all around, covering the mountainside, in places several bodies deep. *"There, little Witch. I fulfilled your demand. Now fulfill mine. Open your mind for my wife."*

Staggered and appalled by the numbers of the dead, Caer fell to her knees, the knife dropping from her hands as she buried her face in them.

"I met your demand!" Boomed again. *"Now fulfill your part of the bargain, little Witch. Open your mind."*

It was more difficult than Caer expected, removing the shielding. The memories locked within her for century upon century struggled to break free.

"We are waiting!" thundered at her.

"Breathe, dear one," sifted like the whisper of breeze through her skull. Dana's voice had returned, as distant as Roisin's but it was there. *"Your voice led you well. You understand the need. Breathe and relax."* The suggestion of relaxing had Caer tensing even more, a headache beginning to form at her temples. *"Take us home. Return us to the beginning so that we may take back our mistake and end the curse."*

Exhausted, terrified that she would fail, Caer slumped onto the ground, her long white hair wicking blood from the pools around Tine and Everbloom as she stared at the night sky, three crescent moons visible.

"We cannot fight as we are." The voice was soft and gentle. Roisin. *"This world is weary of our long battles. The life it once accepted in joy, Slievgall'ion now wishes to reject. Let Nemhain see your mind. As it was before, it is now. You are the power that can accomplish this."*

"I cannot," Caer mumbled; too spent to manage more than a croaked whisper. "The moons are not right. There are too many bodies. I have not the strength."

A new voice rose in the lilt of music. *"The moons here are of no consequence. The power of creating the way lay in the magic of the sisters. They chose the full moon because in our world, it signified the greatest strength of their magic. Here, in this world, magic is stronger. You are stronger than you know. You do not need the enhancement of full moons."* Caer knew this music. Adrian. *"See the way just before you show it to Nemhain. You can do this."*

"Do this," encouraged Roisin. *"And we will release the magic that has carried your body through all the centuries. It may rest, at last."*

"See the dream," Adrian whispered. *"As was done before, do again. This time, let it return us to the beginning."*

Caer breathed out a tremulous exhale and closed her eyes, her hand reaching to the amulet around her neck. The charm once more rested in the hollow at the base of her throat. For a time, the singular twisting of the trinity knot held her mind's focus, the image bathed in red from the glow at the charm's heart. Its pulse gradually settled from its erratic hammering to a solid and steady rhythm. Opening her eyes, Caer noted how her breath frosted in the frigid air; how the ache in every part of her body had ceased; how she was utterly numb. She would freeze to death, lying here in the snow. Death would be a welcome thing. *"The gateway, little one."*

Caer focused once more, struggling to open her mind.

"We are still waiting," thundered again. *"Do you wish another example of how I can twist the souls of those you love?"*

"I am trying!" Caer choked out.

The subtle music carried, *"Close your eyes, Caer. And remember."*

Above and westerly, the light of the moons made an eerie glow through the sweep of clouds moving in. Somewhere in the distance emerged the echo of pipes and drums, the cadence distinct, though the melody remained buried in the clash and tortured screams of a far distant war. One, two, three, four, five, six, seven. One, two, three. One, two, three. Ghosts of age-old memories…of age-old battles. Then came the song.

Come join together, pow'rs old,
Fix the spells as they told.

Heath and dance with magic fold,
Pow'r gained, now must hold.
Fairy realm of magic mists
From Slievgall'ion's magic gifts,
Bless us, show us, let us see
Abundant beauty returned to thee.

The song repeated, joined by a vision of a great blaze lifting skyward from the snow- covered mountainside. In the shadows stood the tall, dark silhouette of a man, bodhran in hand, the lyrics flowing from him, while around the fire danced three sky-clad women. The rhythm drove them, the song stirring the flames ever higher.

The suggestion of yet another chant began to weave subtly in and out of the song, the indistinguishable words seeming to come from only one of the dancing women, her dark hair swirling round her as she lifted her voice in time with her measured tread. As the chant's rhythm melded into the music, a diffuse glow throbbed from the two silent dancers. The illumination emanating from the pair brightened, their dance coming to a halt before the faint, crystalline outline of an arched doorway that appeared, set within the mountain's slope.

This was one of the original returnings – the sisters and Adrian moving back through their gateway from Slievgall'ion to Earth.

"You know what you must do, little one." Dana's words sounded strained and cracked.

Setting the entire image once more in her mind, Caer revealed what she saw.

"I…I see," Nemhain waivered. Her song began, thin and lacking in musicality.

Bring thunder and fire to dance upon us.
Bring gale to speak of our lives.
Join strength upon strength to foster our purpose.
Grant us the power, take us back from our prize.
Bring thunder and fire to dance upon us.
Bring gale to speak of our lives.
Join strength upon strength to foster our purpose.
Grant us the power, take us back from our prize.

Snow swirled in a sudden gale, Madadh's roar bellowing through Caer's head. *"Too shallow! The song is too shallow, you stupid bitch! It is not reaching Aifa's mind."* Nemhain's squeal of pain and anguish grated along Caer's nerves almost as severely as her repulsion to Madadh Mire. *"It is your fault!"* Nemhain screeched. *"You robbed me of too much strength!"*

"It is your voice," snarled back. *"You lost the music!"*

Nemhain screeched again. *"I have not! I have not! It lacks his part."*

"Sing it again," came the faint lilt. *"If it will stop your squealing, I will add my part."*

Distant thunder rolled. Was that a thin flash of lightening Caer saw above Mt. Sorrow?

The song began again, this time Nemhain's voice echoed with more strength and better melody. Aifa heard and repeated in a voice that was dark and brooding, but that held the music. Adrian's rich tenor, faint at the start and gradually growing, melded with it.

"You must pick up my part, Caer. I will give your voice strength."

Struggling to sit, Caer listened, first. As the song repeated, she gained her feet and sang, her voice clear and steady, Aifa carrying Nemhain's song.

Bring thunder and fire to dance upon us	Come join together, pow'rs old,
Bring gale to speak of our lives.	Fix the spells as they told.
Join strength upon strength to foster our purpose,	Heat and dance with magic fold,
Grant us the power, take us back from our prize.	Pow'r gained, now must hold.
Bring thunder and fire to dance upon us.	Fairy realm of magic mists,
Bring gale to speak of our lives.	From Slievgall'ion's magic gifts
Join strength upon strength to foster our purpose.	Bless us, show us, let us see
Grant us the power, take us back from our prize.	Abundant beauty returned to thee.

As the words played out, Caer's mind raced to recall what happened when she opened the way, there on Slieve Na Calliagh; struggled to keep those thoughts shielded and hidden from both Madadh and Nemhain. There was an emblazoned lightning storm across the sky, and then…and then…the explosion of light from within the very ground. That was the moment she held the power to set and open the gateway. She set it around and within herself.

Curled in her grasp, the pulse of the necklace intensified, its heat near scorching. Caer dared not release it. Must hold it. Must concentrate. Nemhain had, on that dark and bloody occasion so long ago, held the way open too long. Allowed too many of her followers to be blasted through with them. Her effort likely destroyed Earth. This time… This time Caer knew what to expect. If she could set the gateway once again, perhaps she could control it.

"I am watching you, Caer DaDhrga," Madadh rumbled through her skull. *"I know that you hold the power. Set the gateway where you will. Nemhain will know its location even as you form it. You will not prevent our going through."*

"This world will be the better once it is rid of you!" Yet, fear and doubt trembled through her. What if Earth was destroyed? Their souls would return to emptiness. So, too, would all the other souls who might flee this world. What would become of them if they were locked in an empty world? And what would become of Earth if the world survived that first battle, only to have the sisters and Madadh Mire, return to it?

"Slievgall'ion belongs to us. Aifa and our warriors will remain to rule it," Madadh gloated. *"Earth, too, will be ours. And other worlds, as well. We will take them, just as we took this one. It will not be my wife, however, who rules. I hold that power. Still, she has her uses. With the memories of her sisters now open to her, thanks to you, she will use them to seek a way to establish a permanent gateway between here and other realms. As with Aifa, I will set overseers in each. Yet I will retain control. My great granddaughter, after all, shares Nemhain's and Maura's contempt of me. She will need regular reminders of my strength. I am sure the same will hold with others."*

Caer barely listened, her attention on allowing memories to flow to Nemhain piece-meal while she fought her confusion and indecision. Perhaps it would be better if she raised her knife once more. Could she cast the banishing on herself as she ends her life? Let Nemhain and the Dog remain locked in Slievgall'ion forever.

"Do not!" came a frantic murmur at the back of her mind. *"We must be the ones to end this! We must break the curse. We cannot do it, here!"*

Stealing herself with a long, slow breath, Caer accepted her fate. Send them back. Send them all back. What happens beyond that would depend on what had become of Earth. She prayed she was not sending the souls of those she loved to a dead and empty world.

Taking one final frigid breath, Caer opened the remaining memories. "We must sing the song one last time," she sighed. "Sing it and see the memories of the dancers. Three sky clad sisters and the singer whose music added strength to the weaving of their magic."

The song began again. As Caer joined it, she saw the vision, just as she had before. The ghostly images of the naked dancers and the silhouette of Adrian as he sang, weaving strength through the magic with the music of his voice. Overhead, lightning flashed. Beneath her, the snow erupted in a blinding light. Caer's eyes closed, her will holding the power, setting the gateway around and within herself, once more. Only this time…this time she would expand the way. A great explosion split the air, the blinding light sweeping the whole of the mountain. The ground rumbled beneath her feet. The rush of an electric charge chased along her nerves as the souls of Roisin and Dana fled, multiples upon multiples of souls following. Nemhain's outraged scream and the roar of Madadh as they realized what she had accomplished carried above the den of more explosions.

A sweep of dark magic rose as Madadh bellowed, *You will pay for this!* The banishing spell was growing around her. She knew Madadh and Nemhain were fleeing through the gateway; knew he was saving the kill and banishment spells for just before he cleared the other side.

The bang rang in her ears, the searing pain of the bullet striking her accompanying Brandel's scream of, "Traitor! You betrayed us! You did not fight! You made no effort to stop them! You opened the gateway and let them through! You gave them new life! And I helped you!"

She braced for the terrible rending of her soul being torn from her spent body; braced for the excruciating torture of Madadh's banishing spell. It would be brief. And then she would be no more. But the lifting came as a gentle thing, like the sigh of a butterfly. There was a moment of grief as she saw her lifeless body lying in the red snow far below. She saw all the bodies sprawled in the red stains, including Brandel's. After killing her, he turned the gun on himself.

There was one more enormous explosion. Mt. Sorrow erupted in broiling black clouds, molten rock pouring down her sides, wiping away all that lay on her bloodied slopes, Aifa's terrified screech sliced through the growing rumble and crack. Silence followed. For an instant, a faint vision lifted. A vision of soft green struggling upwards through blackened rock and ash.

And then there was darkness, the sensation of being slammed, and a terrible hunger.

PRONUNCIATION GUIDE:

Aifa – Eef-a

Ailill – Eye-lill

Alainn – Aalin

Amhranai Fearalite – Oerann Faerallchi

Bavol – Bav ol

Breag – Braeug

Caer DaDhrga – Kyair daa Derga

Car'Adawc – Car ah dak

Ciuin – Kyooin

Damsa Dana – Dowsu Danna

Danu – Daanoo

Deahlan – Deh lan

Dochas – Doe khas

Faolchú – Fweel-khoo

Fedel'ma – Fe-Dell-maa

Ga Gréine – Ga Grane

Grian Geal – Gray un Gehl

Madadh Mire – Madoo Mirri

Nemhain – Noo-wann

Roisin – Roe-ish-Een

Samhradh – Sow-rooh

Slieve Na Calliagh – Slyabh na Calli

Slievgall'ion – Sly-eev-gallion

Stoirm – Sterim

Tanai –Tanee

Tar On Tine – Tar Owin Chinee